MO‘ HON
O .gov.

Strand of Dreams

Strand of Dreams

Audrey Howard

Hodder & Stoughton

Copyright © 1997 by Audrey Howard

First published in Great Britain in 1997 by Hodder and Stoughton
A division of Hodder Headline PLC

The right of Audrey Howard to be identified as the Author of
the Work has been asserted by her in accordance with the
Copyright, Designs and Patents Act 1988.

10 9 8 7 6 5 4 3 2 1

British Library Cataloguing in Publication Data

Howard, Audrey
Strand of dreams
1. English fiction – 20th century
I. Title
823.9'14 [F]

ISBN 0 340 66604 8

Typeset by Hewer Text Composition Services, Edinburgh
Printed and bound in Great Britain by
Mackays of Chatham PLC, Chatham, Kent

Hodder and Stoughton
A division of Hodder Headline PLC
338 Euston Road
London NW1 3BH

I would like to thank Beryl Mulligan for her invaluable help in describing to me certain aspects of the Catholic religion. This book is for her.

The Chapmans and the Broadbents

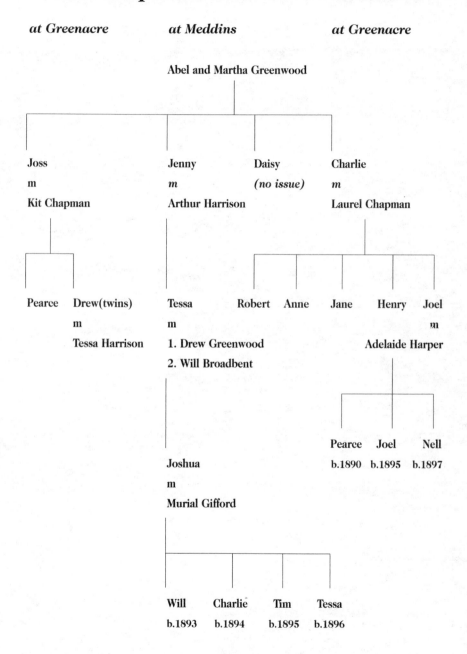

at Greenacre   *at Meddins*   *at Greenacre*

Abel and Martha Greenwood

Joss	Jenny	Daisy	Charlie
m	m	*(no issue)*	m
Kit Chapman	Arthur Harrison		Laurel Chapman

Pearce   Drew(twins)
m
Tessa Harrison

Tessa   Robert   Anne
m
1. Drew Greenwood
2. Will Broadbent

Jane   Henry   Joel
m
Adelaide Harper

Joshua
m
Murial Gifford

Pearce   Joel   Nell
b.1890   b.1895   b.1897

Will   Charlie   Tim   Tessa
b.1893   b.1894   b.1895   b.1896

1

Ask Mary Angelina O'Dowd which was the best day of the week and without hesitation she would tell you it was Sunday since on a Sunday, for a precious couple of hours, she had her daddy all to herself.

Depending on whether they were to take Holy Communion or not, in which case Mammy, Daddy and her brothers would fast from the evening before, the day would begin for the O'Dowds with what Mammy called a proper breakfast. None of the hastily gobbled bread and dripping, or the bacon sandwiches her two sons crammed into their mouths first thing of a morning from Monday to Saturday as they galloped about the kitchen of the small terraced house in Sidney Street in which the family lived.

"Wisht, Mammy, 'ave tha' seen me boots?" Liam would cry in that strange mixture of soft Irish brogue and the harsh broadness of Lancashire which had been passed down through the generations of the O'Dowd and Todd families since the first of their forebears had come from Ireland over seventy years ago. His mouth would be full of fresh bread, his dark, curling hair standing on end, his eyes not yet clear of the deep, dreamless sleep which is the privilege of the young.

"Sure an' aren't they where yer stepped out o't blessed things last night, darlin', an' that's right by't fender," his mother would answer.

"'Ave I a clean shirt, Mammy?" his twin brother Patrick would beg her, the pair of them falling over one another in their mad dash to get to the mill gate on time.

"Holy Mother of God! 'As there ever bin a day when yer'd not one, pet? 'Tis there, airing . . ." pointing to the rack which was pulled high to the ceiling.

"Thanks, Mammy," they'd call in unison, barely stopping to buckle their clogs as they clattered after their father up the narrow hallway to the front door. Mary Angelina and Mammy would smile at one another over the rim of their teacups, two females contemplating the unending but lovable shortcomings of the male. Mary Angelina would not be eight years old until April but she knew exactly what was in her mammy's mind. They were at the last minute for work as usual, her sons, and why couldn't they get up a quarter of an hour earlier when the knocker-up tapped at their window and sit down to porridge, bacon and black pudding, followed by toast and home-made marmalade as their daddy did? Mammy asked them plaintively. Not that there was anything much wrong with bread and dripping, for didn't Róisín O'Dowd make the bread herself on "baking day", usually a Friday morning, and the savoury dripping came from the juices of the cheap but tasty and nutritious cuts of meat she roasted for Sunday dinner. All good stuff and all cooked in the oven next to the kitchen fire, but there was nothing like a proper hot breakfast to set a man up and she said so every day, even on Sundays when they all had one. It was a constant source of worry and aggravation to her, this habit they had of lying in bed until the last minute, and a stranger at her table might have been forgiven for thinking her two handsome, strapping sons were in the last stages of malnutrition.

But it was different on three Sundays out of four. First of all they had a "lie-in" which was lovely, especially in the winter when the icy air of Mary Angelina's bedroom had a strange haze to it as though all the breath which had escaped her lungs while she slept had gathered against the ceiling like the woolly cap of mist over Oldham Edge. Through the half-drawn curtains at the window the lemon translucence of the street lights added to the curious effect and Mary Angelina would hitch down in her little bed, warm and snug and safe. She knew that on the other side of the wall against which she lay, Mammy and Daddy would be awake and cuddled together, kissing, which they did a lot of, smiling and whispering, another thing they did a lot of but which she and her brothers were quite used to. It made her even more secure, for wherever Mammy and Daddy were there was a feeling of love, of warmth, and it wrapped itself about them all like a soft, fluffy blanket.

It was 1914 and the cotton textile industry was booming. Daddy and Liam and Patrick, who had all served their time as "piecers" to the trade, earned good wages at Broadbents Mill in Radnor Street where they each minded "a pair of their own". This meant that they were mule spinners, working in a pair of loose, white corduroy trousers, a thin white shirt and no shoes. They were barefoot because the wooden floor was slippery with oil, dangerous to the sparks which might come from their iron-tipped clogs, and they were always coming home with splinters in the soles of their feet which Mammy took out with her darning needle.

It was hot in the "jennygate", hot and humid like a tropical jungle, Daddy said, though Mary Angelina was never quite sure what that meant, never having been in one. She had been in the spinning room though. Mammy had taken her once when Uncle Fergus had died in a tramcar accident and Mammy had had to fetch Daddy out of his jennygate since Daddy was Uncle Fergus's brother and someone had to go and see to his poor, battered body and Aunty Flo, who was Uncle Fergus's wife, had shrieked that she couldn't do it, no, not for a gold clock!

Mary Angelina had never forgotten the heat in the spinning room that day, and the variety of smells, from the cotton itself, from the oil-soaked pinewood floor and from the mahogany carriages and creels, which were the frames supporting the bobbins of thin rope from which the yarn was spun. Above it all was the whirr of spinning spindles, the shriek of tortured leather straps and the thump of the carriages letting out. And Daddy and Liam and Patrick were barely recognisable in their working clothes since Mary Angelina had never seen them in anything but their dark trousers, their worn jackets and their caps.

The house in Sidney Street, like most of the homes of the decent Lancashire working women of Oldham, was spotlessly clean. On most Saturday mornings those women who worked in the mill from Monday to Friday could be seen on their knees, bums in the air, swaying madly with the strength of their endeavours, scrubbing and stoning their front steps. Róisín O'Dowd was not one of these, for Róisín did not go out to work as many of the women did from Sidney Street and Myrtle Terrace, Waterloo Street and Wellington Place. Róisín had three men in work and so had the luxury and satisfaction of staying at home to keep house for her family, which did not mean that she had time to sit about all day on her bum with a cup of tea in one hand and a fag in the other as some might have done in her place. Róisín O'Dowd had what her neighbours called "fettlin'" fever, for she was at her housework from morning till night. Fettling was a term used in the cotton mill for cleaning under the frames before going home. Róisín Todd had been a spinner before her marriage to Seamus O'Dowd eighteen years ago and "fettlin' under" was removing all the loose cotton hanging about, which was a real fire risk. Aye, well used to fettlin' was Róisín and as Seamus used to say, with justifiable pride in his voice as she donkey-stoned her front steps, "If I was ter let 'er she'd do the 'ole bloody street."

There was no fettling and no spinning done on a Sunday. After their lie-in and the proper breakfast Mammy insisted upon, they would all set off up Sidney Street to walk to St Saviours Church in Shaw Street at the back of Henshaws Blue Coat School to go to eleven o'clock mass.

At the gate they would often meet Uncle Fergus – before his sad accident, of course – and Aunty Flo, all spruced up in their Sunday best, as the O'Dowds were, with their four children shuffling their feet behind them, for like Mary Angelina's brothers, Michael, Dermot and Eamon were mad on football and couldn't wait for mass to be over so that they could tear off to the recreation ground and practise their game. Kathleen, who was the eldest of Uncle Fergus and Aunty Flo's children and courting a lad who worked at Greenwoods Mill, would have her eyes peeled for him in the churchyard, smoothing her skirt and straightening her hat – unnecessarily – when she found him.

Masses started at hourly intervals from eight o'clock to eleven o'clock and only if they were to take communion did the O'Dowds attend the eight o'clock because Mammy said that any later was too long to expect growing children, which included her two lusty sons, to fast from the evening before. A good woman was Róisín O'Dowd, who lived by and for the true faith. Nevertheless she was a woman of some common sense and could see no reason why her children should suffer the pangs of hunger for longer than was necessary, no matter how good it would be for their souls.

She loved going to mass, did Mary Angelina. From the

moment she stepped over the threshold into the entrance porch of the church she felt this wonderful feeling come flooding over her. Ask her what it was and she couldn't have told you, not then, but it was something like the sense of comfort and security she knew when she sat before the kitchen fire with Mammy and Daddy of a night. She was still only seven years old, going on eight and so the words serenity and tranquillity were barely known to her and if they were they were usually associated with the Holy Mother of God, but it was all wrapped up in the same parcel somehow. Mammy and Daddy, the Blessed Virgin and Her Son, the warmth and peace of the O'Dowds' homely kitchen, the blessed sense of refuge in the church, love, a kind of dreamlike gladness that never failed her and which met her at the door of the church, welcoming her into its brooding peace. She would bless herself with the holy water, making the sign of the cross, touching her forehead, her chest, her left and then her right shoulder, murmuring as everyone did, "In the name of the Father and of the Son and of the Holy Ghost", before moving down the body of the church to where she and Mammy and Daddy, Patrick and Liam usually sat. Again you made the sign of the cross, bending your knee before entering the pew.

She and Mammy always wore a hat. Many of the women were poor, really poor and could barely manage to feed their children, let alone buy a hat. Their heads were decently covered with the black shawls in which they were habitually draped. Mary Angelina's daddy earned a good wage and could afford to buy his wife and daughter a straw boater apiece, to be worn only for church, mind, or when they went up town. The rest of the week Mammy folded herself in the traditional shawl, as she had done since she was a mill girl. Mary Angelina was very conscious and very proud of her hat, the daisies on it and the ribbons which fell down her back, despite knowing it was a sin which the nuns and Father O'Toole told her was to be deplored.

The first five minutes of the service were taken up with Mary Angelina's favourite pastime of peeping about her to see who was in church. She had the bright interest her daddy loved and her mammy rebuked her for, but she was curious, nosy Patrick called it, about people and felt a great concern for Mrs McMahon from Myrtle Street who, though she could neither read nor write, followed Father O'Toole's droning voice, out loud, with every Latin phrase word-perfect, just as though she were reading it from the prayer book she had open in her hand. Nobody minded.

There was Nancy O'Leary who had once been Nancy Whittaker and who, without fail, sported a colourful black eye every Sunday which her husband had put there the night before, usually the right eye for he himself was left-handed. Beside her would be a tribe of children, these also, though Mary Angelina was not aware of it, a Saturday night gift from Mick O'Leary.

In the pew nearest the back of the church sat the nicotine-stained, crinkle-faced old crone whom Liam had disrespectfully named Fag-end Lil because of her habit of slipping out periodically during mass for a Woodbine in the shelter of the porch.

Betty Spooner, who was Mary Angelina's special friend and who sat beside her in Standard Three at St Luke's Roman Catholic Junior School, was in a pew nearer the front of the church. Mary Angelina knew Betty did not dare turn round and wave, for Father O'Toole would be bound to notice and report her to the nuns at school next day.

Mary Angelina did her best to follow Father O'Toole's prayers, watching his mouth carefully then looking down at her prayer book to find the place, but it was very hard, for the prayers were in Latin and though she had been coming to mass since she was a baby in Mammy's arms she had not learned to read until she was nearly six. She knew all the prayers, of course, as well as she knew her catechism.

Halfway through the mass preparations began for communion and, as he always did when he blessed the wine, Father O'Toole took a good swig of it, an action Mary Angelina never questioned. Next was the bread, the second part of the blessing called "the hosts". The altar boys swung the burning incense with often less enthusiasm than Father O'Toole would have liked as he raised the chalice containing the wine, or the bread, above his head and the congregation answered the priest's blessing in a rapt undertone.

Mary Angelina knew that at this point of the mass every member of the congregation must keep their head bowed and only look up at the sound of the bell. It was now that you were supposed to pray very hard but every child present, if they had the courage, would sneak a look to the front of the church, feeling very daring if they could manage it without being caught and frowned upon, ready to brag tomorrow at school about how many times they had done it, the boys especially claiming, as seven- and eight-year-olds will, at least five "goes".

There was the sermon from the pulpit next, then more prayers for the sick and dying and dead of the parish. After communion and the patient stream of worshippers who moved to the front of the church, the gospel was read, the congregation recited the Lord's Prayer out loud and it was over. Father O'Toole would drift slowly to the church porch, nodding at Nancy O'Leary and her brood, at Mrs McMahon and Fag-end Lil, at Betty and Mary Angelina, his cassock and vestments, the latter in a lovely shade of green today since it was Lent, swaying as he moved. In the porch he stood to take the hand of every member of the congregation, making a mental note of who was not there, Daddy said. The church was never less than full at all four masses but when it had ended and they had all crossed themselves with what Mammy considered due respect and humility, and though it had been a most satisfying hour, it was lovely to come out into the brightness and ordinariness of the day. They were cleansed, refreshed, uplifted, ready to start another week freed from the small sins Mammy and Daddy had confessed to, though Mary Angelina could not imagine what they might be.

There would be a bit of a chat with Aunty Maggie and with Aunty Flo, with a smiling reminder from Mammy that they were all expected for Sunday tea, while Mary Angelina waited impatiently for the best part of the week to begin.

"We'll be off now, Daddy," the boys would say, pleading with their father to let them go, and since it was nothing more than an innocent bit of practice of the football they worshipped, Daddy would nod. There wasn't a more even-tempered, quietly spoken man than Mary Angelina's daddy and yet he had a great fount of humour, and was a constant source of fun which made him popular among his workmates. He was a man of wisdom, a fair and loving father to his children and the heart and soul of his pretty wife.

"Right, my sons, but mekk sure tha's 'ome by 'alf past, fer Mammy'll 'ave tha' dinner on't table, so she will."

"Aye, Daddy, we promise."

With young Michael and Dermot and Eamon, off they'd clatter in their best clogs, which had been mended only the week before at Chantlers Cloggers in Market Place. She couldn't keep up with them, Mammy complained, blaming it on the inordinate number of footballs her sons kicked about and she didn't care how long they had to sit on the long form in the clogger's cellar, waiting their turn with the rest of the lads who had gone to have their own clogs repaired. It was their fault if they had to spend a precious Saturday afternoon there when they might have been playing for the Broadbent Rovers, the football team got up years ago by old Mr Broadbent and carried on with great enthusiasm by young Mr Charlie, Mr Broadbent's second son who had taken over. But they were good lads, her sons, and she would eye them fondly as they tore off down Shaw Street towards Edge Lane Road and the recreation ground.

For a moment, after farewells so long and fulsome they might not have been going to see them for a month instead of later that day, they would watch Aunty Maggie and Uncle Alf and their brood go in the direction of Wallshaw Street, and Aunty Flo, with Kathleen and her "young man", set off up Shaw Street towards Briscoe Street where Aunty Flo, like Aunty Maggie, lived in a house the exact replica of their own and which was no more than two minutes' walk from St Saviours. Aunty Flo was very devout and that's why she and Uncle Fergus had settled so close to the church when they married, for Uncle Fergus had always done what Aunty Flo told him, or so Daddy said, winking at Mammy.

"Well." Mammy smiled, turning to Seamus and Mary Angelina. "I suppose the two o' thi' are wanting ter be off an' all. Sure an' one o' these fine days I might be invited ter come wid yer." Her smile deepened to let them see she didn't mean it, for hadn't she the Sunday roast to cook and besides, she knew how much this weekly walk meant to Seamus and his little daughter. Seamus loved his sons and was proud of them as a man has a right to be, but as boys do, and should do, and any father knows they will at almost seventeen, they were eager to be off about their own masculine pursuits whenever they could.

There had been two other babies in the nine years between the twins and Mary Angelina, a boy, Rory, who had lived for a year until the dreaded scarlet fever had taken him by the throat and strangled him. Their first daughter, a little scrap of a thing quickly baptised in the faith and christened Caitlin after her grandmother, had barely had time to get a grip on Róisín and Seamus's hearts before she went. Nevertheless she had done so in the few short days of her life and for this reason Seamus was particularly attached to Mary Angelina. The child held a special place in his heart, and he in hers, which Róisín O'Dowd did not begrudge since she knew the strength of her husband's love for herself.

"Oh, go on wid yer, yer pair o' daft 'apporths," as they hesitated politely, "but be back fer 'alf past or I'll skin the pair o' yer."

She gave them both a kiss, bending down to her daughter, stretching up to her husband, then turned and walked along Shaw Street in the direction of home.

"Now then, where's it ter be, Angel?" Daddy asked as he took her small hand in his big one. They had lots of places they liked to go to, special places which were dear to their hearts and which even Mammy didn't know about. Of course it depended on the weather, since they did not want to be traipsing about the countryside in the pours of rain, neither did they wish to be indoors when the sun was golden and warm in the washed blue stretch of sky above the rooftops of Oldham. Only on a Sunday when the mills were closed could you actually see the sun except as a hazed, silvery disc behind the smoke from hundreds of mill chimneys. Today it was fine and though only March and cold, there was a hint of spring in the air. The blue of the sky was slightly blurred with high, almost transparent cloud and all about the churchyard spears of new daffodils swayed and danced. It smelled lovely, sort of new, Mary Angelina thought, unused, ready for her and her daddy to enjoy.

For several minutes they discussed where they might go today. First of all there was Alexandra Park which was just off Park Road and was lovely on a fine day. There was an abundance of trees and glorious flowerbeds, massed with every colour, even in spring, a boating lake with rowing boats and swans gliding on its unruffled surface, a bandstand where the municipal band played stirring martial music and, dividing the smooth lawns, neat paths where folk from all walks of life, high and low, took the Sunday air. There was a conservatory filled with the most exotic flowers, brought, said Daddy, who knew about such things, from places known as equatorial forests and which were so vivid they took Mary Angelina's breath away in delight. There was a pavilion in which you could listen to a quadrille band on a Saturday. Daddy said he and Mammy used to dance there when they were courting, which meant before she was born, even before they were married and where Mammy and Daddy had taken tea. They would go and laugh at the monkeys, Daddy told her, which were still there after all this time. There were statues to be inspected of gentlemen who had made Oldham what it was today, her daddy said solemnly, lifting her up so that she might read their illustrious names, before taking her to the refreshment rooms for a glass of lemonade which they would share. Nothing to eat, of course, since they didn't want to spoil their appetites for Mammy's delicious dinner.

Another of their favourite jaunts was to look in the shop windows in Mumps. Mumps was one of the busiest shopping areas in Oldham and not only that but the most prestigious, which meant splendid, Daddy explained. Why was it called Mumps? Mary Angelina wanted to know, with the total belief that Daddy would have the answer and of course he did, for hadn't the historians written that it originated from the disease, though it was a mystery to both of them why they should name an area of the town after a disease.

Oh, but the shops, the beautiful shops, and what those beautiful shop windows had in them were a constant source of enchantment to her. They were all closed, naturally, it being Sunday but left over from yesterday was the heavenly aroma of coffee from the grocer's in Bottom o' th' Moor where little cylinders in the window went round and round, leaving the smell of the ground coffee.

There was Burrow Brothers which sold the best jam and tea, the slogan in the window said, Jacksons which displayed terribly expensive hats at three shillings and eightpence each, the furrier's, Frank Collins, with what looked to Mary Angelina to be dead animals in the window and past which she and Daddy hurried until they came to the best, the very best, which was Buckley and Prockters Mumps Bazaar. One day he would take her inside, Daddy promised her, perhaps at Christmas because inside was a bedazzlement of lovely things to please and enchant the most particular customer which was what Mary Angelina might be one day. This was where the gentry shopped, like Mr and Mrs Broadbent who owned the mill where Daddy worked and the Greenwoods whose mill was the most modern of its kind in Oldham. But just for now the windows must suffice, enormous windows tastefully arranged with gloves of soft leather, ladies' hosiery, laces, feathers, furs, materials of gleaming satin and delicate silk. Once, right in the centre, had been a salmon pink frock with frills round the sleeves and a deep green sash with rosebuds on the hem and one day, Mary Angelina vowed, she would have one just like it.

Then there was Tommyfield, which was at the other end of the social spectrum altogether with its swings and roundabouts and market stalls, its trade in live poultry, its toffee makers, its preaching ground for what Daddy called "quacks" though again Mary Angelina was not sure what that meant, only that Daddy did not care for them. There were swingboats and shooting galleries, dancing bears and performing dogs and though it was all very exciting it was not one of their favourite places.

When it was raining they visited the Art Gallery in Union Street which was situated above the library. The building had been erected and the Art Gallery opened in 1883 but, due to lack of books, the library was not used by the general public until 1885. Now, twenty-nine years later both she and Daddy were members, going once a week to change their library books.

Again this was not their *most* favourite place!

Today, as Seamus O'Dowd watched his little daughter with soft and smiling eyes, he knew before she spoke where she would want to be off to, taking him with her. She was the treasure of his life, sweet-natured, as pretty as a wild hedge rose with dark, gypsy curls and vivid blue-green eyes fringed with long black lashes which curled at the end. She was bright, intelligent and affectionate but with a quick, hot temper on her which was sometimes difficult to contain. It was usually over some imagined injustice, perhaps not even aimed at herself, but something would spark her off and he'd seen her take a swing at a boy twice her size when they were playing in the street. Aye, even the lads with their games of marbles and "peggy" and those who dared to climb a lamppost to tie a rope round the bar from which they swung, steered well clear of Mary Angelina O'Dowd. She fought with her brothers when they showed their masculine indifference to their "little sister's" demands, acting like an enraged kitten taking on two sturdy terriers. Shriek her hot rage she would, until, suddenly, it would all be over and she'd be sorry, doing her best to give them a penitent, loving hug which they bore bravely.

"Will it be th'ouse then, darlin'?" he asked her, bending down to look into her rosy face.

"Would tha' like that, Daddy?" she said hopefully, knowing, of course, that it was her choice for was she not the apple of his eye?

"Suits me, Angel."

"Well then."

"Well then," and having arranged it all most satisfactorily to suit them both, which meant Mary Angelina, they set off. Through cramped, close-knit streets in which, on other days, children would be "playing out", children who would at this very minute be either at church or chapel or a Sunday school connected with one or the other. There were no balls kicked about on a Sunday, at least not in the street. From behind the closed doors of the houses which stood in neat and, for the most part, well-scrubbed row after row between St Saviours and the edge of town, came the succulent aroma of something cooking for Sunday dinner, even if it was only a simple and cheap herring, or a rabbit off a stall in Tommyfield. The children of the house would be busy at the tasks their mams saved up for them all week, cutting newspapers to the required size to hang behind the "lavvy" door or folding strips of paper, concertina-wise, into pipe lighters for Dad. There were several scruffy dogs lying here and there, wherever there was a patch of sunlight, raising an enquiring head as the man and girl walked briskly by, but except for them and the sad little cat which was always on the doorstep of the last house in Westfield Street, everywhere was deserted.

Turning into Huddersfield Road they passed Greenwoods Mill on their right. It was an enormous, perfectly rectangular building with a tower at each corner and a further one for good measure in the middle of its imposing frontage. There were six floors with thirty tall, narrow windows on each floor, and that was just at the front! The chimney, at least half as tall again as the actual mill, was at the back, along with its engine houses, its yards and outbuildings. It had been rebuilt in 1908 and had a spindleage of 108,636 which was almost the same as at Broadbents where Seamus O'Dowd worked. A modern mill with sprinklers and fire pumps, fire escapes and electric lighting in the workrooms. The average number of bales of good American quality cotton used each week exceeded two hundred and the number of men and women who were employed had just risen to three hundred and seventy-five. A prosperous mill was Greenwoods, as was Broadbents, a fact Seamus noted since the two families who owned the mills were related.

They were leaving the town behind now, reaching the "better" part where the houses were detached and sat in long, neat gardens, and beyond them the open fields lay. The hedgerows were already bursting out into their spring finery, nurtured by the frail sunshine of the past week, and the wild daffodils showed their frilly trumpets above the rim of the ditch running at the side of the lane. Sweet violets, shy and fragile, grew beside them, and celandine, brightening the discoloured winter grass with their beauty. Beyond the hedge a blackbird sang, welcoming the sweet budding of this year which was to shatter the world, as the father and daughter knew it, beyond repairing.

There had been heavy rain a couple of weeks back, lasting for several days and nights without let-up and the gushing sound of the mill race beyond the old sandpit could distinctly be heard on the stillness of the Sunday air. A cow lowed plaintively and from somewhere far off there was the sound of guns and they knew it would be some of the grand folk who came to the game moors each year to shoot at the innocent birds.

But they were nearly there now and Mary Angelina scarcely heard them and neither did Seamus as they walked slowly, dreamily, towards the magnificent wrought-iron gates which were let into the pinky rose stone of the high wall before them.

They stopped, their hands reaching out simultaneously to grip the ironwork of the closed gates. For perhaps five minutes neither spoke as they gazed through them to the house which stood beyond.

"Eeh, darlin'," Seamus sighed, "did tha' ever see owt so grand?"

"No, Daddy, never." Mary Angelina's sigh echoed his own.

2

It was on the day she and Mammy had gone up town to buy the material for Mary Angelina's frock that she first saw Tim Broadbent, or rather young Mr Tim as everyone at Broadbents Mill called him.

The frock was to be worn in the procession on Whit Friday. Whit Friday was a very special day in the Roman Catholic calendar and there would be a positive turmoil of planning and pinning, measuring and cutting in preparation for the making of the dresses the little girls in the procession would wear. The boys, naturally, would be in their usual jackets, trousers and caps, but all brand-new and a far cry from their everyday appearance, the farthings, the halfpennies, pennies and sixpences saved up laboriously week by week over the past year to pay for them.

Aye, a fine sight were the Whit walks, especially the ones which set off at precisely eleven o'clock from each Roman Catholic church in Oldham. Even the traffic was stopped so great was the crush, which the children thought was grand, making them feel very important, for, unlike the Protestants who walked an hour earlier than them, the second procession was quite enormous involving every Catholic child in the town. Some of them would have taken their "payments" for their special outfits to school for weeks beforehand but Róisín O'Dowd, devout as she was and a staunch supporter of the Church and Catholic school her daughter attended, had a streak of stubborn independence in her and liked to see to her children and their needs herself. She would save up for and make her child's dress, her veil, her wreath of ribbons, even the staff of flowers Mary Angelina would carry. The day had long gone when Liam and Patrick, then altar boys at St Saviours, would march in great embarrassment in front of the girls.

The fire banked up, the back door locked, the yard gate bolted but the front door left on the latch so that the lads could get in, Mary Angelina and Mammy caught the tram at the corner of Samson Street and Shaw Road. It was full upstairs and down and they were forced to stand, packed like sardines in a tin with Mammy hanging on to an overhead strap and Mary Angelina hanging on to Mammy. Mammy had put half a dozen large onions under the grate to cook while they were out and when the lads got back from football at the ground next to the mill in whose team they played and Daddy from Boundary Park where Oldham Athletic were playing Everton at home, the onions would be eaten with salt and pepper and butter for their tea. It made Mary Angelina's mouth water just to think of it.

It was a Saturday and the streets which led away from Shaw Road in both directions were deserted, since it was a tradition for those who lived there to go up town on a Saturday afternoon. The majority of the housewives would have already done their buying in for the week, usually at the local Co-op in order to get their "divi", and the trip to town was really a social occasion, a chance to have a look at the shops and visit the market where almost every item on every stall would be examined. They rarely bought anything, though on one Saturday, a year or two back, Betty Spooner's daddy had purchased a piano, which, when it was delivered by horse and cart on the Monday, had caused such a commotion in the street Mr Spooner had threatened to send for the constable. Every boy in the area was determined to have a "tinkle" on the keys before the wondrous thing was taken indoors and more than one had his ears boxed before Mr Spooner and the delivery man had the instrument safely jammed into a corner of the parlour, where Mrs Spooner declared fiercely she couldn't get to her windows for the damned thing and how were they to be cleaned, would Bert Spooner tell her that!

Mary Angelina and Mammy jumped nimbly off the tram at the corner of King Street and Manchester Street. They liked to work their way shop by shop from there into High Street, past the Town Hall, into Yorkshire Street and on to Mumps, making a small detour on the way up Henshaw Street to Tommyfield. Right opposite the tram stop and across the road was Coombes shop and the traffic, even the tram, was held up by the "bobby" on duty as she and Mammy crossed over hand in hand. They wore their hats today, she and Mammy, identical narrow-brimmed, flat-crowned boaters of straw with Mammy's decorated with a wide blue grosgrain ribbon and blue silk violets to match and Mary Angelina's buttercup yellow with white and yellow daisies. Mammy was very clever with her needle and though out and about the streets near her home she wore, like her neighbours, a plain skirt, blouse, shawl and clogs since they were warm and practical, when she and Mary Angelina went up town Mammy would put on her best skirt and jacket. Made five years ago, it was what was known as a walking costume, the skirt just touching Mammy's boots, the jacket clinging to her waist. Very plain and neat in a navy alpaca bought on the market from an end of roll and trimmed with touches of sparkling white. Mammy was small and slim with long, dark curling hair, the same colour as Mary Angelina's, with vivid blue eyes and rosy cheeks and a smiling mouth which turned up at the corners even in repose.

Already Mary Angelina, who was tall for her age, was up to Mammy's shoulder. She too was in her best coat, the one she went to church in and again "run up" by Mammy. A lovely rich blue gaberdine, a purple blue like the sky at night, with a velvet collar but already too short for her, showing the hem of her skirt and the edge of her drawers above her black stockings and boots. But the hat made up for it, tied beneath her chin with broad yellow ribbons. Mammy fastened hers on with an enormous hat pin through the heavy mass of her hair which she swept up high on top of her head in a bun.

Coombes was a bit like Buckley and Prockters in Mumps, a high-class shop, the sparkling windows displaying anything from underwear to gloves. The street was crowded with every kind of shopper, including the obviously better-off ladies in their smart outfits, the skirts shorter and tighter than Mammy's, so narrow and tube-like they could barely hobble. In fact that was what they were called, "hobble-skirts", and though it was said that the north could not possibly hope to parallel London in the world of fashion, these ladies were as stylish and up to the minute as any seen in Regent Street, or even Paris, so it was reported in the *Oldham Standard*. They wore wide, tall hats, like buckets upside down, adorned with great bows, as they tottered in and out of the better-class shops in their high-heeled, tight-laced boots which were revealed by their shorter skirts.

She and Mammy had reached the bottom of Yorkshire Street, just where it turned into Mumps, when Mary Angelina saw the motor car. Well, you could hardly miss it, she told Daddy later as she sat on his knee in front of the kitchen fire. Motor cars were few and far between in Oldham and wherever one was seen it caused a great deal of interest and this one was no exception. But it was not just the motor car which drew a hesitant crowd of men and boys about it, but its colour. Motor cars, the few that had entered Mary Angelina's small world, were always black, or at least some dark colour which was not unlike the carriages, pulled by horses, which were still to be seen on the streets of Oldham. Mr Broadbent, old Mr Broadbent, had been among the first to buy a motor car years ago, the most glorious thing you ever saw which shone like the tinsel on a Christmas tree. She and Daddy had been forced to step to one side in the lane one Sunday on their walk, allowing the motor car to pass. Daddy had told her it was a Rolls-Royce Silver Ghost, his voice reverent as though he were in church, and the name suited it since its silvery passage along the lane was as quiet and drifting as Mary Angelina imagined a ghost to be.

This one was red, a bright, glowing scarlet which seemed to set fire to the space it stood in. It was parked in the road right outside the high, arched doorway of Buckley and Prockters, its top tucked away somewhere in the fashion of a baby's perambulator, all gleaming lamps and sparkling bits from one end to the other. There were only two seats, black leather, and what would happen if it should rain, which it often did in Oldham? Mary Angelina wondered, scarcely able to contemplate the image of the lovely little car filling up with rainwater.

And it was a lovely little car, Mary Angelina decided. Well, perhaps not lovely, but cheeky, cheerful, with a style about it which she considered to be enormously appealing. She found herself, along with the dozen small boys and men in caps or bowlers, standing beside it, even putting out a hand to touch it, certain it would be hot beneath her caressing fingers.

Mammy was engrossed with the magnificent display of

crêpe-de-chine and Jap silk blouses in Buckley and Prockters' window. Their prices ranged from twenty-nine shillings and sixpence to forty-nine shillings and sixpence, which was well beyond Róisín O'Dowd's pocket. Indeed there were men who fed a family for a week on less than that, but the garments were lovely, so elegant and in such beautiful colours, patterned and plain. Mind you, if she could just get her hands on one for five minutes she'd soon have the knowledge in her head on how to make one herself and at a quarter of the price.

So preoccupied was she with the details of the blouses she quite forgot her daughter, whom she imagined to be at her side and as absorbed as she herself was in Buckley and Prockters' window.

They catapulted out of Buckley and Prockters' splendid doorway with such force, like two exploding firecrackers, every head in the vicinity, except Róisín O'Dowd's, turned to look at them. The shop walker in his frock coat, his buttonhole adorned with a white carnation, had opened the door for them, bowing respectfully, for these were the upper crust of Oldham, the aristocracy who had been brought up to expect deference and servility and it was his job to give it. It was what he was paid for. It was what Buckley and Prockters was known for. Its reputation was staked on it. It was a ritual, this relationship between customer and shop assistant. Perhaps these two, especially the young lady, were not exactly pedigreed, for many of the wealthy and influential gentlemen of Lancashire could go no further back than a grandfather who had worn clogs and spun cotton in his own cottage. From humble beginnings was the young man who was laughingly holding the young lady's arm as he guided her down the perfectly unmenacing steps in Buckley and Prockters' doorway.

"Watch your step, Daphne, my pet. Those high heels of yours will get you into serious trouble one of these days. Not that they don't look absolutely scrumptious on you which is why you wear them, I suppose."

"Oh, stuff and nonsense, darling. I've been wearing shoes like this since I was fourteen years old and coaxed Mummy into allowing me a pair."

"Do you get your own way all the time, my sweet?"

"Most times. In fact I cannot remember the last time I failed."

"I can well imagine it but I must admit they look very fetching on you."

The shoes in question were of black glacé kid, court shoes with a high heel and a metal and paste cerise-coloured rose decorating the centre front.

It was obvious to the fascinated crowd that the young man was having a good "scen" at the young lady's ankles, at least a good six inches of which were on view and the male observers didn't blame him one bit, for they were fine and slender and well worth scenning at. She was an exceedingly pretty girl, very smart, daring even in her tight, tube-like dress of cerise silk which allowed them all to see every curve of her magnificent figure, even to the bobs of her nipples which threatened to break through the fine material. The neckline of the dress was modest enough but that didn't seem to matter since every generous curve and shapely hollow was on full display. Her hat, the same vivid shade as her dress, seemed to be nothing but a shimmer of feathers which bounced and jostled as joyfully as her breasts.

The young man carried half a dozen parcels in one hand. They were all beautifully wrapped in Buckley and Prockters' distinctive wrapping paper, parcels which Buckley and Prockter would have been more than happy to deliver in their smart, modern, newly acquired motor van. They seemed not to bother him, though, as he guided his companion across the busy pavement.

He was as handsome as she was pretty, dressed quite casually, casual by the day's standards, that is, where most gentlemen wore what was known as a lounge suit of dark grey flannel with narrow stripes to town. A bowler hat or a Homburg was usual but this young man scorned both, wearing his rather long, fair hair uncovered and curling over the collar of his brown flecked tweed jacket. His corduroy trousers were a soft caramel colour, his immaculate shirt was cream and his four-in-hand silk tie was a loud and dashing mixture of yellow and orange swirls which Mary Angelina thought was quite glorious. His brogues were a rich, polished brown. His face was smooth, bronzed as though his days were spent out of doors, his mouth generous and laughing to reveal even white teeth. He was tall, boyish, his "just grown into manhood" body loosely put together, but graceful, the body of an athlete. He hadn't a worry in the world, his manner said, for his world was just as he liked it. He was rich and healthy and handsome. He had a pretty girl on his arm and a dashing sports car waiting to take them wherever it pleased them to go. His content, his satisfaction with what he had, his sense of wellbeing, his joy of living showed in the merry curl of his lips, the deep glow in his rich, chocolate brown eyes and the way he carelessly shoved his slim horseman's hand through the tangle of his tawny blond hair. He epitomised careless youth, the personification of engaging young manhood and Mary Angelina was bewitched with his carefree male vitality.

"Hop in, Daphne my love," he was saying, scarcely noticing the still figure of the child who was standing beside his motor car which proclaimed itself to be a Singer Ten.

Daphne hopped in, not at all worried by the gawping stares of every man and boy in the street as her skirt slithered up to knee height.

"Where d'you fancy going?" the young man asked her. "Afternoon tea at Monico's or how about Yates's? A glass of red biddy would go down a treat after all that shopping. I hear they've just bought in a fine amontillado which Will says is one of the best he's tasted."

"When did your sainted brother ever venture into Yates's Wine Lodge, Timmy, tell me that? I would have thought it far beneath his dignity, which he prizes above all else, to be seen in such a place. It takes him all his time to play a decent game of tennis for fear he might make a fool of himself."

"Hey, go easy on poor old Will, Daph. He's not that bad." The young man laughed, turning to look admiringly at her. "He's a damn good player."

Daphne pouted prettily in answer, then reached into her handbag, bringing out a lipstick case and powder compact, both of which appeared to be diamond-studded.

"Well, whatever you say, Timmy darling. Now, don't start the engine yet," as Timmy darling put out a hand to turn the ignition key. "I want to put a bit of lipstick on," which she proceeded to do, parting her full lips, dabbing and pouting, making quite sure her companion got a good look at their moist fulness, which he did. Her lip colour was the blatant cerise of her dress, her hair beneath her extravagant hat as golden as a fresh-minted sovereign and her eyes as blue as a cornflower.

The young man leaned forward, placing his forearms on

the steering wheel, watching her performance with total absorption and the very obvious male appreciation of a good-looking female. His eyes narrowed until his long, fair, cinammon-tipped lashes almost meshed and his mouth parted on a sigh which was completely sensuous.

"God, Daph, you're a stunner," he murmured softly, "and if we weren't in the middle of the bloody main street I'd kiss you until you begged for mercy."

"It wouldn't be mercy I'd be begging for, darling," Daph drawled.

"Really, then why don't you tell me what it would be, my sweet?"

"Surely you must know the answer to that by now, Tim Broadbent," she drawled huskily, looking at him from beneath her long, darkened eyelashes.

"Tell me."

"You seemed to know very well last night when you spirited me away to the summerhouse at Mabel's."

"Indeed I did, but you played hard to get . . ."

"Hard to get!" Daphne thrust forward the full curve of her breasts, smiling when his eyes dropped down to them. "You know I adore you, you silly boy."

"Do I?" He grinned. "Perhaps if I were to take you to some more private place you could show me how much." His voice had grown husky and standing almost at his right elbow Mary Angelina bent her head in order not to miss a word of this fascinating but totally incomprehensible conversation between these two divine creatures, the likes of whom she had never before come across.

The movement caught the eye of Daphne.

"It seems we have an eavesdropper, Timmy darling," she said languidly, nodding her bright head in Mary Angelina's direction.

At once Timmy darling turned, his brown eyes widening, his eyebrows rising in astonishment as he looked into the brilliance of the bluest – no, they were green . . . or was it turquoise? – eyes he had ever seen, the bewitched eyes of seven-year-old Mary Angelina O'Dowd.

She blinked slowly, then smiled and for the life of him he could not resist smiling back. It was a charming smile, for Timothy Broadbent was a young man of great charm. It was his nature to be amiable and his gift to have his amiability returned. He responded to pretty women and the little girl who gazed at him was remarkably pretty. Not pretty like Daphne, who had the glitter and brilliance and sharpness of a diamond held under the strong beam of an electric light, but a soft, childish loveliness like a tightly furled rosebud in the dew of the early morning sunlight. The sunlight which rose over the fields and meadows, the pastureland and high moorland about his own home just after dawn, palest pink, lemon and gold, touching the new day with a beauty which was breathtaking.

"And what might you be up to, little girl?" he asked pleasantly.

"Nowt," Mary Angelina answered, just as pleasantly, finding his deep brown eyes much to her liking.

"*Nowt!*" Daphne mimicked, but Mary Angelina merely gave her a scornful look, deciding there and then, with remarkably unchildlike intuition, that Timmy's friend was, as her mammy would say, not a proper lady. Common, she was, despite her vivid good looks and lovely dress, her posh accent and la-di-dah ways.

Tim Broadbent's smile deepened. He was himself slightly irritated by Daphne's contemptuous ridicule of the child, wondering why, for the little girl meant nothing to him. She was exactly like the hundreds of other working-class children in Oldham, the parents of whom worked in one mill or another. Slightly better dressed, perhaps, and quite immaculate in her perky straw hat, her polished boots and the whiteness of the lace edging her drawers which showed beneath the hem of her dress and coat.

The man and the child studied one another intently and in the passenger seat Daphne began to fidget, not at all pleased to have Tim Broadbent's attention diverted from her by this big-eyed waif who was obviously from one of the tightly packed terraces which stood about the area of Mumps. Daphne was not used to it and in fact if Timmy didn't return his admiring, covetous gaze back to her at once he would be inordinately sorry. Daphne Murchison was not accustomed to taking second place to anyone, let alone some street urchin. Daphne Murchison, at seventeen, was a very popular young lady, with not only beauty to her credit but wealth as well, since her father was Murchison's Hardware with branches all across Lancashire of the business he himself had started nearly forty years ago with one small shop in Oldham. A broad-vowelled, down-to-earth northener was Sam Murchison, with only one weakness in his forthright, plain-speaking, iron-willed makeup, which was his doting indulgence regarding his daughter, his one chick, this startlingly lovely girl who had come late in his life. He had taught Daphne to believe that she was unique, a star, *the* star in the firmament, especially his, and she had come to expect the same from every man she met. She and Timmy had been introduced several weeks ago at a party at the home of Daphne's best friend, Mabel Rivington, with whom Daphne had gone to school. An exclusive girls' school in the south of England where, though it had almost broken his heart to part with her, Sam had sent her to be made into a lady. Mabel's father, who was Rivington Brewers, had built a magnificent home to the east of Oldham where all the "nobs" lived, not far from Elmhurst Park, the home of the Murchisons. Tom Rivington had given his mansion the grand name of Rivington Grange, hoping to become acquainted, not only with Sam Murchison but with the Greenwoods of Greenacre and the Broadbents of Meddins, the Holdens of Birch Hall and all the other old county families who lived in the area. Mrs Rivington loved to give lavish parties for her daughter who was of marriageable age, like Daphne, and had set her sights on the Greenwood boys, Pearce and Joel, or the Broadbent three, Will, Charles and Tim. Any one would do. All five were very eligible and as wealthy as Sam Murchison and Tom Rivington and would be a good catch for Mabel or Daphne, Mabel and Daphne's mothers privately agreed.

"Were you having a look at my motor?" Timmy was asking the child and Daphne sighed dramatically.

"Aye, 'tis a grand colour, so 'tis."

"You like red motor cars?"

"I never seen one before." She was not shy.

"Have you ever ridden in a motor car?" he asked her, not even pausing to consider why the child had drawn his attention from Daphne, who promised so much and could be a hellion if offended.

"Eeh, nay." The child drew back a little as though afraid he were about to drag her into the thing, then, changing her mind, stepped forward again, a glowing smile of anticipation on her face which said she really wouldn't mind if he did.

"Would you like to?" he heard himself ask her, astonishingly.

"Not 'alf, but me daddy wouldn't let me, nor me mammy."

"And where might they be?"

Daphne yawned ostentatiously, tapping her long, manicured fingernails – which Mary Angelina was astounded to see were painted the same shade of red as the motor car – on the dashboard.

"Mammy's over there . . ." indicating Róisín O'Dowd who had moved along Buckley and Prockters' window to study a length of shimmering shantung which had been dyed to a rich peacock blue.

"In't that grand?" they all three heard her say to Mary Angelina who she believed was beside her. "Sure an' it'd mekk someone a lovely frock."

". . . an' Daddy's at Boundary Park. 'E follers Oldham Athletic."

"Does he now. A man after my own heart. They're a good team and deserve to win the cup. And what do they call you?" His fascination with this bright and lovely child was quite extraordinary and later he was to shake his head and smile at his own foolishness in chancing Daphne's uncertain temper. But he was like that, diverted with anything which was not of the ordinary, expressing an endearing youthfulness and warmth which drew people to him with no effort on his part.

"Mary Angelina O'Dowd," she told him, then waited, for he was bound to say something spellbinding.

"Lord, what a mouthful." He grinned, a flash of good white teeth in his suntanned face, and she grinned back since she'd taken a great fancy to him. "I suppose they call you Molly."

She frowned. "No."

"I thought all little girls who were called Mary were nicknamed Molly."

She considered this carefully. "No," she said again, clearly mystified.

"Really, darling, are you to stay chatting to this . . . this child for the rest of the day or are we to have tea as you suggested?" Daphne was becoming more than just irritated and it showed in the sudden firmness of her usually pouting mouth.

"Oh, sorry, my pet." He turned the key in the ignition and put the car into first gear with a graceful and competent movement as though, despite his youth, he had been driving for years. In fact, though he was still only eighteen years old he had first got behind the wheel of a motor car nearly three years ago when his father, who had instantly adored the thrill of motoring, brought home an old Rover Eight motor car for his sons to practise on. It was built in 1905 but in 1911 it was already sadly out of date. Tim and his brothers had been allowed to chug it about the estate and not until the eighteenth birthday of each of his sons did Joshua Broadbent allow them a brand-new machine of their own. Will, the eldest, had a natty Prince Henry Vauxhall and Charlie a 1913 Cowey Light car which, he boasted, "rode on air".

But none was painted the brilliant scarlet of Tim's dashing sports car which had brought Mary Angelina O'Dowd to its side.

"We'd best be off then, little Molly," he said to her, winking, as though Daphne's obvious aggravation was directed at them both and was therefore something shared between them.

She dimpled, ready to giggle, for he really was the funniest chap she had ever met, with a twinkle to him which matched her daddy's.

"Right," she said. "Ta-ra," waving her hand as he lifted his in a gesture of cheerful farewell.

When, as the roar of the engine tore apart the quiet hum and clatter of the street, Mammy turned, Mary Angelina was gazing after the red monster which gathered speed and raced off in the direction of Yorkshire Street and High Street where Yates's Wine Lodge was situated.

"Nasty thing," Mammy sniffed, taking Mary Angelina's hand in hers.

3

The O'Dowd family were considerably startled early on Monday morning when, at breakfast, Mary Angelina declared airily that she had decided her name was far too much of a mouthful and from now on she'd like them to call her Molly.

"Molly! MOLLY! I never 'eard owt so daft in me life," Liam declared, pausing for a moment in his mad charge about the kitchen which was the normal course of events in the O'Dowd household.

Molly turned on him sharply. "What's it ter do wi' thi', Liam O'Dowd? If I want ter call messen Molly then I will."

"Nay, darlin', we couldn't call tha' Molly, could we, Mammy?" Daddy protested as she knew he would. "Tha's bin our very own Mary Angelina fer nearly eight year now an' ter change tha' name an' expect us all ter call thi' summat else . . . well, 'tis out't question."

"I don't see why, Daddy. 'Tis a perfeckly easy name, so it is. Molly, go on, try it."

"Nay, I don't want ter try it an' neither does anyone else. What put that daft idea in tha' 'ead?"

"Oh, go on, Daddy."

"I said NO!"

She turned to her mother. "Tha' say it, Mammy. I'm that fed up wi' Mary Angelina this an' Mary Angelina that an' when I come ter write it in me book at school . . ."

"Daddy said no, Mary Angelina, an' that's that."

Daddy didn't often deny her anything. Mammy was the one who was strict, if strictness was demanded, making sure in her firm but loving way that her children followed the guidelines set by herself, by Daddy and by the Church. Of course, Daddy's word was law and was obeyed instantly, especially by his sons, and to the letter, but Molly, as she now thought of herself since her encounter with the captivating "Timmy darling", knew she could, almost without fail, "get round" her daddy, providing what she asked for was not too outrageous, and she went about it the right way.

"Why?" she asked again, her eyes beginning to snap. She had thought of nothing else ever since the little red sports car had roared away towards Yorkshire Street, taking with it the lovely bloke who, she realised now, her daddy worked for, or at least for his father. Daphne had been a pain in the neck, of course, but Tim had been grand and if it was his opinion that the cumbersome Mary Angelina with which she had been christened should be changed to Molly, which was much easier and very snappy, then she could see no reason why it should not be so. It made no difference to them, did it, meaning her family, her best friend Betty and everyone she knew in her young life. Mind you, she was none too sure about Sister Ursula and Sister Kathleen at school but she'd cross that bridge when she came to it.

"Because Daddy ses so, that's why," Mammy answered mildly, placing a bowl of creamy porridge before her daughter in which she had dribbled a spoonful of syrup as Mary Angelina liked it. "Sure me an' Daddy wouldn't know who we were talking to. Now eat tha' porridge before it goes cold. Tha'll be late fer school if tha' don't look sharp. Molly indeed!"

"Great-Grandma was called Molly."

"That's got nowt ter do wi' it. Tha' was christened Mary Angelina an' that's an end to it. Now eat tha' porridge."

Molly mutinously obeyed, stirring the rich, smooth mixture round and round in the bowl until the syrup had melted. She knew it was no good going on about it at this particular moment since Mammy was preoccupied with getting Daddy, Liam and Patrick off to work and she herself must soon be leaving to run up the street and call for Betty. She and Betty walked to school together, sat next to one another in the classroom and played all the endless games girls played in the playground at playtime. It was the season for "whip and top" at the moment but ask any child in the school why it was and who decided it and they would have looked blank. Someone started it and the rest followed, that was all they knew. Daddy would bring her a piece of leather from the belt which drove his machine and which would be fastened securely to a stout stick. The top, bought from the corner shop for a farthing or two, would be patterned with coloured chalk which made a pleasing display as it whirled round and all over the playground, and in the street after school little girls would be seen furiously whipping their tops as though their lives depended upon it.

There was skipping when the light nights came, providing one of them could borrow a washing line from an obliging mam, and following that in its due season, hopscotch, which was Molly's favourite. She was the best in the class at hopping and balancing on one leg, scarcely ever treading on the lines and she was as graceful and poised as the little ginger cat which slept on the rag rug in front of the kitchen fire. There always seemed to be marbles, particularly among the boys who were expert at "Dog out", "Ring" and "Jubby" and who played interminably.

She had the same argument with Betty as she had with Mammy and Daddy. Betty couldn't see why she wanted to be called plain Molly when she'd a lovely name like Mary Angelina, she said. She wished she was called something nice instead of simply Betty. Not even short for Elizabeth, which Betty sometimes was, she grumbled, but if Mary Ang – oh all right – if *Molly* was set on it she'd do her best, sighing dramatically.

She started again as soon as she got home from school, barely over the front doorstep before she attacked Mammy. She'd told them all at school, she reported and they'd all agreed—

"Not Sister Ursula?" Mammy interrupted.

Well no, Molly admitted, being a truthful child, she'd not approached any of the nuns but all her friends . . .

"Friends aren't ones what give a child a name, Mary Angelina. Tha' daddy an' me decided what we wanted tha' ter be called an' that's what tha' *shall* be called an' if I 'ear one more word it's ter bed wi'out tha' tea."

Molly shut up then, deciding to try Daddy again when he got home since Daddy was easier to get round than Mammy.

She began right after tea. "Call me Molly," she pleaded with him, climbing on to his knee and smiling winningly up into his face and when he smiled back, exasperatedly to be sure, but a smile nevertheless, she knew she had won even though there would be weeks of argument and annoyance to follow. She finally got her own way, though it took a long time before

Mammy called her Molly as naturally as once she had called her Mary Angelina. When Molly simply refused to respond when spoken to, stubborn as a goat, Mammy said, and for a bit of peace they agreed resignedly that they'd do their best. Daddy's own grandmother, who had married Michael O'Dowd, the first to set foot on English soil in the 1840s, had, as their daughter pointed out, been called Molly and though it wasn't nearly as pretty as Mary Angelina, they'd give it a try. Molly did notice though, that Daddy took to calling her Angel more often. Moll, Liam and Patrick named her, teasing her unmercifully, driving her into what Patrick called one of her "paddies", pretending she was named Polly or Dolly or even Golly like the little doll on the marmalade jar in the Co-op window.

The spring drifted slowly into early summer, as slowly as it does when you are eight years old with your whole life ahead of you, stretching away as far as the eye can see to where the horizon meets the ocean, which Molly had seen when she and her family had gone to Blackpool on a day excursion last Wakes week. Everyone in Oldham was in a savings club, some run by schools or mission halls, at church or the mill, buying a sixpenny "share", or more whenever they could afford it, and it was one of Molly's errands to run with the money to pay the Wakes Club at the Mill Spinners Club where Daddy was a member. This year Oldham Wakes was to begin on the last Saturday in August and the O'Dowd family were hoping, for the first time ever, to go from Mumps station to Blackpool for a whole week's holiday, "doing their own", of course, which meant buying in as soon as they arrived at the boarding house and catering for themselves. Molly was so excited when she thought about it, a whole week at magical Blackpool, it even interfered with her fading – if she were truthful – memory of that day when she had met the man who had called her Molly.

It was pouring with rain on the first day in August when Molly O'Dowd first heard the word "war" mentioned.

"Fetch Daddy's slippers, our Molly," Mammy called to her from the scullery when she heard the sound of the front door latch lifting in the hall, "an' put 'em by't fire ter warm." Molly was kneeling on a chair at the kitchen table, armed with a pile of newspapers, a knife, a piece of string and a bodkin. When she had cut the newspapers into the correct size she would thread them with the bodkin on to the string which would then be hung behind the lavatory door. The lavvy was at the end of the yard, spotlessly clean, naturally, since Róisín O'Dowd wouldn't allow it to be in any other condition. A flush lavatory which they shared with no one else since the council had installed one to every house in the street, but it was a nerve-shattering experience to use it on a dark, cold night. Sometimes Mammy came with her before Molly went to bed at night, standing dithering in the frosty air, beseeching Molly to hurry up but at the moment, while the nights were light and mild, the trip down the yard was bearable. The paper-threading was a job Molly hated but with the rain pelting on the rooftops and windows and pavement making playing out impossible, she could not avoid it.

"Right, Mammy," she answered, glad to be spared the tedious job, clattering up the linoleum-covered stairs to reach for Daddy's old slippers which he'd left under the bed he shared with Mammy. Drifting about the house was a delicious smell of broth which Mammy had made with cowheel and herbs. She had bought two at the market that morning and the second one, with a pound of shin beef and onions and a great panful of boiled and mashed potatoes, would make a filling and nourishing meal for the family's tea.

Molly knew there was something wrong the minute she entered the scullery with Daddy's slippers in her hand. Daddy had his back to the sink, his bum resting on its edge, his arms folded across his chest, his head bent, his expression grim. Mammy stood before him, looking up into his face, her own worried, and Molly felt the first unease prick her.

She turned in the scullery doorway, looking back into the kitchen where her brothers were removing their wet jackets, placing them on the chair backs to dry before sitting down to unbuckle and slip off their clogs. Her glance was questioning but they merely shrugged and pulled a face as though they were not terribly sure what all the fuss was about.

"Sure an' it's not as bad as that, lad, surely?" Mammy was saying. She took hold of Daddy's strong forearms, shaking him gently as though to gain his full attention, and he sighed wearily as he put his arms round her.

"Nay, 'appen tha're right an' it'll come ter nowt, darlin'." His eyes, for some reason, passed over Molly as though she were not there, resting on his two sturdy sons who smiled encouragingly.

"But what's it about, Seamus?" Mammy insisted.

"Well, it were only what Mr Broadbent were sayin' at dinner. Tha' knows 'ow 'e reckons ter 'ave a bit of a clack wi't lads in jennygate. I asked 'im what the 'ell it were all about. There were such a bloody fuss about that there assassination at th'end o' June . . ."

"What assassination?"

"Nay, lass, don't ask me ter remember t'names. It were in a place in't Balkans, wherever them might be but it seems to 'ave put cat right among pigeons, so it does."

"What d'yer mean?" Mammy begged to be told, frightened, Molly could see, by Daddy's sombre expression and the dragging worry in his voice. She and her brothers remained as still and quiet as birds in a bush when the cat goes stealthily by, aware of the importance of this moment, though they did not understand why.

Daddy sighed deeply. "Well, some'ow Austria and 'Ungary 'ave got involved, an' 'ave declared war on . . . eeh . . ." He scratched his wiry curls with an oil-stained finger, for neither he nor his sons had as yet had their customary strip wash at the scullery sink. "Where were it? That's it" – his face lightened as though he had solved a vexing problem— "aye, Serbia, that's it."

Clearly perplexed, for what was all this foreign stuff to do with them, Mammy echoed the last word.

"Serbia?"

"That's it, lass, an' terday Germany declared war on Russia an' . . . well, I dunno why but Mr Broadbent reckons we'll not stop out of it."

"Never . . . eeh, never." Mammy's face had become as bleached a white as the tablecloth Molly had just spread on the table. "Tha' don't mean . . . us . . . in a war?"

The two boys leaped to their feet. Their seventeen-year-old faces, only just seventeen and barely into the stage when they needed a shave, lit up like the new electric light which had been installed in most of the shops up town. Their bright blue eyes, a replica of those in their mother's face, were alive with intoxication for, like all youngsters, they were overjoyed to be presented with anything that smacked of escape from routine, from the ordinariness of day-to-day living and marching off to fight a war seemed to them exactly to fit the bill. They had no idea what it was all about and quite frankly didn't really care. They had a decent job each, a good home, their football, a bit of "sparking" as they grew into manhood with some of the pretty girls at the mill, all of which had been most satisfactory a few moments ago. But what better way to spend the next few months, or however long it took, than wearing a dashing uniform and firing off a gun at the enemy? What enemy? They didn't know, only that he'd better not tangle with Liam and Patrick O'Dowd who were well known for their courage and prowess on the football field. They couldn't wait, they really couldn't and indeed Liam was already reaching out again for his clogs.

"Sit down, the pair o' thi'," their daddy thundered and Molly felt her heart leap painfully in her chest with the extraordinary strangeness of it. Daddy *never* shouted. He had no need to. They all loved him and respected him too much, believing utterly that whatever words came out of his mouth were gospel; would be right and honest and fair. It made the circumstances even more frightening. The boys sat down and Molly placed Daddy's slippers carefully in front of the fire, pushing aside the protesting cat who always lay where the heat was fiercest. Mammy and Daddy still had their arms about one another, Mammy's face pressed into Daddy's chest and all Molly could hear was her muffled voice which seemed to be begging Daddy to promise her something.

The weekend passed by peacefully enough. They all did what they usually did. Liam and Patrick, ordered by Mammy since it was summer and no football, went off to get their clogs repaired and, while they were at it, Mammy said, just as though it would return things to exactly what they had always been, they'd best get themselves measured for a new pair each. Daddy decided he'd set about that there latch on the lavvy door. The damn thing had a habit of swinging open just when you'd got yourself comfortably settled with your trousers round your ankles and the *Oldham Standard* opened at the first page. Molly and Mammy went up town as usual. It would be Bank Holiday Monday the day after tomorrow and they thought, if the weather was nice, they might take a picnic up on the edge of the moor. To Besom Hill, happen, or even Badger's Edge.

It was on Tuesday as Molly and Betty were trudging from

school up Shaw Road in the direction of home that they heard the newsboy, the one on the corner of Shaw Road and Edge Lane Road, shouting in a high-pitched voice of intense excitement, totally different to his usual bored unconcern.

"British ultimatum to Germany – war at midnight."

They looked at one another in bewilderment, the two little girls, not knowing what to think really, nor how to react. Should they be pleased? Was it what everyone had been talking about for the last four days? Would it affect them at all? Indeed, who were they to fight? On the stroke of midnight were all the English soldiers to be confronted with the enemy soldiers, whoever they might be, since Molly and Betty were not really sure. So many countries had been mentioned, France, Germany and . . . and . . . well, a lot of others. How could they begin the war when their soldiers and the soldiers of the countries they were to fight were so far apart? It was a bit of a puzzle, they decided and so important-sounding. If only they knew what they were supposed to do.

They went home and got out their whips and tops!

Mammy cried the next day when war was declared, tears of fear and worry, of grief and sorrow for what was surely ahead for women with sons. Later in the day, just as Mammy was beginning to worry, for Daddy and the boys were late home for their tea, the sound of the latch on the front door brought her sharply to her feet. It was as though, in her mother's heart, she knew what was to happen.

They tried to be composed, to act like men and not the boys they still were. They tried hard to keep the excited anticipation out of their glittering blue eyes and their young men's voices. They tried hard to be casual, to be manly as though this was something men did but when their mammy began to cry and shake, her hand to her mouth, they fell apart as children will. They loved their mammy and yet they resented her tears, her terror, for it seemed to them it took the bright gallantry out of what they had just done. They were to set off to fight the enemy who were threatening women like Mammy and children like their Molly but somehow at the sight of Mammy's tears they changed back from the soldiers they believed they now were to boys again.

Putting their arms awkwardly about her, with no word yet spoken, they patted her and shushed her and when Daddy came in, his face grey and old somehow, though he was no more than thirty-seven, that was how he found them.

"So," he said wearily, "tha've bin an' done it then?" He sat down heavily in his chair before the fire. Molly knelt at his feet as she always did, undoing the buckles, easing his clogs and socks from his oil-soaked feet, rising again to fetch the bowl of warm water in which he soaked them, but he took her hand, stopping her. Pulling her down on his knee he held her fiercely in his arms so that she could smell the familiar smell of him, of oil and tobacco, of male sweat and a faint lingering waft of the carbolic soap with which he had washed that morning. He kissed her cheek, his lips warm and loving, closing his eyes as he wrapped her in his arms as though to show his relief that at least this one was safe.

"I knew where tha'd gone when I saw tha' mules standin' idle. Aye, and not just yours neither. A score o' lads from our room . . . an' from 'em all. Cardin' an' rovin' rooms an' . . . I ran all't bloody way ter't recruitment office but I were too late. Tha'd already signed on. I never saw such queues. Madness. Bloody madness." He paused and in the silence the cat stretched and made a small mewing sound in the back of its throat. "I could stop thi', tha' knows, don't tha?" His voice was without expression. "Tha're nobbut seventeen an' age fer enlistment's nineteen but I know if I did tha'd only try somewhere else. That's so, in't it, lads?"

They both nodded, looking first at one another then apologetically at their mother. She was doing her best to control herself, for even in her distraught state she knew she was gaining nothing, only causing herself and her family, particularly her husband, more distress. They'd have to go sometime. They all would. Go where? her frantic mind asked. She didn't know. Wherever young soldiers went who were to fight. Oh, Holy Mother, watch over them, all the sons who are breaking their mothers' hearts this day.

Seamus O'Dowd studied his two handsome boys. Standing up, he carefully placed his daughter on her feet. Moving round the table he gently led his wife, still silently weeping, to the chair from which he had just risen. He stroked her dark hair and kissed her tenderly, murmuring against her cheek while their children watched.

"There, there, darlin'. Hush now, fer tha'll only upset them all. 'Tis done now, an' can't be undone. They'll come to no 'arm fer I'll . . . well, they'll not send 'em where there's . . ." He smoothed over the trip of his own tongue, searching about in his mind for something to comfort her. "They're sayin' t'will all be over by Christmas, Róisín, so it will, an' then we . . . they'll be 'ome with thi'. Now, don't be frettin', Rosie, darlin'. See," turning to Molly, "mekk tha' mammy a nice cup o' tea, will tha', Angel, an' you two, get them clogs off an' get thissen washed."

They had all gone to bed, Róisín O'Dowd begging her husband not to be too long, her eyes telling him she needed his strong and comforting arms about her. Seamus sat before the banked-up fire, his mind dwelling on the happenings of the day. Thousands upon thousands of young men were enlisting, so it was said, many of them totally unfit for military life but accepted just the same, for men were wanted at once. Medical officers who were to examine them were overwhelmed by the sheer numbers of men joining up on a great wave of patriotism. The doctors, though the public did not know of it then, had no idea how to measure medical fitness for military service. Examinations were cursory and incomplete and men who had no business being in it were pronounced fit to put on the King's uniform.

Seamus had had a word with old Mr Broadbent a day or so ago when he could see the way things were going, a conversation he had not shared with Róisín since he had not then really believed it would come to it. Mr Broadbent had told him it was his opinion that men in the textile areas would be slow to enlist since the livelihood of their families, which depended on both their own and their wives' wages, would be seriously threatened should they go. Trade had dropped off this last year, Mr Broadbent admitted, due to the international situation and men and women had been laid off in the temporarily depressed textile trade and the men in these areas would be bound to ask how their families would manage if they joined the army. He himself was prepared to help, providing allowances for the dependants of soldiers and sailors, those who had worked for him, and Seamus had his firm promise that when the war was over any member of his family who fought in it, giving him a sad look, would find their jobs waiting for them on their return. Mr Broadbent found himself puzzled, he confessed to Seamus, and somewhat annoyed as though how anyone could have set half the world to fighting without consulting Lancashire cotton was beyond him, but there it was. He knew that the sons of operatives and of cotton men would give their services willingly, and not just sons, again casting a knowing look at Seamus O'Dowd. Cotton wouldn't suffer, Mr Broadbent confided, for once the war got going the demand for it would stiffen considerably. Seamus must have no concerns on that score. None at all. Cotton, and the cotton trade, would always be there.

But what of his sons? Seamus brooded as he leaned back in his chair and reached for his pipe. He had provided for and protected them all their young lives. They had wanted for nothing he could give them. They'd not lived a life of privilege, as Mr Broadbent's three sons had, but they'd never gone hungry or had no clogs to their feet or a warm jacket to put on their back. Now they were to leave the protection and security and love he and their mammy had given them for over seventeen years, boys still with no knowledge of anything beyond the boundaries of Oldham and how would they fare? Aye, boys still but soon to become men and until they did could he leave them to fend for themselves? The war might be won by Christmas, as they were saying, but already today the German army had entered Belgium, and, so it had been rumoured at the mill, the British Expeditionary Force was to be sent to France within the next day or so.

No, he'd done right. He couldn't let his lads go alone and after what Mr Broadbent had said about allowances for the dependants of serving men he'd no worries on that score. He himself was seven years over the upper age limit for enlisting and he supposed he should feel flattered that the recruitment chap, though he gave him a strange look, hadn't argued. Glad to get anyone, he supposed, and they'd not turn big, strong blokes like himself and his sons away, would they? They were all three twelve inches above the required height of five feet three inches and ten inches more round the chest than was asked for. And he'd been told that, being a married man, he'd draw a separation allowance for Róisín and Molly so, with what Mr Broadbent had promised, his wife and daughter would not want.

Standing up, stretching, knocking out his pipe on the bars of the grate, Seamus O'Dowd sighed, then made his way upstairs to break the news to his wife that not only had her sons enlisted today, but her husband as well.

It was just as though all the protagonists, having drawn swords, had decided to sheath them again and go home, Aunty Flo said to Mammy, though not in those exact words since Aunty Flo would not have been easy with such a word as protagonist. As the days went by and nothing much happened, Mammy and Aunty Flo, and many of the women in the Lancashire cotton towns, began to relax, for all their menfolk seemed to do, lacking uniforms and weapons, was to march up and down the football field with broom handles.

When, halfway through August, Seamus, Liam and Patrick O'Dowd, and each of Aunty Flo's sons as well, received an official OHMS envelope inside which was a railway warrant and a letter ordering them to report to the railway station the next day, it came as a great shock.

Right at the last minute Róisín O'Dowd dug her heels in.

"No, I'll not 'ave it," she said firmly. "Tha' can't go, none o' thi'. I've kept me mouth shut an' me thoughts ter messen, so I 'ave, but I'll not 'ave it," just as though they were three schoolboys who must be stopped for their own good from going off on some dangerous jaunt.

It did no good, of course, as she knew it wouldn't. Seamus had explained to her why he must go and she had agreed that the lads needed him to guide and protect them. She was to stay at home and protect their daughter as he was to protect their sons but it didn't make it any easier now that the time had come to part.

"I'm comin' ter see thi' off then, Seamus. Tha' can't stop me," and of course he didn't try. Molly went with them, the five of them sitting poker-faced on the tram down Shaw Road, the three small suitcases belonging to Daddy, Liam and Patrick, which were all they were allowed to take, on the floor between their feet. Mammy and Daddy held hands but Molly could see Liam and Patrick were fairly crackling with excitement which they did their best to hide.

The railway station was crowded with young men and their mothers and fathers who had come to see them off, all jostling about in great confusion, the soldiers doing their best to deal with weeping women and at the same time listen to and obey the red-faced, khaki-clad soldier with stripes on his arm who was trying to get them on the train. It was pandemonium, for women like Mammy were beginning to panic as the truth of it, the certainty of it, was at last made clear to them.

Children wailed and grizzled, uncomprehending, caught up in the emotional crowd, and when at last it was her turn to be hugged and kissed by Daddy and Liam and Patrick, Molly felt quite numb, without any sort of feeling and certainly no tears. She just couldn't believe it. She knew it was happening, her brain told her so, but her heart, which seemed to have become affected with the pain of it, just could not contemplate a life without Daddy in it. Daddy and Liam and Patrick, around whom, she well knew, the house and their life in it revolved. What would Mammy do without the three men to cook and clean and mend for? She still had Molly, of course, but how could one small girl make up for three demanding men? How could she fill the enormous hole her daddy and brothers were to leave behind?

It was then, as Daddy climbed after Liam and Patrick into the jammed carriage of the train, that she saw him. He was further along the platform where the first-class compartments were, with two other young gentlemen, all three in the immaculate uniform Molly instantly recognised as that of an officer. They were so smart, so handsome, all three of them, restlessly pacing, their young men's bodies straining to be away, to have this over. They were straight and lean, warriors going into battle, their peaked caps jaunty on their bright, fair curls. Their uniforms fitted them perfectly. They wore knee-high boots polished to a gleaming chestnut brown and they all three carried a small swagger stick with which they impatiently tapped their own jodhpurred legs. With them was an older woman, very smartly dressed in a rich shade of blue. She was not weeping as the other women were but held her head high as though proud to be sending her sons off to war and seeing no reason to cry over it. Beside her was the figure of a rather bent, white-haired gentleman who, nevertheless, had an air of authority about him and they were all five smiling brightly as the doors of the train slammed shut.

For a second the young officer looked over the heads of the elderly lady and gentleman, his face framed in the open carriage window. He had removed his peaked cap to place a second kiss on the cheek of the woman and when he had done so he stepped back to allow his two companions to do the same and his brown eyes met the smoky blue of Molly O'Dowd's.

"Good luck, O'Dowd," Molly heard the elderly gentleman call out as he saw Daddy's face in the carriage window.

Daddy turned, startled, then he nodded politely.

"Thank yer, sir . . . an' ter thy lads an' all."

As Molly's intent gaze held his, Tim Broadbent smiled, a brilliant smile of anticipation and excitement, just like the ones on the faces of Liam and Patrick and all the other young men who were setting off on the almost holy quest of defending their country. His brothers had moved back into the carriage and for a still moment Molly O'Dowd and Tim Broadbent were alone in a deep pool of silence. His smile became gentle and his lips moved.

"Goodbye, Molly," they said and it was then she began to weep.

4

The battalion, the "Pals" battalion of the First Lancashire Fusiliers, formed in Oldham on the day war was declared and in which Daddy, Liam and Patrick had enlisted, left for France at the end of September. The Broadbent boys went with it.

Aunty Flo came round a lot. Mammy was lonely, Aunty Flo could see that, she said, and wasn't she, Aunty Flo, a woman who knew all about loneliness? Since Uncle Fergus had been killed so tragically under the wheels of a tramcar on its way to the depot at Hollinswood, hadn't she suffered more than her share? Of course, she still had Kathleen, as Róisín had Mary Angelina.

Aunty Flo could not be prevailed upon to call her niece by the name of Molly and could only doubt the wisdom of her dead husband's brother and his wife in allowing the child, sniffing in Molly's direction and narrowing her lips, to dictate to them as she did. Children should be curbed of rebellious tendencies, as her Kathleen, Michael, Dermot and Eamon had been curbed, and Uncle Fergus too, Molly thought derisively, before he went and got himself chopped into mincemeat under the tramcar. Michael, Dermot and Eamon O'Dowd had all departed their mammy's house in Briscoe Street at the earliest opportunity, marching away in the same Pals battalion as Daddy, Liam and Patrick, and, as soon as Tommy O'Brien, another enlisted man in the First Lancashire Fusiliers could get a bit of leave and he and Kathleen could be married, she was to be off too. They had their eye on a house which was to rent in Earnshaw Street. Kathleen would stay on at the mill and Aunty Flo would be lonelier than ever and serve her right, the bloody miserable old cow, Molly said to herself, or to Betty.

Molly had only just learned the satisfaction of uttering the very rude word "bloody" and whenever she and Betty were out of their mammys' hearing they said it constantly, savouring its badness and not even considering the sin of it which they should confess to Father O'Toole.

"When this bloody war's over," was the most endlessly used, which was where they had heard it, for it was on everyone's lips.

"It'll be over by bloody Christmas," was another and so the word was for ever on Molly and Betty's tongues.

"Me bloody top needs chalkin' . . ."

"Mind them bloody marbles, Alfie Bagshaw . . ."

"I've ter go a bloody message . . ."

"I can't play out till I've done't bloody winders . . ."

They had a letter from Daddy the second week after he and the boys left. He said he was writing for all three of them and Mammy had to smile, she said, since the idea of Liam and Patrick putting pen to paper was one she found amusing. Men of action were her sons, at home on the football field and certainly not sitting down to write a letter, even to their mammy. Just the same, when she answered Daddy's letter she begged him to get them to drop her a line. Even a postcard would do.

Daddy said they had arrived at their destination, wherever that was, he didn't say, where a party of soldiers had met the recruits, yes, that was him and the lads, he said, and they were marched for miles, up a long valley in the pitch dark. They didn't know where they were going but ended up in a place with hundreds of small tents and one great big one where they were given bread and herrings and an enamel cup of tea which was so black and strong it was a wonder it didn't tarnish the spoon. There were twelve men put in each small tent which was a bit of a squash when you remembered how big he and the lads were. They lay on blankets on the ground but Mammy wasn't to worry because it was a warm, dry night and they were all together. The next morning some chap blew a bugle and they were told by a sergeant to "fall in" and Liam had laughed and asked what they were to fall into and the sergeant didn't think it was a bit funny. Their Liam'd have to learn to watch that mouth of his. Not that he'd meant to be rude but Mammy knew what a joker he was.

The next letter spoke less of the conditions and the food,

which was what Mammy was dying to hear about, going into great detail about firing rounds and rifle ranges and uniforms in which they all looked a treat but, Mammy asked Molly indignantly, when were they going to get some leave? She wasn't interested in guns, she said to Aunty Flo and what had Michael and Eamon and Dermot had to say about it all? Were their beds comfy and their socks dry when they put them on and what were they eating? Patrick didn't like herrings. Would Aunty Flo ask one of hers, for she could get no sense out of Seamus at all.

There was a big battle at a place called Mons. Mons was in France, that country now called simply "the front", so that was all right, Mammy said, concerned only with *her* men who were stationed somewhere in England. It was not until Aunty Flo with Aunty Maggie in tow, who was married to Mammy's brother, came racing up the street like two out-of-breath racehorses that, at last, the true picture of how it was to be was finally brought home to them.

The street was crowded. The rag and bone man was doing his best to lead his horse and cart through the maze of skipping girls, and to avoid boys who were kicking their footballs, no more than pigs' bladders begged from Bloomers Slaughterhouse on Manchester Street. He would exchange a rubbing stone for a bundle of old rags and sometimes he gave away a balloon if the "rags" were presentable enough to be used again.

Two hawkers, one of them playing a penny whistle, were working their way up one side of Sidney Street and down the other and Aunty Flo was seen to elbow one aside with great irritation as she made her way towards the door of number twenty-two.

Molly and Betty and half a dozen other girls were skipping, the rope borrowed from Cissie Thompson's mam, who was obliging about such things. It was "turned" by Cissie and her younger sister, Elsie.

> All in together girls,
> Very fine weather, girls,
> When I count twenty this rope must be empty,
> Five, ten, fifteen, twenty . . .

At each turn of the rope a girl would leap out of its twirling clutches, only to jump in again when the chanting voice of the caller allowed her to.

Molly was so astonished at the sight of Aunty Flo and Aunty Maggie panting up the street, shooing out of their path children playing hopscotch and peggy, she missed the beat and twirl of the rope and, to howls of derision, was out. By the strict rule of the game she must now take a turn on the end of the rope, but shoving aside Cissie Thompson, ignoring her indignant, "Aye up, Molly O'Dowd," Molly stood stock still.

"It's me Aunty Flo an' me Aunty Maggie," she said, unnecessarily, for didn't the whole of the street know intimately the relationships of every family in every house in it. It was like one big extended family and to keep anything secret, whether it be serious or trivial, was like asking the sun to hide behind a cloud when there was none in the sky.

"What's up, d'yer think?" Betty asked, her voice tinged with the morbid fascination caused by someone else's drama.

"Dunno."

"Shall tha' go an' see?"

"Aye, 'appen I'd better."

It was a Monday, wash day and because for the best part of it the rain had slanted from low, saturated clouds, the kitchen was hung about with lines on which half-dried washing was draped. Mammy's and Molly's undergarments, stockings, blouses, towels, tea-towels, the linen from two beds and indeed anything Mammy could lay her hands on to fill her "dolly-tub", since she felt the absence of her menfolk's shirts quite dreadfully. The kitchen was steamy and felt damp, despite the good fire banked and glowing in the grate.

They all three had their hankies to their faces when Molly stepped hesitantly into the kitchen. They hadn't heard her come in and for a few seconds she was devastated by the cold feeling of sorrow which pervaded the room. Mammy's shoulders were shaking, her hand smoothing the pale ginger fur of the cat who purred on her lap. Aunty Maggie rocked back and forth in the age-old movement of grieving woman and even Aunty Flo's firm mouth was trembling with some deep-felt sadness.

"Mammy . . ." Her daughter's frightened piping brought Róisín O'Dowd to her senses and at once she briskly dried her eyes, sniffing and sighing all at the same time. She threw the cat to the floor, ignoring its plaintive protestations and gave Aunty Flo and Aunty Maggie a warning look. One of her looks which Daddy said would stop a charging elephant in its tracks and it certainly pulled Aunty Maggie and Aunty Flo together.

"What's up, Mammy? It's not . . . not . . . Daddy?"

Immediately Mammy smiled, a bit of a watery smile but enough to reassure her daughter. She drew Molly on to her lap, ignoring Aunty Flo's disapproving look which said surely Mary Angelina was too big for such things.

"No, darlin', oh, no, thank the Blessed Virgin." They all crossed themselves automatically. "No, it's . . . well, tha'll not remember Aunty Maggie's sister, her what lives in Manchester?"

Molly didn't but she nodded her head anyway.

"Well, 'er Benjie's bin . . ." Mammy hesitated.

"What, Mammy?"

"Eeh, it's that sad I can 'ardly . . ." Róisín O'Dowd bent her head to Molly's, fresh tears leaking from her eyes.

Aunty Flo tutted impatiently. "'E's only gone an' got 'imself killed, that's what." She made it sound as if he'd done it to spite them all and that if he'd been more careful he could have avoided the whole thing. Nevertheless there was a compassionate glow in her eyes.

"Where were it, Aunty Flo? Were it a street accident, like . . .?"

Molly had been about to say like Uncle Fergus but stopped herself in time since she didn't want to upset Aunty Flo further.

"No, tha' balm-cake. 'E were at front, weren't 'e? 'E were a regular."

"What's that?"

"I'll tell thi' if tha'll give me a chance."

"There's no need ter be 'ard on't child, Flo," Aunty Maggie said reproachfully. "She's not ter know."

"Well, she will keep chippin' in." Aunty Flo did not care for children who "chipped in".

"Sorry, Aunty Flo."

"I should think so."

"What Aunty Flo's tryin' ter say," Aunty Maggie interrupted impatiently, "is that our Benjie were a regular soldier. Bein' in th'army were 'is job. 'E went over ter France with BEF. Dost tha' know what that is?"

She was not awfully sure what it was but Molly had certainly heard of it, for hadn't the *Oldham Standard* been full of it since the British Expeditionary Force had sailed from Southampton to France in August? Already there were reports of heavy casualties and lists of men killed or wounded in the newspaper. Little boys up and down the country were bewitched by it all, following this regiment or that's progress, reciting to one another what they had heard their daddies say at the breakfast table, those daddies who had not yet "got in on it".

"Well, our Benjie's bin killed an' I've ter get over to our Freda's."

"I'm that sorry, Aunty Maggie," and Molly was, for she had a warm heart and a sympathetic one.

"Aye, I know, love. Eeh ..." She sighed on a long, shuddering breath for her Bill who was married with a two-year-old son and another on the way and who had enlisted, like all the other daft buggers, on the first day. "I can't believe it. 'E were a grand lad, only twenty an' our Freda'll be out of 'er mind. 'E were 'er only boy an' all. Anyroad, what I wanted ter know" – turning to the other two women – "is will the pair o' thi' keep an eye on our Chrissie while I'm gone? Alf's a scone'ead, soft as clarts wi' 'er an' she'll be up ter all sorts o' tricks wi'out me ter watch 'er. Yer know what they're like at sixteen."

No, Aunty Flo's expression said, she didn't. Her Kathleen had been brought up properly and at sixteen had obeyed her mammy and daddy – well, her mammy – without so much as a murmur. Some folk made a rod for their own back the way they fetched their kids up, and Maggie Todd should know better.

Benjie Atkinson, Aunty Maggie's sister's boy, was the first one that they knew to get killed. Well, Mammy knew him, she said. She remembered him at the wedding when Bill, Maggie's boy, had married Jane Broadwood from Waterloo Street, nearly three years ago now and Benjie an imp of a lad then, just the age of Róisín's two sons now. She went all cold when she thought of it and when Aunty Flo and Aunty Maggie had gone flung on her shawl and hurried down to St Saviours to light a candle for Benjie and to say a prayer for Seamus, Liam and Patrick. She went every day to mass, sometimes persuading Molly to go with her but Molly told her that they all said prayers at school for the soldiers and sailors, the brothers and fathers of the children in her class. Father O'Toole was most insistent that now, more than ever, they must pray and pray and pray again to the Blessed Mother and Her Son to keep them all safe.

Molly was a logical child and though she wouldn't breathe a word of it to Mammy, she did wonder why so many of their soldiers kept on getting killed and wounded, whole regiments annihilated, it said, and Molly knew what that meant since she looked it up in Daddy's dictionary and if that was so, were all those who had gone not of the true faith? It didn't make sense, did it, so what was the use of all the thousands of prayers which rose up to heaven, hour after hour and day after day? Nevertheless she still said them, just in case.

She missed her daddy. It was a perpetual, aching sadness inside her, especially on a Sunday when she and Mammy came out of church. This had once been the high spot of the week, this moment when she and Daddy went off hand in hand towards one of their special places. Somehow she hadn't the heart to go to Alexandra Park, even when Mammy offered to go with her and it wasn't the same drifting round the Art Gallery looking at all the lovely works of art displayed there when there was no Daddy to beg her to look at this or get a scen of that and had she ever seen such a lovely colour as that there goblet in the glass case. She and Mammy still went up town on a Saturday afternoon, more from habit really, for it wasn't like the old days when they knew Daddy would be waiting for them at home to tell them all about what the "ref" had done or said and the goal that was offside and the one the goalie shouldn't have let in, but did.

She did still go occasionally to one place and that was to see the house. She could somehow feel her daddy close by when she stood at the gates, almost see him in his good striped suit and the bowler hat he wore only for church.

By, that's a grand sight, Angel, he would say to her, as he had done a hundred times in the past. Just clap yer eyes on them swans, he would add. Did yer ever see such lovely creatures? And see the way the sunlight comes through them leaves. Now what colour would yer say it was? Amber, d'yer think, like them gemstones we saw at the Art Gallery? And yer can't see the grass fer leaves, all rosy and pink and gold and if the old chap catches them gardeners they'd get what for. Holy Mother, it's that lovely it fair makes yer shiver, don't it, darlin'?

And now, though she was all alone but for a goldfinch which, unafraid of her still figure, was feeding on some thistle seed in the ditch beside the gate, she spoke to Daddy, agreeing with him that it was the loveliest place in the world. She told him about the gardeners, at least the younger ones who had gone away to war and those who were left were old and could barely find time to rake up the leaves there was so much to do. A good part of the glorious gardens were to be sacrificed to the growing of potatoes and cabbages, she had heard, since food would be scarce, but it made no difference to the house, the house which her daddy loved. It in no way detracted from its timeless beauty. The leaves which carpeted the ground and drifted in vivid colours of flame and gold across the drive did not mar the loveliness of what lay beyond the gates. Where before there had been faultless perfection, now there was a delightfully carefree look about it. Not orderless or untidy but a charming disarray as though at any moment a horde of rowdy children would come racing round the corner of the house, shouting their high spirits and kicking at the piles of leaves as they ran. The house would not mind the barely perceptible air of neglect for it was the kind of house which would enfold and soothe and cherish its occupants, just as Molly's own kitchen at home and the benediction of the Church enfolded and soothed and cherished.

She wrote to Daddy to tell him about the house and about the blackberries she had gathered for Mammy to make a pie. The hedges were full of them, she told him, just as he had predicted earlier in the year, black and luscious and smelling of sunshine and she wished she could send him some. She did her best writing which Sister Ursula said was vastly improving. Well, it would, wouldn't it, for she wrote to Daddy nearly every day. She described to him the glorious autumn sunset she had seen over the waters of the mill race to the side of the house, which had been as placid as a bucket of water. Peach, it had been, edged with gold, turning to a vivid rosy pink as the sun went down. She had that day caught a glimpse of the lower slopes of the moorland at the back of the house, covered with gorse and blossom, and she wrote it all down for him because, wherever he was, her daddy would want to know about such blessed things.

When, in October, there was talk of a big battle at a place called Ypres, which no one knew how to pronounce, she and Mammy went to mass to pray that Daddy and Liam and Patrick and indeed all the men they knew personally were not in it. It was an important battle Molly heard Uncle Alf say. Uncle Alf was too old at forty-two to fight but he followed the war news carefully and it was thanks to him they knew what was happening. When, at the end of a month of bitter fighting, the British soldiers won and the Germans gave up, Uncle Alf was greatly relieved, he said, though Molly was not sure why. She did her best to understand and not to dwell too much on the anxiety which plagued her and which was that somebody had to be in it and if, instead of Daddy and Liam and Patrick, others were being killed and wounded . . . well, the thought perplexed her, for that meant other families, who must also be praying for the safety of their loved ones, were not having their prayers answered.

Their Christmas, though they shared it with Aunty Flo, Uncle Alf and Aunty Maggie, with Kathleen and Chrissie and Elspeth, who was Aunty Maggie's eldest girl, was just not the same. Not without Daddy and Liam and Patrick. They had heard from them, of course, and Mammy was enormously relieved to read that they were resting in billets behind the line, whatever that meant. All she was thankful for was that they were not in the fighting and surely that was all that mattered.

Just before Christmas some enemy ships had bombarded the east coast, killing civilians in Hartlepool and Scarborough and Whitby but best not tell Daddy that, Mammy said, since he'd only worry. Tell them about Christmas Day in Aunty Maggie's tiny house when eleven of them had squashed round Aunty Maggie's parlour table to eat Christmas dinner and Aunty Maggie's three grandchildren had been forced to sit on upturned orange crates, kept for such an occasion in the washhouse. They had all collected their quarterly dividend the week before, their "divi" which was calculated on the value of the purchases they had made at the Co-op during the quarter and, clubbing together, they had managed a good spread. Aunty Maggie's table had groaned with it and as Uncle Alf had remarked, as he sharpened the carving knife on the steel ready to cut into the splendid turkey it was a feast they'd not be ashamed to invite their Majesties to sit down to. The only sadness was the missing faces, he went on, getting ready to be maudlin about Seamus and Liam and Patrick, about his own son, Bill, about Elspeth's husband, Joe, about Michael and Dermot and Eamon, who were all "at the front" or perhaps, God forbid, at Ypres. Aunty Maggie told him sharply to hold his tongue and get on with the carving or he'd have them all in tears.

Winter dragged on and Mammy fretted dreadfully. She didn't like Seamus's letters at all. She was convinced he was holding something back from her, she told Aunty Maggie and Aunty Flo. Molly was under the table, it being a wet day, playing house with her dolls and the patient ginger cat who was being dressed in a bonnet. The table had a big red plush cloth which was taken off for meals but when it was on it touched the floor. It was dark and airless but when Molly was under there she often heard gossip she wasn't supposed to hear, and barely understood. Who was getting married and about time too. How Nancy O'Leary had got her weekly black eye and, though it wasn't entirely unexpected, Aunty Flo said tartly, "another" on the way. Had Róisín seen Madge Holmes's lass in the baby shop up town? It was anybody's guess what she was doing there and her married less than a month. Buying a baby, Molly presumed, struggling with the ginger cat and keeping out of the way of Aunty Flo's well-polished clogs.

"What's up with his letters?" Aunty Flo asked Mammy.

Well, it seemed that at first they'd been cheerful and full of optimism, even though the war showed no sign of being over by Christmas as had been forecast, but lately they had become . . . well, they were . . .

"What?" Aunty Flo wanted to know, more than a little impatient with her sister-in-law. Her Michael and Dermot and Eamon, like Liam and Patrick, were not much for letter-writing and she depended on what Daddy wrote to Mammy to let her know how things were over there.

"Sure an' I don't know, Flo. It's just summat . . . missin'. Tha' remember what a wag 'e were. Did tha' ever know him when 'e weren't 'avin' a laugh? Saw summat comical in't daftest things, so 'e did, and though 'e ses they're fine, all three of 'em, an' thank the Holy Mother they're still together, there's summat . . . not there."

They had received the parcels Mammy sent and were glad of the warmly knitted socks and scarves and the apricot jam had gone down a treat, Seamus had told her. But Róisín

O'Dowd's instincts were not playing her false. Her husband *was* keeping something back. He did not tell her of the winter he and their two sons, along with thousands of others, had spent in the trenches. The sardines had been very tasty, he wrote, lovely on a slice of bread, and the smell of the soap was grand, not mentioning the stinking sea of mud in which the bodies of soldiers rotted and with which he and their lads were surrounded. The Christmas pudding, bought from the Co-op, had been shared with those in his billet who had not received one, neglecting to tell her that his billet was nothing more than a shelf cut out of the trench wall. He did not trouble her with tales of gas and bullets and the constant hell of the artillery bombardment – their own – which drove men mad and wiped out scores of British soldiers, one of them Kathleen O'Dowd's Tommy, whose mother at this very minute was staring with paralysed horror at the telegram in the hand of the remorseful delivery boy.

"What d'yer mean, not there?" Aunty Flo's down-to-earth nature could not comprehend Róisín O'Dowd's sometimes bewildering attitude where her family were concerned. "Nay, Rosie O'Dowd, tha're talkin' daft, lass. 'E does write ter thi', which can't be said o' many of 'em, my lot included." Aunty Flo sniffed ungraciously but somehow Molly could tell she was upset and worried about the absence of frequent word from her lads. They sent postcards now and again and she'd been made up with them and when she received a letter from Eamon she could barely contain herself as she read it out to them, even if it was so "beggared about with" by the censor she could hardly make head nor tail of it.

The news of Tommy O'Brien's death reached them that evening. It was Aunty Maggie who came to tell them of it, saying she was just on her way to St Saviours to light a candle for the poor lad's soul and would Molly and Mammy like to come. Aunty Flo, of course, was busy with their Kathleen who was in a bad way and could not be left alone. Aye, Aunty Maggie said, shaking her head sadly, it were a sad day and Kathleen was taking it hard. She was twenty-three was Kathleen and with all the young unmarried men of Oldham, and indeed elsewhere, disappearing into the great war machine, her chances to be wed seemed to be disappearing as well.

April came in on a very still, grey day. Molly had suffered a

heavy cold and Mammy had kept her home from school, glad
of her company, for the house was empty without Seamus
and the lads. Molly, who would be nine the following week,
was aware that Mammy was lonely and hadn't enough to
do since she frequently complained about it. Mammy was
thinking of going back to work in the mill, she told Aunty Flo
when she came to tea on Sunday, which was the first Molly
had heard about it. Gradually, as the men enlisted, women
were becoming accepted as substitutes, working not only as
ambulance drivers and on munitions but in banks and offices
and even as blacksmiths, paper-hangers and grave-diggers,
though Mammy and Aunty Flo were not at all sure they
agreed with these last. Both Róisín and Flo O'Dowd had
worked at Broadbents Mill before they were married. They
had been ring spinners and word had got round that with
conscription being talked about, though how true that was
no one knew, many of the women would be welcomed back
with open arms. Lancashire was the biggest supplier of cotton
and cotton goods in the world. It was the world's cotton shop.
They were cotton proud and cotton saturated and the call on
them and their goods would be enormous. Mr Broadbent had
told Seamus so just before he went to the front and if she,
Róisín O'Dowd, could do anything to shorten the bloody war
by taking a man's place in the mill then by all that was holy
she meant to do it.

"What about tha' Molly?" Aunty Flo wanted to know.

"What about our Molly?" Róisín asked, frowning.

Molly, who was in her favourite hideaway under the table
since her cold prevented her from playing out, pricked up her
ears. They were talking about her, having, it seemed, forgotten
her presence. She had barely registered what her mammy and
her Aunty Flo were talking about. She had heard in a vague
sort of way about Daddy and the boys and Mammy's worry
over them but that was nothing new. Soon, surely they would
all come marching home again and everything would be as it
had been before the war began. To be honest, Molly was a bit
sick of the war and she'd said so to Betty only the other day.
It was eight months now since Daddy went, leaving Molly to
her own devices every Sunday morning and now, from what
Mammy and Aunty Flo were saying, it seemed Mammy was
to go somewhere as well.

"'Oo's gonner look after 'er while tha's on tha' frame? Tha' can't leave a lass of eight ter fend fer 'erssen. She'll be up ter all sorts if she's left ter run wild in't streets."

"Give over, Flo. Our Molly'll be fine, so she will. I'll mekk sure o' that. Anyway, she's nine next week an' sensible. I trust 'er. If I'm workin' she can let herself in an' see ter things fer me."

Molly smirked and puffed out her chest and, though it was hard to do under the confines of the table, she lifted her head with great pride. She liked the idea of being trusted with the front door key, of coming into the empty house and "seeing to things" as Mammy did. She could make a cheese and onion pie as good as her mammy and her bacon hot-pot was delicious. Daddy had said so. You put layers of sliced potatoes in an oven dish, sprinkling each layer with chopped onion, sage, salt and pepper. When the dish was full you put knobs of bacon fat, then rashers of fat bacon on top. Popped into the fire oven and left to cook for a couple of hours it would make a grand tea for Mammy to come home to. It would be Molly's contribution in the effort to get this bloody war over and her daddy and the boys home again and everything back to normal.

"Well, I dunno, Rosie O'Dowd." Aunty Flo sniffed disapprovingly, since in all her married life she'd not have dreamed of leaving their Kathleen alone in the house and their Kathleen was a sensible lass, not like Mary Angelina who was as wilful as a basket of kittens, in her opinion. "She's nobbut a little lass. 'Appen she could come ter me while tha' gets 'ome from t'mill," the tone of her voice saying Flo would soon knock her into shape.

Molly almost popped out from under the table, ready to protest hotly, for there was nothing worse she could think of than being forced to go to Aunty Flo's from school each day. It was in the opposite direction to the one she and Betty took and would mean she'd never get to play out in all the endlessly exciting games the lighter nights were bringing. They were planning on borrowing Cissie Thompson's mam's washing line after school and practising their skipping and how, she agonised, could she do that if she were forced to go to Aunty Flo's? Aunty Flo would save up all kinds of awful jobs for her since she did not believe in idle hands. The very thought was almost too much to bear.

She need not have worried. Mammy was most diplomatic

in her refusal of Aunty Flo's kind offer. There was nothing definite yet about her working at the mill, she told her, and besides, she had it on good authority that women with children were to be given the chance to work hours which suited them, so she and Molly would manage fine. Perhaps in the school holidays . . .?

Molly sighed with relief and resumed her game of house.

5

Molly had been to the Premier Picture Palace with Betty. It only cost a penny to get into the Saturday morning show and besides a couple of hours of Pearl White's adventures in *The Perils of Pauline* and the daring deeds of cowboy William S. Hart, all the children were given a toffee apple as they went in. Molly and Betty, sometimes with Cissie and Elsie, loved to go to the pictures and thought with the toffee apple thrown in this was really good value for money. You had to consider it when all you got was a halfpenny a week. So they could only go now and again, of course, which was a nuisance because that meant they would miss an episode of Pauline but their Saturday halfpenny must often be shared with other purchases. But it didn't matter what was on, *The Perils of Pauline*, or a cowboy film, they and the rest of the audience enjoyed every rowdy minute of it, shouting their heads off when the beautiful heroine was in danger as the villain sneaked up on her.

"Look out, 'e's be'ind yer," they'd all scream, standing up and jumping on the wooden forms which were the only seats available to those who had paid a penny.

It had been particularly thrilling today and though the usherette had come round in an attempt to quieten them, it was not until the house lights had been turned on and the film stopped that the heaving, fighting, yelling mass of children calmed down. There had been a deathly hush then for several minutes but as soon as the lights went down again and the chase on the screen resumed, they'd all started shouting at the tops of their voices.

Molly and Betty loved it, though they were often considerably frustrated when Pauline was left dangling over a hundred-foot drop or trapped in a burning building, or trussed up like a chicken on a railway line just as the train puffed into view and "continued next week" was flashed on the screen. Pandemonium broke loose then and had it not been for Molly's fighting spirit and Betty's gift for swearing, which was inordinately admired by the boys, they might have gone down in a welter of clogs and rough masculine handling. There were not many who dared tangle with Molly O'Dowd and Betty Spooner, for not only could they stand up for themselves, they both had brothers who were "at the front" which commanded immense respect among the young male population.

Sometimes, and one of the reasons they couldn't afford even a fortnightly visit to the Premier Picture Palace, she and Betty went swimming at the Central Swimming Baths in Union Street. It opened at seven o'clock on a Saturday morning and though they could barely speak as their teeth chattered with the cold, nor move for goose-pimples, most of the children spent all morning, or at least until the attendant finally chucked them out, in the "duck pond". It was here, helping one another in a sort of floundering, arms flailing, legs wildly kicking motion, Molly and Betty learned to swim. A grand building was the Central Swimming Baths, reminding the two girls of a church, they decided, with two arched doorways and steps leading up to them from the street, dozens of curved and decorated windows and a magnificent roof which soared away like that of a temple Molly had seen in a book about India. And all this to house a simple swimming bath!

They had turned the corner into Sidney Street that Saturday dinner-time thrilling all over again to the remembrance of Pauline's latest dilemma, telling one another, both at the same time, how they thought she would escape, since she certainly would escape, there was no doubt of that, when Molly saw the three soldiers ahead of them. They were walking slowly, heavy-footed, not marching jauntily as she had seen soldiers do on their way to the railway station. Young soldiers going to the front, heads up, arms swinging, whistling sometimes one of the songs they themselves had made popular. She had seen them wink at the girls, herself and Betty included, as they marched by, proud of themselves and longing to get there before it was all over.

The soldiers ahead of her were doing none of these things.

In fact, to Molly's surprise, they looked as though they had all three been dragged through a hedge backwards, spattered with bits of what seemed to be dried mud. They were walking in the same direction as her and Betty. They wore peaked caps and khaki overcoats even though it was June. They each had a kind of knapsack attached to their chest, from which a helmet hung, and a rifle slung on their shoulder. They appeared to have khaki-coloured bandages wrapped about their legs at the bottom of which were mud-encrusted boots. They were big men, broad-shouldered, but slumped as though they were in the last unendurable stages of exhaustion.

There were children playing out as there were always children playing out and though these were not the first soldiers they had seen, they were the first in their street. Most of the small houses had given up at least one son or father or brother, gone off to the glory of defending their country against the foe alongside their "pals" in Kitchener's army. Exactly what that meant none of these children knew and none of their daddies or brothers or husbands had been back since they left, except Freddie Whittaker's dad who'd had the misfortune to go down with a bout of pneumonia just after Christmas and had come home from the hospital in a blue uniform. He'd never gone back and Aunty Flo, who seemed to know everyone's business, said he shouldn't have gone in the first place, not with that chest of his!

The children all stopped what they were doing to stare. A milkman with a rattling float pulled by a thin and dusty horse was on his second delivery of the day. There were two big milk churns on the back of the float and, as he turned to watch the soldiers go by, Mrs Kenny from number eleven came out with a jug in her hand.

"A pint, please, Wilf," she said, then following the direction of Wilf's stare turned to watch as, approaching the O'Dowd door, the three soldiers, as one, miraculously lifted their heads, straightened their backs and squared their shoulders.

"It's me daddy." Molly felt her heart leap gladly inside her chest and with a strangled shout of joy she began to run. Like a bird will fly, Molly O'Dowd ran, her feet scarcely touching the flagged pavement. Her dark, curling hair which, in the excitement of the scuffles at the pictures, had come loose from its thick plait, flew out behind her like an unfurling banner.

"Daddy," she screamed. "It's me daddy." Her high, excited voice tore apart the strange silence which had fallen about the street. Wilf's horse wickered nervously, shifting back a couple of paces so that the float which it had pulled for years without mishap nudged Wilf's back and almost had him over.

"It's me daddy an' our Liam an' Patrick," she yelled at each group of children as she raced past them. In the short time it took her to get from Betty's side and into her daddy's open arms she could feel the delight of it bubble up, for the war must surely be over. Daddy and Liam and Patrick were the first back, apart from Freddie Whittaker's daddy and soon every child in the street would be doing just what she was doing, welcoming back their daddies and brothers and even sweethearts, for Cissie Thompson's oldest sister, Annie, had got engaged to a chap in a Pals battalion from St Helens before he left for the western front. Her clogs clattered noisily on the pavement, then, as she leaped into Daddy's arms, hers tight round his neck, they flew off, leaving her feet altogether.

She felt his whiskers prick her cheek, and the stubble of what looked like several days' growth on his chin. She could hear his voice whispering her name over and over again, his face pressed into the curve of her neck and she felt something wet touch her flesh, but before she could get to grips with the astonishing and frightening phenomenon of her daddy's tears Mammy was there tearing her out of Daddy's arms, desperate to get in them herself.

Molly moved away, for Mammy must have her turn. Her face was creased in a huge grin of rapture and she was ready to fling herself at either Liam or Patrick who stood to one side, hesitant, wary, even a bit scared, she thought, though she couldn't think why. It was as if they didn't know what to do next. As though, having been so long in the habit of jumping to the orders of their sergeant they were not sure how to proceed without him.

Wilf, in a hurry now, for after all he had a business to see to and must get on, dropped the can with which he measured the milk from the churn into his customers' own jugs. It was not much of a clatter as it fell to the cobbled roadway, not enough even to disturb the horse but the effect on Liam was quite dramatic and if Molly had not seen it with her own eyes she would not have believed it. Liam was the star of the football field. Liam was known for his ruthless determination to score goals. He was the one who tore up the pitch caring not a jot for his own safety or any member of the opposing team who got in his way. He'd tackle a herd of wild horses to get the ball, would Liam and it was Liam whom the ref told to watch his step. Liam was the cheeky one, the one who'd take no lip from any lad, be he bigger or older than himself.

He began to tremble and from the back of his throat came a strange moaning sound. He fumbled with his rifle in a desperate attempt to get it off his shoulder and when he had it he began to turn round and round, pointing it first up the street and then down.

"Where are they, Daddy . . . for God's sake . . . where?" Then, as though suddenly seeing the appalled faces of his neighbours for the first time, he threw the rifle down and lurched to lean against his father's compassionate shoulder.

"They've gone, son . . . they've gone," his father said, gripping him in fiercely loving and protective arms.

Liam's rifle lay where it had fallen and not even the fascinated curiosity of every small boy in the street who were longing to get their hands on it could coax them forward. The sight of Liam O'Dowd, whom they all knew and admired as a future player for Oldham Athletic, a grown man and a soldier, being hugged by his daddy, made them strangely nervous and, what's more, embarrassed.

Patrick dropped his own rifle and the pack he carried on his chest and in a strangely gentle way took his brother from his father.

"'Tis nowt, lad, nowt. Only some owd can t'milkman dropped. Tha're safe 'ere. Tha're 'ome, so tha' are, an' see, 'ere's our Molly come ter give thi' a kiss. See . . ." And all the time the gentle voice soothed, the gentle hand of Patrick O'Dowd on his brother's shoulder did the same.

You could have heard a pin drop. There were some sparrows twittering and hopping from the rooftiles to the gutter above the ginnel which led from the street to the back yard and a cat, lying in the shadows, watched them unblinkingly, unconcerned with the human drama across the road. The sun shone weakly from the smoke-laden sky, outlining the rows of chimneys which marched above the rooftops in symmetrical rows. Wilf's horse snorted and, all along the street, women brought to their doorsteps by the excitement leaned against their doorframes, their arms crossed over the bibs of their pinnies.

Mammy had her hand to her mouth, her eyes wide with shock, the lovely glow brought about by the arrival of her sons and husband completely wiped out as she watched her handsome, sturdy boy tremble against his brother. His face was grey, like cement newly poured and the sweat stood out on it. He still shook and twitched and Daddy was beside him with Patrick on his other side and Mammy's own arms were suddenly wide and welcoming as her son stumbled thankfully into them.

Without a backward glance Molly followed her family inside, closing the door behind her, shutting out the gaping faces, the amazed gleam in the eyes of the children she played with, aware that today something dreadful had slithered into what had been the unquestioned security of her home and that it was the end of her unclouded childhood.

They had fourteen days' leave, Daddy and Liam and Patrick, which included travelling time. It had taken them nearly three days to get from the railhead in France to Lancashire. They had been given their pay for the fourteen days, which was three pounds each. They had travelled from London lying in the corridor of the train they were so tired, Daddy explained, doing his best to be cheerful in an attempt to disguise the awful state of Liam's shattered nerves. They were given free tea, rolls and cigarettes when they got to Manchester, but that was northeners for you, wasn't it, he smiled, holding Molly on his knee, breathing in deeply the clean, little-girl smell of her, feeling her wholesome, whole, loving presence in his arms.

"Sure an' 'tis time tha' were in tha' beds, lads," Mammy said briskly as both Liam and Patrick yawned until their jaws cracked.

Daddy laughed, the first real "Daddy" laugh Molly had heard since he left home nearly a year ago. They weren't talking much, none of them and somehow it didn't seem to matter. It was enough all to be together again, though Molly was sorry to hear that the war wasn't over. Mind, Liam's fidgets were a bit unnerving. Still, he seemed to have recovered from his strange behaviour in the street. She pressed her cheek against the rough, scratchy material of Daddy's khaki jacket. She knew Mammy and Daddy were dying to be alone together. Daddy kept catching Mammy's hand as she passed his chair, holding it against his cheek, even pressing a kiss on the back of it. Nobody minded or was embarrassed, for that was how

Mammy and Daddy had always been for as long as Molly was old enough to notice.

"Nay, darlin'." He laughed in answer to Mammy's order. "Sure an' aren't the three of us as lousy as beggars. In fact, Angel, tha'd best get off Daddy's knee or tha'll be as bad as we are." He pushed her gently to her feet. "Fetch in't bath, son, an' get the water 'ot, Mammy, fer the three of us'll need a good scrubbin'."

It was only just over a week they had together since they had to allow travelling time back to France, Daddy said, and apart from the family party Aunty Maggie insisted on having, since they had to celebrate, hadn't they, they kept pretty much to themselves. They didn't need parties, Daddy said, eyeing the still figure of his son Liam. Just a bit of peace and quiet, happen a walk up to the house, smiling at Molly, to see if it was still as it had always been. Patrick went up to the football ground, just the once, to see if there were any of his old mates about but he came back very quiet, saying Frankie Newman, who'd played half-back, and Andy Austin, the goalie, had both been killed at Ypres and it hadn't been the same somehow.

If Mammy was distressed by the strange stillness and tendency to jump at the smallest sound Daddy and her two sons displayed, she had nothing to say about it, though Molly heard her and Daddy's voices in the night in the bedroom next to hers and once there was the sound of weeping. She didn't go to school while they were home and, strangely, neither Daddy nor the boys would go to mass, no matter how Mammy pleaded. They wouldn't say why, none of them and a funny look came over Liam's face and for a moment Molly thought he was going to break down again as he had done in the street. Mammy put her hand on his shoulder and bent to kiss his stiff cheek, for by now both Mammy and Molly were aware of the deep disturbances which were inside their Liam.

"It's all right, my son," she said gently. "I'll say the prayers."

It was as though a key had been turned, unlocking a box in which all the horrors eighteen-year-old Liam O'Dowd had witnessed were stuffed, and before anyone could stop him or soothe his fears, which only Daddy and Patrick seemed able to do, he had slapped Mammy's hand away and stood up with such violence the chair he sat in fell backwards to the floor.

"Why the fuck didn't tha' say one fer Percy then? 'Appen 'e'd not've spent two whole bloody days crucified on't wire beggin' fer someone ter shoot 'im. I'd a' done it meself but I'm nowt but a fucking coward . . ."

Molly was so shocked she felt the blood in her veins drag and run slow. The most peculiar feeling came over her as though her head were too heavy for her neck and might fall off and roll to the corner of the room. For Liam even to raise his voice to Mammy was bad enough but to say that word, that word which was whispered, with a lot of coarse sniggering, by the boys behind the lavvies at school and which none of them knew the meaning of, only that it was bad, devastated her. And who was Percy and why had he been crucified like Lord Jesus?

"LIAM . . ." Daddy's voice thundered.

But it seemed Liam was not yet done. "Or Charlie 'oo blew up in me bloody face. Covered in 'is blood, I were, an' all the rest of 'im . . . 'is brains and . . ."

"*Liam, shut tha' mouth, lad. Now!*"

"Oh, Jesus God, Daddy . . ."

"I know, my son."

"Them pictures in me 'ead . . ."

"I know, I know, but don't bother tha' mammy wi' it. Tha' mammy don't want ter know."

"Nobody bloody wants ter know, Daddy."

"I know, son, but it's not tha' mammy's fault."

Róisín O'Dowd had fallen back from the shrieking figure of her first-born, the words in his mouth an abhorrence to her. He had been put in her arms minutes after he was born while they were waiting for Patrick, who, Daddy had laughed, was always to be late. He was the first child of her own that she had ever held, his lusty cries the first to fall on her rapturously waiting mother's ears, the first to be put to her full breast and take the milk which flowed bounteously there. She had loved with equal measure the five children she had borne Seamus O'Dowd but Liam, her first son, was perhaps to hold a tiny special place in her heart, a heart which was ready to break, as her son's brave spirit appeared to be breaking.

"No, no, Seamus, leave 'im be. See, why don't thee an' our Molly go an' . . . well . . . tekk me purse, lass, an' thi' an' Daddy slip down ter Bentleys an' fetch me a pound o' bacon an' a dozen eggs fer us tea. 'Appen tha' could 'ave a bit of a walk first but don't ferget bacon an' eggs, will tha'?"

Her eyes signalled frantically to her husband to get their young daughter out of the house, for this with Liam was not fit for a nine-year-old. Róisín O'Dowd didn't want to be told what her husband and sons had witnessed, not really, but somehow she must help this child of hers to find his way back from the nightmares she realised at last he dwelled in. She had known right from the start when Seamus's letters had started to come from the front that it was not the neat cavalry charges, the quick and merciful death by bullet, the proper burial with a decent service in the faith they had been brought up in, all the things the public at large envisaged, those who had sons and husbands in the trenches Seamus had described, dry and safe and comfortable he would have her believe. It was a great comfort to those mothers whose sons had died in France, like Benjie Atkinson and Tommy O'Brien, like Frankie Newman and Andy Austin, to think of them going peacefully in a clean white bed, or swiftly, or painlessly, lying in a neat grave with a neat headstone which, when the war ended, they would visit with flowers. But what her own son was babbling, even now, denied this, confirmed what Róisín had feared, not from what Seamus had written or said but what he had *not* written and *not* said.

Molly was white-faced and frightened, ready to cry as Liam was doing and even Patrick had tears on his face though Patrick was quiet about it.

"Come on, Angel, get tha' coat an' thee an' me'll go an' see the 'ouse, so we will. We've not bin yet an' . . . well, I'd like ter tekk a scen before we . . . go back. Now don't upset thissen over Liam. 'E's not bin 'imself just lately but Mammy'll get 'im right an' tha' knows tha' daddy'll look after 'im, just as I want thi' an' Mammy ter look after each other when . . ."

"Daddy . . .?"

Molly did her best to look over her shoulder to where Mammy had her arms about Liam. She was murmuring something to him, rocking him, patting his back, doing her best to tuck his tall frame beneath her chin as she had done when he was a boy. She held out her arm for a moment and when Patrick blundered into the circle the last picture Molly had in her mind was Mammy and Molly's two brothers standing on the worn rag rug before the fire with their arms about one another.

"Come wi' Daddy, Angel," Daddy urged and she went.

The fields on either side of Wood Brook Lane were thickly starred with the vivid crimson of poppies. A glory of poppies, so many and so vigorously growing it looked as though, climbing the gate, she and Daddy could have walked across the fields on their brilliant heads. Everywhere they looked was an abundance of colour, just as though God had painted it especially for her and her daddy on this last day of his leave. The grass was lush, a bright green, moist and luxuriant, the clear sky above their heads the deep blue of a cornflower, or the Madonna's robe in church, fading gradually to a pearly eggshell blue on the horizon.

They stopped to lean on a gate which had a broken latch and Daddy sighed, wishing he'd brought his hammer since he couldn't abide to see a job needing doing which he could fix. He lit his pipe and the fragrance of the smoke about his head and Molly's was a benediction to the child, for it brought back the memory of a crowded multitude of days when there was no war, a memory that would remain until her daddy came home for good. Daddy put his foot on the lowest rung of the gate, his eyes half closed, his face peaceful, his hand at Molly's head. She leaned against him and was comforted, knowing that between them Mammy and Daddy would always put things right, even this dreadful thing which seemed to have fallen on Liam. Mind you, Liam'd probably be as right as rain when they got home, brought to peace by Mammy's tranquillity and soothing words.

The growing corn beyond the gate moved in a graceful swathe as a vagrant breeze caught it and on the far side of the next hedge, down the slight slope on which the field was set, cattle grazed, tiny in the distance, heads down and all facing the same way. Trees edged the horizon where the ground rose again, a dark and lacy frieze against the pearl blue loveliness of the approaching evening.

There had been very little rain in the past weeks and the mill race was quiet, moving along with a deep, contented chuckle between the swaying green reeds on either side. There were nine cows, six black and white, the remainder brown, standing knee-deep in the grasses and clover, grazing peacefully, moving only their tails to swish away the flies.

"Wonder where them come from?" Daddy pondered idly as he and Molly walked slowly by them, hands clasped, the tension which had erupted at home and the strain it had produced ebbing away from him. He looked about him, his eyes resting for long minutes on the cows, the clover which dappled the grass about their hooves and the grass itself, a glistening green from shades of lime to emerald. He studied the full canopy of the oak trees, the gold-washed beauty of the beech, the slow-moving water in which the trees were reflected and the deep blue bowl of the sky towards which their branches reached.

His gaze came at last to rest on the fresh rose loveliness of his child and it was as though he knew he was seeing them all for the last time.

The house her daddy loved was as Molly had last seen it, beautiful and glowing, like a jewel in a crown, the crown itself a glory. Aye, a glory despite the garden's growing air of neglect, the flowers thriving in a bounteous profusion, the trees and bushes unpruned, the grass cut, but roughly.

"Them gardeners'll 'ave their work cut out 'ere." Daddy had his face pressed to the wrought-iron gate. "Will it ever be't same again, d'yer think?" Molly heard him say almost sadly and at once she turned to him, her face frowning with resolve.

"Course it will, Daddy. When t'war's over an' them gardeners get back they'll 'ave it all lovely again, just tha' wait an' see. Anyroad, I *like* it this way." Her voice was stern and her manner that of someone who will remain loyal to what she loves however it looks.

"Yer right, Angel." Daddy sighed deeply, reaching for her hand.

Turning, hands clasped, they began to walk in the direction of home and when they got there Mammy had the tea set out and Liam sat peacefully before the fire, his hand smoothing the ginger cat which purred on his knee.

"Tha're just in time, darlin'," Mammy said to Daddy, some signal passing from her to him and Molly knew it would be all right now. Patrick winked at her, then pointed to the box of snakes and ladders, which stood on the sideboard.

"I'll beat tha' ternight, Mary Angelina O'Dowd," he told her, "see if I don't. I'll bet thi' – what? – the price of ticket fer't pictures."

"Fer me *an'* Betty?" She grinned.

"Aye up, remember I'm only a poor tommy an' not made o'

money. One an' tuppence a day don't go far, does it, Daddy, but go on then. If tha' beat me I'll pay fer't two o' yer."

"Yer on, our Patrick, an' then I'll beat our Liam. 'E can pay fer me an' Betty ter go ter't duck pond."

"Duck pond! Holy Mother, is that place still goin'?" Liam laughed and the last evening the O'Dowd family were ever to spend together was filled with snakes and ladders and cheese and onion pie and parkin, warm with love and soft laughter.

Clare O'Dowd was born in March 1916, the loveliest little scrap you ever did see, Aunty Maggie said dotingly, and the dead spit of their Molly, putting the yelling baby in Molly's arms as soon as her mammy had had a hold of her. Well, with the men of the family away Molly would have to support her mammy all she could with her new sister. After all, Molly was nearly ten now and would be a grand little helper, which Molly realised, for hadn't she been helping her ever since Mammy confided that Clare was coming. Of course they hadn't known it would be Clare then, but just the same Mammy's short-lived return to the mill, which had lasted only three months, had shown Molly, and all of them, what Molly could do in the house to help and hadn't she been doing it for the past six months. She went out to play less and less, for somehow it all seemed a bit . . . well, *babyish*, the skipping and whip and top and hopscotch and hadn't she promised Daddy faithfully she'd look after Mammy. It was Mammy who made her go out to play but she was soon back, anxious, as Mammy got bigger and bigger, that she might need something and Molly not be there to get it for her.

They wouldn't let her into Mammy and Daddy's room on the night Clare was born, Aunty Maggie and Aunty Flo and the midwife from Inkerman Street, but when it was all over and Mammy was sitting up serenely in her bed, her sweet face rosy, her dark hair tied up with a lovely red ribbon Daddy had bought for her, her blue eyes glowed with love for her elder daughter. Mammy hugged her and kissed her and told her she loved her and she didn't know what she would do without her, while Aunty Flo cast her eyes to the ceiling at what she considered to be a quite unnecessary and embarrassing show of emotion, but Aunty Maggie, who had the baby in her arms, smiled and sniffed as she put Molly's sister in Molly's arms.

Clare O'Dowd was three months old on the day her daddy and her two brothers were killed on the first day of the first Battle of the Somme.

6

Mary Angelina O'Dowd crouched in the recess beside the kitchen range where Pikey had cornered her, curling herself up into as small a target as possible, bringing her knees up to her chest and wrapping her arms about them. She tucked her head well down between her shoulders but she made the mistake of glancing up to see how close he was and the calloused palm of his hand, with all his considerable strength behind it, found her cheek. Her head wrenched agonisingly on her neck and tears spurted from her eyes which infuriated her more than the blow, for she had been determined not to let him see her cry. The force of it made her head ring and she thought she might have bitten her tongue, for she could taste blood.

From somewhere in the kitchen she could hear her mother begging Pikey not to be too hasty.

"She didn't mean it, Pikey, did tha' darlin'?" she implored, without even knowing what had been said. "She's a bit quick wi' 'er tongue, that's all but she didn't mean it. Don't 'it 'er again, please. She's a good girl, tha' knows that an' if she said 'owt ter cross yer, then she did it wi'out thinkin' an' she's sorry. She's only a lass, Pikey, please . . ."

Molly heard the sound of a further blow as Pikey fetched Mammy a backhander followed by a sharp cry of pain. Jesus, Mary and Joseph, she'd kill him, so she would. If she had a knife in her hand she'd leap up and plunge it into his grotesquely bloated belly and then she'd twist it and twist it, a saw-edged knife it would be, until he screamed like the pig he was. She hated him, despised him and was terrified of him all at the same time, as they all were, and if she could get away with it she'd see him off and suffer the consequences of purgatory

67

for eternity and be glad of it. He wasn't worth swinging for, but by all that was holy if she could slip something into his tea without anyone knowing of it, or in the beer he guzzled from the minute he got out of his bed until he fell back into it, she'd do it without a qualm.

She didn't dare come out of her corner, not while he was prowling about the kitchen on his way to the bed he shared with her poor oppressed mammy, and for the thousandth time in the last six years the part of her mind not occupied with the all too familiar problem of defending herself agonised over why Mammy had married him.

It was seven o'clock in the morning and Pikey had just come home, since it was his week for the night shift at Cravens Ironworks in Arkwright Street. He was tired and in an evil temper even before he'd set his iron-tipped clog over the doorstep but somehow the sight of her had thrown him into one of those blind rages which were the deep-rooted pattern of their lives. She herself was soon to be away to the Broadbent Cotton Spinning Mill where she "minded" a ring frame spinning machine. The knocker-upper had roused her from her bed half an hour since and she had hoped to be gone by the time Pikey got home but Mammy had sent her to Bentleys on the corner of Sidney Street for half a pound of bacon for Pikey's breakfast and it had held her back.

She chanced a peep from beneath the glossy tumble of dark curls which cascaded over her forehead.

"Don't tha' tekk that tone wi' me, my lass," he was roaring at Mammy who, after all, had done no more than feebly remonstrate with him and had certainly not adopted any "tone" since she knew it was more than her life was worth. She was cowering away from his threatening finger, her hand to her own reddening face, Pikey's no more than inches from hers.

"One more bloody word from either of yer an' I'll fetch me belt ter yer," he went on menacingly. It was no idle threat and the three children, who were no more than little shadows in the room, huddled piteously behind their mother as she flinched away from him. The youngest, Archie, two years old and almost witless in his terror, began to cry soundlessly.

There was silence for a moment as Pikey got his breath back. The room was warm, a fan of radiance spreading out from the glowing, gleaming range which took up most of one wall. Flames leaped behind the bars, orange-flowered, yellow-centred. The range itself was blackleaded and polished to within an inch of its life, mirror-like in its glory, the brass handles on the oven door brilliant as newly minted gold, as was the fender and the hearth tidy.

A large, round table over which was flung a red chenille cloth took up a great deal of space in the cosy room, the cloth matching the fringed and bobbled pelmet tacked to the mantelshelf above the range. There were a couple of sadly worn but comfortable armchairs from which the stuffing did its best to leak, one on each side of the fire, the best one Pikey's, naturally, and on the sepia-tinted, faded wallpaper hung three oval gilt frames and in each one was a photograph of a soldier, handsome but serious as though going to war was not to be taken lightly. Astonishingly, Pikey had not objected to having his predecessor looking solemnly down at him from the wall, nor his sons since they had all died bravely in battle, as *his* mates had done, as *he* had nearly done.

A big clock, ugly with ornamentation, stood in the exact centre of the mantelshelf, ticking slowly and sonorously as though to say there was all the time in the world for what Pikey Watson had in mind. The linoleum on the floor was worn, the pattern and original colours unrecognisable, removed by hard scrubbing and heavy feet. There was a small rag rug in front of the fender made from all the worn-out, cut-up clothing which could be used for nothing, not even dusters, saved and stitched together by the thrifty fingers of Rosie Watson. On it drowsed a small ginger cat which seemed impervious to the storm which raged about it.

Pikey glowered at his wife. "That lip o' thine'll get yer inter serious trouble one o' these days, my girl," he told her menacingly, "an' that there trollop's as bad. Look at 'er . . ." And obediently six pairs of eyes, including his own, turned to gaze at the girl in the chimney corner. "Just look at 'er an' tell me what she's gorron's decent. Go on, woman, 'ave a good look."

It was very evident, not only to the girl in question but to her mother, that Pikey was doing his own share of looking and Molly O'Dowd, nineteen years old and as lovely as a wild hedge rose, did her best to pull down the perfectly decent hem of her cotton work skirt which, when she was standing, was no more than eight inches from the ground. Hemlines were going up all the time, Betty told her, confirmed in the fashion pages of the *Woman's Weekly* Betty purchased from the share of her wage her daddy, who was generous, allowed her to keep. Already skirts were fourteen inches from the ground but Molly had known fine well that she would be in serious trouble with Pikey if she put hers up so high, not because he was incensed by her lack of decency as he was pretending but by his failure so far to get his hand up them!

"She's nowt but a shameless 'ussy," he continued balefully, "an' when I tell 'er so, which I've every right ter do, she gives me a mouthful of bloody cheek. I've a bloody good mind ter give thi' the thrashin' tha' deserve, my girl. Disgraced I am by the sight o' me own daughter wi' 'er skirts 'alfway up 'er bum an' wi' no sense o' shame neither. Aye, a good 'idin's what tha' need, what tha' *all* need."

He glared about him, his maddened eye falling on the three small children. "An' tha' can stop that blubberin', lad," he told his son, "or I'll give thi' summat ter blubber for."

"Please, Pikey, they've done nowt," Rosie Watson pleaded, spreading her arms to protect the children who cowered behind her. "Our Molly might've spoke outer turn an' so did I but little 'uns 'ave done nowt wrong."

Would they dare, her agonised expression asked and Molly could stand it no longer. Clutching the offending skirt about her, she sprang to her feet. The sight and sound of her mammy begging this bullying sod not to thrash his own innocent children, who were scarcely more than babies and cowed to the timid silence of rabbits, was more than her outraged spirit could bear. Her greeny blue eyes narrowed to the brilliance of turquoise chips of ice in her chalk white face, chalk white but for the livid hand print on her left cheek. Her nostrils flared and her soft, full mouth thinned into a venomous line of pure rage. Though she was tall for a girl, she came to no higher than her stepfather's collar stud and with one contemptuous flick of his hand he could have knocked her into the middle of next week, a favourite expression of his and one with which he constantly threatened them. Molly knew it, but her fierce temper, inherited from her great-grandfather who had come as a lad of twelve on an immigrant ship from Ireland, took no account of it. As Michael O'Dowd had once done, she stood up and fought for what she thought was right.

Her eyes never faltered. They were filled with a wild, quite devastating hatred, a hatred so perilous Pikey Watson almost fell back from it. Hot sparks flashed between them like those he himself created in his furnace at the ironworks.

"Tha' touch Mammy again, or them kids an' I swear I'll send Eileen fer't constable," she screeched, beside herself with fury. "'E were standin' at corner o't street when I left Bentleys an' 'e'll still be there, I reckon, drinkin't tea old Ma Bentley give 'im. 'E'd not tekk a second ter get down 'ere so tha'd best watch thi' step. Why don't tha' pick on someone yer own size, tha' great bully?"

"Molly . . ." her mother beseeched her. She admired her daughter's spirit, she really did and wished she could still be the same but it had been knocked out of her years ago and it did no good in the end. He'd get the better of her, of them all. He always did. She'd not even been allowed to keep the name she had been given, since Pikey said it was a bugger to get his tongue round and she'd be known as Rosie from now on.

"An' I'm not thy daughter, Pikey Watson," Molly went on, her voice rising to screaming pitch, "thank the Blessed Virgin, an' if my daddy was 'ere . . . or . . . or me brothers, they'd knock the livin' daylights outer yer fer what tha've done ter this family."

She was ready to weep, the quiver in her voice said. The irony of the last words had not escaped her, for if Daddy was here Pikey would not be. If the "great war" as it was being called, though she could see nothing great about it, had not taken Seamus, Liam and Patrick O'Dowd, Pikey Watson would not now be sleeping in Seamus's bed with the woman who had once been Seamus's wife.

Molly, now that she had escaped from the chimney corner while Pikey's attention had been momentarily distracted by his wife and children, was darting and dancing like a giddy firefly, or a lightweight boxer whose fists are clenched with the intention of landing a telling blow on an opponent. Her eyes glared at him from between the tangle of her long, dark lashes. They were normally a soft greeny blue, like velvet, luminous and glowing, but now, as her fury raged, the black of the pupils had dilated to deep, dark pools. There was the fierceness of a she-cat about her, one trapped in an alley by a tom and her mother was afraid for her. Her cheeks were as red as poppies, both of them to match now and her riot of curls whipped and bounced about her skull like a chrysanthemum bloom in a high wind. She kept just out of Pikey's reach, which was not easy in the small back kitchen, but she was young and agile and Pikey was neither. As he lumbered about the room, like some savage bear which is being baited beyond endurance, she skimmed from one corner of the table to the other but it would not take him long to realise that he had only to overturn it and Molly would be in his grasp. Then again, he might not catch her this time if Molly had the presence of mind to run for her life from the house but Rosie knew that whatever the outcome, now or later, someone would suffer. If it wasn't Molly it would be her or one of the kids. Pikey Watson's temper was short and vicious at the best of times but when he was on nights the disturbance in his sleep pattern made it even more uncertain. For some strange and inexplicable reason it was Molly who seemed to inflame it, not on purpose, her mother was aware. In fact she did her best to keep out of his way when they were in the house together. To efface herself from his notice since what Pikey called "her insolence", which might be no more than a lifting of her delicately arched eyebrows at some question she was asked, was usually what set him off.

But Rosie had noticed over the past year, perhaps even longer if she were honest, though she was reluctant to admit it for fear of where it might lead, that Pikey had taken to giving Molly some nasty looks. Not nasty as though he was mad at her, but nasty sort of . . . coarse looks, those a man gives a desirable young woman he lusts after and Rosie didn't know what to do about it. Molly was nineteen now and the loveliest thing you ever did see, with lads for ever hanging about at the end of the street, lads who watched her with the fascination and longing a beautiful woman arouses in a male. There was none of the nudging and winking that went on over some girls she could mention, like Cissie Thompson who, it was said, would let any man put his hand down her knickers for a tanner.

No, their Molly was different, and a lot like she herself had been when she had married Seamus, God bless his sweet soul, crossing herself surreptitiously so that Pikey wouldn't notice. He didn't like all that daft hocus-pocus she mumbled over, he'd told her when he caught her with her rosary, and *his* children weren't being brought up in it neither and if she didn't stop yapping on about bloody purgatory he'd give her a shiner to match the one she already had.

Once, when she had married Seamus at the age of seventeen, she had been as pretty as Molly, though when she looked in the mirror these days she was hard pressed to remember it. She was forty-six years old now and had given birth to nine children, the last three fathered by Pikey, but she looked old enough and worn enough to be Molly's grandmother and could you wonder with a husband like Pikey to contend with? Six years they'd been married and it was puzzle to her why she hadn't given birth every nine months the way he kept after her, night and morning, but she'd rather he used her like a sixpenny whore in one of the alleys at the back of Union Street than lay a hand on Molly. Mind you, if she wasn't mistaken she, Rosie, had come to that time in a woman's life when nature allowed her to conceive no more children, thank the Holy Mother, so that was one less worry to sharpen its teeth on her. Their Archie would be the last.

She trembled as the pain and longing for Seamus washed over her in great crashing waves. Like her daughter she wondered despairingly why she had ever consented to Pikey Watson taking her beloved husband's place, for that was what Seamus would always be to her, her husband, despite the few, hurried words spoken by her and Pikey in the Registry Office in Oldham. She must have been off her head, still deep in the awful place she had retreated to when they had told her that not only was Seamus gone but her two beautiful sons as well. All three on one sunny day in the offensive on the Somme. They had been in the same battalion composed of working-class men who had worked together, played football together, had a pint together on a Saturday night, fought together and eventually died together in July 1916. Whole streets of them in the chapelry of Oldham and Royston and Crossfold. The telegram boy had been busy that day and as Aunty Maggie said, she being one of them, you could have floated a battleship in the tears that were shed by the hundreds of women they left behind to mourn.

A year after the war ended she had met Pikey at the first Remembrance Day service in Oldham. He had worn his uniform, a sergeant-major, big and strong, a striking man with fierce whiskers who had looked quite devastated as

the roll of honour was called. They were his mates, he had
told her, incredibly distressed, and when he had asked her to
take a little drink with him at Yates's Wine Lodge, which was
eminently respectable and where a woman could safely and
comfortably enjoy a port and lemon, she had agreed. Not on
that day, of course, since it was not a time for jollification, but
the following week. Well, she had felt so sorry for him. A big
chap like him almost in tears over his lost pals, just as she was
over her lost husband and sons, and it was not until after their
marriage, which, if she were honest, she barely remembered
agreeing to, that his true nature was revealed.

The wild colour in Molly's face had drained away to the
almost transparent whiteness of bone china, the temper which
had come down to her through the years from her Irish
antecedents gripping her in its devastating power. It had not
been bequeathed to them all, missing a few here and there,
like Seamus and his brother Fergus who had both been as
mild-mannered and patient as the great Shire horses which
had pulled the waggons at Broadbents. There had been a
Donal O'Dowd who had nearly killed a man, they said, just
for making a remark Donal had not cared for and only the
combined efforts of six of his mates in the alehouse where
they had been drinking had prevented it. Always in trouble
he was and men stepped lightly round him, so they did.

And what about Caitlin O'Dowd who had been Seamus's
mother? A lovely woman with a heart of gold but get her
dander up and she'd be after you with the first thing that
came to hand. And then there was Molly who, from an early
age, had displayed signs that the expression "mad as Mick
O'Dowd" might be applied to her.

Mick O'Dowd had been her great-grandfather and his story
had been passed down through the generations, the story of
how, helped by his parish priest in Galway after the famine
had killed all his family but him, he had stepped ashore
at Liverpool believing himself to be in America where he
was bound. He was an ignorant, illiterate country boy who
had been stunned by the noise and turmoil of "America",
wandering away from the dockside to have a look at this
wondrous place.

Discovering his mistake when he had asked a passer-by
where he might find New York, he had run like the wind,
despite his weakened, scarecrow state, back to the Pier Head

to see the ship he had sailed on from Ireland and which was to take him to the New World half way down the estuary on the tide.

It was said that he was almost locked up that day, so violent had he become and his wild Irish temper had tramped with him from Liverpool to Manchester and beyond to Newtown where the Irish congregated. It was one of the worst slum areas on the outskirts of Manchester, row upon row of cheap, back-to-back houses without ventilation or drainage. The black-haired inhabitants lived cheek by jowl in the appalling mass of human garbage, dirty, noisy, quarrelsome, half starved and completely wild; twelve-year-old Michael O'Dowd had seen no improvement on the conditions he had left behind in Galway.

Taking his temper, which had got him into more scrapes than a bare-knuckle prize fighter, he moved on to Crossfold where he found work in what was then known as Chapman Manufacturing, a cotton mill situated in the south Lancashire heartland.

Aye, mad as Mick O'Dowd and if something wasn't done soon his great-granddaughter would find a weapon, the kitchen knife perhaps, or the heavy iron poker in the hearth, and lay it about her stepfather until she finished him off, or get badly mauled in the attempt.

"Mary Angelina . . ." Rosie screamed, doing her best to dart between her and the sharp corners of the table and at the same time keep a protective eye on the four children who stared, blank-eyed and senseless, at the wild scene which was being enacted, not for the first time, in the kitchen. They had developed a knack of withdrawing, even young Archie, inside some innermost part of themselves, hiding there, silent and still as little mice, until the commotion was over and their father gone when they would creep out and be as other children were, or as least as much as their fear of Pikey and his return would allow them to be.

"Don't stop me, Mammy," Molly shrieked. "I've 'ad enough, so I 'ave, an' so's yerself an' them bairns. Six bloody years . . ."

"Molly O'Dowd!" Even in the midst of this nightmare, habit came to the fore and Rosie felt the need to rebuke her daughter for her language. There was nothing Seamus had abhorred more than coarseness on the tongue of a woman.

"All 'e's done is terrorise us. 'E's given thi' nowt but blows an' them three kids . . ."

"Why, yer little madam! I'll flay bloody skin off tha' back fer that," Pikey thundered. "What goes on between me an' tha' mam's nowt ter do wi' thi'. We're man an' wife an' if a man sees fit ter wallop 'is wife the law ses 'e can. Anyroad, it's not yer mam we're on about 'ere. 'Tis you what needs a seein' to. Yer not fit ter live among decent folk wi' them shameless ways o' thine, flauntin' thissen in front of any man what sets eyes on yer. I've seen tha' prinkin' in front o' them lads at corner o't street an't way they look at yer."

"It's *you* what looks, tha' dirty old bastard."

"Molly, please . . . please, lass . . . give over," Rosie begged, for if this went on much longer there would be murder done. Pikey was literally foaming at the mouth, the white gummy substance about his lips, mixed with his saliva, spraying disgustingly across the table in his madness. His eyes were red, the white filmed with the bloodlust of his fury. He was sweating copiously, his shirt wet through with it, the thick grey mat of springing chest hair which grew right up to his chin dewed with moisture. He stank of it, and the stench he brought home from the ironworks, and Rosie felt her gorge rise, bile filling her mouth, for there was only one way to get these two apart, to put out the frightening power of her daughter's rage and distract Pikey's attention from her.

"Leave 'er, Pikey. Leave 'er be. Tha're on tha' way ter bed so why don't I come wi' thi' fer an 'our or so. We could 'ave us a nice time, a bit o' fun, like." *Fun!* The word sickened her. "She's off ter work, anyroad an' the kids'll amuse theirselves. Come on, lad," giving him an arch look which shamed the memory of her dead husband. "As yer just said we're 'usband an' wife an' what we do . . . what *I'll* do fer thi' is just between ourssen."

Not only did the coarseness of the words distract Pikey, who had the most enormous swelling in the drooping crutch of his trousers caused by his stepdaughter's lovely, wild defiance, it brought Molly back from the edge of the madness which threatened to tip her into a black hole from which she would never climb. She had been beyond reason, beyond any sense of caution of where all this might lead, the gallows for all she knew, since she had been ready to kill him with whatever came to hand. A young girl she might be but the abnormal strength which comes to those in times of great crisis flowed through her veins, pumping her heart, giving her limbs twice the power that Pikey, who was twice her weight and a foot taller, might call up.

Now, with a sentence or two, her mother had taken it from her. She wanted to feel disgust, and she did, shame at her mother's dreadful words, and she did, but more than anything she felt a great wave of pity well up in her for what her mother was prepared to do to protect her children. This beast of a man who had terrorised them for six years was getting worse, was getting out of hand, beyond control, and she, Molly O'Dowd, was the innocent cause of it. He wanted *her*, not her mother, she had known that for months and what she had roused in him was to be perpetrated on her mammy.

Pikey turned to glare at her.

"I've not done wi' you yet, lady, think on. That tongue o' yours needs a lesson an' the shameless length o' that there skirts, an' all." His tone was quite cheerful now. It was not that he couldn't have his wife any time he wanted but it seemed she was going to show him a bit of liveliness in their bed instead of merely lying there submissively as she usually did and it excited him. After all, the girl would be there when . . . well, he was not awfully sure what he meant by *when* but it would come one day.

"Right Rosie, love, lets thi' an' me 'ave a bit of a cuddle, shall we, and then tha' can mekk me breakfast. Tha' knows it gives me an appetite."

Molly watched them climb the narrow stairs, Pikey's hand already up Mammy's skirt and the anguish in her heart was so strong and so painful she felt as though she had been mortally wounded. She could only imagine the full horrors to which her mother was to be subjected in the next hour but whatever they might be she knew Mammy had suggested them to keep Pikey from inflicting them on her, or, if it had not quite come to that yet, at least to stop him thrashing her.

She felt sick and dizzy all of a sudden, her bright spirit crushed beneath the dreadful knowledge that it would never be any different. Her mammy was tied to this foul beast for ever. The woman who had been loved with the sweetness and goodness which had been Seamus O'Dowd was to live in the cruel degradation which Pikey Watson was perfectly at liberty to inflict on her, for she was his wife.

Putting her hands to her cheeks, Molly dragged in a deep draught of air, swallowing it into her lungs and breathing deeply to prevent the bread and dripping which had been her breakfast – no bacon and eggs for Molly O'Dowd or indeed the rest of the family – coming up again on a tidal wave of despair. She looked about her blindly and the four children watched her in that curiously unnatural way of those who have learned exactly what their place is in this household, at least when Pikey was in it.

"It's all right," she said, though of course they knew it wasn't, even young Archie. "Mammy'll be down soon. Don't go near't fire, will tha'?"

They all four shook their heads, even nine-year-old Clare who, like Molly, was not Pikey Watson's true child, solemn as baby owls, their eyes enormous in their pale faces, and she knew they wouldn't. They probably wouldn't even move from the corner where they were huddled, so deeply ingrained in them was the habit of obedience to their father and his belt. The three young ones were not handsome children as Seamus O'Dowd's children were, for there was too much of the coarseness of their father in them, but Molly had a certain fondness for them since they were related to her but she knew her mother loved them and would be devastated if they were hurt.

But she had to get to work. Already she was late. The line shaft would have been turned on with the main lights and the spinners would be stepping up to their frames ready to spin their day's output of cotton. Piecers would be oiling spindles, and minders fussing about their headstocks and every mule and frame would be running except hers. If she didn't get there soon she would be "quartered" which meant the loss of part of her wages and it would be Mammy who would suffer the deficiency. *He* would still have *his* share since, as the master of the house, he insisted that any wage packet earned must be put unopened into his hand.

With a deft movement of her hands Molly dragged her hair up to the crown of her head and threw on the cap which had once been Seamus O'Dowd's and which she had worn ever since she started work. She settled it at a defiant angle on her head, slipped her feet into her clogs and reached for her black woollen shawl. Throwing it up and out like the wings of a bat she draped it about her shoulders, her arms folded in it in the age-old, submissive manner of the mill girl, though her deportment was far from humble as she stepped out into the street and began to stride along Sidney Street.

"Late this mornin', Molly. Betty's gone wi'out thi," Mrs Spooner shouted from across the road, but Molly merely nodded as she walked blindly in the direction of the mill where she had worked since she was fourteen years old. It was quarter of an hour's walk through narrow streets packed with terraced houses, most of whose occupants would already be at their spinning frames or mules.

She didn't know how it came about and somehow realised she didn't really care but she found herself not on Radnor Street where the mill was situated but going past it and on to the Huddersfield Road, the magical road which she and her daddy had taken on so many lovely Sunday mornings. The magical road which led to the house.

The house! The house her daddy had loved with a passion which had passed, without either of them noticing it, from him to her. The house he had loved more than any other though he had never been beyond the gate. He had been like that, her daddy. He could read and write, for he had gone to school until he was twelve but he had known nothing beyond the sprawling labyrinth of houses in which the mills were set, the blackened church spires, the hundreds of mill chimneys from which smoke belched to obscure the sky and pollute the air about the mill town. He had seen nothing of the world which existed over the horizon beyond the moors he loved, except what he read in books he borrowed from the lending library, that is until he had gone to be a soldier and had given his life for his country. That was what they said, "given his life for his country", though Molly was of the opinion that he had not so much "given" it as had it taken from him.

In vivid contrast, encircling the town were the soft rolling hills leading upwards to the high sweep of the moors, the great vault of the sky, the sweet, wind-ruffled air of all that lay about the drabness of Oldham, and her daddy, though she had not been old enough to realise it then, had nourished himself with it. He had a reverence for beautiful things, not just those that were God-given and which were about them for all to enjoy, he had told her, but for the things man himself had made. A well-crafted piece of furniture, the exquisite grace of a crystal goblet, pictures, especially those he told her

were called the "French Impressionists". Ballet dancers and
poppy-filled fields, lilac trees and ladies in flounced skirts and
enchanting hats, lilies reflected in water and golden cornfields
under blue and white skies.

"Look at the arch on that there bridge, darlin'," he'd say
as they crossed a tumbling moorland stream. "Did yer ever
see anythin' so graceful?" and she had to admit that though
she hadn't noticed it until he had pointed it out to her it
was true.

But it was the house which drew him, which elicited in
him that dreaming contemplation for which he had no words.
Through increasingly narrow lanes bordered by hedges in
which honeysuckle and wild roses rioted, as though even
the approach to the house must be no less than perfect. There
were white farmhouses deep in buttercups and clover, neat
cottages, the walk along the mill race with the glorious music
of the racing waters in your head and then you were there.

And then *she* was there.

It was an old manor house of great antiquity, at least two
hundred years old, Daddy said, with circular chimneys which
were typical of the north country and when she asked him
how he knew he had said, vaguely, his eyes clouded with
the emotion the lovely house evoked in him, that all things
were written in books for anyone to read. The house was set
in a bowl of grassy slopes that rose all around it, a house
of soft, pinky-coloured bricks and tiles, an enchanted house
framed by venerable old trees, the whole protected by the
stone wall that surrounded it.

The gates, which were closed, were tall, made of delicate
wrought iron and set between two stone pillars with a carved
pineapple on each one. There was no sign of life, on her side
or beyond the gates, except for a squirrel which darted out
from the trees, stopped for a quivering moment on the drive
as though sensing her presence, then continued its flashing
journey to the trees on the far side.

There was a lodge to the right-hand side of the gateway in
which she was aware lived a gatekeeper and his family, the
building constructed from the same rosy stone as the house.
It had a deserted feeling about it and she shivered, she didn't
know why.

Her hands gripped the gates. Her shawl was draped about
her head and shoulders, screening her face and her whole,

desolate attention, silent and unswerving, was focused on the house and as she concentrated the miracle happened as it always did. She could feel the peace of it enter her heart, her sorely tried heart, a peace and tranquillity which never failed her. It seemed to draw her in, beckon to her, welcome her to its own heart even though she could not accept its call and never would. It was a dream, an enchantment, a glory which was not for the likes of her, but at the same time it was a healer, a mender of broken hearts, for it had been her refuge, even from this side of its gates, when Daddy had died.

But she must get back, back to the terraced house which Pikey stalked, back to her ring spinning frame, back to the life she and Betty shared, she and Betty and all the thousands of other mill girls in Oldham.

The sound was no more than a murmur to start with, a sort of drone like a swarm of bees, coming from far off so that at first she barely noticed it but as she turned her head to listen it came closer and closer, surely that of a snarling beast and beginning to take on a savagery that frightened her. It stuttered from time to time, became silent now and again, then came thundering on, its voice rising and falling until she knew it had arrived, whatever it was, at her back where it became somewhat quieter. She hardly dared turn to face it and might have stood there frozen to the gates until darkness fell but a voice, a man's voice with the cultured drawl of the privileged class in it, called out to her cheerfully.

"Good-day to you. Lovely day, isn't it? Could I be terribly cheeky and ask you to open the gates?"

7

Tim Broadbent had not meant to go to the mill in his brand-new motor car. It was a supremely elegant Vauxhall sports car with a stylishly fluted radiator and bonnet and he had had it sprayed in a vivid, pillar-box red and the temptation to try it out on the narrow lanes from Meddins through Delph and Shaw and then down into Oldham – the long way round – to show off, he supposed, smiling at his own foolishness, had been too much for him.

The startled, even alarmed expressions on the faces of those in the mill yard who saw him arrive in his snarling machine, though by now they all knew of his love of motor cars, had made him smile with the wicked delight of a small boy displaying a new toy, though he was not by nature an unkind man. They had positively leaped, one and all, towards the mill wall, like monkeys reaching out for the safety of the wire mesh about their cage, their eyes wild, their mouths agape as though the Vauxhall were some wild animal which had escaped its confinement and come roaring among them. The huge, docile Shire horses, which still pulled the waggons loaded with Broadbent cloth, shook their heads and stamped their enormous, fringed hooves and men found it necessary to run and soothe them, throwing him the looks of those who loved animals and abominated the infernal machines which had come to terrify them.

Tim already had an open-top Bullnose Morris which he had bought for a hundred pounds in 1920 when he was discharged from hospital. They were used to that and to an earlier model of a Singer Ten, purchased in 1914 when he had been no more than a lad, which was still in the garage at home, both motor cars painted in the vivid red he liked. Both were simple and uncomplicated with a hood which went up and down and a back seat, but this powerful racing machine made the older motor cars look like outdated perambulators.

The Vauxhall, named the Car Superexcellent in the motor trade, was easily capable of *touring* speeds of sixty miles per hour and had cost him the astronomical sum of thirteen hundred pounds and, with the Rolls-Royce Silver Ghost his mother was driven in, made four motor cars in the garage block at the back of Meddins.

"Why do you need another new motor car, darling?" his mother had asked him mildly on more than one occasion. "You can only drive one at a time."

"I know, Mother, and I'm know I'm very extravagant to indulge myself but I couldn't resist it when I saw it at the Motor Show. Besides, we have a dozen or more horses in the stable. With . . . with Will and Charlie . . . gone and Tessa married I am the only one to ride them."

"Yes, you're right, but I just can't bear to part with them somehow. I remember them . . . Will on Prince and Charlie . . . and after all, they do come in handy when we have guests who like to ride."

"I know, Mother." He patted her hand gently. "And I understand, believe me. I'm not criticising but we really do seem inclined to have far more than we need of . . . most things, don't you agree?" He smiled whimsically. "I feel the same way about my motors as you do about the horses," and his mother who, of them all, knew what was in him, had understood.

The men in the yard had crowded round his new machine, quite fascinated, those who loved motor cars as he did and would have given their right arm for his old Singer, let alone this beauty. They were agreed that it was the finest sporting car on the road today with its four-and-a-half-litre side-valve engine, its this and that and the other, terms which were dear to the newly growing band of motor car enthusiasts. Some began to drift away as the talk became too technical for them but Tim was only too happy to explain to those who stayed, mainly youths, this lever and that switch, to talk of speeds and b.h.p, whatever that might mean, but Mr Watson's disapproving face at the office window on the first floor had reminded him, and them, that there was no profit to be made hanging about in the yard when their mules had been turned on and were waiting for them. Business was bad enough as it was without the men wasting their time, and the firm's, in idle chatter. Mr Watson had no control over Tim Broadbent, of course, whose mill it was but he knew that his employer, who was known to be soft-hearted, would not want to see his operatives "quartered" on his behalf. That had been at seven thirty.

At midday a stream of small boys, each carrying a basin covered with a saucer and tied up in a large red and white checked cloth, converged on the big iron gates of the mill. There was a ringing clatter of clogs on cobbles which slowed noticeably as they passed the great red monster of Mr Broadbent's new motor car, the magnificence of which had reached their ears at school during playtime. They stared in awe but dared not linger for they had their dads' "baggin" to deliver before the faltering in the note of the engine which ran the frames and mules warned them that in a moment there would be a mass exodus from the mill of those who went home for their dinner. Most would be women.

At twelve thirty, after five hours of "messing about", as he called it, at his desk, it had been too much for Tim Broadbent, the consuming need to leap into the Vauxhall, switch her on, rev the engine and roar out of the yard to the accompaniment of cheers from the men and small boys who still hung about there. The motor car was fast becoming commonplace on the roads of Britain and these men had grown accustomed to them but none was as splendid, as expensively luxurious, as fast and daring as this one.

They watched him swing out into Radnor Street and heard the roar of the powerful engine as the machine turned the corner on to the main Huddersfield road which headed away from the centre of Oldham. For a period of two minutes they could still hear the howling of it, heading towards open country and the moorland. He would go over Saddleworth way, they supposed, pitting his skill and nerves on the narrow, winding lanes, the tracks and ways which threaded the high moorland. Lucky bugger, being able just to leave the mill and head off wherever he fancied in that glossy machine of his while they had no choice but to return to their jennygates where each minded "a pair of his own".

*   *   *

When Molly turned at last, fearfully, for in her mind were confused thoughts of dragons, monsters and fiends with faces like Pikey Watson who had come to get her, she was considerably startled to see, not a monster but the flashing, shining, gleaming splendour of the biggest motor car she had ever clapped eyes on and behind the wheel the good-humouredly smiling face of Mr Broadbent, the man who was the "maister" of her and Betty and hundreds of other lasses at Broadbents Mill. The noise of the machine had shattered her almost comatose state, created in the tranquillity of the sun-drenched lane where no motor car should be and it had wrenched her from the dream world she was in in a particularly ferocious manner. She did not know why she should feel startled or in any way confused, for after all this was where Mr Broadbent lived and he had a perfect right to drive up to his gate, to go beyond the gate, which it seemed he intended to do.

But shouldn't he be at the mill at this time of the morning?

As she should! Dear Lord, as she should. What the devil was she doing here loitering about as though she were as grand a lady as this chap's mother, or sister, with no need to bother with such things as spinning frames, or rovings and spindles and bobbins. The doffers would be moving about the machines taking off the empty bobbins and replacing them with full ones and they would all be asking one another where Molly O'Dowd was this morning. Betty, who worked in the next frame to hers and with whom she shared a cup of tea at ten o'clock would already be wondering why she had not called for her on the way to work, and would be discussing it with the other spinners, speculating on what was up with her since they had called out a cheerful "Ta-ra" to one another at the end of the shift yesterday with no presentiment that tomorrow would not be exactly the same as today.

"Are you all right?" she heard Mr Broadbent call out as he half stood in the motor car. He was not in any way put out to see her there, it seemed, which he had every right to be since it was his gate she was leaning against. His voice had none of that patronising tone the gentry often affected. It appeared he was prepared to wait amiably until she was ready to do as he had asked. She was a black-shawled woman, a mill girl like any of the thousands who worked in the cotton towns of Lancashire. God alone knew what she was doing staring through his gates, he would be thinking, but she seemed harmless enough.

She did not answer and Tim Broadbent was ready to leap out over the side of the Vauxhall which, though it had a door, he rarely opened. She was elderly, that was obvious, dressed in her shawl and clogs, and he began to feel uneasy. She must be unwell, surely, and what was he to do with her if she collapsed?

From beneath the edge of her shawl Molly saw the concern in his face and could you wonder at it, finding a half-witted woman, for that was how she would appear, hanging about outside his home. Deaf as well. Daft and deaf, and with that she threw back the shawl, removed her cap, shook out her curls and grinned at him to show him she was neither. Pikey Watson might call her names and threaten her with his belt end. He might try to put his ham-like hands up her skirt and promise her a "present", his word, if she were a good girl, meaning just the opposite, of course, but he'd not get the better of Molly O'Dowd. Nobody would.

The wide grin said it all and though it was not actually aimed at him but was a confirmation of Molly's resolution to be taken down by no man, Tim Broadbent got the full, blinding glory of it.

"I'm champion, Mr Broadbent," she answered, as blithe now as she had been sad a moment ago. "I'll soon 'ave them gates open fer thi'."

Tim Broadbent sat slowly back in his seat, not even breathing, he realised later, staring at the vision which appeared from beneath the shawl, his strong hands gripping the steering wheel as the girl, she seemed no more than that, turned to the gates.

She wrestled for perhaps ten seconds with the latch, just as though her hands were paralysed by some emotion and were too excited to obey what her brain was telling them to do, then, with a gesture of pure rapture, a reverence which implied a worshipper approaching the altar, an awestruck wonder which Tim could not, for the life of him, help but marvel at, she pushed the gates wide, her face to the house. She simply stood there in the middle of the drive, oblivious to anything but the serene beauty of what lay before her. He and his motor might not have existed, might have been swallowed up at the back of her for all the heed she took of him. She was quite still, like a graceful young doe which scents danger deep in the forest, but it was not fear that held her fast but something else he could not name.

The day was warm and sunny and bright and the slight breeze moved her hair, ruffling through its darkness, its gleaming, polished darkness. The sun in the azure-tinted blue of the sky touched it, placing sparks of russet and gold and chestnut in it. It was short, thick and curling, tumbling in wind-blown disorder over her brow and neck, the skin of which was a pure, alabaster white and as fine as rare porcelain. Tim Broadbent could not wait another minute to look properly into her face, which he had only glimpsed as she had turned away. He wanted, more than anything he had ever wanted before, to see what colour her eyes were.

She still remained where she was, her hands at her breast lightly holding her shawl and cap to her, then, suddenly, as though she had become nerveless and boneless, no longer capable of holding it, she let the shawl slip down her back to fall in a dark pool about her feet. She was dressed in a simple white cotton blouse with short sleeves above her elbow and a cotton skirt of some neutral tobacco shade which was somewhat longer than the ones the ladies with whom he was acquainted were wearing now. She wore no stockings and on her feet were a pair of buckled, iron-tipped clogs.

She made no attempt to retrieve her shawl but continued to stand, tall and graceful and still, absorbing, he could think of no other word, through her eyes and through the pores of her skin, the dreaming, sunlit loveliness of his home.

Climbing from the car he moved towards her and picked up her shawl but did not offer it to her since he seriously doubted she would even notice. Her eyes were blue, deep and lucent, or were they green, he asked himself as he stood beside her and looked into her rapt face. They were framed by long, dark lashes which, amazingly, were dewed with tears. She was very pale, like someone in shock – and he had seen enough of those to know – except for her mouth which was a full, poppy red.

He said nothing. It didn't seem appropriate somehow, not at this unique moment. He had the strange feeling he must not disturb her, for coming from her, surrounding her, holding her firmly, was an emotion that was quite indescribable. He did not take his eye from her face, though, as she gazed, beginning to shiver, he noticed, at the house where he had been born and in which, apart from the war years, he had lived all his life. He did not need to look away from her to see what she saw.

Meddins, it was called, though no one knew why and if it was not grand, nor imposing as some old manor houses were, it was, quite simply, the most hauntingly beautiful house he had ever seen and he had travelled extensively, not only in England but in France and Spain and Italy. It was constructed of old-fashioned bricks which were small, each one a fractionally different shade ranging from the palest rose to soft ochre, shell pink, beige and carnation. The house appeared to rest in a bowl of gently sloping green lawn. Before it, and holding it in a gracious half-circle, was a lake on which swans glided and ducks quarrelled and where once three boys had dived and swum and larked about as boys do, and he knew, for he had been one of them. There was a small wooden jetty to which an old rowing boat was moored and all about it, except for the wide gap which allowed the house to be seen, was a graceful curtain of weeping willow trees. Leading up to the lake, where it parted and ran to the right and left of it, was the smoothly raked, honey-coloured gravel driveway on which they stood.

It was said that centuries ago a prosperous farmer had built himself a house on the site of an earlier building and in the seventeenth century a rich Liverpool merchant bought the property and restored it to its present beauty, creating a home for himself which was no less than perfection. Tim's own grandfather, Will Broadbent, had taken it over and the surrounding land when the then owner fell into financial difficulties in 1866. He had married the fabulously wealthy widow Mrs Tessa Greenwood, though he was not, as they said in Lancashire, short of brass himself. Unable to live in his new wife's home of Greenacres in Crossfold, which had been built by her first husband's great-grandfather, he and his wife had moved to Meddins where Tim's father had been born a quite indecent seven months after their wedding.

The arched windows were set deep with lead-latticed panes and wrought-iron casements, all flat to the wall and surrounded by the vibrant blue of climbing wisteria. The main door, which was to the side of the house because of the lake and the need to direct the gravelled drive round it, was sheltered by a wide, overhanging porch set with a coat of arms, a rich finial to the apex of its roof with carvings of stags and other animals so worn they were barely recognisable. There was a date, 1642, blurred and indistinct, set among them.

The chimneys, a dozen of them, were cylindrical, tall and slender, with delicate crenellations at the top like the battlements of a tower. The roof tiles were the same pale rose tint of the bricks with which Meddins was built and the whole was set in a garden of stunning loveliness. As they watched, gardeners were working on the smooth lawn and the well-ordered borders which edged it. It had been watered earlier in the day and crystal droplets still clung in the shade of the trees where the sun had not yet reached, to the scarlet of fuchsia bells, the pink and blue and yellow of lupin, to hollyhock and columbine all nodding in perfect harmony with one another, dewing the roses which glowed from the palest ivory to the deepest crimson. There was an enormous tree standing in front of the house, masking some of its windows. On one side of it where the sun shone it was a bright and vivid green but where it was shady the leaves were darker and they rippled like sea water as the wind caught them. The smooth grass led away to the left and right of the house ending at the woodland in which the whole estate was set.

The girl sighed and shivered with what appeared to be delight.

"It's the first time I've ever seen it wi'out gates between," she said at last. "It fair tekks tha' breath away, don't it?"

"Yes, I suppose it does, especially when you look at it through someone else's eyes." Tim turned to look at the house and then back at her, waiting for her to return his gaze but it appeared she had eyes for nothing but her surroundings. They had narrowed and she raised a hand to shade them, the movement lifting her young breasts which he was instantly and painfully aware of. The colour had returned to her face, pinking at her cheeks and she was smiling. Not the smile of someone who has just been told an amusing anecdote but that of a dreaming contemplation of something which brings unbelievable pleasure. It lifted the corners of her mouth in a way which was quite involuntary.

"Daddy loved it." Nothing more, just as if he should know

exactly what she meant and though he didn't, he answered her, his voice soft.

"I'm not surprised. It's said that my grandparents fell in love with it the moment they saw it and I must admit I'm fond of the old place myself." He paused, lounging indolently beside her, his hands in his trouser pockets, his eyes full of her and her young, vibrant beauty and if she had said it was a grey rainy day and she was the Queen of England he would have agreed with her, so totally bemused was he. "And you say your . . . your father . . .?" His voice rose questioningly.

"Oh, aye, an' 'e made me't same. Not that I needed any persuadin', mind." Her smile deepened.

"No, of course not. They say beauty is in the eye of the beholder though in this case that's not true."

"Do they? What does it mean, d'yer reckon?"

"Oh, that some eyes see a lovely thing and do not recognise it."

"Daddy recognised it. We used ter come out 'ere on most Sundays, me an' 'im, after mass. It were our favourite walk."

"I can imagine. And where would that be from?"

"Oldham. Me daddy worked in tha' mill. 'E minded a pair of 'is own. That was before't war, o' course."

"Of course." Wasn't everything? Did not every lovely thing, every lovely happening and event and feeling date back to that glorious time about which every man and woman who was old enough to remember described simply as "before the war"?

There was a slow-moving herd of cows in the field at their back and one called plaintively, wanting to be milked and evidently of the opinion that the two human creatures were to be about it. From somewhere in the direction of the house a dog barked and several others joined in, then, their disapproval proclaimed at whatever it was that had disturbed their peace, they settled down again. A horse whinnied and above the house swallows wheeled in a thrown veil of movement, disappearing over the lovely winging roof. Doves cooed and a blackbird sang triumphantly and the enchantment of it all was a drug to their senses.

It was the man who broke the silence again. "You sound as if you might come from further away than Oldham." His voice was diffident, not really wanting to break the spell.

It seemed so natural somehow to be standing here talking to this beautiful girl as though they shared, if not the same background, then some special thing which did away with the need to consider it. She was unimpressed with such things as rank, with the fact that he was one of the wealthiest men in Lancashire and that she lived among the poorest. She spoke with the broad-vowelled northern dialect of her people and yet in her voice there was something else, an intonation, soft and musical and lilting.

"Oh, no, I were born an' bred 'ere but me great-grandfather come from Ireland."

"Aah, that explains it then."

"What?" She had still not dragged her eyes away from the house and the gardens, the fountains and pergolas and trellised archways over which roses climbed and tumbled. The trees, the lake, the swans upon it, the reflection of it all in the unruffled water. She was hypnotised by its enchantment, for could you describe it in any other way? He wanted, incredibly, to take her hand and hold it. To stand with her in the perfect harmony of two people simply worshipping Meddins, for it seemed she felt the same way about it as he did.

There was a smile in his voice as he answered her abrupt question.

"The Irish brogue."

"What?" she said again.

"You have the brogue of Ireland in your voice. Only very faint but it's there."

She looked at him then, turning her head on her long, slender neck, her greeny blue eyes studying him. One of them, the one which had been furthest from him, was set in a livid, darkening bruise.

His mouth dropped open in shock. "Jesus . . ." It was out before he could stop himself and yet why should he try? he thought. Wouldn't any man react with horrified disbelief to see such . . . such raw brutality imprinted on the face of a lovely young woman, on the face of *any* woman? Wouldn't any man demand to know who had done this to her and, with a snarl of outrage, set about giving the brute the same treatment?

If he expected her to drop her gaze, to flinch and put her hand to the cheek Pikey Watson had struck he was disappointed, for that was not Molly O'Dowd's way. Daddy had taught her to lift her head proudly, to meet any man's gaze steadily, to square her shoulders and stand up for what she believed in, which was how she'd got the damned thing in the first place. If she had done nothing wrong then she had no need of guilt or shame. She had "spoken up" to Pikey this morning and tried to defend Mammy and the little ones and she'd do it again if she had to.

"Yes?" she asked warningly. She wanted no man's sympathy her truculent expression told him, and he'd no need to think she might weep or faint or whatever it was ladies of his class did when they were hurt. Mind, there weren't too many of them had a Pikey Watson in their lives and, by all that was holy, she wished she was one of them.

"I'm sorry, I didn't mean to be rude but your face . . ."

"Yes?" she said again, daring him to go any further and if he did she'd not be pleased, but Tim Broadbent had been brought up as a gentleman and in his world, men, most men, did not strike a lady. They were taught to believe that their mothers and sisters, and their friends' mothers and sisters, were made of fragile stuff and were to be defended, honoured, respected and adored at all times. Again the war had proved that women were not the frail creatures gentlemen believed them to be. They were tough and durable. They had been employed in what had previously been considered a male territory, freeing men for the trenches. They had driven trams and trucks, worked on munitions and in factories. They had gone to France with the men, nursing in conditions which had flung soldiers into the state known as neurasthenia, or shell shock, and they had survived. Women over thirty had the vote now. They were independent and emancipated and, some would say, men of course, if they got hurt in the hurly-burly of what was essentially a man's world then they had no one to blame but themselves. But still, there was a bloody limit, he told himself savagely as he gazed at the abused face of this unusual girl.

"I can see you don't want to discuss it," he said, his face hardening, "but the man . . . . I presume it *was* a man who gave you that bruise, should be horsewhipped and if you'll give me his name, by God I'd be happy to oblige." His voice was cold, his elegantly smiling mouth smiling no longer. It was as though he were furious with her for having sustained the blow but Molly, whose impish sense of humour often got her into trouble, especially with Pikey, at once saw the funny side of his words. The image of this lean and graceful man taking a horsewhip to the mountain of flesh who was her stepfather was just too ludicrous for words.

"Yer what?" She began to smile, for not only did he have a somewhat . . . old-fashioned . . . view of the world, at least her world, and a way of speaking which came from a place she knew nothing about, she could see he was deadly serious. This gentleman, for he was that, was ready to take up arms in defence of a lady in distress, incensed by what happened regularly in her class. Some men, not all, got drunk every pay day and thrashed their wives before climbing on them and giving them another child. But it should not be put up with, his expression said, as, presumably, she was prepared to put up with her own abuse. He wanted Pikey punished, which was a real laugh for the law took no account of "domestics" as they were called, unless they led to murder.

For the first time she really looked at him. She'd seen him before, of course, years ago in town and at the mill. He had moved on the periphery of her vision when she was spinning, for she'd no time to glance away from her machine for more than a second, but he was the maister, the owner of the mill, though it was rumoured he put in a lot less time there than he should. He was so far above her and the other be-shawled and be-clogged spinners he might have been the King up in London. Now she had a good scen at him, unselfconsciously studying him, her slanting, cat-like eyes not wavering as they moved across his face and now, despite his anger, it was his turn to smile.

He was very handsome with a long, curving mouth and a whimsical half smile which lifted its corners. His eyes were a deep chocolate brown, warm with humour, narrowed now against the sun and his skin was bronzed as though he spent as little time as he could indoors, which she supposed would be true in that infernal thing he drove. When he smiled it was to reveal excellent teeth. He was tall, half a head taller than she was, his frame loosely put together, with crisp fair hair cut in short curls. There was a cleft in the middle of his chin. Though he had just come from the mill he was casually dressed in a rough tweed jacket and flannels.

"Well?" he said, beginning to fidget under her steady gaze, "Will I pass muster? No one has given my appearance such close attention since I stood before my house master at school. I feel I should apologise for not having combed my hair." He grinned endearingly.

"Nay, tha' look grand," she said, for Molly O'Dowd's daddy had also taught her the obligation of truthfulness.

He laughed out loud then and the gardeners on the far side of the lake lifted their heads, wondering who the devil Mr Tim was talking to. A great one for having a right good laugh, was Mr Tim, and he and his brothers, God bless 'em, had been right little beggars, always into some devilment, years ago.

"May I know your name?" he asked engagingly, his eyes all crinkled at the corners, for he was quite old, twenty-eight or -nine, Molly supposed.

"Mary Angelina O'Dowd." She lifted her head proudly. "But they call me Molly. They 'ave done ever since t'day tha' give me't name."

He blinked. "I beg your pardon?"

"Tha'll not remember, o' course. I were no more'n eight or nine, just a kid. It were before't war. Tha' were comin' outer Buckley an' Prockters wi' a right pretty lass . . ."

"Daphne . . ."

"Aye, that were 'er. Well" – she grinned – "bein' a right nosey little madam I were standin' next ter tha' motor." She glanced back at the Vauxhall and his eyes followed her gaze. "That were red an' all. Thi' an' Daphne were off ter . . ."

"Yates's Wine Lodge."

"Aye, well, anyroad, tha' spoke ter me, though Daphne didn't like it an' asked me me name an' when I said it were . . ."

"Mary Angelina . . ."

"Aye, tha' said, do thi' call thi' Molly?"

"I remember." He sighed, a long painful sigh of deep regret as though that far-off day had been one of immeasurable loveliness, one that had gone for ever, erased by what had passed since then.

"Well, Molly . . . I may call you Molly, mayn't I?"

She nodded.

"I am—"

"Yes, I know 'oo thi' are, Mr Broadbent. I work fer thi'."

The statement was made flatly, telling him that Molly O'Dowd and Tim Broadbent had nothing in common and had no right to be standing gossiping on the driveway of his beautiful home. That she was already late for work and if he should take it into his head to mention it to the overlooker that he had found her strolling the lanes about Oldham instead of minding her frame she could be in trouble.

"Anyroad, I'll 'ave ter go. It must be near dinner . . ."

He glanced at his watch as she spoke.

"It's half past two, Molly. Dinner will . . ."

"Saints preserve us, an' 'ere's me standin' about jawin' as though I'd nowt ter do all day."

She sprang to life, turning savagely in the direction of the gates beyond which still stood the Vauxhall, the sun reflecting on every polished surface so that she was dazzled. "I'd no idea what time it were . . . I were that upset . . . what with . . ."

Now she put her hand to her face, ready to weep, not over it but over the possibility of losing her job, of getting into trouble, of having a cut in her wage which Pikey counted out, matching every penny to the hours she worked.

"Molly, don't run away. Stop, there's no need, really . . ." He turned after her as she plunged through the gateway and up the lane in the direction of Oldham. Hedge parsley and nettles stood waist-high in the ditches, bending gracefully towards the narrow lane as Molly passed by, the full green foliage moving like fronds beneath water in the gentle breeze. The stems and leaves of shining cranesbill, seen against the bright sunlight, assumed a translucent beauty of scarlet and crimson but Molly was aware of nothing now but the urgency of getting herself back to her spinning frame.

"'Appen if I was ter go by't fields," Tim heard her mutter and it was then that the shot rang out. It was no more than a crack really, and Molly did not even hear it, or if she did it meant nothing to her, but the effect on the man was appalling.

"Oh, Christ," he said, "oh, Christ," and in a moment of terrible, total panic he threw himself down on the dusty ground, curling into a ball, his arms about his head, his face pressed into his chest, giving the impression of a man protecting the more vital parts of his body from some dreadful attack only he could see coming.

Molly had been about to claw her way through the hedgerow along which a positive explosion of sweet cecily grew. There was a scent of aniseed hanging sharply in the air and in the ditch the sting of nettles but it couldn't be helped. If she could cut even fifteen minutes off the time it would take her to walk, run, to the mill it would be worth a bit of nettle rash.

She turned at the strange sound of Mr Broadbent's voice, her mouth popping open in surprise when she saw him curled up like some . . . some . . . Mother Of God, what *was* he doing? Why had he fallen down, there was nothing . . . no one . . .

"Oh, Christ," he moaned, his mouth muffled against his chest. "Oh, Christ . . ."

She walked back to him hesitantly, since she could hardly leave him like that, could she, standing over his curled-up figure, half her mind registering that he had some cow-shit on his lovely pale grey flannels, the other dwelling on his bewildering behaviour. She was not at all sure she wanted to be mixed up with this . . . this whatever it was. Not when she should be on her way to the mill where she might be able to make some excuse . . . Mammy was not well, which, by now, might not be a lie! Was Mr Broadbent drunk or what? But he couldn't be, could he? He'd been as right as rain a minute ago.

Some memory fluttered at the edge of her mind. A memory which went back to Liam, her big brother . . . he'd been on his last leave with Daddy and Patrick . . . and . . . there'd been something . . . a noise and though he'd not fallen down like Mr Broadbent, he'd certainly acted very strangely.

She turned on her heel, shading her eyes, looking up the driveway in the hope of catching the attention of one of the gardeners but they had all gone.

"Oh, Christ," he said again, and then again, as he had said it on that day seven years ago in the Battle of Meuse-Argonne, when, after four years of bloody trench warfare in which every soldier in his battalion had been killed but him, his mind had decided that it could stand no more.

Molly knelt down beside him and put a reluctant hand on his shoulder, feeling the taut trembling in his body, but he seemed not to notice or even be aware that she was there.

"Sir," she said. "Mr Broadbent, are thi' not well?" which she knew was a daft question since the poor chap was lying in the dust shaking like a leaf and curled up like a baby in a cot.

"Mr Broadbent . . ." She knelt closer to him, sliding her arm beneath his head, for surely he should not have those bright, boyish curls pressed into the dust and when he turned his face up to hers she was appalled. His sun-bronzed flesh was grey now, half eaten away by the great black smudges spreading beneath his eyes which looked as though they stared into hell.

"Mr Broadbent . . . Tim, what is it?" With a compassion which was strong and at the same time gentle, she drew him up against her, holding his head to her breast, some instinct telling her he was a child again, a child who needed his mother and was this not what mothers did? Was this not what Mammy had done for Liam?

"Oh, Christ." His teeth chattered and he was soaked in his own sweat and his arms clung about her as he burrowed his face into the haven, the comfort, the protection only a woman's body can bring to an injured man.

"It's all right, there, there, it's all right." She rocked him as she had seen Mammy rock Liam, smoothing his fair, sweat-soaked curls from his forehead, stroking his sunken cheeks and even dropping a kiss or two, as one would with a child, on to his brow to help ease him from whatever had him in its grip.

The blackbird continued its song, oblivious to anything but its search for a tasty worm and in the wood a squirrel scampered along the branch of tree in its search for its own meal.

Molly had no idea how long she knelt there in the lane, cradling Mr Timothy Broadbent, owner of Broadbents Mill, in her arms and it didn't seem to matter now. All that mattered was his need of her and her capacity to meet that need which it seemed she did. He began to relax, still pressed in her arms but throwing off whatever it was that ailed him.

"It was the bloody rifle," he mumbled. "I wasn't expecting it . . ."

"It doesn't matter. Tha're gettin' better now," she murmured, as though he were a child recovering from an illness, one she must humour and calm. He still held on to her in an embrace which was vice-like.

"I'm sorry . . . Jesus, I'm sorry . . . for this to happen now. It's been over a year since . . . I thought I was over it at last. Jesus, I'm sorry."

"It's all right." She had not the faintest idea what he was talking about but that was all right too, as she held him protectively in her strong young arms in the lane in front of Meddins.

8

He was waiting in the mill yard at seven thirty the next morning as she and Betty clattered arm in arm through the gates. He was leaning against the bonnet of his vibrantly red motor car, his hands shoved deep in the pockets of his flannel trousers, his tweed jacket, the same one he had worn yesterday, unbuttoned to reveal the immaculate laundering of his cream shirt. His tie was a livid glare of red and gold, lemon and what she could only describe as shocking pink, swirls and circles and drifting spirals and once more she was taken back to that day outside Buckley and Prockters. Was it the same one he had worn then? Dear God, it was hideous and yet it was so endearingly him!

Again it was a sunny day and though, being early and the sun low, most of the yard was still in shadow, he and the automobile stood in a square of sunlight. The windows, upwards from the second floor of the six-storey mill building where the sun caught them, winked as though a thousand candles burned behind them and the bright light picked out the bold design of the name on the factory chimney. BROADBENTS SPINNING, it said. Its rays caught Tim Broadbent's fair cap of crisp curls, striking gold from them, and there were many lasses who glanced appreciatively at his long, lean frame, his cheerfully smiling, handsome face from beneath demurely lowered lashes. Some were not so demure. One of those was Betty Spooner. She grinned and nudged Molly who had her head resolutely lowered. Betty was very much of the opinion, one openly conveyed, that Mr Broadbent was a right "looker" and she would not have said "no" to a spin in his splendid motor car. Betty could not have been more surprised when Mr Broadbent's smile deepened into an answering grin though it soon became amazingly apparent that the grin was not directed at her.

"Good morning, Miss O'Dowd. Have you got a minute to spare?" he called out, causing every jaw in the vicinity to drop and every pair of eyes to turn speculatively in Molly's direction. Even above the ring of iron-tipped clogs on cobbles they heard him and Molly wished the ground would open and swallow her up. Or, better still, him and his bloody motor car.

Broadbents Mill covered many acres of ground on the outskirts of Oldham. The area had once been known as Crossfold but as the spinning town of Oldham spread outwards Crossfold had been engulfed in it. The mill had been built in the 1860s by Tim Broadbent's grandfather Will. Grandfather Will had married Tessa Greenwood, widow of the son of one of Crossfold's wealthiest mill owners, but being an independent sort of a chap with a bit of brass of his own he had broken away from the Greenwood side of cotton textile manufacturing and built his own small empire.

Further across town there still remained a concern known as Chapman Spinning and Weaving which was begun in the latter part of the eighteenth century. Chapman's granddaughter Katherine, who inherited it from her father, had become involved with the family of Joss Greenwood, the man she had later married and who was an elected radical member of parliament almost a hundred years ago. Perhaps because of him, for it was said she adored him, and her own compassionate heart she had converted her mill and her workers' hovels into places where men and women might live and work decently.

Her mill, Chapmans Spinning and Weaving, had been run by her husband's brother Charlie, passing through the years to its present owner Joel Greenwood, who was a distant cousin to Tim Broadbent. Both men were known, as had been their forebears, for the decent conditions in which their hands were employed, for their fairness, their good wages and the hours they required their spinners to work. Since 1919 these had been cut from fifty-seven and a half to forty-eight each week. Seven forty-five to five thirty with an hour's break for dinner, five days a week and finishing at twelve thirty on a Saturday morning. Life in the jennygate was hard and the incidence of cancers in the spinners who had worked on the mules for twenty years or more was high. Cancer of the scrotum, believed to be caused by the faint spray of mineral oil blended with animal and vegetable oils used to lubricate the spindles.

Both Mr Broadbent and Mr Greenwood had introduced a specially refined oil in an attempt to lessen the danger of this affliction and it was well known in Oldham that employees of both mill owners who had suffered the disease were well looked after and their families, if they had any, did not want. Aye, good men and good employers, both of them, but Molly could have wished hers to the far side of Besom Hill at this moment.

She had spied him lounging by his motor car but had not for a moment expected the daft beggar to address her in front of all her workmates and was astounded when he did. Astounded and mortified, for what interpretation would they put on the owner of the mill singling out one of his own spinners, and in the yard! Cissie Thompson, who was at her back, began to snigger, whispering something behind her hand to their Elsie, then prodding Betty between the shoulder blades. Molly wanted to turn on the three of them and give them the rounds of the kitchen. They would think the worst, of course, colouring and exaggerating the incident until it was all round the mill she was Mr Broadbent's "fancy piece". And, of all things, calling her Miss O'Dowd as though she were a person of importance. He was still smiling, grinning like a bloody Cheshire cat, really, standing away from the motor car, the sun placing a gleam of gold in his deep brown eyes as he waited for her to detach herself from the gawping crowd.

He'd been a damned nuisance yesterday afternoon as well, once he'd recovered from whatever it was that had ailed him.

"I'll run you home," he announced as he got shakily to his feet.

"Tha'll do no such thing. Tha'd do better ter get thassen ter tha' bed, Mr Broadbent."

"I'll run you home, Molly. After what you have just done for me it's the least I can do." He smoothed his hand over his tumbled hair, then brushed the dust from his flannels. "Anyway, I'm better now, really I am."

They were both embarrassed and could you wonder, Molly thought, remembering his face pressed between her breasts, his arms drawn tight about her. No man, as yet, had touched

Molly O'Dowd and though Mr Broadbent had not done so in any way that might be described as . . . well, impure, she could still remember the feel of him in her arms, the faint aroma of lemon soap and cigarette tobacco which clung to him and – Mother of God – the kisses she had pressed on his forehead.

His face was drawn and spent and his hand had still trembled. Molly had watched him carefully, wondering what was wrong with him. There were tales of men coming back from the trenches in a right old state, declaring they could see their dead mates grinning at them on every street corner, ducking and diving at any sudden noise, just as he'd done, but surely that couldn't be what was wrong with him. The war had been over for nearly seven years now. He was so . . . so . . . healthy-looking, so perfect, so . . . well, it sounded barmy, but he was beautiful, in a completely masculine way, of course. The lines and planes of his face were covered by smooth, sun-browned flesh – or had been until his funny turn – and his eyes, such a lovely brown, were surrounded by a sweep of thick golden lashes tipped with cinnamon. Lashes any girl would envy. His smile was sweet and his expression honest, engaging, cheerful. He was tall, finely proportioned and as far as she could see completely uninjured and yet something had sent him spinning into a black hole in which he had cowered for ten long minutes.

But the idea of coming to a roaring halt before the door of number twenty-two Sidney Street in the magnificent splendour of the machine behind her; of having every net curtain at every window twitched to one side, faces peering out in amazement, including Pikey's, watching, mouths open as Rosie Watson's lass, black shawl and clogs, climbed out of it, made her want to laugh quite hysterically.

"No . . . oh, no, sir, I'll not let thi'. It's not far an' yer not fit."

"I'll decide if I'm fit enough, Molly. I wouldn't dream of letting you walk all those miles to . . . to wherever it is you live. Now hop in and behave yourself."

Her face was agonised. "Oh, sir, I can't let yer. Tha've no idea what would be said about me if I was brought 'ome in tha' motor car."

"I can't see why." His voice had become sharp, the voice of a man who was not used to being argued with, his jaw squaring, his eyes narrowing beneath his dipping eyebrows.

"Don't be daft . . . sir. I'm a mill girl and tha're me boss an' if we was ter be seen tergether they'd add two an' two an' mekk five. Before I knew it they'd 'ave thi' an' me . . . well, yer know what I mean. I've me reputation ter think on . . ." just as though she was some grand personage who could not afford the slightest scandal to tarnish her good name.

"That's bloody ridiculous."

Her own jaw squared ominously. Her mouth tightened and a glint of her snapping temper showed in her slanting cat's eyes. She'd not be sworn at nor argued with, her truculent expression said.

"No, it isn't an' tha' knows it. I'll walk an' that's that," she snapped, and as if to emphasise that she'd not have another word said on the matter she began to step out, head high, back straight, in the direction of St Matthews Church and the stile which led over the hedge and into the fields. A short cut skirting the sandpit and Cloggers Pond, crossing several fields until she reached the football ground, the cricket pitch and the recreation ground on the edge of Oldham. Across the main Ripponden Road and then into the labyrinth of squalid streets which led to Sidney Street and if he could follow her on *that* route in his grand motor car then her name wasn't Molly O'Dowd!

"You're a stubborn woman, Molly," he had called after her, beginning to laugh, accepting that she had beaten him, making no attempt to follow her and when she turned at the stile he was standing where she had left him, watching her. He lifted his hand and, forgiving him, she waved back.

Now would you look at him, grinning like some daft schoolboy, pleased as punch with himself in the knowledge, she supposed, that here he could order her to do whatever he wanted her to do, and she would have to do it, or so he thought.

She threw him an incensed look, hoping he would interpret it, understand and turn away. Leave her alone, at least here where everyone in the yard was watching with goggle-eyed fascination. What was going on, they were asking one another, nudging those who had, incredibly, not noticed. What did Mr Broadbent want with Molly O'Dowd who had no truck with any man and more than a few of them had tried!

Damn him to hell and back! If he must show her up then she'd let no man or woman see that it was bothering her, she told herself as she wrenched her arm away from Betty's. Least of all him and she'd make it quite plain that it would not do. Although she had come from whimsical, light-hearted Irish stock there was a sharp streak of practicality bred in her by several generations of down-to-earth north country women who admired and respected a bit of common sense and who passed down this trait to their daughters. She was a woman and what woman does not recognise and is flattered by the attentions of a personable man, but this was going too far and she'd have nothing to do with it, or him! It was not that he'd said or done anything that might be considered in the least offensive, now or yesterday, but surely the soft devil realised what a pickle he was putting her in. Well, if he didn't now, he soon would!

She wore no shawl today but her sturdy black clogs rang on the cobblestones as she pushed her way through the press of workers who were to spend the next ten hours at their spinning frames and mules. They made way for her, only sorry that, with the engine turned on, they could not afford to linger in the yard and see what was to happen between her and Mr Broadbent.

"Good morning, Molly," he said when she reached him, his smile warm, his eyes glowing with bright good humour. "I just wanted to make sure you had arrived home safely yesterday and to enquire after your eye which I see has developed into a real corker. I haven't seen one so fine since my older brother gave me one when I cheeked him."

By all that was holy, would you listen to the man, going on about her eye, which was nothing to do with him in the first place and within earshot of several latecomers! And anyone'd think she'd not been finding her way about Oldham and the countryside surrounding it ever since she was five years old. With Daddy at first, of course and when he went to war when Molly was still only eight, all by herself. Who did he think she was? One of those delicate ladies she'd seen traipsing about the posh shopping area of Oldham who could go nowhere without a man's arm to support them? Or was he having her on?

She gritted her teeth so hard she could barely speak.

"Listen 'ere, Mr Broadbent . . ."

"Do you think you could call me Tim, Molly?" he asked

her softly and she could have sworn that for a moment he intended reaching for her hand. "You did yesterday," he went on and so she had but only in the emergency of the moment when she had thought him to be almost unconscious. The operatives who were still scrambling to get to their machines on time were inclined to stumble over their own feet as they stared at Molly O'Dowd. Everyone knew her, for she was an attractive girl with a fine figure, good-hearted too, though it was known her temper could be tricky if you displeased her. She was dressed as all the women were and they found nothing unusual in that, except that she was engaged in what looked like furtive conversation with the mill owner, Mr Broadbent himself.

She reared back from him as though he had made some obscene suggestion.

"No, I could not," she asserted roundly, "an' if it's all't same ter thi' I'd be glad if tha'd not order me over ter speak ter thi' in't yard in front o' me friends. What they'll be sayin' don't bear thinkin' about. I know tha've a right ter . . . speak ter me, if tha' 'ave to, that is, about spinnin' or summat o' that sort but tha' should do it through't overlooker not shout across yard full o'people."

Her face was a rosy red with her fury.

He slapped the palm of his hand to his forehead and the pleased expression on his face turned to one of agonised remorse.

"Molly, oh Lord, I'm sorry. I didn't think. I should have done, I know, but it was just that you were so . . . so kind yesterday and then you dashed off before I had a chance to thank you properly."

"That's as may be," she answered primly, not noticing that he was doing his best not to smile, nor giving him a chance to finish, "but that were yesterday an' now, if that's all, I'll be on me way. Me frame'll be turned on an' me not there ter see to it."

"Of course, forgive me." His deep brown eyes told her he could not be more sorry but despite his contrite expression there was a twitch at the corner of his mouth which she tried hard not to respond to.

Someone was whistling an out-of-tune rendition of "The Sheikh of Araby" in the far corner of the yard and a man's voice complained that some daft beggar had taken the wrong bales of raw cotton from his waggon and there'd be hell to pay when they reached the scrutching machine. "What's goin' on?" another voice shouted, then it all faded away, leaving nothing but the stamp and crash of the horses' hooves on the cobbles and the mild sputter of one of the new trucks which were beginning to take the animals' place.

"Well, as long as tha' know," Molly continued loftily, her own soft coral mouth beginning to lift at the corners, for Mr Broadbent's lovely smile was very difficult to resist. She found she was reluctant to move away for some reason she could not identify.

"Oh, I do, Molly and I promise I shan't . . . approach you again."

"Right then."

"Unless you're alone."

"What does that mean?" Her tone was suspicious.

"Well, I presume you are giving me this ticking off because I had the temerity to speak to you when your friends were about, or that is what you are implying. In which case it seems to me you are saying you would have no objection to my speaking to you when they are not."

Molly did not know what "temerity" might mean since it was not a word she had heard before but she did know when she was being teased. He had somehow twisted her words about so that it seemed she would not mind a bit of a chat when they were alone, and, though it was completely out of the question, naturally, she found the idea quite . . . novel. He was years older than her and from a different class altogether but he was so . . . so . . . likeable you couldn't help but warm to him. His eyes twinkled now, narrowing in a smile, a smile so sweet and funny you absolutely knew he meant her no harm, and by that she meant as Pikey did.

"Well . . ." Molly found herself at a loss for words. For five years she had worked in the mill and had successfully deflected the banter, the cheek, the good-humoured, inoffensive repartee which the men in the jennygates aimed at any girl with the slightest claim to good looks. She could give verbally as good as she got and found no problem in "wiping the floor" with any lad she considered had gone too far. She liked a laugh, a joke, as long as it was not dirty, but she would stand no nonsense. She stood up for herself and anyone else who might need the sharp edge of her Irish tongue and quick wit, but this man somehow seemed to have a way of . . . well, she could only describe it as "getting round her". He made her want to smile all the time and yet she had really only known him for less than twenty-four hours. She'd seen him about, of course, in the past five years, but since she had spoken to him yesterday, gazed at the beauty of his home, stood in peaceful harmony with him on the driveway and held him in her arms when he fell into that funny fit, he had, she was honest enough to admit it, been in her thoughts far more than she thought was good for her. She had liked him, which was a gormless thing to say, but it was true. He was very likeable, even if he was a bit soft in the head, by which she meant expecting to hold a conversation with her in the mill yard without every operative in the mill conjecturing about it. You'd think a man in his position and of his obvious intelligence would know it would cause no end of talk and yet that was just it, she suddenly realised. There was an honesty, an innocence almost about him that saw no reason why two adults, despite being of the opposite sex and of a different class and culture, could not address one another even beneath the eye of every employee in the mill. They were doing no wrong, no harm to anyone, were they, he would reason, if it occurred to him to question it, but still, for her own sake she must put a stop to it now before . . .

"Will you come for a spin with me, Molly? Perhaps this Sunday?" he said suddenly, leaning forward to look intently into her face. At the office window on the second floor where he had been curiously watching the exchange, Tim Broadbent's cousin, Joel Greenwood, frowned.

"A spin? What's that?"

"In my motor. We could go up on to the moors. I know a splendid spot for a picnic. It's called Badger's Edge and rumour has it that one of my ancestors, a rebel by the name of Joss Greenwood, used to meet my . . . well, I suppose she would be my great-grandmother . . ."

"Eeh, no! Eeh, I couldn't . . ." Her rosy mouth, which was just about to tell him that he must not single her out again, fell open in dismay and her rosy face became even rosier. Her eyes widened quite dramatically and Tim was fascinated by the way the green and the blue lay almost in stripes from the pupil with a narrow ring of black about the iris, like a cat's.

"Why not? You know I would not . . . hurt you, don't you, Molly. I like you too much for that."

He liked her! How strange that they should both have the same feeling for one another and that feeling should be "liking".

"Nay, sir, that's got nowt ter do wi' it, likin' or not. It just wouldn't be . . . be . . ."

"What, Molly? Why shouldn't you and I . . .?"

But this was going too far and too fast for Molly O'Dowd and she whirled away from him, watched by dozens of wondering eyes.

The house was empty when she got home at just gone six o'clock. She had clung like a limpet to Betty's arm as they clattered through the mill gate and into Ceylon Street, glancing over her shoulder as though the devil himself was at her back. She refused absolutely to discuss, even with Betty who was her best friend, what the maister had wanted with her, simply because she was too embarrassed to admit that she had found it . . . welcome. Let Betty put what interpretation she wanted on it, which would be that a man of Mr Broadbent's position was using it to get Molly O'Dowd into a compromising situation. What else would a man like Mr Broadbent want with a girl like Molly? That's what "gents" did. Chased mill girls and factory girls, shop assistants and waitresses, wooing them with presents and a "good time" until the inevitable happened. Mind you, Betty remarked cheerfully, give her half the chance and she'd snap it up so fast the poor man wouldn't know what had hit him. A well-set-up chap like Mr Broadbent and if that's what he'd been after she thought Molly was cracked not to take him up on it. She'd no need to let him . . . well, you know, she went on, slyly nudging Molly in a way Molly abhorred. A kiss or two, happen, which was quite acceptable, but she'd best not let Pikey know or he'd give her a "mouse" to match the one she already had. Betty was only too familiar with the situation at number twenty-two Sidney Street and was always ready to commiserate, since this was not the first time Molly's stepfather had landed her one.

At the mention of "a kiss or two", Molly turned venomously on her friend.

"Tha've a mucky mind, Betty Spooner, an' one o' these days tha're gonner trip up an' fall in it."

"Well!" Betty put her hands on her hips and glared. "You listen 'ere, me girl. There's no need ter tekk that attitude. I were only . . ."

"No, *you* listen. 'E's not like that . . ."

"'Ow dost tha' know if this mornin's first time tha've spoke to 'im?" Betty's expression said she was not born yesterday.

"Tha' mind tha' own business, Betty Spooner," Molly cried in desperation, not knowing what else to say, "an' I'll mind mine."

"Well . . ."

"An' I'll walk rest o't way on me own," which she did, or rather ran, as fleet as a deer along Huddersfield Road and through the maze of streets which led to Sidney Street, not awfully sure what she was running from, Betty's questions or the expected sound of the lively red motor car driven by Mr Broadbent.

She was glad Mammy wasn't in. It gave her a bit of time to pull herself together, to recover from the awful day she'd had, for try as she might she could not get the smiling eyes and whimsically tilted mouth of Mr Broadbent out of her mind. She'd worked like ten men, calling out time and again to the team of "doffers" who stalked the machines taking off the empty bobbins and replacing them with full ones.

"We can't keep up wi' thi', Molly," one grumbled. It took five minutes for a good team of doffers to change the bobbins and Molly fidgeted about as they did it, scarcely able to wait to get back to work in order to keep her mind from the incredibly lovely picture of herself and Mr Broadbent and that wondrous machine of his roaring out of Oldham, her in her best frock and hat with her new silk stockings, up into the high moorland which, though she had been surrounded by it all her life, she had never really seen.

She made herself a cup of tea and sat down to drink it before the fire which rarely went out. It heated the ovens in which her mother cooked and baked and the water with which she did the family's weekly wash. It warmed and comforted them on a bitter winter night and was the very heart of the house.

She placed her toes on the fender, wriggling and stretching them in the crackling warmth of the flames which tinted her white skin to cream and peach and rose. She wondered where Mammy had got to. Wherever it was she must have met Clare from school and taken her with her. She sometimes went up to Father O'Toole's at St Saviours and did a bit of scrubbing for him. There were not many folk who would employ a woman who dragged young children at her skirts, especially one as old as Mammy but the parish priest was a kindly and understanding man who knew of Mammy's circumstances, meaning Pikey, and Mammy's struggle to keep faith with the Church. He did his best to see that Róisín Watson's children were brought up in the true religion despite the difficulties which arose from her disastrous second marriage. He often put a bit of work Mammy's way, knowing that the money she earned went on her children and not down her husband's throat.

Molly herself had not been to mass for weeks, nor to confession. She often found it hard to reconcile the loss of her daddy and brothers and the appalling introduction of Pikey Watson into her and Mammy's life with the teaching of the Church, but she knew it upset Mammy if she lapsed and didn't Mammy have enough on her plate already without thinking her daughter's soul was damned to hell for all eternity? She supposed if she did go she would have to tell Father O'Toole about Mr Broadbent although she had done no wrong, none at all. She was tempted. Dear sweet Mary, she was tempted, but Betty had put nasty thoughts, her *own* nasty thoughts, into Molly's mind, making what had been as sweet and unblemished as a flower about to open into something . . .

The hands on her shoulders froze her for one heart-stopping moment into the depths of the sagging chair. Her back was glued to the cushions Mammy had made, and her feet, still up on the fender, made it difficult for her to escape. She sat there, paralysed with shock and the hands moved down inside the neck of her blouse, one to each naked breast, thumb and forefinger finding the bobs of her nipples and pinching them cruelly. They were huge, those hands, kneading and twisting at her soft, vulnerable flesh. There was the sound of grunting like a pig at a trough and, with a scream of outrage which took the owner of the hands by surprise, Molly was released from the half-dreaming state which Pikey had found her in. She leaped up to face him, tearing her blouse as his hands were cast off. Without thinking, her instincts rushing to defend her woman's body from a male predator, she grabbed the heavy, brass-headed poker from the "tidy". Taking a stance somewhat in the manner of a player in the game of rounders she had enjoyed at school, swinging it to and fro, she moved from bare foot to bare foot on the cold of the linoleum.

"You bastard . . . you bastard . . ."

"Now then, me lass," Pikey smirked, "there's no need fer that. It were only a bit o' fun. An' don't tell me tha' weren't willin'. Them titties o' thine were stood out like door knockers. Tha' let me get right up to't chair, an all, wi'out even turnin' round so . . ."

"Tha' filthy bastard . . . tha' dirty, filthy bastard. I didn't 'ear tha' come in. D'yer think I'd play some daft game? Holy Mother o' God, don't tha' dare say I were . . . that I'd let tha' put tha' . . . Dear Jesus, I'd kill messen before I'd let thi' touch me an' I'll kill *thee* if tha' try it again."

Her face was dough white and sweating and her teeth snarled at him from between her flat, parted lips. She was shuddering violently, her eyes wild and hot and hating. Her breasts, even after no more than fifteen seconds of Pikey's rough handling, were sore and she trembled deep inside her where the untouched core of her womanhood, that which he had threatened, recoiled in horror. She felt filthy, marked, unclean, ashamed and frightened. The poker seemed to hold no fear for him. Indeed he grinned playfully as though it were all part of the "game" they were playing, taking several small, darting steps, first one way then the other round the chair in which she had been sitting.

For some unaccountable reason the face of the man she had spoken to for the first time yesterday swam into her vision. Though she was glaring into Pikey's coarse, grinning features, those of Tim Broadbent, humorous, mouth curling in a smile, eyes deep and admiring, but kind, honest with something he felt, overlaid her stepfather's and at once, again she could not explain why, she felt a calmness come over her. She saw again the sun-hazed serenity of the house called Meddins, heard the lazy drone of the bumble bees among the flowers, even smelled the flowers and it was as though the man, the man for whom she worked, spoke to her.

"Tell me who it was who hit you and I'll see he's horse-whipped," he had said to her, his smiling voice suddenly dangerous.

"Tha' put one finger on me again, Pikey Watson, or on me mammy or them kids an' I'll report thi' ter Mr Broadbent."

Pikey's face was a picture. She might have told him she was off to inform His Majesty the King who'd have him clapped in the Tower before you could say "half a pound of tripe and two cowheels". His chin dropped and his mouth fell open. Molly felt the satisfaction move in her, though she had time to wonder what Mr Broadbent would have to say if he knew she was using his name to threaten her stepfather.

Then Pikey grinned and her satisfaction ebbed away, for the grin was not pleasant. Though she was not sure how, or why, she knew she had made a mistake.

9

The cricketing weekends, the tennis weekends, the shooting weekends which were his mother's way of bringing as many attractive, well-bred and marriageable young ladies to his attention as possible were, more often than not, Tim Broadbent conceded, a great deal of fun and, in that respect, enormously successful. Perhaps his mother would not think so a few weeks later when it would become apparent to her that not one of those young ladies had caused the slightest alteration in the steady rhythm of his heartbeat. It was sad, he understood that, none better, for he was only too unhappily aware that there was nothing more in this world his mother longed for than to see him "settled" – dreadful word – with the right girl from the right background, of course, married to a young lady with at least twenty good years of childbearing in her. She longed to fill the empty nurseries which had once resounded with the shouts and laughter of Will and Charlie and himself and though she did her best not to put pressure on him, knowing his own delicate balancing act, a heritage of the Great War, there was only himself, Tim Broadbent, who could do it for her.

He had a sister, Tessa. Tessa was married to Hugh Addington, an ex-officer like himself and who, also like himself, had managed to get through the war with nothing worse than a bad case of the "jitters", his sister's description of the mental scars her husband bore. Tessa and Hugh had three children, all girls, and every so often they came over from Hugh's place in Surrey, but though Meddins was filled again for a little while with children's voices, they were little girls' voices, Addington voices and nothing at all to do with the Broadbents. Muriel Broadbent longed for little boys, Broadbent boys, to fill the agonisingly empty hole the death of her two eldest sons at Ypres and Loos had left and if Tim didn't fill it no one else would. He was the last of them and with him would die the name which had been respected in cotton, and out of it, for over a century.

Every few months she had what once had been cumbersomely called a "Saturday to Monday", inviting the daughters of her friends, some of them a bit long in the tooth, Tim murmured sardonically to his cousin Joel, since the war had deprived a whole generation of them of husbands. They were eager to be married to him; to Joel who was also considered to be a good catch or to any suitable gentleman, as eager as his mother was to see him married to them. He would himself like to find a pretty, personable wife, to have the children his mother longed for. But his heart must be stirred, he admitted sadly to himself, before he could contemplate spending the rest of his life with one of them.

And then, of course, there was his "trouble", though thankfully, as the years passed, it was beginning to ease, but would one of the "bright young things", the "flappers" as they were called, be able to understand and sympathise as, a small but persistent voice inside him kept on telling him, young Molly O'Dowd had understood and sympathised? He could not get it out of his mind how safe he had felt that day as she had wrapped him in her arms in the lane at the gates of Meddins, as he pressed his face and uncomprehending, terror-stricken body to her breast. He had been back "there", where his nightmares had begun, a survivor of the ravages of shell shock, mustard gas, trench foot, shattered bodies and shattered nerves and she had soothed him, calmed him, been a steady rock in the maelstrom of destruction which had swept over him. She had been ready to tear off across the fields in, he supposed, the direction of the mill, his mill, where she worked, shaking herself free of the strange, almost hypnotic trance he had found her in. But she had come back when the shot rang out and with the compassion of a woman, a real woman, and not one of the "modern" girls he was accustomed to, had returned him to normality, or as normal as he was ever likely to get.

He had not seen her since the following day in the mill yard.

The weekend weather had been spectacularly glorious

113

and the chaps, some of them, like him, veterans of the trenches who had been unable to settle to anything that might be called steady, had played cricket on the pitch his father had put in at the back of Meddins before the war, utilising an orchard where the apple trees were past their best. The chaps had adopted the enthusiasm which they had shown over ten years ago on the playing fields of the public schools they had attended and the ladies had watched and clapped, or yawned, depending on their age and disposition. The cricketers were all about his age, having gone, in 1914, straight from school to war, starry-eyed with idealism, as he and Will and Charlie had been. These men had gone through hell and now all that concerned them was to wring every last drop of pleasure from their lives. They had arrived in their Mercedes, their Hispano-Suizas, their Aston Martins, fast motor cars driven by fast men, accompanied, each of them, by a bevy of pretty, modern young women whose shingled hair, painted faces and short skirts vastly disconcerted his mother. She might have invited a dozen or so but they turned up in droves, inspired by the prospect of some fun. It seemed the old-fashioned courtesy of answering invitations and writing "thank-you" letters had been swept away by the war years, many of which these younger girls barely remembered. The older ones, those who were approaching thirty and to whom Tim was unfailingly kind and courteous, had been brought up in the way Muriel and their mothers had been brought up. They were modest, most of them, self-effacing, conforming to the rules of their class, of pre-war society, reared to marry and give birth to the next generation of landowners. Now they must remain single or do their best to catch the eye, in a ladylike way, naturally, of those men who were still available. Many of them had chosen the former.

There were all kinds of "high jinks" over those weekends, the sort got up to by the dashing Prince of Wales whose main purpose in life, or so it seemed to Muriel Broadbent's generation, was the pursuit of pleasure. They danced the night away in the drawing room at Meddins which was stripped of its expensively luxurious Aubusson carpet, each guest doing their own version of the latest dance craze from America which had, Muriel's generation decided, the most odd names. The breakaway, the black bottom, the conga and the charleston, to name but a few. In a blare of smoky jazz from the records played on the gramophone, their eyes glazed with alcohol, they swayed and stamped and had a ripping time and Tim Broadbent often found he was yawning with boredom even before midnight struck. His mother would put on a superb meal once she had ascertained how many were to sit down to it, for with the advent of the motor car one was never sure where one's guests might disappear to.

But best of all Muriel Broadbent liked to give dinner parties, sending out invitations to local society of which her friends and their daughters were a part. A dinner party was predictable. The guests arrived and drank sherry for half an hour before going into dinner. They ate her superbly cooked and served meal, conversing amiably and in a civilised manner with one another until she gave the signal for the ladies to leave the gentlemen to their port and cigars. The ladies wore elegant evening gowns which reached the floor and the gentlemen were correct in the immaculate black and white of their evening suits. It was terribly old-fashioned, she knew, but at least there was none of the bright and witty repartee which passed for conversation among the young. There were none of the "shimmy" dresses, the gleaming caps of short, flat hair, the smoking, the drinking of cocktails, the noisy music, the horseplay which she was forced to endure on the "Saturday to Mondays" she arranged for her son's sake. In one way or another, she didn't care which, she meant to find him a suitable wife.

Many of the guests she invited to her dinner parties were what were called "new society", the families of self-made men, a great many of which had sprung up during the war years. Her own husband's family, a century or more ago, had been such men, but, by marrying well and wisely, educating their sons with the sons of gentlemen, they had become gentlemen themselves. Considering the new society, one was selective, of course, but most of them were eager to be accepted and had learned how to conduct themselves properly. Many of them were charming, elegant, courteous and all of them very rich which, at the moment, counted for more than Muriel liked to admit. The new rich had made their money from brewing or shipbuilding, army contracts or tobacco, but they had acquired polish and the social graces which seemed to dovetail with what Muriel called her friends from the old days.

There was, naturally, the exception, like the dreadful little man Sam Murchison who had made millions, it was rumoured, during the war and he had been enormously wealthy before. His wealth had bought his daughter a title and Daphne was now the Countess of Erinfield, her husband the only surviving son whose inheritance and family home would have been eaten up by taxes had it not been for Sam Murchison's generosity. Sam and Ada, his mouse of a wife, though they were invited to many of her friends' homes since they were so enormously wealthy and one could not really afford to ignore it since they had two unmarried sons, had never set foot in Meddins.

The dining room at Meddins had a high ceiling and, like the rest of the rooms, like the rest of the house itself, was exquisitely furnished. It was large and spacious and had tall windows which looked out to the terrace and a long vista of rolling lawns and flowerbeds which led down to the lake. The walls and ceiling were a pale washed green with intricate mouldings of white plasterwork in the shape of fleurs de lys, leaves entwined with lover's-knots, squares and rosettes which stood out in delicate detail. The floor was a mirror of polished wood and in the centre of it was an enormous square carpet on which the dining table and chairs stood. The furniture was fine, elegant, the table long and rounded at its corners, the chair seats covered in pale green damask. Beneath the window was a backless couch, its arms delicately curved, and standing against one of the walls of the room was a fine Chippendale, serpentine-fronted side table from which the butler served and on which stood an abundance of gleaming silver, candlesticks, decanters, a silver rose bowl and numerous serving dishes. There were bowls of fresh cut flowers on small tables and tastefully arranged on the wide mantelshelf above the marble fireplace. In an alcove, painted in a darker green the better to show her off, was a statue of Diana the huntress glancing over her shoulder as though keeping an eye on the guests.

Tonight there were thirty of them, sixteen ladies and fourteen gentlemen, which Muriel thought was a splendid achievement in this day and age especially as eight of the gentlemen, including her son and her nephew, as she thought of Joel Greenwood, were single. There were the Herberts, Helen and Percival, with their eighteen-year-old, Angela, a pretty, shy child who had only just returned from her finishing school in France and was far too young for Tim but you never knew with men. Perhaps her demure innocence and freshly blooming youth might appeal to him, though her total lack of conversation, despite her expensive education, could be a disadvantage.

There were the Knights, Maurice and Beatrice, with their Laura whose fiancé, a school friend of Tim's, had been killed on the Somme; the Ropers, William and Charlotte, Totty for short. The Ropers had three unmarried daughters, Anne, Dorothy and Mae, all under twenty-five but all painfully plain. Still, Willy Roper was a gentleman, and rich so perhaps their complete lack of what today was considered to be smart, attractive and witty might be overlooked.

The Davidsons, Arthur and Joan, had managed to persuade their two sons, Justin and John, eighteen and nineteen years old respectively and who were far too young yet to be considering marriage, to partner their sisters Ellen and Agnes, who, at ninteen and twenty-one, were not. Peter and Delia Bowman with their pert daughter, Sarah, who was a mite too daring for Muriel's taste, but kind-hearted and even-tempered and, in a way, Muriel's favourite for Tim since she was pretty, well bred and would be enormously rich one day. She was twenty, a perfect age for a bride. The Bowmans had brought their nephew, George, who was staying with them, a handsome young man who, to his vast disappointment, or so he told everyone, had been just too young to fight in the war. He and Sarah kept up a scintillating exchange of witticisms which Muriel neither cared for nor understood but Tim seemed to find it amusing.

Owen and Hilda Forrester had been Muriel's lifelong friends since she and Hilda were girls. They had come with Kathleen, their daughter of twenty-seven, bringing her, against her will, Muriel was aware, since Kathleen was resigned to spinsterhood. Nevertheless Hilda would not give up, dragging her from one party after another in the hope of finding her a husband. She would, apart from her age, make an excellent wife for Tim, having been tutored from childhood to be wife, hostess and mother. Josephine, her sister, still had a chance, it was thought, at twenty-two. Fifteen when the war ended, she had developed into a striking young woman and it was noticed by more than Muriel that a great deal of interest was taken of her by George Bowman.

Owen and Hilda's son, Oliver, a few years older and a damaged survivor of the war, having lost an arm at Neuve Chapelle, escorted his sisters and Muriel knew that Hilda, like herself, was longing to see him set up with some kind and pedigreed young lady and perhaps here, among Muriel's guests, he might find one.

Tim's school friend, Rupert Lucas, had "dropped in", his words, to see his old chum a day or two before the dinner party, roaring up the curved gravelled driveway to the house in the kind of flaunting sports car all young unmarried men seemed to favour these days and Muriel had no choice but to invite him to stay. He was a gentleman. He had known Will and Charlie and was happy to share Muriel's quiet remembrances of the days when he and her sons had climbed trees, swum in the lake and ridden their fine horses about the estate at neckbreaking speed.

And then there was Joel. Joel Greenwood who was almost Tim's cousin, since Joel's grandfather had been brother to Tim's great-grandmother. It was all a bit complicated, involving Chapmans and Greenwoods and Broadbents but, like Tim, Joel was the only son to come back from the war to run the cotton mill some far-off Chapman had begun. He was a quiet, one even might call him brooding man, dark as the Broadbents and Greenwoods were, apart from Tim who had inherited his streaked blond hair from her side of the family. Joel was tall, three inches over six feet, a big man with broad shoulders and an arrogant tilt to his head which said it would bow to no man and it was perhaps this, or some characteristic he had had passed down to him from his sturdy, north country forebears, which had brought him unscathed – or so it appeared – through the war years. His hair was thick, tumbling with rich brown curls on to his forehead. It was often in need of a barber since he was a busy man and had little leisure for such niceties, he had remarked in his coolly courteous way when Muriel, feeling she had the right as his aunt, had remarked on it. His eyes were so deep a brown they were almost black and they were set in thick dark lashes which drooped lazily, though there was nothing somnolent about Joel Greenwood as any of his business competitors could tell you. He was well educated, as Muriel's boys had been, at a first-class public school and it had been remarked upon in the Penfold Valley and in

Oldham itself that it was not exactly the training a lad who was to go into his father's mill might be expected to have. Nevertheless, when old Joel, his father, had died and Pearce, Joel's elder brother, had been killed at Gallipoli, Joel had, like Tim, stepped into the shoes he had not been expected to wear and made a damn fine job of marching about in them. His mill, Chapmans Manufacturing Concern, though many cotton mills were going, or had gone, to the wall, was quietly ticking over, it was said, and it was his astute mind and "feeling" for the cotton trade which kept it so.

After dinner they played bridge, the older generation, and when Sarah suggested that Tim might like to put on the brand-new gramophone she had heard he had purchased, Muriel sighed inwardly. Surely Tim would not allow a dancing party to be got up when he knew how much she enjoyed a quiet dinner party followed by the bridge her generation were used to, but he could hardly refuse a guest, could he, his rueful smile in her direction asked her as he led the young set towards the music room. All but Kathleen, who was partnering Muriel, went with him.

The gramophone was exclaimed over by the giggling girls. It was a table gramophone with a pleated diaphragm, right up to the minute and before long all but Tim and Joel were "jazzing it up" to the rhythms of New Orleans and Chicago, which were the "rage". Strains of the music drifted out of the music room, down the wide hallway and into the drawing room where the bridge game was in progress. Willy Roper and Arthur Davidson had wandered off through the open French doorway to the terrace to smoke their cigars and talk a little business. They were both in cotton.

"Business all right, Arthur?" Willy asked, blowing a perfect ring of smoke into the warm, rose-scented air, the complete picture of a man who is casually interested in another's concern but no more, though both men knew it was not so. From 1914 to 1918, India, deprived of cotton by the lack of shipping from its usual source, Lancashire, had been manufacturing its own and by the end of the war had added an amazing thirty per cent to its own production. It was the same in China and Japan where they had also been affected by the loss of Lancashire cotton. Lancashire, naturally, did not expect to get back to the phenomenal yardage it had exported before the war immediately that war ended and as they said on the Exchange, the Manchester Royal Cotton Exchange, things must be given time to readjust themselves, but most agreed that the enormous profits of 1917 were a thing of the past.

In 1923, after five years of troublesome, worrisome times the cotton men of Lancashire said to one another, "Wait until we get shilling cotton." For a few months from summer 1924 to spring 1925 trade had picked up but now the Indian connection was less than half what it had been and the Chinese less than a third. There was hope of "tenpenny" cotton in this summer of 1925 which was the price of raw cotton and might give some alleviation, but it was all very disquieting though not many would admit to it. Lancashire *was* cotton and had been for centuries and must surely recover.

"Gradely, thanks, Willy," Arthur replied, which was a lie and Willy knew it. From supplying seventy per cent of the world's cotton in 1913, Britain's output had fallen by half and was continuing to fall.

"Any cutbacks in your labour force?" the first man asked. "Only I heard Dickinson's let another fifty go and what's left are working only thirty-five hours a week."

"Jack Dickinson never had a head for business. It was his father who was the force behind it all."

"That's true, and it needs a strong hand to keep from going under."

Willy Roper took another deep draw on his cigar, then, leaning over the balustrade, stubbed it out in one of Muriel Broadbent's graceful urns of geraniums. There was no moon but the stars cast a glow on the waters of the lake and it shimmered like a moving ripple of pewter silk. A breeze tangled in the long fronds of the weeping willow, making them rustle and sway and dip their leaves into the water.

From the open windows of the music room came the staccato beat of the dance called the tango which an American movie star by the name of Rudolph Valentino had revived and made the craze among the young generation. It seemed Sarah knew how to do it and was giving a lesson to the others. Her voice could be heard begging someone to "hold me properly . . . no, not like that, you idiot, or I'll fall flat on my back . . ." and there were shouts of male laughter overlapping the excited giggles of the Davidson girls. Their father frowned. Willy heard his own daughter Mae, who should have known better, call someone a damn fool, begging whoever it was to look at the state of her skirt. He wondered for a moment what had happened to it and hoped Totty hadn't heard her. The young today really were becoming more unmanageable by the minute, especially the young women. They had no figure to speak of and what they had was shamelessly on display beneath their short, tight shimmy skirts. His own daughters had been kept strictly away from what he considered the decadence of the age but they must be brought out to find husbands, for what else were they to do with themselves if not marry? And the music! Where were the melodious strains of the Strauss waltzes and the graceful dances he and Totty had once performed?

There was a crash and a shriek which must have been heard in the drawing room and sure enough Totty and Muriel and Beatrice Knight could be heard a moment later begging to know what had happened.

In less than half an hour most of the guests had taken their leave, Josephine and George Bowman whispering together for a moment before Josephine climbed into her father's Rolls-Royce. Rupert, Tim's friend, with a faint smudge of lipstick on the corner of his mouth put there by who knew which pair of pouting lips, waved innocently to Sarah Bowman and everyone except Muriel agreed it had been a splendid party.

"A brandy before you go, Joel?" Tim asked, reaching for the decanter and raising an enquiring eyebrow in his cousin's direction. Muriel had gone to bed.

"I might as well, thanks."

There was silence for several minutes as the two men, easy in one another's company even when there was no conversation since they were the same age and had known one another from birth, sipped their brandies. They lounged, ties loosened, jackets removed, in deep chairs, one on either side of the fire in the drawing room.

Though it was July a fire had been lit in the fireplace. It had been allowed to die down, the applewood logs falling in wisps of smoke into crumbling ash, the aroma of them pleasant in the room, which was already redolent with the scent of freshly cut roses. Tim's old labrador who had once, as a puppy, romped with three boys in the grounds of Meddins, sprawled at his feet and when he stirred the animal with his foot the dog rolled his eyes in ecstasy. He was fifteen years old and crippled with arthritis but wherever Tim went and Albert was able to follow, he did so, lumbering painfully to his feet as though he was not about to let this one out of his sight lest he disappear as the others had done.

It was very peaceful and Tim thought he might drop off. Joel's voice roused him from his delightful torpor.

"A good party, lad, though that Sarah's a bit of a handful, I'd say."

"Oh, she's not so bad. Young, you know."

"Aren't they all, even the older ones," which was an oblique reference to what they had seen during the war. Though they were not yet thirty they were both elderly in experience.

"I suppose so. Mind you, Mother's got Sarah lined up to be the next Mrs Broadbent if I'm not mistaken." Tim grinned wryly and pushed his hand through his short cap of curls.

"So I noticed. She and Mrs Bowman had their heads together, casting smug glances in your direction when you took her into dinner. You'd best watch out, cousin, or you'll find yourself caught hook, line and sinker and in the basket before you know what's happening to you. Sometimes I'm almost glad the old man and Ma are dead or Ma would be doing the same routine on me."

"Lucky dog."

Silence fell again, then: "That was a damn pretty girl you were talking to the other day, old chap. Anyone I know?"

He could see his cousin stiffen quite visibly. A kind of drawing in of himself, a reflex of self-defence which was well known to anyone who had been a soldier. It was as though he were trying to make himself into as small a target as possible, as they had done in France, and Joel felt the first twinge of alarm.

Tim's head turned slowly and his stare was blank. Though he knew exactly who Joel meant even though it had not been the other day, as Joel had said, but several weeks ago, he pretended ignorance. He did not want his private thoughts, whatever they might be, of Molly O'Dowd aired by anyone, or to anyone, but something in his manner and tone of voice gave him away at once.

"What pretty girl's that then? There aren't many of them about these days." His voice was deceptively casual but his face had a look of strain on it and Joel wondered why. "They're either sweet sixteen and never been kissed or heading for spinsterhood like poor Kathleen Forrester. God, I can remember when I was seventeen and she'd be . . . what? . . . fifteen? I thought she was the bloody cat's pyjamas but now life has passed her by and it's a damned shame. I feel bloody sorry for women, really I do. The older they get the less we want them and yet the same can't be said about us. There's poor Kathleen . . ."

"Don't try to distract me with the sad tale of poor Kathleen, Tim, my lad, though I must admit I agree with you. You know who I mean and you know what I mean. It was in the mill yard but it seemed to me it was not an employer – employee kind of conversation, which the pair of you obviously were, employer and employee, I mean, but a conversation of a different sort altogether. If you ask me . . ."

"I wasn't aware that I had asked you. Bloody hell, man, what the devil's it to do with you? You're not my damned keeper and if I want to talk to one of my mill hands in my mill yard I bloody well will."

"I see! Like that, is it?" Joel smiled in the way men do when they are discussing a woman who is not a lady.

"No, it's not bloody well like that." Tim's face had become flushed and he narrowed his eyes dangerously.

"Really, then if it's as innocuous as you are making out why in hell's name are you getting so worked up about it?" Joel Greenwood's temper was beginning to fray a bit and his snapping voice said so.

"I'm not, as you so quaintly put it, worked up about anything and if you've finished your drink then you'd better sod off."

Joel was seriously alarmed now. He had known his cousin to be involved with more than one attractive young lady but he had never seen him leap to his own, and the young lady's, defence so impetuously. He did his best to make his voice smooth.

"Now, now, Timothy. If you've got something going with one of your girls who am I to criticise? Good luck to you. What else can I say, or think . . ."

"You can bloody well think what you like but keep your thoughts to yourself, lad, for I'll have no . . . no muck cast at this . . . at . . ."

Tim's face was turning an even darker red, dangerous and threatening. His mouth was curved in what could only be described as a snarl, showing his eye teeth which, though

123

Joel knew it was a trick of the light, appeared to grow longer, almost like fangs.

"Look, Tim, I meant no slur. If you want to have a lark with—"

"A lark! What the bloody hell does that mean?"

"Oh, come on, Tim, don't play the innocent with me." Though Joel, unlike Tim Broadbent, was not disposed to smile a great deal, he did so now. "You were leaning on your car, the picture of elegant young manhood, smiling fatuously at one of the prettiest girls I've ever seen. A spinner, if I'm not mistaken, in your own mill and you'd hardly be discussing the number of spindles on her frame, would you? You can't expect me to believe—"

"I don't give a bugger what you believe."

"Tim, come on, boy." Joel put out a conciliatory hand and his smile deepened, lightening the darkness of his face. "I'm sorry if I—"

"I'm not a boy, and certainly not yours."

Joel Greenwood's anxiety grew at the fraught state into which his cousin seemed to be falling. He knew, none better, the hell through which he and Tim and hundreds of thousands of other survivors of the trenches had suffered, but Tim had less . . . well, he supposed it could only be called strength of mind than he himself had. Their experiences in the trenches had affected them in quite different ways. He had become withdrawn, sombre, surly, some said, inclined to be unsociable, whereas Tim never stopped laughing as though life were one big joke, cheerful and light-hearted with everyone he met, just as though if he stopped he might fall into a chasm of terror from which he would never escape. His cousin had been a courageous officer and had never wavered when heroism had been demanded of him but his mind, unlike Joel's which had taught itself to turn away, to go blank, to empty itself of the horror, had retained it for many years and when he was distressed, as he was now for some reason, he began to lose control.

"Bloody hell, I'm sorry, old chap. I meant no offence and if I've given any, I apologise. I've put my big foot right in the shit again, haven't I, but you should know by now that's my style. No finesse, that's me." He grinned, becoming younger, lighter, engaging, a look which would have amazed many of those who knew him, in business and out of it. "Charlie used to call me the most tactless bugger in the county. Remember that party we all went to at Daphne Murchison's, right at the beginning of the war? We were all in uniform and some cousin of hers was in civvies."

"Jumped-up little prick he was." There was a sketch of a smile about Tim's mouth as he relaxed in the memory.

"I believe that's what I called him."

"And then Will said you should apologise. Always was a perfect gentleman, old Will."

"He was that. God bless him."

"Good times, Joel."

"They were that, boy," and this time Tim took no exception to the show of what was a deep affection between the two men. They were all that was left of five handsome, lively, vigorous boys and their friendship was more than that of cousins. They were not at all alike, for as they had become men and soldiers what had happened to them had altered them. Tim had always been sunny-natured, endearingly cheerful, carelessly generous with everything he had, from his horses, his motor cars, his great wealth, his girlfriends, and himself. He had come back from France outwardly just as he had gone but he clung to these youthful characteristics now where he should have matured into a man. He clung to himself as he once had been and allowed nothing, not even what little work he did at the mill, to ruffle him, to separate him from the safe, warm corner of life he had made for himself. Give you his last sixpence, would Tim Broadbent. Everybody liked him but Joel knew he could not be depended on in a crisis.

He himself was also outwardly the same. He had always had a quick temper, an arrogance, a stubbornness, a defiance which had kept him steady. It had not allowed events, feelings, of grief or sorrow or rage, at what was done to himself and those about him to weaken him. There was a quietness in him now which had never been touched, just as his heart had never been touched by any woman, a deep well of resilience which had kept him sane in the trenches where others had gone mad, or become, in defence of it, like Tim.

And this girl. The one at the mill. He had not cared for Tim's unusually fierce denial of her importance, or even her relationship to him. Mind your own business was what he had said, which was strange because if he was having some sort of light-hearted . . . well, *affair*, for want of a better word, why had he become so incensed about it? It seemed she meant more to him than she should and it worried Joel. There were a number of attractive young women working in the mills, most of them decent, hardworking and honest. But now and again there would be one who would let you see quite shamelessly that if you were interested she might be willing to do more for you than earn her wage at her frame. Good-time girls, he had heard them called and he had, in the past, availed himself of their generosity, giving generously in return. None had suffered at his hands, or through his loins come to that and there had been no animosity or repercussions, on or from, either side when it was over.

He might make it his business to find out who this girl was and what she was after. He was not about to let Tim Broadbent become more damaged than he already was.

10

Molly remembered it was Friday because the insurance man had just been. Friday was the traditional night in every household when the collector came, or rather the collectors, for there was always more than one to be paid and the street was a bustle of bowler-hatted men, some on bicycles, with notebooks in their hands in which to record payments. A family knew that it was only practical to put a bit by each week for some unexpected doctor's bill. You never knew when a child might be poorly, or a man, the breadwinner, be involved in an accident at work and best be prepared for it the sensible among them agreed. And then there were the pennies and tuppences on insurance for one's own funeral since everyone was entitled to a decent burial. It was the fear uppermost in the minds of most that they might not get a decent burial.

There was the watchman to be paid, and the knocker-upper who, though he was often not necessary in this modern day of alarm clocks, was still required by some. He always liked to know what time he should knock you up next week and he put it all down in his notebook, the time and what he was owed for it.

Pikey was in an exceptionally good mood for some reason and though Molly did not trust it, or him, she made the most of it, as they all did. He was doing his best to make Mammy smile as he stamped about from kitchen to scullery, getting himself up "posh" as he called it in readiness for his Friday night out at the Old Soldiers Club. He would have a drink with his old mates, those who had gone through the war with him, or at least if not with him then in a Lancashire battalion of some description, reliving it, going over and over the battles, the "pushes", the offensives, remembering the men who were gone, and Molly wondered sometimes why they continued to do it, to relive that dreadful war in which Daddy and Liam and Patrick had died with millions of others and she could find no answer. You'd think they'd want to forget it, she'd said to Mammy, after all it had been over for nearly seven years but Mammy had only shrugged, thankful that he was to be out of the house, Molly supposed. He went out drinking on most nights, if not to the Old Soldiers then to the Legion or the Queens Head at the corner of Marine Street, coming home as sober as he went out, though he consumed vast amounts of beer and his "beer gut" testified to the fact. He had a drinker's head and it was only very occasionally that he let the ale get the better of him. He was a man who did not get merry or good-humoured when he'd had a few but became cold and nasty, especially if someone rubbed him up the wrong way. To Molly he always seemed to be in that state.

At the moment the house was a haven of calm. Mammy was darning, her glasses on the end of her nose, her lips pursed as she created the exquisite workmanship which was her gift with a needle. She still bought roll-ends from the stalls at Tommyfield, running up little dresses for Eileen and Gracie and Clare, and even a frock or two for Molly who, after Pikey had taken his share – the major share – of her wages, had little money to chuck about on shop-bought clothes.

The plump cat, who was a descendant of the one which had purred on Daddy's lap ten years ago, did so now on Mammy's, undisturbed by her movement with the darning needle and Pikey's sock.

The clock bonged the hour and Pikey glanced at it before bending over his wife in what Molly though was a particularly foolish way, grimacing with what he evidently thought great good humour. He was in a sleeveless vest and vast tufts of grey hair erupted from it, at the neck and from under his armpits, along his shoulders and down his arms. He looked like an ageing monkey, she thought contemptuously, making an idiot of himself, and the worrying part was why?

"Now then, chuck, I'm ter be off soon," he was saying to Mammy. He had just come through from the scullery, where he had been shaving, to fetch his clean shirt which was airing by the fire, "so give us a kiss. In fact I've a good mind ter 'ave one off the lot of tha'." He had shaving soap lathered across the lower half of his face, the brush still in his hand. He rubbed his soapy cheek across Mammy's, laughing uproariously, then gave her a smacking kiss. Mammy did her best to laugh too, for it was only wise when he was in this mood to respond to his sudden joviality, for if she didn't he was just as likely to turn churlish, calling her sour-faced, and worse. She didn't know what had got into him, she really didn't, her eyes signalled to Molly who was sitting at the table with the little ones. From the few bob Pikey allowed her to keep she had bought each of them a colouring book and a few coloured crayons and the three girls, tongues out, heads bent, hair falling in a curtain across their absorbed faces, were busy beside her. Molly was helping Gracie, who was only just three, to keep inside the lines, advising her on the best colour for the clown's hat and the little boy's ball. Archie, the youngest, was already in bed and soon it would be the turn of Eileen and Gracie but Clare, who was nine, was allowed to stay up until eight o'clock. Normally she would be out skipping with her friends, Minnie Haydock, Beryl Openshaw and Bunty Thompson, who was Cissie Thompson's young sister but Pikey had taken it into his head to forbid it tonight, for reasons best known to himself.

Clare, who had known no other father but Pikey, since she had been only three years old when Mammy married him, called him Daddy, as the three youngest did and every time Molly heard it on her lips it made her flinch. She had to clench her teeth sometimes to prevent herself yelling at her little sister that Pikey wasn't her daddy. That her real daddy was with the angels up in heaven. Clare had heard of the angels, of course, because she learned about them at school, at Sunday school when Mammy could get her there, at mass, again when Mammy and Molly could spirit her and the three little ones out on a Sunday morning while Pikey had a "lie-in". The memory of their real daddy, hers and Clare's, still stabbed Molly to the heart at times, even though it was more than ten years since he had left them. Swearing Clare to secrecy, since she knew it would go hard with them all if Pikey knew that the memory of Seamus O'Dowd was being kept alive in *his* house, despite his strange tolerance of Daddy's picture on the wall of the kitchen, she often whispered to her of Daddy and Liam and Patrick and had even taken her to see the house a couple of times.

Pikey's soapy face was thrust into those of his own children who, afraid of him and not experienced enough to know that this time he was "playing", cowered away from him but he merely laughed, not at all concerned, for in his opinion all three, including his son, were nothing but "nambie-pambies" who were fearful of their own shadow. It did not occur to him that it was he who had made them that way.

"Gerron wi' yer, give yer dad a kiss." He laughed, lifting the blank-eyed figure of Eileen into his arms and tossing her into the air. Rosie Watson had her hand to her mouth as the child's head touched the ceiling, longing to stand up and snatch her daughter to safety but knowing how dangerous that might be. Sometimes Pikey could be just as perilous in a good mood as he was in one of his violent tempers. When he was mad you kept out of his way. He was predictable then. Sometimes you got it wrong, of course and were rewarded with a back-hander, but when he was like this it was very tricky, for you never quite knew what to expect next.

"Oh . . . mind 'er, darlin'," she murmured.

"She's all right, aren't tha', chuck?" he told his daughter as though they were the best of friends. He kissed her rosy little mouth before dropping her roughly back into her chair. He reached for Gracie who looked as though she might be about to have a fit, throwing her roughly over his shoulder, catching her as she slid head first down his back, kissing her soundly then tossing her into her chair. Molly felt her gorge rise.

"Now then, 'oo's next?" he chaffed, leering at Molly and winking but he was wary of Molly now. Since the day she had threatened to report him to Mr Broadbent, or to someone in authority, her manner had implied, when he had tried to have a bit of fun with her, he had not touched her.

"Tha' lay a finger on me an' tha'll regret it," she said now, her voice icy, her young face the colour and texture of white marble. "Tha' can keep tha' bloody kisses fer them as wants 'em an' Clare's too big ter be chucked about like a sack o' potaters."

"Yer right, our Molly, she is," he answered softly, "so I'll just give 'er a kiss instead. Like one o' me own she is, aren't tha', sweetheart?" knowing this remark was guaranteed to make Molly wild. "Give tha' daddy a kiss then," he went on to Clare, kneeling down by the child in what Molly thought was a very strange manner. It brought his face on a level with Clare's who stared at him with the blank-eyed vacancy of a rabbit cornered by a stoat. She did not flinch. Indeed she made no movement at all as he laid his loose-lipped mouth in a curiously gentle fashion against hers. Her soft, childish lips were parted and for the space of five long seconds his mouth covered hers, moving against it, then he leaped to his feet and, before Molly and her mother could get to grips with whatever it was they had seen, he strode back into the scullery. He began to whistle as the cut-throat razor he used scraped away at the iron grey stubble on his face.

Molly hardly dared turn to Mammy. The three little girls all sat in the peculiarly rigid pose Pikey had left them in. There was soap on all three of their faces, but somehow though they had all been subjected to Pikey's attentions Molly had the feeling that there was something . . . different . . . unusual . . . *nasty?* about that which he had offered Clare. She couldn't really say there was anything out of the way in Pikey's behaviour except that he had kissed them at all. It was not his way to show affection, if indeed he felt any, but he had kissed them, his own children and Clare and . . . and Molly had not liked it. As he had strutted from the kitchen and into the scullery he had glanced in her direction, a strange glance of what looked like triumph. A glance Molly had not understood, though it seemed to her there had been a message in it.

At last she chanced a look at Mammy and there it was, the reflection of her own doubting thoughts, whatever they were and however jumbled they might be. As plain as day on her mammy's face was an expression of the unease she herself felt, unease backed with a growing dread. Dear sweet Mary Mother of God . . . Molly's eyes held her mother's in a desperate question and Mammy nodded as though she understood. That was as far as either of them were prepared to go at that moment, for it was just too horrible to contemplate and too much for them to manage. They weren't even sure what they had been witness to and Clare had never . . . had never complained of . . . Of what? their eyes asked one another and though nothing was said it was as though it had. As though, since words could not be spoken for they were too foul, an agreement had been made between mother and daughter.

There was always someone with Clare from that day on, either Mammy or Molly. Again, though they did not speak of it or make any specific arrangements, it was accepted that she was never left alone in the house with Pikey. She went directly to Aunty Flo's or Aunty Maggie's from school if Mammy was working and, strangely, neither Aunty Flo nor Aunty Maggie questioned it. It was six years since either of them had set foot in the house in Sidney Street, for right from the start Pikey had made it quite clear that he wanted no interference in *his* house from Seamus O'Dowd's relatives and they were not welcome. Mammy and Molly and the children went as often as they could to see them but their visits were short, their eyes on the clock in order not to be out of the house, which would have to be explained, when Pikey returned. Hurried visits with which, having known from the very beginning how it would be with Pikey and Seamus's widow, Aunty Flo and Aunty Maggie understood and sympathised.

"Send them young uns round 'ere ter play wi' our Jane's two," Aunty Maggie told Mammy, looking particularly at Clare who was Seamus's child and though not Aunty Maggie's niece by blood, her Alf was Rosie's brother. Jane's two were Aunty Maggie's grandchildren, her Billy's son and daughter and, since they lived close by and were always in and out of her house, what could be more natural than their Rosie's children coming to play with their Jane's? Jane had never remarried, though Aunty Maggie had confessed to Mammy that she'd had a few offers and Aunty Maggie was right fond of her daughter-in-law who had remained faithful to the memory of Aunty Maggie's son for nearly nine years.

Elspeth and Chrissie, Aunty Maggie's daughters, were married and had left home, both with children who regularly filled Aunty Maggie's small house with their din and what difference would a few more make, she added philosophically. Privately, she thought that Rosie's four children with their quiet ways, big eyes and unchildlike solemnity needed to be in the company of some rowdy, normal children where they could escape for a while from Pikey Watson's dominance.

Aunty Flo was not quite so generous. Of her three sons only one had come back from France and, as Aunty Maggie said, it had fair taken the snap and ginger out of Flo O'Dowd. She was quieter, letting Kathleen, who had never married after the death of Tommy O'Brien, more or less run the house. Eamon had wed a lass from over Delph way, a farmer's daughter and had gone to live with her family. Taken to farming in a big way, had Eamon, watching crops and vegetables grow as though the contrast with the bloody war he had fought in, living things instead of dead, had healed his wounds and returned him to sanity. They were all a bit barmy, he had told Aunty Flo, those who had come back from the trenches and the farm work, moving with the seasons, predictable and each day exactly the same, suited him down to the ground. But it was a long way to Delph and Aunty Flo didn't see much of him and his wife, nor her grandchildren, the only ones she had. Her house was quiet, polished scoured and immaculate as she and Kathleen liked it to be and though Rosie's children were as silent as little mice and with none of the tendency of Maggie's grandchildren to tear round like whirling dervishes, and were just as Flo liked children to be, she was never quite sure what to do with them.

But Clare, who was an O'Dowd, was a little beauty. A real O'Dowd to look at, she seemed to find Aunty Flo's peaceful, shining house and Aunty Flo's peaceful, shining kitchen where, being such a quiet, tidy child, she was allowed to help in the baking of bread and scones and biscuits, a very satisfying place to be.

"There's no men at Aunty Flo's," she said one day to Molly as they walked home hand in hand down Briscoe Street and Molly had asked her if she had had a nice time. Molly had taken to picking her up on her way home from the mill. It saved Mammy the walk, especially with the little ones. Archie was only two years old and had to be carried and it was a fair walk along Shaw Road for the two little girls.

"What dost tha' mean, darlin'?" Molly bent to look into Clare's grave, childish face. She was a lovely child, dark hair in a halo of tossed, glossy curls, eyes the colour of an azure sky, deep and clear and set in a frame of long, silken lashes. She was thin, the bony thinness of a nine-year-old with shoulder blades which stuck out in vertical ridges and shoulders like coat-hangers. Her fragile bones and the delicate tracery of her veins showed through her pale, fine skin. She had not Molly's wild rose beauty, nor Molly's vitality and courage since she had been terrorised by Pikey for six years, but, if left to mature in the peace and security which is every child's birthright, would make a sweet-natured and comely young girl and woman.

"Well, it's right . . . quiet an' theer's . . . no mess. Aunty Flo don't shout an' . . . an' Kathleen's nice."

"Is she, darlin'? How?"

"She . . . she lets me read me library books wi'out . . .'

"But tha' can do that at 'ome if tha' want."

The child's face closed up and the small flush of interest ebbed from her face, leaving her pale once more. Her eyes became shuttered and the uneasy feeling which had settled in Molly on the day Pikey had kissed her little sister ran through her veins like spiders on a window. Her skin prickled and she wanted to kneel down and draw Clare into her arms. Question her. Ask her what it was that . . . that what? What did she want to ask her? Clare had always been quiet, at least as far back as Molly could remember. For three years after Daddy and the boys' deaths she and Mammy had not been themselves and in those three years, before Mammy met Pikey, Clare had been an infant, a toddler, a small girl growing up in a house of sorrow and loss. Could you expect her to be anything other than the way she was, poor kid?

"Is owt wrong, our Clare?" she asked her, brushing Clare's hair back from her forehead, studying the closed-up face of her sister, doing her best not to sound too concerned. "At school, 'appen? 'As someone bin bullyin' thi' or summat like that?"

"No, nowt's wrong, Molly, 'onest, nowt's wrong."

The words were spoken with such force Molly was startled. She stopped, drawing Clare round to face her as they turned out of Briscoe Street into Bacup Street. They were approaching Oldham Edge across which was a short cut from Aunty Flo's house to Sidney Street. When they had crossed the Edge they would nip through an alleyway between a row of houses in Edge Lane, across another patch of rough ground called Higher Moor and on to Shaw Road which, at this time of day, would be bustling with people and traffic, some of it motor traffic and bicycles, though horse-drawn vehicles were still to be seen.

"Sure an' tha'd tell me if . . . well, if there were owt troublin' thi', wouldn't thi', darlin'? Anythin' at all. Tha' know I'd let . . . well, if anyone were . . . 'urtin' thi' . . . or owt like that, I'd give 'em what for, tha' know that, don't tha', Clare?" she asked anxiously.

"Aye, Molly."

"Promise?"

Clare was looking away from her, her eyes on the last house of the terrace, the end wall of which was plastered from the pointed gable to the ground with bright, large-lettered posters. OXO, one proclaimed in brilliant scarlet. EFISCA LAMPS, said another. THE OLDHAM CHORAL SOCIETY, THE COMMERCIAL INSTITUTE, IRON JELLOIDS, CLAYMORE WHISKY, MACINTOSH TYRES and QUICK QUAKER OATS vied with one another for attention and Clare studied them with the thoroughness of someone who must make up her mind which of them she was to sample.

"Clare, look at me, darlin'," but Clare shook her head. Pulling herself free from Molly's restraining hand she began to run. Wiry she was and quick, with the sure-footed grace of a young deer, a young deer which is being pursued and must find safety before the predator catches it. Molly, alarmed and bewildered for a moment, watched her go, then sprinted after her, her iron-shod clogs clattering on the flagged pavement and echoing between the houses of the narrow street.

There were the usual children playing, dogs lolling and women gossiping in the hazy warmth of the sunshine. They all stopped what they were doing to watch her go by and several of the dogs began to bark. They knew her, of course, the women, since her Aunty Flo, Flo O'Dowd, lived round the corner and they called out to one another, speculating on what was up.

Oldham Edge, bordered on one side by quarries and the disused boiler works and on the other three by streets of terraced houses, was not wide and Clare was across it before Molly was barely halfway.

"Clare, give over, tha' daft beggar," she shouted as her sister vanished into the alleyway which led on to Edge Lane. "Wait fer me, please," but she was shouting into the wind and other users of the short cut stared at her in astonishment.

"Bugger it," she muttered under her breath. Though she was young and healthy she was not used to running flat out in her clogs and she was badly winded by the time she was through the alley and into Edge Lane. Not only into Edge Lane but halfway across it before a terrifying and painful screeching of brakes and tyres and the hoarse shouts of men brought her back to reality and the consciousness of a steady stream of traffic, trams and carts, bicycles and motor cars which threaded their way along the teeming road.

"Dear God, woman," someone shouted. "Look where you're going. And get off the bloody road. D'you want to get killed?"

She was dazed and though not touched, badly shaken. A shining strip of chrome attached to the brilliant scarlet bonnet of a motor car was an inch from her hip and all about her women in shawls and men in caps stopped and stared as they made their way up Edge Lane. Cyclists whistled in appreciation, whether of the pretty girl or the dashing sports car which had almost knocked her down. A police constable, whistle at the ready, hurried up, prepared to bring some sort of order to the traffic which the young woman had seriously snarled up and all the while Molly was aware of nothing but the strong arm about her shoulders, an anxious face bent to hers, sweet breath in her nostrils, a warm, gentle hand holding hers as she was led to the pavement.

"Sir, tha' can't leave that vehicle there," the constable protested hotly and a soft voice murmured in her ear to wait there, he'd be no more than a minute. Other arms held her steady, there was a familiar roar of an engine then, thankfully, she was back in the protection of Tim Broadbent's arms.

"Come, we'll sit in the car," his voice said soothingly. "I'll put the hood up."

Though it was still noisy, all abustle with the home-going crowds, there was peace at last and Molly sank into it and into Tim Broadbent's comforting arms as he held her against his chest. She could hear the rapid beat of his heart and her cheek rose and fell on the force of his agitated breathing, but he smelled nice and she felt vastly comforted. He didn't speak, just patted her shoulder and rested his cheek on the top of her head, waiting until she had recovered, quite prepared to wait for ever, it seemed, if that was what it would take.

At last she sat up, though she didn't want to and, to her own amazement, immediately began to pat her hair into place. Her cap, which had fallen off as the traffic whirled about her, was on her lap where someone had tossed it and her hair, which was ready for a trim with Mammy's cutting-out shears, sprang about her head in a mass of gleaming curls, framing her heart-shaped face and tumbling in disarray almost into her eyes. She was pale, blanched with shock, since she had been so nearly taken under Mr Broadbent's wheels and her eyes were bright with unshed tears. They were like blue-tinted diamonds in her face, brilliant, the pupils dilated to no more than pinpricks. Only her mouth had colour, a full soft poppy which trembled over her even white teeth.

"Jesus, Mary and Joseph, that were close," she said tremulously.

"Indeed it was, Molly," Mr Broadbent said gravely, his own mouth inclined to be serious.

"Them's good brakes."

"They are that, thanks be to God, but don't you think you might give the driver of the motor car a bit of credit?" His eyes, now that the emergency was over, were beginning to twinkle, narrowing as he smiled, fine lines fanning out from the corners. The vertical grooves on either side of his mouth deepened as his smile did.

"Oh, o' course, Mr Broadbent," Molly said hastily. "I'd a' bin a gonner, else."

"Well, it could have been nasty. I'm glad there was no harm done. There *is* no harm done, is there, Molly?" Almost dreamily he pushed back a curl from her cheek, tucking it behind her ear and she ducked her head in what looked like shyness. "You must take care when you're crossing a road, you know," as though to a child. "There are more and more motor cars about."

"I know."

"And just out of interest, Molly, where were you going in such a tearing hurry? You seemed to come from nowhere. One minute I was driving along wondering what I should do with myself tomorrow, it being Saturday" – his grin deepened – "and suddenly the very person I was thinking about flings herself into my path and is almost sitting on the bonnet of my motor. It was a bit unnerving and not exactly what I'd hoped for at our next meeting. Still, it was very timely."

"Pardon?"

"Never mind, we'll speak of that later. First I'd best get you home so if you'll direct me . . ."

"Oh, no, sir . . . no. I'm all right, 'onest."

He had reached out to switch on the engine, reluctantly removing his arms from about her but as she spoke he leaned back and sighed.

"Dear Molly, surely we are not going to go through all that again, are we? The last time I offered to give you a lift home you said—"

"I know, an' I'm sayin't same now as I did then. It were my fault, runnin' in't road like that but I'm not 'urt an' I only live over theer," waving a vague hand in the direction of Higher

Moor across which . . . In the name of God, across which Clare had vanished at least ten minutes since. Mammy was working and Pikey, who was on night shift, would not yet have left home and Clare would be alone with him!

"What's the matter, Molly? You've gone even whiter than you were a minute ago. What is it? Is something wrong? Are you hurt?"

"No, oh no, sir," she babbled, "but I've gorrer get 'ome. Me little sister's—" She bit off the words with a snap of her jaw.

"What? What is wrong with your little sister?"

"Nowt, but I've gorrer get 'ome."

"That's what I'm saying so sit still and I'll take you there."

"NO!" She reached for the handle of the door, ready to jump out and dodge through the traffic in her frantic haste to be home but the car's engine had roared into life and leaped forward with an eagerness which terrified her. She'd never been in a motor car before and in normal circumstances would have thrilled to the excitement of suddenly going so fast, of the roar and clamour, of the people who turned to stare but all she could think of was Clare.

"Which way, Molly?"

"Sidney Street. Turn right at Edge Street then left inter Adelphi. Sidney Street's just off it."

Bugger it, what did it matter as long as she got home quickly, she thought frantically. She could walk it, or run it in just over five minutes but this way she'd be there almost before Clare was and surely that was all that mattered? Dear God, who cared what the neighbours thought? She'd rather lose her reputation than let that sod touch Clare. They weren't even sure, her and Mammy, if he had touched her. They had never seen it, except that revolting kiss and Clare had insisted that there was nothing bothering her. Nevertheless, that denial of hers had seemed to Molly to be too fervent somehow, though she was not altogether sure what she meant by that.

The street, like all the terraced streets of Oldham at this time of day, was packed with screaming, jostling, laughing children, skipping, playing hopscotch, marbles and football. Women in aprons leaned in doorways, watching and shouting to one another across the street and in their midst Clare O'Dowd whirled Bunty Thompson's mam's washing line, on the other end of which was Bunty herself. Beryl and Minnie were waiting to "jump in".

Molly let out her breath, which she had not been aware she had been holding, on a long shuddering sigh and Tim Broadbent looked at her sharply, suddenly conscious that there was something going on in this girl's life that was threatening her. Her quick relief was very evident though he could not have said what had caused it.

"Stop 'ere," she told him sharply and he did, pulling over to the side of the road in front of number eleven where Mrs Kenny was about to mop her front step. Mrs Kenny faltered, her mouth dropping open, her bucket of hot water in one hand, her brush in the other. As she said later to her next-door neighbour, Mrs Wainwright, she nearly wet her drawers she was so flabbergasted. Molly O'Dowd in a bright red motor car, the like of which had never before been seen in Sidney Street. And what was she doing in it? Mrs Kenny wanted to know, and with what could only be called a "toff", though of course the answer was as plain as the nose on your face. She was shocked, shocked, she told Mrs Wainwright since Molly had never been seen with any lad, let alone one with a motor car and if that stepfather of hers caught her he'd give her a good leathering. Sat chatting as bold as brass for at least ten minutes, she did, as though she didn't care who saw her and when she got out she was smiling and so was the toff!

11

He took her to the top of the world that first day, or at least the top of their world; had she seen anything more beautiful? he asked her. He was looking at her when he said it.

Mammy had been horrified, terrified, mortified, for surely Molly knew what a man like Mr Broadbent wanted with a girl like Molly.

"Dost tha' know 'im, Mammy?" Molly asked, her voice cold, probably the first time it had ever been so with her mother.

"Course not. I don't 'ave ter know 'im ter catch what 'e's after and if tha'll stop an' think fer a minute tha'll know I'm right, so tha' will. Holy Mother o' God, girl, 'e's gentry."

"What does that mean terday, Mammy?" Molly's voice had contempt in it, not for her mammy but for the stupidity of conventional society which said that Molly O'Dowd, daughter of the best man who had ever lived, Molly O'Dowd who had done nothing of which she might be ashamed, who worked hard and was decent and respectable, could not have an afternoon out, an *afternoon*, mind you, not an evening, with a man from a world which considered he was better than her.

She had not thought of it like this at first. At first her mind had travelled along the same line as Mammy's. What did he want with her, she had asked herself, coming, as Betty had done, to the inevitable conclusion. What did he hope to get out of Molly O'Dowd that was not obtainable among his own sort? What did he see in her? Why had he waited in the mill yard that day, his admiration clear to more than Molly, if his intentions were . . . well, she didn't know the word which might properly describe them, not one that didn't sound barmy, but dishonourable came close. But when she had made it plain what her feelings were he had stepped back. He had not deliberately sought her out, had he? He'd respected her wishes and let her alone so that no one could tarnish Molly O'Dowd's good name with sly innuendos and glances which told of thoughts which were not charitable. She had spoken to him on three occasions and each time he had been respectful, ready to smile and joke, but not be coarse, and his manners had been exemplary. He had treated her as though she were his equal. He had not been patronising or in any way tried to put her in her place, her place as his class would see it, but had shown her nothing but civility and goodwill. He liked her, he had made that obvious, and she liked him and if he wanted to take her for a run in his motor car, then why shouldn't he? It would lead nowhere, she was well aware of that, for despite what she told herself the classes did not mix.

But did that matter when all they were offering to one another was friendship? Liking. The sort of relationship which, though it would not end in the way relationships her kind expected, which meant marriage, would be very pleasant. They were both free adults, harming no one and she was surprised at Mammy for not trusting her to be the good girl she and Daddy had brought her up to be.

"'Tis not thee I'm concerned about, darlin', it's 'im, so. I know tha'd do nowt ter dishonour thissen, or tha' daddy's memory, but men, some men aren't ter be trusted, lass, and this un's tha' employer."

Mammy's voice was anguished. Pikey had left the house two hours since, his night shift beginning at six. The children were in their beds, the three little ones top and tail in the one Liam and Patrick had shared, Clare tucked in with Molly where she had been since Archie was born two years ago, since four children in one bed was too tight a fit and though Molly and Clare were a bit squashed, they made do. Clare clung to Molly like a limpet on a rock, even in the depths of sleep, turning when Molly did, her face in Molly's back or her back pressed against Molly's breast.

"Mammy, 'e means me no 'arm. I know 'e doesn't. 'E's a gentleman."

"That's just what I'm tellin' thi'! A gentleman an' tha's a mill girl an' when it gets about tha's . . . tekken up wi' 'im, they'll all be whisperin' about thi'."

"Let 'em. I don't care. There's none as bothers me, Mammy, only thee and tha' know I wouldn't do owt wrong."

Rosie Watson studied her daughter. Molly's face was bold but it had a freshness about it, a frankness which took no account of social taboos, of intolerance and prejudice. She tossed her head defiantly and her hair, which Rosie had just cut and washed, rippled and bounced like ripe corn in a wind. In the light from the lamp and the fire it took on the colour and glow of a burnished horse chestnut. Her eyes flashed, a dangerous and deep blue-green as though to warn anyone who might doubt it that Molly O'Dowd was afraid of no one and would put up with no nonsense. She would have her own way in this since it would harm no one.

Rosie felt her heart clench with fear for her lovely girl.

"And what about . . . Pikey?" It was out at last.

There was a long, deep silence. The clock ticked musically and the fire crackled. The cat stretched and rumbled on the rug and from the front of the house came the shouts of the children who were still playing out. The two women stared at one another. There was nothing Rosie could do to stop Molly having a day out with Mr Broadbent and if she could she doubted that she would. She knew her Molly. She was a good girl and could be trusted. She had been brought up in the true faith and though she was not such a regular churchgoer as she once had been, she would never compromise it. She was sensible, not giddy like Cissie Thompson who would get herself into trouble one of these days. Molly was well aware of the consequences of allowing a chap liberties which should come only within a marriage. She'd never so much as gone to the pictures, or taken a walk with any lad, and her nineteen, and just as well, really, since Rosie couldn't see Pikey allowing it. But she'd got to start sometime and who was there round here who could match her Molly in looks, in taste, in intelligence or sheer style? They were decent working-class lads, most of them, but their interests were fags and football and Molly was special. Her daddy had been special and he had made Molly the same way. You only had to see the books she brought home from the library. Not trashy novelettes but books with lovely pictures in them of faraway places, glossy pictures of works of art, splendid houses, great people of the past in whom Seamus, and now Molly, were interested. She seemed to find great satisfaction in reading what Rosie knew were called "classics" by writers such as Charles Dickens, Jane Austen and some sisters who were named – now what was it? – yes, that was it, Brontë. She kept them hidden from Pikey since he would only have taunted her about her pretensions of grandeur, though that was not the phrase he would use, reading them by the light of a candle in bed, or in the kitchen when Pikey was out.

Rosie didn't know this Mr Broadbent though Seamus had thought highly of his father. A good man who had seen many a family through the war years, hers included, with allowances for those in need. He'd lost two sons, as she had, and had died soon after, leaving it all to this one lad; well, you could hardly call him a lad since he must be approaching thirty. They said of him that he neglected his duty at the mill, leaving it all in the hands of men his daddy had trusted, which didn't sound as if he were as stable as he should be but Molly liked him, trusted him and Rosie trusted Molly's judgment. That was all she could do.

"'E'll not like it, darlin'," Mammy said at last, meaning Pikey, of course. "'E'll not let tha' go, tha' know that, don't tha'?"

"We'll not 'ave ter tell 'im then, will we?" Molly clenched her jaw ominously. Now that she had made up her mind to it there was nothing she wanted more than to go out with Mr Broadbent in his zippy little motor car. She'd wear her new frock, the one she and Mammy had made while Pikey was out, and the new cloche hat which matched it. Bought off the market, as had been her shoes which were of black patent leather with a bar across the high arch of her foot and two-inch cuban heels. Her hat was plain, like a helmet pulled down over her eyebrows, with a high crown and on the left side of the tiny brim she had sewn a small bunch of artificial violets. The hat was a pale, cornflower blue and so was her dress which was very simple with short, magyar sleeves and the waist sitting neatly on her hips. The hemline was exactly fourteen inches from the ground. Her art silk stockings were the colour of smoke and had cost her one and elevenpence halfpenny which was more than the hat! She had no gloves and could not afford them but her small handbag matched her shoes and she could not wait to put on the whole stunning outfit. It had been meant for church really, when the weather was suitable and when Pikey had gone off to the Old Soldiers Club which sometimes had a domino match on a Sunday morning.

Now, by God, she would wear it tomorrow. She didn't know how she was to get past Pikey if he was at home but she'd deal with that problem if and when it arose. Fortunately, being on night shift, he would probably be in his bed and she prayed fervently to the Blessed Virgin that that was where he would stay until she'd left the house. Mr Broadbent had promised he would wait round the corner in Shaw Road, for she had impressed upon him the necessity of keeping their meeting a secret.

"Very well, for now, Molly," he had agreed solemnly and though the way he said it, *for now*, sounded a bit strange and had bewildered her, she had been satisfied.

It had gone so smoothly Molly wondered why she had been worried. Pikey had come home from his night shift at the ironworks, getting into bed beside Mammy at half past six and, after paying his usual grunting, energetic attentions to her for ten minutes which he made no attempt to conceal from the rest of the household, had fallen into a deep, noisy sleep in which, by noon, he was still fast. She and Mammy and the children had crept round as stealthily and silently as the cat, speaking in no more than whispers. Of course this was normal practice when Pikey was in his bed, for let one of them waken him and there'd be ructions. They were all obedient to his brutal rule, the four young children, and though their eyes popped out like marbles on stalks and their faces were aglow with wonderment at the splendour of their Molly and her lovely hat and frock, they made no sound, showing their admiration in small, silent jumps and pretend clapping until Molly felt like crying. Poor little sods, they couldn't act like normal kids, letting out their excitement, infrequent as it was, in a show of spirited exuberance, but must do it in hushed whispers, their big eyes constantly turning towards the ceiling as though expecting their father's roar of disapproval to fall about their ears.

"What'll tha' say, Mammy?" Molly had asked her mother the night before. "'E'll 'ave ter be told summat."

"I bin thinkin' about that, darlin' an' best place'd be church, may the Blessed Mother forgive me. It's the only thing 'e'd accept an' 'e'll not like even that. Tha' know 'ow 'e is about . . . well, Bridie O'Connor's gettin' married, tha' remember 'er, she were in tha' class at school. Aye? Well, if tha' was goin' to 'elp wi't flowers, then t't service an' 'appen even ter't th'ouse afterwards I don't see as 'ow 'e can object, can thee?" She smiled shakily and Molly knew she was afraid. "It's the only thing I can think of, darlin', ter give thi' all afternoon. I'll put pot dog in't winder bottom, so I will, when 'e goes out, an' don't come in until tha' see it there. Holy Mother o' God, if 'e doesn't go to't club I don't know what we'll do though 'e always does on a Saturday. An' if anyone sees tha' an' tells 'im . . ."

"Don't worry, Mammy, it'll be all right, so it will. I'll stand up to 'im, if 'e gets ter know."

"That's what I'm afraid of, darlin'," her mother said sadly.

He was there where he had said he would be, smiling broadly, leaping out of the car as she came quickly round the corner, opening the car door for her, his eyes glowing with admiration, ready to tell her how wonderful she looked, she knew, and wasn't the day grand, but before he could speak she flung herself into the car begging him to be off at once. She could feel eyes looking at her from every corner of the street, from every window and doorway and from the moment she had stepped out of the doorway of number twenty-two she had been subjected to appreciative whistles and shouted demands to know where she was off to, tricked up like a dog's dinner as she was! How could she possibly have imagined she could get away with this, she agonised as Mr Broadbent, without saying a word, started the motor car and raced off up Shaw Road towards Brownlow.

But the sheer exhilaration of sitting in the open sports car; of going at the unbelievable speed Mr Broadbent seemed to find not at all out of the ordinary; of seeing people turn to stare; of houses flashing by so that she barely got a glimpse of them, whipped all thought of Pikey and the trouble this day might cause from her excited mind. Her eyes, though she was not aware of it, were wide and as brilliant as turquoise-tinted crystal caught in a ray of sunlight and her cheeks became as poppy red as her mouth. She loved it. She was not afraid. She just loved it and the vivid glances she turned on Tim Broadbent told him so.

He turned right at Bullcote Lane and at once they were in the country. They called Oldham "a town in the countryside" and it was true, for no matter which road out of town you took within minutes you were on meandering country lanes, narrow, and in summer, deep between hedges which were submerged in a rising tide of growth. Hedge parsley and coltsfoot, sweet cecily fragrant with the scent of aniseed, waist-high and blocking the ditches on either side of the lane. Full green foliage and a profusion of blossom brushed the side of the motor car as it sped by and Molly, holding on to her hat had time to pray they wouldn't meet anything coming the other way. It wouldn't really matter if they did, she knew that with a certainty, since Mr Broadbent would handle it as he was handling the dashing red sports car. With a confident turn of the wheel, smiling that impudent smile of his that she was getting to know so well, he would have them out of any danger that might present itself.

Birds, she didn't know of what sort, for the car went too fast for her to identify them, rose in panic from the hedgerows and suddenly, since she was young and pretty and had a handsome man beside her, a man whose smiling glances told her he thought she was something special, she threw back her head and began to laugh. Her hat tipped backwards so she took it off and threw it into the small space behind her.

"What?" Mr Broadbent shouted above the roar of the car's engine and the sound of the rushing wind then, pulling over on to a small square of rough grass in front of a gate, he stopped the car. He said nothing, just looked at her and she looked back at him. They smiled at one another and she knew she had never been as happy as this since the days when she and Daddy had gone off on their Sunday outings.

She told him so, letting him see for a few seconds her treasured memories of those days and the man who was a part of them, memories she had shared with no one else.

"I'm glad, Molly, and honoured that you should feel you can tell me about them, for I can see what they meant to you. Your father must have been a rare kind of man for you to love him and his memory so much." His voice was kind, his face grave as though he knew full well this was not a moment for levity.

"'E was. Rare. That's what 'e was."

Their eyes clung and neither was embarrassed or awkward, sharing this intimate space in time with the ease of old friends.

His voice was husky when he spoke again.

"Have you any idea how lovely you are, Mary Angelina O'Dowd, have you?"

"No." Molly cleared her throat. "An' fancy yer rememberin' me full name."

"I can never, will never forget anything about you, Molly. You are unique and your beauty is flawless. Not only the beauty people can see, but inside you."

"Oh, no, Mr Broadbent." Now she was embarrassed.

"Yes, Molly, and if you don't call me Tim I promise I shall be seriously offended. We are friends now and besides, your Mr Broadbent makes me feel as ancient as that oak tree by the hedge. I'd say four hundred years, wouldn't you, and I definitely do not feel four hundred years old. In fact I feel like a boy again. Like the boy who . . . who went off to war without a care in the world and . . . well, you know what I mean, don't you, Mary Angelina? So how about Tim, please?"

She could not look away from him and did not want to. His eyes were so gentle and warm, filled with the honest truth of what he was saying, with what he believed. Gone was the engaging humour, the sense of fun, the laughter, the careless flippancy which was the face he had shown her on their previous meetings.

"Say it, Molly." His voice was low.

"Tim," and so was hers as though this moment was a milestone in their short relationship.

"Molly," he repeated dreamily. "You are truly . . . the most . . . the most . . ."

"Tim, tha' must not set me up ter be summat I'm not."

"I'm not doing that, Molly. I'm saying what I believe to be the truth. What I see in you. You are . . . I can't find the words, not now, not yet, so I'll not try. We are going on a picnic which is supposed to be fun." He grinned infectiously as he reached for the ignition key. "Nothing serious is allowed today, you hear."

"Yes, Tim," throwing back her head again so that her hair rippled about her head.

Tim's hand stayed for a moment on the key. "God, your hair is glorious with the sun on it and . . . there I go again, Molly, but that's the effect you have on me so let's get going before I . . ."

"What?" Her eyes were warm on his face.

"Never you mind." He grinned and started the engine.

The land, the high land he took her to was benevolent now

as summer held it in her gentle hand. As they got higher it rolled away endlessly as far as the eye could see, an uplifting, billowing land, stretching itself under blue skies on which a few white, curling clouds were painted. Saddleworth Moor, and Molly could not help but dwell on how Daddy would have loved it. It was awesome, majestic, shaded in a dozen colours from the palest green and lavender, to gold and bronze, softened by trees down in the valley which looked like a carpet of multicoloured lace from where they sat. There was bracken from which skylarks lifted and sang. The sweet, wind-ruffled moorland grasses were soft and springing beneath their feet as they made their way upwards from the track where Tim had parked the car and the sun beat down on them as he pointed ahead to the sprawl of rocks where they were to picnic. He had a rug and carried a basket of a sort she had never seen before and when he had seated her with great ceremony on the rug he opened it to reveal plates and cups and gleaming glasses and cutlery, all fastened in with little leather straps. It was a marvel and she was enchanted and when he handed her one of the exquisite glasses filled with a pale amber-coloured liquid with bubbles in it, she had her first taste of champagne. There was something he called "patay", come from a duck, he said, though for the life of her she couldn't imagine which part of the bird had produced it. He spread it on thin slivers of toast before handing it to her on a plate so fine she could see the outline of his fingers through it. Delicious plump rounds of crumbling pastry with shrimps and mushrooms in them, again with a name she didn't know: *volo* . . . something or other. Cold chicken legs with crispy skins, tiny pies of such flavour and flakiness they melted in her mouth. Strawberries, ripe and fresh, cheese, celery and an apple pie which she was too full to eat, she told him apologetically.

"I know what you mean. Forbes has done us proud."

"Forbes? Who's Forbes when 'e's at 'ome?"

"He's our butler." Butler! Holy Mother, what the devil was she doing here with a man who had a butler, for God's sake, ready to withdraw into herself the person Tim Broadbent had drawn out, but he seemed to find nothing unusual in having a butler, or her reaction to it, if he had even noticed it.

"I told him I was to take a very discerning young lady on a picnic today and that only the very best would do for her."

"What does that mean?" she asked cautiously.

"What does what mean?" He had been lying on his back on the rug, his jacket tossed to one side, his colourful tie loosened, his hands linked behind his head, his eyes closed. He looked perfectly relaxed, his long legs crossed at the ankle and she studied him, hardly aware of what they were saying since her mind was too preoccupied with the vexed question of what she was doing here with a chap like him. Oh, it was lovely, so lovely and perfect she never wanted it to end. The breathtaking beauty of this rugged land, *her* land which she had not known existed. The warmth and absolute stillness, the shrill of some bird fluting on the air, the butterflies which danced and whirled above a bush studded with white blossom, but what, if she was honest, was she to make of it all and how was she to feel when it ended? He was so . . . God, she didn't know how to describe him except to say he seemed to melt something inside her, but at the same time he gave her a feeling of such wonder it was indescribable. In repose his sun-tinted face was like that of a sleeping child. Like Archie's, she thought, vulnerable, with his mouth relaxed into a slight, curving smile. His lashes lay on his cheek in a thick fan and yet his face was in no way feminine. It was manly, clean cut and in it was something which spoke of a memory of pain.

"What does discerning mean?" she went on, watching his smile deepen, feeling it tug at her own mouth. "An' what does a butler do exactly? I've read about 'em, o' course, but I never met anyone 'oo 'ad one."

He sighed in what appeared to be deep content. "Discerning means a lady or gentleman of great taste."

"Them pies were tasty."

"Well, it doesn't mean exactly that, Molly. If someone shows discernment they perceive clearly, with their minds and with their senses, what is good and what is bad. They have insight . . . you know what that is?"

"Yes."

"I thought you might. They have insight, quick and true and can tell the real thing when they see it. I sound a pompous ass trying to explain myself which doesn't matter if I'm making myself clear?"

"Oh, aye, an' what about that there butler o' thine? 'As 'e discernment?"

"Molly, you're priceless, and yes, he has discernment, for he knows the difference between an ordinary picnic and a superb picnic and today's was a superb picnic. It was, wasn't it? You approved? Shall I tell him so?"

"Aye, tell 'im Mary Angelina O'Dowd like his patay and 'ad a particular fancy fer them . . . whatsits . . . volo . . . whatever. What else does 'e do? Apart from gettin' up superb picnics?"

"He looks after my mother's household."

"Cleanin'!"

"No." He laughed out loud at the idea of this superior being doing anything so lowly as cleaning and Molly watched the white flash of his teeth in his brown face. "He oversees everything that goes on, makes sure that the other servants do their work properly, that kind of thing. Mind you, apart from some of the menservants, those we employed when the war ended, most have been with Mother so long they need no supervising. Dear God," he mused, "I suppose Forbes must be over seventy and Mrs Ogden . . ."

"'Oo's she?"

"She's the cook and must be as old as Forbes."

"'Ow many are there?"

"What, servants?"

"Aye."

"Lord, I've no idea, Molly, and by the way, since that moment in the car when you pleased me by calling me by my christian name you have avoided saying it again. Why?"

"Nay, I 'aven't. It's just . . . never come up."

"Would you believe me, Molly O'Dowd, if I told you it isn't in you to lie, which you have just done. What is in your mind is reflected in your face, so be careful what you think."

Molly felt her heart lurch and her stomach did the same, disturbing the lovely feeling of the picnic she had just eaten. It was a lie and she didn't know why she had said it except that she somehow couldn't bring herself to call Mr Broadbent by his first name. It just didn't seem to come easy to her and yet she didn't like to be called a liar, neither.

She scowled. "I 'aven't. Don't tha' call me a liar. I never . . ."

"You have. Everything you think shows plainly on your face, Molly, whether you are speaking the truth or prevaricating as you are doing now. And before you ask, prevaricating means telling a lie, or at least a fib. And you look simply adorable when you scowl like that, particularly when it is accompanied by a blush."

Her mouth popped open and she turned away from him lest he read anything else in her expression, conscious that while they had been talking she had been getting closer and closer to him. She had thought his eyes were shut as she leaned towards him, staring raptly into his face.

He sat up abruptly and reached for her hand. The champagne, though he had allowed her only one glass, saying it was far too expensive for any more, joking, though she did not know it, had made her feel deliciously dreamlike and she felt a great desire to lie back and simply stare up into the great blue bowl of the sky. Her hand lay passively in his and she wanted to go no further than this. Lord, oh Lord, he was so lovely and she though it would be grand if he kissed her, which it seemed he was about to do but she knew that if he did she would never forgive him. She liked him too much, that was the trouble and if he kissed her things would be different. They could no longer be friends because a kiss would change them and she couldn't bear it if things changed.

As though he read her thoughts he smiled. "I'd like to kiss you, Molly," he said softly, "but I'm not going to because if I did you and I would never be the same to one another again."

She stared at him in wonderment because her thoughts were coming out of his mouth.

"Have you ever been kissed, Molly? The truth, because I shall know if you tell a lie."

She shook her head, her hair swirling in a glow of burnished curls and was bewildered when he smiled with what looked to be satisfaction.

"You will one day, and very thoroughly, or my name's not Tim Broadbent. You are a woman who should be loved thoroughly and often and that will come too, but you're very young . . ."

"I'm nearly twenty," she said indignantly, wondering why she was allowing this man to speak so freely and so intimately to her on a subject which surely should only be shared by two people in love.

"Oh, and when is your birthday? I should like to take you out to celebrate."

"Well . . . April."

"So you were nineteen last April, then?" He released her hand and lay back on the rug, closing his eyes so that she could not see the expression in them, though he doubted she would

understand it if she did. He sighed again in deep content, aware
that she was watching him with great puzzlement and he was
not displeased by it, for Molly O'Dowd, though she was brave
and honest and open-hearted, was not yet ready for what he
wanted.

"I shall be thirty on my next birthday which is at Christmas,"
he told her lazily.

"Oh dear," she commiserated with him and he smiled.

Molly lay down next to him and her thoughts turned to
Daddy who would have loved all this. He would have liked
Mr Broadbent, too . . . Tim . . .

He watched her sleep, brooding over the soft, childish curve
of her cheek, the flush on it, the length of her lashes which
fluttered as though she were dreaming and the full curve of
her poppy mouth which parted slightly to reveal her white
teeth. She made a small sound in the back of her throat and
he leaned forward, thinking she was going to speak but she
turned her head away from him. Her hair was tumbled about
her head and fanned out beneath it, the sun putting streaks of
pure copper in it. Leaning on his elbow he touched it gently,
lifting a rich curl which twined itself about his finger, just as
she had twined herself about his heart. It would take time,
Jesus, a long time, for she was not the woman he would
have picked and his mother would be devastated, he was
not fool enough to think otherwise, but Molly was young,
clever, adaptable and she liked him, he knew that. She was
not overawed, nor overwhelmed by the small pieces of his
world he had shown her. She had a great sense of fun and, at
the same time, propriety and had even joked about Forbes who
must be like an alien from another planet to her and she'd not
even met him yet. He'd not miss that meeting for the world, he
smiled to himself, wondering what the old chap would make
of this beautiful girl he had found working in his own mill.
He watched the lovely swell of her full breasts rise and fall,
the bobs of her nipples clearly discernible beneath the fine
crêpe-de-chine of her dress. She was a child and yet she was
a woman, and one day he meant to have the right to show
her the difference and in the meanwhile he'd best move away
from her or the painful swelling which tightened the crotch
of his trousers would be clearly visible should she wake.

He was sitting on the edge of the rug, his back to her, his
arms about his bent knees when she woke, though it had

been a scramble to get there when she began to stir. He gave the appearance of having been admiring the view the whole time she slept, turning to smile at her as she sat up.

Evening was approaching fast. A crimson sun hung in the sky above the swell of the hills and shading from it down to the horizon were glorious colours of orange and pink and lemon and lavender. Three birds flew across it, black and mysterious, making their way to their nests, the sound of their wings causing a hum in the air. There was a wisp of cloud edged with apricot and gold and the sky turned to a milky blue at their backs as they absorbed the enchantment of it. It was quiet, still, empty, with no movement anywhere but for the birds.

"We'd best get you home, Molly O'Dowd, or your mother will wonder . . ."

It was as though he had touched an exposed nerve with a red-hot iron. She leaped to her feet with a savage cry.

"Dear God in heaven," she began to moan. "What the devil am I doin' lollin' about 'ere when I should've bin 'ome 'ours since? I promised Mammy I wouldn't be late, so, an' will tha' look at me. Mother o' God, where's me shoes? Don't just sit theer wi' tha' mouth 'angin' open . . . come on, come on."

She was running down the slope, the rug trailing after her, her shoes in one hand, the half-finished bottle of champagne in the other, the first things that had come to hand. Her expensive stockings were laddered beyond repair.

"Molly, for Christ's sake, what is it?" he shouted at her back. "It's only just gone half past seven and there's at least an hour of daylight left."

"I'll 'ave ter say I were kept at Bridie's," he heard her babbling. "She was . . . there was . . . Oh, God . . . what excuse can I give an' what about me frock an' me stockin's?"

"What about your frock and your stockings? They look all right to me."

He was clearly bewildered but doing his best to understand and when, in Shaw Road, she leaped from the car without opening the door as she had once seen him do many years ago, he watched her pelt down Sidney Street as though the devil himself were at her heels.

He did not know, and neither did she, that the devil was ahead of her, in her own cosy kitchen.

153

12

It was on the third day when his surprising tour of the mill, surprising to his manager, Mr Watson, that is, failed to reveal what he was looking for that he sat down at his desk, rang the bell and asked his clerk to fetch a ring frame spinner to him by the name of Molly O'Dowd.

"Molly O'Dowd, sir?" the man queried, as though Mr Broadbent had spoken to him in a foreign language. "Which room's she in?"

"I don't know. Surely you have records or . . . or you could ask someone. I wish to speak to her on . . . on urgent family business. Her family . . ." since he must have some reason for summoning one of his operatives to his office. Since Monday he had stood at this window watching the men and women flood in at his gate and stamp across the mill yard, searching among them for the tall, straight-backed, gracefully swaying figure of Molly O'Dowd. It had turned cold and wet and many of the women had their shawls pulled close about their heads, huddling down in them against the wet but Molly wore a jaunty cap, her father's cap which Mammy had altered to fit her, she had told him, and certainly would not walk in that shuffling, bent-backed attitude many of the women adopted.

"She's not in," the clerk told him when he came back half an hour later. He was not used to going into the spinning rooms where the din caused by the machinery had given him a headache and the exotic atmosphere of the humid heat had caused him to sweat profusely inside his suit. He had nearly slipped on the oil-soaked floor and when he got to the machine where the girl was supposed to work she had not been there.

"Wheer's Molly O'Dowd?" he had shrieked at the young woman on the next frame.

"Nay, don't ask me. Their Clare fetched a note an' give it me mam ter say she weren't well. I told overseer."

"Why didn't he tell me?" the clerk asked her in exasperation, since it would have saved all this "to-do". There was bound to be oil on his boots, if not on his good working trousers.

"Not in?" Mr Broadbent said accusingly as though it was all his fault. "Where is she then?"

"I couldn't say, sir. Girl in next frame said as 'ow she were poorly."

"Poorly? What does that mean?" Tim could feel his heart begin to thump erratically and for some reason he felt a great need to fling himself under his desk and cower there, as he had done so many times in the past. But this was Molly and he had no time to be dwelling on his own weaknesses when she might need him.

"Bring the girl here," he told the clerk curtly.

"What girl, sir?"

"The one who works next to Miss O'Dowd."

"What . . . here?" remembering the sweated state of the young woman on the spinning frame.

"Yes, and quickly."

Betty Spooner hovered in the doorway of Mr Broadbent's office, her heart going ten to the dozen. She wiped her sweaty palms down her overall then fiddled about with her hair which, as she worked, had fallen in wisps about her face. She was not scared of Mr Broadbent, for it was said he was a nice chap, pleasant and not over-facing but Betty had never been in this part of the mill before, none of the operatives had that she knew of, and the splendour of it overwhelmed her. There was a carpet on the floor so deep your clogs sank into it. In fact it seemed a bloody shame even to walk across it. A lovely deep blue it was, the colour of the Madonna's robe and the huge desk was so highly polished she could see the reflection in it of different objects that stood on its top, but ask her what they were and she couldn't have said. Was that silver on the mantelpiece framing photographs of three young lads, and those pictures on the walls of flowers and trees and clouds were lovely.

And so was Mr Broadbent. He actually stood up when she moved hesitantly across the carpet and that smile of his, such lovely teeth, and on either side of his mouth there were indentations which might, on a woman, be called dimples.

There was another in his chin which was just deep enough to fit the tip of a woman's finger. She shivered delicately at the thought. His eyes were the deepest brown she'd ever seen, like the treacle toffee her mam made and in them was an expression of such great worry she felt herself go soft all over, wishing she had the power to comfort him. Holy Mother, Molly O'Dowd was a lucky cow! His hair, which was a sort of dark and silver blond mixed, was curly, falling over his forehead and as she watched he pushed a hand through it in what appeared to be great agitation.

"Aah . . . come in, come in, Miss . . . er . . ." he said, doing his best to smile, she could see that, waving her to one of the leather chairs which stood before his desk. "Won't you sit down, Miss . . . er . . . I'm sorry I don't know your name . . ."

"Betty, sir."

"Of course, Betty. You work in the next frame to Miss O'Dowd, I believe."

So that was it, and not completely unexpected, Betty thought with grim satisfaction. He'd been after Molly for ages now, or at least he was a few weeks ago, though things seemed to have died down a bit recently. Showed her up in the yard and Molly had been livid but what was this all about then? Surely to God he wasn't going to ask her, Betty Spooner, to act as . . . as messenger? Jesus, that would be a laugh and no mistake and she'd tell him so too. No, on second thought, best keep her trap shut or she might lose her job. Folk were getting turned off at a lot of mills at the moment, business was so bad it was said, and Betty had no intention of being one of them, not if she could help it.

"Yes, sir?" was all she said.

"And you are . . . a friend of hers?"

"Aye, she lives a few doors down from us."

"In Sidney Street?"

If Betty was surprised that Mr Broadbent knew where Molly lived she did not show it.

"Aye."

"She is . . . I believe you told my clerk she was not . . . well." Tim licked his lips and wondered what in hell's name he was up to but something, something in Molly's behaviour last Saturday filled him with unease and he must get to the truth. If she had a cold or some such thing this girl would know and tell him and he could leave it alone, stop making a fool of himself, but he must know.

"That's right. 'Er mam sent mine a note. I were ter tell overseer she weren't well—"

"What is wrong with her?" Tim interrupted sharply.

It was Betty's turn to lick her lips and look away in some confusion. They all knew in the street what was up with Molly O'Dowd and her mam, poor sods, and that bugger who lived with them, Molly's stepfather, should be reported, but it was the habit of folk in their community to mind their own business. To respect the privacy of their neighbours unless asked to do otherwise and there was not much anyone could do about a chap who knocked his wife about when he was drunk. A lot of them did it and were sorry afterwards but Pikey Watson was a cold-hearted bugger with a temper on him, and fists on him that could stop an ox. Nobody had seen Molly and her mam, or even the children, but Mrs Haydock who lived next door to them said there was a right old hullaballoo on Saturday night.

Betty sighed deeply. Perhaps she ought to tell him. Perhaps he could do something about it. She and Molly had been friends for as long as she could remember. Gone to school and church together, pictures, swimming, up town, all the things children and young girls did and she'd not like to see her get seriously hurt, which she would one of these days if that sod wasn't stopped. Betty had said so to her dad on Sunday. Keep out of it, girl, her dad had said, for though Bert Spooner wouldn't dream of leathering his own kids, nor his missis, what other men did was nothing to do with them.

"You must tell me, Betty," Mr Broadbent said quietly.

So she did.

The door was opened to him by a thin child of eight or nine, he supposed. Only a fraction, as though not even the air in the street must be allowed to creep through the gap into the house. Her attitude, so blank and unchildlike, alarmed him more than anything else could. For a fraction of a second she looked beyond him to his motor car and into her eyes came a strange expression as though she had connected it to something, then they returned to him, clouded and vacant.

"Is . . . Miss O'Dowd in?" Tim asked her politely, doing his best to see into the narrow hallway. There was no sign of life in it, nor indeed anywhere. The net curtain shrouded the windows and they did not twitch to indicate that there might be someone behind them. The house felt empty, as though the child were all alone in it.

She shook her head, ready to close the door but he put out a hand to stop her. She was so – strange. So utterly still and . . . not there! Empty. Hollow. Withdrawn from the world in which she existed and he must find out why. It was not his practice to force his way into another man's home but surely, after what Betty had told him, if only on purely humanitarian grounds, he was entitled to find out.

"Can I come in, child?" he asked her gently but firmly, beginning to push open the door and it was then he saw the figure lurking in the doorway at the end of the hall. It was very dim, for the rain still fell and very little light reached inside the narrow passage. The child stood passively, the door knob still in her hand as though waiting for further instruction.

"Molly?" he ventured, peering up the hall, trying to see who it was who leaned there. "Is that you, Molly?"

"Aye, it's . . . me . . . all right, Mr Broadbent . . . but tha'd best be . . . on tha' way. Theer's . . . nowt 'ere fer thi'." Her voice was hoarse, rasping, only just recognisable as Molly's but Tim felt a great thankfulness wash over him despite her words, for after what Betty had told him he had thought to find her seriously injured.

"Molly, I came to see if you're . . . all right. Betty said you weren't . . . well."

"Jesus, Mary and Joseph," he thought he heard her whisper as she sagged heavily against the doorframe.

"Pardon?"

"Not well, is it? Dear . . . dear God in . . . heaven!" Her hand lifted and fell.

"Let me come in, Molly. Perhaps I can help. I don't mean to interfere . . . but . . . you see . . ." He would have to be careful. It was getting away from him, the hold he had on the frenzy of his rage and hatred, all the emotions he had felt when Betty had told him of the violence of Molly's stepfather. Dear Christ in heaven, he hadn't even known she had one. She had sported a shiner several weeks ago but she had not told him who had given it to her. He had let her talk him out of doing anything about it and now look what had happened. The brute had probably given her another! He had known nothing about her or her family, her home life, brothers, sisters and yet in the background had lurked this beast who, presumably, had been here when she returned from her innocent outing with himself on Saturday and again he had taken his fists to her. It was *his* bloody fault. Tim Broadbent had caused this and goddammit to hell he was going to do something about it this time.

"I'm coming in, Molly, and if I need to I shall send for the constable. From what your friend said . . ." As he talked he moved slowly up the hall, watched by the vacant-eyed child, towards the figure at the far end who had begun to back away from him.

"No . . . no, Tim, please . . . there's no need . . . really. Don't come in. We're all right." She even tried a small, heartbreaking laugh. "'Tis nothin', so 'tis. Tha'd best go . . . please."

"I'm not leaving until I'm sure you're . . . you're not . . . badly hurt, and I swear . . ."

"No . . . oh, please, Tim . . . leave us alone. We're all right, Mammy an' me. Go 'ome, Tim," she begged him in the strange, harsh voice that sounded as though she had something stuck in her throat. "In the name o' God, please go 'ome . . . there's nowt tha' can do . . . don't come in." She was weeping now, great tearing sobs that seemed to hurt her, for in the dark of the hallway he saw her pale hand go painfully to her breast. "Oh, please . . . please . . . I don't want tha' ter see me . . . what 'e's done ter me. Don't . . . oh, please don't . . ."

"Hush, hush now, sweetheart." His voice was soft, soothing, speaking as one would to an overwrought child but the anguish in it was clear.

"Aah . . . Tim . . . 'e 'urt us . . . me an' Mammy an' . . . an' Clare."

"I know, my dear love, but he'll not do it again, I promise you. Won't you let me . . ."

He saw her then. She had retreated so far the light coming through the front room doorway fell about her and had it not been for her voice Tim Broadbent would not have known he was looking into the broken face of Molly O'Dowd.

"Jesus . . . oh, Jesus," he began to moan. "Oh, Jesus . . . Molly, my love . . . my love . . . what has been done to you?"

"'E 'it me, Tim," she said simply. "First Mammy an' then me an' then 'e . . ."

"Don't, sweetheart. Come . . . come here and . . ." He put out a hand to her, his heart breaking for her pain, her shame, for that was how she felt, he knew. He knew her as he knew himself, even after such a short time, and her lovely shining spirit, as well as her flesh, had taken a beating. He wanted to hold her, kiss her lovingly as one would hold and kiss a hurt child, comfort her, show her his true, deep feelings for her which nothing would ever change.

She seemed to stiffen. "Don't touch me, Tim. I . . . I think summat's broken inside an' Mammy's badly . . ."

Tim sagged against the stained wall for just a moment, his head hanging low. He was drained of everything but two emotions. One was hatred and a need for revenge, the other was a deep, despairing compassion. The two emotions fought with one another for precedence, since there was nothing Tim Broadbent wanted and needed more at that moment than to find this girl's stepfather and sink his fists into any bit of flesh and bone that was handy. Beat him to a bloody pulp as *he* had beaten Molly's face. Knock him down, kick him and stamp on him until his blood ran in the gutter, then pick him up and start again.

But there was Molly, Molly injured and beaten herself, the bravery taken from her, her pride and lovely defiance diminished by a bully's fists. Molly, whom Tim Broadbent loved and who needed, not to see the man who had beaten her beaten himself, but to have transferred to her some of his own strength to bear her up, to get her through; to know compassion and tenderness, and understanding of the terrible state she had been reduced to. Vengeance, retribution, justice, could wait.

The whole of Sidney Street was at its door that day, swearing they had seen nothing so entertaining for years. Mrs Haydock, Minnie's mother, who lived next door and had never before used one of the revolutionary things, was goaded into running up the street to telephone for an ambulance! Her, speaking into a telephone and the voice that came out of it gave her the biggest shock of her life, she told Mrs Openshaw later. Her Ernie, who was eleven, eager to be of help to this chap with the grand motor car, ran off at great speed to look for a bobby. They hung about, waiting for the next thrilling event, not wicked, not even thoughtless, just ordinary folk who found a bit of drama, so long as it was not their own, most entertaining.

Even the slanting rain which drifted like smoke along the street could not keep them indoors, fetching old Granny Jamison creaking to her doorstep to see what all the fuss was about, and her ninety-two next birthday.

They watched as Molly O'Dowd and Rosie Watson were carried out on stretchers and tucked into the ambulance, gasping, those who were close enough, at the sight of Molly's face, speculating on where they were to be taken. They watched as Flo O'Dowd and Maggie Todd, both flushed and flustered and grim-faced, arrived, summoned by the police, it was rumoured, to tuck the four frightened children and a battered suitcase or two into the back of a taxi-cab, and they watched as Pikey Watson strutted along Sidney Street later that day to be met at his own door by two constables.

Molly wakened to a clean white world that smelled of disinfectant, carbolic soap and roses. She was strapped down to something hard which rustled when she moved her feet, the only part of her that didn't hurt and even to move them was difficult she was trussed up so tightly. She was comfortable, though, and despite the pain which spread from the top of her head down to somewhere on a level with her knees, in a state she could only describe as "dreamlike". She could hear voices far away, though not what they said and soft, rubber-soled footsteps hurrying somewhere but it didn't seem to matter because somehow, at last, she knew, don't ask her how, but she knew she was safe. God, her arm itched and she longed to scratch it but she couldn't move, not one bloody inch, she was so securely tied up, but the itch got worse and she struggled to get her arm free.

"Don't move, Molly. Lie still, I'm here," his voice said and she knew then why she felt safe.

She opened her eyes. Well, she tried. They had been firmly gummed together for days now and she had been forced to creep about the house blindly with only Clare to help her, as she did her best to look after Mammy. Mammy was worse than Molly was because it had taken a long time for Pikey's fists to extract from her the exact truth of Molly's whereabouts. It seemed he had not believed Mammy's story about weddings and flowers and this . . . this beating they had both suffered was the result. Pikey had returned home earlier than usual, she mumbled, and of course she herself had been late, which explained why she had forgotten the signal arranged between herself and Mammy.

"Tim?" she ventured, croaking. Her mouth was dry and swollen and she felt as though her face was the size of the balloons the rag and bone man gave out. Mother of God, she must look a bloody sight and with Tim Broadbent sitting next to her an' all. She could feel, sense, the state of her and she knew it was appalling to look at but he was looking at it, and not minding. She couldn't speak properly and she wondered why, for she had managed it this morning when Tim knocked at the door. Why did she feel so drowsy and though she hurt, why did the pain not seem to bother her?

"Yes, I'm here, my darling," his voice said, rich with tenderness and on her closed eyelids she could feel his light breath as though he were leaning over her.

"Drink . . ." she rasped.

"Just a sip, Mr Broadbent," another voice said firmly, and Molly was startled since she had not known there was anyone else in the room, wherever the room was. "I'll give it to her through this straw," the voice continued. "After an anaesthetic we must take great care. We don't want to be sick, do we, and damage our stitches?"

Who was she talking about, Molly wondered drowsily. Stitches? Who had stitches and if it was the woman who spoke why wasn't she in bed like Molly?

"Of course, nurse, I'm sorry, but don't ask me to go," Tim's voice pleaded.

"But you've been here such a long time, sir. Would you not like to go home and rest?"

"Not yet. Not until she is . . . recovered."

Molly sipped the straw which the nurse – the nurse? – held gently between her lips, feeling the cool water flow down her bruised throat. It revived her and she spoke more clearly, more strongly.

"Where . . . is this?"

"Don't talk, dear," the female voice said. "We need all our strength."

"Where . . .?"

"Let me just speak to her, nurse. She knows me. Please let me have a few minutes then I promise I'll go home."

Someone tutted, presumably the nurse. The sheets – that's what held her so securely – were drawn back slightly and Molly felt fingers on her pulse, then she was made tidy again and she felt too weak to argue. The nurse moved away, doing something in the background and she thought she heard someone moan.

"Tim . . ."

"I'm here, my darling." She could sense his hand hovering at her face, almost see it through the blood red slits which had once been her eyes but he did not touch her.

"Tell . . . me . . . where . . . Mammy . . . the . . . children . . . where . . . how long . . ."

"You've been here three days, sweetheart."

"Three days . . . Oh, Jesus an' all his . . . angels . . ."

"Mr Broadbent, I shall not be pleased if you tire my patient. Doctor Taylor was most explicit in—"

"Yes, nurse, two minutes only. I must put Miss O'Dowd's mind at rest. Surely that can only do her good?"

"Very well. Two minutes."

"Mammy . . .?"

"Is fine, my love. She's here, in the next bed to you. Now don't speak again or the gorgon . . ."

"Gorgon?"

"The nurse." His voice dropped to a conspiratorial whisper and she knew he was smiling. "I'll explain what that is when you're better because I'm sure you'll want to know. You have the most enquiring mind . . . even now in the . . ."

"Mammy . . .?"

"She was . . . badly beaten, Molly. As you were. She has a broken arm and ribs and . . . slight concussion but Doctor Taylor has X-rayed her and says she will mend. You . . . your ribs were . . . cracked and you have . . . Christ, Molly, I'm finding it very hard to . . . I must not lose control or I swear I'll kill that bastard."

She could hear him taking deep, convulsive breaths and she wished she could get her hand out to comfort him, then he grew calmer. "You have . . . extensive bruising. Both of you had surgery."

"Surgery?" God, she was tired. She wanted to turn her head and look at Mammy but though her spirit was willing, nay, eager, longing to see how Mammy was, her weak flesh . . . so weary . . . she could not.

"Yes," Tim was saying, "to mend your broken bones and . . . sew up . . . your face."

"My . . . face?"

"It was . . . badly cut . . ." She could hear him choking again, or was he weeping? If only she could get her arm free to put her hand to his face but it was beyond her.

"The . . . children, Tim . . . please . . . Clare . . ."

She could sense he was making a great effort to get a hold of himself. This must be hard for him for though he'd said nothing much on the matter she knew he'd spent a long time in hospital when the war finished. Look how he was the first time they met. So cracked up and over nothing. She'd give anything to see him, to smile at him and tell him she didn't feel so bad, not now, not now that he was here but it was all she could do not to drift off up to the ceiling, the funny way she felt.

"The three little ones," he said at last, his voice stronger, "I'm sorry, I don't know their names . . ."

"It's all right. I do," she said dreamily.

"They have gone to Aunty Maggie's and she says you're not to worry about them. They'll be fine with her."

Bejasus, as Daddy used to say, what would Aunty Maggie have made of Tim Broadbent, she wondered, wishing she could smile. What was he up to with their Molly? she could just imagine Aunty Maggie demanding to know. The same with Aunty Flo, who, if Aunty Maggie was there, so would she be, bewildered, distressed of course, and shocked by this chap they didn't know but whom Molly did, taking over Pikey Watson's family.

"Yes . . . they will . . ." she managed, "and Clare?"

"Aunty Flo, I believe. Is that right?"

"That's . . . exactly right. Clare likes . . . Aunty Flo. There's no . . . men . . . at Aunty Flo's."

She and Mammy were in a private nursing home on the outskirts of Oldham, Tim told her, brought in an ambulance summoned by him and when she was feeling better and sitting up, both she and Mammy would have a good laugh about Mrs Haydock running down the street to the telephone kiosk on Shaw Road. Mrs Haydock, and indeed most of the women in the street, had never seen an electric light, except when they went up town and had never had any experience with things that were run on the magic of the "electricity". As for the telephone, that was a mystery none could comprehend and how anyone could talk at the end of Sidney Street to the man at the ambulance station in town was beyond their understanding. Still, Mrs Haydock had managed it and when they got home she'd thank her personally, Rosie murmured a few days later, though the prospect of going home to the house where Pikey had done such bad things to them was very daunting.

Mr Broadbent had told her and Molly about Pikey. He had been charged with grievous bodily harm and both Mr Broadbent and Doctor Taylor were to testify to what he had done to her and Molly. Doctor Taylor had even examined their Clare to see if . . . well, to see if she was damaged. Pikey had taken her into the bedroom that night and kept her there while she and Molly had floundered, only half conscious, in their own blood, but it seemed he had done nothing "down there", thanks be to the Blessed Mother who watched over small children, though Clare was not right. She had always been afraid of him, weren't they all, but now, even the doctor and kind Mr Broadbent caused her to cringe away as though any man's hand terrified her, pressing herself against Flo's protective bosom. Funny about Flo. She'd been such a disciplinarian with her own four but now she fussed and fretted over Clare, asking her if she was warm enough, calling her sweetheart, sitting her on her knee possessively when they came at visiting time to see her and Molly, and you could tell the child was the better for it. It seemed Flo and Kathleen made much of her, welcoming her into their totally female world and Doctor Taylor said it was best to leave her there for now. Rosie had watched Flo relax quite visibly as he spoke.

"There, love, tha's ter stay wi' yer Aunty Flo. Will tha' like that?" she crooned to the child, hugging Rosie's daughter to her when she nodded. It broke Rosie's heart, for Clare was Seamus's last gift to her but could she deny her little girl a bit of peace, affection and a reprieve from the fear under which she had lived for six years?

The other three? Well, Maggie said, not bringing them on that first visit, for God alone knew what they might get up to in this splendid and expensive place, Rosie'd not know them. Getting really cheeky was young Archie, even in such a short time and it just showed what a relief from fear and tension did for kids. They soon forgot, didn't they? She'd bring them on her next visit, she promised, casting a look round the immaculate room in which Molly and Rosie lay side by side. Private rooms they could have had, one each, but Mr Broadbent had thought they'd do better together. He was paying for the whole shenanigan, so he was, and a pretty penny it must be costing. There were even pictures on the wall, carpet on the floor, lovely curtains of velvet at the window through which Molly and Rosie could look out on a garden so big and so colourful it put Alexandra Park to shame. The room was filled with flowers. Maggie had never seen so many and when Molly pressed her to take some home she did, for there must have been a dozen bowls and vases overflowing with roses and carnations and sweet peas and some Maggie had never seen before and certainly could not name. Hothouse flowers, Molly said they were, come from Mr Broadbent's place which was called Meddins.

Maggie didn't know what to make of Mr Broadbent and their Molly and this was not the best time to be questioning her, or Rosie, about it. There was something going on, though. You'd only to look about this room filled with more flowers than the florist in Yorkshire Street and see the way he looked at her niece. Nice chap, polite and grateful, he said, for all her and Mrs O'Dowd's help. He didn't know what he would have done without them, he told her and Flo, smiling in a way that . . . well, it was a kind smile, a good-hearted smile, a smile that made you take a shine to him, but he was the owner of the mill where Molly worked and everyone knew what was said about mill girls who associated with those above them. It was this association, apparently, which had goaded Pikey to do what he had done, though that was no excuse, of course.

Molly healed quickly. She was young and fit and now that the spectre of Pikey was gone from their lives was filled with the joy of simply being alive, of being safe and feeling better, of having Mammy and the children safe and she was soon chafing to be up and about. Her ribs had healed and though her body was still a livid map of fading bruises, they would soon be gone. There was only her face and how that was to turn out was still to be determined. By some great good fortune she had lost none of her teeth, though her lips had been mashed and split against them by Pikey's mindless fists.

A flap of skin above her left eye, torn away by Pikey's signet ring in the shape of an L, had been sewn neatly back by a surgeon who, Tim said, had dealt with men come back from the war with dreadful facial injuries. The trouble was that the wound had been left unattended from Saturday to Wednesday and had begun to heal in a puckered ridge and the surgeon had been forced to reopen it and begin again. She would bear a thin white scar for the rest of her days but it mattered not one iota to him, Tim told her. She would be just as beautiful as she had always been, he said, able to touch her cheek now and with Mammy listening as well, though he didn't seem to care and neither did Mammy. The rest was time, Doctor Taylor said, time and rest, good food and . . . good company, turning to smile in a constrained manner at Tim who was in his usual place beside Molly. Tim didn't notice. Tim noticed nothing unless it was happening to Molly O'Dowd.

It was three weeks before Doctor Taylor declared Molly well enough to leave, though he would like to keep Mrs Watson with him a little while longer. She needed more rest, a time to gather her frail strength about her before returning to her life, whatever that might be, though he did not voice this last. She was a trifle withdrawn, he confided privately to Tim Broadbent and he was worried. What was to become of her and her children? he asked, but Mr Broadbent had reassured him that there was nothing to be worried about there. He would take care of them all, especially Molly, his eyes said as they turned to look at her where she leaned lovingly over her mother.

Doctor Taylor raised his eyebrows and walked away. It was nothing to do with him but how was this working-class family with its broad accents and uncultured ways to fit into the elegant world of Muriel Broadbent, whose physician he was?

Muriel Broadbent was just about to find out.

13

"I want to bring someone to meet you, Mother," Tim said at breakfast. "Would you have a free hour tomorrow?"

Forbes exchanged a glance with Parsons as he handed her the hot breakfast plates and Parsons raised her eyebrows. Forbes and Parsons, Doris Parsons, the elderly housemaid, had been serving breakfast to the Broadbent family for over thirty years. Mrs Broadbent had been a new bride, come from a Cheshire family of impeccable pedigree to marry old Mr Joshua who had been young Mr Joshua then. Mr Will Broadbent had still been alive, and his wife, Tessa, but when the babies had begun to arrive, Master Will in 1893, Master Charles a year later and then Master Tim in 1895, the old gentleman and his still beautiful wife had moved out of Meddins and gone to live in Torquay where the air was mild, almost Mediterranean, it was said.

Forbes could remember as though it were yesterday, Master Will and Master Charles, with the small boy who had grown into the man at the breakfast table tagging along behind them, catapulting into the kitchen from the yard shouting for Mrs Ogden's muffins and biscuits at teatime, their faces rosy, young, smooth, alive with the belief, as they all had been, that it would go on for ever. Master Will, "missing, believed killed" which, Forbes was aware now, meant that he had been blown to pieces by a shell with not enough of him left to identify. Master Charles had been shot and died instantly and that was all anybody was told, despite Mr Joshua's "pull" at the War Office in Whitehall. In those last months before the war the boys had been going to mend the small jetty from which they had all once dived but it had not got done, falling into worse disrepair with no one to care until

Mr Tim had taken it in hand a year or two ago. Not himself personally. You could tell he hadn't the heart, but a jobbing carpenter had fixed it up and they all waited patiently, the servants, for the next generation to come along and bring it to life again.

So who was this "someone" Mr Tim wanted his mother to meet? Forbes and Parsons waited, their elderly hearts beating more quickly with anticipation.

Muriel Broadbent put her napkin delicately to her lips and her own heart skipped a beat, for though she had waited, or so she told herself and all her friends, with great eagerness for Tim to bring home some suitable young lady for her inspection, now that it could be about to happen, she was not so sure she wanted to share her boy with another woman. It must be a woman. He was so serious and yet, now she looked at him more closely there was an air about him of . . . of what? She couldn't really say. A tenseness, not a nervous tension, but one of excitement and at the same time what could have been apprehension. He'd been acting strangely these last few weeks. Oh, not the strangeness he'd brought back from France with him, thank God, but distracted, away from home a lot, overnight at one point and when she had questioned him about it, diplomatically, of course, since young men were entitled to their little . . . flings, he told her a friend of his had had an accident. No one you know, Mother, he'd added hastily and he'd tell her all about it when he had a minute.

"Of course, darling," she answered now, "I have no engagements tomorrow. I did tell Beattie Knight I might telephone her today to fix up some bridge with Totty and Hilda but it can wait. Who is it, dear? The friend who had the accident?"

"How did you guess?" He leaned towards her and Muriel Broadbent's heart contracted with love for this one son of hers God had allowed her to keep. Who was this person who had caused Tim to look so frantic, so desperate, so worn out and even ill at times over the last few weeks? She had been worried, she had to admit, and puzzled too and it had taken all her considerable resolve not to demand to be told. He could not abide to be what he called "fussed over" and got quite rattled when she did, but just when she was about to insist on knowing who this "friend" was, he'd suddenly looked better, more cheerful, in fact his usual endearing self.

"Ask him to lunch, dear. Why not? Then we can get to know one another. I'm longing to meet him. You know any friend of yours is more than welcome in our home."

"It's not a chap, Mother. It's a girl."

There was a deep and strange silence as Muriel did her best to control her sudden urge to say that after all she believed she was engaged for tomorrow. That she found she could not bring herself to meet any young woman her son brought home, since she did not want her place as mistress of Meddins and sole companion of her son to be taken from her, but of course she did not. This situation was what she had told Tim, her friends, her daughter and indeed everyone she knew, sighing resignedly, she had longed for ever since Tim came home, but now it was here it frightened her. She did not show it, naturally. The girls and young women she had dragged through this house, paraded before his polite but disinterested gaze and now he had found one for himself. If it was to happen she had hoped for the daughter of one of her own friends, or at least a girl she knew personally and now it appeared he was to introduce her to a perfect stranger. Someone it seemed he cared about, she could sense that, someone special to him, someone he wanted her to meet which could mean only one thing.

"Darling, how lovely, a girl . . ." and Forbes and Parsons smiled at one another in gratification. "Who is she? Do I know her? Where is she from and who are her people?" She managed a smile. It was really no more than a cool glimpse of her teeth but Tim seemed not to notice in his own delight.

"Now hold on, Mother." He laughed, turning to the servants, raising a rueful eyebrow as though to say what was a chap to do with a mother like his, but he should have known her first questions would be to do with pedigree. "I haven't known her long."

"How long? Where did you meet? Aren't you the dark horse keeping this to yourself and you know how I've been longing for you to meet some girl of good family."

"Mother, please, give me a chance."

"I'm sorry, darling. You must forgive me. I'm so . . . excited."

"Really, Mother?"

"Of course, please do go on."

"I'm going to tell you nothing. I want you to judge her yourself without any preconceived ideas of what . . . of what someone I care about should be like."

"I see. You . . . care about her then?"

Her son looked surprised and the servants, perhaps catching a whisper of the dismay in their mistress's mind, exchanged glances.

"Of course I do, Mother. I would not be bringing her to see you if I didn't. I want you to . . . well . . ." He began to fiddle with his knife, his eyes lowered and when he raised them it was almost shyly.

"I . . . love her, Mother."

Muriel Broadbent's heart plummeted and she felt a strong urge to put her hand to it.

"And . . . her? Does she feel the same?"

"I believe so."

"You don't know?" There was a faint gleam of what might have been hope in Muriel Broadbent's eyes and she lowered them hastily.

"I will tomorrow and so will you. Now, no more. Not another word. You shall see for yourself what . . . what a delight she is."

"A delight." His mother's face was unreadable.

Molly had been staying at Aunty Flo's for a fortnight now, going into the hospital to see Mammy every day, sometimes taken by Tim who seemed able to leave the mill whenever he pleased, sometimes on her own on the tram. Informed by Betty, who had come to see Molly in the hospital – against Betty's dad's advice who said she'd be better off out of it – on when Pikey was at work, Tim had driven Molly over to Sidney Street. Without a glance left or right, as though she could not abide a minute more than was absolutely necessary in this place of suffering, Molly had stuffed some clothes, hers and Mammy's into a suitcase borrowed from Aunty Flo, tossed it in the back of Tim's car and been driven away at speed. She knew Tim was restive under the restraint the law had put on him regarding Pikey and, conscious of the inquisitive eyes of the neighbours who would never cease to be amazed at Molly O'Dowd's courage, or was it bare-faced cheek, she had urged him to "put his foot down", an expression she had heard him use on that first day she had ridden in his motor car.

The suitcase did not contain the lovely blue dress and hat she had worn that day.

It was nearly six weeks since the event following the picnic up on Saddleworth Moor and though she herself was completely restored to health, Mammy still lingered in her bed at the hospital. Molly and Tim had both impressed on her that she never need see Pikey again. That Tim had found them a dear little house on the road which led out of Oldham towards Meddins and they were all to move into it as soon as Mammy was better. Pikey, though Tim and the doctor had done their best to get him a prison sentence, had merely been bound over for a year to keep the peace. The judge, who had seen neither Molly nor Rosie, was not at all sure that the "walloping" – the word he used to his wife later that day – these sort of chappies gave to their families warranted a stay in prison. Pikey was back living in Sidney Street, working still at Cravens Ironworks and keeping his nose clean. He had made no fuss or objection about his children remaining with relatives, nor about being arrested, and Tim was of the opinion that he had learned his lesson. He still wanted to give him a good "pasting", he told Molly, as they sat in the increasingly autumnal garden of the hospital but, grinning widely, being a sensible fellow who knew his own limitations, and having now seen Pikey's enormous build, he thought he'd better leave it to the law.

That was before Pikey went before the judge and it had taken several days, and many tears, before Molly had persuaded him to let it drop. It was over. Their life with Pikey was over and they must start their new one, her and Mammy and the children with nothing from the past hanging over them. If he killed Pikey or Pikey killed him how would she feel, she begged him to tell her. She would never forgive herself, and so he had let himself be persuaded.

It was a Saturday and Molly was dressed in the lovely new outfit Tim had insisted she let him buy for her, since it was his fault in the first place that Pikey had ruined the smart blue dress and hat she had worn on the day of the picnic. She had brought nothing from the house but a plain skirt, a blouse or two, Mammy's elderly costume and serviceable brown winter coat, her own new patent leather shoes, a pair of clogs apiece and a change of underwear.

She had argued hotly with Tim over the three-piece suit of

almond-coloured cashmere, saying she could not accept any more money from him, not after all he had spent on hospital bills and what he gave Aunty Flo and Aunty Maggie for the upkeep of the children.

He had been very serious when he answered her. Did she expect her aunts to bear the cost of feeding and clothing the children? he asked her gravely, and until she could manage it herself she must allow him to . . . well, if she preferred to call it a loan, then a loan it was. Neither of her aunts was well off, wasn't that true? Aunty Flo was a widow and Aunty Maggie's Alf retired and, for God's sake, didn't he himself, without appearing to boast, have more money than he knew what to do with and surely she could not be so mean-spirited as to deny her own mother decent medical attention and her brother and sisters a bit of food in their mouths and new shoes to their feet. Aunty Maggie was only telling him the other day, with no ulterior motive, Molly was to understand, for Aunty Maggie wasn't like that, how young Archie's clogs were for ever at the menders.

"Heaven preserve and bless us! Sure an' whenever did Aunty Maggie an' you discuss our Archie's clogs, Tim Broadbent?"

"Sure an' the day before yesterday, Molly O'Dowd, while you and Mammy were in with the doctor."

"Tha're mekkin' fun o' me, so tha' are."

"Me? Never. Would I dare?"

"Tha' would so."

Though he was laughing he was looking at her in that way that was becoming increasingly familiar to her, a way she found she liked enormously and yet at the same time dreaded. In fact, she more than liked it, for one day it would end and how could she bear that? He'd been that good to her, and to her family, all of them, and she didn't know how she would have got through it all without him. But then, if it were not for him none of it would have happened, would it? Not that she blamed him, the Holy Mother knew that, but sometimes she was of the opinion that she and her family might have been a damned sight better off if he had not come into her life.

But would she, if she were honest, could she really admit, even to herself, that that was what she wished? That Tim Broadbent had not come into her life? He was so . . . special and she was not unaware that he thought her to be the same. Even his face seemed to change shape when his eyes were on hers. It appeared to smooth out, become younger and, though it was a lean, masculine face, softer. His eyes narrowed slightly and became a darker brown. His lips curled at the corners, not exactly in a smile, but almost. They looked as though they were about to form themselves into words of some importance though that was probably her imagination.

Pressing a dramatic hand to his heart his grin deepened. "Me! Make fun of you," he went on. "Make fun of Molly O'Dowd who, when she gets her dander up is as mad as Mick O'Dowd."

"'Oo told tha' that old tale?" she squealed, her face scarlet.

"Aunty Maggie, who else? Mad as Mick O'Dowd, she said, though happily I've yet to meet it. Mind you, you were pretty miffed that day in the yard when I had the effrontery to speak to you in front of your friends."

They smiled at one another in remembrance and all about them the squirrels scampered among the fallen leaves of the beech and hawthorn trees which surrounded the hospital garden. The sun shone mildly, warming the sheltered bench where they sat and around their feet the ground was strewn with empty shells and ripe kernels the squirrels were gathering. The foliage of the beech trees was beginning to turn its rich golden red and the horse chestnuts, the same shining colour of Molly's sun-dappled hair, had long since donned their autumn glory of burnished darkness.

They had just returned from up town, where, in Buckley and Prockters' splendid store, the Mumps bazaar into which Daddy had promised he would one day take her, Molly had been treated as though she were the greatest lady in the land. Naturally Tim was well known there. His family had an account with them, he whispered to Molly, pulling a comical face at the retreating back of the lady floorwalker who had begged them to follow her. His mother and sister regularly shopped there and, he added fiercely, would she please stop skulking about behind him as though she were a shoplifter who was about to get "pinched".

They were treated with great ceremony, the floorwalker asking after Mrs Broadbent and her daughter, Mrs Addington, the assistant she summoned eyeing Molly's rather short brown coat which belonged to Mammy, the black skirt which fell about three inches beneath it, her black patent leather shoes which matched neither and her tossed mop of hatless, glowing curls, with astonished misgivings. The scar above Molly's left eye did not go unnoticed and were those the remains of a "shiner" about each of her wide, somewhat startled blue-green eyes? Her face had a curious lopsided look to it, the floorwalker and the shop assistant agreed, sotto voce, as they hurried away at Mr Broadbent's command to bring something "fetching" for him and Miss O'Dowd to see. What? Well, they would leave that to them, wouldn't they, Molly, he said to the young lady he had brought in and Molly nodded speechlessly.

It took a long time for Mr Broadbent to choose exactly the right outfit for Miss O'Dowd, and for Miss O'Dowd to agree with him. It seemed, odd as she was, and as oddly dressed, she had a very decided idea of what she liked and disliked. Red she would not have, nor a certain shade of pink. She did not care for eau de nil though she agreed the dress was lovely. Mauve, which was "in" at the moment, oh no, not for her but it would look well on Aunty Flo, she said to Mr Broadbent who laughed and agreed with her. Tangerine, violet and chartreuse, though pretty, she said politely, would not suit her at all. She liked almond, pale apricot, biskra, cedar, heather, ivory, jade, mole grey, pale grey and white as long as the last three had a hint of colour about them. Rose beige was lovely, so were sahara and sand, which turned out, astonishingly, to be the new season's colours. She spoke with the broadest Lancashire accent, mixed with something the floorwalker, who was from London, could make no sense of.

The transformation was quite extraordinary, she and the shop assistant agreed and, you could tell by the light in his eyes, so did Mr Broadbent. She had been a good-looking woman when she came in despite the faint blemishes on her face, but now she was quite glorious. She had chosen almond. A skirt, straight and just touching her kneecap, a short-sleeved top and a long-sleeved open jacket, again straight, and without buttons. The outfit was perfectly plain except for three narrow bands of contrast in a pale coffee colour round the neck and the welt of the under top. There was a cloche hat to match, from under the narrow brim of which her eyes sparkled. Her unruly curls disappeared, giving her, the assistant said, exactly today's look. Plain, almond-coloured gloves, a small coffee-coloured handbag and court shoes and she might have stepped from the pages of *How to Dress*, a magazine in which Lady Cynthia Hammond wrote the fashion page, she twittered.

Tim didn't speak and neither did Molly. He told the assistant to send the bill personally to him and not to his mother, aware of the knowing looks which passed secretly from one to the other of the women. They thought him to be the usual high-class gentleman with the usual working-class paramour, though most did not bother to dress them at Buckley and Prockters, and if they did, they did not bring them into the shop so blatantly, and still in their working clothes, to purchase a new outfit.

"I'm sorry, Molly," he said abruptly, his tone of smiling banter changing to one of sudden and unusual seriousness.

"What about?"

"About those girls in the shop. They were thinking the worst. About you and me, I mean, and I suppose you can't blame them. But you were very . . . restrained. After Aunty Maggie's revelation about mad Mick O'Dowd I wouldn't have been surprised, nor would I have blamed you if you'd landed a fourpenny one on the damned supercilious nose of that floorwalker. She put the wrong connotation entirely on the friendship you and I share, and yet . . ."

"What does connotation mean?"

He delicately took her hand in his. Her bag and hat were on the bench beside her and she had removed her gloves. They had just come from visiting Rosie Watson and the look Rosie had given him as she stared at the vision who was her daughter had been one of great alarm, but he had smiled and nodded briefly at her while Molly did a twirl to let her mammy see her grand new outfit and Rosie had relaxed, recognising what was in Tim's face at last, what Molly had as yet not been allowed to see.

Rosie had nodded back at him, letting him know of her approval, satisfied, her pale, worn, sad face, not so quick to heal as Molly's, gentle with love and peace, since she knew her girl was to be all right.

"Connotation means . . . well, meaning! It means to imply something which is perhaps not correct. Those shop girls looked at you and me and decided—"

"It's all right, Tim. I know what tha' mean now, an' what they thought." Her young dignity smote him to the heart.

"I'm sorry, Molly." He appeared to shake himself as though he were wandering from the matter in hand and must get back to it at once. He cleared his throat and took a deep breath.

"I've someone I'd like you to meet, Molly," he said quietly, looking down at her rough, work-scarred hands which had got that way in her labour at her spinning frame. They were clean but the nails were short, one or two broken and not the hands of a lady, nor did they match the elegant outfit she wore, but it was only by these small details that the difference between her class and Tim's was marked.

"I don't want you to speak until I've finished," he continued. "There is a lot of it but I must ask you to promise you'll hear me out right to the end."

He did not look up and Molly studied the top of his head, the thick, wavy mass of streaked blond hair, the parting of which had vanished as it always did when he pushed his hand through it. He was never exactly neat though his clothing was of excellent cut and quality. He had a sort of rumpled look as though his appearance was not of great importance to him, like a small boy who has just come in from play, engaging and lovable. He favoured rough tweed jackets, sports jackets with patch pockets and a centre vent at the back. Today he wore dark grey flannels and a deep cream shirt, a yellow silk, four-in-hand tie with a printed pattern on it in colours ranging from tangerine to cherry, from aquamarine to cornflower blue. It was so vivid it almost hurt the eye to look at it and Molly wondered where he got them from. Surely he must have them made to achieve such a degree of hideousness. It was just like the one she had seen him in all those years ago outside Buckley and Prockters which as a young male he might be expected to wear but it seemed he still fancied himself in them. Then, as a child, she had thought it very fine. She admitted to herself that his appalling taste in ties only served to endear him to her all the more.

He looked up at her then, his deep brown eyes very soft.

"We've known one another a very short time, Mary Angelina O'Dowd. Three months, is it, and in that time, as it says in the best romantic novels, I believe, I have come to hold you in high esteem." He did his best to smile, to lighten the serious tone in his voice and Molly felt an uncontrollable urge to place a comforting hand on his cheek. He did that to her. Brought out a feeling that was protective, as though inside her was something that could not bear to see him get hurt.

"We have barely got to know one another in those three months. We've spoken a time or two and had a picnic up on the moor. Nothing else, and yet I know . . . perhaps I'm being presumptuous" – she resisted the urge to ask him what presumptuous meant – "in thinking . . . hoping, especially since you were hurt, that we have become . . . close. You are very dear to me, Molly. Oh, dammit, dammit . . . I must say it even if it alarms you. I love you, Molly. Jesus Christ, I love you so much."

His whole body was tense with something she was beginning at last to recognise and his words, though they seemed at the moment to make little sense, were important, even welcome to her, for what woman would not be enchanted to be loved by Tim Broadbent?

Her heart was beating in great rhythmic thuds but she did as she was told and did not speak, though by now he was looking beseechingly into her face.

"I've been drawn to you ever since that first day, Molly, when you held me while . . . you remember . . . outside the gates of Meddins? I kept thinking about you and wondering why I was thinking about you, remembering that day and the next one when you hauled me over the coals for seeking you out of the crowd. I embarrassed you and I was sorry and I made up my mind that what you had said, about you and me, I mean, was only good sense. I ignored every instinct in me that told me . . . told me you were something remarkable and I wanted to find out why. I did as you told me and stayed away" – he smiled beguilingly and Molly's heart melted in the most delicious way— "but again, as they say in romantic novels, fate intervened and threw you, literally, across my path. God, all this sounds a load of piffle. Trite and . . . and mawkish but I knew then, as you stood like a trapped rabbit, trembling on the bonnet of my car, your eyes wide and shocked – I have never seen such a brilliant colour – I knew I loved you. So, I began to woo you, my darling. I began the pattern, the customs, if you like, that a gentleman pursues with the lady of his choice and which eventually lead to . . . marriage."

She could stay silent no longer.

"Marriage?" she quavered.

"Yes, that's what I want and I hope you feel the same." He shrugged ruefully. "I know I'm a great deal older than you . . ."

"Only ten years." Her voice broke a little.

"So you don't mind . . . an elderly gent like me?"

"Tim . . . I . . ."

"No, no more, my love. I only want to add that I was going to go slowly, take my time. Let you, and your family, become accustomed to me . . . calling, taking you about. I had such plans. Dinner now and again, the theatre, shows, meeting my family . . . all the things a lady would expect."

Not in my world! Not in my world!

"But then . . . this happened," lifting his hand vaguely in the direction of the hospital at their back. "It's knocked all my plans for six, or so I thought but then, perhaps, it has only brought forward what is inevitable, that's if you agree, and that is for you to become my wife. Will you, Molly? I cannot live my life now without you in it. I shall look after you, and your family and if love . . . Jesus, I love you, Mary Angelina O'Dowd, I love you."

He was trembling, his face set pale with deep emotion. There was moisture in his eyes and he blinked rapidly and again Molly experienced that soft melting in the bones of her, for he was so . . . appealing, was that the word? Irresistible. He had been her strength, where she got her strength from, over the last weeks. Kind to them all, to Mammy and the children, even to Aunty Flo and Aunty Maggie, cheerful, once he had known she herself was to heal properly, keeping their spirits up with his smiling good humour, the flowers he brought and it had all helped Molly to recover. To get back her spirit and her pride and her self-esteem. She had known, of course, that his gaze was admiring, that he found her company pleasing, that he . . . well, he liked her, for he had as good as told her so on Saddleworth Moor.

But marriage! Holy Mother of God! Marriage between this gentleman, this handsome, wealthy gentleman who must be one of the most sought-after bachelors in Oldham and herself, daughter of the man who had once worked in a jennygate for his father, a girl who ran a ring spinning frame in his mill. Why, it was laughable! They were poles apart in absolutely everything. Culture, class, religion, speech, background, family . . . everything and how could they possibly bridge the gulf that separated her people from his? She knew the outfit she had on immediately disguised who she was and where she came from. Had they met someone from his world on the pavement outside Buckley and Prockters after they came out there would have been smiles, pleasant greetings, perhaps even a look of approval because she knew she had looked well, but the moment Molly O'Dowd opened her Irish-Lancashire mouth their smiles would have frozen on their faces and Tim would have been in no doubt as to their feelings.

"My darling." His voice was rich and deep, almost husky as he allowed her to see the truth and depth of his love for her. "Look at me, Molly." And she did so and saw it there. "You know I am quite serious, don't you?"

"Tim, sure an' tha' don't know what tha're askin', lad."

"Oh, but I do, Molly. Do you imagine I think it will be easy for us? For you especially, but for me as well, and yet are we so different? My grandfather was what was known as a 'pauper brat'. He was taken from the orphanage to some mill in Lancashire when he was no more than five or six years old and, unable to read or write, he worked there and in other mills, dragging himself up until he was a mill owner himself. My great-great-grandfather was a spinner like you. He was killed at the Peterloo Massacre. Have you heard of it?"

She shook her head numbly.

"Then I shall tell you all about it and about many other things to do with my family. I will teach you, my love, guide you through the ways, many of them foolish and time-wasting, which my . . . people get up to. Do you think I would allow anyone to hurt my wife, the woman I love more than anything on this earth? Dearest Molly, say you will. My mother is waiting to receive you . . ." or at least the woman I love, he told himself, which was not quite the same thing. He brought her hand to his lips, bending his head in a gesture of courtly gallantry, placing a kiss on it of such tenderness she felt again that well of warm emotion rise in her and she was shaken by it and by her need to put her other hand to his hair and smooth it. Was it love and if it was, would she survive the tempest, the storm of protest, not only from this man's family but the whole of his society? They would take up arms against her. She was a mill girl and though, as Tim had just told her, there were dozens of men in the Penfold Valley whose forebears, perhaps no more than two generations back, had been spinners, weavers, carders, doffers, barefoot and illiterate, this would not influence their judgment of her. In the name of God, what was she to make of Tim's . . . Tim's proposal of marriage and, more to the point, what was she to do about it? She liked him so much. He made her laugh and they had become easy and relaxed in one another's company. There was never, when they were alone together, any sense of strain, of the "swank" so many of his kind put on. He treated her and her family with thoughtfulness which in no way smacked of condescension. They had all taken to him, even Aunty Flo. And she liked him so much!

And then there was Meddins.

Aah, beautiful, beautiful Meddins. Daddy's house, or so she always thought of it. Dreaming in the warm sunshine of summer, serene and protective in the bitter winds of winter, flowering each season into a different kind of loveliness, for she had seen them all come and go. The house never changed. It seemed to smile and beckon, to invite and welcome and could Mary Angelina O'Dowd, who had loved it since she was a child of no more than four or five, resist it?

She felt helpless in the grip of something she could not name, nor escape, some excited Irish spirit which called to her to step out on the road Tim was offering and yet at the same time a caution, born of the blood of generations of practical northern women and which ran warningly through her veins.

Her face was white and strained with plum-coloured thumbprints beneath her wide, frightened eyes. She bit her lip and he watched her, his own face as pale as hers. She put her other hand to the one he held between his own and at once it was folded away protectively, as she knew, to the best of his ability, he would always protect her. He loved her, she did not doubt it. It was written clearly on his pleading face. A good-humoured, gentle face, vulnerable, and in it was his need of her, of Molly O'Dowd who, though she had been badly hurt, badly shocked by the beating Pikey Watson had given her, had risen up again, strong and unbreakable. So she always would be.

"Molly?" His voice was no more than a breath in his throat.

She sighed. How could she say no, to him who wanted her and to Meddins which was her dream?

She said yes.

14

They drove through the open gates of Meddins, the roar of Tim's motor car lifting the heads of several gardeners who were clearing the beds of the summer annuals, raking leaves from the lawns in readiness for the bonfire and preparing the graceful Grecian urns which lined the terrace for the planting of geraniums, calceolarias and jasmine. Primroses, polyanthus, violets, iberis, arabis and a mass of colourful wallflowers would be put in the empty flowerbeds so that even in winter the wide gardens of Meddins would glow with colour and beauty.

The interest in the sports car and particularly its female passenger was keen. Some of the men were old soldiers, given their jobs by Mr Tim who was known to have a soft heart and they were intensely loyal to him and intensely interested in the young lady who, if what was being whispered in the kitchen were true, might be their new mistress. Though Forbes and Parsons and Mrs Ogden were upper servants and had been so long with the family, it was perhaps the latter which had led them, in their excitement, to let slip the uniqueness of Mr Tim's guest. A young lady coming to meet Mrs Broadbent and, though it was not how things were done in the old days when the families of the couples concerned would probably be acquainted anyway since their sort hung together, what did it matter if, after all these years Mr Tim had found a suitable bride. That is if she were to be his bride. How far along the courtship had gone was a matter for fierce conjecture. Had Mr Tim spoken to the young lady's father, whoever he might be, and when, if this should turn out as they all hoped, were her family to meet Mrs Broadbent?

Molly wanted to drink it all in in one great gulp, absorb it

into her flesh and fill every hollow place in her body with it as
the tyres of Tim's car crunched up the gravel driveway. It was
no more than two hundred yards from the gate to the front
porch, which turned out to be at the side of the house, but
she merely got an impression of old trees with wide trunks,
their branches, some of them, still dense with autumn foliage,
meeting and entwining above their heads. Of water to her
left, glossy with the reflection of the house in it, half a dozen
ducks squabbling at its edge. Of broad green lawns, more
trees against the house with garden benches beneath them,
splashes of vivid colour here and there, bronze and gold and
white of what looked like chrysanthemums. There was a thin,
pale drift of cloud, high and streaked, through which the sun
shone hazily on the house, on the old rose and beige and
cinnamon of the bricks and as she drew nearer she felt the
sureness, the absolute rightness of it, of being here, and an
excitement within her that could not be described. It was the
most beautiful house she had ever seen. She had thought so
from the other side of its gates; now, the closer she got to it,
the lovelier it became and the more she wanted it. It went
straight to her heart, making it jump and skitter in her chest
and she wanted to hold her breath in case it was an illusion,
come to her of her own dreams when she was a child.

There was an old dog sprawled in a bit of sunshine which
had been captured in the porch and as Tim drew up to it and
turned off the car's engine it heaved itself to its feet and padded
slowly towards his side of the car. There was an old man in the
open doorway, old but still erect and with his head held high,
wearing what looked to Molly to be an evening suit and white
gloves and behind him an elderly woman in a grey print dress,
immaculately starched apron and a frilled cap, which Molly
was to learn later was her morning uniform. They both stared
with the interested familiarity of old servants at Molly, a look
which was inclined to be approving, she thought.

The dog pushed its head against Tim's knee as he got out
of the car and he put a casual hand to its broad brow.

"Hello, Albert, have you come to meet her too?" Molly
heard him say, then he was at her side of the car, opening
the door, giving her his hand to help her out. She distinctly
saw her lovely new court shoes emerge and touch the ground
followed by the length of her slim, silk-stockinged legs from
ankle to knee then the hem of her cashmere skirt which, with

the top and jacket, had cost a staggering sixteen guineas. The shoes alone were forty-nine shillings and the handbag thirty-five and the hat, in a fine bangkok and lined with crêpe-de-chine, eleven and ninepence. Twenty-one pounds eleven shillings and ninepence which, at the mill, would be six months' wages for girls like her and Betty Spooner. All spent on one outfit which Molly was well aware Tim had bought for her to impress his mother. She didn't blame him, of course, for it was unlikely he would want Mrs Broadbent to see her future daughter-in-law for the first time dressed in a shawl and clogs. But she did wish she could have worn the simple blue dress and hat she and Mammy had made. The one she had put on with such thrilled anticipation to go for a "spin" in Tim's little red motor car. The dress Pikey had torn in his frenzy, torn and splattered with Molly's own blood and which had been ruined beyond repair. Aye, she would have liked to have been wearing her own clothes. It would have been more honest.

She could see the growing satisfaction, the pleasure in the eyes of the couple by the front door as they lingered for a moment on her face before moving, discreetly, of course, to the smart and obviously expensive outfit she had on. The man held the door wide and the woman hovered behind him, for what function Molly could not say.

"Good morning, sir. Good morning, miss. Mrs Broadbent is in the drawing room," the man said politely.

"Thank you, Forbes, we'll go right in."

"Of course, sir."

The man in the evening suit creaked forward and Molly smiled at him, ready to shake his hand if it was required of her but he merely closed the front door behind her and Tim, then majestically moved across the wide hall and opened another, holding it open just as though she and Tim were incapable of performing such a task for themselves. Molly saw Tim wink at him and the man – Forbes, the picnic man, of course – must have seen it, for his face twitched slightly.

The woman who was sitting on the velvet sofa was dressed as Molly was dressed, fashionable and expensive, in a well-cut day dress, plain and in a shade known as cocoa, the sash of embroidered satin on her slim hips, her only concession to her age the longer skirt which almost reached her ankle. She had an exquisite three-strand rope of pearls about her neck which fell to just below her breasts and as she lifted her hand the light caught the diamonds on her fingers.

She did not get up but waited impassively as Molly and Tim crossed the broad stretch of deep pile carpet. She had snow white hair and Tim's deep brown eyes but they were cool, assessing, without that look of good humour which was so natural in Tim.

"Mother, I'd like you to meet Miss O'Dowd. Molly, this is my mother," Tim said, his eyes on Molly's face, his smile so proud and loving and unaware, or so it seemed, of what was to come, Molly felt a little spurt of irritation. Surely he knew his mother, though smiling politely now, would, in a very few moments, have that cool smile wiped completely from her face. Tim was acting as though Molly was exactly as his mother was, as his sister was, as all the ladies of his acquaintance were, all except Molly.

"Miss O'Dowd." Muriel Broadbent bowed her head, declining to offer her hand. She had no idea who this young woman was or who her family were but at first sight she was at least presentable. A beautiful young woman with the most unusual eyes somewhere between blue and green, a complexion as smooth and flawless as a rose petal except for . . . dear Lord, was that a scar over her left eyebrow, almost hidden beneath the brim of her chic cloche hat? Now how had she come by that? A hunting accident perhaps, still with no presentiment of what the next moment was to bring. Dark, she appeared to be, from the tendrils of hair which could be seen doing their best to curl up over the brim of her hat. She had a pleasant enough smile and good teeth and her figure was superb, tall, straight, strong and looking, Muriel was quick to note, as though she might have a whole nursery of lusty, handsome children within a year or two. Young, of course, and now she only had to ascertain her pedigree and Muriel might find it in her heart to accept this young woman who was not of her choosing but who was Tim's.

"Molly," the young woman said, leaning forward to pick up Muriel's flaccid hand, gripping it firmly in the way men did.

"Pardon?" Muriel ventured frostily.

"Sure an' I'd like it fine if tha' was ter call me Molly. Everyone does. Me name's Mary Angelina but can tha' imagine tryin' ter get tha' tongue round that?"

Muriel distinctly felt the warm blood in her veins become

cold and sluggish and even, she thought, here and there, turning to ice. Tim was still smiling at the woman, holding her arm possessively, but as she stopped speaking he turned his gaze on his mother and in it was the awareness of exactly what she was thinking. Yes, she is not a lady as your understanding of a lady means, it said. She has not been presented at court as you were but she is the woman I love, the woman I will have and you had best accept it. There was no harshness in his eyes, no animosity, no doubt, nothing but the simple truth of it and, if he and she were to remain friends, she must make Mary Angelina O'Dowd welcome, they told her.

"Miss . . . O'Dowd." In Muriel Broadbent's eyes was the undeniable evidence of her position, her belief and conviction that her son had totally lost his mind, but that could not be discussed here. Despite her . . . her rank, which was sadly lacking, Miss O'Dowd was a guest in this house and was, for that reason only, due a civility which Muriel had been raised to recognise. Her composure was badly shaken but not broken. It would take more than this to break Muriel Broadbent. She was a lady even if this woman wasn't, but strangely, she was amazed to see, Miss O'Dowd, which was unusual in one of her class, was not at all disconcerted, gazing about her with a look of such joy, such enchantment, Muriel was quite taken aback.

"Would tha' mind if I just . . . just 'ad a peep out o't winder," she said, turning her joy on Muriel while Tim stood quietly to one side, since he knew exactly what was in Molly's mind. "I've never sin it from this side. The 'ouse, I mean, nor't gardens. Me daddy an' me used ter stand at gates like a couple o' kids wi' our noses pressed ter't toffee shop winder, so we did. Well, I were a kid when I first saw it an' . . ."

Suddenly, as though remembering her manners, she turned to Muriel, her face contrite. "I'm that sorry, Mrs Broadbent. 'Ere's me babblin' on but I were . . . overcome, tha' might say, by't loveliness of it. 'Tis even better 'n I expected."

Muriel's heart hardened even more and though her face showed nothing of her thoughts, they were not pleasant. Of course! It was as clear as daylight now. Even after such a short time the girl had given away exactly what it was she was after and she was only surprised Tim had not seen it. Look at her gloating, her eyes darting all over the drawing room, no doubt assessing the value of everything from the brass fire tongs in the hearth to the cloisonné enamel clock on the mantelshelf above it. And to be so blatant about it! Could not Tim see it? Well, she thought grimly, he soon will when I'm done with him. Longing as she was for grandchildren she'd sooner see Tim unwed and the line die out than have them from this common hussy. The outfit she had on was superb, simple, elegant and obviously costly and just as obviously bought by her son, for she could not imagine a woman such as this one having the taste or the money to buy it for herself.

Unaware of Muriel Broadbent's hostility since at the moment it was well hidden, Molly stood at the window, longing to ask if she might look round, explore the grounds, poke about in every part of the fascinating garden which, now that she was on this side of the gates, seemed to stretch on for ever. You couldn't even see the walls and Tim had told her that at the back of the house, beyond the stables and kitchen gardens, where the land sloped up to a woodland, there were fields full of horses. Holy Mary, Mother of God, it was so beautiful she wanted to rush outside and then back in again, rummage in every room, study the view, look inside cupboards, touch and smell and fill her eyes with what she knew would be a glory she could not even begin to imagine, but she couldn't, not yet. In fact she had no idea what came next so she waited quietly, her inherent good manners warring with her youthful curiosity. She looked at Tim and waited, her face grave.

"Well, if you have seen all you want to, Miss O'Dowd," Muriel said politely, "perhaps we might have a chat before lunch. I thought, since it is just the three of us, darling," turning eyes which were so like his on her son, "we might eat in the small dining room. I hope Miss O'Dowd will not mind." The irony was heavy.

Miss O'Dowd was too busy looking at everything her eye could capture to notice it.

"We'll have a sherry first, I think, Forbes," Mrs Boadbent was saying to the butler who had mysteriously appeared. The room they were in was done in colours of the palest green and rose, with a plain cream carpet and bits of dainty furniture about which looked so fragile a careless hand could have smashed them all to pieces with no trouble at all. The sofa on which Mrs Broadbent sat bolt upright was in rose-beige and there was another in cream. There were portraits on the wall, one of a young girl in a white dress and feathers in her hair, another of four children, three boys and the same girl, the boys somewhat awkward as though they would rather be off doing something else, up a tree perhaps, or in a boat on the lake. There was a piano, the size of which Molly had never seen before – it certainly put the Spooners' in the shade – standing in a corner so that the daylight fell on it. On its polished surface was a copper bowl filled with white roses and, crowding against it and on all the small, scattered tables which were about the room, were tiny snuff boxes and miniatures in silver and bronze, and porcelain figures from Dresden, ivory figurines, fans and dozens of silver-framed photographs of babies, boys, young men, one of whom was Tim.

Leading from the room was what looked like an enormous, fairy-like fretwork glasshouse from which came the warbling notes of birds and a rich, exotic smell of flowers which was strangely familiar to Molly, since it must have been from here that Tim had brought the bunches which had crowded the hospital room.

"Please, do sit down, Miss O'Dowd." A command not a request. Mrs Broadbent indicated a chair to the side of the fire which roared halfway up the chimney. The fire was set in what looked like marble, Molly thought, remembering those far-off days when she and Daddy had visited the museum in Union Street and where there had been statues fashioned from the stuff.

"Sit here beside me, darling," Tim said, patting the seat of the cream sofa, then sitting down beside her and Muriel winced since she knew her son was establishing the pattern of what was to come. He was to marry this low-born working girl, this person who spoke with the dreadfully coarse voice of the northeners, this well-dressed and lovely young woman who was, despite her looks, not a lady and never would be. His mother would not sway him to the contrary, he was telling her. She might do her damnedest to put Molly in her place, as it seemed she was intent on doing with her continued use of Molly's surname, but this was to be Molly's home. She was to be mistress here. He was to be her husband and his mother, like it or not, must accept Molly, Miss O'Dowd, as her daughter-in-law.

Molly, not knowing any better and with a naturalness which Muriel called ignorance, removed her hat and shook out her short curly hair which she had done her best to coax into the waves and "spit" curls to the front of her ears which were all the rage. It refused absolutely to conform. It had a glowing, glossy life of its own, looking exactly like a dark dandelion clock, one of those which, when blown on, disintegrate and drift away. She was not making a good impression, she knew that. The only way she would make a good impression would be if she kept her trap shut. By closing her bloody cake-hole and keeping it closed. For ever! Her appearance was perfect – Mrs Broadbent's eyes had told her so as she walked towards her across the drawing room – but now, now that she had spoken, even what she had said, had turned Tim's mother into a cold-eyed but very polite "grande dame". If she kept her gob shut she could pass as a lady but how could she? What of her, the real Molly O'Dowd who lived inside this smartly dressed young woman and who could only come out when she spoke? Her ideas, her ideals, her opinions, her memories, her family, her sorrows and joys, her hurts and grievances. Only in expressing them, talking about them, would people know her and she meant to be known.

She took Tim's hand in hers and smiled into his loving face. He thought she was something rare. He had told her so and with him in her "corner", so to speak, how could she fail? She couldn't. She bloody well wouldn't!

"Them birds mekk a right old row, don't they?" she said brightly. "When we've 'ad us lunch 'appen I could 'ave a look at 'em, if tha' don't mind. I've never seen birds in a 'ouse before."

"Really!" What else could Muriel say, she reflected, she who was an expert in what was known as "small talk". They sipped the sherries Forbes had poured before vanishing silently and Molly cast about for something to say. She was pretty sure, as the hostess, that Mrs Broadbent should be engaging her in conversation. Not that she knew what the hell the gentry did. She only knew that if Mrs Broadbent came to her house she wouldn't just fiddle with her glass, saying nowt.

"Of course you can, Molly," Tim answered, casting a cool glance at his mother, since surely she had realised by now, though nothing had been said in so many words that what they had talked about yesterday was to happen. "In fact after we have eaten I mean to show you over the house and grounds."

"Will tha'? Really?" He might have said he was to give

her the crown jewels for her very own, Muriel thought contemptuously. He probably would, at least the jewellery which had been passed through the family down the years. Pieces bought by Katherine Chapman's father for his wife, old-fashioned now but very valuable; by Joss Greenwood for Katherine, with Katherine's money since, as a Member of Parliament, he had none of his own; by Will Broadbent for his wife Tessa who had once been married to Katherine's son, and by Joshua, Muriel's own husband, all the lovely diamonds, emeralds, rubies and sapphires which the women of this family had worn and which, apart from Muriel's own, brought with her on her marriage to Joshua and which would go to her own daughter, Tessa, would pass to Tim's wife. *Tim's wife.* Dear God in heaven. Not this dreadful, working-class girl . . . this plebeian creature who came from another world to theirs and whose voice and manners would not be out of place in Tim's own mill.

"And where do you come from, Miss O'Dowd?" she managed to ask at last.

"Me name's Molly, Mrs Broadbent, as I said, an' I were born in Oldham." She deliberately pronounced it "Owdham" as true "Oldhamers" did. "I've lived 'ere all me life in Sidney Street which is just off Shaw Street. By't recreation ground."

"Oh really, I can't say I know it."

"Well, tha' wouldn't, would tha'?" Molly smiled forgivingly and sipped her sherry which she thought was delicious and if that chap came back she'd ask for another.

"And your . . . father? Is he in business in Oldham?"

"No, me daddy's dead. An' me two brothers. In't trenches. The Somme. 1916."

The words were clipped with pain and for a moment Muriel's face softened, for had they not all suffered the loss of loved ones in the war to end all wars. Tim pressed Molly's hand encouragingly and when she turned to him, blinking a little, he smiled.

"Another sherry, my darling?" His voice was caressing, warming and it made his mother cringe, for her own husband had never once spoken to her like that, not even in private. Molly relaxed, her shoulder resting against his.

"That'd be grand, Tim," she said, holding out her empty glass to him. "'Tis lovely, so it is."

"Lunch will be ready, I think," Muriel admonished, as though to warn this ill-bred young woman that ladies drank only one glass of sherry before lunch and a small one at that, but neither she nor Tim seemed to hear her.

"Do ring for Forbes, Tim," his mother added icily as Tim stood up to reach for the sherry. "After all it is his job."

"Oh, come on, Mother. Surely we can have a drink without dragging poor old Forbes in to do it for me. You know how bad he is on his feet."

Mrs Broadbent lifted one delicate eyebrow, an expression which spoke volumes, then turned again to Molly.

"And what of you, Miss O'Dowd?" she enquired, as Tim sat down again. "So many young women of today seem to have jobs, don't they?"

Without waiting for Molly to answer she turned to Tim. "Do you know what Kathleen Forrester has done? Really, you will never believe it. I know I didn't. She has gone to train as a nurse. Can you imagine it? That lovely young woman doing menial work. Her mother is devastated."

"Well, Mother, if you want my opinion, I can only say good for her. If she is not to marry, and it seems she's not, far better to do some useful, satisfying work."

"How sad, though. She would have made some man a wonderful wife."

You for one, her manner said.

"Proably, but we must not talk about people Molly does not know. It is scarcely polite."

"Eeh, I don't mind," Molly said cheerfully, the effect of the second glass of sherry, to which she was not accustomed, making her glow. "I work at mill, Mrs Broadbent," confirming Muriel's worst fears. "I'm a spinner. Ring frame spinnin' like me mammy before me. Dost tha' know what that is?"

"Er . . . well . . ."

"Before that, when I'd just left school – I were fourteen then – I were put ter doffin', that's tekkin' off full bobbins an' puttin' on empty ones. It were 'ard work."

"It sounds it, Miss O'Dowd."

There was a discreet knock at the door and it opened to reveal the quiet presence of Forbes.

"Luncheon is served, madam," he announced and Muriel Broadbent rose thankfully to her feet. She was certain this girl was deliberately and defiantly being provocative. She was not pretending a part as a woman from the lower classes, a woman who worked for a living in the Broadbent Mill would pretend, but she was "putting it on" as Muriel had heard it described, exaggerating her own lack of pedigree. Usually it was the other way round, those who were from the lower orders doing their best to be genteel but Miss O'Dowd was being just the opposite, smiling as she did so at Muriel's son who seemed to think it a great joke.

On the short walk from the front door to the drawing room, and now from the drawing room to the "small" dining room, Molly did her best to get a grip on everything her eye fell on, since she wanted to have each object clearly in her mind so that she could describe it to Mammy. The idea that a house might have not one but two dining rooms was so novel to her who had lived in a house with none, she could barely imagine it but she did not say so. She wished she could think of some word other than "beautiful", "lovely", "glorious" to describe the objects she saw and not only the objects she saw but the setting they were placed in. She had an impression of space and light from great windows with coloured glass in them which ranged along one wall, windows which were draped with ruby red velvet curtains. The floor was of wood, the colour of polished honey, scattered with rugs, and everywhere were flowers, in large copper bowls and in fragile-looking crystal vases. There was porcelain, pictures on the plain white walls and a fireplace in the hall so large and so filled with merrily burning logs you could have sat a "guy" in it and, with a few fireworks, called it "bonfire night".

They ate a simple meal. Melon garnished with leaves and flowers, the slices cut lengthwise and then into small cubes. It looked very pretty and tasted delightful and Molly said so, nodding at the startled Parsons as though the housemaid had prepared it. There was fish, salmon in caper sauce, with small portions of what turned out to be something called broccoli which Molly had never tasted before and said so, followed by a chocolate soufflé. Molly had two helpings of that, admitting guilelessly that she had an awful "sweet tooth" and telling Forbes she had never tasted anything so delicious in her life.

For a moment Forbes's seamed old face almost broke into a gratified smile though the soufflé was Mrs Ogden's creation. She was a real beauty, this young woman Mr Tim had brought home and you could see he doted on her and thought every word she spoke and every natural gesture she made quite miraculous. She was completely unsuitable, of course, and unsuited to be the mistress of this glorious house and you could tell madam thought so, too. Well, he could tell since he'd served her for over thirty years. She'd invited young ladies by the score to parties and dances, dangling them in front of Mr Tim, pretty, brainless young things, ladies, naturally, but trained to be the wife of a gentleman like Mr Tim. It had done no good though. She might have saved herself the trouble for he'd gone out and found his own and God alone knew what was to happen. Perhaps it would be the making of him. She was a down-to-earth, north country lass with a quirky sense of humour by the look of it, for you could tell she was playing up to madam for all she was worth. Nothing offensive, of course, for she'd natural good manners and . . . well, he could only call it charm, none of which cut any ice with Mrs Broadbent.

"You have worked in the mill since you left school I believe you said, Miss O'Dowd?" Muriel asked coolly, since something must be said and all Tim seemed capable of was gazing at this young woman as if she had just stepped down from her place among the gods.

"Aye. Five year last April." Molly smiled at Tim's mother, doing her best to hide the fast beating of her heart and the slight nervous tremor in her hand, for despite her show of confidence she was tense and self-conscious in this vastly new and frightening world Tim had brought her to.

"And where did you go to school?"

"Our Lady and All Saints in Bracken Street."

"Our Lady . . .?" Muriel blanched visibly and even Tim frowned, for neither he nor Molly had discussed their religious beliefs, or even if either had any.

"You are a Roman Catholic then, Miss O'Dowd?" Muriel carefully placed her knife and fork on her plate. She dabbed at the corner of her mouth with her napkin and her eyes moved to Tim, beseeching him to consider what this might mean if he were serious about this girl. Dear heavens, it was unthinkable. The Broadbents, though not particularly fervent about their religion, were members of the Protestant faith and were attenders at St Matthews Church on Hall Lane.

"Oh, yes, Mrs Broadbent." Molly lifted her head and her gaze did not falter, ready, should Mrs Broadbent say something she did not care for, to defend her faith to the last.

"I . . . did not know, did you, Tim?" Mrs Broadbent's voice was soft and somehow triumphant, for surely this would make a difference.

Forbes and Parsons, unobtrusively hovering by the sideboard, exchanged glances. Not only a mill girl with Irish antecedents but a Catholic as well! But what did it matter, their eyes asked one another. She was a bit nervous, you could see that and who could blame her, but she was bearing up courageously beneath their mistress's probing. She'd got guts and spirit and perhaps that was what this sorrowing house needed, a young woman with a bit of spunk in her, a bit of sense. One who was obviously not overwhelmed by the perfection, the grace, the special quality that was Meddins. She was dying to have a look round, she was saying now and madam didn't like it one bit.

"I hardly think this is the time to be doing a tour of the house, Tim," Mrs Broadbent stressed frostily. "I'm sure Miss O'Dowd will understand that the servants will be busy and—"

"Nonsense, Mother. Molly and I won't disturb them at all, will we, my love?" Though his smile was disarming there was a steely glint in it which his mother recognised. "After all," he went on smoothly, "Molly will one day be mistress here. Yes, Mother, that's right. She has done me the honour of promising to become my wife. I told you I had hopes yesterday and . . . well, she has agreed."

He pushed his hand through his hair in that boyish way he had but it flopped back over his forehead, then he reached out to take Molly's hand. "I . . . we wanted you to be the first to know, though I dare say it will be all over the house within half an hour," dashing an impish grin in the direction of Forbes and Parsons. "We have not even told Molly's mother yet and of course we have not yet picked a date for the wedding but it will be soon, won't it, darling? The sooner the better, I say. We have not known one another very long. Was it June, Molly? Yes, I thought so, but there seems to be no reason to wait since we're both of the same mind, aren't we, darling, and I don't want Molly to go back to the mill. Not now. We hope we have your blessing, Mother." He grinned disarmingly. "After all, you have been telling me it was time I married for years now." He stopped speaking abruptly and his face altered to the one with which Molly was becoming very familiar. "Is she not the loveliest thing you ever saw, Mother, and can you blame me for feeling the way I do?"

The whole time Tim was speaking Molly O'Dowd and Muriel Broadbent looked at one another and the antipathy in Muriel's eyes was plain to see, at least to Molly. Tim's mother did not want her for her son and her expression said so, though the besotted man whose eyes were full of the girl he loved did not see it. Muriel Broadbent was not a particularly unkind woman. She had lost two of her three handsome sons in the war, and soon after the husband of whom she had been fond. She would have endured almost any woman for her Tim, since he had to have one eventually, no matter how much she personally disliked her, providing she was suitable, meaning of their station in life, but this was beyond endurance. She would be unable to hold up her head as the whole county whispered of the mill girl Tim Broadbent had taken up with. Could he not just have had his . . . his fun with her without bringing her into the world in which his family moved? They would be disgraced. Tim, perhaps because he had never married, and despite what he had suffered in the trenches, was still a boy to her and boys, and young men, got up to all kinds of mischief with women of a certain sort, but they did not marry them. Dear God, how was she to introduce this . . . this earthy creature to the Herberts, the Forresters, the Knights, to bring her into their society which still had its strict rule of etiquette, into her home when at table she didn't even know which knife and fork to use. She had made no show of herself, Muriel admitted, eating with the delicacy of a cat at a saucer though with good appetite. She had been discreet, watching what Tim did as the salmon was put before her, but her free and open smiles directed at Forbes and Parsons, who had been seriously startled by her friendliness, were not acceptable. Firmly, kindly but distantly was the way to treat a servant, not as though they were equals, which, in a way, Muriel supposed they were to her guest!

Muriel Broadbent was not to blame for these thoughts and no one would have blamed her for them. Society and her upbringing had made her as she was but she despaired that society, as she knew it, would ever take Tim's wife, this . . . this creature whose gaze was as bold as she was herself, into their fold.

"And where is the marriage to take place?" she asked her son though she did not look at him.

"I'm not sure."

"Come now, darling, Miss O'Dowd, being of the Catholic faith, will no doubt want it to be at the church of her choice and you, following the traditions of the family will—"

"In the name of all that's sensible, Mother, does it really matter?"

"I would say so, Tim. There is bound to be conflict."

"No conflict, Mother. None at all. We shall marry wherever Molly chooses."

"Tim . . ."

"No, Mother, it—"

"But surely—"

"No, Mother . . . *no!*"

Dear heaven, it was obviously going to be even more horrendous than she thought, but she could hardly go on arguing with the girl sitting there as mim as a mouse. Pale as the petals of the white roses in the centre of the table she was, having the grace to look devastated by this argument.

Muriel clamped her mouth shut. Tim was waiting for her to speak again, his manner defensive, for though he might be determined on this course he was taking he was not such a fool as to think she would approve. She would accept, his manner told her stringently. Molly was a resourceful, brave and intelligent young woman, quick to learn, adaptable and would very soon pick up the niceties of polite society, the manners and speech of what were known as gentry. Even her faith would not interfere with her position as his wife. Given half the chance and with his mother's goodwill, or even without it, his resolute expression told her, his young and inexperienced wife-to-be would become as expert as herself in managing this household and the servants in it. She would learn to entertain, to do all the things Muriel did and had done so well for thirty-odd years. She would grace any gathering with her beauty, her sense of humour, her integrity, her unique brand of earthy charm which was in no way coarse. She had an impish good humour which came from her Irish side and a strength of character which was particularly of England's north country. Molly could take care of herself in any company, of that he was sure. She needed . . . polish, not too much, for he did not want her altered. She needed guidance and that could only come from his mother.

There was the soft chink of one plate against another as Forbes and Parsons went about their efficient, unobtrusive work at the sideboard. The dog, which had ambled into the dining room at Tim's heels, snuffled and yipped in his sleep as his elderly brain remembered what his puppy body had once performed.

"Mother?" Tim's voice was deceptively light but challenging. They were both surprised when Molly spoke.

"Tim, don't rush it, lad. Give tha' Mammy time ter get used ter me, an' ter idea o' thi' an' me gettin' wed. 'Tis not every day tha' son brings 'ome 'is intended, is it, Mrs Broadbent, no matter 'oo she is. I'd like ter go an' see my mammy now, if that's all right, Tim. Tell 'er . . . about us. If tha'll excuse us, Mrs Broadbent."

With grave dignity Molly stood up, both Tim and Forbes leaping to help her from her chair.

She grinned at them wryly. "Nay, I've bin standin' up on me own fer nigh on twenty year now an' I reckon I can manage a few more yet. That were a lovely spread, Mrs Broadbent, thank you, an' I only wish I could cook like that."

She spoke as though Tim's mother had prepared and cooked the meal herself and both Forbes and Parsons were seen to turn away as though in smiles.

"Thank you . . . Miss O'Dowd," for no matter what the provocation a lady must always show courtesy.

"Molly," Molly emphasised as she moved gracefully, and under the fascinated gaze of Forbes and Parsons, from the room.

15

When the news reached Sidney Street they could not have been more amazed if Molly O'Dowd had announced that she was to marry the thirty-one-year-old Prince of Wales who was known to be wilful, irresponsible and daft enough to do such a thing. In their eyes to aim as high as Mr Broadbent who owned one of the biggest mills in Oldham was not that much different to aiming for their future king and not only to aim for it but to hit the bloody bull's-eye! She was wearing a ring, a diamond, Betty Spooner said, that Mr Broadbent had bought her at Whittakers in Manchester Street. The "Ring Specialist" the jeweller's advertised itself as, their speciality diamond and wedding rings and, if Molly O'Dowd's ring was anything to go by, what they said was true. As big as one of the marbles Ernie Haydock and his cronies played with in the street and how she lifted her hand to brush her hair was a mystery, Betty stated, with the thrilled satisfaction the raconteur of a drama knows in the recounting.

Her wedding ring, which of course Betty had not yet got a scen at, matched her engagement ring, Molly had told her and if you'd seen the "get-up" she had on you'd have thought she was off to take tea with the Prince of Wales's mother, the stately Queen Mary herself!

The next big shock, following on the news that Molly was to marry Mr Broadbent – lucky cow, Cissie Thompson remarked acidly – was that everyone in the street got a handwritten, gilt-edged invitation to the wedding which was to take place just before Christmas at St Saviours Church in Shaw Street and afterwards to the reception at Meddins which was where Mr Broadbent lived. Cissie and Elsie Thompson who had played skipping with Molly since the three of them had been steady enough on their infant legs to "jump in"; Betty and her mammy, of course; Netta Haydock who lived next door to Molly and who had done such sterling work on the day Mr Broadbent had sent her to telephone for the ambulance and, if he cared to, even her son, Ernie; Mrs Kenny and Granny Jamison who had not been over her own front doorstep for five years. They were more than gratified, agreeing among themselves that though Molly was going up in the world she was not apparently to forget her old friends as so many would. They'd certainly go along to St Saviours to see the lass wed but perhaps they might not bother with – where was it? – Meddins, that's right, for it seemed to them to be as far removed from their world as Buckingham Palace!

Pikey was still there, of course, at number twenty-two though they doubted he would have had an invite, tittering among themselves, eyeing him as he marched steadfastly along the street to work each day, coming home at the end of his shift, giving no trouble, nor "lip" to anyone, which was not like him. Shout some insult as soon as look at you, would Pikey and they had all of them kept out of his way, especially after they had seen what he'd done to Rosie and Molly, but quiet as a mouse he was now which was almost as unnerving as his bluster. There was no doubt that the judge's order binding him over to keep the peace for a year had something to do with it, but whatever it was he was certainly keeping his nose clean.

Molly was still living at Aunty Flo's, sleeping like two spoons in a case in a single bed with Clare who had blossomed like some delicate flower lifted from a dung-heap where it had struggled helplessly for life. Sometimes Molly thought that the dreadful beating she and Mammy had suffered at Pikey's hands might have been worth it in some odd and gruesome kind of way. Look at the good it had brought. Apart from the obvious joy she herself knew in the goodness of Tim's love, it had rescued Clare, Eileen, Gracie and Archie from the nightmare of living under the same roof as Pikey. Aunty Maggie reported that the three youngest, Pikey's own children, were as rowdy and mischievous as "normal" children, by which she meant her own grandchildren. They were to remain with Aunty Maggie and Uncle Alf until it was all settled where Mammy was to live, which would, their Molly implied, and who could blame her with such a wealthy husband, be in better circumstances than they had ever known before. They, she and Tim, had looked at several neat and well-built little houses on Huddersfield Road, she told Aunty Maggie and Aunty Flo and as soon as Mammy was up and about she had only to say which one she liked and she and the four children could be moved in to it. She was aware that Aunty Maggie and Aunty Flo were deeply shocked that she had taken up with a man like Mr Broadbent, as they still insisted on calling him, even if he was going to marry her. He was a lovely chap and had been so good to Molly and her family but he was not their sort. What was going to happen between Rosie and Molly when Molly was wed, for instance? There would be none of the cosy running in and out of one another's kitchens as there would have been had she married "one of them"; the family get-togethers which were an integral part of their world. Oh, she'd have brass and knowing Molly she'd fling it about like there was no tomorrow but it wasn't the same, was it? How could they be comfortable with him, no matter how pleasant he was, and really, though they didn't say as much to Molly, they couldn't see it being a success, they told one another, for once in complete agreement.

Róisín was still not exactly herself yet, having been moved to a private convalescent home on the outskirts of Oldham. She was completely healed but she needed rest, peace, good feeding, the doctor said and as long as the wealthy Mr Broadbent, who, astonishingly, was to marry the lovely and charming but definitely working-class daughter of his patient, was to pay for it, she could stay for ever, though he did not voice this last.

It was several days later when Joel Greenwood roared up the gravelled driveway of Meddins in his sleek, racing green Mercedes-Benz Coupé, coming to a halt in front of the porch with a heart-stopping panache which threw a shower of gravel a foot into the air. George, who was the gardener's lad, which meant he did all the jobs none of the others wanted to do and who was turning over a flowerbed beneath the breakfast room window, flung him a disgruntled look, for it would be him who would be sent running for the rake to smooth it all out again when the visitor had gone. Mind you, it was a grand-looking motor car, George thought. Perhaps not as dazzling as Mr Tim's scarlet Vauxhall but a corker just the same. Long and low and racy with a black hood which could be folded away when the weather allowed it. A two-seater, all a'sparkle with chrome, even to the two fluted horns at the front. A leather strap was fastened across the bonnet, though the reason for it was not clear to young George but he supposed it must be to hold the bonnet on.

"I believe Mr Tim is in the paddock, sir," Forbes told Joel in that suave, courteous but slightly disdainful manner butlers seemed to cultivate. Joel didn't have one at Greenacre since there was only himself and he rarely entertained at home, making do with an excellent cook-housekeeper and half a dozen housemaids to look after his home. He had a couple of stable lads, a handyman and two gardeners and his house and surrounding gardens, though not as uniquely lovely as Meddins, were well kept, and he lived in a comfortable luxury comparable to the Broadbents. His life almost exactly mirrored Tim's in that his elder brother Pearce had died in the mud of Flanders, his younger sister was married, but whereas Tim's mother still lived both Joel's parents were dead. Joel had survived the horror of the war simply because it was his nature to be a survivor. He was a fighter, warding off stoically the blows under which other men had foundered. All those young men who had been captains and majors in the first year of the war, thinking it to be an extension of the playing fields of the splendid public schools they had only just left, had vanished in their first battle and those who did get through it were never the same again. But in Joel, though he had been brought up as they had, with the same education and background, ran the blood of Abel Greenwood who had died for his beliefs at Peterloo, and Abel's son Joss who had fought his own battles to bring equality to men nearly a hundred years ago. There was a core of strength in Joel, a resolve, what his forebears would have recognised as sheer bloody-mindedness, that had brought him through, if not unscathed since he still had a bit of shrapnel in his shoulder that hurt like hell when it rained, at least with a whole mind.

Unlike his cousin.

"Joel, lad, what in hell's name are you doing out here on a weekday?" Tim joked. "Won't Chapmans grind to a halt without you crouched over your desk or poking your nose into every bloody machine in the mill? I can't believe it. Joel Greenwood strolling up my paddock on a Wednesday afternoon, and dressed for riding, if I'm not much mistaken. Had a brainstorm, old lad?"

Tim was standing next to his stable lad, legs apart, hands slung low on his hips, studying a fine, long-legged mare the colour of a pale grey dove. Her mane and tail were a silvery white and she tossed her head coquettishly as though she knew full well how pretty she was.

Joel smiled amiably and at once his brooding face fell into boyish lines to reveal a faint likeness to Tim, who was his cousin twice or three times removed. He was a big man, the same age as Tim, heavy and broad-shouldered with none of Tim's leanness or whippy grace. He was vigorous, dark, with a skin the colour of amber and eyes which were the rich brown of treacle toffee. He was shrewd, hard, keen, cunning, all the characteristics his cousin lacked. He had a reputation for being a "loner" with a capacity for hard-headed business dealing, and it was said at the Cotton Exchange in Manchester, where such things were known, that even with the slump in cotton which was so badly affecting many mill owners, Joel Greenwood, with irons of varying sizes in so many fires, was not likely to be one of them. He knew every thread that was spun in his mill, how much it cost to spin it and how much he was likely to get for it, which could not be said of his cousin who left it all to his managers and spent his time driving fast motor cars, riding fast horses and generally drifting from day to day in a delightful haze of good-humoured euphoria.

"That's a fine-looking animal, lad," Joel remarked mildly, not at all put out by his cousin's good-natured insults. "Must have cost you a pretty penny, by the look of her, and I *have* been known to take an hour or so off now and again. You know what they say about Jack. All work and no play . . ."

"Your name's not Jack and I don't believe a word of it. You've come over here for some reason and as I'm not the fool some folk make me out to be I can guess why. I suppose Mother's been droning on, begging you to try and talk some sense into me but it won't do, Joel, so, as my grandmother used to say to me, save your breath to cool your porridge, right?"

"I suppose the mare is for her?"

"Who, mother or grandmother?"

"No, you bloody fool. The bride. I got my invitation this morning, by the way, and I shall be delighted to attend."

"As my best man?"

"I should be insulted if you were to ask anyone else, old lad."

"Thanks, Joel."

"Don't mention it. Can she ride?"

Tim looked surprised. "Dear God, your mind's like a damned butterfly, darting from one thing to another and then back again. I can't keep up with you but yes, the mare is for Molly and no, she cannot yet ride but Wilf here is going to teach her. She's having breeches made along with her wedding frock or whatever it is women wear for these affairs and as soon as they're ready, the breeches, I mean, she is to come over for her first lesson. At the moment Molly spends a lot of time with her mother who's been ill. She's devoted to her and, I might add, if her mother had not approved I would have been turned down flat."

He smiled wryly at Joel as though he were sure his cousin would find that hard to believe.

Joel raised his eyebrows and grimaced. "Really!"

"Yes, really. Now then, the mare's name is Isolde which in its Welsh form means, 'of fair aspect', which could describe not only the mare but Molly and if you have anything further to say on the matter you'd best get it over and done with and then, depending on what you say, naturally, as you are in your gear perhaps we could have a gallop up the back and on to the moor."

"Mistress of Tristram, wasn't she?"

"What?" Tim looked perplexed.

"Isolde. She was an Irish princess betrothed to an elderly king. She drank some potion and fell in love with a young knight called Tristram, with tragic consequences, so the legend goes."

The stable lad shifted uncomfortably from foot to foot, looking from one face to the other, his master's flushed and intense for some reason, his master's cousin's quite expressionless. They had really said nothing that he even understood, let alone that might be construed as argumentative or conflicting in any way, and yet both men were steely-eyed, their chins thrust out in a way which declared their family link.

"I'll just put 'er on 't lead, sir," he mumbled and, since neither man seemed to hear him, he gladly escaped.

"Say it, cousin, and then clear off," Tim said coldly. "I assume you are to take me to task on the subject of my choice of bride. That I am marrying beneath me and—"

"You said it, lad, not I, and yes, Aunt Muriel has bent my ear somewhat, and so has Tess who gets constant and distressing telephone calls from your mother regarding your forthcoming nuptials. You are a wealthy and personable young man . . . yes, I said young, and could have your pick of the county and Aunt Muriel cannot be blamed for thinking this . . . this . . ."

"Yes, this what, Joel, and you'd best mind how you answer."

Joel Greenwood had, as he had promised himself he would, made discreet enquiries about Molly O'Dowd and her family and though he had dug deep and gone back to Molly's childhood he had found nothing to indicate that she, her father and brothers who had died in the defence of their country, were not perfectly decent, hardworking and honest folk, the sort who were known to be the backbone of the country. There was nothing to tarnish their name. There was nothing linked with Molly that might indicate she was what his aunt believed her to be – a common, gold-digging trollop. She was nineteen and all those who had spoken about her had had nothing to say but good. She had only one flaw and that was she was not born in the same class as Tim. There was nothing he could honestly hold against her, but just the same she was not for Tim and he had promised his Aunt Muriel that he would do his best to make Tim see it.

"She works in your mill, Tim."

"No, she doesn't."

"She doesn't?"

"No, she left the mill when her stepfather smashed her face and her ribs several weeks ago simply because I took her on a picnic. A perfectly innocent bloody picnic."

"Well, I must admit I did hear something of the sort, but can you blame the man for thinking that you were playing fast and loose . . ."

"Fast and loose! Don't be so bloody ridiculous, man." Tim's voice was filled with contempt. "Jesus, I hadn't even kissed her and even if I were playing fast and loose as you so decoratively call it, that's no reason to beat her senseless. If you'd seen the state of her, and her mother when . . . Dear God, she still bears the scars. For any man to inflict such injuries on a defenceless woman is unforgivable and

Molly, for one, and me for another, will never forgive him. And all he got was a year's bloody probation. He should have been horsewhipped."

"Yes, I'm sorry, that wasn't very well put. No man has the right to—"

"Dear God, I should never have let her talk me out of . . . of shooting the bastard."

"Steady on . . . hey, steady on, old man." Joel put a placatory hand on Tim's arm, for his cousin's agitation was beginning to alarm him. This talk of shooting and horsewhipping was worrying. He had come at his aunt's pleading to see if he could "talk some sense", was how she put it, into her son since she herself had failed lamentably. It was making her ill, really it was and how was she to go on living at Meddins if that coarse creature . . . oh, yes, very pretty, she agreed, but Muriel Broadbent could not possibly hand over her lovely home to a girl who lived in the poorest part of Oldham, worked in a mill, spoke like an Irish navvy and who was only after her Tim for what she could get out of him. She was used to nothing, and it showed. Tim was besotted with her and if only Joel could speak to him. He was throwing himself away on some trollop. How could he demean himself, and his family? She called her mother *Mammy* for heaven's sake, his Aunt Muriel moaned and she could barely imagine what the creature must be like. Meddins would be overrun with Irish and Lancashire layabouts, all scrounging off her son and on and on and on . . .

"I mean to have her, Joel, with or without my family's blessing. Almost from the first moment I saw her she unlocked something inside me that was frozen, though I didn't know it was frozen until she thawed it. I felt as though I had been pinned to the wall with an arrow through my heart. I love her deeply. She is the loveliest woman I have ever known and I don't just mean to look at. She is kind-hearted, funny and generous. Spirited, you know, and after what that brute did to her she could not have been blamed if she'd lost that brave spirit. She was nervous with Mother who won't have her in the house again, she says, though I have gone ahead with all the arrangements for the reception to be held at Meddins. But though Molly was . . . awkward she conducted herself well. She didn't eat peas with her knife or blow her nose on her napkin as I could see Mother expected her to do and . . ."

"Tim, lad, it's all right. I'm not condemning—"

". . . she stood up to Mother. I don't mean in a presumptuous way, but quietly, bravely. She was completely herself, natural, you know? Some girls would have tried to put on airs and graces, pretending a refinement they didn't have or done their best to . . . to alter the way they spoke, but Molly didn't. And she's bright and clever and will soon learn. God knows who'll teach her if Mother remains awkward but Meddins is my house, my home and I'm entitled to bring the bride of my choice back to it. Christ, Mother's been nagging me for years to get married and now, when I'm about to do so, she spends all day playing the tragedy queen, swearing she'll not come to the wedding."

He paused. He had been striding back and forth in front of Joel who stood quietly waiting for the tirade to finish but now he stopped, looking directly into his cousin's face.

"Molly's a Catholic, did you know?"

"I did wonder when I saw where the wedding was to take place."

"She wanted a nuptial mass but of course it was not possible as I'm not of her faith. I wanted a Church of England do so we compromised, we had no choice, I suppose, so we shall be married in her church but without the mass. Am I making myself clear?"

Joel indicated that he was.

"Dammit to hell, Joel, when I told Mother you would have thought I was suggesting we were to live over the bloody brush. We've not discussed children and God knows what religion they'll belong to but do you honestly think I care? Molly will make a wonderful mother, that's all that matters, surely? You should see her with her brother and sisters. Jesus, Joel, I love every hair of her head."

"So it seems," Joel answered drily, his voice low.

"She's an angel, so strong, resourceful . . . staunch, you know, and she'll not be broken, not by Mother nor her cronies. Not by anybody or anything."

So that was it! That was the powerful attraction which had drawn the endearing, charming, merry but vulnerable man who was Joel's cousin to the woman he was to marry. Her strength! Her ability to defend and support his weakness, the weakness which he and so many other young men had brought back from France. Many had lost limbs, their sight, their virility. Defiant, bitter, disillusioned, faith gone, youth gone, they had been broken in body and mind and though Tim was, on the surface, as well as any man, he had lost his nerve. He was afraid and Molly O'Dowd had shown him that she had enough for both of them. She was a lovely looking woman, Joel knew that, for he had watched her that day in the mill yard when Tim had spoken to her. Joel had driven over to Broadbents Mill to see Tim or, failing that, Mr Watson, who was one of the managers of the mill, on a bit of business and, as he watched her in the yard he had himself been drawn to her young and flaunting beauty. She had tossed her head in what looked like temper and Joel had smiled to himself, thinking his cousin had made some suggestion that she did not care for. He had seen nothing to suggest anything but a man, a man of wealth and position, using both to tempt one of his operatives to a "bit of fun", which was how it was described. But it seemed he had been grievously wrong and in a few weeks' time that same mill girl who, he remembered, had worn what looked like a man's cap, a shawl and clogs, was to become mistress of Meddins. It was a position many girls had coveted – the man and the house – girls far more suited to be the wife of the former and mistress of the latter than Molly O'Dowd. For years they had cast acquisitive glances at this handsome cousin of his but, it seemed, none of them had touched that special place all men have within them, a place which is ready for the right woman and which knows when she arrives. Not until this Molly had found it, unlocked it and curled herself up there like a kitten who unexpectedly comes across a silken-lined basket which it finds to its taste. A scheming minx as his Aunt Muriel seemed to think, or a sainted young woman who genuinely loved and cared about Tim? How was Joel to tell? He had never met her. Never spoken to her and if he did was he wise enough, detached enough to tell the difference?

The paddock drowsed in a ground-level, autumn-scented haze in which the lovely horses seemed to drift, their fine heads dipping into it to search for the sweet grass. Joel could smell the apples which weighed down the trees in the orchard at his back. He had walked through it to get to the paddock, through the gnarled old apple trees, carefully avoiding the windfalls which were scattered on the rough-cut grass. The mild autumn sun lit the falling leaves to flame and a light breeze rustled them. What a beautiful time of the year it was, he remembered thinking, and how much more beautiful it all seemed in the quite exquisite setting of Meddins. Michaelmas daisies were massed in the big flower borders to the side of the house, lining the wide path down to a clematis-covered pergola, filling his eyes with rich colouring, pale and dark lilac, strong purple, pure white and a pale green foliage. And the girl who had caught his cousin's eye was to have it all. Who was she? What was she? What was in her that had captured this man's heart and mind and soul? Or so Aunt Muriel would have it. He was no longer in his right mind, she said tearfully to Joel and to look at him, stamping about in uncontrolled agitation, his eyes quite wild, his face working over some dreadful inner storm, Joel was almost ready to believe it.

"Look, old chap, why don't you . . .?"

"Bloody hell, not you as well, for God's sake. Can none of you believe I know my own mind? Jesus, I'm thirty next and surely should be old enough to decide for myself who I'm to marry without this damned farrago you and Mother have created."

"Calm down, lad. Nobody's trying to stop you marrying this girl."

"Well, you could have fooled me." Tim's voice was derisory.

"Let me finish, will you? As I said, nobody's trying to stop you, we only want to be absolutely sure *you're* absolutely sure that she's the right one for you."

"Goddammit to hell! What else can I do to make you see how much she means to me? Haven't I just opened up my bloody heart to you?"

"Yes, you have." Joel's voice was carefully neutral. "And I accept it and so will Aunt Muriel . . . oh, yes, she will eventually. She might give you hell now, and the poor girl you're to marry, but when she sees how happy you are she won't give a damn if Molly's a half-naked Hottentot."

"You don't know Mother. She's absolutely obsessed with me hitching up with a girl who's 'our sort' and if she imagines—"

"Chuck it, Tim. Let's give it a rest. Here, have a cigarette and stop pacing about like a caged beast." Joel put his hand in the pocket of his tweed jacket and drew out a packet of Woodbines and a rather battered cigarette lighter.

Tim relaxed and smiled affectionately. "I see you still smoke those atrocious things." He knew that the "fags", which were the ones most ex-soldiers smoked, were a heritage of the war. The lighter was made of gunmetal, the pattern of it worn away with usage and with several dents in it as though it had, like Joel, been through the wars. It had been given to him on his eighteenth birthday, just before he went to France, by a young lady of whom he had currently been fond and though it was old, one of the first "striking" lighters, its case filled with cotton wool soaked with a few drops of petrol, he had never felt the need to change it for a more modern one. A Dunhill, say, or a Ronson. It had a wick, a flint and a steel cap. When the cap was struck against the flint a spark was produced which lit the wick.

Tim took a cigarette, put it between his lips and bent his head to the lighter Joel held out to him, cupping his hand round it to protect it from the breeze. Joel could have kicked himself later, for he knew the bloody old thing was temperamental and even as his thumb pressed down the cap he had this awful feeling, like a premonition, or a film at the cinema which runs at the wrong speed, moving slowly on with the performers going at a languid, almost motionless pace.

The cap struck the flint, a spark flashed and the wick lit up in a tall thin flame, reaching out viciously for Tim's eyes, his eyebrows, his hair, licking at his face in snarling venom before retreating and dying back to nothing more than a tiny red, smoking dot on the end of the wick.

The effect on Tim was devastating.

"Jesus . . . oh, Jesus, keep your bloody heads down, lads," he screamed at the top of his voice, throwing himself flat on his belly and burrowing his face in the sweet grass of the paddock. The horses, panicked by the high-pitched terror in his voice, threw up their heads, eyes rolling, tails flaunting and raced madly this way and that as his voice continued to shrill its warning. His body twitched in a regular convulsive spasm as though to the beat of something only he heard, and Joel knew, his heart anguished, for had he not been in the same appalling conflict, that Tim was reliving the horror they had both survived at Verdun. The Germans had first tried out the dreaded *Flammenwerfer*, the flamethrower, in 1914 but it was not until two years later that liquid fire was used extensively and both he and Tim had witnessed the dreadful sight of their men turned to human torches by the monstrosity.

He knelt down to his cousin and with the compassion and ease the soldiers of the war – for only they had experienced it – show to one another, he drew him into his arms, cradling his head against his own broad chest, brushing back the tangle of his sweat-drenched hair. He murmured some incomprehensible but soothing sound as though Tim were a child who was lost in the dark of a nightmare. Though the day was mild Tim was shivering violently, locked in a paroxysm of terror that could, and had in the past, caused him to lose control of his bowels and bladder.

Joel held him comfortingly, keeping up the murmur of reassurance until, gradually, the ferocious shaking eased, warmth returned to the stricken man and he was no longer blind and deaf with remembered horror. He sat up, putting his arms about his bent knees, hanging his head between them, exhausted, angry and horribly ashamed.

"Christ almighty," he muttered to the bit of grass between his legs, "you'd think by now I'd be over this damned nonsense, wouldn't you?" His voice was bitter and for several minutes he cursed fluently and obscenely on the subject of the woeful disability he had brought back from the trenches. He cursed all the things he had seen, and suffered, all the things he had seen other men suffer until at last he fell silent.

"All right, lad?" Joel asked mildly. "Will you have that cigarette now," smiling, holding out a strong brown hand to haul his cousin to his feet. "I promise not to take your eyebrows off this time."

"Bloody hell!" Tim dabbed at his face anxiously. "Are they still there? I can't walk up the aisle with no eyebrows."

"No, all is intact, even your beautiful golden curls."

"It's time you bought yourself a new lighter, cousin." Tim was pale, sunken-eyed, strained about the mouth but he was recovered enough to attempt a grin and to accept another cigarette which he lit himself with a match. "Perhaps I'll buy you one, gold, I think, since you are to be my best man and I believe it's customary for the bridegroom to buy his best man a gift."

"Now hold on. I'm very attached to this old lighter. Josie Dickinson bought it for me . . . remember her?"

"God, how could any man forget her? She'd the biggest—"

"Now, now, Timothy, I was also very attached to Josie."

"We all would have liked to be attached to Josie, my lad."

"Good days, cousin."

"Aye, good days. Now then" – Tim shook himself – "where were we? Aah, yes, I do believe that you and Molly will get on like a house on fire. Daft as it sounds, you're strangely alike. She . . . one day . . . months ago now, she saw me have one of my . . . attacks and, well, she was splendid. She'd no idea what was going on, poor kid, but she wasn't afraid as many women would be. She made no fuss. She . . . held me, as you did, until it was over."

The confession was evidence, if evidence was needed, of the reason, perhaps not the only one, but a strong one, why Tim Broadbent was possessed with the need to marry his young mill girl and Joel quietly put away his doubts, for did not this damaged man need a strong, compassionate woman to share his life with him?

16

The blow fell a week before the wedding and at first Molly thought Mammy was joking, kidding her, though she should have known better. Would Mammy joke about something so vital, so terrible, so life-threatening, for that was how Molly saw it, and of course, the answer was no. Mammy didn't joke any more. Mammy didn't tease any more. Mammy didn't laugh as once she had done when Daddy and Liam and Patrick were alive. Her face, healed now, was pale, resigned, patient, showing only a vague interest in all the exciting and sometimes alarming things Molly was experiencing as the fiancée of Tim Broadbent. Mammy sat in the comfortable velvet chair in the luxury of the private room Tim was paying for, her toes to the leaping, red-hearted fire in the fireplace, her hair, which had once been as dark and gleaming as Molly's, brushed back into a grey-streaked bun at the back of her head. She wore a one-piece dress of rose-beige wool and the colour suited her, putting a little warmth into the lined sallow flesh of her face and neck. The dress was neat and simple, what Molly was aware Mammy would think of as suitable to her station in life. Molly had chosen it, buying it at Buckley and Prockters with the "allowance" Tim had insisted she, as his future wife, was entitled to, though Molly knew it would take her a long time to become accustomed to it.

"You cannot keep on asking me for money, my darling," he told her gently.

"I know, that's what I keep tellin' thi'," shamefaced. "'Appen I should go back ter't mill until we're wed."

"That's not what I mean, Mary Angelina O'Dowd, and you know it so don't play that game with me."

"Sure an' it's no game, Tim."

"My love, will you stop arguing with me. You and I are to be married in December. As my wife you will have an allowance of your own to spend as you wish. You can blow it all on your brother and sisters and cousins and second cousins and all those relatives you appear to have and I shall not complain. It is your money. So if I choose to start it now before we are married, which, dearest Molly, is when you most need it, humour me, will you? I have opened an account for you at the Allied and Union Bank in Manchester Street and I shall deposit . . . well, what d'you think? Fifty a month, will that do? Will it be enough?" He frowned in deep thought and Molly, who was struck speechless, watched his face with the fascinated awe of someone who cannot quite believe her own ears. "Shall we say that if you run short you have only to tell me. I want you to buy whatever you need, to wear, of course, and to see to the needs of your family but . . ."

"Fifty pounds a month?" she managed to croak, putting out a trembling hand and placing it on his arm where he immediately covered it with one of his own.

"Yes, my darling," he said anxiously. "Is that not enough?"

"Holy Mary Mother of God! Enough! 'Tis more'n I earned in a bloody year at mill. Tim, tha' don't know what tha're sayin', lad. I can't tekk all that."

"You'll be my wife, Molly. You must dress well and I know you want your mother and the children to have a nice home. Isn't that true?"

"Aye, but . . ."

"No buts, Molly. If you are to help them you must have money to help them with and who else are you to get it from but your husband? Yes . . . yes, I know we're not married yet but that is merely a matter of time. You are your family's support and mainstay and I am yours. They are to be related to me by marriage and would I want to see part of my family in need? You should know me better than that, my love."

"Tim, yer that good ter me . . ."

"No, I'm not. I want you to be happy because when you're happy so am I. I am an amazingly selfish chap, my love. Now I realise after even this short time your pride and fighting spirit do not take kindly to having to ask for what you might see as . . . charity. Perhaps that is the wrong word but . . . well, all the ladies . . . like . . . well, like my mother and sister, have their dress allowances and so will you. Now take that troubled look off your face and come and give me a kiss."

That was another thing that took a bit of getting used to. Not that she objected to it, of course, for she liked Tim's kisses. At first they had been slow, soft, tender, undemanding, his lips almost like those of her little brother when he put them against hers, but they were becoming more ardent as their wedding day drew closer. Whenever they were alone his arms would go round her and his body would press along the length of hers so that she could feel every inch of him from knee to shoulder. He would put his hand in her hair at the back of her head, holding her still as though afraid she might turn away from his kiss, from his warm lips, his probing tongue, his passionate need of her which he was beginning to let her see. His mouth would travel across her face to her eyebrows, her closed eyes, her ears, along the line of her jaw and down the arched length of her throat, pressing against the swelling curve of her breast.

One bright day, a cold December day on the top of Saddleworth Moor, he unbuttoned her coat and blouse, pleading with her not to stop him and when she didn't, for he seemed to have a kind of despair in him, he pushed aside her clothing and pulled down her lacy chemise to reveal her white, rose-tipped breasts. His hands cupped them with what was almost a reverence. He sighed, his hands moving to stroke and fondle, his thumb and first finger rolling her nipples then, when she made no objection, bending his head to take them in turn into his mouth, nuzzling at them like a suckling child. He sighed again then rested his cheek on their soft fullness, breathing deeply as though to draw into himself the womanly smell of her. He was smiling. She could feel it against her flesh and when his hand dipped into the top of her skirt and down across her flat belly to where her pubic hair grew thickly she could feel not only his fingers but a delicious feeling starting to tingle and throb, a warmth she had not felt with him before and she wanted to beg him to go on. She was willing to allow him to strip her naked and lay her on the coarse grass if he wanted to, since it was the only way she could think of to thank him for what he had done for her and her family, but he went no further which she supposed was just as well for the temperature was almost at freezing point. He seemed content to kiss and caress her breasts, sighing with what appeared to be delight over her white skin, the feel of it which he said was like a rose petal, licking her nipples until they stood out like rosy marbles, smiling, for it seemed Molly's response pleased him.

"I could take you now, Mary Angelina," he murmured against her naked breast, "for it seems you are as disposed as I am to be loved."

"I . . . I'd like it, Tim, if tha' want."

"No, my darling. I want you to be an immaculate bride, a virgin when we meet at the altar of that church of yours. Though no one will know of it but you and me it means a great deal to me. I love you, Molly and before them all you will be my pure and faultless bride."

"Not if tha' keep doin' that, Tim Broadbent," she gasped.

He laughed joyously, putting her together again, smoothing her hair and cheek, drawing her blouse, her coat and muffler about her and hugging her close to him in the confines of the little car, which was a bit tricky since there were so many knobs and levers between them.

If that was what he wanted it was a good job they seldom got a chance to be alone together, she smiled to herself on that Saturday exactly a week before her wedding as she knocked on the door and entered Mammy's room at the nursing home. She had discovered she was a warm-blooded woman, a woman with great love to give, pleased to find herself responsive to his maleness, his handsome, narrow-eyed desire. It would be a sin, of course, outside marriage but if the opportunity occurred how could she refuse him, this disarmingly attractive man with his dry, quick-witted humour which made her laugh, his warm, fathomless brown eyes in which she felt sometimes she might drown, his lean strength, his vulnerable smile, his generosity, the blaze of his love for her which held her steady when she thought of what was ahead in the months to come.

She kissed Mammy's cheek and hugged her and told her how much better she looked and how cold it was outside. Had she seen the children and how had they been and weren't the roses lovely which Tim had sent over from the Meddins hothouse?

She talked and Mammy seemed to listen. "We're goin' ter spend a few days in London, Mammy. Can tha' imagine me going ter London? Then guess what, we're ter tekk the ferry

over ter France. Paris! Can yer believe it, Molly O'Dowd from
Sidney Street in Paris but Tim ses everyone should see Paris
even if it's wrong time o't year."

She did not add that Tim had promised her that he had
booked a room with a view of the Eiffel Tower so that she
could get a look at it, since she would not be allowed out
of the room, never mind the hotel, so it didn't really matter
what time of the year it was! They'd go again in the spring
when the trees along the "Chance . . . Cham . . . Champs . . ."
whatever it was Tim had called it, were in bloom, providing
she wasn't pregnant by then, he had added, narrowing his
eyes and winking suggestively, and he certainly intended to
play his part in that direction, he murmured, licking and biting
the lobe of her ear until that newly discovered part of her,
deep in her belly, began to throb.

"Nay, darlin', 'tis a wonder so 'tis," Mammy answered
absently.

"But before that there's t' wedding ter be got through. I
know every girl's supposed ter think 'er weddin' day's the
best of 'er life but 'onest, Mammy, this 'un can only be like
Fred Karno's circus."

Róisín, roused out of her introspective trance, spoke in
dismay.

"Child, what are tha' sayin'? Every lass's weddin' day's
special. Mine an' yer daddy's was. I'll never forget it." Her
eyes clouded in remembrance and her lips softened and then
tightened again as though in pain.

"I know, Mammy, but thi' an' Daddy 'ad tha' two families
an' . . . well, tha' knows what I mean."

"But so will thi', darlin', an' tha' friends an' all," though
the thought of sitting among all the elegant acquaintances of
the well-bred Mrs Broadbent was something Rosie Watson
dreaded and pushed firmly to the back of her mind every
time she thought of it. Of course she would have Flo and
Maggie with her, Maggie's husband Alf, Flo's Kathleen and
Jane who was Maggie's daughter-in-law and many of her old
friends from Sidney Street which, though it should comfort
her, actually made it worse, for only the Heavenly Mother
knew what they might get up to. She was only thankful it
was to take place in her own church of St Saviours where,
prior to Pikey's brutal attention, she had attended mass several
times a week. It would have been grand if Molly's fellow had

been a Catholic, though, and a nuptial mass heard. Father O'Toole came regularly to the nursing home to see her, to say a prayer, to bless her, to hear her confession and give her Holy communion but she would feel better in herself, shake off this dreadful listlessness once she could get to her knees before the altar at St Saviours.

"Oh, I know, Mammy," Molly was saying, echoing Rosie's own thoughts, "but can tha' imagine the likes o' Cissie Thompson wi' Tim's friends? Yes, I invited 'er so it's me own fault an' I've yet ter meet any o' Tim's friends but I suppose they'll all be like 'im. Not as kind, 'appen, in fact, not near as good as 'e is. 'Is Mammy's not come round yet an' when Tim said 'e wanted a party so that 'e could invite 'is friends ter meet me she told 'im she'd not be there. So it were called off. Apparently it's not done to 'ave a party wi'out an 'ostess so Tim ses we'll 'ave ter wait until we're wed then *I'll* be 'ostess . . . hostess. Lord knows what the ceremony an' reception'll be like though wi' Mrs Broadbent's frozen face at me back. Tim ses Mrs Ogden's all of a dither because she's 'ad ter tekk orders from 'im instead o' Mrs Broadbent. Well, 'e don't know what ter order, do 'e, so 'e's told Mrs Ogden, she's the cook, by the way, ter do't best she can. Same as Tessa 'ad – that's 'is sister – when she were wed . . . married, 'e . . . he told 'er . . . her."

Molly was making a great effort to improve and refine the way she spoke. Being with Tim so much of the time and having a quick ear and a talent for mimicry, she was beginning to do well, but she only had to be back with Aunty Maggie or Mammy or Aunty Flo for five minutes and she lapsed into her old way of talking. She was not ashamed of who she was or how she spoke but she wanted to please Tim more than anything in the world. She wanted to "fit in", to be part of his world, to have him be proud of her. She knew her appearance was impeccable. She knew how to dress and even, with Tim's help, how to conduct herself at the restaurants he delighted in taking her to. It was just when she opened her mouth to speak that her origins were revealed, though not by a flicker of his eyelashes did he register disapproval.

"Tha'll be Mrs Broadbent then, darlin'. Mistress of Meddins an' tha' mustn't forget it," Róisín told her daughter sternly, but her eyes were warm, loving, proud and had a touch almost of relief. "Tha'll be wonderful at it, darlin'. I only wish tha' daddy was 'ere ter see thi' on tha' weddin' day. Now tell me about yer frock again."

Molly spent a lovely half-hour describing the exquisite lace wedding dress she was to wear. It was to be very high at the neck with long sleeves and a "handkerchief" hemline which meant it swirled about her ankles in points six inches from the ground. Her veil, in the absence of a train, was long and diaphanous, trailing several yards behind her and Clare who was, to her rapturous delight, to be her only bridesmaid. Clare was also to wear white, a replica of Molly's dress but with the palest of pink rosebuds at her waist and in her dark hair. Both the dresses were ready, covered in masses of tissue paper and hanging in Aunty Flo's wardrobe, and Molly could only pray that they would not attract the strong smell of the mothballs Aunty Flo scattered among her own clothing.

"But we've summat . . . something else to talk about, Mammy, so we 'ave, an' if we don't look sharp I'll be off on me 'oneymoon without you an' the kids properly settled. The agent's only waitin' . . . waiting on your word about which o' them two 'ouses tha' . . . you like best. Remember when we took yer . . . you a couple of weeks ago in Mrs Broadbent's Rolls-Royce?" Molly grinned in wicked glee, wondering what Tim's mother had had to say about Molly O'Dowd and her mammy riding in the luxurious depths of the beautiful silver machine Molly had seen with her daddy gliding by in the lane fifteen years ago.

"We've got ter get tha' . . . you moved in this week. Doctor ses tha're . . . you're fine now, Mammy, and Aunty Flo'll stop wi' thi' fer a few days until you're settled. I've bin ter Buckley an' Prockters" – with whom she was now on good terms, for, recognising her importance and the amount of money she was spending, they treated her like the Princess Royal – "I told thi', didn't I, and I've ordered the furniture an' they said they'll come an' measure up an' 'ave . . . have the curtains at the winders before the week's out. Tha' can move in on Friday an' on Sat'dy Tim'll send a car to pick up you, Aunty Flo an' Kathleen an' fetch thi' ter't church. The seamstress from Buckley and Prockters's comin' 'ere for a final fitting fer tha' frock, but the most important thing, Mammy, is ter get tha' in thi' own house. There's not much time. We should be—"

"Pikey's bin ter see me."

The words came at her like a below-the-belt blow from a

boxer and Molly felt as though a fist had thumped her right in the middle of her stomach, halting the flow of blood to her heart. An icy, breathless paralysis came over her so that she could neither move nor speak nor even express horror on her chalk white face. Her eyes stared in widening terror at the calm face of her mammy and when Mammy reached out and took her dead hands within her own she was surprised at how warm they were.

"'E's bin a few times, darlin', but I were afraid ter tell thi', so I was, fer I knew tha'd be upset. 'E ses 'e's that sorry an' 'e'll never do owt like it again, never. Oh, I know 'e means it now an' they say a man can't change 'is ways, especially an 'ard man like Pikey but . . . oh, Mary Angelina, darlin', 'e's me 'usband an' a woman must bide wi' 'er 'usband, so."

Molly couldn't speak. Her throat was clogged with the torrent of tears which threatened her and she felt the bubble of despair swell in her chest. Mammy, her gentle, patient, loving mammy was looking at her with an expression of sadness so deep it could not be fathomed and yet there was also a resolve, a quiet determination in them that told Molly she would not be moved.

Released at last from rigid shock, Molly began to shake her head in denial and the tears which had found their way to her eyes and were welling there flew about in bright diamond droplets caught in the light from the fire. Her hair, which Tim had begged her not to cut again, swirled about her head in glossy, russet-tinted curls and her mouth opened on a wide wail of protest.

"Oh no . . . oh no . . . Mammy, tha' can't. Tha' can't mean ter go back to 'im. Not after what 'e did ter thi'." Her attempts to improve her diction were completely forgotten in her devastation. "Tha' knows 'e's a brute, an' 'e'll not change, never. I won't let yer, Mammy, I can't. Please, Mammy, don't . . ."

She gripped Róisín's hands frantically, kneading them until Róisín flinched. She fell to her knees before her mother's chair, her eyes blinded by her tears which washed in a flood across her blanched face. "An' what about our Clare, Mammy? Tha' knows 'e did summat to 'er, don't thi', Mammy? Please . . . Mammy . . ."

She was babbling now, desperate to make her mother see that this was madness, a lunatic move which would be dangerous for them all.

"'E 'ad a go at me, Mammy, did tha' know?"

"I guessed, my angel girl." Her mother bent her head in great remorse.

"Then please, Mammy . . . don't do it. 'Tis not safe. I do believe 'e could kill thi'."

"No, no . . . hush, darlin'." Róisín's hands moved lovingly about her daughter's distraught face, brushing away the tears, smoothing back the tumbled mass of curls which fell over her forehead, kissing her cheek, doing her best to calm her child with her own sure calm.

"Clare'll stay at Aunty Flo's, darlin'."

"There, yer see, yer know there's summat ter be afeared of or tha'd tekk 'er with yer." Molly's voice was triumphant.

"No, she's 'appy at Aunty Flo's. They love 'er, Flo an' Kathleen an' it'd be a shame ter disturb 'er."

"Tha're lyin', Mammy. Tha're leavin' 'er at Aunty Flo's because tha' can't trust that bastard ter keep 'is filthy 'ands off 'er. An' wharrabout little 'uns?"

"Oh, no." Róisín frowned and shook her head. "'E'd not touch 'is own children, Molly. 'E's their daddy an' . . ."

"They're terrified of 'im, Mammy, you know that. Like little birds 'idin' away in a nest while cat's about, they were, but look 'ow they've bin since they went ter Aunty Maggie's. Lively, playin' like kids should. I seen Archie sit on Uncle Alf's knee an' 'e were medd up wi' it. 'Ave tha' ever seen 'im sit on that bastard's knee? No, an tha' never will. Archie's too feared. Oh please, Mammy, don't do this ter me. Not now when I can 'elp yer ter lead a decent life wi'out that bugger for ever at yer. I can't bear it, Mammy, I can't bear it an' if Daddy—"

"Don't tha' speak o' tha' daddy, Mary Angelina, or tha'll feel the flat o' me 'and, so tha' will. 'Tis bad enough, 'avin' ter . . . ter . . . well, wi'out tha' fetchin' up Daddy's blessed memory ter spike me through me 'eart. I'm ter go back, Molly, an' that's that so dry tha' tears an' get off back to tha' Aunty Flo's. Tha've a lot ter do before next Sat'dy."

Rosie Watson's face had closed up and become as hard and unyielding as granite. Her blue eyes which, over the past months seemed to have faded, or become washed out with the scalding, secret tears she had shed, were steely and her soft mouth was suddenly firm as she stared fiercely at her daughter who was, she could tell, about to continue the argument.

"'Tis all settled, my lass. Pikey's me 'usband. I know we wasn't married in church but 'e's me 'usband just the same an' I belong wi' 'im. After't weddin' on Sat'dy me an' the children'll move back ter Sidney Street. Now don't thee fret, darlin'," bending to peer into Molly's stricken face. "We'll be all right, you just see. 'E's learned 'is lesson an' now that tha're . . . well, 'e knows Mr Broadbent'd not like 'is mother-in-law knocked about."

She did her best to smile and Molly bowed her head, though not in acquiescence.

She ran all the way to Meddins, her well-shod feet thumping on the hard, frost-bitten ground like hammers on an anvil, her breath gasping in and out of her laboured lungs and curling for a moment about her head before being snatched away by the ferocity of her movements. She had left her hat in Mammy's room but she did not miss it. Her mind was stunned by a sense of her own inadequacy and all she could think of was that she must get to Tim as soon as possible.

Forbes's face was galvanised from its usual cool expression of imperturbability into one of amazement when, in answer to her frantic knocking, he opened the door to her. She didn't give him a chance to perform his accustomed task of enquiring who it was she wished to see, of showing her into the drawing room and telling her, as he would any casual visitor, that he would see if whoever it was was at home. She simply strode in, pushing past his portly form and flung herself to the bottom of the stairs which seemed to her to be the central point of the house and where her voice would be heard.

"Tim?" she shrieked. "In God's name where are thi'? Tim, Tim, it's Molly an' I must see thi' . . . Tim . . . please, Tim."

"Miss, I beg of you," Forbes began, ready, if not exactly to lay hands on Mr Tim's intended bride, then at least to edge her diplomatically into the drawing room but she did not wish to be edged anywhere and her tense, overwrought face told him so.

"Leave me alone, you idiot," she howled. "Go on, get back ter't kitchen or wherever it is tha' 'ides when tha's not mekkin a nuisance o' thissen. I want ter see Tim an' I want ter see 'im now an' if tha' can't fetch 'im to me then bugger off. I'll find 'im messen."

Forbes was mortified and since he had never heard the

phrase "mad as Mick O'Dowd" he put both his elderly feet right in it, up to the knees in fact. He was not about to be spoken to as though he were one of her class, his expression said. This quite glorious-looking woman, even if she was to become Mrs Timothy Broadbent next Saturday, was revealing that she had the manners and breeding of a peasant and he would tell her so too. He had been butler to the Broadbents for three decades and though he was a servant he was used to being treated and spoken to with courtesy.

"Miss O'Dowd," he barked, so ferociously Molly turned to stare, though it did not alter the madness in her eyes. She herself felt as though someone had removed her brain and returned it to her head in the wrong position. Nothing made sense any more and there was only one person who could put it right as he had put right all the other emergencies in her life since they had met.

"You cannot come stamping in here, shouting at the top of your voice, young woman," Forbes continued, glaring at her, icy-faced, as he did to the parlourmaid when her work had displeased him. In fact this young woman was no better, nor higher in the social rank than the parlourmaid, his tone and expression said, which is where he made his first mistake.

Molly took a step towards him, her eyes no more than brilliant bluish green slits in the blank whiteness of her face.

"Can I not?" she hissed. "And who are you to stop me?" Her diction was suddenly perfect. "I am looking for Tim, Mr Broadbent, my fiancé and your employer and if you don't have him here in the next thirty seconds or tell me where he can be found I shall make sure your employment is terminated within a week after our marriage. Do I make myself clear?"

Her hair bristled about her head like the brush the chimney sweep used on the flue.

"Don't threaten me, young woman." Forbes's neck swelled wrathfully but his voice was dangerously quiet. He was so incensed he went so far as to forget his position and his usual sangfroid which had never, in the total span of his life as a butler, been shattered.

"I'll threaten who I like, you old fool." Her scowl was so ferocious Forbes fell back from it, seeing what was in her and beginning to wish he'd kept his mouth shut. "And I'll shout as much as I like as well. I want to speak to Tim. Now."

A cool voice from the top of the stairs halted Molly's flow

of angry, frustrated words and she whirled about to stare up into the contemptuous but totally ladylike face of Muriel Broadbent.

"My son is not at home, Miss . . . er . . ."

It was this that finally snapped the last shred of hold Molly had on her hot temper, tearing it loose from the quiet peace where it had been tethered ever since she had become engaged to Tim. This pretence on Mrs Broadbent's part that she was a nobody, a nobody whose name she could scarcely remember and it sent her over the edge of reason. She had not been far from it when she ran from Mammy's room as though all hell had been let loose behind her, for that was what Mammy was going back to. Now Muriel Broadbent's withering voice snapped that last hold she had on her white-hot temper, a temper fanned by fear.

"Where is he? I've to see him at once. It's urgent." She did not know how she got the words out, or even made them sound comprehensible, her jaw was clamped so tight.

"I'm afraid I don't know but if you care to leave a message . . .?" Muriel Broadbent raised haughty eyebrows.

"Where the bloody hell is he, that's all I want to know, never mind leaving bloody messages. Tell me and I'll find him. I need him and I need him now. I've run all the damned way from the nursing home and I'll not be put off by some bad-tempered old biddy . . . aye, that's right, that's you . . . and this . . . this jumped-up old fart in a monkey suit. Tell me where he is. Tell me or I'll scream the bloody place down."

The strange thing was all the time she was screaming and swearing Molly was conscious in some dim, appalled recess of her mind that she was making a show of herself and that should Daddy be watching her he'd be appalled too. Swearing was something he had never liked, especially in a woman and really, did it do any good but somehow she couldn't stop. A demon had got her, a demon of loathing and terror which had sprung up when Mammy had told her about Pikey and which could only be exorcised by the loosing of this rage within her.

"You are quite the most impertinent young woman I have ever met, forcing your way into my home like some common thief and really, your language is quite detestable. How my son imagines he can introduce you into decent society is beyond me."

"Sod decent society. Where's Tim? If you don't tell me I'll go screaming round this house and the gardens until I find him. And if I don't find him here I'll do the same at the mill and let me tell you this, you silly old woman, in case you'd not realised it, he'll be as mad as me when he hears you've stood in my way."

Muriel knew it was true but it did not deter her. She was not afraid of this strumpet who, today, was showing herself in her true colours and in a way she wished Tim was here to see it. But this was her house, at least until next Saturday.

She curled her lip, signalling with her eyes to Forbes. It seemed she was telling him to get rid of this creature, as they would any interloper Mrs Broadbent did not care to have in her home, and to do it in any way he thought fit.

Forbes hesitated. Surely she did not intend him to use force? She was Mr Tim's fiancée after all and to be chucked out like a . . . a wandering tinker? Even he, who was livid himself, would not dare to contemplate such a thing. She was a devil of a woman was Miss O'Dowd and he felt sorry for this family of which she was soon to become a part but Mrs Broadbent could hardly ask him to . . . to . . .

But it seemed Molly had intercepted and interpreted the look and she began to laugh and as she laughed it cooled the hot blood of her temper as laughter has a habit of doing.

"Eeh, Mrs B, tha're an eejit," she said, ready to make up just as easily as, minutes ago, she had been ready to spit and snarl. "Dost tha' know 'ow much tha' son loves me, dost tha'?"

An expression of disgust twisted Muriel's face. Not only did she object to this upstart calling her Mrs B as though they were cronies, but also the indignity of discussing something so private as feelings in front of a servant. She did not answer but her eyes told Molly what she thought.

"Nay, I don't think tha' does," Molly went on, "but let me tell thi' this. If it come to a contest between thee an' me dost tha' think tha'd win? Dost tha'?" She was deliberately assuming the thickest of Lancashire accents now, knowing how much it infuriated her future mother-in-law. For a moment she had forgotten the reason for her mad dash to Meddins, her need to pour her sorrow out to Tim who would surely make it right for her and she raised her tousled head pridefully, a younger woman telling the older that she was no longer the keeper of her son's wellbeing. He was Molly's now. This house was

Molly's now and Muriel Broadbent had best accept it. They had met only once in October when Tim had brought her here to meet her and since then Mrs Broadbent had steadfastly refused to have her in the house again. Molly was aware that she could have forced Tim's hand, persuaded him to invite his friends so that Molly could be presented to them but if Mrs Broadbent refused to be present there seemed no point in stirring up bad feeling between herself and Tim's mother whose home she was to share. Let them, after the wedding, live together, find a common ground which surely was Tim's welfare and in the fulness of time agreement would come. She would do her best to win her round, to let her see that she, Molly, would make Tim happy. That she would learn to be the woman, the lady, Mrs Broadbent wanted for her son. There would be a child perhaps and this cold-faced, haughty woman would be its grandmother. Dear Mother of God, could she not see what she was depriving herself of if she kept this up? And what about Saturday? What about the wedding? Was she to carry on this antagonism right up to the church door itself or was she not to come at all?

"Mrs Broadbent," she said placatingly, putting out a hand as though to invite her to come down the stairs, "can't we just . . .?"

"Show this person out, Forbes, if you please," Mrs Broadbent said icily. "This is my house until next Saturday and it is my privilege to have in it who I please. Good morning, Miss . . . er . . ."

17

She met Joel Greenwood for the first time on her wedding day. He was standing just to the right of Tim at the altar as she came up the aisle on Uncle Alf's arm and as their eyes met through the misty folds of her veil she was startled by the feeling which leaped in her heart. It was what she imagined an electric current would be like, though she couldn't really say she'd had much to do with electricity. It had been installed at Meddins, Tim had told her and she supposed it could be very dangerous if you messed about with it and, for some reason, as she handed her bouquet of white, hothouse roses grown at Meddins into Clare's trembling but careful hands, she knew that Joel Greenwood would be exactly the same.

What a curious thought to have on her wedding day, her mind marvelled, just at the very moment when she should be wholly concerned with Tim and the vows they were about to exchange, but even as Father O'Toole began to speak she was acutely conscious of him on Tim's right-hand side. She could sense his reflective gaze on her and wished to God he would look away for this was no time to be studying his cousin's bride as he seemed intent on doing. She had had no more than an impression of darkness as she approached the two men, of hair and eyes and skin, of a large man, powerful, a broad back over which his immaculate grey morning coat seemed to strain, then Tim's hand found hers, hidden in the folds of her layered skirt and everything was all right. She turned to smile at him, to warm herself in his glowing adoration and for the rest of the ceremony which, without nuptial mass, was shorter than usual, she was conscious of no one but him.

At her back the church was crammed, not only with her

friends and relations, and Tim's friends and relations, but with every spinner and weaver from Tim's mill who could squeeze themselves into the church, with those who regularly worshipped at St Saviours and with curious women who lived in and around Shaw Street and Hobs Hedge, which was a working-class area, and who had never seen a "society" wedding. They had come to watch Molly O'Dowd, once one of them, change, on her wedding day, into a lady. A rich lady, and there was not one woman there who would not have cheerfully changed places with her, even if her handsome, smiling bridegroom had been as poor as a church mouse!

The fluting, triumphant sound of the Wedding March brought the congregation to its feet as she and her husband, vows exchanged, rings exchanged, the paraphernalia of forms and certificates the registrar insisted upon, this being a Catholic wedding, over and done with. They stood for a moment, their backs to the altar, their smiling faces turned to those in the body of the church who had come to wish them well. Molly picked out Betty's awestruck but sincerely pleased face, her eyes as wide as her mouth. She wore her best frock in a quite fascinating shade she later described proudly to Molly as "chartreuse" which was neither green nor yellow but a bilious mixture of the two, with a hat which consisted of as many birds as could possibly perch there. It had a froth of yellow ribbon and a small yellow veil which reached the tip of her nose. Her outfit was the very latest fashion, she told Molly enthusiastically, the hem of her skirt brushing her kneecap, the waist gathered at her hip with a large yellow artificial flower purporting to be an orchid. She resembled an exotic and highly coloured bird of paradise among the modest browns and blacks and greys, the navies and mauves which were the "Sunday best" of Molly's family and what those from Sidney Street considered suitable for a wedding. Hats were decorated with a new feather or a bunch of cherries in honour of the occasion but an outfit especially for this one day was beyond the pocket of most of them. Aunty Maggie and Aunty Flo were respectably turned out in the sensible hats and coats they had worn since they were girls, though Kathleen and the younger women of the family shivered in the unsuitable flowered prints they donned in the summer.

Only Mammy was smart, chic even, though in a dignified way, for her chestnut brown two-piece, her cloche hat in a paler shade but to tone, her small fur tippet had been chosen and paid for by her daughter, now Mrs Timothy Broadbent. She had her three young children beside her, the girls in well-made grey flannel coats and pretty crimson velvet berets, subdued and overcome by the splendour and beauty of their Molly, though Archie, accustomed by now to the somewhat careless discipline his Aunty Maggie doled out, was beginning to make a nuisance of himself. At least the elder Mrs Broadbent thought so as he pulled faces at the fastidiously turned-out children on the bridegroom's side of the church.

Molly felt a great desire to laugh out loud as it was all so . . . so hilarious somehow. Not the wedding ceremony, nor Tim's kiss, nor his clear and confident promise to love and protect her until death separated them, but the spectacle, now she could get a good look at it, of Mrs Broadbent and her family and friends trying to appear as though they were not aware of the rag, tag and bobtail assembly who crowded not only on Molly's side of the church but Tim's, or if they had noticed then they were certainly nothing to do with them. It was as though two weddings were taking place, one the good-humoured, sentimental, simple joining together of a man and a woman like herself, like Mammy and Aunty Maggie, like Aunty Flo, like Uncle Alf, the other the elegant, detached, ordered union between the ladies and gentlemen of Muriel Broadbent's class. They sat, aloofly withdrawn, Mrs Broadbent herself, her daughter Mrs Hugh Addison, Mrs Addison's husband and her three well-behaved daughters. Gentlemen in impeccably tailored, impeccably fitted grey morning suits carrying grey silk top hats. Ladies in intricately cut, expensively acquired gowns of silk, and hats of such magnificence they looked as though they were all off to Ascot or to a garden party at Buckingham Palace. They were superior, disdainful, letting it be known by their manner that they had condescended to come only for the sake of their dear friend Muriel Broadbent who surely needed all the support she could get on this dreadful day. They understood not one word of the wedding service, much of it in what they supposed to be Latin, looking askance at the genuflecting, curtseying absurdity half the congregation got up to.

Nancy O'Leary, another "bun in the oven" plainly displayed and obviously kicking beneath the tent of her maternity frock, the one she had worn for each of her many pregnancies, was jammed into a pew next to the terribly smart and highly indignant Mrs Delia Bowman. Nancy was of the opinion that little Molly O'Dowd had done right well for herself, didn't Mrs Bowman agree, and may the Blessed Mother watch over her and keep her for she'd need all the help she could get marrying into "that lot".

Mrs Spooner in the pew behind wiped a gratified tear from her faded eyes, for what was a wedding without a bit of a cry, she said eloquently to Mrs Totty Roper who could do nothing but sit in mortified silence. Girls were a worry, she was sure Mrs Roper knew that, eyeing Anne, Dorothy and Mae who sat beside their mother, and she only hoped her Betty would do as well though there was fat chance of that!

Towards the back of the church, again on the bridegroom's side, was the be-shawled, be-clogged figure of Fag-end Lil who must be a hundred years old by now, Molly thought, slipping out before the rush to get at her Woodbines.

At once Liam was there, his impish face young and hopeful as it had been when he had given the old woman her whimsical nickname. Patrick, with Daddy behind him, smiling in the hazed shadows to the side of the church, his arms draped about the shoulders of his sons. Molly's eyes flew to Mammy, their thoughts interlocking and one half of the congregation were fascinated, not to say deeply embarrassed, when the lovely bride dropped her husband's arm, picked up her drifting skirts and ran down the two steps to the pew where her mother sat. She drew her into her arms and kissed her soundly and only Róisín heard the words she whispered.

"They're 'ere, Mammy, all three o' them."

"Aye, I know, darlin'."

Wordlessly they stood then, wrapped about together in the love and strength Seamus O'Dowd had bequeathed to them both.

"Go back ter tha' 'usband, child. A woman's place is wi' 'er 'usband," and Molly was forcibly reminded that later when the reception was over and she and Tim were on the overnight sleeper to London, Mammy would lie once more beside the brute who was her husband.

Tim stood quietly and waited for mother and daughter to draw apart, aware of what his new wife was suffering, letting it be known that he thought this behaviour not in the least awkward or unusual, that he was ready, should he be needed, and his wife knew it, to protect them both, and she was comforted.

She turned and, to his, and indeed to the consternation of every member of the congregation, moved in a dignified way vastly at odds with her previous impetuosity, towards her mother-in-law. Smiling, she put her arms about Muriel Broadbent's stiff and furiously embarrassed figure and hugged her. Muriel did not respond.

There were more crowds outside the church, for it was not often a wedding such as this took place in Shaw Street. It was a Saturday afternoon. The mills were closed and everyone from the dozens of narrow streets which radiated out from St Saviours, north to Oldham Edge, east to Edge Lane Road, south as far as Yorkshire Street and west to Tommyfield – which must have been deserted – had come to see one of their own marry Mr Broadbent of Broadbents Mill. It was like a fairy story and she was like a fairy princess, they shouted to her, since they had no inhibitions, not at all put out by the pursed lips, the disapproving frowns on the faces of the gentry. They threw confetti with great enthusiasm, nudging one another and smiling slyly but with great goodwill, on what a lucky beggar the bridegroom was, or would be later that night. They were so thickly congregated Molly and Tim could barely get through to the silver Rolls-Royce which was to take them to Meddins, and Mrs Broadbent senior was heard to remark to her friend Totty Roper, who had had her hat knocked over one eye, that she had never been so humiliated in her life.

The reception was lovely. All those from Sidney Street who had been courageous enough to brave it thought so, as did several of Molly's fellow spinners from the mill whom, with reckless generosity, she had invited to come back to the house for a glass of champagne. They trooped up the gravel driveway, as out of place as sparrows in a cageful of haughty eagles, not caring really, for this was an opportunity of a lifetime to see how the "other half" lived. They stared in open-mouthed wonder at the grandness of the house, filling the hallway and the reception rooms with their noisy admiration, telling one another that they'd never seen owt like it in their lives and Molly O'Dowd had fallen on her feet, no mistake. They had a certain dignity, the dignity of the decent, hardworking, practical northeners they were, even Betty Spooner and Cissie Thompson who had never drunk champagne in their lives and might have made fools of themselves. They had a good laugh afterwards, of course, recounting to one another stories of the airs and graces of the posh guests, the marvel of the indoor lavvy, of which there were three, the fine calves on the footmen who served them something called caviar which they didn't like one bit, pitying poor Molly who was, apparently, to be eating the detestable stuff for the rest of her days. When it was over and they were back in their own environment, they let their hair down as they had not done in front of Molly's new friends, or what they supposed were to be Molly's new friends, poor cow.

It was noticeable to Joel Greenwood, who watched the bride from a secluded corner of the elegant dining room, that not one of his Aunt Muriel's friends spoke to her. They shook hands with her and with Tim, with Muriel Broadbent and with Tessa Addison who were in the receiving line, their faces only becoming animated when they addressed Tim or Muriel, Tessa or Tessa's husband, Hugh, who was one of them.

His cousin's wife of an hour was quite the loveliest creature Joel had ever seen. She appeared to be unaware of the cold, polite looks, the frosted snubs, the general impression of being unaware that she even existed. She was enchanting in her virginal white, though her flushed, poppy cheeks and her vivid greeny blue eyes which reminded Joel of the seas he had seen off the coast of Cornwall, the glossy wings of her slightly dishevelled hair, did not convey the picture one usually associated with a pale and submissive bride who was to be taken very soon to her husband's bed. Her figure was rich and womanly, with high, rounded breasts, a narrow waist which he was sure he could span with his hands, and generously curving hips. She laughed out loud, drawing glances to her, showing her perfectly even white teeth and the tip of her moist pink tongue. She held Tim's hand and leaned on his shoulder, to his mother's obvious disgust, gazing up into his face, shamelessly, you could tell Muriel thought so. She was ready to kiss him right there and then, her attitude said, so much in love with him no one could be in any doubt of it.

And Joel could not get out of his mind that bravely defiant but contrite act of appeasement she had prof-fered to her mother-in-law before her own and Muriel's contemporaries. She had courage, spunk and a generous heart, that much was obvious, but Muriel had spurned her for everyone to see.

Muriel had made a grave mistake, Joel was certain.

As he watched her he would have been considerably startled to know that the new Mrs Tim Broadbent was as conscious of his narrow-eyed attention over the heads and from behind the shoulders of the guests as he was of her.

There was no dancing, no "knees-up", which frequently happened at the weddings of humbler folk. No music, no "sing-song" and, after an hour or two, having had enough of the restrained conviviality which passed for a good time in the gentry's world, the Spooners and the Thompsons, the Haydocks, the O'Dowds and the Todds prepared thankfully to take their leave. The men had been sorry at the absence of real ale since sherry and champagne were not to their taste. Mrs Haydock, finding herself somehow or other in conversation with Molly's new brother-in-law whose accent was so genteel she couldn't tell a word he said, confiding to her husband later that she thought he might be a foreigner, had a slight but quiet attack of hysterics. Rosie Watson, whose Archie, after six months of living cheek by jowl with Maggie's lively grandchildren, had begun to be naughty with boredom, decided she'd best get him home, she told Molly.

"Mammy . . ." Molly's eyes pleaded in one last attempt to persuade her mother to be taken in the Rolls to the house in Huddersfield Road which was still waiting for her.

"No, darlin', don't . . . it's all arranged. Pikey'll be waitin' . . ."

Even now, after all that had happened and despite being the mother-in-law of one of the most influential men in Oldham, it seemed that six years of Pikey Watson's rule could not be swept aside. "The 'ouse 'as bin cleaned, though not as I'd do it . . ." Rosie tried to smile into the stricken face of her daughter.

"Oh, Mammy, please . . ."

"No, Mary Angelina . . . no. But I promise if . . . if 'e turns . . . nasty again, I'll . . ." She bent her head for a moment as her voice broke then lifted it in a faint resemblance of the woman she had once been. "I'll . . . I'll come ter thi'. Now, see, tha' 'usband's waitin' fer thi' an' tha've guests . . ."

Indeed all about the wide hallway Muriel Broadbent's well-bred friends, sipping their champagne and wondering, now that the bride's "party" were leaving, whether things might all get back to normal, tried not to notice that Tim's bride was weeping and that her "Mammy" – dear God! – was doing her best to comfort her, though it was anybody's guess what she was saying, her accent was so broad.

They had gone, all Molly's side of the family, and for the first time in her life she was left without the loving support she had always received from them. Even Aunty Flo would have been welcome, Aunty Flo who once, before the death of her sons, would have made mincemeat of this lot, but even now was fiercely loyal and protective of her own. Sharp-tongued, brusque, ungracious at times, she was generous and open-handed with those she thought deserved it. She had always had a great deal to say about Róisín O'Dowd's madness in marrying Pikey Watson, about the way she brought up her children, at least the children of her first husband, about Molly who had not attended mass as often as Flo thought fitting, but let anyone outside the family criticise and she would jump down their throat to defend those she loved. She would stand beside Molly now against all the furtive, speculative, contemptuous looks which were being directed towards her. Molly knew, and was thankful for it, that she must go and change soon, for she and Tim, to whom she still clung, were to be driven down to the station on the first leg of their journey to Paris but in the meanwhile she must not let these stiff-necked, self-confident members of Lancashire's privileged society see that she was overwhelmed by them. She must find a way to talk to them as she would her own people.

"I think it's time your wife and I were introduced properly, don't you, Tim, lad? We can't count that brief handshake earlier, can we? After all, we are related now and I believe there is a custom at weddings where a gentleman is allowed to kiss the bride."

The slow, deep voice took her by surprise. It came from behind her and when she swung round, relieved that at least one of Tim's relatives was willing to address her, she found herself looking up into the unsmiling face of Tim's cousin. Joel Greenwood, who had been best man and though, as he said, he had bowed over her hand in the receiving line, his dark, stern face had been gone before she got more than a fleeting look at it.

His dark eyes captured hers, as deep and as dark as the waters of the tarn she and Tim had found up on the moors of Saddleworth and she felt her senses drown in them and was suddenly afraid.

Tim put his arm about her, a possessive arm but strong and supportive and she found herself nestling close to him as though she were a child.

His voice was soft with love, and with pride.

"Darling, this is Joel who is my cousin, or second cousin, or third cousin twice removed or something. He and I grew up together and . . . well, since the war we have—"

"Mrs Broadbent," Joel interrupted, with what looked to be a small gleam of humour in his eyes, "your husband is about to get sentimental and remind us of things that are best forgotten. I have heard that bridegrooms get like that on their wedding day so we'll forgive him, shall we? I came over merely to make myself known to you and to claim my cousinly kiss and then I must be on my way."

"Not yet, old lad," Tim protested. "Won't you wait and see us off? You know how these things are. The chaps acting the goat and Molly and I will be in need of some support, won't we, my darling?"

Tim's eyes were on Molly as he spoke, as deeply brown as his cousin's but warm, the warmth of a polished chestnut, filled with his love and with the anticipation of what they would do when they were alone together. The other man saw it, knew what it was, for desire is difficult to hide, and was badly alarmed by his own reaction to it.

"Isn't she absolutely divine, Joel?" Tim was saying, placing a reverent fingertip on Molly's cheek. "Have you ever seen anything quite so lovely?"

"No, I can't say that I have, old man." Joel's voice, like his face, was quite without expression and, Molly thought, if nature had planned it she could not have created two men who were such direct opposites to one another. Both handsome, of course, but one so dark and forbidding, without humour, the other light, finely moulded, open, endearing, his face alive with goodness and joy and love.

"You're a lucky devil," Joel continued, "and how you managed to capture the heart of . . . of such a beauty is a mystery to me." His wide mouth managed a small smile. "I hope you will have a long and happy life together, but now, I really must be off. You know I am an unsocial creature . . ."

"Please stay, Mr Greenwood." They were the first words Mary Angelina Broadbent, as she now was, spoke to Joel Greenwood and his large frame, though it did not move in any way that might be considered unusual, seemed to quiver.

"It's Joel, my darling," Tim laughed. "You can't call him Mr Greenwood. You're related now."

"Aye, tha're right. Joel, won't tha' stay . . . fer Tim's sake an' 'is mammy's . . . mother's," she added hastily, wishing for some strange and unnerving reason that this large, brooding man would take himself off home as he intended.

"Thank you . . . er . . . Mary Angelina. Is that not what the priest called you? Yes, I thought so, but I must be off."

Tim grinned broadly and hugged his wife closer to him. "Joel, old chap, no one calls her Mary Angelina. She's Molly."

"But the priest . . ."

"Well, of course she had to have her full name for the marriage ceremony but . . . well, I christened her Molly many years ago, didn't I, my darling?"

Joel looked startled for a brief moment.

"*You* did?"

"Yes, she was no more than child. We met . . . before the war."

"I had no idea." For some reason not understood nor even acknowledged by themselves, Joel Greenwood and Molly Broadbent had begun to avoid one another's eyes. "I must admit to a . . . a liking for Mary Angelina," he murmured, his voice as cool as the champagne which kept on flowing into every empty glass.

"Yes, so do I but . . . well, it's a long story and one we'll recount to you when you ask us to dine at Greenacres on our return. You do intend to invite us, don't you, Joel? I do believe Molly and I will be in need of some friendly support when we settle in at Meddins. Mother is not yet reconciled to the fact that I have married a girl almost young enough to be my daughter."

"Fiddlesticks, Tim." Molly's voice rose sharply and several heads turned in her direction. "It's got nowt ter do wi' my age or thine an' tha' knows it. If I'd bin fifteen an' tha' fifty she'd've bin made up as long as I'd a pedigree ter match thine. Not that it matters now, nor never did. I mean ter make thi' a good wife, so I do, an' learn ter run this 'ouse as well as tha' mammy does. An' even if tha' mammy can't bear me ter . . . ter touch 'er, ter show me affection which I would if she'd let me, as any normal, warm-blooded woman'd do, then that's 'er loss."

She glared about the spacious room and from the grouped, perfectly turned-out figures of Muriel Broadbent's friends, a dreadful, refined silence flowed. They did their best not to stare, to pretend that Tim's common little wife was not behaving with the atrocious manners one associated with her class and which had been so much in evidence today, but how could one not be dismayed and concerned for the success of this awful mismatch.

"I'm not afeared of 'er, nor them," Molly declared stoutly, and Tim's arm tightened about her, though he did wish she had not chosen this particular moment to confront his mother, his sister, and their family friends with her challenge.

"After livin' wi' Pikey an' 'avin' ter put up wi' 'is bullyin' all these years, this 'ere'll be like bein' in 'eaven, so it will."

The silence that followed was short-lived and it was broken by Joel Greenwood.

"Good for you, Mary Angelina Broadbent," he said, and Molly was bowled over by the warmth and beauty of his wide smile.

When the bride and groom had been sent on their way in the polite but decidedly cool manner the bride's appalling behaviour seemed to have generated and when the rest of the guests had departed for Cheshire and Yorkshire and various points in Lancashire, Hilda Forrester, Helen Herbert, Beattie Knight, Totty Roper, Joan Davidson and Delia Bowman, all Muriel's special friends, settled down in her small, private sitting room and prepared to commiserate with her on her son's choice of wife. Their husbands, as husbands do, waited patiently in the billiard room, wreathed in the smoke from their expensive cigars.

"She's very young, my dear. Perhaps you'll be able to make something of her," Helen offered tentatively. Helen had a kinder heart than the others and had been quite taken with Tim's new wife who had shown remarkable courage in standing up to them all.

"If one could only be sure that all those dreadful relatives will keep away from her there might be some hope, Muriel. She herself is quite . . . presentable."

"Until she opens her mouth, Totty," Muriel said icily.

"I know, but perhaps if a good teacher might be found. To train her to speak properly, I mean."

"Dear Lord, what am I to do? Did you see that appalling little man, her Uncle Alf, I believe she called him." Muriel shuddered delicately. "He . . . he actually scratched his . . . his crotch and I saw him fumble about with his fingers to the back of his mouth to find . . . Oh heavens, what is one to do?" Muriel bowed her head in despair.

"What is to happen with the servants, do you suppose?" Beattie sighed in great sympathy for the trouble of her friend. "As Tim's wife I suppose we can only presume . . . indeed, as she told us," referring to Molly's outburst, "she will expect to run this house."

"Heavens above! Can you picture her giving orders to Forbes and Mrs Ogden?"

"Yes, I can actually, Muriel. You must admit she's not short of nerve and girls like her, you know, those who have come up in the world, won't allow anything or anybody to hold them back. And Tim is so . . . so besotted—"

"It won't last, Delia," Muriel interrupted coldly. "It is a purely physical thing. Anyone can see that. The thought of my poor boy at the mercy of that . . . that gold-digger, I believe they call them, that common little trollop, breaks my heart and I will never, never hand over my position as mistress of Meddins to her, that I promise."

"Won't Tim have something to say about that, dear?"

"Oh, no, not Tim. You know how good-hearted he is. He will not see me ousted by that . . . trash."

"Muriel, she is his wife," Helen said gently.

"Helen, can you see her arranging and then presiding at a dinner party?"

"No, not yet, but – with help – I think she might surprise us all."

"Helen Herbert, how can you? I thought you were my friend."

"Darling, I am, but you must not underestimate that young woman. She has captured your Tim despite all the pretty and suitable young ladies who were paraded before him, including my Angela, and I'm sorry about it but there are things that cannot be changed and this is one of them. My advice to you is to make the best of it and accept—"

"Never! *Never*! She will be unwelcome at Meddins until the end of her days."

Several miles away stood a grand old house by the name of Greenacres. It had been lived in by Chapmans and when the daughter of the house married, by Greenwoods, for well over a hundred years. Now there was only Joel Greenwood and, until he took a wife, he lived the life of a bachelor there, not caring what his servants did as long as he was warm, comfortable, his shirts immaculately ironed, his suits immaculately pressed and splendidly cooked meals were on his table when he came home from the mill, no matter what time of the day or night that might be. He paid well for this service.

His cook, Mrs Hebden, was mortified when he sent his dinner back untouched, the first time he had ever done so since she had started work at Greenacres in 1905.

"What's up wi' 'im?" she demanded of Lily, the parlourmaid, as though, whatever it was, Lily was to blame.

"Nay, I don't know. 'Appen he et summat at Meddins what upset 'im."

"Never! Mrs Ogden's as particular as me about what she serves."

"Then I can't say, Mrs 'Ebden. 'E's just sat at winder smokin' them Woodbines of 'is starin' out inter't garden, though 'e can see nowt in't dark."

"Eeh, I 'ope 'e's not sickening fer summat."

"Nay, not 'im. Never ailed a day in 'is life, 'im."

The man they were discussing stood up with such violence the small rough-haired terrier dozing at his feet sprang up, hackles rising, ready to snarl, thinking he and his master were being attacked. He glared about him, then, seeing nothing unusual, leaned adoringly against the man's leg. A hand came down to scratch behind his ear and he stretched ecstatically.

The man sighed. "What's to be done, eeh, Woody?" he asked the animal, then, in a whisper he spoke her name. "Mary Angelina . . ."

Somewhere between Oldham and Northampton Tim Broadbent made Mary Angelina truly his wife. As he said, laughing and puffing and pulling the most extraordinary faces his wife had ever seen, there was not much room in the berth but she must agree it was better than the Vauxhall where they had almost consummated their love. The mad rocking of the train did nothing to interfere with his endeavours. He was loving and tender, his embrace retaining a certain wondering quality that spoke of his intense emotion, his hands and mouth paying great attention to all areas of her willing body. There was no pain, merely a moment of discomfort, then a long shuddering cry of what seemed like despair before Tim collapsed on top of her. She had been stirred to warm anticipation by his caresses as she had several times before, but her body was puzzled by a strange sense of disappointment as though it asked, was this all there was to this act by which men set such store?

Nevertheless she gathered him to her in what she, and he, failed to recognise as a maternal gesture, kissing his rumpled hair, smoothing his cheek and forehead with a loving hand, holding his head to her full breast.

"I love you, Molly," he murmured, more than half asleep.

"I love you, Tim," she answered him, knowing it was true, then was startled when Joel Greenwood's face smiled sardonically against her closed eyelids.

18

Molly Broadbent's doting husband bought her her own little motor car several weeks after they returned from France despite the fact that there were already four in the garage at the back of Meddins.

"I could drive one o' them, Tim," she protested, pointing to them, since her upbringing in a household which had never had much cash to spare had made her thrifty. The O'Dowds had not starved but they were careful, watchful of every penny and Tim's open-handed and casual flinging about of good brass was an amazement to her.

"No, you couldn't, my darling. The Singer is over ten years old and the Bullnose is not suitable for a lady. No, I think an Austin Seven will do admirably to start with."

"To start with! Am I ter 'ave a fleet o' the things then, like you? Anyroad, I can't even drive yet."

"Molly, driving is the easiest thing in the world to learn, isn't it, Herbert?" he said to the groom-cum-chauffeur who drove the senior Mrs Broadbent wherever she wished to go in her Silver Ghost Rolls-Royce. "And the Austin is just right for you. 'The Motor for the Millions' they're calling it but there's a special edition which I fancy you'll like. The Swallow, it's called, and we'll have you zipping about the grounds within a day and by the weekend you'll be driving to your mother's or Aunty Flo's and begging them to come for a spin with you. It's as easy as falling off a log."

"Aunty Flo! In one o' them things! Tha're jokin'."

"No, she'll love it, and so will you. I taught Herbert here in no time at all and he can vouch for how easy it is, can't you, Herbert? Go on, tell her," he ordered the groom, at the same time reaching forward to kiss his beautiful young wife on her parted lips. She had the grace to laugh blushingly and push him away, telling him to behave himself, that he would embarrass poor Herbert, but Tim didn't seem to care. The servants had become used to it, even after only four weeks of marriage and they were all learning to look away patiently and wait for him to get back to whatever it was he was about before his new wife's hair, or mouth, or hand, or neck caught his attention. Devoted to her, he was. Couldn't keep his hands off her and Atkinson, the footman, had reported that madam, meaning old Mrs Broadbent, had threatened to take her meals in her room if Tim could not confine his "activities", that was the word she used, to the bedroom. Not that he ever did anything . . . offensive, for he'd been brought up a gentleman, but it seemed he just could not stop displaying his affection for his wife, even in public.

They had come from the stables where, after an invigorating gallop through the woodland which surrounded Meddins and out into the fields and lanes, they had just unsaddled Isolde and Major. Molly had taken to horseback riding with great enthusiasm. She had an easy, erect carriage and though she was not yet ready for riding out with the Hollins Hunt where jumps were involved, Tim told her, she was progressing well. She loved her pretty little mare and was only sorry that since, as she had hoped, Mammy had not gone to live in Huddersfield Road, she could not ride over there and show her off. There were a lot of things she might have done if Mammy had not gone back to Pikey, she often thought bitterly.

Things were not good at Meddins since Mr Tim had married, they all sadly agreed. It was like a bloody battlefield at times, Mrs Ogden reported tearfully, and her not one given to swearing. The trouble was the servants were used to taking their orders from old Mrs Broadbent and the first time young Mrs Broadbent had gone against her it had caused such an upheaval, Mr Tim had had one of his funny "turns".

It seemed that young Mrs Broadbent had made up her mind that she did not care for the bedroom at the back of the house where old Mrs Broadbent had put her in with the master. It was dark and rather small for two people, she said politely enough and, without putting anyone to too much trouble and since no one else was occupying it, she thought she and Tim would be far more comfortable in the big bedroom at the corner of the house. The bedroom with two windows, one overlooking the lake, the other part of the flower garden. Since she had not been invited by Tim's mother to look over Meddins and choose her own room before her marriage, she added, cool as a cucumber, she felt this was not an impossible request.

"Do you not . . .?" Muriel had been about to address her daughter-in-law by the title she had used before Tim had married her but even she could see that "Miss . . . er . . ." would be out of place now so she called her nothing, since as far as Muriel was concerned she was nothing.

"Is there some reason why me an' Tim can't 'ave it, Mrs Broadbent?" Molly continued, noticing the way her mother-in-law winced as she spoke. She did her best to speak in the polite and careful way she was slowly learning from Tim, though sometimes it was bloody hard just to keep her temper, never mind being polite and careful.

"It's a guest bedroom. It always has been." That was the end of the matter as far as Muriel was concerned and she returned to the letters she had been writing before Molly so rudely interrupted her.

"Then, sure we'll not be disturbin' anyone, will we?" Molly said cheerfully. "I'll get one o't maids ter give me a hand. Happen it'll need airin' and I were . . . was . . . thinkin', the room next to it, a dressin' room, Tim said it was . . ."

"Have you been prying about this house without my permission, miss?" Muriel was clearly scandalised. Her face turned an alarming shade of puce and though she was long past that stage in a woman's life when such things happen, she felt the hot tide of blood flood her body.

"What's wrong wi' that?" Molly asked, clearly puzzled. "I live 'ere, don't I?"

"Indeed you do, girl, more's the pity, but may I remind you that I am mistress here and that it is not only ill-mannered, but incomprehensible to me that anyone would wander about someone else's home without being invited."

"That's just it, yer not."

"I beg your pardon?"

"Tim's bin explaining it ter me. Tha're not mistress now." Molly could feel the irritation begin to ruffle her skin and she narrowed her brilliant eyes, a warning signal her mother would have at once recognised. "When the master of the 'ouse gets married, *his* wife is mistress. Now I'm not suggestin' I should do what tha' does 'cos I don't 'onestly think I could, not yet.

Not until I've found me way round and learned t'ropes, like. Until then, if tha're willin', I'd appreciate it if tha'—"

"You little upstart." Muriel's voice was icy. "How dare you speak to me like that. You will allow me to run my own home, is that what you were about to say, but only until you are qualified to take over. Well, let me say this. It takes a lady, a lady born and bred to it, to be mistress of a house such as this and you will never be one of those. Oh, you dress well and conduct yourself soberly enough. You are an . . . an attractive woman and my son can't leave you alone for more than five minutes," sneering, "but you will never qualify to be mistress here. Not until I'm dead and even then . . ."

"Tha're a daft old woman, so tha' are," Molly heard herself say through clenched teeth, horrified by her own rudeness, you could call it nothing else, for Mrs Broadbent was really only defending what she thought of as her own position. She was doing her utmost not to fall into one of her hot-tempered rages, for she knew it would upset Tim when he got home from the mill where he had been summoned to sign some papers, the only active part he seemed to take in its running.

"How dare you . . ."

"Tha've said that once, mother-in-law, an' yes, I dare. Tim ses it's all right so I'm off ter't kitchen ter fetch Agnes and Flora who, I was told, are housemaids. Tha' see, I'ave learned summat . . . something since I came ter live at Meddins, an' I'll tell 'em they're ter turn out that there spare bedroom an' move mine an' Tim's stuff into it an' when Tim comes 'ome I'm gonner ask 'im if we can't 'ave next door medd inter our own bathroom."

"A bathroom! I suspect you never used one until you married my son. Now you're blithely talking about . . ."

"Aye, a door knocked through an' . . ."

"No . . . no, never."

"Tell me 'ow tha' can stop me, Mrs Broadbent? 'Ave me chucked out?"

"You insolent baggage . . ."

"Be careful or tha' might say summat tha' might regret. One o' these days me an' Tim'll 'ave a child an' when we do tha'll be sorry tha' got on't wrong side o' me."

Molly softened suddenly. She didn't want to be for ever fighting with this gritty old lady, upsetting her, tearing her well-ordered world apart but Muriel Broadbent must be made to accept that Molly was Tim's wife. That Molly's children would one day romp and play about the house and gardens, as once Muriel's had done.

"Don't let's fight, Mrs Broadbent," she said gently. "Can we not be friends? We're . . . poles apart, I know that, but we both love Tim an' want—"

"Don't talk to me about Tim and love in the same breath, miss. Love has nothing to do with what he . . . he wants from you and it's not Tim you love but his money, this house. The standing you hope to have."

"No."

"Oh, yes, but I'll fight you every step of the way. Tim is my son. His children will be my grandchildren but you are nothing to me and never will be."

Molly shook her head as though it were full of buzzing bees. She didn't want to say such dreadful things to her mother-in-law since it was not in her nature to be unkind or harsh. She had been brought up to respect the elderly, to allow them their small idiosyncracies – and who had more than Aunty Flo? – but this was just too much. Like a spitting, furious cat she could feel it rising in her, that state known as "mad as Mick O'Dowd" and now she let it go, not caring what was said or who heard it.

"Yer stupid old woman. 'Ave thi' any idea what I mean ter Tim, 'ave thi'? If I was ter say the word tha'd be outer 'ere quicker than that bloody racehorse 'e's got in't stables. 'E's mad fer me an' I could do owt I liked if I set me mind to it. Knock this 'ouse inter any shape I liked."

"Don't be ridiculous, girl."

"An' that's another thing. If yer keep on callin' me 'girl' an' 'miss' I'm gonner get really mad an' when I'm mad I lose control an' God only knows what might be said or . . ."

Muriel reached for the bell, not sure what she meant to do when Forbes arrived but determined she would not put up with this . . . this termagant for a moment longer. Not in her own house. Not in her own drawing room. She had taken just about as much as she could of the degrading manners this girl displayed and, as she would any ill-bred person who invaded her house, she would have her removed at once.

"When are thi' goin' ter realise I'm Tim's wife?" Molly panted. "Tim's *wife*, fer God's sake, an' if I took it inter me 'ead I could 'ave the very bed tha' sleep in. Tha've no idea, 'ave thi'?"

Forbes opened the door but neither of them noticed him. He was so dumbfounded he failed to close it behind him and for five minutes the horrified servants were treated to the sound of the two Mrs Broadbents going at each other hammer-and-tongs and it was not until Mr Tim returned to find his wife and his mother almost at blows and, at the sight of it, fell heavily into the deep sofa, that they stopped shouting. Well, young madam was shouting, old madam hissing like a snake, arguing even then over who was to see to him.

The next time was even worse and for weeks afterwards the servants talked about it in whispers. Young Mrs Broadbent, after a canter along the back pasture and round to the front of the house to the lake, then back to the stables, had wandered from the stable yard through the arched doorway and into the back yard where the laundry maid hung the washing.

Tim had again been called to the mill office, this time over some nonsense to do with cash which had been overdrawn from some account, but he would not be long, he had told her, kissing her with that urgent passion she aroused in him, pulling her shirt from her breeches and taking her breasts one to each hand. He began to breathe heavily, drawing down her doeskin jodhpurs and gripping her naked buttocks, pulling her even closer to him.

"Tim, have we time?" she gasped as he hurriedly began to undo his own clothing.

"We've always time for this, my love," he murmured hoarsely, picking her up and laying her on the bed where he proceeded to prove it was true.

Now, after her canter, she was relaxed and dreaming, her thoughts still dwelling on that moment. The kitchen door was open and from it came the sound of laughter. It drew Molly towards it and she realised that since she had married Tim there had been little laughter in her life. Of course, she and her husband giggled and fooled about in their new bedroom, love play that always led to love-making, but she had never once had a good laugh, the sort she and Betty and Cissie had enjoyed. Women's laughter, sometimes a bit coarse, saying the sort of things they would not say before a man.

She stepped inside and at once all sound and movement stopped.

"Oh, tekk no notice o' me," she said, smiling at Kitty who was the scullery maid and the youngest. Kitty, knowing no better, smiled back but Mrs Ogden's face was quite blank, offended even.

"Can we help you, madam?" she asked politely. "If you're lost that there door leads through to't hallway," pointing to the far corner where a green baize door was a barrier between the servants' world and hers. "Perhaps Agnes could fetch you some coffee?"

"No, ta, Mrs Ogden. I think I'll just 'ave a scen round't kitchen if that's all right wi' thi'?"

Well, how could it be anything but "all right" with Mrs Ogden who was nearly sixty-five years old and did not fancy, should she get on the wrong side of the new mistress of Meddins, looking for another job at her age. Not that that was likely, but Mrs Tim would one day have a say in things so best be discreet. You never knew with a new, young mistress how she was going to be and this one had already crossed swords with old Mrs Broadbent over the bedroom. Got her own way an' all. The builder was coming in on Monday to look at the transforming of the dressing room next to her and the master's bedroom into a bathroom. Mind you, you could see why the master was so taken with her. Beautiful she was, in a rich, ripe way, her figure all curves but with no fat on her, smiling and friendly too, with a skin on her like peach bloom and eyes as green as the velvet lawns of Meddins. Or at least they were today. Mrs Ogden had seen them when the light seemed to turn them to a brilliant turquoise blue, like those of the cat which stalked the stables, but they were always bright, always vivid, alert, curious, as though they reflected the sharpness of their new mistress's mind. Her hair was tossed about like living waves of dark silk and she fascinated them all, there was no doubt about it, but she'd no right to be in Mrs Ogden's kitchen. Mrs Ogden, who took her orders from old Mrs Broadbent and no one else.

"Well, we're a bit busy at the minnit, madam, gettin' ready for dinner."

A real mistress, a real lady brought up to such niceties would have understood at once. In fact she would not have been there in the first place but would have summoned Mrs Ogden to her sitting room if she needed to speak to her. Things were different now, of course, since the war, with girls who had once been glad to be in service, for it had been the only employment open to them, doing all manner of things in what had once been solely a man's province. It was hard to get decent girls and when you did they demanded this and that and the other and as Mrs Ogden remarked on a daily basis to Parsons, she didn't know what the world was coming to. Thank heavens she still had most of her old servants, those who had been with her for years, elderly and trained in the old ways. Atkinson, the footman, had been one of Mr Tim's soldiers, wounded somewhere in France. With a serious leg injury which caused him to limp, he had been overjoyed to be offered the post. Kitty, only sixteen, was the daughter of Jack Hailey from the home farm, a bit "slow", not employable anywhere but in the scullery but a good little worker none the less.

Forbes and Atkinson were in the small butler's pantry off the kitchen. Forbes, who was, of course, in charge of Mr Tim's wine cellar, had just brought up a fine bottle of claret which he was about to uncork and allow to breathe in readiness for dinner in a couple of hours' time. The crystal decanter upon which Atkinson was bestowing a last meticulous polish with a soft cloth scintillated in his hand, but both men froze, staring at Mrs Tim, as they called her, at least among themselves in order to differentiate between her and the master's mother, with open mouths.

She wore the pale buff breeches that had been made for her before her marriage from the finest doeskin. They clung to every curve and crevice of her lower body, to the flatness of her belly and the long shapeliness of her legs. Her boots, again handmade, were polished to a glassy shine only that morning by Billy, the boot boy, though there was what looked like mud and manure clinging to them and Mrs Ogden frowned disapprovingly. She had on a warm tweed jacket and a red woollen scarf twined about her neck, kid riding gloves and carried a small crop. If it had not been for the man's cap, somewhat old and faded, which she slapped against her leg, Mrs Ogden confided to Parsons later, you'd have thought she'd come from some great family and not the teeming streets of industrial Oldham, her background of Irish-Lancashire working-class culture completely eradicated by her superb appearance.

Polly had been chopping vegetables and, with a stern look from Mrs Ogden, she returned to them, at the same time doing her best to keep her eye on the strolling figure of Mrs Tim.

Agnes and Flora were checking the table mats, the silver, the crystal goblets, the candlesticks which they had just buffed up to a fine glow, the bowls of flowers all of which, by now, Molly was aware would provide the exquisite setting for the evening meal she and Tim would share with his mother. After several weeks of living at Meddins she knew the routine. Dressing for dinner, drinking sherry in the drawing room until Forbes came to announce dinner was served. Mrs Broadbent, as the senior lady, would take her son's arm and would be led into the dining room and seated while Molly trailed behind and had to make do with Forbes's ministrations. It was a performance she thought of as maddening and – if she had known the word – pretentious. A waste of time and effort which could be better spent in a nice cosy family dinner in the breakfast room but this was Tim's way of life and she must learn to share it with him. Do what he and his people did. At dinner Muriel did her best to cut Molly out of the conversation completely by chatting about Helen and Percy, Maurice and Beattie, of Katherine Forrester who had gone up to London to train as a nurse and had Tim heard from that charming friend of his who had dined with them . . . Rupert Lucas, that was the one. What a gentleman he had been and what a splendid evening . . .

Always Tim gently and courageously led the conversation back to Molly, asking her about her mother, about Aunty Maggie and Aunty Flo, earning his own mother's disapproval. Was Clare doing well at school now that she lived on a permanent basis with Aunty Flo and Kathleen? remembering the names of all Molly's relatives. Was Molly looking forward to her new motor which would arrive by the weekend and would she like to go with him to the "meet" on Saturday? Not to go out with the hunt, of course, but to see what took place. Be introduced to some of his friends, perhaps walk with some of the ladies who did not ride, over part of the countryside.

When Molly answered Muriel fell silent, aloof, attending to the food in front of her as though she were alone, looking at no one, ladylike, haughty, just as though she were overhearing the conversation of a servant and one in which she had no concern, or interest.

But now Molly felt quite at home. "What are thi' makin' fer dinner ternight, Mrs Ogden?" she asked the cook. "It smells right good."

All those in the kitchen turned to Mrs Ogden, their faces amazed, their mouths and eyes round with wonder as to what the cook, who had never been visited by her mistress in all her years of service, would do.

"Carrot and stilton soup, madam," Mrs Ogden replied through stiff lips, "followed by pheasant."

"Pheasant? I don't think I've ever et pheasant."

"Really, madam."

"Where does it come from?"

There was a strained silence.

"Mr Joel sent it over. He shot it."

"Mr Greenwood . . . shot it!"

"Yes, madam."

"Jesus, Mary an' Joseph, sure an' I don't know whether I like the sound o' that."

"No, madam?" Mrs Ogden stared somewhere over Molly's shoulder, her eyes a mite glazed.

"'Ave . . . have yer ever tried rag puddings, Mrs Ogden? Me mammy used ter mekk 'em. Yer . . . you put in raw minced beef, onion, parsley, herbs, then top it wi' a suet crust. Yer mix it together before crust goes on, o' course, wrap it in a damp cloth, tie it up an' boil it fer two to two an' a half hours. Mind, yer've ter keep fillin' it up wi' boilin' water or it'll boil dry. Served with taters . . . potatoes an' a good thick gravy it mekks a right good dinner. Sticks ter tha' sides on a cold day."

Mrs Ogden blinked. As a matter of fact she had cooked rag pudding many and many a time before she went into service. It was a popular Lancashire dish, one eaten by the lower classes, since it was cheap, nourishing and tasty but it was not a dish she had made for the Broadbent table.

For a moment her stiff face melted, for this girl had a lovely natural way with her. Forthright and without "side", which was a condition detested by northeners. She talked to whoever she fancied talking to and said whatever came into her mind without considering the wide gulf between mistress and servant. But it wouldn't do. Next thing she'd be chatting to the housemaids as they went about their work, treating them as though they were friends almost, and when madam heard that Mr Tim's wife had been down here poking her nose where it shouldn't go, there'd be ructions.

"I'd best get on, madam," Mrs Ogden said woodenly. "Polly,

them veg should be chopped by now and bring me that pan from the shelf, Kitty. I'll need stilton from't larder an' a pint of cream . . ."

Molly took no offence. It was like being back home in the kitchen in Sidney Street with Mammy swirling round and about as she concocted one of her wholesome dishes. The smell was lovely and, without thinking, she reached for the big brown teapot in which the servants made their tea.

"Is there one in't pot?" she asked affably and, finding there was, poured herself a cup, adding sugar and milk from the bowl and jug on the table. She flung herself down in what was Mrs Ogden's own special chair with a sigh of sheer content, for she was among her own here, placed her booted feet on the fender and began to sip her tea.

Forbes put on his jacket and left the kitchen. Three minutes later he was back. He stood before her, his face impassive and in the cool tone he saved for those he considered inferior to himself, told her that madam would be glad of a moment with her in the drawing room.

"Rightio, I'll just finish me tea," she answered airily, but they could all tell she knew exactly what she was in for. She'd done it again. She'd displeased the mistress and her a bride of only a few weeks and how were they all to get through it, their exchanged glances asked, for neither of these two strong-willed women was prepared to give way to the other. The mistress was of the old school, and so were they really, trained to believe there should be no intercourse between master and servant, except that of master and servant. Old Mrs Broadbent was mistress, had been mistress for over thirty years and would be hard to dislodge, by anyone, even one of her own class, and this one, the one sipping her tea with such apparent unconcern, was not fit to govern this household, not trained for it, not brought up in the ways of the gentry. And madam was not about to help her achieve that position, not if she was put to the torture!

Molly stood up and smiled. She straightened her back, squared her shoulders and lifted her dark head. She caught the admiring glance of the scullery maid and winked, then strode towards the door which led to the hallway.

"Good afternoon to you all," she sang out, "an' by't way, Mrs Ogden . . ."

"Yes, madam."

"Per'aps one day tha'll make rag pudding fer me an' me husband. I reckon he'd like it."

"I reckon you're right, madam," Mrs Ogden replied, amazingly.

Her voice rose higher and higher and louder and louder as the next hour progressed. They could not hear madam's voice, naturally, since she never raised it, but they could imagine the cutting phrases, the icy contempt, the imperious words with which their old mistress tried to rope and break their master's young wife. Mind you, the new one gave as good as she got, by the sound of it, probably telling the old lady that if she and her husband fancied rag pudding and Mrs Ogden was able and willing to cook it, then rag pudding they would have and if Mrs Broadbent didn't like it then she could eat in her room as she was always threatening to do. She would not be changed, they heard her shriek. Tim loved her as she was and if Tim was happy then the rest of them, meaning Mrs Broadbent and her friends, none of whom had yet invited her to their homes though madam dined out a couple of times a week, then they could go to the devil for all she cared.

But she did care. She wanted Tim not only to love her and possess her every morning and every night in their bed, but to be proud of her. Oh, he was that now. When they dined out at restaurants, or went to some public function in Manchester or Oldham, he was made up with the admiration and envy he saw in other men's eyes but it was the women, the ladies, their wives, she wanted to impress, to please, to befriend her and she longed to prove that she could do exactly what they did, given half the chance. She was doing her best to gentrify her speech to please Tim, though it was a damned hard task, and to please herself as well, since she had come to realise how coarse hers had been, but she absolutely refused to change herself, to change the Molly O'Dowd her daddy had shaped, into a false replica of Muriel Broadbent and her friends.

They made love that night and almost, *almost* Tim brought her to the edge of that shimmering precipice which something told her would be electrifying if she tipped over it. The feelings shivered from between her thighs down every nerve to her toes and up every nerve through her stomach to her breasts until she thought she would stop breathing but somehow it eluded her, skimming away and shrivelling to nothing as her husband cried her name out loud and collapsed on top of her.

She was almost asleep, a bit restless as Tim's love-making seemed to leave her, when he spoke drowsily in the curve of her shoulder.

"Darling . . ."

"Mmm . . .?"

"I believe you and Mother had a spat today while I was at the bank."

"I suppose she told you all about it."

"Well, she was a bit upset. If you could just be a little patient . . ."

"*She* was upset. Jesus God, will she never let me do what I want to do in her precious house?" Molly sat up abruptly, pushing Tim to one side, then sprang from the bed, striding about in great agitation, her long, lovely body gleaming like rosy pearl in the dancing flames of the firelight. "I only went into't bloody kitchen fer a minute an' 'ad a bit of a chat with Mrs Ogden."

"And a cup of tea."

"That bloody Forbes. 'E does nowt but slink about spyin' an' tellin' tales. And if I did 'ave a cup o' tea, what's wrong with that?"

"Sweetheart, they are servants and you are . . ."

"Yes . . . yes?" She stopped pacing and glared at him.

"Their mistress and as such . . ."

"You see . . . you see!" she shouted in triumph. "You accept it. I am their mistress, mistress of Meddins, and the sooner your sainted mother realises it the better. Besides, all this arguin' an' carryin' on's no good fer me. A woman in my condition shouldn't be crossed!"

19

Molly went up to Sidney Street almost every day, choosing a time, of course, when she knew Pikey would be out. She had shown Mammy how to use the telephone at the end of the street, since she knew she was hoping for miracles if she expected her mother to allow her to have one installed at number twenty-two. Besides, if Mammy consented to it, Pikey would probably wreck it or hit Mammy with it out of spite. So, instead, Rosie would run to the end of the street to the telephone kiosk on the corner, ask for the number at Meddins and within ten minutes Molly would be on the doorstep. They would kiss and hug and smile and Molly would wave to Herbert who ran her over to Sidney Street in the Bullnose – not even Molly had the nerve to risk asking to use the Rolls yet – and tell him to pick her up in an hour's time.

Sometimes when he was home and not riding to hounds, or enjoying one or other of the odd pursuits Molly had discovered gentlemen of his class got up to, Tim would take her in the Vauxhall, going inside with her for a cup of tea and a chat, bestowing on his mother-in-law one of his amiable hugs, and Molly was often almost brought to tears by the difference between her husband who was so warm and funny with everyone, no matter what their station in life, and his mother who wasn't.

Mammy adored him. She would glow and come to life as she had not done since Daddy died and Molly was aware that she thanked the Blessed Virgin every day for the gift of Molly's happiness and security with Tim Broadbent.

Pikey, it seemed, was on his best behaviour, Mammy reported, and had not once raised his hand to her and the kids, though it had seemed only sensible to leave Clare at Aunty Flo's where she was flourishing. Eileen, Grace and Archie would be there, of course, though Eileen would be starting school soon. They were no longer the noisy tearaways Molly had heard they were at Aunty Maggie's but then they had not again become the terrorised little creatures they had been last year. Pikey ignored them, Mammy said. Pikey was well aware that Molly visited regularly and sometimes her husband, too. Her husband counted for something in Oldham, Molly made sure he knew of that and of her own immediate availability should he threaten her mother with violence. Mrs Haydock next door, being, in her opinion, an old hand at the telephone now, something she allowed no one to forget, would be up the street at the double, she asserted stoutly, if Pikey got up to his old tricks and had Molly's telephone number propped up behind the clock on the mantelpiece in case of emergencies.

When Molly got her own little motor car, which Tim had had sprayed in the scarlet he loved so well since it must match the others, he said whimsically, she would pack Mammy in beside her and the children in the back and whirl them up to Aunty Flo's or Aunty Maggie's, delighting in their half-frightened, half-enchanted expressions as they gasped and clutched at one another during the drive. She was a "nippy" driver and Tim was always begging her to go more slowly, half sorry, now that she was pregnant, that he had allowed her the vehicle at all.

"Tha' shouldn't be sittin' in the thing, let alone drivin' it," Aunty Flo declared. "God knows what them vibrations'll do ter that poor babby an' I'm surprised that 'usband o' thine allows it. It'll come out all funny, I shouldn't wonder, poor little soul. See, come inside an' fetch them childer. Kettle's on an' Clare's medd us a bit o' parkin, 'aven't tha', chuck?" indicating fondly the bright and lovely child whose dramatically changed appearance and manner she took full credit for, which was only right, Molly and Rosie both agreed. She was still thin as a stick but she'd lost that look of a hunted animal and though pale it was the delicate paleness which has nothing to do with ill-health. She stood to the side of Aunty Flo's immaculately white table, "her" parkin on a fancy doiley, Aunty Flo's best china and teapot set out before her, even paper napkins folded in a neat row, her passion for order and cleanliness clearly satisfied.

Every surface, horizontal and vertical of Aunty Flo's parlour was polished until you could see your face in it. In fact Daddy had remarked on one occasion, before Uncle Fergus died and they used to go regularly, it fair put him off his tea to see his own face grinning back at him everywhere he looked. He was sure that even Uncle Fergus got a polish and a shine to show him off at his best before visitors arrived.

There wasn't a thing out of place from the snowy chair backs and arm covers which were washed and ironed every week, to the glossy leaves of the aspidistra, the stems of which were arranged by Aunty Flo and didn't dare move from the position they were placed in, Daddy joked. Her nets were like driven snow and woe betide the speck of dust which had the temerity to alight again when Aunty Flo had "bottomed".

Clare herself was just as flawless in a pretty, frilled lawn dress, a pale and flattering blue which was her best and which Molly had bought her, as she bought most of the children's clothes now, from the generous allowance Tim gave her.

"Tha' pour, our Clare," Aunty Flo told her, smiling and nodding and though it almost broke Molly's heart to watch the way Mammy was doing her best not to let them see her own anguish since this was Seamus's child whom Pikey had forced out of her own home, she knew that deep down Mammy was glad to see her younger daughter as well set up as her eldest.

Clare did it beautifully, her manner sweet and hesitant, looking constantly at Aunty Flo for encouragement which was freely given.

At the last moment she clung to her mammy as though she knew she was hurting and she was sorry about it but both of them knew, though nothing had ever been said about Pikey, that she could never live at twenty-two Sidney Street again.

"Now next time I'm sendin' t'Rolls ter fetch lot o' thi' to 'ave tea wi' me. Aunty Maggie an' all," Molly announced as she hugged Aunty Flo's stiffly corseted figure. "Now that I'm in't family way I reckon the old besom'll see 'er way ter lettin' me do what I like, within reason, o' course."

"Eeh, our Molly, dost tha' think tha' should?" Mammy wrung her hands and stared pleadingly into her daughter's face. Molly looked so lovely in her good, warm, three-quarter-length coat which had a deep fur collar and cuffs. It was a rich shade of chestnut brown, the fur a pale coffee colour and Molly looked a picture. Her hat was fur as well to match that on her coat, pulled well down over her eyebrows, from beneath which her rosy face beamed.

"Oh, don't worry, Mammy, 'er ladyship'll not be there. She'll mekk sure she's out callin' on 'er friends when I tell 'er I've callers of me own. But don't fetch little 'uns, ay, not just yet. There's ter be a nursery suite on't top floor, well, it's already there but I want it decoratin' ter suit me an' when it's ready I'll put some toys in an' kids can mekk as much row as they want up there."

They listened to Molly talk so confidently of what she intended to do at Meddins, their faces bemused with it, overcome with the novelty of it. Not that their Molly was boasting or anything like that, for it was not her way, but she took it all so much for granted as though she had been born to it. A whole top floor to be made into a suite of rooms for one baby, could you credit it? They certainly couldn't.

Muriel Broadbent, though she certainly could not have been said to thaw towards her daughter-in-law at her son's news that she was to be a grandmother – that was how she described the coming birth – and so soon, was less inclined to treat her as though she were as noticeable as a chair or a table, and definitely not as useful. She managed to nod stiffly whenever they met and to ask after her health. She must see Doctor Taylor regularly and use the Rolls whenever she needed to go anywhere, she told her coolly, since she was sure she no longer intended dashing about in that dreadful little car Tim had bought her.

"I'd certainly be glad of't big car, Mrs Broadbent, but not fer meself." She smiled winningly. "I'm only just two months gone an' can still drive t' Swallow. It's ter fetch Mammy an' me aunties ter see me. Tha' don't mind, do tha'? It's a bit of a walk fer them at their age."

Tim glanced warily from his wife to his mother, hoping this was not going to turn out to be one of those sharp contests of will which could spring up so easily between them. He had thought that now, with Molly carrying his mother's grandchild, they might be easier with one another, but Molly seemed all the more determined not to allow his mother to dominate her.

Muriel winced, casting a warning look in Atkinson's direction where he stood by the serving table. Muriel took her breakfast in her bedroom, but now and again she and Molly and Tim met at the luncheon table and she was often mortified, and at the dinner table too, when the "girl" came out with the most inappropriate remarks. To talk of her pregnancy in front of a manservant, not to mention her awful family intending to visit, was just too much and must be stopped at once.

But then Muriel could not quite forget that awful day when her daughter-in-law had spoken of a child, children, and the threat that had been implied. Not that Tim would allow his mother to be kept from her grandson and would probably be only too relieved to let her oversee his upbringing, since this creature would have no idea how to go about it. Still, best be careful for the time being.

"Very well, providing I myself am not requiring it."

"Of course, thank you."

The visit to Meddins by Mammy, Aunty Flo, Aunty Maggie, Clare and Kathleen – on a Saturday afternoon when Kathleen was not at work since she did not want to miss a chance to get a good look at how the privileged classes lived – was not a success. The trouble was, they were overwhelmed by the grandness of it all. The lofty elegance of the drawing room with its pale, soft-piled carpet, the lovely silk-covered walls, the deep sofas of rose-beige and cream which would show every mark, Aunty Flo's pursed lips said, were too much for them. The portraits of past Broadbents on the walls, one of a beautiful dark-haired lady with a bold laughing face who put Aunty Flo in mind of Molly, she said. She wore a vivid amethyst-coloured gown with a vast crinoline and a low neckline which revealed more than was decent of her breasts. The masses of flowers in a dozen vases and bowls, the mirror-like piano, the score of scattered ornaments so delicate they were afraid even to glance in their direction and the silver-framed photographs of three small boys and a pretty girl. They had seen them before, of course, on Molly's wedding day but then there had been a multitude of smart and intimidating guests crowding the room, which had discouraged them from even looking up from the strange and wonderful food and drink which had been pressed into their hands.

Now they gaped about them, plain decent folk dressed in plain decent hats and coats and sensible shoes, their best, of course, and wondered how their Molly coped with it all. Of course, she'd always been a bit different to them, made so by Seamus O'Dowd who had led her to believe she was a princess, a confident child who had feared no one and had her nature not been so sweet and warm she'd have been a little madam!

"Isn't it lovely, Mammy?" she murmured, hugging her little mother to her, leading in the hesitant, careful figures of Aunty Flo and Aunty Maggie, who acted as though Her Majesty the Queen was about to be ushered in to take tea with them.

"Aye, lovely . . ." her mammy quavered, while Aunty Flo fingered the velvet curtains as though she was pondering how much a yard the material cost and was quite sure it had not come off a stall at Tommyfield.

"That's Tim's grandmother on't wall. Tessa she were called," pointing to the laughing lady in the portrait.

"Oh, aye . . ."

"An' Tim says he's goin' to 'ave one of me done after the baby's born."

"Oh, aye . . ."

"Come an' look at conservatory," and they followed obediently, eyes wide, mouths agape, into a world filled with birds and flowers, white wicker chairs and gaily patterned cushions, wishing to God they were at home in their own snug little kitchens. They drank tea from wafer-thin porcelain teacups, tea as pale and bland as water, not at all as they were used to it, you could see from Aunty Flo's face, and ate little cakes that hadn't got one decent bite in them, served by a blank-faced woman who clearly resented their common, working-class presence in her mistress's splendid drawing room.

Only Clare seemed at ease, which was strange when considering her nature which was shy and uncertain, self-doubting, even despite the great improvement since she had lived with Aunty Flo. Her pointed little face which was usually as pale as a moonflower became flushed. Her eyes, like the deep blue velvet of an evening sky, were everywhere, glowing with excited interest and she even rose from the sofa where she sat with Aunty Flo and wandered quite naturally across the room to stand beneath the portrait of the flaunting Tessa Broadbent. It was seen that the maidservant didn't like it, probably thinking the child was about to create mayhem, not knowing any better, among her mistress's lovely things but Clare was quiet and restrained, touching nothing, the expression on her face almost ethereal in its wonder.

They watched her for a moment, exchanging marvelling glances, but she seemed unaware of them so they continued the sporadic and unnatural conversation that had begun the moment they came through the door.

"Mrs Broadbent out then?" Aunty Flo said tartly. "Gone up town, 'as she?"

"Er . . . no, I believe she's . . . restin'." Molly avoided Mammy's worried eyes.

"Oh, aye . . ."

"Yes, so she said. Seein' as 'ow I had the Rolls she couldn't go out."

"Didn't fancy tekkin' tea wi' us, then?"

Molly felt ashamed, hanging her head like a rebuked child and Aunty Flo relented. She leaned forward and patted Molly's hand.

"Never tha' mind, chuck. I'm as eager ter tekk tea wi' 'er as she is wi' me."

They all laughed then and even Parsons had to turn away to hide her smile.

They did not come again.

It was the following day when Tim suggested a dinner party. Molly had been to mass, alone, as she did most Sundays. Today she had gone to the eight o'clock so that she could take communion, fasting from the evening before, earning a dressing-down from her mother-in-law who didn't give a damn if Molly starved herself to death but whose grandson was being put at risk. Molly had set her face against the cold-eyed comments that it was unpardonable for a woman in her condition to act as she was doing and what kind of men were these . . . these priests who dictated such nonsense when everyone knew that a woman should be eating for two, never mind starving herself for nearly twenty-four hours? She hoped Tim was going to be firm with his wife, she told him, since it was his child as well and she sincerely hoped he was going to make his wife eat a decent breakfast before . . .

"I'll eat as soon as I get 'ome, Mrs Broadbent." Molly had done her best to be patient as Tim had asked her.

"But that means almost a full day with nothing inside you except what you had last night at dinner. Really, I am amazed that more women of your . . . your faith don't lose their children in the first weeks of pregnancy."

"Mother, stop it."

"No, I will not stop it. This is my grandchild we're talking about and I for one wish to see it healthy."

"And I don't? Is that what you're sayin'?" Molly jumped to her feet and so did Albert, Tim's old dog, who had been dozing by the fireplace. "Jesus, Mary and Joseph! May the blessed saints in heaven give me patience for sure an' I find it 'ard ter come by these days. D'you want me ter lose me temper, do you? D'yer like provokin' me?"

"Molly, darling, Mother is only concerned for you and for your child. Now eat up like a good girl and then everyone will be happy," which was all Tim Broadbent asked. That everyone should be happy, no matter what compromise must be made to attain it.

It was as they dined that evening that the matter of the dinner party was brought up.

"Now then," Tim began with great enthusiasm, "how about giving a dinner party? What d'you say, Mother? Molly and I have been married almost three months and none of our friends have met her, apart from at the wedding. It's ages since the Herberts and the Forresters and the rest were over at Meddins. I saw old Joel this morning . . ."

Why did her pulse leap and why had she the most urgent need to drop her gaze from her husband's as though she had been caught in an act of deceit? She didn't know what came over her whenever Joel Greenwood's name was mentioned, really she didn't and was only thankful that it didn't happen very often.

She loved Meddins. She could never quite believe that it was now her home and she spent hours on her own going from room to room, caressing the polished surfaces of the lovely furniture, trailing her fingers in a dreamlike way across the bedheads, the windowsills, the dressing tables and footstools, the chairs and sofas and every exquisitely made piece of furniture the Broadbents had gathered and treasured for over a hundred years. She roamed the nursery floor, empty now of children but still cluttered with rocking horses and toy soldiers and even a doll or two, and echoing softly with the voices of three small boys, one of whom was now her husband. She even ventured into the attics where, to her amazed delight, she found, carefully wrapped in tissue in a trunk, the very gown worn by Tessa Broadbent in the picture on the drawing room wall.

She spent hours on horseback, and on foot, with Albert padding stiffly beside her, exploring every corner of the estate, placing her hands on the ridged bark of the trees which had stood for hundreds of years before the house was built. The gardeners were often considerably startled to come across her just standing, her arms crossed, her back to a tree, her eyes narrowed, doing nothing at all that they could see, communing with nature, they supposed, but then she was in the family way and everyone knew women in pod did daft things. She could sometimes feel the presence of Daddy beside her and she would smile and turn her face to the skies, welcoming him into this place which he had loved so well and whose love for it she had inherited.

She was happy. She loved Tim more and more every day and would never cease to be grateful to him for loving her. He was so good to her, so loving, so generous, encouraging her in her efforts to fit into the role of his wife and making nothing of the faux pas she committed now and again and the numerous occasions she lapsed into the dialect of her childhood. She would never erase the broad northern vowels in her speech, nor the sudden lilt of Ireland which came from nowhere, but she pronounced her words correctly for the most part and did not hesitate in her choice of them. And it was Tim's love that had given her this perfect life. It was Tim's love that had given her Meddins, the dream she had had since she was a small girl and because of it, and because of her own growing attachment, she knew she would never feel for any man what she felt for Tim.

So why did her heart miss a beat and her face feel as though it was flooded with colour when Joel Greenwood's name came up? She barely knew him. Why did she feel the need to question Tim about him, which would not be out of the way, of course, if it were the careless questioning a woman newly married might make of her husband's cousin? Would he be invited to this dinner party Tim was talking about? The thought filled her with dread and with a strange feeling she could not describe except to say it was not one Molly Broadbent should be feeling about a man not her husband.

Tim was proud of her, he told her so again, and again, and

if this dinner party was what he wanted then she could only agree to it. His one wish, the only cloud in the perfect sky of their union was the "spats", that's what he called them, that sprang up between his mother and Molly. Oh, he knew his mother was mainly at fault, he admitted, since she was finding it hard to accept the woman Tim loved. She had wanted one of the Roper girls, or Sarah Bowman who was young but a favourite of his mother's since Delia Bowman was her dear friend. But she'd come round, you'll see, he told Molly, when the baby was born. He was so pleased about the child since surely it would mean an end to this disunity. He himself had never felt so content, he told Molly. His adoration of his young wife never abated. She was everything to him and though as yet he had not been called upon to choose, he knew that if a confrontation arose in which a choice must be made he would not hesitate to support his wife. He was extremely fond of his mother but Molly was the very heart and soul of him. He wished that he could remain at home more, with the baby on the way, but somehow, in the last few weeks, things seemed to be getting in a muddle at the mill and old Watson, the manager, was for ever calling him out on some errand or other. There seemed to be some cash flow problem which Tim, who really had no head for figures, could not quite understand and, if he got the chance, he might ask his cousin to have a look at the books for him, he had said on one occasion to Molly. It was not that he did not trust George Watson, or the team of accountants who looked after his money, but Joel had a good head on him and Tim trusted him without question. There seemed to be some trouble with the miners which, Joel had said when he spoke to him, might cause problems but Joel was a bit of a pessimist and no doubt it would all come right in the end. He must, of course, be invited to the dinner party and perhaps they could get him fixed up with some pretty woman, for Tim could only admit that the state of marriage was a wonderful, blissful thing and it was time old Joel settled down to it.

His mother was looking at him as though he had suggested she should put on an orgy and Molly drew back in her chair. She hadn't the faintest idea what went on at a dinner party, though it sounded quite fearsome. How many would be there? Would they all come, those frosty-faced ladies who had looked at her on her wedding day as though she had arrived at the church in her shawl and clogs? She had seen the thought in their faces, the one that asked how she had the nerve to snaffle one of the most eligible bachelors in Lancashire from under their very noses and it was something they would never forgive her for. They had despised her then and they would despise her now and how could she possibly dress up and walk among them, speak to them, smile and chatter as Mrs Broadbent and they did so confidently?

All her previous determination began to drain away. The meal? Who would choose the meal? For some reason rag pudding came into her mind and she wanted to laugh hysterically.

"I don't think it's appropriate, Tim darling," his mother was saying, turning to stare pointedly at Molly. "After all, with a child on the way it can hardly be proper to . . ."

If Muriel Broadbent had purposely considered the one reason guaranteed to stiffen Molly's spine and make her hell-bent on giving a dinner party – whatever that entailed – she could not have better succeeded. If Muriel was against it that was good enough for Molly. She had no idea how to go about planning it and without her mother-in-law's help, which she was certain she would not get, she might possibly – would probably – make the biggest fool of herself and shame Tim into the bargain, but when had a challenge, particularly one thrown down by Muriel Broadbent, stopped Seamus O'Dowd's daughter?

She began by sending for Mrs Ogden, asking her to come to the small sitting room used by Mrs Broadbent for such purposes.

Mrs Ogden approved, you could see that, and Molly was aware that she had taken her first step, as it should be taken. She had not barged into the kitchen ready for a cosy chat over a cup of tea, which was her natural inclination, but had acted as a lady should. Propriety had been observed and Mrs Ogden was a stickler for propriety.

"I've asked you to come here this mornin' because I need yer help, Mrs Ogden," she began, not certain whether to ask the elderly cook to sit or not, then, shrugging, for could she, a young woman, loll in her chair while a woman old enough to be her grandmother stood to attention, waved her to a chair.

Mrs Ogden sat thankfully.

"My husband wants me ter give a dinner party, Mrs Ogden," she began, "and since me mother-in-law does not feel able ter guide me in this I'm turnin' ter you for 'elp . . . help."

Mrs Ogden looked aghast. "Me, madam?"

"Yes, yer must have seen a few in yer time so I'll need ter . . . pick your brains since there's no one else." Molly was brisk but pleasant, her manner saying she meant to do this thing and do it well and if Mrs Ogden, who was employed by Molly's husband and surely had some loyalty to him, could not or would not help her she would be forced to turn elsewhere.

"Madam, I'm not sure . . ."

"Yes?"

The servants and Mrs Ogden in particular had begun to see a side to their young mistress they quite liked. She was a feisty young woman who, no matter how many times Mrs Broadbent put her down, got up again to fight. They were made up with the news of the coming baby, naturally, and couldn't wait to hear a child's voice again and the sound of running baby feet. To see perambulators and ponies, toys to trip over, see the house come alive as this young woman's already fertile body promised. She'd done well to get herself in the family way so soon and it would surely make a difference with old Mrs Broadbent to whom they were all devoted.

But that was the problem. Despite their growing regard and admiration for young Mrs Broadbent who was trying so hard to fit in, their duty and obedience lay with their old mistress. How could they go against her? It seemed she had no objection to this dinner party or Mrs Tim would not now be in Mrs Broadbent's sitting room beginning to plan it, poor little beggar, and all on her own. Had she ever been to such an event in that working-class street from which she came? Did she even know what one was? And, should she get past all these obstacles, would they come, those guests who would be sent an invitation without old Mrs Broadbent's name on it?

"Well, madam . . ."

"Yes, Mrs Ogden?" Mrs Tim leaned forward eagerly.

"I suppose I could give you a few pointers . . . an' p'raps Mr Forbes . . ."

"Oh, Mrs Ogden, if yer only knew what that means ter me." Mrs Tim's face bloomed like a rosy apple and for a dreadful moment Mrs Ogden thought she was about to leap to her feet, skim round the table and hug her in that spontaneous way she had. Of course, Forbes would check with madam first to see that this really was to take place and perhaps Mr Tim would help his wife since he doted on her and would not want to see her take a tumble. But if that was all right there was no reason why a menu should not be drawn up, wines chosen, invitations sent out on madam's specially headed notepaper. The two parlourmaids, Agnes and Flora, had been setting the table for dinner parties since they were no older than Mr Tim's young wife and could do it blindfold. With a bit of – well, she hoped Mrs Tim wouldn't mind – but a bit of instruction on the correct behaviour of a hostess which Mr Tim would know about and give every assistance with, and her own natural charm Mrs Ogden could see no reason why it should not be a big success.

"You are to go ahead with this madness, then," Muriel Broadbent said distantly to her daughter-in-law at lunch the next day. She chose a moment when her son was absent and the servants had withdrawn. "You realise that you will make a show of yourself, don't you? That you, and through you, my son, will be made laughing stocks."

Molly drew a deep breath and clenched her fists beneath the table. She had been prepared for this. As yet she had barely discussed it with Tim and he, who could not believe that his mother, if only for the sake of her own pride, would not guide her in what to do, had been delighted that she was to go ahead. She would do splendidly, he told her, kissing her upturned face. He loved her, could see no wrong in her and their guests would feel the same, he was certain.

"No, I don't know that but your help would make it easier."

"My help! My dear girl, you chose to be Tim's wife and you must, now that the bed is made, lie in it. This is your dinner party and if you want to shame Tim, show him up in his friends' eyes as the fool who fell for nothing but a pretty face and figure, in other words he lost his reason over a girl who is no better than she should be, then that is your affair. I shall, of course, attend, since this is my house and Tim is my son but I shall let it be known from the start that the whole dreadful farrago is none of my doing. They will come, there is no doubt of that, because of Tim and because of me, but don't expect it to be easy, miss. They will tear you to shreds and quite frankly I shan't be sorry. There is nothing to be done about it now. You are married to Tim and carry his child but I am hoping this will show him the mistake he has made in marrying a nobody."

"Why are you such a harridan?" Molly asked pleasantly, using a word she had read for the first time only last week in a book from the Meddins' library. "How could a cold-hearted bitch such as you have given birth to a warm and loving man like Tim? I can hardly believe he came from your belly . . ."

"Why, you ill-mannered slut. How dare you speak to me like that? Yet should I be surprised when one considers who you are and where you came from."

"A better place than you, madam." Molly rose to her feet, cool and unruffled, the first time Muriel had ever seen her so after one of their confrontations. For a moment she was seriously alarmed. She always enjoyed pricking this young woman to the peak of her red-hot Irish temper while at the same time retaining her own cool, well-bred manner, but today something had gone wrong.

"If you'll excuse me I must go and consult with Mrs Ogden and Mr Forbes. We are to discuss the menu and I believe Tim and Mr Forbes are to decide on the wines. A week on Friday it is to be, if that is convenient to you and if it's not, then bugger it, and you!"

Molly moved serenely towards the door and Muriel was disconcerted, she didn't know why, to see Albert heave himself to his feet and follow her.

20

He was the first guest to arrive and she was not to know that he had planned it deliberately, for he had hoped to speak to her alone before the others came. She looked absolutely exquisite in an ankle-length sheath dress of perfectly plain layered chiffon. It was in shaded colours of the palest aquamarine, peacock blue and sea green, caught on the hip with the narrowest crystal beaded belt. Her shoulders and arms were bare, the neckline of the bodice cut low enough at the front to reveal a shadow of the deep cleft between her breasts and down to her waist at the back. She wore satin high-heeled shoes and fine silk stockings dyed to match her dress. In a band across her forehead and threading through her dark hair, which was arranged in a casually tumbled Grecian style, was a turquoise satin ribbon. She wore no jewellery and had rejected the big feathered fans and floating scarves which were the rage.

Tim stood proudly and protectively beside her in the wide hallway, one arm about her waist, and behind them Forbes and Atkinson were waiting to take the gentlemen's coats. At the foot of the stairs Parsons was ready to show the ladies to the luxurious bedroom on the first floor which Mrs Ogden had told Molly was always used on such occasions.

"Joel, old lad, good to see you, and first here, I'm glad to say. You can stand on Molly's other side to give her some moral support when the hordes arrive."

Joel's dark face moved in what might have been a smile. "Tim, you look well. Marriage obviously agrees with you." He turned courteously to Molly, no hint of what might be in his head showing on his face. "But I must admit you are completely overshadowed by this beautiful wife of yours. Of course you will know that by now. Good evening, Molly. May I say I don't think I have seen a lovelier gown but it fades into insignificance beside your own loveliness."

"Hold on, old man, this is my bride of barely three months you're talking to. Save your compliments for the 'gels' who are coming tonight, though I must admit none will compare to my own Irish rose."

Molly began to laugh and as she laughed she relaxed the stiff and unnatural body posture she did not even know she had assumed.

"Mind your own business, Tim Broadbent. If Joel feels the need to pay me such compliments don't you dare stop 'im. I need 'em tonight and anythin' else anyone can give me, an' all, to get me through this evening. Me legs're like jelly an' me insides feel as though I've had a jar of butterflies chucked down me gob. Oops . . ." She put her hand to her mouth but both men laughed, Tim with that full-throated delight his wife always aroused in him, Joel softly as though not used to it.

Joel could feel his heart doing the foolish things he had heard hearts did in romantic novels and his throat was so dry he wasn't sure he could swallow but he did his best not to let his extraordinary feelings regarding this remarkable young woman show. Not that that was hard to do since he knew he had the expressionless face of a poker player and not a few ladies had told him so. He did not think he had ever met such courage as this wife of his cousin's was displaying. She had not been brought up to this. To this opulence, to this way of life, to the ways of those who lived it and yet she was prepared to meet them on their own ground and not only that but to laugh about it. He had worked beside men and women from her world for most of his adult life and he had found them to be – most of them – good-humoured, hardworking, honest and brave in the face of adversity, putting up with hardships which would fell a great many of those who would be here tonight. But not one of them, man or woman, could tackle head-on, as Mary Angelina Broadbent was doing, the often cruel ways of what was known as "good" society to those whom they considered interlopers, and it was perhaps this which had aroused the bizarre feelings he was experiencing now, or so he told himself.

Not that he quite knew what his feelings might be towards his cousin's wife, only that now, on their second meeting, he was as dazed by them as he had been at their first.

"A united front is what is needed, Joel, old lad," Tim was saying, "since this is Molly's 'do'. Oh, yes, Mother has given her carte blanche to do as she pleases," which Joel was aware meant that his aunt had washed her hands of the whole affair and Mary Angelina was to stand or fall on her own efforts and what would a mill girl brought up in the back streets of Oldham make of that?

"Between us we should be able to put up a show for them, Molly," he told her drily, taking his place at her side, letting her know that should Tim, as host, be separated from her, he would be there to protect her.

Molly wondered why she should think that, looking up into his dark, unreadable face, searching for some spark of warmth, or humour, but there was none. Nevertheless she knew, though she did not know how she knew, that she could rely on him as surely as she relied on Tim.

"You're very kind, Joel," she told him hesitantly as Tim turned to speak to Forbes.

"Nonsense. I can't resist a pretty woman, Molly, and you're the prettiest I've seen in many a long day." They were the words expected of a gentleman to an attractive woman, slightly flirtatious, meaning nothing, but there was something in his voice, in his eyes, in his grave expression that said there was more to his words than what was actually spoken. For a long moment their eyes locked and Molly felt the slow thump of her heart rise into her throat.

There was a small commotion at the door as a sleek Rolls-Royce drew up and Herbert, smart and scrubbed and in a full evening suit as correct as Forbes and Atkinson, marched forward to open the car door.

The first guests moved beneath the porch and into the hallway, smiling at one another and speaking of the cold and how particularly lovely the house looked tonight and, as though she had planned it, Muriel Broadbent came down the stairs.

"Arthur, Joan, how lovely to see you and don't the girls look divine in those dresses. Really, the pair of you have grown into the most enchanting young ladies and get prettier every time I see you," she enthused to the perfectly plain Ellen and Emma Davidson. "Could not Justin and John come? Oh, what a shame, but never mind. Young men have their own lives to lead. See, Tim, kiss Joan and the girls and Joel . . . darling, I did not see you there. Come through to the drawing room with us. Yes, Parsons will see to your wraps. Now then, Joel, you shall entertain us by telling us what you have been doing with yourself since Christmas." She was ready to take Joel's arm and draw him away from the frozen figure of her daughter-in-law who had just been totally ignored by her, by the Davidsons and by their two daughters.

"Kind of you, Aunt," Joel said, his facial muscles moving into what in him passed for a smile, "but I am just renewing the acquaintance of my new cousin here," putting his arm through Molly's. "We have not met since her wedding and I believe it is the same for you, Mr and Mrs Davidson. No, Molly, you will not remember the Davidsons for what bride sees anything but her new husband's face on her wedding day. Tim . . ." He drew his cousin into the circle and the Davidsons had no choice but to take Molly's hand and murmur a greeting. "I shall be through directly," he added, raising one sardonic eyebrow in the direction of Muriel Broadbent, his mouth twitching.

"Well, I must say, Joel Greenwood," his aunt murmured, turning to her guests and leading them towards the drawing room, but it was not vouchsafed to him, or to Molly, what she meant. Perhaps that she could not believe that one of her own could take the side of this intruder who was her son's dreadful wife.

"Thank you." Molly's words were scarcely audible.

"My pleasure." Joel inclined his head unsmilingly.

"Thanks, Joel, old lad. I didn't realise Mother had come down. I'm sure she didn't mean to . . . to . . . well . . ."

"'Tis all right, Tim, really. Sure an' didn't I expect something like it, so. It'd take more than these owd trouts to upset Molly O'Dowd . . . Molly Broadbent, so it would."

But they did upset her, over and over again. They took their cue from Muriel who acted as though Molly did not exist but at the same time making no effort properly to steer the guests, their conversation, the course of the evening and what they were to do in it, as a hostess naturally would. It was as though she herself were a guest, waiting for her hostess, who was never where she should be, to guide her through the intricacies of pre-dinner drinks, the groups of guests who must be skilfully broken up and re-formed so that everyone had a chance to speak to everyone else. It was a hostess's duty to move about, to chat briefly, to fling small snippets of laughing conversation into one that flagged, to smile and introduce those who were not acquainted, to make sure no one was left alone. She must have eyes everywhere and be everywhere, drawing this one forward and tactfully carrying off those who were a mite tedious, to bore another group. Muriel Broadbent did it to perfection, but Molly Broadbent, who did her best and looked stunning doing it, was overwhelmed by it all on that first evening, despite the gargantuan efforts of her husband and her husband's cousin.

Whenever she shyly joined a group of laughing people, who all seemed to know one another so well, they simply stopped laughing and drifted away to form again somewhere else. It was she who had to be introduced by Tim who was having his work cut out by being not only host, but hostess, doing what his mother normally did. Molly was circulated about the room, looked up and down, or through, by Muriel's friends, only the gentlemen inclined to be slightly less frosty since gentlemen find it hard to resist a pretty woman.

At dinner, knowing where she was to sit, for Forbes had gone through the seating with her, she was at the head of the long, polished table and Tim was what seemed a hundred yards away at the other end. She was surprised and immensely relieved to find Joel on her right, though she could have sworn he had been placed halfway down the table when she and Forbes had made the seating plan.

It wasn't so bad during dinner. The guests all chatted to one another and there was a great deal of male laughter at Tim's end of the table which, though she was not aware of it since no one had thought to advise her, she should, as hostess, tactfully put a stop to. This was not a bachelor party and the conversation must be the sort no lady could take offence at. Helen Herbert was seen to glance at Molly who should have done something about it but the young hostess was shyly conversing with Rupert Lucas who was on her other side, and Muriel was in smiling conversation with George Bowman, her attitude saying it was not her place to intervene since she was not hostess. Helen shook her head sadly.

The courses came smoothly and miraculously, one after the other. The food was superb, as was the wine and, apart from the untoward hilarity at the host's end of the table, everything was running as it should. Joel talked to the young lady on his right who had been introduced to Molly as Miss Dorothy Roper, including Molly and Rupert in the smooth exchange, making it easy, keeping it flowing, introducing his own brand of dry humour to ease her way. It seemed Rupert had gone to school with the Broadbent and Greenwood boys and though again Molly could have sworn he had been placed at Tim's end of the table, she was glad to have him as one of her "partners". He was pleasant, polite, recounting tales of their shared schooldays, his eyes admiring, and Molly found she was enjoying herself, glad that she had such pleasant company around her though Miss Roper was a bit on the cool side.

". . . and why they cannot understand that unless the owners lower their wages our goods will be too expensive for the foreign market, I shall never know. The war is over, years over and we cannot be expected to pay them the high wages they earned then."

The voice came from about halfway down the table though Molly had no idea who it was who was speaking.

"True, true," another male voice answered. "When the government ran the coal industry they could afford to pay the miners over four pounds a week but those same miners must be made to understand that those days are gone. Unemployment has dropped, certainly, since 1921, but they must realise they are lucky to be in work at all. We have to pay our way in the world. Unemployment can only be reduced further by increasing exports and bringing down prices."

General conversation ground to a halt and the guests looked expectantly at Muriel Broadbent to bring it back to the light, frothy chatter which was expected at a dinner party. Politics, religion, commerce, anything of a serious nature must not be brought to the table, that is until the ladies had left the gentlemen to their port and cigars.

Muriel gazed in front of her and all eyes slowly turned towards Molly, all except those of the gentlemen beyond Muriel who were becoming somewhat heated on the matter of the coal miners and their preposterous refusal to have their wages halved at once.

"Baldwin said it last year. All the workers of this country have got to take reductions in their wages to help put industry on its feet."

"It's not as if their families cannot manage on what they are paid. Nearly two pounds a week and another hour on their working day is not much to ask."

"I agree and if it should come to it there is absolutely no reason why—"

"Would you like to live on less than two pounds a week, sir?" a high female voice from the end of the table asked, and in the appalled silence that followed every eye in the room, including those of Forbes, Atkinson, Parsons and Flora, stared at Mrs Tim Broadbent. Her face was flushed, a heated rose of indignation at each cheekbone and her fine eyes flashed. She had no idea of the names of the gentlemen who were so carelessly disposing of the lives of millions of workers and their families and she didn't care. Her family had never suffered want but she had seen Mrs Haydock at number twenty slipping out on a Saturday night to buy the cheap leftovers at Tommyfield when her husband was out of work. Poverty stalked all working families should the slightest mishap disturb the tightrope of their budgets. She had watched the gratitude glow in Mrs Haydock's eyes when Mammy had "lent" her a bob or two until the weekend, and the shamed droop of her head that she was forced to accept it if she were to feed even these scraps to her brood of children.

As usual she let her heart rule her head, her sensible head which had told her earlier that she must, this evening, be quiet, calm, polite, unassuming. But they were speaking of men from her world, men who had already had their wages reduced and reduced. Mine owners had no skills. They did not share the danger the miner knew, nor did they share the profits the miner made for them. She had heard Daddy say so time and time again, for Daddy had been a strong union man.

"Young lady," the gentleman protested condescendingly, "surely we . . .?" He had been about to back down and say that she and the gentleman with whom he had been in conversation should remember where they were and stop right now. He was at fault, his bow in Muriel's direction said and he was ready to apologise, but Molly rarely backed down from anything.

"It's always the same," Molly went on hotly. "The workers of this country get a poor deal when it comes ter wages. Me daddy an' brothers all worked in a jennygate fer Mr Broadbent, old Mr Broadbent, that is, an' he was a fair man. Paid decent wages fer a decent day's work but—"

"Molly, darling," her husband's voice came mildly from the other end of the table, "we must . . ."

"There's mill owners in this town an' I could give yer names, an' all, who pay low wages fer long hours. Me friend Cissie Thompson once worked at Knights in Agnew Street . . ."

There was a murmured gasp, for at the very table, no more than six feet away from Molly, sat Maurice Knight who owned that very mill in Agnew Street.

". . . an' with stoppages fer bein' even a minute late, petty things like that, she barely brought 'ome enough ter live on."

She could feel the big warm hand gripping hers and from somewhere came a sense of warning, a silent voice from her right which told her she must not do this thing. Not here. Not now, for it would be she who would suffer. The hand held hers so hard it hurt her, cracking the bones and she turned defensively, all caution gone, ready to snatch her hand away from the cruel grip but it would not let her go. Deep, deep brown eyes bored into hers, steady and commanding and suddenly she came to her senses.

"Oh," she said in a small voice. "I'm that sorry . . . I shouldn't've . . ."

"It's all right, darling," Tim said, springing up from his chair, almost tipping it over, almost running the length of the table to get to his wife and, in Joel's opinion, making the situation even worse. Left alone, bad as it was, the incident would have been smoothed over. Conversation would have resumed, dinner would have resumed and though they would have gossiped among themselves later about poor Tim Broadbent's ill-mannered wife, the party would have continued to its end. Instead Tim plucked Molly from her chair, put his arms about her and petted and consoled her as though she were a child who had been rebuked.

The company was stunned and Muriel looked about her, exchanging glances with her horrified friends, her expression sad but dignified, as though to say they could see now what she had to put up with.

"It's all right, Tim, 'onest it is," Molly's muffled voice was saying. "I'm fine. There's no need ter make a fuss. Go an' sit down an' . . . an' . . . Forbes can serve . . . Oh, I dunno, whatever's ter come next."

"But sweetheart, let me . . ."

"No, Tim, stop treating me like a babby. I know I'm to have one but if I can't manage a . . . a discussion with a gentleman in me own house it's a poor do."

"But it's not really . . ."

"Holy Mary, Mother of God, will yer not go an' sit down, Tim Broadbent, an get on wi' yer dinner," and Tim had no choice, short of making even more of a fool of himself, than to obey.

Sometime later Molly knew something else was wrong. They had all resumed their conversation, pretending that there was nothing wrong and if there was they themselves hadn't noticed it, if only for poor Muriel's sake, but now the ladies were glancing from Molly to Mrs Broadbent and the gentlemen were doing the same, only more forcibly, becoming somewhat restless. Several cleared their throats, almost as though in warning and Forbes was piercing her with his eyes.

"In the name of all that's holy, what've I done wrong now?" she hissed through gritted teeth but only Joel heard her.

"I think it's time for the ladies to leave," he murmured casually, his left hand deep in his pocket, his right fingering his glass of wine. He found he could no longer meet her gaze. For some inexplicable reason the disclosure that she was pregnant had struck him a sorry blow though he could not for the life of him think why. Jesus, she was his cousin's wife. Tim obviously worshipped the ground she walked on and presumably she felt the same way about him, since Joel knew without knowing how he knew that Molly Broadbent was not the sort of woman who would marry for anything other than love. In which case, was it any wonder that this pair of love-birds should be about to produce another to share their nest? Christ, why did he feel so bloody bitter? he asked himself disgustedly. It was nothing to do with him. She was nothing to do with him except that he felt a great and abiding admiration for her pluck, her bravery in bearding this particular pride of lions in their own den. She was dazzlingly beautiful . . . no, not dazzlingly since her loveliness was soft, warm, almost childlike it was so perfect. But it seemed it had the power to touch him, to make him want to protect her, to save her from the hurt which his own kind would inevitably inflict – and had – already inflicted on her.

"Leave? Where are they goin'?" she asked him suspiciously

as though she suspected some further trick to embarrass her.

"It's the custom, you know . . ." indicating with a slight nod that she must stand up and lead the way.

"What?"

"The gentlemen drink their port and smoke their cigars and the ladies go to the drawing room."

Daylight dawned. Yes, she remembered now. Mrs Ogden and Mr Forbes had said something about it and she had made a mental note of it but somehow it had slipped her mind.

She cleared her throat and stood up, moving slowly towards the door which Atkinson sprang to hold open for her, hoping to God they would all follow her, thinking that if they didn't she'd march right out of the front door, collect her motor from the garage and go home.

Home! Home? Where was that if not right here at Meddins?

The thought gave her strength and before the astonished gaze of the gathered company she crossed to her husband where he had risen to his feet with the rest of the gentlemen and kissed him soundly on the mouth.

"Don't be long, sweetheart," they all heard her say and Joel Greenwood turned away to hide the expression on his face.

She got through it. Through sheer, unflinching bloody-minded willpower, through teeth-clenching resolution and blind determination not to let any of these narrow-eyed, mean-spirited women see how badly wounded she was, she got through it.

She was so nervous she spilled coffee in every saucer as she poured it for the ladies. She had practised it all one afternoon with Mrs Ogden until she could have done it blindfold, handing out cup and saucer, offering sweetmeats, managing beautifully then, but the bitter knowledge that her mother-in-law watched her every move and smirked at every mistake made her even more clumsy. Muriel's finely modulated voice could be heard above the others as she spoke of Mildred Harrington whose Prudence was to marry in April. A baronet, no less, and what a catch. Surely a joy to fill every mother's heart. And had they heard about her own Tessa? Yes, her voice dropping for a moment, another baby on the way and how lovely it would be to become a grandmother again, while her daughter-in-law, in whose womb Muriel's grandchild grew, filled and refilled fragile China coffee cups, handing them out with shaking hands and gritted teeth, and prayed for the gentlemen to return.

The babble of voices rose and fell as the smartly dressed women, following Muriel Broadbent's lead, gossiped and laughed and totally ignored Muriel Broadbent's daughter-in-law.

They played bridge later, those who had a taste for it, forming into tables of four, brushing ignominiously past Molly, smiling warmly at Tim who stood beside her. He had his arm about her, telling her she had done well and the worst was over. He was proud of her and if she'd just come into the hall for a moment he'd show her how much. He made her smile and then laugh out loud as he whispered some rather intimate remark into her ear which concerned the technicalities of what he meant to do to her when he got her into their bed that night.

As she laughed some of the guests, ladies among them, were seen to look at Tim Broadbent's young wife who, unlike others who would have run from the table in a flood of tears, had managed not only to get through this evening, which must have been terrifying to a girl not brought up to it, but at the end to be still laughing. After all, Muriel had been a bit hard on her and could you blame Tim Broadbent for falling for her? She really was a stunner.

The younger ones, as they always did, drifted off to the music room where Tim's gramophone was soon in full throat and though Angela Herbert, Josephine Forrester, Laura Knight and the rest of the young ladies were inclined to cluster together, giggling over nothing, and, like their mothers, endlessly talking about people Molly did not know, Molly hardly cared. Tim's arms were about her as they drifted round the room to the haunting strains of "Let the Rest of the World Go By", and, when Tim finally gave way, there were Rupert and Bunny, Guy and Freddy and Robbie all ready, eager even, to whisk her about the floor, particularly when it was discovered that she knew every one of the latest dances and could perform them better than any lady there. The black bottom, the charleston, the breakaway, the tango which they were not to know she and Betty, Cissie and Cissie's sister, Meggie, had practised in their dinner hour in the yard at the back of Broadbents Mill. She had been to see Rudolph Valentino in the film *Blood and Sand* where he had brought women to their feet and men to declare it was disgraceful with his sensual performance of the mesmerising dance. She and Betty had learned every step, turn and beat ready for the time when Molly might be able to avoid Pikey and get to the Roxy in Eccleston Street where the other three girls went almost every Saturday night.

Now she danced it with Bunny who turned out to be the best dancer among the gentlemen. Jerking and twitching, flaunting and gliding, tossing her head, narrow-eyed and smouldering, she over-exaggerated the movements, since she was enjoying herself for the first time that evening. With a rose between her teeth, she kicked up her shapely legs at every turn, as Valentino's partner had once done in a film, until the gentlemen were beginning to breathe rather more quickly than they should and the ladies to whisper to one another that it was true what they said about working-class women being no better than they should be.

The success of it all went to Tim's head. He drank too much and became so boyishly comical, so endearingly amusing he had them all, even the somewhat strait-laced Roper girls, giggling helplessly as he tried to imitate his wife's energetic charleston and the noise of it drifted through to the drawing room where the game of bridge was just ending.

The fun in the music room was by now fast and furious. They had been drinking, at Tim's insistence, one of the new-fangled cocktails he had taught Forbes how to mix and the concoction had gone to the heads of almost everyone in the room. It had been decided that they should play hide and seek. The gentlemen were tired of cavorting about, they said, all of them wanting only to dance with Tim's spiffing little wife who had turned out to be such fun, though Tim's spiffing little wife, who had declined the cocktails, not caring for what they might do to the tiny embryo growing inside her, was not so sure she liked the idea. Was this what the gentry got up to at parties? Grown men and women playing kids' games? And she was sick of being handled by all these red-faced, mumbling, wild-eyed chaps who had begun to fall over their own feet. What was the matter with Tim? Why did he not tell them, as her daddy would have told them, to grow up and behave themselves? Rupert had even tried to kiss her behind the curtains where he had dragged her. She had smacked him in the face, of course, which she would with any chap who got over-familiar. She was not tired, but she was tired of all this horseplay and she longed to take Tim's hand and draw him up the stairs to their room.

"What is going on in that music room?" Muriel ventured at last with a smile which did not quite reach her eyes. Everyone was aware, of course, that it was certainly not the first time this had happened, whatever this turned out to be. The old people played bridge, the young people had some fun, good clean fun, naturally, and inevitably there was a certain amount of revelry to follow.

This time is was not so clean, not so good, the fun which was discovered when Rupert Lucas, thwarted in his endeavours to get his hands on Mrs Tim Broadbent who, by his code and her class, should have been more than willing, took the seriously drunk Sarah Bowman into the gentlemen's lavatory where the two of them were found, she totally naked and almost senseless, he with his trousers round his ankles, in what could only be called a compromising position.

Delia Bowman fainted. Peter Bowman, Sarah's father, hit Rupert on the jaw and it was not until Joel Greenwood, who had partnered Joan Davidson at bridge since Arthur did not play, had taken charge, bundling Sarah up in his own jacket and thrusting her into the arms of a blank-faced Parsons, and Rupert had been flopped on his back on the billiard table, that order was restored.

"This is your fault," Muriel hissed at the white-faced Molly. "No hostess would allow such goings-on in her home. No decent hostess, that is. You are finished, you realise that, don't you? Those young girls" – who were all older than Molly – "should have been properly chaperoned and how am I to lift my head in decent society when this gets out?"

Molly's mouth popped open. "Holy Mother of God, am I ter be blamed fer everything that goes on in this bloody house?" she answered hotly, her face the colour of a wild red rose. "'Tis not my fault that Sarah Whatsername couldn't keep her hand on her halfpenny, nor Rupert his John-Thomas in his pants where it belonged. I'm fed up ter the back teeth with the lot of yer, so I am an' I'm off to me bed. Tim, are yer comin'?"

And so saying she marched up the stairs, her back as straight as a poker, though her hips were not quite so restrained. The shocked guests stared in open-mouthed fascination, especially the gentlemen, and Joel Greenwood, as he watched her go, had the most amazing desire to applaud.

21

Molly and Tim Broadbent's son was born nine months and one week after their wedding day. He was christened Seamus Liam Patrick, what else, but called Liam by his doting parents.

Muriel Broadbent was beside herself.

"No grandson of mine will be given such outlandish names, Timothy Broadbent and you had better inform that wife of yours—"

"Oh, Mother, haven't you learned by now that that wife of mine will be told nothing she doesn't want to hear and will certainly not listen to it. Those are the names of her dead father and brothers and I can see nothing wrong with them."

"No, you wouldn't, would you? You can see nothing wrong with anything she does, that's the trouble. I appreciate her wish to remember her father and brothers but surely it would be more suitable to have just one of them as a second name. He is a Broadbent, after all, and there are several family Christian names to choose from. What about William Seamus, or Joshua Seamus?" mentioning the names of Tim's grandfather and father.

"Mother, stop it. I have no intention of trying to persuade Molly to change Liam's name."

"Liam . . . pah . . ." His mother's tone was disgusted. Tim took not the slightest bit of notice.

"Besides which, I like it," he continued. "Liam Broadbent has a handsome ring to it and you must admit he's a handsome boy."

"The image of your father, of course."

"Molly thinks he favours the O'Dowds."

"She would! And I suppose they will all be beating a path up to Meddins before the day is out. Droves of them, I shouldn't wonder. You know how they are, these families. A wedding, a funeral, the birth of a child and they quite lose control of themselves and how I am to cope with it is beyond me. I noticed Herbert speeding away in the Rolls a moment ago without even so much as a 'may I?' That wife of yours seems to imagine she can order my chauffeur and my motor car to run her family hither and yon whenever she pleases and I wish to make it quite clear . . ."

Tim knew that his mother, more from habit than from any great expectation that her words might be heeded, would grumble on as long as anyone would listen to her. The truth of it was that slowly, almost without Muriel being aware of it, Molly was becoming the true mistress of Meddins.

She had taken a giant leap last night when Seamus Liam Patrick was born and his cries had echoed lustily from the first-floor bedroom, along the hallway and down the stairs to where the servants hovered.

A boy! The first boy to be born at Meddins for over thirty years. The first child to be born since Mr Tim had come into the world, Mrs Ogden said, wiping away a sentimental tear, for she remembered the event so clearly, as did Mr Forbes and Parsons. There had already been two in the nursery then but Mr Joshua, bless him, had been as pleased as a dog with two tails saying a man couldn't have too many sons though a daughter would be nice next time. Now those two little boys were gone and the third, whose own health had been precarious after the war, was now a father himself. The house was to come alive again and did Parsons think she could persuade that there nurse who had helped to deliver Master Liam to fetch him down to the kitchen to let them all get a look at him for a minute?

"Certainly not," snapped the nurse, almost slamming the nursery door in Parsons's face. "Baby cannot be exposed to the germs and goodness knows what else might be lurking about down there," which, when reported to Mrs Ogden, made her see red.

"Right," she snapped, "that does it. I'm going up to see her."

"What, the nurse?" Flora, who had met the person in question, was appalled.

"No, yer daft happorth, the mistress," and they all knew by now that Mrs Ogden didn't mean the old lady.

They were all in Molly's bedroom when Mrs Ogden knocked on the door. Mammy, Clare, Aunty Flo, Aunty Maggie and Aunty Maggie's daughter-in-law, Jane, confirming Muriel Broadbent's worst fears. Jane had happened to be at Aunty Maggie's when the silver splendour of the Rolls-Royce drew up at Aunty Maggie's door, after first collecting the others, and though it had been a bit of a squash since Archie could not be left at home alone, Jane could not resist the temptation to get a scen at Molly O'Dowd's new home.

The few-hours-old baby Liam was being worshipped by his grandmother, Rosie Watson, when Mrs Ogden stepped inside the room. It was the first time the cook had been in here since all the fuss about Mrs Tim's determination to change from the back bedroom where madam had put her son and his new bride to this sunny suite at the front. And it was a suite now. God almighty, what a row that had caused but Mrs Tim had had her way. Of course Mr Tim could deny her nothing, standing up to his mother in a way that had astounded them all. The upshot was Mrs Tim had three adjoining rooms with connecting doors. The bedroom was on the corner of the house with big windows looking two ways, south and west so that it got the sun, when there was any, for most of the day. The bathroom, and what a bathroom it was, and where, it was whispered, Mr and Mrs Tim actually bathed together, was to one side of the bedroom and on the other was a sitting room. Flora had overheard Mrs Tim remark when she thought no one was listening that she must have some private place where she could be herself. She did her best of an evening to engage her mother-in-law in the sort of small talk Mrs Broadbent liked, in Mrs Broadbent's drawing room and at the dinner table, but she needed a place of her very own, to share with Tim, of course, she told him, wrapping herself quite outrageously about him, Flora thought, and it must be made plain to Mrs Broadbent that it was out of bounds to her unless invited. A place where her own family could gather and not be overwhelmed by the grandness of Meddins. Mind you, the room was grand by their standard but in a simple, unfussy way. Though it was summer a small and cheerful fire burned in the fireplace of wood, the surround of which had been painted white and inset with pretty, rose-imprinted tiles. There were small tables on which shaded lamps stood, the new electric lamps, naturally, two deep and comfortable sofas in cream linen strewn with pastel-tinted cushions, a rocking chair before the fire which only recently had been fitted with a polished brass fireguard like the one in the nursery. There was a pale patterned carpet in musky pinks and creams, draped cream curtains of heavy silk, plain walls on which Mrs Tim, raiding the attic, had hung prints of ballet dancers painted by some French chap. Warm, comfortable, almost, one could say, like the parlour of a working man's home – well, not quite but more homely than the drawing room downstairs – and her family, once they'd got past Forbes and the splendour of the staircase, were at home in it. When Mrs Tim, at Mr Tim's firm command, was no longer able to drive the Swallow to go and see them, she sent the Rolls at least once a week to pick up her mother and any other member of her extensive family who cared to come, not caring at all, it seemed, about Mrs Broadbent's disapproval.

Mr and Mrs Tim's bedroom was large and airy, sunny today, a kind of golden bower in the midst of which their young mistress and her child seemed to glow. It had been done out in white and lemon and old gold. The bed was quite enormous with white gauzy draperies drifting down from what looked like a crown in the ceiling and covered with a white lace bedspread lined with lemon silk. Say what you liked about her young mistress, Mrs Ogden thought admiringly, she had lovely taste considering she'd not been brought up to it. There were several comfortable chairs, not large but sturdy enough to support Mr Tim's weight, though Mrs Ogden was of the opinion he did not spend much time sitting about in the bedroom he shared with his wife. The carpet was a sort of creamy white and what would Master Liam make of that when he started crawling, the servants had asked one another, since Mrs Tim did not strike them as being the sort of mother who would keep her child restricted to the nursery. There had already been ructions over the hiring of a nursery maid. She would not have a nanny, they had all heard her declare, since she saw no reason to lower her voice, tossing her head, no doubt, in that particular way she had. She'd nowt else to do with her time, anyroad, she'd added passionately, falling, as she did at times of stress or argument, into the dialect and broad vowels of her north country upbringing. She had finally agreed to Elspeth, thanks to the persuasive powers of her husband, a young girl from out Grasscroft way, recommended by Parsons who knew the family and who could guarantee – to Mrs Tim – that the girl would be biddable and unobtrusive, there when she was needed and would not "take over", as an older and more experienced nanny would be inclined to do.

They all looked up and smiled as Mrs Ogden closed the bedroom door behind her, recognising a woman of their own class. Mrs Tim's young sister was draped across the lovely bedspread, since Mrs Tim did not concern herself unduly with such things as creases or crumplings, her little chin in her hands as she absorbed every detail of her new nephew's rosy face. The one called Aunty Maggie was begging Mrs Tim's mother for a "hold" and the other one, Aunty Flo, was tutting irritably and telling them they'd drop the blessed child if they weren't careful and best let her nurse him. And should that lad be swinging on those curtains like that and if he was hers she'd box his ears for him. Nobody took any notice of her and she didn't seem put out. The fifth visitor, who Forbes said was a cousin or something, was staring raptly through the door which led into the bathroom, a look on her face as though she were being given a glimpse of heaven.

Mrs Tim looked surprised to see her and could you blame her, for the cook was the last person a newly delivered mother expected in her bedroom.

"Yes, Mrs Ogden? Is there something wrong?"

"Well, yes and no, madam."

She saw the visitors exchange glances and she supposed they were not used to hearing one of their own being so addressed.

"Then what is it, Mrs Ogden?" Mrs Tim smiled encouragingly and Mrs Ogden felt herself relax, for if anyone understood it would be this young woman.

"Well . . . it'd just that . . . well, yes, there is something wrong," she went on, becoming furious all over again. She folded her hands over the bib of her snow white ankle-length apron, at the same time doing her best to get a glimpse of the tightly wrapped bundle in his grandmother's arms. "It's that there nurse."

"What nurse, Mrs Ogden?"

"That there nurse who's in charge of Master Liam."

"Oh, what's she done?"

"Well, madam, it's been a long time since we had a baby

in this house. Thirty years and this little'un's ... well, with
Mr Charles and Mr Will both gone, he's special, you see
and ..."

"Oh, Mrs Ogden, of course he is. But what's troublin'
you?"

"We, the servants, want to see him, madam. Especially me
and Forbes and Parsons, begging your pardon, remembering
those that have gone, like ..."

"Mrs Ogden, of course you do."

"But that there nurse won't let us. She says there's germs
an' such in my kitchen just as if the little lad might catch
something ..."

"What!"

"Yes, madam, and we were wondering ...?"

Mrs Tim turned to her mother, her face bright red with
indignation.

"Mammy, I want you to go down to the kitchen with
Mrs Ogden and take Liam with you. Introduce him to them
all, for they are to be his friends. And don't forget Herbert
and Wilf and Jud and all the other men who work outside.
Anyone who wants a hold let them, for if there's something
a child can't get enough of it's hugging. Take your time and
if the nurse hears of it and comes down to object refer her
to me. In the meanwhile we'll have tea, Mrs Ogden, if that's
all right, and some of your hot scones. Sure an' you're not
in any hurry, are you, Aunty Flo, Aunty Maggie? No? Good,
then off you go, Mammy."

If anything was needed to put the final stamp of approval
on Molly Broadbent, at least in the eyes of the servants, it
was this generous offer to share her son, the heir to this great
estate and to the mill which had been in his family for three
generations. The nurse, naturally, nearly had a fit, threatening
to leave that very day, instead of staying the customary three
weeks ladies of quality needed to recover from a confinement.
Mrs Tim told her to do so. She and Elspeth, with Mammy's help,
would manage just fine, but Mr Tim smoothed it all over, as he
usually did and a fitful peace was restored.

It had been a somewhat stormy nine months and yet Molly
had been increasingly happy, happy that gradually, as the
weeks passed, she was slowly becoming accepted, not only
by the servants but by a small circle of people to whom she and
Tim had been introduced by Joel Greenwood. Mrs Broadbent's

friends were still cool with her whenever Mrs Broadbent gave a dinner party, which was about once a month but Molly made no attempt to play hostess after that first fiasco. She knew that she could do it perfectly now, if she chose. It had been too soon. You learn by your mistakes, Daddy had often told her, and she had survived a tough lesson but the truth was she no longer cared, leaving that role to her mother-in-law. She chatted to whoever was seated beside her, unconcerned if they did not respond, but it was noticed that one or two of the older gentlemen seemed to find her manners and looks, her direct and straightforward approach quite taking and she was never left to stand alone for long as she had done in February. The experience seemed to have had no lasting effect on her self-confidence, instead it grew with every attempt on her part to mingle with her mother-in-law's guests. It was also noticed by Molly, and by several others, that Muriel Broadbent no longer invited her nephew Joel Greenwood, though of course he was known for his reserve and unsocial nature which perhaps explained it.

Molly still did not care for Mrs Broadbent's friends, she was forced to admit, although one or two had given the impression that had they not been forced to take sides they might warm to her. Helen Herbert for one, who had written a polite thank-you note after the first party and had hinted that perhaps, in the future, when Molly's baby was born, she and Tim might care to come over and play tennis at Parkfield House. There would be a young crowd. Their Angela, of course, and Laura Knight who was good natured and therefore apparently willing to overlook Molly's poor beginnings; Sarah Bowman, whose engagement to Rupert Lucas was to be announced shortly, and some pleasant young men and women Molly had not yet met. She would keep in touch, she said, and hoped Molly would continue in good health during her pregnancy.

It was two weeks after the party that Molly met Joel when she was out riding. Tim had gone over to the mill to try and sort out some complexity which had again arisen over money, though why they should think he could solve the problem was beyond him, he said cheerfully to his wife as he leaped into his Vauxhall after kissing her warmly goodbye in the porch.

There were in Lancashire at least four hundred thousand men and women working fewer than thirty-five hours a week with no dividends to speak of for the mill owner. In fact yarn and cloth were being produced at a loss at the moment and many spinning mills and weaving sheds were going under but it would not last long, he told her. Broadbent Mill had been building on its reputation for three generations, their name stood high, their credit would be extended, the fame of their cloth going to the very ends of the earth itself. Molly, having no idea what he was talking about, since all she knew about cotton was how to spin it, had run cheerfully up the stairs to put on her riding breeches, which would not fit her for much longer.

She went further than she intended, going north of Oldham, then east, keeping to quiet lanes and bridle paths, moving higher and higher up towards Badger's Edge. It was hard, the tracks stony and in places marshy but, keeping to the bridleways, she had no difficulty leading Isolde up to the Edge itself. The lower slopes had been made up of grass heath and heather moor but as she went higher there was a rapid growth of bilberry, bracken and evergreen crowberry. Fast-flowing streams had carved out tightly wooded, steep-sided cloughs, crowded with silver birch, rowan, mountain ash, willow. She noticed what, later in the season, would be the blossom of guelder rose, dog rose, milkmaid, marsh marigold, celandine and already the delicacy of wood anemone nestling among the roots of the trees.

It was said that a "badger", or travelling salesman, so far back in time no one could even remember when, had fallen to his death here in a snowstorm and since then there had been little or no change. A great stretch of wildly rolling moorland sweeping down and down into the valley where a grey blanket of smoke hid the town of Oldham. The land was wide and uneven with folds of growing bracken, gorse and heather which in summer would be thick and burgeoning in colours of green and yellow and purple but which now was still the dun colour of the edge of winter.

Molly dismounted slowly, speaking gently to Isolde, rubbing her soft nose with her gloved hand, for she had become inordinately fond of the pretty little mare since she had started to ride her. She was still only a novice, she knew that, and the ride up here which had seemed so short and easy on the day they had come in Tim's motor car, had taken it out of her. She would sit for an hour and rest, let the mare crop the tufty grass before she tackled the return journey. She was warmly dressed with a woollen jumper under her tweed riding jacket, a scarf wrapped snugly about her neck and her daddy's cap pulled well down about her ears.

She let the mare go, knowing she would not wander, watching for a moment as she lowered her head to the tough, windswept grass.

A lark rose up from behind her, disturbed by something and Molly turned to stare upwards into the wide bowl of the blue sky, watching until the bird was out of sight though she could still hear its tuneful song. She sighed and sat down, her back to a grey pitted rock thick with moss, looking out over the somewhat bleak landscape. Not by any stretch of the imagination could it be called beautiful, Molly reflected, but it had a powerful majesty which appealed to her. An unwelcoming land really, at this time of the year, impossible to plough or cultivate, useful for nothing but a few scattered sheep and the abundance of its water which fed the valleys and the mills which had made men rich. Hostile sometimes, to those who did not respect it, intractable and cruel, but today it was mild and dreaming in the pleasant springlike air. It was worth the hard ride to get up here, she told herself, gazing over the now familiar landscape which stretched as far as the eye could see on either side and high at her back to where the moors rose up and away towards Yorkshire. She would not be able to come here much longer once the baby began to show and if Tim knew she had ridden this far today, and alone, he would be furious.

She smiled at the thought of her humorous, good-natured husband being anything but just that. He had this disarming way of laughing her out of any temper she might get into, usually over his damn mother, and she could not imagine him being furious with her for long.

From somewhere behind her she heard a small sound, the chink of stone against stone and her heart quickened as she peered cautiously round the rock. There were men about, unemployed, desperate men who would steal her boots for the cash they would bring, but to her relief a small, rough-haired terrier suddenly appeared. His short tail was going round and round like a miniature windmill and his ears were pricked with astonished interest as though the last thing he expected was another living creature up here in this deserted moorland.

"Hello, where did you spring from?" she asked, holding out a hand to him. He seemed to smile, his tail going even faster. He sniffed her hand, then, finding it to his liking, began to lick it, and then her face, with great enthusiasm.

"He's with me," a man's deep, slow voice said and her heart, which had slowed at the sight of the dog, somersaulted in her breast, for the voice was that of Joel Greenwood.

He put her in such a flurry she could hardly get to her feet, but when he put out a hand to help her she recoiled from it as though it were a hooded cobra.

"I'm sorry, Molly, I didn't mean to frighten you. I saw your mare, she's very distinctive, you know, from further down the clough. I was not sure whether you were . . . well, I thought I had better come and investigate. You might have come off and in your . . ."

"Thanks . . . thanks . . . but I'm fine . . . really." Their combined embarrassment was a torment to them both and yet neither was sure what created it.

He was dressed in well-cut but old riding breeches and a jacket which had seen better days. He wore no gloves but his boots were polished to a high gleam. He looked at her steadily in that piercing way he had, his dark eyes seeming to bore right into her head with their scrutiny. His face was sombre, unsmiling and she found herself wondering if he had ever had a damn good laugh. He was kind, she knew that, for she was aware now that he had altered the seating arrangement at the dinner party so that she would have easy-going, sympathetic partners beside her at the table, but apart from that his gaze was cool, unconcerned, polite but disinterested.

"Woody is a blighter and I'm sorry if he startled you. He is only young and cannot bring himself to believe that everyone is not totally overjoyed to have him leap all over them."

"I don't mind. I like dogs. Me an' Albert have become good friends."

"Albert. Tim's old dog, that's nice."

"Aye, but he's too old to come up here."

"Yes, I suppose he would be. I remember the day Tim got him. It was just before the war began. None of us had any idea that we were to . . ." His jaw set suddenly, his mouth drew to a thin line and he seemed to shake himself. "Well, there was this wriggling scrap of golden fluff going begging at Home Farm. Tim was always a sucker for helpless creatures. He slung it up before him on his saddle . . . God, we were only lads – fifteen or sixteen, I suppose – but really, I'm babbling on and I'm sure you're not interested . . ."

"Oh, but I am. Tim does not speak of the past much and I'd love to hear about him . . . and you and his brothers."

"I had a brother, too. Name of Pearce."

"Did he . . .?"

"Oh yes, there's only me and Tim left."

"My . . . daddy and brothers . . ." She could not go on and when he leaned towards her this time and took her hand she did not resist.

"I know, Molly, Tim told me."

"I miss them still."

"Yes, we all do . . ." meaning every soldier who had not come back from the war.

"Do you ride up here often?" she asked him, totally and painfully aware that her hand was still in his but for some reason unwilling to let go.

"Yes, I do. There seems to be something up here, besides the awesome landscape, that draws me. An ancestor of mine was involved in riots and machine-breaking when the Luddites and then Chartism was alive. Have you heard of it?"

She shook her head, hoping he would go on.

"The men involved marched over these moors, cotton spinners who were deprived of their livelihood by the new factories and the machines inside them."

He stopped and looked down into her absorbed face, his hand still holding hers and his heart moved painfully and hopelessly in his chest. With an abrupt movement he let go of her hand and shoved his own, the one that had clasped hers, deep in the pocket of his old breeches.

He scowled, his eyebrows dipping fiercely.

"I don't wish to appear rude but should you be up here?" In your condition, he was plainly saying and Molly felt the embarrassment return and flood her whole body. For some reason this man had a way of making her aware of him as a man. Her pregnancy, unlike those of women of her mother-in-law's generation, genuinely did not disconcert her. She was aware that the men working about Meddins grounds knew she was to have a child but their respectful glances, their warm smiles, their sincere enquiries after her health did not trouble her. Only this man made her cheeks flood and her heart race and her eyes want to look anywhere but at him. His concern was genuine, somehow she knew that, and entirely courteous, but something in her, amazingly, did not want him to see her as a pregnant woman. A woman carrying another man's child and the thought astonished and frightened her.

"I'm . . . I'm . . ." How could she say I'm not due until September and this is only March? How could she let him know that Tim had made her pregnant in the first week or so of their marriage and she'd not been visited with the "curse" since? How could she even contemplate telling him that this would probably be the last time she rode Isolde since she herself knew it was unwise. She couldn't. She couldn't talk about such things to this man. Not this man who was regarding her so gravely.

"I was wondering if you and Tim were free to dine a week on Saturday," he said abruptly, right out of the blue and at once she looked up at him, her heart beginning thankfully to slow, her eyes to narrow and gleam, as she smiled with genuine pleasure, then, just as abruptly the smile slid away.

"Who'll be there?" she asked, her frankness curling the corners of his mouth.

"Oh, none of those who were at Meddins a fortnight ago. Some friends of mine from Chadderton. He's a doctor, she's a teacher."

"Really!"

"Yes, really." His mouth twitched. "Perhaps my mill manager who has a pretty young wife whom I'm sure you'll like."

"That sounds grand," beginning to beam, for these friends of his seemed nothing like the stuffed shirts and high-toned ladies who had come to the Meddins dinner party.

"And I thought Sarah Bowman and her fiancé, Rupert Lucas."

Molly's mouth dropped open and she stared into Joel's face then she began to laugh.

"Blessed Mother of God, not . . ."

"Yes, I thought it was time someone forgave them."

"You're a spalpeen, so you are."

"I'm not sure what a spalpeen is, Molly, but I take it you approve."

"Of Sarah and Rupert?" giggling like a child.

"Of asking them to my dinner party. I know I can rely on you to be kind to Sarah."

"Well, I'll do me best," thinking that Sarah had not been very kind to Molly Broadbent.

She had a lovely time, she told Tim when they finally fell into their bed at almost three o'clock on the night of the party. Doctor and Mrs Chard, Millicent and Robert, as Molly was to call them they insisted, had been as friendly and down to earth as any of Molly's own people and she meant that as a compliment. Robert was about thirty-five and had served in France where he and Joel had become friends and so he, Tim and their host had a certain bond, unspoken, of course, of those who had fought in the war. Robert had a practice in a not very smart or lucrative part of Chadderton where he worked among those who were hard pressed to keep up the insurance they paid each week for his services. Molly got the impression he did not turn them away should they fall into arrears. Millicent was younger, a teacher in a council school where much of her work included the making of enormous pans of broth to supplement her pupils' diet, the collecting of children's clothing from the better-class areas about the school and the perpetual fight she had to ensure her children got their free school milk. She and Robert had no children of their own.

Mr and Mrs Thomas, Andrew and Laura, Mr Thomas being mill manager at Greenwoods Mill, were just as pleasant. Laura – "call me Loll" – was a little out of her depth and constantly turned to Molly for guidance which made Molly feel quite grand. Loll was sweet and charming, like a kitten wanting to be friends with anyone who was kind to it, so consequently everyone was.

As for Sarah and Rupert, the change in them, at least in Sarah, was quite dramatic. Molly confided to Tim that she thought Sarah was ready to get on her high horse at first, prepared, should anyone say anything she considered snide, if Tim knew what she meant, which he did, to cut them dead. Since no one at the party but Molly, Tim and Joel knew of the incident in the lavatory at Meddins which had led to their immediate engagement, and when it was apparent that Molly wanted nothing but to be sociable, with no memory of that awful evening, Sarah thawed and even asked Molly if she'd care to take tea with her at the Café Monico next week.

The conversation was an exhilarating mixture of serious discussion and flippant small talk. They spoke of the social iniquities of the day of which Sarah knew nothing; the likelihood of the miners striking and where it might lead, a subject Millicent and Molly thought quite in order for ladies such as themselves to give an opinion about which impressed Loll no end.

They talked of films and theatre and music, of sport and the chances of Oldham Athletic winning the cup, indeed of anything under the sun that anyone cared to throw into the conversation, even Loll's innocent revelation that she had paid fourteen guineas for the dress she wore, a red chiffon velvet with a silk fringe round the hem.

For a moment Molly was aware that Sarah was appalled, for it was frightfully bad form to speak of money and how much one had paid for a thing but how could anyone be cross with Loll who meant no harm? She and Andrew, who was Mr Greenwood's right-hand man, she confided to Molly in the lovely bedroom put aside for the use of the ladies, had not been married long and she'd be thrilled if Molly and Tim would dine with them one evening. She didn't know many people since she came from West Derby in Liverpool. Did Molly know it? Her parents had a house there and perhaps she and Molly might drive over there one day in the zippy little motor car Andrew had just bought for her.

The people she met at Greenacres, the friendships which were developing from that visit had done much to ease Molly Broadbent into her new role as Tim's wife and mistress of Meddins. Now she had another, she reflected that night as she suckled her new son under the admiring gaze of her husband.

And she had Meddins!

22

"Not a penny off the pay, not a minute on the day", the miners said and so on May 1st, 1926, they were locked out. A national strike was called at midnight on May 3rd and every union member in the country came out with them, transport and railway workers, workers in heavy industry, in building and in gas and electricity undertakings. It was so instinctive that the voluntary recruitment of the war, almost twelve years ago, and the strike of 1926 were likened to one another. Both acts of spontaneous generosity and both without parallel. The strikers wanted nothing for themselves, they said, they merely wanted the miners to have a decent living wage and it was then that the "class war" began. Volunteer drivers for trams and lorries were called for. Special constables were recruited from among ex-army officers and from universities and when Tim, whose operatives had walked out en masse from Broadbents Mill, and having nothing else to do, he said cheerfully, wanted to offer his services as a tram driver, Molly's temper flashed and crashed about the house with such violence everyone in it was convinced she would lose the child she was then carrying. These were her people who were fighting for a decent life for themselves and their families. No, there were no miners among the O'Dowds and the Todds but they were all working men and women and if Tim did anything to aid the cause of the owners she would never, never forgive him!

There were violent industrial disputes in London and it was feared troops might have to be called out. Buses were obstructed and even wrecked and altogether about four thousand people were prosecuted for violence or incitement to violence. In other parts of the country, and in complete contrast, police and strikers formed teams and played football against one another!

The government was hampered in appealing to public opinion by its own act of calling out the printers, and when an attempt to penalise the strikers and the unions was called for, a stop was put to it by no lesser person than His Majesty King George V who described himself as an ordinary little man who recognised that these were all his people and good people at that.

It all came to nothing. The miners were driven back to work six months later by starvation and in November when Liam Broadbent was two months old all talk of a further general strike petered out.

Nevertheless, Robert Chard agreed on the occasion of the first dinner party Molly and Tim attended after the birth of their son, the working man's lot was slowly, very slowly, mind, improving. He had hopes that the rates of benefit for the unemployed and the sick would soon be raised. A contributory old-age pension would double the income of the aged needy, of whom there were a great many in his practice. Education was improving, so was public housing and Great Britain was fast approaching a welfare state. Income tax had been reduced to four shillings in the pound and gross poverty was slowly on the decline. Wages had risen – except for the miners, of course – and large families were no longer usual. Despite the seriousness of the General Strike and its after effects there would be new ideas in economic planning. Unemployment would fall and the working man would regain his proper place in the order of things, and his pride.

An idealist, was Robert Chard, and Molly would sit, her chin in her hands, her face rapt and rosy, drinking in all his wonderful words, for had not her daddy said exactly the same thing all those years ago? As she watched and listened and sighed at the wonder of it she was unaware that the man at the head of the table, his face lost in the shadow beyond the candles placed there, watched her with the same wondering, total absorption with which she listened to Robert Chard.

It was at Christmas that Muriel Broadbent told her daughter-in-law that she would have no objection if Molly would prefer to remain in the background and let Muriel do all the arrangements for the Christmas festivities that went on at this time of the year.

She had confided to Helen Forrester, who was her special friend and whose daughter Muriel had wanted for Tim, that she might have accepted Tim's dreadful wife more easily if she had not put herself forward so much, but one only had to look at her as she flaunted herself, particularly since she had become the mother of the heir to Meddins, to know what a disaster it would all turn out if left to her alone. There was a traditional party given at Meddins every Christmas Eve and the little upstart seemed to think, now that she was making friends – of sorts – from among those odd people Joel entertained at Greenacres, indeed some of them had been invited to the party, that she was now part of decent society when everyone knew that she was accepted – just – only because of Tim and herself, Muriel Broadbent. She was making a fool of herself and would soon come a cropper.

The way she was with Muriel's grandson was an example. No proper nanny but some young girl who was allowed to watch over Liam – I know, dreadful name – when his mother was out in that monstrous motor car visiting those excruciatingly common relatives of hers, or up on the moor exercising her mare, which she seemed to do a lot of these days. Surely it could not be good for a woman to . . . to . . . well, to sit astride a horse so soon after having a child? Muriel had never ridden and had never wanted to, but the latest thing, which Tim agreed with, could you believe, was riding to hounds. Yes, Tim had taken her to the Hollins Hunt only last week where, it was reported, she had done well and to cap it all Tim was talking of buying her a hunter of her own! They already had four horses in the stable, including her daughter-in-law's mare, all eating their heads off – just as though the Broadbents were down to their last penny – not to mention three grooms. It was quite disgraceful. A girl who scarcely more than a year ago had worn a cap, clogs and a shawl and worked on a ring spinning frame in her husband's mill to be hunting with the Hollins which was known to be one of the finest in the county.

The girl in question, who had agreed amiably enough that Muriel, for this Christmas alone, though she did not voice it, should continue with her usual preparations, was engaged in a game of musical chairs, which, it seemed, had become part of the warp and weft of the Broadbents' Christmas Eve party for the past thirty years. Muriel insisted upon it, as she insisted on every small detail of how Christmas had been ever since she married Joshua Broadbent. Even during the war years when he and she, the Herberts and the Forresters, the Knights and the Ropers, the Davidsons and the Bowmans, sadly missing the young men, of course, had done their best to retain the Christmas spirit.

It had been a perfect day, cold, clear, lightly frosted and Tim and Molly had ridden out on Isolde and Hal in the morning, getting as far as Badger's Edge, though Molly had been keen to turn back before they got there which had surprised her husband since she was mad about riding and would gallop on and on long after he had had enough. They had met Joel who said he often came up here and yes, he would see them that evening at Meddins but his voice had been cold, his expression withdrawn.

"He's a funny chap, is Joel," Tim mused as he followed his wife and her mare on their way home, picking his way carefully, for the clough side down which they rode was steep and rocky. "He's a few months older than me and yet he's shown no sign of ever taking an interest in any lady. As opposed to a woman, I mean, since he's had plenty of those."

"Has he?" Her voice came back at him, sharp and somewhat constrained but then she was concentrating on the path.

"Oh, yes. He confided in me when we were fifteen that a girl in Oldham, a mill girl from Austins, had made a man of him."

"A mill girl, really?"

"Yes. Christ, I was envious and begged for her name and short of that a description of what she had done to him but he wouldn't tell me. Her name or their endeavours together. He's like that. Deep, close, you know."

"I'd noticed."

They had reached the lower slopes and with a shout Tim dug his heels into Hal's side, urging the bay on to a gallop.

"Come on, Molly Broadbent, I'll race you home."

It was still rough and uneven, going downhill, occupied by rabbit and stoat, curlew and magpie, fit only for small animals and birds but Molly needed no second bidding. With a cry to Isolde and a touch of her heels in her side she was off, soaring away into the winter sun, the frozen grass crisp beneath the mare's hooves, the blue sky wheeling dizzily, her heart thudding, her breath harsh in her throat. She was still somewhat tremulous at the unexpected sight of Joel up on Badger's Edge. She hadn't wanted to go that way in the first place, knowing it was a favourite spot of his but Tim had cantered on, shouting behind him to her to keep up and she had no choice but to do so. She and Joel met at dinner parties, not just in his home but in Andrew and Loll's pretty little villa at Wood Brook; at Meddins, now that Muriel had forgiven him for what she considered his interference at the dinner party in February, but there were always half a dozen or more other guests which seemed to dilute the breathlessness which came over her at the sight of him. He looked at her so coldly at times, his eyes hooded, his strong face serious, even disapproving, and she wished she knew what he was thinking, but as Tim said he was a deep and enigmatic man who, her common sense told her, was nothing to do with her.

She and Tim leaped as one a drystone wall which surrounded a pasture called Two Acre, racing, their faces to their mounts' necks, leaping across Shiloh Lane and on over Thurston Clough Brook. The brook was wide and shallow, the water clear and cold, easy to wade, studded with smooth, wet stones which gleamed like gunmetal in the sunlight.

They slowed then, neither conceding defeat, first to a canter and then a walk, moving slowly along lanes frozen and deserted, the ground hard and silvery, until they reached the gates of Meddins. The gatehouse was empty now since old Evans had retired and Tim had thought it unnecessary to employ another man just to open and shut the gates as Evans had done. Carriages then, of course, and not motor cars.

They had both been glowing and exhilarated as they dismounted, handing over their mounts to Wilf. Molly felt the rhythm of her heart begin to slow, to fall into that state of peaceful calm Meddins always had on her and she sighed, secure in the knowledge that this was where her place was. It had been waiting for her ever since that day Daddy had first brought her to its gates, and she had loved it then, child as she was. Now its dreaming, tranquil beauty rested her in its heart's core, its mellow walls seeming to glow with welcoming warmth against the stark, bare silhouettes of the trees which surrounded it. There was a thin film of ice on the lake, easily broken by the irritable, squawking ducks, a skim of sunlight across it turning it to gold. White with frost, gold and pink and russet, her surroundings in their beauty made her feet falter and her breath quicken again.

"Darling?" Tim enquired softly.

"Nothing . . . only I love you," meaning not just her husband but this house which he had given to her.

"I would hardly call that nothing, my love, and I love you."

They walked towards the side door hand in hand then made their way to the nursery where, they told one another, their baby son already recognised them and smiled a welcome.

The house was a positive Christmas grotto of tinsel and holly, well-placed mistletoe and a Christmas tree reaching to the ceiling in the high hallway which the menservants had decorated to Muriel's liking, standing on tall stepladders to reach the top branches. It had red candles, tinkling gold and silver bells and was crowned by an angel a foot tall. Under it were heaped dozens and dozens of brightly wrapped parcels to be given out later and to which Molly had added her own. Those left tomorrow would be opened with great ceremony by the three of them before lunch, Tim, Molly and Muriel Broadbent and by the servants who would be lined up in the hall just as though it was still as it had been before the war.

The game of musical chairs waxed fast and furious. Katherine Forrester, home from her nursing studies for Christmas, and a talented pianist, good-naturedly played all the latest tunes while the guests, the young ones, plunged recklessly round and round the double row of back-to-back chairs. There were howls of laughter from the ladies who, in Muriel's opinion, had had too much sherry, particularly that dreadful Loll who had become such a close friend of her daughter-in-law, and who won, shrieking like an excited child. Muriel and her friends were playing the inevitable bridge since the high jinks – which seemed excessively heated to her and which she blamed on Tim's wife, of course – were not for them. There was to be dancing after supper, and Rupert and Sarah Lucas, married last May and not a day too soon in Muriel's opinion, were shouting for sardines of all things.

"Charades would be nice," Laura Knight suggested tentatively but she was shouted down by the Davidson boys, Justin and John, by George Fraser who was Delia's nephew and by Oliver Forrester, all flushed and overheated – in more ways than one, Muriel privately thought – and should have known better. She would have to go and tactfully restore order, as a proper hostess should, if they did not quieten down soon. Yes, she knew it was Christmas but decorum must be applied at all times.

"Who's to be 'it', then?" Sarah wanted to know, smiling in that provocative way she had, and not at her husband. "Let me, oh, do let me." Most of them had been coming to Meddins since they were children and knew every hiding place in the house and it was the greatest fun to slip away, leaving the rest to count to a hundred while the one who was 'it' found some hidey-hole, not too hard to find, and waited for the first person, hopefully some dashing young man, to squeeze in with her.

"Molly. Molly must be 'it'. It's the first time she's been to a Meddins Christmas party" – she had still been on her honeymoon last year – "so it's only fair."

"Oh, not me, please," she protested. "I know I'll get lost and no one will ever find me except for my mouldering bones."

"Rubbish."

"Off you go, Molly."

"Go on, darling. I won't let you get lost. In fact I intend to find you first," her husband said huskily, since the neckline of her dress was cut very low, at the back and the front. Though it was no more than three hours, indeed when she was attempting to put it on, since he had made love to her, his hot brown eyes told her exactly his intentions.

The dress was made of layered smoke grey chiffon, a straight sheath with handkerchief points which barely touched her knees, drifting and folding about her restored slender figure. It skimmed her full breasts, clearly showing the bobs of her nipples, then clung to her hips, rippling and floating as she moved. She wore a narrow band of diamanté about her forehead and her hair was loosely brushed to the back of her head in a tumble of dark curls. Tim had bought her a triple strand of exquisite pearls for Christmas which she had obligingly tried on for him – with nothing else – last night but she had declined to wear them tonight since they did not go with her dress. Instead she had on a long pair of silver earrings which almost reached her shoulders and half a dozen silver slave bangles. She looked exotic, the excitement, or was it the sherry, flaming pink flags in her cheeks and turning her eyes to the brilliant blue green of a turquoise.

"Well . . ."

"Oh, do get on, Molly, I'm starting to count to a hundred," Rupert shrilled, meaning to be the first to find her, since he had still, despite his married state, an itch in his pants for Tim Broadbent's glorious wife and this might be his chance to get it scratched!

From across the drawing room where he was leaning beside the wide doors which led into the conservatory, Joel Greenwood watched her through the haze of the smoke from the cigarette he had just lit. His eyes were narrowed, his expression inscrutable but when she was turned, still protesting, towards the door which led into the hall, no one noticed him slip away through the conservatory and out into the garden.

Molly, her heart beating for some reason, like a soldier's drum, whirled about at the foot of the stairs, wondering which way to go, while from behind the closed door of the drawing room voices could be heard chanting, "Ninety-five, ninety-four, ninety three . . ."

"This way," a voice said curtly and when she turned, bewildered, towards the front door, she saw it was slightly ajar, held open by a man's strong brown hand.

"Be quick or they'll be after you," the voice added, more gently this time, and indeed, going faster and faster, the chanting voices in the drawing room were down to forty-six.

She went, she didn't even wonder why, only that the voice, the man, told her to. Perhaps she had a curiosity to find out what it was he meant to do with his cousin's wife who was out of bounds to him, or how she would respond to whatever it was. Ever since she had met him on her wedding day he had seemed to have the power to quicken her breathing, to make her body tremble just a little, to cause her heart to miss a beat and her gaze to lower itself before his. To dry up her mouth so that she could hardly speak. To make her feel like some blushing schoolgirl to whom an older man has just spoken. She loved Tim devotedly but Joel Greenwood seemed to have some fascination, some potent, hypnotic charm which she was afraid of. It was not that he did anything which might be called an enticement. He was civil to the point of boredom.

He treated her, whenever they met, as he did every other woman, including her mother-in-law, with courteous, almost chilling respect, but whenever she was in his company she seemed to feel his eyes on her, though when she looked in his direction they never were.

After Liam was born she had gone up to Badger's Edge on a number of occasions and had found him there, leaning with his back to the same tall rock where they had met in March.

"Good morning," he would say politely. "A fine morning."

"Aye . . . lovely," she would answer just as politely, both of them carefully avoiding one another's glance and she wondered why she had ridden this way in the first place. Sometimes she thought he didn't even like her very much, his face was so set and stern, as though she were intruding on his peace. His eyebrows dipped ferociously as he scowled away over the golden bracken and the deep purple of the heather and when, after several silent minutes, she said she must be off, he had seemed almost relieved.

So what was he up to now?

"What . . . where . . .?" she managed to stammer as he threw a warm cloak – where had it come from? – about her shoulders.

"You want somewhere to hide, don't you? Somwhere that will take them a long time to find?"

"Yes, but . . . but shouldn't you be looking for me, not hiding with me?"

"Let's just say I am about to find you first."

"But . . ."

"Mary Angelina, you really are the most argumentative young woman I have ever met. I noticed it from the first and I'm sure Aunt Muriel would agree with me. Now, do you, or do you not want to win this daft game?"

"How do you win?"

"By not being found then simply walking back into the drawing room without disclosing where you have been."

"But where . . .?"

"In here."

"But it's the coachhouse."

"Exactly and there is the elegant old brougham which used to convey my aunt about the countryside on her social calls over twenty years ago. Is it not charming and . . . romantic and does it not seem to you to be the most perfect place to hide?"

"Yes, but aren't I supposed to stay in the house?"

"I don't believe I know of any rules to that effect."

"Yes, but . . ."

"If you say that again, Mary Angelina, I shan't answer for the consequences."

"Yes, but . . ."

He sighed deeply and, as though it were something he had no power to resist, he drew her towards him, holding her by her shoulders, but lightly so that she could escape should she want to. Gently he put his mouth against hers. A bolt of lightning struck her and when he took his mouth away she almost fell, so he returned it, but more vigorously this time.

"I must be mad," he murmured against her lips, which did their best to cling to his, for now, with that one kiss, Molly Broadbent knew what it was that had slept and awakened at last between her and Joel Greenwood.

"Yes," she answered, no more than a whisper in her throat as her body edged closer to his. Her mouth opened of its own accord, since Molly O'Dowd and her practical good sense had been lost somewhere between that first kiss and this moment. Carefully and with great deliberation, her tongue began to flick and probe the soft inside of his lips in a way that instantly brought him to a desperate, hungry need for her.

The cloak slipped back as his arms reached beneath it, falling in a graceful black shadow about their feet. The stone floor of the coachhouse was immaculately swept and scrubbed and each week the handsome brougham was cleaned and polished. When Joel opened the door and lifted her inside she could smell the sharp tang of soap and faintly overlaying it the aroma of some long-forgotten perfume worn by the young Muriel Broadbent. The padded seats were of a pale-coloured velvet, difficult to recognise in the dark and there were neat little curtains at the windows, Molly had time to notice, wondering on the state of the human mind which could register such things at a time like this.

"Joel," she murmured huskily, turning to him, reaching out for him with that electric bolt of passion which the touch of him had generated in her.

"Jesus, I've waited for this . . . watched you . . ."

She didn't know what she was doing and barely who she

was doing it with. She was aware that it was Joel, naturally, but this hard-breathing man whose hands were at her face and neck, whose lips explored the outer curve of her ear, whose tongue probed the softness inside it, making her shiver in uncontrolled delight, whose mouth nipped the lobe with not very gentle teeth, was a stranger to her. Exciting her, enslaving her, mesmerising her, totally overwhelming her with rapture and the absolute certainty that it would last for ever. Time had skipped a beat and she was agonisingly aware that nothing would ever be the same again.

"I can't see beyond you . . ." His voice groaned in anguish as though he were racked with torment. "Can you understand that, Mary Angelina, can you? You block my vision of any other woman . . . do you know? This past year . . . ever since your bloody wedding day . . . Oh, Jesus . . ." His voice was shaking. "Oh, my darling . . . my love . . . my love," and the enormity of what he was saying, what his hands were doing to his cousin's wife forced them apart as nothing else could.

There was silence for several minutes. Molly could not stop trembling and he opened the carriage door, reached down for the cloak and wrapped it about her, careful not to let his hands touch any part of her naked flesh. Her beautiful grey chiffon dress had somehow slipped down, or been dragged down, to expose her breasts and he turned his head away with great delicacy as she attempted to rearrange it.

"I'm sorry . . . I should not have . . . I suppose we had best get back." His voice was stiff and though Molly couldn't see his face she knew it would be set in its usual forbidding lines.

"Yes."

"I'll take you to . . ."

"Thank you . . . yes."

"Find somewhere for you to . . . to hide . . . pretend . . ."

"Yes . . . thank you."

Then, in a voice harsh and explosive, turning violently towards her so that she cowered back from him, he told her, "No, I'm *not* bloody sorry, Mary Angelina. I should be, I know that. I didn't plan this, whatever you may think. Jesus God, I could have . . . have kissed you any time up on Badger's Edge. I wanted to, Christ, I wanted to. You were so cool . . . that prim, pursed-up look to your mouth. I wanted to make it warm, moist, eager for mine . . . but I didn't. I was a perfect bloody gentleman, in fact." He lowered his head and put his hand to his mouth, then lifted it again, turning to look directly into her glittering eyes which were staring unblinkingly into his. "You and I . . . you were meant for me, you know that . . . not him. We are a perfect match and . . . and he . . ."

"Tim's . . . a good man." Her voice rasped in her dry throat.

"Dear God in heaven, d'you think I don't know that? He is my brother . . . since . . . If you were any other man's, I'd take you away from him. I know I could, but Tim . . ."

His voice faded away and he hung his head again in hopeless resignation. "Tim would not survive it if . . ."

"I know."

"So . . ."

"Yes?"

"You know I love you, Mary Angelina."

For a luminous moment her heart sang with joy, then shrivelled away as though in a little death.

"Why do you call me Mary Angelina?" Her voice was as empty as his.

"Because no one else does."

"Joel . . ."

"Yes?"

"Kiss me."

He put his hands carefully on her cheeks, cupping them, then brought his mouth down just as carefully on hers, as one would kiss a child. It lingered there as though to retain the feel and taste of her in his mind. As though he would never see her again.

"Thank you," she said quietly.

"Go now."

"Yes."

"Through the side door and into the boot cupboard."

"They will have looked . . ."

"There's a cupboard within the cupboard."

"Joel?"

"Oh, my love, my precious love, go . . ."

She wept silently that night as her husband slept beside her. They had not found her and when she had judged it was time she had left the boot cupboard and made her way back to the drawing room, praying to the Holy Mother that he would be gone. The Holy Mother answered her prayers and she was surrounded by open-mouthed and unbelieving guests who demanded to know where she had been, aggrieved when she would not tell them.

The next day, Christmas Day, when she went to mass with Mammy, Aunty Flo and Aunty Maggie, she lit a candle. She didn't know why, really, for it did not seem appropriate but she prayed wildly, despairingly, that somehow the Blessed Mother of God would give her the strength to resist this joy, this madness that had come upon her. Reason told her it was madness but her heart struggled against it and her woman's body, which Tim had never completely satisfied, wanted to run, fly across the miles and throw itself into Joel Greenwood's willing arms.

They ate Christmas lunch, at great length, and with only sporadic attempts at conversation. A traditional roast turkey with chestnut stuffing, and plum pudding flamed with brandy and soaked in rum sauce and afterwards they handed out their presents, to each other and to the servants.

Liam was brought down and only then, as Molly nursed her son, did the black, desolate cloud lift a little from her heart.

"Should he be allowed to lie on the drawing room carpet without his napkin on?" Muriel asked, since her daughter-in-law seemed not to care about such things.

"He's just filled one, Mrs Broadbent, so we're quite safe," Molly answered, aware of the disdainful expression on Muriel's face. Despite Muriel's joy in her grandson, who was bright and handsome, she was of the generation that believed a child should be kept in the nursery and not be allowed to lie about her Aubusson carpet as her grandson was doing and where he was bound to bring up his milk, or even worse!

"I'll take him upstairs then," Molly said, lifting the baby up in the air where he kicked in delight, his little penis bobbing merrily, his rounded pink bottom on display for all to see, "and then I think I'll get out Swallow and go and see Mammy. I promised her and Aunty Maggie and Aunty Flo when I saw them this morning that I'd try and get over there this afternoon. I've presents for them and . . . well . . ."

Anything to get out of this house which she loved so well, though it was not the house but the atmosphere of genteel refinement which bowed her down. Where a baby's rear end was looked on as something nasty and her son's gurgles disturbed his grandmother to a pained silence. And anything to get away from the memory of last night, a despairing voice inside her whispered.

"Do you think you should, sweetheart?" Tim asked anxiously. "After all, that man will be there."

"He'd hardly lift a hand to me now, Tim. Not to Mrs Tim Broadbent," and for some reason, though she hadn't meant it to, her voice sounded scornful.

"I'll come with you. In fact we'll take the Rolls. It will be more comfortable with Liam."

"I wish you wouldn't, Tim dear," Muriel Broadbent drawled. "After all I might need it later if I decide . . ."

"Decide to what?" Her son was clearly astonished.

"To go somewhere. It seems it is reasonable for your wife to visit her friends and so why not myself?"

"Today? On Christmas Day? Where would you go? And besides it is Molly's family she wishes to see."

"Delia did say that if any of us cared to drop in for a glass of champagne . . ."

"It's the first I've heard of it and anyway surely it's unfair to drag Herbert out today of all days?"

"He is my chauffeur, dear. That is what we pay him for."

"Mother, I'm sure . . ."

He got no further. Leaping to her feet, the smiling baby tucked beneath her arm like a badly wrapped parcel, Molly was white-faced with some emotion neither her husband nor mother-in-law recognised. Her eyes flashed and her lips curled and her voice was high with angry defiance.

"Oh, for the love of God, keep yer bloody Rolls. I'll tekk me own car."

"Molly, sweetheart."

"Don't sweetheart me, Tim Broadbent. It's about time you stood up to this awful old woman and until you do I'll go alone."

She knew herself that this was totally unfair, for hadn't Tim being doing just that but Molly was way past any point where logic reigned.

She did not take the Swallow and she did not go to Sidney Street.

He was there when she galloped wildly up to Badger's Edge an hour later and as she leaped from the saddle his arms reached out for her hungrily.

307

23

On New Year's Eve Pikey Watson took a drop too much
at the Old Soldiers Club. He stumbled home after agreeing
with several other old soldiers that things had never been the
same since the war ended, a war which he personally had
thoroughly enjoyed. His mood was self-pitying and morose.

He was in a foul temper when he crashed across the
threshold of his home in Sidney Street. Aware that next
door the old cow would be on the alert, ready to report
to that bitch up at the grand house should he threaten his
own wife, he tried to be quiet as he set about her cowering,
terrified figure but she would keep on screaming. He felt like
knocking her into the middle of next week, really he did and
in fact he raised his fist to do so.

As he lifted his hand the pain struck him full in his chest and
leaped down his left arm and before he could heave himself
to his chair the world went black. He was dead before he hit
the floor.

When the soft tapping began on the bedroom door Molly
was in that state of almost drugged sleep that Joel's love-
making had induced in her. A sort of dreamlike, anaesthetised
state that, though it caused her to be languorous, unfocused
on what was going on around her, also made every nerve end,
every pulse beat, every tender inch of her skin acutely alive.
She and Tim, Andy and Loll Thomas, Robert and Millicent
Chard, the Lucases and several dozen other like-minded
people – in fact as many as he could cram in for added
cover, he said – had been guests at Greenacres where Joel
had put on an informal New Year's Eve supper dance. He
wanted nothing grand, he said, since it was New Year's Eve,
a time recognised as one for having fun, whatever that might

mean. He was only having the blasted thing as an excuse to get her into his bed, she did realise that, he had scowled as he kissed her almost to the point of insensibility behind the grey rock on Badger's Edge. She was shivering violently and so was he, for they had almost undressed one another and the temperature had been hovering on zero that day. He had cursed and groaned as he put her together again with trembling hands since she seemed incapable of doing it herself, holding her as she almost fell, soothing her, petting her, calling her his dear love, crooning into her tumbled hair the sort of unintelligible sounds one makes to a distressed child and apologising to her for rousing her to a peak of violent passion and then being unable, because of the intense cold and a lack of somewhere to lay her, to satisfy her need.

He would have to think of another way that they could be together, he had murmured to her as he cradled her against his broad chest and brushed back the wild tangle of her hair from her face.

There was plenty of champagne that night, bottle after bottle of it which Joel pressed on his guests, good champagne they couldn't resist, a superb buffet, dishes piled high with cut-up lobster and fricasséed chicken, prawns in a rich sauce, delicate pastry cases filled with mushrooms, raised game pies and an ornamented tongue. There were salads, oyster patties and roast pheasant, fruited jellies and custards in fragile glasses, Swiss cream and tipsy cake and in the centre of this feast an epergne filled with every kind of fruit imaginable, all grown in the hothouses of Greenacres. They were all dishes which could be comfortably eaten standing up, though after a couple of hours of dancing and billiards for those gentlemen who fancied it, Joel's guests found seats wherever they could in the most informal fashion, in the hall lounging in the deep leather chairs before the enormous log fire, scattered about the dining room where the food was arranged, in what had been Joel's great-grandmother's winter garden among the cages filled with exotic birds and ornamental pots overflowing with magnolia, hibiscus, bougainvillaea and camellia, so heady with perfume it blunted senses already clouded with champagne. They sprawled in the drawing room and the small parlour and for an hour, as Joel's efficient maidservants refilled every glass as it became empty, as the conversation swirled, as laughter became even more hilarious and where no one knew the exact whereabouts of anyone else – except for those in their immediate vicinity – Joel Greenwood took Molly Broadbent up to his room and in the bed where they had first made love showed her again the true meaning of sensuality, of need, of lust. Over and over again he brought her to a frantic climax of love until she was limp and helpless, boneless and senseless, so that if Tim had walked in on them she would not have cared. Dangerous, cruel, immoral even, for she was committing adultery and yet Joel's caressing hands sliding deep into the rift of her buttocks, his mouth devouring her breasts, his powerful body pounding on hers gave her no time to consider it. This was love, she knew it as the blood tingled at her fingertips and his movement inside her was an exquisite torture. This was what she had been created for, this man and what this man did to her.

"I love you," he cried as, at the last, he went with her, crashing together like waves on a rock before being sucked down into the soft and formless depths of their shared passion.

Yes, it was a dangerous game they played, they both agreed sadly as they lay for a precious moment in one another's arms, nevertheless reaching hungrily for one another's mouths again and if they should both be missed and two and two were put together and added up correctly to four it would cause devastation to many lives. They knew it. They admitted it and they could do nothing about it.

"You won't let anything come between us, will you, Mary Angelina?" he whispered into her hair, a strong man forced to beg and not liking it. "I won't let you. You . . . you're . . . you belong to me now and I mean to keep you. It's no good saying you did not intend it to go this far" – though she had said no such thing— "because it has and one way and another I mean to keep you, my precious love. I'll not allow you to turn back now. Dear God, it consumes me . . . *you* consume me."

She could barely say his name. "And Tim?"

"Don't, for Christ's sake don't speak his name in my bed."

"Joel . . ."

"What?" His voice was a snarl of jealous outrage, for already his possession of her was being forced into a corner of their lives which no one must see and he was not a man to accept it. She could do no more than stop his mouth with a savage kiss.

They had not been missed though they had been gone for over an hour. When Molly slunk downstairs – she could think of no other way to describe it – they were all chattering like a flock of starlings, their laughter the high, wine-induced laughter which notices nothing unusual in anything. Tim was flirting with Sarah – or was it the other way round? – and when he saw her he even managed to look a little guilty which curled her up inside in shame.

But the shame and guilt did not last. They danced. She danced with every man there, including Joel and though they did their best not to press their bodies too close together in the slow foxtrot someone had put on, their bodies cared nought for decorum, remembering the hour upstairs and she could feel his hardness press against her and was not surprised when he excused himself and hurriedly left the room.

As the tapping increased in volume she came out of bed on a surge of breathless agitation, dragging herself from beneath Tim's heavy arm. He mumbled and turned but did not wake and she wondered what it was that had wakened her.

The tap became a knock and from the other side of the door Forbes spoke.

"Madam, there is a telephone call for you."

Oh, Blessed Mother . . . Joel . . . no, not Joel, for God's sake, for would he be likely to waken the whole house at – she peered at the clock on the bedside table, her eyes blurred with sleep – at three o'clock in the morning? It was only an hour or even less since she and Tim had fallen, quite literally, into bed. Tim had been so drunk Herbert had to be summoned to drive them home in the Rolls and then help him upstairs to their bedroom.

"Who . . . who is it, Forbes?" she quavered as she pulled Tim's warm woollen dressing-gown about her, since she could hardly let the butler see her in the pale, drifting, transparent garment of rose-coloured smoke that Tim liked her to wear.

"It's a Mrs Haydock, madam. Shall I tell her you'll come to the telephone? She says it is most urgent," or at least that is what Forbes thought she had said, the woman on the other end of the line being so excitable.

Mrs Haydock! Who the devil was Mrs Haydock? she asked Forbes, who looked a complete stranger to her in his own

311

checked dressing-gown and slippers, as she ran ahead of him down the wide and curving staircase.

"I'm afraid I couldn't say, madam." Forbes followed more slowly as he believed in keeping up a certain standard no matter how unusual the circumstances.

It was Minnie. Minnie Haydock whose presence at number twenty Sidney Street, whose stalwart promise to fetch Molly at the first sign of trouble had allowed her to live without the constant fear of what Pikey might do to her mammy and Molly not know about it. It had relieved Molly's mind when Mammy had declared her intention of sticking to her marriage vows and returning to Pikey Watson on Molly's own wedding day.

When she put down the receiver Forbes was amazed to see the rapturous glow of joy which flooded his young mistress's face. Evidently good news, he reflected, since Mrs Tim looked as though she had just been told she had won the pools and was filled with an elation which not only had her lifting her head in a peal of laughter but dancing a little jig, her bare feet beating a soft tattoo on the polished wooden floor.

"Good news, madam?" he ventured.

"The best, Forbes, the very best. My stepfather has just had a heart attack and died."

It was a simple affair, at Rosie's request, since there was no one, apart from a few of his old soldier pals, to mourn Pikey Watson's passing. Since Pikey was not of their faith he was laid decently to rest at St James's Church off the Huddersfield Road, reposing in a coffin the grandness of which would have surprised him and paid for by his delighted stepdaughter who wanted to have a party when it was all over. But more to support Rosie than from any inclination to honour Pikey, they all clustered about his grave in their best black. Aunty Flo and her Kathleen, though Eamon could not make it and had no wish to, he had privately told his sister. Uncle Alf and Aunty Maggie, their dead son's widow, Jane, and their Elspeth and Chrissie and as many of Aunty Maggie's grandchildren who were old enough and could be prevailed upon to attend. Cissie and Elsie Thompson from number two and Betty Spooner with her fiancé who was a tram driver for the corporation and had only consented to come in order to get a look at the posh "skirt" who was, or had been, Betty's best friend.

"Ashes to ashes, dust to dust . . ." the minister intoned as the coffin was lowered into the grave and only Tim Broadbent heard his wife mutter, "Aye and good riddance to bad rubbish." Rosie had refused Molly's offer to pay for the actual funeral – apart from the coffin – since she had been putting her few pennies of "policy" money away for such a contingency as this ever since she and Seamus were first married. This was the first time it had been called upon since the War Office had kindly seen to the disposal of her first husband and her two sons. Seamus, Liam and Patrick, God rest and keep their sweet souls, were buried in France and now that Pikey had gone, she could go with her daughter to visit the place where they, and thousands of others, were buried, Molly had promised her.

"Well, considerin' what a bugger 'e were tha' give 'im a proper send-off, Rosie Watson an' I fer one can only admire thi' for it."

Coming from Aunty Flo this was high praise indeed and for the first time in eight years Rosie felt the desire to smile broadly. She winked at Molly, who winked back and Molly knew that her mammy was herself again. She had undeservedly suffered the fires of purgatory with that bullying bastard, as they all had, for all these years and now she was free, and now, no matter what anyone thought of them, she and Mammy were to rejoice in it.

They all went back to Sidney Street and it was more like a New Year party, a celebration, than a wake, with Uncle Alf handing out pints of best bitter to any male hand which presented itself, and there were more than a few. The old soldiers who had stood to attention at the graveside had been only too pleased to accept Pikey's widow's invitation to come back to the house and have a drink or two in his honour and half the men in the street, though they had feared and detested him, became quite maudlin as they did their best to say something pleasant about him.

The house was packed from rooftop to cellar, for Rosie Watson and her girl, the one who had married the toff, did not stint on their hospitality. There was a table groaning with grub. Brawn and fresh bread, both made by Rosie before the funeral. Potato cakes hot from the oven, pressed beef and haslet, pickled onions and cheese and an enormous pan of lentil soup, it being such a cold day. Of course all the women in the street, as was the custom when one of their community passed away, had brought a dish of this or a plate of that.

Apple pies and custard tarts, rich fruit cake and girdle cakes and malt loaf and what with the sherry and port that husband of Molly O'Dowd's kept handing round they decided it was the best wake they'd ever been to.

Mrs Kenny from number eleven and old Mrs Wainwright from number thirteen could remember every detail of the day the dead man had smashed poor Rosie and Molly to broken dolls and they became so upset at the memory they cried drunkenly on one another's shoulders.

Aunty Flo and Aunty Maggie did a few choruses of "Nellie Dean", which was their party piece, accompanied by Willie Haydock on his mouth organ, and Minnie, who in her own opinion was the star of the show since it was she who had run to telephone Molly, acted as though this grand party would never have taken place but for her.

The children ran in and out, the little ones scarcely aware of what it was that had brought about this excitement, this wonderful rejoicing and infectious good humour, only Eileen, who was now six and had recently become as quiet and withdrawn as her half-sister Clare had once been, inclined to cling about her mother's neck. Of course, Pikey had done his best to kill any spirit his three children might have had and though they had perked up wonderfully in the six months they had spent at Aunty Maggie's they had all reverted to tiptoeing little mice when they had been returned to Sidney Street.

Only Clare herself was missing, refusing absolutely to enter the house again, even though at ten years old she fully understood that Pikey Watson was dead and Molly and Rosie were sadly aware that the damage done to her would never be mended. She would be eleven in March and was as lovely a child as Mary Angelina had been, her Aunty Flo was heard to remark, though not half as lively, of course. She had begged to stay with Mrs Monihan who lived next door to Aunty Flo, whilst the funeral party was held and they had no choice but to allow it.

It was a week later when Molly pulled up outside her mother's house, parking her little motor car by the kerb as neatly as a fledgeling attaching itself under its mother's wing. She was dressed in a warm, woollen coat in a rich shade of chestnut brown, tubular in style with one button at the fastening on the hip and with a creamy, spotted fur at the collar, the cuffs and the hem. It came to halfway between her knee and her ankle and she wore a "helmet" hat in the same material as the coat. Her shoes were brown with two-inch heels and an instep bar with a right-angled piece running down the foot to give a T effect. Her gloves were of rich brown suede. Beside her on the seat was a strong, lined wicker basket in which her four-month-old son was firmly and warmly strapped.

It was almost two years since the day Tim had brought her over to fetch her and Mammy's clothes after Pikey had beaten them, and what a difference between then and now. The threat which had hung over them all was gone and from now on Molly meant to see that her mammy lived in comfort and peace for the rest of her life. Not in this house, of course, since Molly could afford better and besides, might not Clare be persuaded to live with Mammy again if she moved to another place? The sooner Mammy, and the children, were got away from bad memories the better, which was why Molly was here today.

The front door flew open and Mammy's smiling face was there, almost rosy now and Molly could have sworn that even in a week she had put on some weight.

"Come in, darlin', come in. See, Eileen, mash tea, will tha', there's a good girl. Gracie, get out cups an' saucers, so, an would yer tekk a look at this bright-eyed little feller, me lad. Come ter tha' granny, me lovely. Come ter tha' granny, me little Liam . . . Liam . . . oh, Liam."

Scarcely before the door was closed she had Liam out of his basket, lifting him to her face, kissing him and tickling him until he crowed with laughter. He was an even-tempered child, as his father had been, his Broadbent grandmother was fond of saying, though she made no attempt to cuddle and kiss him as Rosie was doing. She loved him, naturally, since he was the son of her son, though his maternal blood did not please her, but she would not have dreamed of taking him from his nursemaid's arms when, at teatime, he was brought down to see her, and would certainly not have dreamed of visiting him in his nursery. She admired him from her drawing room chair, questioning the girl on his health and progress, doing her duty as she saw it.

Liam allowed himself to be divested of his wrappings, watching the movements of the other children, since none of them had yet returned to school. Archie, whose nature it was to be as bright as Molly's, if let, leaped about, showing off to the wide-eyed baby who did his best to keep him in his slower-moving vision. It seemed Archie was already aware that the dreadful shadow of the man who had been his father was no longer about. He showed the infant his new marbles, explaining their colours and names, even demonstrating to him on the table top how to play and Liam crowed his approval.

"He's lively, Mammy," Molly remarked, raising her eyebrows as Archie ran round and round the table and the chair where his mother nursed the baby. Liam was almost cross-eyed, trying to keep this fascinating person in view and his interest made the older child even more boisterous.

"Aye, an' can I stop 'im, Molly? 'E's lived fer four years in terror of . . . well, e's only a baby 'imself an' scarce knows what's happened but 'e seems ter realise . . . that summat's got better."

"Aye, I suppose you're right but what about her?" nodding her head in a discreet way at Eileen who was doing her best to share her mother's lap with Liam.

"Oh, she's a bit . . . well, it'll tekk time ter . . ."

Rosie fiddled with the ribbons on Liam's white matinee jacket, her gaze unable to meet Molly's and for a moment Molly was bewildered, then she felt the blood in her veins begin to thicken and turn to ice.

"Mammy?"

"Don't . . . don't, darlin'. 'E . . . 'e didn't touch 'er. I wouldn't let 'im even though 'e give me . . ."

"Gave you what, Mammy?"

"Well, a clip round the ear a time or two . . . no more. She saw it 'appen . . . watched when 'e . . . used me. It were the only way I could stop 'im." Rosie's lovely colour had faded and she hung her head in shame.

"The blackhearted bastard," Molly hissed venomously. "May he rot in hell for all eternity. If he was alive I'd kill him all over again and I'm only sorry he died so quickly. Why didn't you tell me? Why didn't Minnie hear him and tell me?"

Her blood, which had slowed in horror at the picture her mother's words had painted, began to pound and thud about her body, making her heart beat so hard it shook her like a rag doll in her chair. She jumped to her feet, almost stepping on the cat who had resigned itself to being leaped over by

Archie, seriously impeding Archie himself as he entertained her son. The young child came to a skidding halt at the sudden upsurge of her temper and edged closer to his mother.

The children, even her own, stared at her with big, wondering eyes and Liam's lip began to quiver.

"Stop it, stop it, Mary Angelina. Please, darlin', not in front o' them. Don't frighten 'em like 'e did. Don't shout . . . not in front of 'er." She put her arm about Eileen and drew her close to herself and the baby, who was Eileen's nephew in a roundabout way. Molly looked at her, at Eileen and Archie and then Gracie, wondering again at the somewhat weasel-faced appearance of her half-brother and -sisters. They had none of the handsome Irish looks of her side of the family. Their eyes were set close together, a pale, washed-out blue and though Mammy put the girls' hair in curling papers every night it wisped about their heads in fine, lifeless strands. They were not bad children. Their father had made them secretive and withdrawn with none of the open candour which is the nature of young children. And yet they were her mother's children, a part of her mother and as such deserved Molly's care and consideration. He was dead now. There was nothing he could do to them anymore and she must be thankful for that. She must not look back, only forward.

There was a loud clatter from the front door and, as is the way in northern homes where keys are turned only at night, when Aunty Maggie and Aunty Flo entered the fire-lit warmth of the kitchen it was no surprise to Molly. They had called, not because they thought Rosie would be lonely, raising their eyebrows and work-worn hands at the very idea of anyone missing that beggar, but because Father O'Toole had asked them to pass on a message. They'd just come from mass and the priest wanted Rosie to know she was to bring the three children to see him tomorrow to talk about their official entrance into the Catholic Church. They needed to be properly baptised and Eileen would be ready soon to be confirmed since she was nearly seven.

"An' about time, an' all," Aunty Flo sniffed, looking at the three children with such remorse you would have thought they were about to be dragged down to the hobs of hell this very minute. Leaning over Rosie's shoulder and without so much as a "by your leave" she lifted the astonished Liam out of his grandmother's arms and on to the only capable and reliable knee in the kitchen, her own naturally, and proceeded to examine him as though he were a leg of mutton she was thinking of buying.

"Will I take his clothes off for you to have a better look, Aunty Flo?" Molly asked mischievously, winking at Aunty Maggie, but Aunty Flo, who had looked up to receive a cup of tea from her sister-in-law, caught it and her face hardened.

"Don't tha' tekk that tone wi' me, Mary Angelina O'Dowd, fer what I want ter know is when is this poor lamb to be brought to the true faith? In mortal sin, 'e is . . ."

"Mortal sin! At four months old. Don't be ridiculous."

"Ridiculous, is it? An' what if, God forbid" – crossing herself vigorously which they all copied— "anythin' should 'appen ter't poor little mite an' 'im not . . ."

Molly stood up and snatched the poor little mite from Aunty Flo's arms, holding him tightly to her as though Aunty Flo had personally threatened him.

Aunty Flo would not back down. "Go on, then," she went on, her face as red as the cloth on the table, "tell us. 'As 'e bin baptised yet, at any church?"

"No, not yet. It's the custom among Tim's people to wait."

"Wait! Wait fer what?"

"It's none of your business, Aunty Flo. It's mine an' Tim's."

"Molly darlin', sit down," her mother begged. "Aunty Flo didn't mean anythin', did yer, Aunty Flo? Sure an' she's only concerned wi't little chap's soul."

"And I'm not?"

"O' course y'are, darlin', an' as soon as it's right tha'll fetch 'im ter church. Eeh, lass, we're only thinkin' of 'im."

Molly turned towards the door. "I'm off. I'm not listening to any more of this claptrap."

"Claptrap, is it, Molly O'Dowd? Tha' didn't think so until tha' married that chap up at Meddins. Tha' went ter mass every Sunday an' took communion an' now look at tha'. Dolled up like some . . . some . . ."

"Yes?" Molly's voice was dangerous and, as though sensing the menace in her, her son strained away from her, looking in alarm up into her face.

"Flo!" Rosie Watson's voice was like a whip cracking about their heads. "I'll not 'ave this in my 'ouse, an' I'll not 'ave it said ter my daughter, neither. Molly's bin best daughter in't world ter me, so she 'as, an' only the Holy Mother knows where I'd be wi'out 'er. She's a good lass, ter me, an' ter everyone an' yer can't deny it an' she mun do what she thinks is right, fer 'er and 'er child. Sure an' there's nowt I'd like better than ter see 'er an' babby at mass but she's a 'usband ter consider an' 'usbands come first. Tha' all know that . . ." and none more so than Rosie Watson who, for a principle in which she believed, her marriage vows, had sacrificed herself to Pikey Watson's brutish demands.

"Sit thi' down, Molly," she pleaded. "Don't fall out wi' Aunty Flo. I couldn't bear it, not now when we're just . . ."

"Nay, lass, say no more, an' same goes fer thi', our Flo," Aunty Maggie put in mildly. Always more easy-going than Flo O'Dowd, Aunty Maggie put her cup and saucer down and reached out her arms to the big-eyed baby. "An' it's my turn fer a cuddle, in't it, my lamb? See, come ter Aunty Maggie. Eeh, 'e's a lovely lad, our Molly, an' the spit o' tha' daddy."

At once all four women were taken out of themselves as they gazed first at the baby and then at the likeness of Seamus O'Dowd which had hung on the kitchen wall for twelve years. Neither Molly nor Aunty Flo were the sort to harbour grudges. They had had their say and now they let it go, and they joined together in the whole-hearted adoration of the newest addition to the family as though nothing had been said.

Contrary to Aunty Maggie's declaration, the baby looked nothing like his grandfather. At least his grandfather O'Dowd. His hair was thick and curling on his small skull and of a fairness that was almost silver. His eyes were brown, like Tim's, but they all admitted that the shape of them and the set of his eyebrows was Seamus O'Dowd all over again. A few tears were shed and blinked away. The children played quietly on the floor beneath the red chenille cloth that covered the table, as once Molly had done, and Liam Broadbent, after a snack from his mother's full breast, fell fast asleep.

"Well, I'd best tell you my news," Molly began, and they all leaned forward expectantly as she laid her son in his basket. "I came over especially, to see you, of course, which I can whenever I want to now, thanks be to the Holy Mother, but also to let you know that the house is still for rent and I've told the agent to hold it."

There was an interested silence and Flo and Maggie exchanged glances before turning them on Rosie.

"What 'ouse is that, our Molly?" Aunty Maggie asked mildly, since Rosie seemed incapable of speech.

"The one on Huddersfield Road, you remember, Mammy? The one I wanted you to have before I married Tim. It's only a mile or so from Meddins and half a mile out of Austerlands. It's a bit further from town than here but I can take you any time you want to go. There's fields all round it, lovely for the kids and the lavvy's inside, think of that. You saw it, Aunty Maggie, didn't you?"

"Aye, lass, a lovely 'ouse that's fer sure."

"You liked it, didn't you, Mammy? Well, it's not been let and all the curtains and carpets and such that were ordered from Buckley and Prockters are still in store just waiting until . . . well, until . . ."

Her voice died away. The three women watched her, then Aunty Maggie and Aunty Flo turned to Rosie again. She licked her lips as though they and her mouth had suddenly gone dry. She was obviously on the horns of some dilemma, a dilemma of overwhelming proportions, one she had no idea how to get over and she continued to stare at Molly. Then her eyes slid away and she bent her head, resting her cheek on Eileen's mouse brown hair, hugging the child to her though she still did not speak.

"What's the matter, Mammy? You did like the house, didn't you?"

"Yes, darlin', 'tis a lovely 'ouse."

"Well then?"

"I don't know what ter say, darlin'. It's . . ." Rosie squirmed in her chair, her eyes looking everywhere but at Molly.

"What yer mammy means is it's a big decision," Aunty Maggie began in that equable way she had, but Aunty Flo was not so tactful.

"What's up wi' this 'ouse, Molly O'Dowd? It were good enough fer tha' daddy an' mammy when they wed. They was as 'appy as two little rabbits in a burrow an'—"

"It's got nowt ter do wi' you, Aunty Flo, so I'd be glad if tha'd keep tha' nose outer this. This is between me an' Mammy an' no one else, so it is. Same as what she an' Daddy did's got nowt ter do wi' you."

Her accent broadened and became clipped as her agitation

grew. Her face was flushed, not only with indignation at what she saw as Aunty Flo's interference but with her mother's obvious lack of gratitude and enthusiasm. Her eyes had turned to the vivid turquoise brilliance which was a sign of her temper, snapping and narrowed and she tapped her foot in a rapid and dangerous tattoo on the stone-flagged floor. Lately Molly Broadbent had become accustomed to having her own way in most things. Her mother-in-law she rarely saw, since they each had their own circle of friends and when they did meet at the dinner table they were polite, for they were the mother and grandmother of Tim Broadbent's son. And of course Tim could deny his wife nothing, giving way to her in that engagingly flippant and endearing manner that was typically his. Her word was law simply because what made her happy, made him happy. He did not cross her because on most occasions he agreed with her, believing she could do no wrong. She was bright and clever and shrewd so she must be right in all things. It was a dangerous principle to adopt.

Aunty Flo did not agree with him.

"That's enough from you, young lady. Tha's not speakin' ter that soft 'usband o' thine now, tha' knows. Everythin' tha' wants 'e gets yer but this is tha' mammy's 'ouse an' I'm tha' mammy's sister-in-law an' I'll not be spoken to like that. I've a perfect right ter 'ave me say . . ."

"Tha' always do."

". . . when it's my family what's involved. Tha' mammy's 'ad troubles enough."

"D'yer think I don't know that? Anyroad, I'm not goin' ter trouble 'er, if tha'd only listen. I'm tryin' ter get 'er in a house what most people'd give their eye teeth for. A detached house wi' four bedrooms an' a proper bathroom with a garden full of bloody flowers."

"Don't you swear at me, yer little madam."

"Well, 'appen if tha' kept tha' nose outer what don't concern thi'—"

"Well! I never 'eard owt . . ."

"That's enough!" Rosie Watson shrieked. "Stop it, our Molly, an' you, Flo. By the Blessed Lord an' all 'is saints, will yer be quiet, the pair o' yer. Can I not speak fer messen, our Flo, an' you, Molly O'Dowd, tha' should be ashamed ter speak ter tha' Aunty Flo like that. She's bin like a sister ter me . . . these last years an' . . . an' what she's done fer our Clare, though it grieves me that I couldn't . . . well, I'll never give over thankin' 'er. An' you, lass. Tha've a good 'eart, so yer 'ave, but eeh . . . Molly, can yer not see? This last eight years 'ere wi' . . . wi' 'im don't mean owt ter me. All I can remember now 'e's gone is before, when tha' daddy was alive . . . an' tha' brothers. They're 'ere, our Molly. All I 'ave o' them is 'ere. I can't leave 'em behind, darlin'. I've only ter close me eyes an' I can see our Liam gallopin' about shoutin' fer 'is clean shirt an' yer daddy . . . well . . . I can't give that up, darlin'. Tha' can't ask me. I'm that sorry about the 'ouse. It were a fine 'ouse but this is me 'ome an' I mun stay in it."

24

They gave a garden party in June, for it was Muriel's birthday and again it was a tradition that had been carried on for over thirty years. The sun shone for Muriel, who was known for her determination in such things, since she would allow it to do nothing else, the garden was perfection, everyone agreed, and the gardeners were to be applauded for their efforts. The sunlight washed the house and its surroundings with gold-edged brilliance. The fuchsias were at their best, frothing in scarlet and white profusion and in the wide beds beyond the terrace delphiniums in every shade of blue raised their proud heads as though they were aware of the importance of the occasion. Roses from the delicate pink of Constance, a pink so pale as to be almost without colour, through all the shades to the deepest scarlet of Skyrocket, a newcomer to the rose beds of which Jud, the head gardener, was justifiably proud. Hanging baskets of verbena trailed at each side of the open conservatory doors and on the terrace were a score of terracotta pots filled with petunia, begonia and geranium.

But to have a well-filled garden is not enough, Jud often told young Mrs Tim who seemed to take a great deal of interest in such things, which he found very encouraging. It must also be planned as to colour, the outline of the beds, the shape and height of the plants themselves and though it had taken some time after he returned from the trenches in France to restore it to its former glory, he thought he had managed to harmonise it, at least to his own satisfaction, and hers too, so she told him. She had often peeped through the gates during the war years, she informed him wistfully, a declaration which surprised him, and she had been sad to see the neglect that had taken place but thanks to him it was all as it should be now. She was like that, was Mrs Tim, always ready to give credit where credit was due and it gave a chap a right lift to be thanked for his efforts.

The rolled and mowed perfection of the lawn, which Jud watched somewhat anxiously since many of the ladies wore high heels, had been set out with little tables on which were placed white lace cloths, those of them not arranged in the shade of a tree protected by wide canvas umbrellas. Flora, Agnes, Parsons and Atkinson, supervised by the ever-watchful eye of Forbes, moved from table to table, offering fragrant tea from silver teapots, passing round paper-thin china teacups and saucers and plates on which were arranged a vast selection of Mrs Ogden's "fancies". Queen cakes and snow cakes, dainty sponge cakes iced in delicate colours, plain buns for the children, Victoria buns since Mr Tim was known to like them, almond cakes and coconut biscuits, macaroons and ratafias of such delicacy they melted on the tongue.

For those who liked something to cut at there was rich chocolate cake decorated with chocolate cream and glacé cherries, and a coffee walnut cake which was Mrs Ogden's speciality. There were cream ices and water ices and straw-berries and thick whipped cream and for those who did not fancy tea, champagne in tall, fluted glasses. There were gifts for everyone, personally chosen by Muriel at Buckley and Prockters and all beautifully gift wrapped by the department which specialised in such arts.

Muriel, like royalty, had her own table, a big oval table of white-painted wrought iron around which all her own special friends sat. Dear Helen and Delia, Beatrice and Hilda, Totty and Joan, while their husbands stood or sat about the lawn with their cigars. As a concession to the heat their hostess had smilingly suggested that they might remove their jackets or blazers, which they thankfully did. Several of them were observed surreptitiously wiping a sweated face with an immaculate handkerchief and Arthur Davidson was heard to ask Maurice Knight, sotto voce, when he thought they might reasonably ask to go home, or failing that get out of this damned heat into the cool of the billiard room?

Most of the gentlemen wore flannels of white or grey. Some of the younger men, given an inch so taking a mile, had taken off their ties and rolled up their sleeves, which Muriel did not approve of, for beyond the smooth lawn, on the pitch Muriel's husband had had laid, a vigorous game of cricket was being played.

The ladies were engaged in croquet, those who could neither be described as young nor old. They wore what Molly called their "garden party frocks" long, floating, in shades of lilac or primrose with large, floppy hats tied about with ribbons and decorated with large bunches of artificial flowers.

To the side of the house Rupert Lucas and Tim were playing tennis, a game of mixed doubles with Sarah and Molly. Rupert partnered Molly and Tim was with Sarah. They were all good players, for it seemed that whatever Molly took up she excelled at.

Appallingly athletic, Muriel described her as, making no attempt to hide the fact that she thought it terribly unladylike. Tim had even insisted she had lessons and the professional who had taught her was impressed with the strength of her forehand and the power of her serve, which Muriel thought was something she, as a lady, would not care to have said about her. From a bad start, Molly and Sarah had become friends, a friendship Muriel did not care for, not because Sarah was unsuitable but because her family went even further back than the Broadbents and her uncle, Delia Bowman's brother, was a baronet, all far too good for the woman Muriel's son had married. What on earth was Sarah thinking of, taking up with a woman like her daughter-in-law, she beseeched Delia Bowman to tell her, since Sarah was Delia's daughter but Delia, who had never forgotten the sight of her naked, drunken daughter in the gentlemen's lavatory at Meddins, had nothing to say on the matter.

"And she does nothing but gallop about the countryside on that mare of hers," Muriel told the sympathetic faces round the table, "and it's no wonder she does not conceive another child. Liam is nine months old now and should have a brother or sister well on the way and do you know what Tim said when I challenged him with it?"

They shook their heads in unison.

"I hardly like to repeat it."

They begged her to.

"He said it was not for want of trying. There, what do you make of that?"

They didn't know what to make of it but they were not surprised. It was well known that Tim Broadbent was mad about his beautiful but common wife and could see no wrong in her, and the sooner Muriel came to terms with it the better, though they did not say so.

There was quite a crowd about the tennis court, for it seemed Rupert and Molly were just ahead in the third set, no more than forty-thirty at five games to four, having won one set as had Tim and Sarah.

Molly was serving. There was no doubt about it, those about the tennis court told one another, Tim's wife was certainly a stunner. As she skimmed the court, stretching to reach a ball or lifting herself to snatch at an overhead shot, she seemed to float effortlessly like a white butterfly. And would you look at those long, slim legs. What was Tim thinking about allowing her to show so much of herself? Was it modest? the ladies asked. Did they care? the gentlemen replied. She wore a pleated white tennis skirt which should have reached to just below her knee but didn't, since she had asked the seamstress at Buckley and Prockters to shorten it, to her mother-in-law's horrified despair. She had nice knees, Molly said hotly and what was wrong with showing them and her knickers were particularly modest if Mrs Broadbent would like to examine them, at which Muriel, hand on heart, left the room like the lady she was. Molly wore no stockings, just a pair of short white socks and plimsolls, or pumps, as she called them. About her forehead was a Lenglen bandeau, named after the popular ladies tennis champion and which kept her abundant hair out of her eyes.

It was a perfect serve to Tim, almost defeating him but he managed to get it back. Rupert was at the net and with a deft flick of the wrist returned the ball, which was just in and too far away for Sarah to reach.

It was game, set and match to Rupert and Molly.

They all exploded, Rupert and Molly and the watching crowd. Tim and Sarah shook hands resignedly, smiling across the net to where Rupert was boldly embracing his partner, kissing her enthusiastically and though Tim frowned, for he did not care for it – after all there were half a hundred spectators to witness it – he made no fuss.

The man leaning against the broad trunk of an enormous cedar tree which shaded the court pushed himself away from it and his eyes narrowed menacingly. He was tall, broad of shoulder and chest but narrow of hip and with a flat belly. His sun-darkened face was strong, aggressive in its masculinity and, but for the scowl which marked it, would have been pleasantly handsome. His hair was a deep chestnut brown, curly and far longer than was fashionable, falling over his forehead and ears, reaching his collar at the back of his neck. His eyes were thickly lashed, a dark brown which in the shadow of the tree was almost black.

His face was like a thundercloud and it was perceived, or would have been if everyone had not been looking at the tennis players, that he was doing his utmost to restrain some inner turmoil. He had just scored a triumphant seventy-nine runs in the cricket match which still played on but instead of mingling by the cricket pitch with his team who were batting, he had been drawn by the shouts and laughter, the crack of the tennis ball against the racquet, the whip of it over the net and the laughter of one of the women who were playing.

Joel Greenwood had driven over just after lunch from Greenacres, already dressed in his whites for cricket since it seemed Bunny Armitage had commandeered him for his team. He hadn't wanted to come. He never wanted to go anywhere where the woman he loved to desperation would be surrounded by either her mother-in-law's friends and their families, or her own small, but growing coterie of acquaintances, that included the ones he himself had introduced her to last year. They weren't here, of course, since this was Muriel Broadbent's party and only her own circle came to Muriel's parties but all the rest were applauding and shouting congratulations and Rupert Lucas, who still had his arm proprietorially about Molly's waist, bent once more to kiss her, since the opportunity to do so did not come his way very often.

"Well done, Rupert." Tim's voice had a slight edge to it making its deepness higher than usual. "Indeed, well done, but my wife is not the prize, you know."

He was smiling when he said it but those about him were aware that it was not a smile of pleasure. He was a gentleman and gentlemen were beaten at cricket or tennis or football and made nothing of it, congratulating the winner with great good humour. Good losers, in fact. Tim Broadbent was a great sport, an excellent player of the games these upper-class ladies and gentlemen enjoyed so much but it seemed he did not care to see his wife handled as Rupert was so openly doing.

He began to look quite strange. His face seemed to slip, or at least the flesh of it, and his mouth, which was smiling, opened wide though no sound came from it. He dropped his tennis racquet and his arms wavered in mid-air as though he was not sure whether to drop them to his sides or wrap them about his head. His eyes became deep pools of brown, dead and lifeless, and he lost every vestige of colour, not only from his face but his neck and bare arms as well.

Before anyone had time to do more than gape in shock, Molly was over the net and at her husband's side. Her arms went round him, round his body and his faltering arms, holding him firm against her, holding him upright, holding him together. Her face was close to his, her lips moving from his silently screaming mouth to his eyes, his cheeks, his quivering jawline.

"Darling, I'm here," she said over and over again, making him look at her, making him aware that he was in her arms. That she was his as he was hers.

"Tim darling, look at me, sweetheart, look at me. It's Molly. Come, come with Molly, darling . . ." and when Joel Greenwood reached her side, ready not only to hold his cousin, his soldier cousin whose gallantry in defence of his country had reduced him to this, but Molly as well if she needed it in his strong and protective arms, Tim was coming out of it.

"Christ," he said. "Christ, Molly, I thought . . ."

"Darling, it doesn't matter. Lean on me. Lean on Joel. Joel's here."

"Good . . . good man, Joel . . ." and his teeth chattered so violently he was in danger of biting his own tongue in two. "Get me inside, my darling . . . Joel, help me. Jesus, in front of . . ."

"It doesn't matter, darling. They are all your friends here and know what . . . what you did in the . . ."

The men standing about were nodding, for many of them suffered something of what Tim did and several of the ladies had their handkerchiefs to their eyes. Tim Broadbent was a fine man but it seemed his little wife knew just what to do for him as her words told him.

"Darling, I'm here. I'll always be here . . ."

"Yes, thank God . . . thank God!"

Doctor Taylor gave him a sleeping draught and then one to

Muriel since she appeared to be on the verge of a breakdown. It was many years since she had seen her son in that awful state of what was known as "shell shock", but she had hoped, believed that it was over. He used to tell her he saw his old pals, those who were dead and lost in the rotting sea of mud and bodies in France and once, soon after he came home from the sanitorium at the end of 1919 he had screamed that a decaying corpse sat in the chair opposite him at the dining table. What a furore that had caused, with Parsons having hysterics and Forbes trembling violently with an old man's shock, since neither had seen their young master in such a state. She had often wondered why Joel had not suffered in the same way since she happened to know he had seen, and fought, the same battles as Tim. Perhaps because he was a good bit steadier than her Tim, who had always been light-hearted, absurdly reckless and endearingly lovable and had never in his young life had to face anything more violent than the kill at the end of the hunt.

When Tim was asleep Joel and Molly went into the nursery where Liam was sleeping, sending away the good-naturedly smiling Elspeth. The guests had all dispersed, kindly urged on their way by the pale-faced cousin of the lovely but sadly injured son of the house. Yes, he would let them know . . . of course. Please do ring but don't bother Molly. I will . . . Yes, very sad but Tim is a good lad and would be right as rain . . . so kind . . . such a pity but he was sure . . .

The nursery was filled with the inestimable peace which surrounds a sleeping child. It was a charming, cheerful room, walls lined with shelves on which books and toys leaned companionably together. An enormous fireguard on which small garments were airing protected the young baby from the small fire burning in the grate and at the windows which looked out over the paddock at the back of the house were bright curtains with nursery rhyme figures on them.

"Go and have a cup of tea with the others in the kitchen, Elspeth," her mistress told her. "I will watch over Liam for an hour. Do take an hour, Elspeth, if you don't mind, for I feel the need to sit with my son."

Elspeth, who had heard about what had happened, as who had not in the house, nodded wisely, for it was a well-known fact, at least she knew it, that the presence of a child was a tonic and a restorative. Nine-month-old Liam Broadbent was no angel. He was lively and mischievous, into every blessed thing now that he was crawling, almost walking. His mother and father loved and watched over him and she had become used to their frequent visits to the nursery and to the walks and drives on which they took him, sometimes all day, which left her with very little to do. Like Muriel, she would be glad when another little one was added to the nursery. This one was the centre of his parents' world and in danger of being spoiled, which was right in a way for it did a child no harm to know it was absolutely loved. She knew that the minute the master woke he would be calling for his wife and son and that was right too, for they were the centre of his world.

The door closed behind her and Joel put his back to it, holding out his arms. Molly walked blindly into them, pressing her face into his neck beneath the curve of his chin. She moaned slightly as though in pain and he bent his cheek to her hair, smoothing her back and shoulders in an excess of loving tenderness. He murmured deep in his throat, small, incomprehensible sounds of comfort but his eyes were blank and sightless at they stared at the cot in the corner where the baby slept.

They had been lovers for six months.

"Dear Blessed Mother in heaven, what is to become of me?" her voice whispered against his throat. "What is to become of us all? How can we go on – you and I – knowing what he would become if he found out?"

"Don't ... don't, my precious love ... don't torment yourself," and me, his anguished expression said, for he knew if he were to lose this treasured woman he would lose himself. That first time, when she had come to him at Badger's Edge on Christmas Day he had swept her back to Greenacres, terrified that she would refuse, terrified that her passion would diminish if she had time to consider it, to think of Tim and her child back at Meddins. His servants, like those at Meddins, were having their own Christmas Day celebration, indoor and outdoor staff crowded into the kitchen, knowing he was out riding, believing, as was his habit, that he would not be home for hours. They would not be looking for him. They had served him his solitary Christmas dinner, eager to be off back to the kitchen, believing, correctly, that they would not see him until darkness fell.

Tying their mounts to a tree in the woodland set about the

three acres which was his garden, he had hurried her, almost carried her, through the side entrance and up the back stairs to his own bedroom. The door locked, he had stripped her, then himself, no tender gesture of gallantry, or even of gentleness but a rough need to be quick, to possess her before she could change her mind. There would be time for making love later. She had wanted it as much as he did, urgent in those first moments, her body burning, pleading and when they were both naked, gasping and clutching and biting, devouring one another until, with a fierce penetration which made her gasp and cry out in rapture, she was his.

They had lain in silence, recovering from what had been almost a battle. Their breathing had been fierce, harsh, taking a long time to slow, then, they had drawn apart, turning, he on his right side she on her left, to face one another. He had traced the curve of her hip and the neat nip of her waist, moving up to cup her breast, his face absorbed, dreaming with his love and wonder.

"You'll be mine always now, you know that?" he had said, meaning it, putting up a gentle finger to push back a sweated strand of dark hair from her cheek, tucking it behind her ear as though to make her tidy again. "You must love me, I reckon, or you wouldn't be here, for you're not a light woman, my Mary Angelina, and you must know I never let go of what is mine." His hand went tenderly into her hair, moving to the nape of her neck. "What we have just done, it was need, you realise that. Do you know about need, Mary Angelina?"

"I do now."

"Then let us make love," and they had, slowly, tenderly, her body turning and arching under his exploring hands and tongue, a dreamlike process that had brought something alive in her, something that had until that moment been dormant. She felt his life flow into her, pour into her, warm, vital, strong, filling her with love that could not be measured, a man's love for his woman. The lordly lift and thrust of his loins made her moan in depthless pleasure. His face in the winter light was strong and uncompromising until the moment of his climax when it broke into vulnerability, a youthfulness that amazed and enchanted her.

She loved him. She told him so then and on all the other occasions, not enough, they told one another feverishly, when they were able to meet, to hold one another, to make love.

At first, in those early days, it was enough for both of them to know the physical possession, the physical joy of loving one another and as the new year progressed, as spring rejoiced in its rebirth and summer followed, they were too dazzled, too lulled by the dangerous, sensual abandonment of their bodies to be cautious, to think about anything but the ecstasy they made for one another.

But it was not enough for him as, deep inside her, she had known it would not be enough for him and jealousy sank its poisoned fangs into his heart.

"How much do you love me?" he would ask and she knew she must answer carefully. This was no idle question but the demand of a unique and complex man who found himself in circumstances he did not like and, worse, could not change.

"Tell me, Mary Angelina . . . tell me . . ."

"I love you."

"And . . .?"

"What?"

"More than . . ."

"I love you best, my darling, more than anyone else."

"More than anyone?"

"Yes, oh yes, more than I could ever love any man."

"Liam . . ."

"Joel, it is quite different. Liam is my child."

He would bend his head in great pain, ashamed of himself, resting his forehead on hers, not apologising for this weakness since that was not his way, hating himself for being weak, his body slumped in misery, in gritted anger that, despite who he was, he could not have her for his own.

"Come away with me," he would say. "I have a house up Ullswater way. It belonged to my mother and father. We could stay a whole night together, perhaps two. Mary Angelina, do you realise I have never made love to you in the morning? Surely you could get away if you wanted to."

"Joel, I can't go away with you." She had been horrified, terrified. "What would I tell Tim? And Liam . . . how can I leave him. He's only a baby."

"You could say you were visiting friends."

"What friends? I have none, only those Tim knows about and certainly none who live far enough to keep me away for two nights. Glory be on high, this is madness, madness . . ."

"Aye, madness. Christ, why didn't I fall in love with some woman who would not only be a suitable wife but would love me as . . . as I need to be loved?"

"Oh, Joel, my darling, I love you as you need to be loved. I cannot bear it when you talk like this. Perhaps – it'd be better if . . ."

"No . . . no, I know what you're going to say, and No." She could feel the tight clenching of his body as he did his best to control the frustration his own emotion engendered, this passionate love which had come to him at the peak of his manhood. He wanted a wife. He was of an age to be married. He wanted children and this woman, who was wife to his damaged cousin, stood between him and them.

He stayed for no more than ten minutes in the nursery. He was aware that the servants must be allowed to see him downstairs, perhaps speaking to Forbes who was beginning to see to the clearing-up of the uneaten food, the half-empty bottles of champagne, the pretty tables and all the detritus of his mistress's disastrous party. There must be no talk, not even a whisper, to unbalance further the delicate mind of Tim Broadbent, and deep inside him something moved and seemed to break. He loved this woman with a depth and strength of passion not even she realised. She could destroy him if he let her and yet what could he do about it?

Holding her against him pensively, his eyes went over her head to the sleeping boy, and then on through the open window beyond to where Molly's mare, Isolde, kicked up her heels in the long sweet grass of the paddock. Across the fields at the back of Meddins he could see the square tower of the church where the Broadbents and Greenwoods had worshipped for over a century. There were clouds, fleecy and white but edged with a fine line of pearl grey, gathering above the treeline which lay along the boundary of the estate and he had the idle thought that it might rain before the day was out. It was so still in the limpid sunshine, so calm and lovely, so totally opposite to the war which raged inside himself.

Again he asked himself what he could do about it.

Nothing . . . nothing, his agonised mind told him as he kissed his love softly, put her from him and left the room.

They did not see one another for two weeks and then it was no more than a frantic half-hour of loving which left them both restless and dissatisfied, inclined to be sharp with one another in their frustration. It was high summer up on Saddleworth Moor but it was not there they met but in a small, detached, four-bedroomed house with an indoor lavvy, a villa set in half an acre of garden on the Huddersfield Road where once Molly had hoped to house her mother. The nearest house was half a mile away on the outskirts of Austerlands and if anyone saw Molly Broadbent there and mentioned it to her husband he would not be surprised, since he was well aware that she still had hopes of enticing her mother to live in it one day. She would not give up hope, she had told him, that soon Mammy and the children would enjoy the comfort she had created for them but she knew she was lying. The carpets and curtains ordered from Buckley and Prockters two years ago were all in place, she told him, and would Tim mind if she put in one or two pieces of furniture she had seen and liked and which she knew Mammy would like when she came to live there. She knew she was lying even as she said it.

"My darling, I told you before we married that your allowance was yours to do with as you liked. To spend on your family, on whatever or whoever you fancied. Fill the house, sweetheart. Make it comfortable for your mother and perhaps, one day, if you can coax her to come and see it, she will change her mind."

He had been surprised and deeply distressed when she began to cry. Not the soft sound a woman usually makes when she is upset but an ugly noise, like someone sawing wood. She knelt at his feet and slowly bowed her head, until her brow rested on his knee and when he tried to draw her up into his arms she resisted.

"Sweetheart . . . oh, my love, what is it? What is it? What have I said? I did not mean to . . ."

"Tim . . ." She could not speak, it seemed, continuing to sob, helplessly and loudly, so that Albert, who lay before the fire in her sitting room, a place he sought despite the painful obstacle of the stairs, raised his head and stared at her, his tail moving sympathetically.

"Molly, tell me . . ."

"I can't . . ."

"Of course you can. You can tell me anything, my darling. There is nothing you could do which would offend or annoy me . . ." at which she cried the harder.

"Molly, lovely girl, I shall weep myself if you don't . . ."

"Blessed Mother, you are the . . . the best man I know."

"Well," grinning, "if you want to think so, my love, but that is rubbish."

"Truly, and I love you . . . more than you know."

"Well, that's all right then," his grin deepening, trying once more to lift her into his lap, folding her against his chest, tucking her head into his shoulder, dabbing at her face with his handkerchief. She was still trembling with the force of her weeping and he held her close, gently brushing back her hair which tumbled over her forehead.

"Better now?" he murmured, as he did to his small son who, now that he was up on his feet, was always tumbling against something.

She sighed. "Tha're so good ter me, Tim, so kind an' generous, so tha' are. I don't know anyone what's more warm-hearted an' sweet-natured . . ." He knew she was badly upset by her reversion to the speech of her childhood but he only smiled.

"Whoa, whoa there, Mary Angelina Broadbent. You make me sound like some maiden lady who goes about doing good works and expects no reward except what she will get in heaven. So how about showing your appreciation right now by coming with me into our bedroom? Or shall I make love to you here? Albert won't mind, will you, Albert?"

She found no hardship in obliging him and never had, for he touched nothing in her that was Joel Greenwood's. She gave him her body, her warmth, her loving kindness and he was satisfied.

He was overjoyed, and not surprised at her recent weakness, for it explained it all when she told him she was to have another child.

25

It was two months later when Mr Barton, manager of the Allied and Union Bank in Manchester Street and Mr Watson, who held the same position at Broadbent Mill, reported to the owner, Mr Timothy Broadbent, that since 1920, when his spinners margins had been forty-three shillings and threepence, to December 1926 it had dropped to five shillings and sevenpence. The margin represented what the spinner had to work on for all production, costs and profits. For a spinning firm to remain in business it required a margin of sixpence to sevenpence per pound, so for the last year, and probably a lot longer, Broadbent Mill had been running at a loss. Without question, any spinner or manufacturer who could survive such a severe aggregate loss must be either wonderfully lucky or extraordinarily shrewd. It seemed that Tim Broadbent and his manager were neither.

In 1920 Mr Broadbent had a one hundred thousand spindle mill, a working capital of one hundred and twenty thousand pounds, a personal capital of one hundred and seventy-five thousand pounds and a sizeable gilt-edged stock investment. Mr Barton studied Mr Broadbent's uncomprehending face from the other side of Mr Broadbent's desk where he had been seated and told him that not only had his capital vanished, drifting away over the years like mist dispersed by a wayward breeze, but he now had a considerable overdraft, and nothing else. Except Meddins, of course, which, fortunately, was not encumbered. If it was any comfort to him, fifty spinning companies, thirty manufacturers, eleven spinning and manufacturing firms and seventy-nine merchants in Oldham were to go into liquidation, or would have to come to forced terms with their creditors. How many more were keeping out of the bankruptcy court rather by their wits than their assets remained to be seen.

"So what are we to do, Mr Barton?" Mr Broadbent asked equably, confidently, optimistically, his serious manner meant to convey to the bank manager that whatever it was he was willing to do it.

"Do, Mr Broadbent? There is nothing to be done except put up your mill and the land it stands on for public auction and sell your house which might then cover your debts."

Mr Broadbent smiled as though Mr Barton were joking. "I can't do that, Mr Barton. It would put hundreds of men and women out of work and as for my home, it has been in the family for generations and I would not part with it for the world."

Mr Barton ignored the question of the house for the moment. "I appreciate that, sir, but a business cannot be run at a loss. It used to be said, and it was true, that Lancashire men could spin the world's cotton needs before breakfast and the rest of the day was nothing but pure profit. That was before the war, of course, but since then Japan, India, China and other countries have taken our trade. The war did it. When we could not supply them with the cotton they needed they decided to manufacture their own. They stole our ideas, our technical skills, our very machines and for seven years our fortunes have fallen so low I fear they may never pick up again. Earlier we thought the depression would not last but we were mistaken. And please, don't speak of further loans to keep you afloat. It cannot be done. I hesitate to say this, sir, but . . ."

"Yes, Mr Barton?" Tim's politeness was exquisite and had Mr Watson not heard what had just been said he might have thought his employer was being sarcastic.

"Over the years . . . you . . . your personal expenditure has been quite considerable. The household . . ."

"I have a family to support, Mr Barton. Certain standards to keep up and Meddins itself must be looked after. It is an old house."

"I understand that, Mr Broadbent, but, if I might say so . . ."

"I don't think you might, Mr Barton. Just tell me what is to be done and I will do it."

"There is nothing to be done, sir, other than what I have just told you."

"Sell the mill?"

"Yes, sir, and the house which is apparently eating up your resources faster . . ."

"Impossible." Tim evidently considered responding to the last part of this statement unnecessary. "I cannot simply throw hundreds of people out of work. Some of them have been with the firm for all their working life. Forty years and more. It would be unthinkable." He raised his head in an imperious manner reminiscent of his mother.

"Mr Broadbent, you can do no other. There is no money to pay their wages. I have been urging you for two years to be prudent, to cut back. If you had halved your workforce, gone on short time . . . well, you would not listen and now you must file at once for voluntary liquidation. That will tie up pressing loan holders. There will be no opposition from the bank. In fact in a debate in the House of Commons last week it was stated that at least two hundred mills in Lancashire are in the power of the banks."

"If we were to bring our prices down, Mr Barton, perhaps?" Mr Watson chipped in, for it was his job on the line as well as hundreds of operatives.

"Every cotton man in Oldham is trying to sell a shade lower than the fellow who is getting trade ahead of him, Mr Watson. It must stop somewhere. There is no profit to be had, Mr Broadbent, believe me. You have no choice but to sell. There is simply no point in keeping your mill doors open hoping something will turn up because it won't."

Molly was at her mother's when her eyes were opened and it was Betty Spooner who opened them for her.

She and Mammy had drunk a companionable pot of tea between them, speculating idly on the gender of the coming baby, hoping it was a girl, for, as Mammy said fondly, looking at Molly, daughters were special. Not that Mammy regretted having three sons, she didn't, for they gave something special in their own way, but daughters were a boon and a comfort to their mammies.

Liam Broadbent, chasing the protesting cat about the room, fell into the red folds of the floor-length tablecloth.

"Oh, sweetheart, did he fall then? Let Mummy kiss him better," but Liam struggled purposefully from his mother's arms and made for the cat which had paused for a breather.

In desperation, it sprang up on to the second shelf of the dresser, delicately avoiding Rosie's best china and Liam began to howl.

"See, play with Archie, darling. He has a lovely rocking horse just like yours at home," which in fact Molly had bought for Archie when she had ordered Liam's from Buckley and Prockter's toy department. The room was strewn with toys, dolls for the girls, a train on tracks, picture books and colouring books and crayons and Aunty Flo had been heard to remark that it did no good to shower children with such things when they had not been used to it.

"No," Liam said firmly, or what purported to be no, shaking his head positively and scowling.

"Well, it's no good, Mammy, I'd best get him home. He's tired and ready for a sleep."

"Sure an' isn't 'e still a babby." Rosie smiled, giving her grandson a resounding kiss.

The difference in Rosie Watson since her old man "popped his clogs" was absolutely amazing. She was plump and as rosy as her name, bobbing her head and smiling, ready for a chat with anyone, and everyone in the street commented on it. Of course, that daughter of hers kept her in the lap of luxury, only last week bringing her a wireless of all things, a wonderful contraption miles from the old crystal set which was the rage earlier in the decade. It was all encased in fancy wood with a cut-out "sunrise" on the front and an on/off knob, a tuning knob and a wavelength knob on its side. Rosie loved it and had invited a few of her favourite neighbours to listen to one of the thrilling plays that were on, and a programme on which the BBC's 2LO band played lovely music. It was all very technical, like that telephone which had pride of place in her parlour. Not that Rosie ever used the thing since she knew of no one, except her daughter, who had one and when it rang, the only caller their Molly, she nearly had a heart attack, she told Aunty Maggie and was convinced she would get an electric shock from it. Had she not known it was bound to be Molly she wouldn't answer the dratted thing.

And Molly, who never forgot her humble beginnings, it was said of her, was for ever bringing little dresses and such for Eileen and Gracie, a sailor suit of all things for Archie which Rosie didn't dare put on him for he'd be bound to be teased by the children in the street. Even before they were in need of new there Molly would be on the doorstep, parcels and boxes all about her, saying there had been a sale at Buckley and Prockters or she thought this warm coat would just do their Archie for the coming winter and Rosie herself had a wardrobe stuffed with dresses she never wore. Boxes of groceries, fruit, even flowers arrived regularly at number twenty-two, delivered by Buckley and Prockters' smart van, and Mrs Kenny at number eleven said to Mrs Wainwright at number thirteen she bet Buckley and Prockters' driver had never been called upon to deliver in the back streets of Oldham before. Mind, Rosie was generous, sharing her good fortune with anyone who would let her, handing out apples and oranges and bananas and pomegranates to kids playing in the street, most of whom scarcely knew what a pomegranate was, nor what to do with it.

Betty Spooner was leaning in the doorway of her house when Molly stepped outside Mammy's front door, her arms folded across the front of her flowered apron. She was talking to Cissie Thompson, laughing about something, and somehow it never crossed Molly's mind to wonder what the two of them were doing home on a Wednesday afternoon. Molly and Betty sometimes met on a Saturday afternoon "up town", Molly careful to wear her plainest clothes since the expensively elegant suits and dresses she customarily wore when she took morning coffee with Sarah Lucas would only serve to show up the difference that now yawned between her and Betty. Not that in the past, even before Molly married Tim, she and Betty had dressed alike. They had both worn cheap, ready-made or home-made skirts, blouses and dresses but where Betty's had been colourful, often too short and what Pikey would have called "tarty", Molly's outfits had been simple of style and colour. But they had looked what they were, two working-class girls having an afternoon up town.

Since then, whenever they met for a cheerful "cuppa an' a chin-wag" as Betty called it, it seemed Betty bore no resentment nor felt envy of Molly's good fortune, since Molly herself made little of it, but still the difference between them had become very obvious, not only in their appearance but in the way Molly now spoke. Betty knew she would never be invited to Meddins, at least to a party, though now and again, give her her due, Molly did beg her to have tea at her home. Betty had not taken her up on the offer.

"Hello, Betty, Cissie," Molly shouted, hiking the baby up on her hip as she opened the car door. "What's the joke?"

They both turned and the laughter slipped from their faces like melting jelly.

"No joke, Molly O'Dowd, not fer the likes of us, anyroad." Cissie's voice was sharp and spiteful.

"Oh, what's happened?" Molly began to walk slowly along the pavement towards the house at number ten where Betty lived, Liam still on her hip. For some reason Mammy tried to grasp her arm, begging her in an anxious voice to "Come away in, darlin' . . . I'd wanted ter say summat but I'd been waitin' fer you ter speak," but Molly shook her off.

For the first time she was aware of the unusual number of men and women who were hanging about the narrow street, men without jackets or caps, women, like Betty, in aprons. The rag and bone man was making his slow way between a screaming horde of small children, those not yet at school, his cart rattling and clattering, its contents shifting and lurching and ready at any minute to tip off into the road. Mrs Wainwright stopped him, offering him something in exchange for a donkey stone, and the bony, sway-backed nag which pulled the cart came thankfully to rest.

But all eyes, except those of the rag man who was concerned with nothing but his own profit, were on Molly Broadbent.

"Betty?" she asked enquiringly, smiling. "What are you doing at home? And Cissie? Has the mill gone on strike?" ready to laugh.

"Tha'd best ask that fine 'usband o' thine, Mrs Broadbent. Ask 'im what all us lot're 'anging about 'ere for, our frames standin' idle an' nowt goin' inter our pockets 'cept what dole money them up at Labour'll give us. 'Undreds, Molly Broadbent, 'undreds wi'out a job an' not even a bit o' notice. Get yer cards an' bugger off, is what we were told. Don't come back 'cos . . ."

"Betty, for God's sake, calm down. I don't know what you're talking about. What are you talking about? You must be mistaken or . . ."

"Oh, don't talk so bloody daft, woman. Tha' don't mekk a mistake like that. Tha' knows when tha've bin laid off, lass. Dost tha' think we're all barmy, the lot of us" – waving a hand to indicate the listless men and women on doorsteps and leaning their backs against house walls – "an' a lot more beside—"

"It's all right fer some . . ." Cissie interrupted, her eyes going greedily over Molly's fine cashmere suit, her antelope-skin laced shoes with a Louis heel which had cost Molly three guineas, her suede cloche hat which exactly matched the coffee brown stripe in her suit. "There's some what don't give a damn if they see what once were mates thrown outer work on t'ot streets which is likely where me an' Betty'll end up."

"Tha' speak fer thissen, Cissie Thompson." Betty, who was to marry her tram driver in the spring of next year, glared at Cissie but Cissie merely shrugged. "Now then, Mary Angelina O'Dowd, 'appen tha'll explain why that chap tha' married 'as chucked us lot out like a pile of old rubbish? Forty year, some of 'em 'ave bin there, wi' old Mr Broadbent 'oo'd never 'ave done this to us, not in a million years . . ."

Betty's words drifted off somewhere into the pale September sunshine which fell here and there between the row of terraced houses, lifting and fading over the rooftops. Molly could still hear her but she made no sense. It was like the twittering of a bird or the burbling sound her son made which he thought of as conversation. She knew she had lost every vestige of colour from her face and even her body, for she felt as cold as ice, frozen in this strange dreamlike world which had come upon her so suddenly and so menacingly, but she couldn't just stand here and wait for it to go away, since something told her it never would.

She cleared her throat painfully. "Betty, please . . . I don't know what tha're talkin' about, 'onest. What can I say?"

"What is there ter say? We've bin given sack, every last one of us so gerrin that bloody motor an' go an' ask that chap o' yourn what 'e's playin' at," for it had begun to dawn on Betty that Molly was as bewildered as they were. "Go on, go an' ask 'im why Broadbents Mill is up fer sale an' when tha's done that come back an' tell us fer we'd like ter know, wouldn't we, Cissie?"

"You wouldn't understand," he said when she asked him, pushing his hands through the fair cap of his hair.

"Try me," she answered, her face still white with shock, her eyes glittering.

"Darling, I'm not sure I understand it myself. It's something to do with profit, or lack of it. I've no head for figures, Molly, you know that, no head for business. There have been . . .

emergencies, again I'm not sure of what kind, over the last two years. I don't know . . . cash flow, old Barton called it, but now it seems there is no cash to flow so I'm forced to sell the mill to pay my debts."

"But didn't you realise what was happening? Didn't tha' see from – I dunno – ledgers, records, accounts, that there was summat wrong?"

"Molly, if I had seen them they would have meant nothing to me. I left it all to my managers. And I'm not the only one to go under, Barton told me. God, I forget the exact number but scores of firms are going bankrupt. I'm to undergo a public examination in bankruptcy at Oldham Bankruptcy Court."

"What does that mean?"

"Do you know, I'm not awfully sure. I only know that I am now a bankrupt and I can no longer trade."

"But didn't Mr Watson realise there was summat wrong? Surely as manager 'e should've known an' 'ave warned thi'."

"He probably did, Molly, but . . . not realising the seriousness of the situation I took no notice."

"'Appen if tha'd spent more time there instead of . . . of . . ."

Tim looked desperately away from her accusing face, staring out of the sitting room window over the mellowing beauty of the gardens, wondering how he was to tell her that not only the mill was to go, but perhaps Meddins as well.

It was almost the end of September and leaves were beginning to shake themselves free from their summer resting place, drifting on to the immaculate smoothness of the lawns as fast as Jud and Albie swept them up. The sky was a pale grey, like ruffled pigeons' feathers but it was bright as though at any moment the sun would shine through. As he watched, his son came from round the corner of the house, his sturdy legs going so fast he could not keep up with them. He measured his length and at once both the gardeners sprang to lift him up, their faces smiling fondly, eager to see to the little lad who had brought such joy to them all. He held his hands out to them and Jud took out his handkerchief, wiping the small palms which had some soil on them. The child beamed up at him then, seeing Elspeth coming after him, squealed and set off again on his hurtling path down the lawn and the men watched him go, telling each other what a grand little chap he was, speculating on the one which was to come in the new year.

"How long have you known?" she asked him coldly.

"A . . . a week."

"A week! In the name of all that's holy, a week! When were you goin' ter tell me, Tim? Or did tha' just think it'd all blow over?"

"Molly . . . Jesus, I'm sorry. I don't know what to say. I'm hopeless at anything that . . . I can't bear to be shut in. Perhaps if Will or Charlie had lived . . . I was never cut out to be a mill owner, you see. I'm making no excuses. I know my father spent every waking moment at Broadbents and perhaps that's why it was so successful. My grandfather Will was the same and I believe my grandmother Tessa had a good business head. It was understood that my brother Will would carry on – he was the eldest – and Charlie was interested as well, but I never was."

His eyes became unfocused as he turned back to those golden, dreamlike days before the war. Thirteen years ago now and who had he been then? A boy brought up to believe that it would go on for ever, this halcyon time of peace and plenty, these days of fun, of boundless health and luxury he scarcely noticed it was so taken for granted. The sun had always shone then. The girls had been pretty and eager to make Tim Broadbent think he was a hell of a fellow. His father had been indulgent, after all he had three sons, and his mother doting, urging him on to enjoy himself since he was scarcely out of boyhood. Eighteen he had been, born with what was known as a silver spoon in his mouth, favoured by the gods with health, wealth and good looks. He would do something one day, that was understood as his brothers, Will two years older, Charlie a year, began their apprenticeship by their father's side. Perhaps he might go on to university, read languages or something or other, though what that something or other might be was not absolutely clear and did it matter when he was enjoying life so much?

The war had seemed the very answer, a gallant cause to which he and his brothers had nailed their colours. His father, at the last moment, had begged Will not to go, perhaps sensing that of them all, Will was the one to carry on the great tradition of cotton spinning which had been begun one hundred and fifty years ago by a distant ancestor called James Chapman. Barker Chapman. Katherine Chapman who married Joss Greenwood. Tessa Greenwood who had married

Will Broadbent and whose son had been Tim's father. He was the sixth generation and now, it seemed, it was all to end in the ignominious defeat of the bankruptcy courts.

"I'm trying to blame it on the general decline in the cotton trade, Molly." He turned to her in his misery, longing to have her put her comforting arms about him, to take away that dreadful look of accusation from her face. She had never, in the years he had known her, looked at him with other than love, approval, smiling recognition that in her eyes he could do no wrong. Now her expression was hostile, a dreadful expression which he could not bear, an expression which sent the trembling shock waves he dreaded to his mind which cowered away from them.

"It has been falling away ever since the end of the war, even I know that." He did his best to be steady. "Did you know – or so Mr Watson informed me, for I didn't – that in 1914 Lancashire's share of the market was two thousand . . . Oh God, I can't remember but it was millions of pounds a year. That was raw cotton and our annual cotton cloth exports equalled that figure. Since then they have halved, or so Mr Watson tells me, and every year fall even further. Lack of investment during the war." His voice was vague. "A shortage of workers who were lost in the trenches . . ."

His voice trailed away and he turned away from his wife's narrow-eyed gaze, the shocking whiteness of her face, the tense, clench-fisted rigidity of her body, looking again to where his son played on the lawn.

"I'm sorry, Molly. I don't know what to do."

"Neither do I, but I'm sure as hell going to find out." Her voice was so harsh it surprised even herself.

"What? There's nothing left. We have an overdraft of . . . I don't know the exact sum, or even if the bank can compel us to repay it. I've no head for figures, Molly."

"So you said." Her voice was crisp, allowing for no further drifting into self-pity. "But there are men who have."

"Mr Barton said . . ."

"To hell with Mr Barton. What about Joel? Is his mill to stop trading?"

Tim turned to her in surprise and a look of distaste came over his face.

"I couldn't borrow money from Joel, Molly."

"I'm not asking you to borrow from him. Just talk to him,

ask his advice, see if he has any suggestions on how you can get out of this mess. There must be something."

"Well, there is Meddins."

She became completely still then, as though she wished to merge silently into the shadows which were beginning to reach into the corners of the room. Like an animal which senses danger and must freeze to avoid it. She moved not a muscle, not even to blink. Then she swallowed.

"What does that mean?"

"Well . . ." It seemed he had difficulty speaking.

"Yes?" Her voice had deadly menace in it.

"It could be . . . mortgaged."

"What does that mean?"

"It means we can borrow money against the house from the bank and use it to repay some of our debts."

"And?"

"And what?"

"What becomes of it?"

"Meddins?"

"Yes." She was having the greatest difficulty in stopping herself from hitting him full in the face.

"We would have to find the money to repay what we borrowed or the bank would foreclose."

"Foreclose? What does that mean?"

"It means it will belong to the bank. They can sell it to recoup—"

"No! No! No!" She almost knocked him over as she sprang at him, her nails, he thought, ready to reach for his eyes. He just managed to grasp her wrists, rearing away from her as she fought to get at him, not sure what she meant to do to him when she did, and neither did she.

"*N . . . o . . . o . . . o.*" Her voice rose to a scream and beyond the open window the two gardeners raised their heads, turning to look at the house, uncertainty in their faces since they were not sure what it was they had heard.

"Darling, don't . . . don't. Please, Molly, calm down."

"If there's one sure thing in this whole bloody mess, Tim Broadbent, it is that Meddins will not be sold, nor be tampered with in any way. This house is ours. It belongs to our son and our son's son. Broadbents" – and O'Dowds, her heart whispered, for Daddy's blood ran in Liam's veins – "who have lived here for . . . well, I don't know for how long,

346

but it's not going to be taken over by strangers. There is no house like Meddins, Tim, not even remotely . . ."

"Molly, stop howling like that. The servants . . ."

"Bugger the servants."

"Molly, darling, please."

"Tim, I love this house, you know that." She was quieter now, more in control of herself, ready to speak reasonably, not only on the subject of Meddins but on what they were to do about the mill. Joel must be consulted and if the prospect of going with her husband to ask her lover what she was to do about the house which, feeling a pang of guilty shame, meant more to her than any other consideration, daunted her, she showed no sign of it.

"Yes, I know." Tim's voice was expressionless and his face empty. It was as though he could read her mind and for a moment she was filled with remorse. But it was no good standing about agonising over what had happened. This had been a shock, a bitter blow from which she would find it hard to recover, but recover she would. Tim had been . . . negligent. God! what a word to describe his actions, his complete lack of responsibility, his absolute refusal to see what was happening and take steps to avoid it. She had no idea what they were, those steps, she only knew that if she had been in charge of one of the most prosperous mills in Lancashire she would not have let it slip through her fingers like water through a sieve.

"Molly, I'm sorry, I really am. I was too trusting."

Well, if it made him feel better to think of it that way then let him. It did no good to berate him, to scold him as though he were a child who had lost the errand money. He was beginning to shake, his face drawn in that particular shade and shape which she had seen it take on when an attack was imminent and with a murmur of comfort she took him in her arms.

"It's all right, sweetheart. It will be all right. Don't tekk on, lad, we'll work it out somehow. We'll not lose Meddins, trust me. This mortgage thing . . . we'll ask Joel about it an' if I've ter work me fingers ter't bone I'll find money ter repay it. We've a son ter consider, and another on't way," which she was perfectly well aware could be Joel Greenwood's, "an' we'll let no one tekk their inheritance, choose how."

His reply was muffled in her shoulder as he clung to her and she sighed.

"Come on, lad. Let's get over ter Greenacres. Or will Joel be at the mill?"

"The mill, I suppose."

Yes, she supposed so too. It was where responsible mill owners were to be found at this time of day.

26

Molly Broadbent's second son was born at Meddins as she had been determined he would be. It was his ancestral home after all, the place where five male children had been born since 1867, six now with this one. A week later she and Tim, with Elspeth and Mrs Broadbent, moved into the gatehouse.

The past five months were to remain in Molly's mind as the worst, the most punishing, the most hopeless – and yet the most hopeful – of her life, perhaps even worse than Pikey and what she and Mammy had suffered at his hands. Later she was to be afflicted with pain, far deeper and more cutting than she could ever imagine, but the months before her second child was born were carved, like symbols in stone on her stone-like heart.

Joel had got them through, got her through, for he had given her hope and her heart had overflowed with thankfulness that he should be there, just at her back, or, more literally, at the end of the telephone whenever she needed him. And the ironic thing was that now they could be seen together, he pulling up outside the porch at Meddins, she thundering up the wide driveway of Greenacres, sometimes with Tim but most often on her own, without a hint of gossip or tittle-tattle whispered about them. Well, they said, those who saw them constantly together, he was settling Tim Broadbent's affairs for him, since it was well known that Tim Broadbent was incapable of settling them himself. In fact it was doubtful he could add two and two and make it come to four which was probably one of the reasons he had lost his mill. Joel Greenwood could not help in any financial way, naturally, since his own concern was sailing close to the wind in this day of tumbling cotton prices and fading cotton markets, but he had helped to arrange the auction of the Broadbent Mill and the land it stood on, the disposal of the Broadbent machinery, which, though he would rather have seen it broken up than go abroad to those who were stealing Lancashire's cotton trade, had fetched a fair price. He dealt with solicitors and bankers, men who, without him to protect them, would have had Tim and Molly Broadbent on toast for breakfast, and at the last finding buyers for Prince and Hal, for Isolde and Major and for the fleet of motor cars which were garaged in the old coachhouse at the back of Meddins. The beauty and grace and elegance of the Silver Ghost Rolls-Royce which had been queen there for over twenty years, the old Bullnose Morris, the Singer Ten, Tim's first car, the two which had belonged to Will and Charlie, his dead brothers, Tim's Vauxhall and Molly's Swallow.

She had wept bitterly that day, for the Swallow had been a kind of symbol, a token of the gigantic step Molly O'Dowd had taken, and been successful at, and of which her daddy would have been so proud. Joel arranged the auction of the motor cars and of the horses, sending Molly and Tim away in his own splendid, racing green Mercedes-Benz Coupé, telling them sharply to take their son and go and have a day in Blackpool or New Brighton, knowing his cousin would be unable to manage in his delicate state of mind the sale of his beloved machines, of the beautiful animals which had been a part of his life since he was a child. They must go, Tim understood that, if they were to survive, if Meddins was to survive, for there was no money now for such luxuries, nor for the wages of the grooms who had looked after them, but it took all Molly's strength and dogged determination to keep him from wandering into that state of black depression which had oppressed him after the war and which had returned. Every penny was needed, Molly told him, and since Meddins was not to be touched, Joel had assured her of that, not one object sold from it, since it must all be there waiting for them when they returned to it, Molly declared vehemently, everything else that was not absolutely needed must go.

"We will buy bicycles, my darling," she said to him gaily when she found him leaning morosely on the coachhouse door where the motors had been garaged, or hanging over the door of the empty stable as though still studying the glossy animals which had once filled it. "One each. We shall fix something up so that Liam and the 'bump' can come with us, though it will no longer be the 'bump' by then and when we feel like a gallop we shall climb on to our trusty steeds and go up to wherever . . . well, wherever we choose. Uphill one way, downhill coming home."

With the horses gone and her little car gone she could no longer get up to the moor to meet Joel. From the moment he had known of her pregnancy he had not made love to her, for what man can stomach the idea of lying with a woman who might be carrying another man's child, she had understood that. They had not been to the house on Huddersfield Road again, not for five months and now it had gone, rented to someone else, since Tim could no longer afford to pay her allowance and she could no longer afford to pay the rent. Joel knew he could have offered to keep it up but there was no way it could be arranged without Tim knowing of it and since there was now no chance of Rosie Watson and her children living there, Molly had moved out the carpets, the curtains, the simple furniture she had bought and put them in the gatehouse.

Their only contact was during one of the business meetings or discussions which took place between September and February. In consideration of Mrs Broadbent's condition, Mr Barton had called at Meddins to finalise the signatures for the mortgage and the arrangement for the repayment of it, and of the interest which would naturally accrue. Mr Barton did not ask, since he was a gentleman, and, besides, Mr Greenwood was to stand as guarantor, but he did wonder how the lovely Mrs Broadbent was to achieve all this, since it was obvious that Mr Broadbent would be neither use nor ornament as the saying went in Lancashire. Meddins had been put in her name, with her husband's consent, of course, since Mr Greenwood had urgently advised it.

It was all coming to an end, the nightmare of losing their children's inheritance which had haunted her and now all she had to do, Molly reflected bravely, squaring her shoulders which, despite her pregnancy, were thinner than they had been, was to find some way to earn the money with which to repay the mortgage. There would be a tiny allowance each week on which they must all survive, Joel had told her, less than Tim had paid his butler and certainly not enough, even if none of them ate, to pay the interest they owed, never mind the mortgage itself, but at least Meddins was safe for the moment and she would find some way to earn the rest, dear sweet Mary, she would.

Tim had absented himself, saying he was going for a walk up past Badger's Edge to Motherhead Hill. He might call at the farm, the Home Farm which had once been part of the Broadbent estate and which had been sold along with hundreds of acres of farmland and moorland which his grandfather, Will Broadbent, had acquired when he bought Meddins. Horace Tinsley, who had rented it, and his father before him, had somehow scraped together the necessary capital, overjoyed to be given the chance to own it and Tim wanted to . . . well, he thought he'd just look in on Horace. He had this idea that perhaps he might get a job – since he couldn't accept Molly's declaration that she would find work – and farm work, outdoor work might just suit him. He'd see her later, he told Molly, kissing her on the cheek.

"He's grieving, Mary Angelina," Joel said when Molly told him about it. "He's not as strong as you. He has been a wealthy man all his life and to lose what his family has built up has been a bitter blow. You must be gentle with him."

"You don't have to tell me that, Joel Greenwood. But who is to be gentle with me?"

"Aah, don't, my love. I am here . . . if you would let me be."

They were in the drawing room since it would not have been prudent to take him to her private sitting room. The bright, flickering flames of the fire coloured the pale walls, the carpets and furniture to gold and orange and apricot and gave Molly a false glow of health in her pale cheeks. Joel stood up and drew her to her feet, awkward since this was her house and her servants might at any moment come knocking at the door. He put his arms about her but her swollen belly came between them and she knew, since she loved him and understood him better than anyone, that in his despairing mind was the awareness that this could be Tim Broadbent's child between them since she had never denied that her husband still made love to her.

He held her for a moment, his cheek resting on her hair, then gently sat her down again. He drew his chair up so that they sat knee to knee, leaning forward and holding her hands.

"If you would let me I would take you away, you must know that. I'm a man of business and find great satisfaction in what I do. I am extremely attached to Greenacres for my family have lived there since the late eighteenth century but I would chuck the whole bloody lot in the River Tame if you would come to me, Mary Angelina. Come away with me. Let me take care of

you. Start a new life with me far away from here. You and
the boy and . . . the new one," who might be my child, his
anguished expression told her. "You're shaking your head
already and really, did I expect anything else?" His dark face
closed in a scowl and the strain of what had happened in the
past few months, and his part in it, was clearly written there.
It stained his eyelids and engraved lines Molly had never seen
before from beside his mouth to his chin. This strong, proud
man was suffering because of her and his feelings for her. It
was not his nature to take second place, to beg for crumbs
from any man's table and she knew what it must have cost him
to share her love with his cousin who was her husband.

"I don't know why I'm asking you this since I know it
will come to nothing, my darling. As my mother used to say
when I pleaded for something she would not allow, I might
as well save my breath to cool my porridge. But, my dearest,
it's hard for me to understand Tim's cavalier treatment of his
inheritance. What happened to him, happened to me. I lost
my older brother in the trenches. Pearce was to have control
of the mill but I was forced to take over when he died. I
went through a war, like Tim did, but . . . Dear God, why am
I saying these self-pitying things? I suppose I am just pointing
out to you that what has happened to Tim has happened to
others. Even my father, who was the youngest brother, lost
his two older brothers to some fever, some ailment which
struck down children in those days. He took over, carried
on . . ."

"You are saying that Tim should have done what you and
your father did?"

"Yes." His voice was low, barely more than a whisper. "If
he was . . ."

"A proper man?"

"Yes . . . yes, then I would not hesitate to . . ."

"Take me away from him?"

He bent his head in despair, bringing her hands to his
lips and kissing them with a pain she could feel inside her
own breast.

"If only I could," he said sadly. He stood up, tall and so
compelling he seemed to charge and fill the room with his
power.

"Oh, Mary Angelina, my heart is breaking with loving
you."

The room was empty, hollow, almost echoing when he had gone.

It would have been so much easier without her mother-in-law. Muriel Broadbent would never give up Meddins, she said loudly, imperiously, her voice ringing from room to room a dozen times a day.

Home! Would someone tell her how she was to make her home in the cramped gatehouse which her daughter-in-law insisted they were to move into? she asked fiercely. She for one could not see why they could not stay on at Meddins since it was not to be sold, and, privately, neither could her son. Though Joel explained time and time again about the cost of the upkeep, the heating and lighting of the many vast and lovely rooms, the servants needed to run it and the absolute and total lack of money to pay for all these things, Muriel Broadbent was not convinced. It was bad enough that her friends should be privy to the Broadbents' state of financial affairs which were printed in the financial section of the newspapers for anyone to read. They had all rallied round, of course, begging her to feel welcome to call on them at any time and naturally she would continue to be their guest at dinner parties, bridge parties, even weekends, indeed any social function that might be put on, but how was she to accept if she could not get about, having no motor car, and was unable to return their hospitality, she demanded of her daughter-in-law.

"You can have them here whenever you like, Mrs Broadbent. Me an' Tim'll clear off somewhere or other."

"Here?" swinging round to stare in horror at the small living room in the gatehouse where she was now expected to spend her days. Her bedroom upstairs, one of three, was just as minute, the smallest, since there were two of Molly and Tim, Molly said through gritted teeth and there would be three in the "nursery" when the new baby came so it was only fair that Elspeth and Liam should have the largest of the three. But Muriel's bedroom was next to the nursery and how was she to sleep through the child's crying and babbling? she asked, and really she did not think she could cope with it all. She didn't know how Tim could have lost so much money in such a short time and really, could he not do something about it? Perhaps Maurice, or Albert or Peter Bowman could help, and she was sure Mrs Ogden and Forbes would willingly take a cut in their wages and stay on at Meddins to serve her as she had always been served. Wages? Yes, well, she admitted she knew nothing of wages, naturally, since someone else had always seen to that.

The servants were badly shocked, the older ones at least, since Mrs Ogden, Forbes, Parsons, Wilf in the stable and Jud in the garden had been with Mrs Broadbent since Adam was a lad and where were they to get jobs at their age?

Joel saw to that, as Molly knew he would, patiently finding places for the younger ones, since good servants were hard to come by these days and were in great demand. Mrs Ogden, Parsons and Forbes were retired to a couple of cottages on Greenacre land and with their old-age pension and what they had saved and the bit of cash in hand they earned now and then helping out Mrs Hebden, who was Joel's cook and housekeeper, they managed nicely.

Jud refused absolutely to budge. They'd have to get the bobbies to shift him, he said, setting his seamed old face in Mrs Tim's sad young one. He didn't want no wages. He was settled in his rooms above the stable and he was staying there. He had a few bob put by and if anyone thought that there garden could manage without him, then they were barmy, if Mrs Tim would pardon his rudeness. Aye, it'd be hard work on his own. Three men and a lad'd take a bit of replacing but he'd manage, thank you very much, ready to stump off and show her how.

"Perhaps my husband might help?"

Jud turned in amazement, his pipe almost falling from his mouth as it dropped open.

"Mr Tim?"

"Why not? He's been saying he wouldn't mind outdoor work. You see, Jud, now that the horses have gone and the motor cars, not to mention the mill" – which Jud wouldn't anyway since Mr Tim never went there – "he's going to be at a loose end and . . . well, I don't know why but I have this feeling he might be quite good at it. He likes the outdoors. I'll sort of . . . put it to him, see what he says, but if he offers, will you let him? I had the idea, you being such an expert, you might be able to grow . . . well, vegetables, which you do already . . . but to sell. Make a bit of cash for us all. What d'you say?"

She was a lovely woman all right, was Mrs Tim, doing her best to make a new life for them all, including the old lady who was a proper handful and had been nasty with her right from the start. Mrs Tim was trying to find something for Mr Tim to occupy his time with, carrying it all on her shoulders and her with another babby on the way. Of course, Mr Joel was a rock to them all and so he should be, for he was family but if she asked him Jud'd do owt' for Mrs Tim, even if it meant taking on the well-meaning but cack-handed master of the house to play havoc with Jud's garden.

They called him Joss, the new boy. Joshua Drew Broadbent since Drew had been a family name years ago and the minute Mammy put him in her arms Molly knew he was Joel's son.

"Well, tha'd never know they were brothers, 'im an' Liam, would tha'?" Mammy remarked fondly, bending over her new grandson whose dark hair lay in damp little corkscrew curls all over his skull. Joss Broadbent yawned, raising one eyebrow as Molly had seen Joel do a dozen times after they had made love, turning his face to her breast. He was, in Molly's appalled but bewitched eyes, a mirror image of his father and yet Mammy, who knew Joel by now since she had often walked up to Meddins in the last five months, seemed to see nothing out of the way in her grandson's darkness. "Mind, 'e's got a look o' tha' daddy about 'im," she added, as though that explained it, her eyes soft, "just like Liam, but Liam's so fair an' this 'uns so dark. But 'andsome, 'andsome as a little prince. We've ter wait ter see what colour 'is eyes are," turning to smile at her son-in-law who was hanging over the bed in an effort to get his new son in his arms.

"Who cares?" Tim said, cradling the baby to him, then grinning wickedly over his head at Molly. "Blue or green, I don't mind since his mother has one of each."

"Eeh, 'ow can tha' say such a thing?" Rosie remonstrated with him, still somewhat unsure of how to treat this gentleman who was married to her daughter, but ready to be his friend should he need it, for hadn't he been a friend to her. Molly, bereft as she was to be leaving Meddins, knew a moment of pure happiness, for their misfortune, their loss of Broadbent wealth and position in Oldham had brought Mammy from Sidney Street and into Molly's home just when she needed her, so something good had come out of it.

Rosie never met Muriel, of course, going straight up the stairs and along the landing to her daughter's sitting room with growing confidence, even speaking a word or two with the formidable butler who seemed not to mind. Yesterday, when the telephone had shrilled and Molly's voice had told her her waters had broken, she had dumped her three children on the obliging Aunty Maggie and come to act as midwife, as was only natural, at her grandson's birth. Doctor Taylor had been there, of course, but then she and Doctor Taylor were old friends, greeting one another with great cordiality. Doctor Taylor was unable to get over how well she looked, he told her, and when the boy came shouting into the world, not at all sure he cared for it, Rosie was the first to hold him in her arms. Doubtless this setback of the Broadbents was going to affect the standard of living she and her children had got used to but she would manage as she always had managed in the past. There was always work to be had for strong, willing women and, thanks to her daughter, Rosie was both.

Molly and her new son were alone in her sitting room, her chair pulled up to the good fire, when Joel called the next day and she knew by his face that he had first enquired of Forbes, who was to go to his cottage at the end of the week, the cottage which stood next door to that of his old friends Mrs Ogden and Parsons, whether Tim was about.

He closed the sitting room door quietly behind him, standing for perhaps twenty seconds with his back to it, his eyes steady on hers and she could not look away. She held his son in her arms and she dared not tell him. Perhaps he would see it in her eyes but she could not look away. There was so much love in his expression, a desperate, hopeless love, the love of a strong man who would deny it if he could, if he could only find the strength.

"Mary Angelina," he said, his voice so soft, so tender she felt the tears start to her eyes. "I came as soon as I decently could and for a moment only. Forbes said Tim was . . . somewhere."

"Yes, he's taken to helping Jud in the garden." Her voice was husky with longing and her eyes clung to his.

"You're well," he went on, moving slowly across the room towards her. "Yes, I can see you are. You look like a . . . a madonna . . . beautiful. And your son?"

He had an enormous bunch of hothouse roses in his hand, a conventional thing to join all the other conventional massed vases of flowers, most come from Meddins' own hothouse and showered on her by her husband. He dropped them on the table next to her, then went down on his haunches at her feet, bowing his dark head as though to a queen and she put a hand on it, then lifted his chin so that he looked up into her face.

"Joel . . ."

"Yes, my darling."

"I'm glad you came. I missed you these last weeks," for since the settling of the financial and legal arrangements to do with the mill and its sale, the mortgaging of Meddins and all the other things he had dealt with on her behalf, she had not seen him since the new year.

"I've missed you too, my precious love." He did not look at the boy who was swaddled in a fine woollen shawl, an anonymous bundle, and she made no attempt to display him. In fact he had the feeling that she was deliberately keeping the child's face covered. The boy would be as fair as Tim, as fair as his brother, and Mary Angelina, not wanting to give him, Joel, any more pain than she must, was keeping him hidden.

He rose to his feet and cleared his throat uneasily, for the atmosphere was one of a sick room. He had longed to see her but now he was here he was fidgety, out of his depth. He had come because he knew it would be expected of him. His aunt would expect it of him. Tim would expect it of him but he longed to be away now. She was not his now, his love. She was Tim's wife and the mother of Tim's son in this room. Soon, when she was recovered, they would resume their relationship, become lovers again, he supposed, his heart drumming ecstatically at the thought and at the same time dropping joylessly, for where was it all to lead? Could they go on deceiving Tim, deceiving each other that they were content with this hole-in-the-corner affair, since after all it was all they could have, all they would ever have, he thought despairingly.

"I'd best be off then."

"Yes," she answered sadly.

"I'll . . ."

"I know, my love . . . soon, when . . . when . . ." She began to smile a little and he found himself responding to the hint of humour in her. "When I can ride a bicycle. Oh, aye, me an' Tim, we're to have a bicycle."

"Not a bloody tandem?" The expression of dismay on his face was comical.

"No, you fool." Then she became serious. In her eyes was the look he had come to know so well, one he was aware was meant only for him. It had the glowing depth of her love for him in it but she allowed him to catch a glimpse of the need, the hunger she had for him as a man, as a woman needs a man. She was his, totally and for ever, her eyes said, despite what stood between them.

He felt himself become calm and she smiled again, a smile with a hint of pain in it though he was not aware what caused it.

She could have told him. The child she held in her arms was barely a day old and this was his father and if circumstances had been different they would have had the right to lie together on her bed, she and Joel, the one she had insisted on leaving despite Mammy's pleading, the baby, *their* baby between them, and tell one another how clever they were, what a handsome boy they had made, how they loved one another and that soon, in view of the pleasure it had brought them, they would do it all over again.

Now she was forced to conceal him, their child, keep him hidden for as long as possible from the man who, she was absolutely certain, would know his own son when he saw him. They said it was a wise father who knew his own son, or was it the other way round, she'd forgotten, but Joel would recognise him as she herself had done. And if that happened God alone knew what he would do. Claim him for his own . . . Jesus, Mary and Joseph, it did not bear thinking about, but she knew as surely as she knew the sun rose in the east and set in the west, he would not easily be persuaded to give the boy up. What father would? And could he be blamed for it? Tim's despair, Tim's health, even Tim's life would go to the devil for all Joel Greenwood cared if it meant he could publicly acknowledge that Mrs Tim Broadbent's second son was also Joel Greenwood's. She could only hope that, as Mammy had said, Joss's darkness would be attributed to his O'Dowd heritage. That Joel would accept it. That that shrewd instinct of his, that intuition he seemed to have that recognised the truth, be it in business or otherwise, might be blunted when he looked at the boy he believed was Tim's.

"I'd best have a peep at him, I suppose," he said

unenthusiastically as he bent over to kiss her. "Mrs Hebden would never forgive me if I could not describe him to her in minute detail."

Instinctively she drew the lacy shawl more closely about the baby's face and head, looking up at Joel with a false smile.

"He's just gone to sleep, Joel. I don't want to waken him."

"I promise I won't waken him, darling. Anyway, I thought infants were supposed to sleep through the last trump. Not that I know anything about it, of course, since I've never" – he paused, and a flicker of uncertainty passed across his face – "had one," he continued, "or . . . or have I, Mary Angelina Broadbent?"

She knew she should make some appropriate, perhaps comforting remark but what that might be she had no idea. Her throat appeared to have closed off and her mouth be full of dry dust. How, in the name of all the saints, could she deny this man who loved her his own son? her harrowed heart asked, but she must if they were to keep their world, meaning, of course, Tim's world, from shattering into a thousand unmendable pieces.

But it seemed it was too late. His warm, brown eyes turned to flint, a deep, dark, stony flint that took every gleam of light from them and yet, lurking in their depths, like a fish that idles at the bottom of a murky pond, was a glimmer of something which would, in a moment, be understanding. Different expressions touched his face. Doubt, disbelief, hope, something that could have been joy and something else that could have been anger.

"Mary Angelina, I'll take a look at your son now." There was no question in his voice, just a tone that said he would be obeyed.

"Joel, really! When were you ever interested in babies?"

"I must admit, my love, never, until this moment. To me they have always seemed vastly over-rated. A necessary bane the human race must put up with if it's to survive. My own nephews and nieces, Nell's children, are very trying but somehow this one, this infant you are doing your best to conceal beneath that shawl, interests me greatly and I would be obliged if you would let me get a look at him."

"Darling, please . . . I'm very tired," she managed to say, her arms tightening about her son.

He was hawk-faced and keen now, a look about him she had never seen before and yet he was wary. He fumbled in his jacket pocket and withdrew a battered packet of Woodbines from it. The Woodbines he had smoked in the trenches with his men and which he had never changed to the expensive cigars other prosperous businessmen smoked. He lit one with his old lighter, drawing in a deep lungful of smoke then blowing it out towards the ceiling. It was a measure of his defencelessness that he had not asked her permission to smoke it. After that one drag he threw it violently into the fire.

"And very stubborn. I was under the impression that new mothers were only too eager to show off their offspring, in fact could be bloody boring about it. Now then, why should you try to hide this child who is yours and . . . and whose? Whose boy is he, Mary Angelina? Who fathered your son? Whose is he, Tim's . . . or mine?"

His face was quite blank and Molly cowered away from what was to come but she did not give up.

"He's Tim's, of course."

"There is no 'of course' about it. You and I have been lovers for over a year and I would say that he is just as likely to be mine as Tim's. I don't know why it hadn't occurred to me before."

"Please . . . please, Joel." There was desperation in her voice and in some strange way it conveyed itself to the child in her arms who began to stir. A tiny starfish hand thrust itself out of its wrappings and clutched at the air and before Molly could put it back Joel was there, bending over her and the baby, an enquiring finger pushing aside the shawl. The smooth, honey-coloured skin, the arch of the dark eyebrows, the length of the equally dark lashes and the brown fluff of curls were revealed. A rosebud mouth opened on a prodigious yawn and Master Joshua Drew Broadbent opened his eyes to look up into his father's face for the first time. They were unfocused, inclined to wander but they gave the impression that the boy was vastly interested in the brooding face above his own.

"His eyes are blue," Joel said in a reverent whisper. He knelt again before mother and child as though in homage.

"Like mine," Molly said determinedly, doing her best to divert him but it did no good.

"With some green in them."

"Well . . ."

"But for all that he's a Greenwood."

"No . . . no, he's not, Joel. Can't you see that look of Tim in him?"

"God almighty, woman, don't be so bloody ridiculous. He's no more Tim's son than . . . than . . ."

"Oh, please, Joel, don't. I beg you, you mustn't . . ." Her voice rose on a peak of pain which he ignored.

"Let me have him."

She stared at him in growing horror, clutching her son to her in a fiercely protective gesture. She began to shake her head and her mouth opened on a silent wail of denial.

Joel frowned, a grimly dark frown, then sighed impatiently.

"For God's sake, Mary Angelina, I don't mean to take away, I mean to hold."

"Joel, please, if Tim should come in . . ."

"Bugger Tim. This is my son and I mean to . . . Oh, God, my dearest love, what do I mean to do? I can't . . . I want . . . I want to have him . . . and you . . . Oh, Jesus."

He was becoming distraught and she put out a hand to him. The firelight played on his strained features, drawing deeper the lines on his face. His eyes begged her for pity since this was his son but she bent her own head and her voice was muffled.

"Joel, we cannot . . ."

"I know." His voice was bitter. "We cannot hurt Tim but good God alive, what about me? He's mine . . . mine . . . and so are you, both of you."

Getting to his feet he gently lifted his son against his chest, his arms closing about him as naturally, as hungrily as any father's would. He looked into the baby's face, his own a mask of granite, only his eyes alive with the pride a man knows in his first-born.

Molly was often to wonder what might have happened had Elspeth not knocked at the door at that precise moment. Would Joel, in his new-found joy and pain, the joy and pain of fatherhood, have gathered his son to him and proclaimed him to the world to be a Greenwood? Would he have destroyed Tim and herself in his powerful, instinctive resolve not to give the child up? Who would ever know? Certainly not she who loved and understood him more than anyone. In that moment, as

Elspeth came into the sitting room, Liam's hand in hers, his childish voice piping incoherently of Mummy and the new boy who, it seemed, he wanted at once to come and play with him, there was a space in time in which Joel Greenwood floundered like a man drowning. Molly could see it in his face, the unspeakable anguish of knowing that, if he kept quiet another man would bring up his son and if he spoke up that man would not survive it.

"I came to see if I should take little 'un ter't nursery, madam," Elspeth said. "I thought tha' might be tired."

"No, I'm not tired but you can take him if you would. I think Mr Greenwood has had a good look at him, haven't you, Joel?"

If there was a certain tension in her voice only Joel Greenwood heard it. He did not answer, continuing to gaze down into the baby's face and for a moment Elspeth could have sworn he was rocking the child, as a woman might do, then he turned.

"Yes, I've had a good look at him," he said in the strangest voice, "but I shall need another. I may come again, mayn't I, Molly?"

Elspeth smiled, since there was nothing strange in the request, was there? Mr Greenwood and Mr Broadbent were cousins of sorts and though Mr Greenwood had not taken a great deal of interest in Liam, perhaps this one, coming in the midst of the upheaval which had rocked Meddins from attic to cellar, was to be different. Special.

"Yes, of course you may, Joel," Mrs Broadbent was saying, a bit on the cool side, Elspeth thought. "Now, if you don't mind I think I'd like to go back to bed. If you would give Joss to Elspeth."

"Joss?"

"Yes, Joshua Drew."

"Both Greenwood names. My grandfather's brother was Joss and Drew was Joss's son."

"Yes, Tim did say . . ."

"Joss . . ."

Elspeth was startled when Mr Greenwood smiled. A smile of such sweetness it lit his face as Elspeth had never seen it before, then, without the awkwardness gentlemen usually showed on such occasions, bent his head and placed a kiss on the child's forehead.

27

If Betty Spooner was surprised to see Molly Broadbent on the doorstep of her home in Sidney Street she did not let it show in her cool expression. She merely raised suspicious eyebrows, folded her arms across her breast and leaned one shoulder on the frame of the open door.

"Yes?" she said truculently, letting it be known right from the start that the great Mrs Tim Broadbent, who had once been plain Molly O'Dowd, was not particularly welcome.

"Hello, Betty," Molly said, trying out a placatory smile. The last time they had met had been on this very doorstep when Betty had told her of the closure of the mill and the appalling memory of it still haunted her. She could still see Betty's bitter – and rightly so – hostility, and Cissie Thompson's readiness not only to be hostile but downright vindictive. She could remember as if it had only been yesterday her own bewilderment, her disbelief and then her own rage for, like them, she felt she had been betrayed, and by her own husband. That's when it had begun, the nightmare, right here in Sidney Street at number twelve, next door to Cissie's and it seemed only right and proper somehow that this was where she meant to begin the measures that would end it.

She would never forget it, of course, not if she lived to be ninety. It was all mixed up somehow with memories of her daddy, for it was his unusual love of beauty – unusual for a man of his class and culture, that is – that had led her to Meddins and the enchantment, the bewitchment, the spell it had cast over her from the moment she saw it. It was as though, should Meddins be lost so would her clear as clear evocation of her daddy and the lovely Sundays they had spent together. Daddy had never been inside the house, nor even the gardens, but he had seen them, seen the beauty and experienced the serenity through her, his daughter, who surely, in her silent, unconscious conversations with him every day of her life, had told him of them. If she thought about it, which she did now and again, she knew it to be fanciful, but through her, and her sons who were his grandsons, Daddy lived on so that it was only right that one day, as soon as she could manage it, they must all be returned to their rightful home, even Mrs Broadbent.

Only this morning she had taken the keys from their hook at the back of the kitchen door in the gatehouse and slipped out through the bit of garden at its back and into the stand of trees beyond.

The rest of the household was still asleep since it was barely dawn, Mrs Broadbent, she supposed, tossing fretfully in the "pokey" room, as she called it, she had been allocated. Tim had been breathing lightly as though he had been about to break free from dreaming, the two babies, who had both been up in the night, and Elspeth, cramped together, two cots and a narrow single bed which was all the bedroom would hold.

She had told no one, not even Elspeth herself, why she had been kept on when the rest of the servants had been dismissed and she supposed they wondered, since it was well known that Mrs Tim Broadbent, Molly O'Dowd that was, was perfectly able to look after her own children. She was certainly capable of keeping every room in Meddins as immaculate as they had always been, going over every day to "fettle", they had heard, doing what once Agnes and Flora had done, to Muriel Broadbent's eternal shame.

This morning, when she came downstairs, Albert had risen laboriously from the mat in front of the blackleaded range, greeting her with a snuffle at her hand and a slow circling of his tail and when she went out he had followed her, questing now and again into an interesting bit of foliage. Albert could not get used to making his home in the gatehouse, like the rest of them, Molly supposed, and had been brought back a dozen times by Jud who had found him waiting patiently to be let in at the side door of the house.

It was March. It had been a mild, wet winter and already the damp earth was thrusting forth the green spears of daffodils, the buds showing golden in the early morning light. A great yellow mass of primroses and the blue and white of sweet violets rioted among the roots of the trees. The sun shone low between the branches, a brilliant silvery gold in stark contrast to the bare silhouettes of oak and beech and elm, and everywhere, just as though the absence of humans except for the old gardener had made them bold, birds chorused. A thrush, quite unafraid of her quiet presence, repeated again and again his song to the coming spring and, not to be outshone, a blackbird poured golden notes into the still air.

Molly had felt her heart swell painfully. It was all so perfect still, even though the house, the stables, the woodlands and paddocks and most of the gardens were deserted now. She knew that Jud would be up and about, watching over his solitary domain, perhaps standing in a cloud of fragrant smoke from his pipe as he decided what he and Mr Tim were to do today. He had, over the past few weeks, done his best to explain patiently, since that was his nature, a smattering of garden lore to Tim and, strangely, Tim was turning out a dab hand at it. He seemed to find soothing the eternal digging, the turning over of the fertile soil in readiness for the vegetables they were to plant. A compensation for the loss, not of his own work since he had never really had any, but his horses, his motor cars and the life he had led which had revolved round them.

The side door had opened easily as she turned the key in the lock since she had asked Jud to keep it well oiled. Jud did not just labour peacefully about the garden and the land but had taken it upon himself to act as caretaker of the house. There was, of course, the conservatory, which led out of the drawing room. The birds and their cages had to be seen to, he told Mrs Tim firmly. Nay, he said, it cost next to nowt for a bit of birdseed, and then there were them exotic plants, as though he knew that there was in his young mistress a desperate need to have everything remain exactly as it had always been at Meddins. Happen Mrs Tim or Mrs Broadbent might fancy an hour or so in the conservatory come summer, he had added, so he'd best keep it in good order for them. Of course, without any heat in the house during the winter he couldn't guarantee the plants would survive, nor those in the rows of greenhouses he and George, Albie and Ernest had looked after, but happen he could fix something up and he'd do his best, she could be sure of that.

The slow and dreamlike wandering through the house,

the dog padding silently at her heels, acted as a kind of healing on Molly Broadbent's spirit. She went alone, apart from Albert, since neither Tim nor Mrs Broadbent could stand it, they said. It lifted her sorely tried heart, not only to wander about in absolute silence but to clean and scrub and polish, to keep in pristine immaculacy the home she would one day come back to. Where her husband became depressed over his loss and her mother-in-law vituperatively hostile, Molly never failed to feel the tranquillity, the gentle calm, the beauty and graciousness of Meddins lap about her in a wave of welcoming love. Whenever she stepped through the door she knew that the old house was glad she was there. The house knew that though it must lie quietly alone for a while, its mistress, who loved it almost as much as she did her sons whose inheritance it was, would bring it all to life again, would put back what it had temporarily lost, would return the family which was its heart and that was why she was here standing on Betty Spooner's front step.

"'Oo is it, our Betty?" a voice Molly recognised as Mrs Spooner's asked from within.

"Nobody, Mam." Betty's eyes were hard and unforgiving and Molly flinched, but she must not fall at this, the first damned fence, for if she did she might just as well climb on her bicycle and go back to the gatehouse, for good! She might as well telephone the manager at the bank and tell him to find a buyer for Meddins since Molly Broadbent hadn't the guts to do what she had sworn to do.

"May I come in, Betty?" she asked politely, but for some reason, though she knew Betty was perfectly reasonable in her belief that she, and hundreds of her workmates at Broadbents Mill had been treated unfairly in the way they had been summarily deprived of their jobs, she felt a small spurt of irritation run through her. Betty was looking at her with the hostility she might show some draggle-tailed gypsy selling pegs at the door and it was not fair. After all it was not Molly's fault that the cotton trade had all but vanished, nor that the mill, because of it, had had to close, though she supposed the blame must to an extent rest on bad management, which meant Tim. True, there were still mills where cotton was being spun and cotton goods manufactured. Joel's for one, and others who had been shrewd enough to see it coming and taken evasive action. There was only one way to overcome the tragedy of the lost cotton industry, Joel had told a totally uninterested Tim only last week when he had invited him and Molly, with Robert and Millicent Chard, to dine with him.

"Oh, and how is that, old chap?" Tim had asked, unfailingly and charmingly polite.

"A cotton control board, such as that set up during the war. Equity between master and worker is essential, for more than ever Lancashire fortunes depend on the goodwill of her operatives. They must have a voice, Tim" – and Robert had nodded in agreement—" and of course a control board would put a final stop to the underselling which is what is crippling what remains of the trade."

"I'm sure you're right, old lad." Tim had smiled engagingly. "But I am no more than a simple gardener now and can have no concern in such portentous matters."

"Of course, I'm sorry. Let's change the subject for it must be boring for the ladies." This despite Millicent Chard's vigorous interest in reform and the welfare of the working classes. "Now, Molly, how is that fine son of yours – both your sons, in fact? I have a gift for them which I intend to bring over at the weekend if I may. Oh, no, I shan't tell you what it is," and Molly was completely aware, as Tim was not, that the gift, whatever it was, was no more than an excuse for Joel to drive over to the gatehouse and marvel at the progress of his son.

Now, as the irritation Betty had generated began to grow into sharp exasperation, edging towards the hot flare of temper Betty herself had witnessed, had even been on the sharp end of a time or two, Molly narrowed her eyes and tutted, holding it in as best she could.

"Oh, for God's sake, Betty Spooner, I've not come begging, nor to ask you to be my friend again though I'd like it if you would."

"What! Friends wi' thi' after what that 'usband o' thine did ter me an' me mates."

"That was nowt ter do with me, Betty, an' if you'd get down off that bloody high horse o' thine and let a bit of sense into that thick skull you'd see I'm right. I knew nothing about the mill. D'yer think I was allowed ter stick my nose in—"

"'Course not. Not Mrs High an' Mighty Broadbent 'oo 'adn't even time ter say ''Ow do'."

"That's not fair, nor right, Betty Spooner. You an' me used

to meet in town, and if you'd shown the slightest interest yer could've come up ter Meddins."

Betty hooted. "Oh aye, ter one o' them grand affairs what master o't mill puts on fer 'is swell friends. I can just see me wi' me gob full o' broad Lancashire, droppin' me aitches an' puttin' me foot right in it."

"Like I did at first."

"Tha're owner's wife, lass. It mekks a difference," Betty said scathingly.

"It was still bloody hard, Betty Spooner, but I did it."

"Aye, well . . ." Betty was running out of steam, besides which her curiosity was beginning to overcome the rancour the surprising appearance on her doorstep of her one-time friend had aroused. Molly did not look quite as smart as she usually did. She wore what appeared to be a pair of sand-coloured riding breeches and high polished boots, a warm woollen jumper to match the colour of her pants and a tweed jacket in a mixture of oatmeal and chestnut brown which was much too big for her. Betty was not to know it was Tim Broadbent's. Round her neck was a brown scarf above which her face was rosy and her eyes a vivid, aggrieved aquamarine. Her hair was stuffed in what Betty recognised as her daddy's old cap. She looked as though she had been out riding, which she had but on a bicycle not a horse.

Betty eyed her up and down, sniffed, flounced a bit more, hitched her arms more tightly about her and tossed her head. Molly and she had been friends since their first infant steps together in the playground of the street; since they had sat side by side on their mammies' doorsteps nursing their dollies and eating jam butties and watched with awed admiration the daring of the older girls with the skipping rope. They had gone to school together, spent their Saturdays either floundering about in the "duck pond" in Union Street or screaming at *The Perils of Pauline* at the Roxy. They had been confirmed together, taken their first communion together and still sat most Sundays only a few pews apart at mass. Betty was to be married soon, Molly knew that and perhaps her own bold plan would wither and die before it breathed life but there was no one else she wanted to be at her side when it began. She trusted Betty. They had always got on, sharing a good laugh and sometimes, when they were younger, a good cry. Now, at the most important point in Molly's life she needed Betty's outspoken, no nonsense practicality, her shrewd northern common sense, her good humour, her hardworking application to whatever task was put in front of her, providing she was paid for her labour. Already there were several overalled women leaning, as Betty was doing, in their doorways. They had seen her wheel her bicycle from Mammy's house up to the Spooners and she was well aware that they were already miming to one another – being ex mill girls and able to lip read – across the street on what Molly O'Dowd was up to now. A bit of a come-down from that fast little motor car she had driven to the old bicycle which was propped against the wall of the Spooner house and which had been found, though they were not to know it, in the junk at the back of the stable. There had been two others, all ridden by boys, two of whom had died in the trenches of France.

"Jesus, Mary and Joseph, are you going to let me in or not?" Molly hissed, aware of the interest she was creating, "'Cos if yer not then I'm off. I'll not stand here ter be sniggered at, not by you or by them," aiming a thumb in the direction of the spectators.

Betty hesitated, then with great show of reluctance and a pantomime of shrugging shoulders for the benefit of her neighbours, she grudgingly stepped back into the narrow, linoleum-covered hallway.

"Oh, all right, but it'd better be good. I'll not forget that—"

"Oh, give it a bloody rest, Betty, for God's sake. I've got the picture. You've no need to go on about it."

"Well, if that's the way tha're gonner be . . ."

"Come on, Betty, give over. Go an' mekk us a cup o' tea," she begged as she moved up the passage, Betty a step behind her.

"Well . . ." Betty was still aggrieved and not at all sure she liked being ordered about in her own home by this uppity young woman who had once shared her life, but she snapped her mouth shut with an almost audible click.

"Never mind, I'll do it meself," Molly continued. "I've made enough cups o' tea in yer mam's kitchen ter know where everything is," not aware herself how far she was lapsing into the accents of those about her.

Bea Spooner's mouth opened as noisily as her daughter's had closed when Molly walked composedly into the kitchen.

"Oh, hello, Mrs Spooner," she said, as though they had met only yesterday. "How are yer then, an' Mr Spooner? Both well, I hope."

"It's Molly, Mam," Betty told her mother unnecessarily.

"I can see that, our lass, an' after all tha've 'ad ter say about 'er I'm surprised tha' let 'er over't doorstep."

"Now, Mam, I promised 'er I'd let 'er 'ave 'er say, whatever it is an' it'd better be good. She's got five minutes, that's all."

Betty lifted her chin as did Mrs Spooner, a mannerism that proclaimed them to be mother and daughter. They folded their arms, Mrs Spooner still seated, Betty standing by the door from the kitchen into the hallway as though, since the encounter would be a short one, there was no need to venture further into the room. Nevertheless it was evident she and her mam were waiting with poorly concealed interest to hear whatever it was Molly O'Dowd had to say to them.

Molly took a deep breath then let it out slowly, noticing as she did so the misted vapour which drifted from her mouth. The kitchen, which she remembered as warm, cluttered, filled with the aroma of Mrs Spooner's savoury ducks and girdle cakes, was barely warm. Achingly clean, of course, and smelling of the carbolic soap the Spooners used – as did all the women in the street who had any claim to northern spit and polish – for everything from scrubbing floors to scrubbing backs in the weekly bathtub before the fire. A pot of tea was mashing on the range and two cups and saucers stood waiting on the table. The milk jug and sugar basin were not in evidence.

"Well?" Mrs Spooner said ominously, much as her daughter had done. She and Rosie Watson were still good neighbours, friends even, and Mrs Spooner, who "did" for Mrs Knight who was known to be pally with Molly's mother-in-law, had promised to see if there was anything going in that line for her. This young woman, who had once been their Betty's friend and had been in and out of Bea Spooner's house for as long as she could remember, or rather this young woman's fine husband, had brought a lot of people down when he shut and sold his mill, including Rosie Watson who could no longer rely on Molly for her well-being.

"Well?" Betty said, echoing her mother.

"Can I not sit down, Betty?"

"If tha' must, but don't be long. Me an' Mam's about ter 'ave us a cup o' tea."

"Tea. That would be nice."

"There's only two cups in't pot." Betty's voice was sharp, to the point, telling Molly to be the same.

"Shall I run up to Ma Bentley's and . . . and . . ."

"Yes?" Mother and daughter spoke in unison.

Molly had been about to say she would run up to the corner shop and fetch a quarter of tea since it was very obvious there was none to spare but the implacability in the faces of both women stopped her just in time. Hard up they might be, in fact it was very evident that they were, but just mention what they might think of as charity and she would be back outside on the pavement so fast she'd not have time to catch her breath.

"Well, I'll sit down if I may?" she said instead, and did so, perching herself on the edge of an ancient armchair into which she had seen Mr Spooner lower himself a hundred times in the past.

"Is your daddy well, Betty?" she began, hoping she could crack the wall of mistrust and resentment which these two women had erected.

"As well as any man what's outer work. 'E were at Broadbents an' all, tha' know, workin' in't yard. 'E's down the Labour right now seein' if there's owt goin'. I bin this mornin', me an' Cissie an' Elsie but tha' might as well stop at 'ome. There's nowt round 'ere, not in cotton mills. Mr Greenwood took—"

"Joel?"

"Oh, aye," Betty sneered, "'e's a relative o' thine, in't 'e? I forgot."

"What's he done?"

"Took on as many as 'e could but there's only so much work an' . . . well . . ."

Betty shrugged and moved further into the room, the general plight of all of them causing her, for a moment or two, to forget her animosity towards Molly. Deep in her heart, which was loyal and steadfast, Betty Spooner knew perfectly well that Molly was not to blame for her own misfortune. She was well aware, as all those in Oldham were, that there were dozens of cotton mills going under and hundreds of operatives being thrown out of work. In one way she could not stop herself from accusing Molly of causing the mill's downfall since the evidence of her husband's charming but careless disregard for money, or rather the way he chucked it about, was there for everyone to see. On Molly's back, in that smart little car of hers, the Rolls-Royce which had ferried Rosie O'Dowd, Flo O'Dowd and Maggie Todd wherever they wanted to go. Four gardeners, *four*, there had been at Meddins and countless servants in the house. Horses by the score frolicking in the fields at the back and you only had to get a good look at Molly's engagement and wedding rings – which she hadn't got on today, strangely – to realise that there must be boxes full of diamonds and emeralds back at Meddins for Molly O'Dowd to hang about herself. Like the bloody Queen of Sheba she had been one night when Betty happened to be passing the Grand Theatre and had seen her and her dazzling friends drifting from their chauffeur-driven motor cars into the foyer. It was that picture more than anything which stirred the coals of smouldering affront into flames of bitter fury, for it had seemed to her that had the Broadbents, including Molly, been a trifle more prudent, and with a bit of goodwill on the operatives' part, had they known what was coming, it might all have been avoided. Not that Betty had any head for business but it just seemed common sense.

In the silence that followed, Molly heard the milk cart clattering past the house and the long-drawn-out wicker of the horse as it pulled up at the kerb. There was a clink of jug on urn and the muted sound of a man's voice.

"I'm sorry," was all she could think of to say.

"Aye, well, sorry don't pay no bills," Mrs Spooner said, eyeing the pot of tea with longing, a look Molly could not fail to notice.

"Eeh, please, Mrs Spooner, drink tha' tea. Don't bother about me. I 'ad one before I set off an' then another at Mammy's," which was a lie for she was very conscious now of her mother's changed circumstances.

"Well . . ." Mrs Spooner, in whom the north country woman's habit of hospitality was strong, suddenly stood up and reached for a third cup and saucer. "I don't know about thi', our Betty, but I can't see no one in my 'ouse go wi'out a cup o' tea. Specially as it's just bin made. See, Molly, put a drop more 'ot water on it then it'll go three ways."

"Mrs Spooner . . . really . . . I can't . . ."

"Oh, shurrup, Molly O'Dowd," said Betty, drawing a chair from the table and turning it round to face the small fire. She sat down, her face still inclined to show her disapproval, "an' give over talkin' in that posh voice tha've picked up since tha' were wed. This is me, Betty Spooner, tha're talkin' to, not bloody Lord Mayor. See, drink tha' tea, well, if tha' can call it that. 'Maidens water' me Dad ses it is but it's all we got so gerrit down thi'. An' there's no milk nor sugar, neither."

"Oh, Betty, I'm that sorry . . ."

"We don't want tha' sympathy, do we, Mam?"

"No indeed, our lass. We've managed afore when things were a bit . . . short. I can remember me an' tha' dad. It were just after we was wed an' I'd started wi' our Ernie so that'd be – eeeh, don't time fly – 1904, 'cos our Ernie's twenty-four. Tha' dad were put off. 'E were a bricklayer's labourer wi' no skills an' earned no more 'n eighteen shillings a week. Five bob a week fer't rent an' all. God in 'eaven, we was 'ard up but we managed an' then when 'e were laid off this last time . . ."

"Yes, yes, Mam," Betty said somewhat impatiently, for now she had got over the shock and resentment the sight of Molly had caused in her she couldn't wait to find out what had brought her here. It was something, she could see that. Something that had Molly in a right old tear, fidgeting about in her dad's chair, nodding and smiling at Mam, turning the cup of what was really no more than hot water round and round in her slender white hands. Aye, Molly's hands had changed the same way Molly herself had since that day over two years ago, two and half to be exact, when the beating her stepfather had given her had driven her, for that was how Betty saw it, into the arms of that poor sap who was her husband. A lovely man, oh yes, even-tempered and with a sense of fun which was made evident by the twinkle in his eye and the cheeky grin which curved his mouth. God, how they'd envied her, the girls at the mill, not only for the luxury in which she was to live out her days, but for the handsome, wealthy, good-natured chap who was to share it with her. But, as her Granny Spooner used to say, "handsome is as handsome does" and look where they'd ended up on account of him. Molly still had him, of course, and the two lads he'd given her but instead of the beautiful house she was living in a poky cottage which was scarcely bigger than this, and, it was rumoured, with a mother-in-law who would turn cream sour. Nice surroundings, of course, out in the country but what a job she'd taken on with what was really *four* kids dependent on her to keep it all together.

"Any road," she said sharply, "what's up? What's brought thi' ter my door, Molly O'Dowd? Tha's up ter summat, I can tell. I know thee. I should do, since we shared same old pram almost, an' there's summat on tha' mind. Now I know tha's not come ter borrow a bob or two though I've 'eard tell tha' could do wi' it."

"You listen 'ere, Betty Spooner. My money, or lack of it, is nowt ter do wi' you. What's happened ter me an' Tim is our business an' yer can keep yer nose out of it. I've not come here to be insulted, nor sneered at, so if that's all yer can do then yer can shut yer gob."

"All right, all right, me gob's shut so gerron wi' it. Me an' Mam's better things ter do than sit about passin' time o' day wi' thee."

"Eeh, Betty Spooner, that mouth of your'n 'll get you inter trouble one o' these days."

"It already 'as, chuck, a time or two."

It was enough. Molly's complete reversal to the accent of her childhood, her slightly insulting but friendly repartee with which Betty was very familiar, had thawed Betty's ungracious acrimony and the two young women grinned at one another. It did not mean Molly was forgiven or that the abrupt closure of the mill by Molly's husband was forgotten. There would be an underlying bitterness in their relationship which would take more than a smile to get rid of. But they had arrived at some neutral ground where they might possibly communicate with one another and for the moment it must be enough.

"Well?" she said, almost accusingly. "What are thi' after?"

"D'you 'appen ter know where I can get me 'ands on a good, second-hand knitting machine? Cheap?"

28

The gift was a puppy, a golden labrador like Albert, delivered the following Saturday by Joel.

"The little bugger's eaten half the bloody upholstery in my car," he snapped, ready to chuck the ecstatically wriggling bundle over the nearest hedgerow, which was not far away since the gatehouse looked out directly into the lane.

"Oh, Joel, he's sweet." Molly held out her arms and the puppy, knowing a soft touch when it saw one, became even more rapturous, its rough tongue licking enthusiastically at every inch of bare flesh it could find, paying particular attention to her earlobes, this time with its sharp teeth.

"Sweet! Bloody hell, Molly, sweet! And it's not a he but a she."

"A she!" For several minutes Molly forgot the dreadful muddle of her life, if muddle could describe her frantic efforts to scrape together the necessary sum of money each month with which to repay the mortgage raised on Meddins, the constant battle she had each day with Muriel Broadbent to make her understand that she could not take over for her own use the space in which six of them must live, and the watchful, worried eye she cast about her husband to ensure he did not slip into the deep depression he had known periodically since they had moved out of Meddins. Would she ever become again the young and carefree woman she had been six months ago? Would her face ever light up once more with that youthful exuberance which had been its natural expression then? She knew she had taken on a permanent look of hunted anxiety and sometimes, when she caught an unexpected glimpse of herself in a mirror she would stop in surprise, wondering who that troubled woman was.

But now she squealed with laughter and the puppy, as though taking this strange sound as an invitation for more intimacies, draped herself about Molly's neck, a panting bundle of unconditional adoration.

Joel watched her, unaware of his own expression of unconditional adoration. He leaned on the side of his motor, his tweed jacket unbuttoned and his hands pushed deep in the pockets of his grey flannels. Beneath the jacket he wore a polo-necked jumper of soft cream cashmere which enhanced the dark smoothness of his freshly shaven face. He looked very handsome as he smiled at Molly. One heel was placed on the running board of the car and though he had just spent what he would scowlingly call the worst fifteen minutes of his life with the damned dog doing her best to send the motor and Joel into the ditch, it was worth it to see the glowing pleasure in Molly's face. Oh, there was no doubt that within the hour she would be cursing him as the animal systematically began to destroy her home. To shatter what little peace existed in the gatehouse. To drive his Aunt Muriel to utter for the thousandth time that she could not and would not live in such close and confined quarters for a moment longer, those which had been forced on her by her son's carelessness and her daughter-in-law's wilfulness and if the animal was to stay then she would get Elspeth to pack her suitcase and go. Molly wished she meant it. Albert was bad enough, Muriel would say, under her feet all day long, but at least he was quiet; the addition of a puppy to the chaos caused by her grandsons, who not only took up a great deal of space, but made a great deal of noise from which she could not escape, would be the last straw. Joel knew he was adding more aggravation to the home Tim and Molly, or more accurately Molly had made of the gatehouse. It was really no place for a young puppy, with a tiny living room, no more than a parlour but given the grand title of "drawing room" by Mrs Broadbent, who had taken it over for her own use and Molly had refused to argue. The square, squat building had low oak beams and thick stone walls and had been furnished with all the unremarkable bits of furniture bought for the house in Huddersfield Road where Rose Watson was to have lived, plus odds and ends culled from the attics at Meddins. Molly would not hear of any of the exquisite and completely unsuitable pieces of furniture which still filled the lovely rooms of the house and which she meticulously dusted each week, being brought across, saying it would be out of place, and besides, it was where it should be, waiting for them to return. The slope-ceilinged bedrooms had flowered curtains, comfortable beds, a chest of drawers apiece and a wardrobe, perfectly adequate for their needs at the moment.

The kitchen, the one warm and cosy room in the house, had a pine table, a dresser filled with sturdy crockery, a row of copper pans and a couple of rocking chairs, one on either side of the range fire where Tim and Molly Broadbent nursed their sons before bedtime. It was where Molly cooked bacon hotpot and potato pie, "duck" hash and Scotch broth, bread and butter pudding and fatty cake, parkin and rice pudding, all the dishes her mammy had taught her, cheap and nourishing, and which, since she was adept at no other, the family now ate round the kitchen table. Muriel had hers on a tray in her "drawing room" to Molly's eternal thankfulness. Tim said he loved her rabbit casserole, loyal as always, and her fruit cake was the best he had tasted and though Muriel said nothing, her eyebrows raised in astonishment at such peculiar dishes, she always cleared her plate, Molly noted!

Though Molly was not aware of it, Muriel Broadbent told her friends contemptuously that her daughter-in-law was reverting to type and she, personally, was not a bit surprised.

Molly would not have cared had she known. They had a solid roof over their heads, she told herself resolutely, and if she cared to step out into the driveway which ran beside the gatehouse, just inside the wrought-iron magnificence of the gates, she could feast her eyes on her beloved Meddins which serenely waited for her. The walled garden at the back of the gatehouse where Liam Broadbent played with Elspeth, and Joss Broadbent dreamed in his perambulator in the strengthening spring sunshine, gave evidence of purple clematis about the kitchen door, or so Tim told her from his growing knowledge imparted by Jud, honeysuckle round the windows and what, so Jud said, were apple trees and cherry trees and which, soon, would be awash with blossom. An old-fashioned cottage garden with a profusion of clove-scented pinks, marigolds, hollyhock, columbine and sweet pea in their right season.

The gate let into the wall at the back led out into the woods where, Molly knew, since she had seen it last year, a carpet of bluebells would soon stretch to clutch at her heart and her senses.

They had shelter, her family, the family which depended on her, though she was not sure they were aware of it, and probably never would be, to take them back to their rightful place at Meddins and that was enough. She had, without anyone knowing, had a quiet word with Mr Whittaker at Whittaker's the jewellers, who, though he was astonished to see her and on such an errand, had agreed to buy back her magnificent diamond engagement and wedding rings, the deal including a plain gold band to replace them. The money she received had been put into an account in her name from which each month the specified amount for the repayment of the mortgage was to be withdrawn and in a safe at the same bank she had a box in which were the few remaining pieces of jewellery Tim had given her and which were her umbrella for that rainy day that might come along.

For the moment she felt she could relax.

"I brought her over for the boys," Joel said now, his voice resolutely casual. "I was at Birch Hall, you know, the Holdens' place."

"No." Molly was still doing her best to avoid the squirming tangle of legs, the sharp claws and cold nose, the eager tongue of the puppy. The feel and smell of the small animal enchanted her. Molly was laughing, fighting her off, hugging her, squealing again as the sharp, excited puppy teeth made free with her flesh.

"Well, Sybil Holden . . . she never married, you know."

"No, I didn't."

"She breeds them, labradors, I mean and she let me have the pick of the litter. I couldn't keep her at Greenacres or Mrs Hebden would have been in a real tizzy."

"Tizzy."

"What?"

"That's what I'll call her. Tizzy."

"Very well, but the thing's supposed to be for Joss . . . and Liam."

"I know, but they are still a bit young to be entrusted with a puppy. And then there's Albert—"

His voice was harsh as he interrupted her. "Oh, for God's sake, Molly, put the damned thing in the house and come and walk with me. Have you any idea how beautiful you are with the sun in your hair? It's turned to copper fire . . . and your skin looks like . . . the cream on . . . Jesus, how I ache to hold you in my arms. How long is it? I can't sleep nor eat for wanting you and yet I'm forced to go through this bloody charade every time we meet, smiling through my teeth in case anyone's watching. I can't see past you, Mary Angelina. I've no future, nor do I want one without you and the boy in it. My boy."

"Joel . . ." Her cry was softly despairing. "Don't . . . it's no use talking like that. I can't just walk away from . . . Please, I'll arrange something when Joss is . . . he's only just six weeks old and it's . . . awkward. Oh, God, Joel, don't look at me like that. I can't bear it . . . to hurt you like this."

"I can't help it. I don't know how else to look at you. I love you so desperately and need you. Oh, Christ, those hours we spent together last year . . . how can I describe what they meant to me?" His voice was husky, urgent, a desperate whisper. "And it was as much a delight for you as it was for me, don't deny it. We are matched, my beloved girl. Your heart understands my heart. You are my heart, Mary Angelina. Please. Jesus, I'm not used to pleading, to taking second place. I can't stand much more of this, this waiting for God knows what. My whole bloody life revolves round when I can decently call and see you. And now there's . . . the boy. Oh, don't look at me like that or try to tell me he's Tim's because we both know differently. He's mine, my son, and I don't intend to sit calmly by and let Tim . . . I was never very good at waiting, Molly."

His voice was deliberately cruel, hard and was meant to hurt, as he hurt, and as he spoke his face closed like an iron glove, hard and clenched. He turned away with sudden savagery, leaning with both hands on the bonnet of the motor, bending his dark head in a gesture of utter despair.

Molly looked hastily about her, for if anyone should see him they would know at once that something was wrong. He was beating with his right hand on the polished surface of the car and Molly felt the tears rush to her eyes and she yearned to go to him, put her arms about him, lean against his broad back and tell him it would be all right, but how could she when they both knew it wouldn't? That Molly Broadbent and Joel Greenwood would never have more than this and how were they to live with it?

The puppy, young as it was and sensing something with the uncanny awareness of its kind, had become quiet in her arms, now and again looking up at her anxiously and licking her chin. Joel kept his back to her and she felt the hurt inside her flare up, a constant hurt which was with her every hour. Her expression was haunted and the dread of what lay ahead of her settled like heavy armour on her body but she knew she had no choice but to go on.

She looked about her again, aware that she must do, or say something before Joel's strange manner was seen, perhaps by Jud or Elspeth who would wonder at it.

She said the first thing that came into her head and, without realising it, she chose the only thing which, at that moment, would draw Joel's attention, with its very singularity, from his anguish.

"I'm . . . I'm looking for a knitting machine, Joel." Her voice was high, strained and her face worked awkwardly as though she were trying to speak in a foreign language. "I wondered if . . . if you knew where I might find one. I remember you telling Tim there was machinery going for next to nothing. Being sold abroad . . . and, well . . ."

He turned slowly and stared at her as if she *had* spoken in a foreign language.

"What?"

"I want a knitting machine, or perhaps two if they're not too expensive. Betty an' me . . ."

"What?" he said again and she was relieved to see the strange, blank expression had left his face. His eyes had cleared and there was almost a smile about his well-cut mouth. "I have the feeling you are trying to distract me, Mary Angelina but what the bloody hell with I can't fathom. There is something ahead of me which I have the feeling I'm not going to like, so I suggest you get it over and done with and tell me at once. A knitting machine? And who is Betty, may I ask?"

He leaned his buttocks on the bonnet of the car, folded his arms across his chest and waited. The day was bright with spring sunshine. The trees in the last few days had become gauzed with the first timid emergence of new greenery, each branch studded along its length with unfurling buds. The grass about the lake was a fresh, juicy green, speared from the drive to the water's edge with a shifting carpet of daffodils. The sun floated, a pale lemon disc, just above the roofline of the gatehouse and its rays touched the dark hair of the man and woman, putting a russet gloss there that was strangely similar. There was a sharp breeze, come from directly across the Pennines and it had whipped a rose into Molly's cheeks. A curling tendril of hair flicked across her mouth and she raised a hand to tuck it back behind her ear. Joel watched her, his eyes dazzled, his face flushed, as she moistened her lips and cleared her throat.

"Betty Spooner. She was my friend . . . before I married. We played as children, went to school and worked in the mill together. When Broadbents closed she was thrown out of work."

"And what has that to do with you and – what was it? – a knitting machine?"

"I want, with Betty, to make stockinette dishcloths."

"Dishcloths!"

"Yes, I've been to all the hardware stores in town, spoken to the managers, even Woolworths and they've all promised to look at what I make, what we make, me and Betty."

"Hell's teeth, woman, do you know anything about—"

"I know nothing about anything but I can bloody well learn, Joel Greenwood. I've worked a ring spinning frame and though I know it's different I'm used to machinery and I'll soon get the hang of it. There must be someone in the trade who can show me. I'm going to install the machine, two if I can afford it, in the stable and Betty's coming to work for me. Joel, I must do something to get . . ." Her face became set in a grim determined expression, her eyes a brilliant blue-green, like a turquoise, between the narrowing lids. "I mean to get Meddins back. To live in, I mean. I want my sons to have the life Tim and his brothers had, to have ponies and . . . and . . . the schooling and to do this I must have money to repay the mortgage for a start. Then there is . . ."

Joel put out a hand, laying it on the puppy's head.

"Does Tim know?"

"Not yet."

"Then put the dog in the kitchen, my love," he said, so low she could hardly hear him. "If we are to discuss knitting machines it would be as well if we were to move away from here. I have the feeling Muriel's hovering at the back of the curtains."

"She's out. Totty Roper's chauffeur picked her up to take her for lunch."

"Really." His voice was like honey. "And Tim?"

"Joel, when you look at me like that, I cannot think."

"I don't want you to think, my darling. Just put the pup in. Is Elspeth there?"

"Yes, in the kitchen."

"Good, then you can walk with me and tell me about the knitting machines, and Betty."

The puppy was greeted with such rapture by Liam and dismay by Elspeth, Molly felt a pang of guilty misgivings at leaving her. Even Joel had the grace to look slightly shamefaced as the boy, Tim's boy, as he had unconsciously begun to call him as opposed to *his* boy, grabbed the small animal and began to tow it across the kitchen floor.

"Oh, heavens, madam," Elspeth squeaked from her chair, lifting her feet from the stone flags as Tizzy scrambled at her skirts. "Oh, heavens, Master Liam . . ."

"They'll be all right, Elspeth. They'll get used to one another," Joel assured the startled nursemaid, "and we won't be long. She's called Tizzy, by the way," grinning at Molly.

They were still laughing as they opened the gate at the back of the garden, in that moment as blithe as two children who had escaped the schoolroom. If they had not been fearful that they might run into Jud they would have held hands as they fled through the wood, leaping fallen trees which Jud had not yet "got round to", jumping strangely shaped branches, careful not to tread on and crush the massed clumps of wild daffodils. The ground was soft and squelchy from the wet winter and their boots left imprints in it which filled up with water.

He stopped her as they reached the perimeter of the wall which surrounded the estate. The trees were old, enormous, clustered thickly together, sheltering them from any eyes that might be watching.

"Tell me about it," he ordered, "but first . . ." Taking her wrists in his strong hands he held her arms above her head, then leaned to kiss her, his mouth like velvet on hers, and had her life, or Tim's, depended upon it she could not have stopped him. His lips travelled along her jawline and she threw back her head to accommodate them as they slipped down the pure white, graceful column of her throat. She had on a silk shirt, open at the neck and, unwilling to free her hands, he worried at the top button with his teeth, managing to undo it and then another. The deep valley between her breasts received the attention of his mouth, his tongue and his hard male body, erect and arrogant, held hers against the trunk of the tree. His face was flushed, handsome, vitally alive, the colour in it racing beneath his amber skin. His eyes, narrowed and predatory, telling her he meant to have his way, were so dark they were almost black and she could feel and taste and smell the sweetness of his breath which had a faint linger of the Woodbines he smoked on it.

"Mary Angelina . . . my heart . . . my love . . . my beloved girl . . . let me love you . . . Dear Lord, it never fails to amaze and delight me when I see you come alive . . . help me undo the rest of these buttons . . . there, good girl . . . let me see . . . Oh, Christ . . ." He bent his head and his lips went in turn to each exposed breast. There was a faint milky smell and taste to the nipples which excited him further, for it was his son she had recently suckled and when the clear liquid jetted into his mouth he groaned in indescribable ecstasy.

It was at that moment, as he delicately lapped at her hard, peaked nipples, that Albert began to bark. Quite close by, by the sound of it, and, further away, Jud's voice calling him.

"Come on, tha' daft bugger," he was saying. "There's nowt out there at this time o' day. Besides, tha's too old fer this kind o' mularky. Come on along wi' me an' we'll go an' check them beans in't glasshouse. It'll be warm in there."

Hurriedly, and with desperately trembling fingers, as though Jud and Albert were to appear round the trunk of the wide oak, Molly did up her buttons, fastened the old jacket of Tim's she had taken a fancy to, wound her scarf securely about her throat and stepped away from Joel. The pit of her stomach had begun to flame and throb and melt and her woman's body, which didn't give a damn about Jud or Albert, the searching wind, the rough texture of the tree trunk at her back, nor, if he should care for it, the squelching wet leaves on the ground where Joel might lay her, protested hotly at the interruption. She would splay her legs like any common whore, her excited body told her, but her mind was filled with pictures of her husband, her babies, even her mother-in-law who she knew, quite without doubt, would not manage without her.

Joel's face, losing its colour, was grey and closed as the low banked clouds which suddenly shut out the sun. His mouth, which had been soft as silk, full and sensual with his love, was clamped so tightly shut it was no more than a thin white line. He was shaking, sudden short bursts and his voice, when he spoke, was like fingernails down a blackboard.

"It's a long time since I made love to a woman, Molly. Long before my son was born."

"Please, Joel, I beg you, don't . . ."

"And that woman was you. I have never, since I gained manhood, gone long without . . . without . . . well, you will know what I mean. I'm not a man to be celibate and I tell you, this . . . this is tearing me apart. I only want you, you see. My body needs your body. It seems I cannot simply go out and buy the release I need. It has to be *you*, woman, so what the hell am I to do, tell me that?"

"Joel . . . Holy Mother of God, if only I could give you an answer."

"Won't you . . . come somewhere?"

"Where?"

"I don't know . . . there must be a place where I can . . . Dear God, I am dying of this."

"Joel, my love . . . my love."

He turned towards her and his look had softened.

"There is, remember, the coachhouse?"

"Joel, we couldn't . . ."

"No one goes there."

"Joel . . ." but already her body was screaming at her to stop being such a bloody fool. Mrs Broadbent was at the Ropers. Tim had taken his bicycle and ridden over to Birch Hall to see if Sybil, the same Sybil who had given Joel the puppy, would lend him a mount since he longed for a gallop, he had told Molly wistfully, and Jud was in the greenhouse.

He closed the coachhouse door quietly behind him and backed her up against it, then, holding her arms out as though she were nailed to a cross, he began to kiss her. Both of them were moaning deep in their throats, though they were neither aware of it. He was gentle at first, just a brushing of his soft, parted lips on hers, their breath, which was plainly visible in the cold air, mingling and sighing from mouth to mouth. Molly felt the throbbing, pulsing warmth in her belly grow and spread and she began to struggle, not to escape from Joel's mouth and tongue and hard, demanding body but to clutch it more closely to her. He released her hands and her arms went round his neck and her hands gripped his hair in the nape of his neck so fiercely he cried out.

Someone tore off her jacket and scarf – was it him, was it her? – tossing them on the floor which was now not so clean as it had once been. Then with great deliberation, as though he had waited a long, urgent time for this moment, he tore open her shirt and pulled it down over her shoulders. Her pretty, lace-trimmed chemise fell about her waist and in the dim, misted light of the coachhouse her breasts gleamed white, full and rose-tipped. They seemed to spring into his eager hands and he bent his mouth to them, his enraptured mind so full of her and her shadowed beauty he did not consider the risk they were taking.

He had found an old horseblanket, rough and smelling of the many horses over whose back it had been flung, wrapping their naked bodies up in it as later they drowsed, curled up together on the padded blue velvet seat of the elegant carriage.

"I love you, Mary Angelina, I wish I didn't but I do."

"I know, my darling, I love you."

His hands under the blanket were at her breasts, the brown strength of his fingers fitting about the soft, curving fulness of them, becoming urgent again, demanding, refusing to be denied though no such denial had been offered. He lifted her on to his lap, turning her towards him, her legs apart, and when he entered her for the second time their minds were mesmerised by the beauty and joy their joined bodies had created for one another. A luminous, joyous beauty that blinded their eyes and all conception of the world about them.

When the door of the coachhouse opened, letting in a shaft of light which, though it was not brilliant, contrasted sharply with the dimness within, neither of them noticed. Molly's white back was arched like the curve of a bow, Joel's brown hands gripping her waist. Her head was thrown back and her arms were floating, like white strands of seaweed beneath water, in the dusty confines of the carriage. Joel's face was hidden, his mouth at her breast and they were both groaning as though in agony.

Tim Broadbent's brain, though his eyes told him exactly who it was who shared the act of love in the carriage in which both his mother and his grandmother had been driven, would not accept the image they sent to it. His face was totally without colour or expression. His lips were parted and from the moment his eyes fell on his wife's naked body and recognised the man in whose arms she moaned, they did not blink. They wanted to. They wanted to close for ever and never see again the passion, the love that was slowly and unendurably driving cruel nails into his heart. The love and passion, and yet the tenderness which Joel Greenwood and Molly Broadbent felt for one another.

At last his dead brown eyes blinked. He held a puppy in his arms. He had been smiling as he went in search of Joel and Molly who, Elspeth had told him, had gone for a walk, ready to thank his cousin for his splendid gift to Tim's sons. Albert was too old for children's teasing and romping and Tizzy, as Elspeth had wonderingly told him the young labrador was called, would make a great pet for them. Boys should have a dog. He and Will and Charlie had always had a dog, even before Albert.

So he had smiled but now he knew he would never smile again. The puppy gave a short excited yelp, Joel lifted his head from Molly's breast, Molly turned towards the door and for the three of them the world came to an end.

The puppy fell from Tim's lifeless arms, crying sharply as she landed heavily on the flagged stone floor. She whimpered, then stood up shakily and began to totter towards the feet of the man who had dropped her, making, in her distress, towards the only source of comfort she knew, but as she advanced Tim Broadbent slowly retreated. He walked into the frame of the open doorway, flinching as his shoulder struck it, continuing to move backwards, his eyes on the paralysed, naked figures of his wife and his cousin. He saw his wife's mouth open and the word "Tim" form but if she had shouted it he would not have heard her.

Stumbling, he turned and with faltering, uneven strides began to run towards the archway which led out of the stable yard, turning in the direction of the front of the house.

"Oh, Jesus Christ." Joel was the first to come to his senses, beginning to babble, God knows what, to the frozen, appalled, terrified woman in his arms. They were like a pair of disjointed puppets in the hands of an inexperienced puppeteer and Joel had a moment to consider bitterly what comical, pitiful fools they must look as they struggled to get back into their clothes.

It was like a French farce and he might have found it amusing had it not been so bloody tragic. He could not find his left boot and his flannels which he had flung off so eagerly an hour ago had somehow got turned inside out. Molly was weeping and shaking convulsively, a great blinding wash of tears drowning her face and falling on the silk shirt her shaking fingers could not button. He wanted to say something, comfort her, for this was all his fault but some instinct told him there was no time for that now. He and Molly no longer mattered. All that mattered was to get to Tim. What in hell's name he would do, or say, when he found him, he'd no idea. I'm in love with your wife and she's in love with me, which is what he had dreamed of doing for months but which now, of course, could never be said. It was true, but it could not be said, not now.

"Joel . . ." Molly was leaning against the carriage, her face an incredible greenish white in the shaft of light which streamed from the open doorway, then, folding up from the waist, she began to retch. Again he wanted to go to her, do all the things a human creature does for another in distress but there was no time.

"Molly . . ." His voice was anguished.

"Go, catch him."

"Oh, dear God in heaven . . ."

"Catch him."

They heard it then. The powerful roar of Joel's motor car as someone brought it to life. It sounded like the deep-throated growl of the Vauxhall which had been Tim's pride and joy and which Molly had first heard nearly three years ago. It had been at the gates of Meddins then, as this was now, coming closer and closer then but now it was doing the opposite, snarling away into the dying afternoon, getting fainter and fainter until at last it died away to nothing. To silence. To emptiness. To nothing.

They did not look at one another. Molly picked up the crying puppy which appeared to be unhurt, holding it tightly to her as though for support, then, closing the door carefully on the tragedy of their love, they began to walk back towards the gatehouse.

29

They found Joel Greenwood's motor car the next morning
at the bottom of the disused Broadside Quarry. Tim's body
was not inside it but lying quite peacefully twenty feet away,
looking as though he'd just fallen asleep, the walkers who
found him said, except for the strange and awkward angle
of his head. The car had been horribly smashed to pieces,
but the poor gentleman wasn't, thank goodness, they added,
though it was supposed it made no difference to him since
he was dead. They had been going to walk up to Badger's
Edge, the spokesman for the small, slightly hysterical group
of young men and women from the rambling club in Leeds
told the constable who was first on the scene and it was
the broken quarry fence which had alerted them. It wasn't a
particularly dangerous bend on the road so it was a mystery
to them how the poor gentleman could have come off it. Of
course, it was a very powerful machine he was driving, the
young man said, and he should know since he was himself
a motor mechanic. A Mercedes Coupé with the capacity to
go at one hundred and nine miles an hour, though in the
opinion of those who knew about such things, including
himself, the speed it could go was far in excess of the safe
limits of the chassis. Perhaps this had caused the accident,
he said helpfully to the constable.

The constable, who knew at once who the dead man was,
had the good sense to alert the Oldham Constabulary, who
in turn had informed him that the dead man's cousin, Mr
Joel Greenwood, would be along to identify the body since
they could hardly summon the dead man's widow or mother,
could they? Mr Greenwood was the only male relative who
was available. A dreadful, dreadful accident, though there

were those who asked themselves what Tim Broadbent had been doing in Joel Greenwood's powerful motor car up on the moors at that time of night. There were farms close by whose occupants, when questioned, had confessed to hearing the roar of a motor car's engine several times as though poor Mr Broadbent, such a nice fellow, had gone back and forth between Oldham and Delph, and several pedestrians swore to a terrible fright as the great green monster had gone by them, so fast it had been no more than a blur. Forced them into ditches, it had, and even, one said, over a gate which led into a field.

Muriel Broadbent was upstairs in the tiny bedroom she had loathed from the moment she had been allocated it, heavily sedated, a nurse in attendance, one summoned by Doctor Taylor, for his patient would need a great deal of care. Three sons, three fine sons all dead now, and how was she to bear up under that? The small drawing room in which Elspeth had lit a fire seemed to be crowded from wall to wall with all Muriel's dearest friends, gathered, Joel Greenwood was inclined to think, like crows behind a storm, come, they said, to offer comfort and support to dear Muriel, at least until her daughter Tess arrived to take over. Where had Tim been going at that hour, he was aware they were asking one another, and in Joel Greenwood's car?

But really, how thankful dear Muriel and her daughter-in-law must be to have Joel to take care of all the appalling details at this terrible time. They drank the sherry the Broadbents' nursemaid offered them, and accepted a sliver of fruit cake the dead man's wife had made only the day before.

It was as though there were two men being mourned, Joel thought. His mind was too stunned to dwell on it much, stirring only enough to get him and the two Broadbent women through what had to be done. There was Muriel Broadbent's son whose people, the right people, gathered in their own charmed circle in the drawing room to offer their condolences. They were calm and proper and quite controlled as they had been trained to be since childhood, for it was not the thing, no matter how one felt it, to show an indecent amount of emotion. They were the county families of which the Broadbents had been a part for one hundred and fifty years and would not dream of intruding in Muriel's kitchen where presumably the one servant she had left was attending to her duties.

And then there was Molly Broadbent's husband whose death was genuinely grieved and wept over by the warm-hearted women, and one or two men, who were gathered in the kitchen about his widow. There was Loll Andrews and her husband, Loll in tears and begging to do anything which might ease Molly's pain, she said. Robert and Millicent Chard, quiet but letting it be known they would be there at need. Sarah Lucas, whose husband was in the drawing room, uneasy in such surroundings since she had rarely sat in a kitchen, but there nevertheless. Mammy, Aunty Maggie and Aunty Flo seemed to blend in with them as though the tragedy of Tim's death had drawn them all together and made them the same in some strange way. Tim Broadbent had been kind to them, generous with the loan of his splendid motor car, with his time and his money, when he had it, simple and warm-hearted and yet brave, defending Molly and Rosie when Pikey's cruelty had threatened them. Smile, he always had a smile and joke, a real teaser, he was, or had been, as mischievous sometimes as a schoolboy, but who could not help but like him?

They clustered protectively about Molly in the kitchen which was like home to Molly's relatives, keeping the fire stoked, making endless cups of tea, for sherry was not particularly to their taste, the dead man's elder son comfortably ensconced on his Aunty Flo's lap, his eyes big and wondering, his thumb plugged in his mouth. Aunty Maggie nursed the baby, for really that poor girl of Molly's was run off her feet answering the bell the posh folk in the drawing room would keep on ringing.

Joel found himself drifting between each room, the only man there when the Chards and Andrews left, doing his best to split himself into two people. The one who was needed by Helen and Delia, Totty and Beattie, who thought it was his duty, as one of them, to tell them in grave but steady tones how this dreadful thing had happened, and the other who mourned his cousin and yearned for the woman who sat like a granite-faced frozen statue in the rocking chair in the kitchen. The women of her family, not knowing him, at least only as one of the gentry, hovered protectively, suspiciously about her, prepared to fling him out on his ear should he make a move towards their Molly which might upset her.

They were seriously concerned about Molly, Joel could see that, though she had a perfect right to be dazed, shocked, grief-stricken by the loss of her young husband. She seemed to withdraw further and further into herself and away from them with every passing hour. He had brought them over early this morning in an old black motor car which would not have looked out of place in a funeral cortège, Aunty Flo said, then clapped her hand to her mouth in horror, though at the time their Molly's husband's whereabouts were not known, only that he was missing. Molly needed her family about her, he had told them, stony faced, since there was no one but a flustered nursemaid and her hysterical mother-in-law at the gatehouse.

They would never forget the appalling scene which had taken place when the constable had come to inform them that Mr Broadbent's body had been found. Molly had staggered back as though someone had shoved her, falling down in the hallway against the banister, giving her cheekbone such a crack Flo O'Dowd was convinced it must be broken. Springing up before anyone could reach her, she had begun to smash her head repeatedly against the solid wood. Again and again until Flo and Rosie had dragged her into the kitchen, leaving Maggie and Elspeth crouched helplessly over the crumpled figure of Molly's mother-in-law. Molly's face looked as though Pikey had been at her again, Flo thought, a rapidly closing eye and a large inflamed contusion on her cheek from which blood had begun to flow.

Since then she had said no word, nor even moved from the chair they had put her in, appearing even to be unaware of Doctor Taylor who knelt at her feet to attend to her abused face. The baby was grizzling, indeed his grizzle was becoming a full-throated roar since he was not used to being kept waiting for his breakfast.

Not knowing what was to happen next in this nightmare world which had descended on their Molly, Rosie and Flo and Maggie sat and waited for whatever it might be.

Maggie shook her head as she put the baby to her shoulder.

"Tha'd best send that there girl to't nearest chemist, Rosie. This babby's 'ungry an' it don't look as though our Molly's got owt fer 'im."

"I'll go," Mr Greenwood said from the kitchen doorway, surprising them all, for what did men know, or care much, for other folks' children. "Tell me what to get and I'll get it."

He didn't like it much, Joss Broadbent. He was used to the

sweet, full taste of his mother's nipple and the rubber teat and what came out of it offended him, but his mother continued to stare bleakly at a spot somewhere to the right of the dresser, her attitude saying he could starve for all she cared.

Tessa Addington, once Broadbent, and her husband arrived during the afternoon. The ladies who had awaited patiently to pass over their dear friend into some trustworthy hand since the widow was insensible, it seemed, and incapable of even rising from her chair by the kitchen fire, left for their respective homes, the sound of their respective chauffeur-driven motor cars which had clogged up the driveway for hours, harsh and discordant in the hushed air of misery which lay about the little house.

Again it was a house divided, with Tessa and her husband in the drawing room and Molly and Rosie in the kitchen. At their request, Joel had taken Maggie and Flo home, since there was hardly room for them all but they would be back in the morning, they said, as they kissed the frozen figure of their niece and hugged Rosie silently, thanking the Blessed Virgin that it was not them who were to stay here in this house of fragmented sorrow. It was not natural for a family to be so set apart. They were all grieving for the same man, wife, mother, sister and yet they were severed, distant, unable to communicate with one another, nor share the pain of it.

If Molly was aware of the days which separated Tim's death from Tim's funeral she gave no sign of it. Some time during the afternoon of Tessa Addington's arrival she allowed her mammy to divest her of the clothes she had put on yesterday morning. Her torn silk shirt which, strangely, had two buttons missing, her crumpled breeches stained with something her mother did not recognise, though it smelled remarkably like horse, Tim's old tweed jacket and her boots which, incredibly, were on the wrong feet and if Rosie remarked on it Molly did not hear her. Rosie put her in the bath and washed her hair, then dressed her decently in a black dress before replacing her in her chair beside the kitchen fire. The children were kept out of her way and later, as night fell and there seemed nothing else to do, Rosie took her daughter's flaccid hand in hers and drew her gently to her feet, leading her upstairs to the bed she had shared with Tim Broadbent. She undressed her and put her in the nightgown which was under one of the pillows, then, taking off her own skirt and blouse, lay down beside her. She could hear small sounds from downstairs as though, now that she and Molly were out of it, someone was doing something in the kitchen. There were footsteps on the stairs, hushed voices from Mrs Broadbent's room and once, the cry of the baby, but it seemed Molly heard nothing.

The funeral was at the church where Molly and Tim were married. There was a big attendance. A bad business, everyone was saying, agreeing with one another that Tim Broadbent was an excellent fellow, speculating on what he had been doing on that road and in his cousin's motor car.

It was a bleak March day with a bitter wind blowing and the young widow was seen to shiver, though apart from that she made no movement, nor sound, nor even shed a tear. She was surrounded by a positive army of decently clad, plain working folk, keeping well to their side of the open grave. Her hand was held on one side by her mother who crossed herself conspicuously, as they all did, and on the other by a heavy-set, kindly-faced man who was addressed as Uncle Alf by the family's younger members.

Across the grave Muriel Broadbent, invisible beneath her old-fashioned mourning veils, leaned heavily on the arm of her nephew, Joel Greenwood, who also supported Tim's sister despite the presence of her husband. Like Molly Broadbent, Muriel was hemmed in protectively by her close friends and relatives, a poignant figure, fragile and ready to fall had it not been for the steadfastness of Joel Greenwood. Thank God for Joel Greenwood, they said to one another, for how would they all have got through it without him? A tower of strength, he had been, though he himself looked quite dreadful.

The interment over and those terrible shovelfuls of earth beginning to fall, Molly was led away jerkily, obediently, blank eyes fixed and unblinking, by the kindly hands and comforting arms of half a dozen of her women and when, in a convulsive moment she fell to her knees and was violently sick behind a gravestone, no one noticed Joel Greenwood, who turned away as though in great distress, his own face ghastly, his own body shaking with tremors which threatened to have him off his feet.

There was some confusion at the gate of the churchyard, with people milling about and getting in one another's way and again it was left to Joel Greenwood to sort it out, to unravel the complexities of it, to explain to those concerned what was happening and to make fresh arrangements since those he had made – for who else was there? – were now obsolete.

He spoke quietly to two of the women who were hovering defensively about the widow and they were seen to frown and become grim-faced, their eyes hardening, their expressions saying that an insult had been offered them and they were affronted. Muriel Broadbent was already deeply ensconced in the back of the gleaming funeral car, her daughter beside her, her daughter's husband ready to climb in when he was told. There were a dozen such motors and a long parade of private cars, Rolls-Royces and Bentleys and Daimlers, cars of the rich, and one by one they were filling up and beginning to pull away.

"What is it, Flo?" Rosie asked anxiously, desperate to protect her daughter, who surely must be seriously deranged, from any further distress.

"They're all off ter some friends o't old lady, 'e ses. I dunno where an' 'e's not sayin'." Flo O'Dowd's mouth was clamped to a grim, furious line.

"But . . .?"

"Nay, Rosie love, what's use?" Maggie, leaning somewhat tiredly against Flo's shoulder, shook her head resignedly. "They don't want us no more, nor our Molly. Funeral's over an' done with. The poor chap's bin decently put away an' it were 'im what 'eld 'em together, 'is mam an' Molly. Now 'e's gone an' 'is lot's off to do wharever it is they do in their world. Mr Greenwood ses 'e's sorry an' if there's owt else we want we've only ter say. Them cars is fer us," nodding towards the half a dozen which remained, their chauffeurs standing patiently by the open doors.

"But . . ."

"An' the old lady's goin' back wi' 'er daughter to wherever it is she lives which, if tha' want my opinion, is best news our Molly's 'ad fer days."

Joel watched her being led away towards the waiting line of cars. Grief was choking him, not for the man they had just buried, even though he knew he had killed him, but for the death of his love. He couldn't live without her, it was as simple as that, and just as simply, he knew he must. His vision blurred so that he could no longer see her and in that moment he felt his heart break. She had not looked at him.

Her eyes, so clear and lovely a blue-green, and yet so dead, had gazed somewhere beyond him, and her face, as white and cold as the new marble of a headstone at her back, had been completely without expression. Her mouth, poppy red, the mouth he had kissed so hungrily less than a week ago, was slightly parted as though she might speak but she did not look at him.

He bent his head and the keen wind ruffled his dark hair, the hair she had laughingly told him would trip him up if he didn't get to the barber's before the weekend. He did not believe in God but if he had he would have given Him thanks for the rare woman who had loved him. He had loved her well but she was lost to him forever and he couldn't endure it.

It was two weeks before Molly became aware again of her surroundings. It was April now and in the garden at the back of the cottage a willow tree, covered all over with great golden catkins, was busy with bees gathering the pollen. The sun shone a clear and delicate lemon from the washed newness of the pale blue spring sky. The clematis and honeysuckle were beginning to show signs of vigorous growth. Anemones of all colours were bursting their vividness against the garden wall, crowding beside golden crocus and blue hyacinth and on the scrap of ragged lawn Liam and Tizzy, who had got each other's measure now, were dragging one another back and forth, Liam's battered teddy between them. Elspeth sat in a sheltered corner by the wall where the sun had some warmth, Joss on her knee, while beside her his grandmother, who had not yet gone home since she could not leave her grieving daughter, waited patiently for her turn to nurse him. He was sucking vigorously at his bottle, having at last become used to it and Rosie watched him with that besotted look that is common to grandmothers. The look said she could not believe how clever he was, how incredibly intelligent and him only two months old and if his nursemaid didn't give him up soon she would have sharp words with her. She missed her own children who were staying with Aunty Maggie and prayed every night to the Holy Mother, and in the morning as well, to make their Molly strong again. It was not like her to go under like this, to give way and give up even if she had lost the husband she had loved so desperately. Give her time, Doctor Taylor said. She'd had an emotional breakdown, whatever that was, but Molly had children who were her responsibility, and her own life to see to and Rosie could not stay here for ever.

The subject of her thoughts sat beside her, there in body, present but gone away, gone to some place where pain, grief, guilt, remorse, shame could not reach her. She was in the pretty, strawberry-coloured woollen dress her mother, finding it in her wardrobe, had put her in. It had a single embroidered lapel and a tie sash belt. The sleeves were long and tight with buttons from the elbow to the wrist. It was one she had bought soon after she and Tim were married and was longer than the fashion of today but the colour suited her and seemed to reflect its lovely glow in the thin paleness of her face. Her hair had been washed the night before and was heavy and curling, glossy with the life Molly lacked.

Tired of the game – or was it that instinctive canine knowing which recognises pain? – the puppy lolloped over to Molly and, rearing up, put her front paws on her knee, looking up into her face and wagging her tail.

"Eeh, mind that dratted animal, our Molly. She's mud on 'er paws," Rosie admonished, but Molly bent to lift the puppy to her lap, her face assuming an odd expression as though the animal were reminding her of something.

Rosie turned back to her grandson.

"'Ello, anybody at 'ome?" a cheerful voice shouted from inside the house. "Front door were open so I just let messen in. Where is everybody? 'Ello, Mrs Watson, Molly, it's me."

They all turned as Betty Spooner appeared in the kitchen doorway, even the baby. Betty's arms were filled with brown paper-wrapped parcels. She was smiling uncertainly, since after all this was a house of mourning, but at the sight of her, as puppies do, Tizzy jumped from Molly's lap and launched herself at Betty.

"Oh, God, mind me silk stockin's, tha' little bugger," she shrieked, then, conscious of the interested toddler on the lawn, put her hand to her face.

"Sorry," she mouthed, pulling a face as she advanced into the garden. She was dressed in a skirt and jacket in a shade which could only be described as tangerine with a violet-coloured blouse beneath it. Her shoes, cheap from the market, were of black fake kid with an elaborate pearl buckle and her hat, which sported a tall, straight feather, was a black velvet cloche. She at once took off the hat and threw it backwards into the kitchen where, Rosie hoped, it would land on the table for God help it if the puppy got hold of it. Betty's hair, which in the past few years she had worn shingled, bobbed, Eton cropped and permanent waved, was growing longer than when Rosie had last seen her, loosely covering her ears with curls falling over her forehead. It suited her and, strangely, so did the tangerine outfit.

Betty moved slowly across the grass until she reached Molly, where, in a warm-hearted gesture which brought tears to Rosie's eyes, dropped to her knees before her, unconcerned about her silk stockings, it seemed. She placed her parcels on the grass and reached for Molly's hands, looked up sadly into her face.

"Eeh, our kid, I don't know what ter say, 'onest. I'm that upset fer thi' an' so's me mam. She wanted ter come an' see thi'. We both cried when we 'eard," which was more than Molly had done, Rosie reflected. "The 'ole street . . . well, we 'ad a collection fer a wreath. We wanted yer to know we was thinkin' about thi'. I 'ope yer liked it, an't message."

Molly's expression did not change since the wreath, all the wreaths and flowers had gone unnoticed.

"We meant it an' all," Betty continued. "Not many of 'em knew 'im an' neither did I really. I just remember 'im that day 'e 'ad me in his office when Pikey . . . well, I'll say no more except I'm 'ere now. I give thi' a fortnight which Mam said was only right an' then when Mr Greenwood turned up wi't machines I decided . . ."

It was almost like a mechanical doll which a child has left lying in a toy box, then, on taking it out again, has decided to wind up. Round and round goes the key and, slowly at first, jerkily, the doll begins to function. An arm moves, the head turns and there is life where there had been stillness and silence.

Molly blinked as the last sentence reached the closed circuits which led to her brain, opening them up, giving them energy, flooding them with a pain she could scarcely contain but which must be contained or she would be lost for ever, her suddenly awakened senses told her. It was his name that brought her back, his beloved, *hated* name. A wave of anguish broke through her, so acute she knew she had moaned, for Betty flinched away and Mammy stood up.

"Betty . . ." Her voice was hoarse with disuse and swallowed tears which had not yet fallen for the man who was dead.

"Aye, lass, 'tis me. Did tha' not expect me?"

"Expect you?"

"Dost tha' not remember what we talked about a few weeks back, before . . . well, a few weeks back?"

"Talked about?" She was dazed, disorientated, still trying to get back into that snug hiding place she had whipped herself into when they had told her Tim was dead. She could remember the pain of her gashed cheek and the thudding blows to her head which she knew she herself had inflicted. There were tiny memories, small, like pieces of a jigsaw puzzle. The dog, Tizzy, huddling close on her knee. Her sister-in-law's face, cold and hating as though she knew that Molly had killed her brother, which of course she had. Arms about her and Aunty Flo's face wet against her own. Joss crying, but not being much concerned, an open hole in the ground and a cold biting wind and on the very edges of her mind's eye, *his* face. The face she loved beyond all others but which, because of what they had done, she would never see again.

Now here was Betty, babbling nonsense, saying his name and she could not bear it. She wanted to creep back to where she had come from but it was as though Betty, perhaps not so "soft", that's the word they used in her world, as Mammy and the rest, knew her thoughts and quick as a flash she reached for the parcels beside her. Tizzy had been nosing them but Betty pushed her away.

"Gerroff, tha' little . . . tinker," she said, diluting her language for the sake of Molly's son. "Now then, look at this, Molly. Mr Greenwood—"

"Stop . . . stop. I can't . . ."

"Yer what? What yer talkin' about, Molly O'Dowd?" Betty fell back on her heels, her face agape with amazement. "'Ere, were tha' not serious when tha' talked me inter – what were't words? – goin' inter business wi' thi'? Were it just idle chatter, because if it were then I'm ashamed o' thi'. Me an' me mam, an' me dad an' all, seein' as 'ow there might be summat 'e can do, couldn't stop talkin' about it that night an' when we 'eard about . . . about Mr Broadbent . . . well, Dad ses, 'Looks as if it's all off then,' but I wouldn't 'ave it. Never, I said, not Molly O'Dowd. When she ses summat she means it. When she mekks a promise she keeps it. Me an' Molly shook 'ands on it, I told 'im, an' that's good enough fer me. Now then, me lass, are tha' tellin' me tha's goin' back on tha' promise, are tha', because if that's so then tha' can go to 'ell in a 'andcart, Molly O'Dowd."

"Betty, I can't . . . not now."

"Why? 'As tha' lost use o' tha' 'ands?"

"It's not that. I just . . ."

"'Appen there's brass involved then? 'As 'e left thi' well off, Molly, is that it? Tha' don't need me any more . . ."

"No . . . no, Betty . . . please, there's no money, that I know of . . ."

Molly hung her head and the tears which were flooding her heart and her face, her throat and every corner of her body, tears which were for Joel, for herself, but mainly for the sweet and loving man they had killed, began to surface.

Molly's mammy would have stood up and reached for her but Betty was having none of it. Molly could weep when she had gone, and she hoped she would, for it might take away that awful look of utter despair from her. Molly was in the grip of deep, racking grief for which there were no words of comfort, no physical thing which could ease it. Her expression, now no longer blank as it had been when Betty came in, was haunted with a pain which threatened to overwhelm her. Something must be done and if Betty was to have her way, which she fully intended, there was only one way to go about it. Brusquely, briefly and with none of the morbid sympathy which folk assumed at a time like this.

"Come on, Moll, wait till tha' see what I've got in these parcels. I've bin all over wi' Mr Greenwood since 'e knew where it was ter be found, 'im bein' in the trade, so ter speak."

"What?"

"Samples o' yarn, that's what. Now you an' me's ter decide what we want. What quality an' what price we're willin' ter pay an' then we've ter order it in whatever quantity we think we'll need. Bloody 'ell, our kid, what d'yer think? We're talkin' 'undreds o' yards 'ere, 'appen even thousands."

"Betty . . ."

"Oh, fer Christ's sake, Molly O'Dowd, if tha' say Betty once more I'll bloody clock yer one."

"My children are not used to swearing, Betty Spooner."

Betty's face split into a huge grin and she leaned forward to shine it into Molly's.

"That's the spirit, Moll. Now then, we'll 'ave us a look at this yarn an' then, are thi' ready fer this?"

"What?" The faintest whisper of a smile touched Molly's lips.

"There's a van outside wi' two knittin' machines on it an' two 'efty lads wantin' ter be told where ter put 'em."

30

Molly and Betty went together to the polling station a year later in May 1929 to cast their votes in the first election that put men and women on an equal footing for the first time in history. The voting age for women in Britain had been lowered from thirty to twenty-one in the same month that Betty and Molly had gone into business and it seemed to them a sign, an auspicious omen that women could do just as well as men, given the chance, in the field of enterprise.

They were elated when Labour got in, since that was the party they had voted for and again it appeared to them, with their frail and infant cottage industry just struggling to its feet, that it was an indication that it was to continue to progress. They were working women. Labour was the party of the working class. They liked the look of Ramsay MacDonald. After all it was his second time as Prime Minister so he should know how to go about things in a way which would be advantageous to the working man. A nice steady-looking chap in his sixties, with horn-rimmed spectacles and white hair, and Molly and Betty, quite intoxicated with their newly won power as enfranchised women, thought they'd put their trust in him.

They had made a good beginning. The tack room at the back of Meddins had been cleared of its tangle of harnesses and reins and the accumulated clutter sixty or so years of caring for horses had created. Thank God the Broadbents had put in electricity when the house was done, Betty said to Molly, or the cost would have been beyond them. The place had been whitewashed half a dozen times by Bert Spooner, who was only too glad to have something to do, he said, and anything else the two girls wanted they'd only to ask. He was proud of his Betty who, though God alone knew where it came from, was showing a clear-sighted grasp of business matters, which was just as well since Molly was still a bit hesitant. Mind, you couldn't blame the lass, could you, what with her losing her husband like that and with two little lads to fetch up.

The machines had been set up, a pair of Watts' Patent Griswold Domestic Circular Knitting Machines and hardly used by the look of them, and where Mr Greenwood had found them and at such a low price was a mystery, Betty enthused to Molly, but she for one wasn't going to look a gift horse in the mouth. Queer-looking things which were nothing like the ring frame spinning machines she and Molly were used to, but easy to work, the woman who was going to show them how said. It had a multi-feeder circular latch needle, she informed them cheerfully, and there was nowt to it, at which Betty pulled a face at Molly as though to say it looked and sounded bloody complicated to her.

It was Betty who provided the force, the enthusiasm, the sheer bloody determination in those first weeks, going boldly into the mill where the yarn for the stockinette was manufactured, choosing the quality and quantity they required as though she had been at it all her life. She spent days retracing the steps Molly had already taken before Tim's death, calling on hardware shops and department stores, displaying samples, once they had got the hang of how the machines worked and could run up a few, discussing prices and costing, delivery dates and discounts, promising all manner of things if only Mr Jones, or Smith or Brown would give them a chance to show what they could do by placing an order. Betty gave away scores of free samples to be tried out in this or that store, confident they would sell like hot cakes. Mr Smith or Jones or Brown had only to compare the quality with what he was already selling. No, she had no wish to belittle it, they did the job they were intended for, but the ones she and Mrs Broadbent were offering were far superior.

It might have been the Broadbent name and the strange mystery surrounding Mr Broadbent's death. It might have been Mrs Broadbent's tragedy which they all knew about. It might have been the bold and confident flamboyance of Miss Spooner who was so enthusiastic about her own product, or it might have been the product itself which was well made, a reasonable price and was delivered when it was said it would be. Whatever it was, by the end of 1928 business was so good Betty had decided it was time to purchase another machine and put Cissie Thompson to work on it, and Molly Broadbent, who still went at least once a week to clean some rooms at Meddins, watched with a thankful heart the account at the bank from which the mortgage was repaid growing until the incomings were in excess of the outgoings.

Meddins was safe for the time being.

The man and woman faced one another across the desk in the luxurious office and from her expression it seemed that what they were discussing was not to the woman's liking. It was not the first time Betty Spooner had been here in the last twelve or so months, nor would it be the last, but six months should see it over and done with, thank God. She wasn't dismissing it, mind, for Mr Greenwood had, quite literally, put Molly's and Betty's business on its feet and she was grateful to him, but lately, and she didn't know why it had taken her so long to arrive at the conclusion, she had begun to think there might be more to the secret help, support and sound business advice he had given them than had at first been apparent. The last question, the one about Molly's sons, had seemed to her to have nothing to do with Mr Greenwood's and Betty's business dealings, though of course he and Mr Broadbent had been related so she supposed he was entitled to ask after Mr Broadbent's lads. It was also the way he asked, with a peculiar strain in his voice, a tension in his large frame, an air of almost holding his breath after he spoke and a hooded watchfulness in his dark eyes which made her uneasy.

He had knocked on her door in Sidney Street the day after Mr Broadbent's funeral. She knew who he was, naturally, since he owned the biggest mill in Oldham, but to find him, just after eight o'clock of an evening, on her doorstep, had given her an awful shock and frightened her poor mam half to death. Men of Mr Greenwood's position did not knock at the door of a terraced house in a working-class area of the town. If they wanted to see anyone they simply summoned whoever it was to their office, making them stand to attention while whatever it was he wished to say was said.

She had stared at him in amazement. The light from the street lamp fell on his face and she had been genuinely shocked at what was in it. Not that she knew him well enough to judge but there was an expression of such . . . well, she didn't know how to describe it, only to say that he looked as though he had lost someone so dear and precious to him he could not bear it. Drawn, it was, bleak, deeply grooved like that of an old, old man and him no more than thirty-four. Etched with something which made her want to put out a hand and draw him into her own comforting kitchen. Surely the death of his cousin, even in such dreadful circumstances, would not affect a grown man to such an appalling extent? It didn't seem natural somehow, but who was she to give an opinion since she had known neither of them and certainly the ways of the gentry were a mystery to her.

"Miss Spooner?" he asked, polite as polite.

"Yes." She looked over his shoulder but there was no sign of the motor car gentlemen like him drove about in. Mind, it was his vehicle that poor Molly's husband had smashed to smithereens in Broadside Quarry the other night so perhaps that was why he had walked it.

"Might I have a word with you?"

"Wharrabout?"

"It is rather . . . private. If you could spare me half an hour I would be grateful."

"Well, me mam's . . ."

"It won't take long, Miss Spooner, I promise you." His voice was cool, distant but still polite.

He wanted to help Mrs Broadbent, he said, sitting on the edge of the very chair in which Molly had perched a few weeks ago, while her mam, overcome with the uniqueness of his visit, crouched back in her chair as though he were about to threaten her very life. Mrs Broadbent had said, when last they met, a hideous spasm suddenly rippling across his face, his voice faltering, then, as he got control of himself, becoming stronger, that she wished to go into business for herself and Miss Spooner's name had been mentioned. Did Miss Spooner know what he was talking about?

He looked even worse in the slightly yellow light of the gas mantle, his face like a death mask in which his brown eyes were sunken and blank-looking.

"Oh, aye, me an' Molly were . . ." Suddenly suspicious Betty stopped speaking while her mam's eyes flickered uneasily from one face to another. "But what's it ter do wi' thi', Mr Greenwood?" she asked tartly.

"She is . . . not herself at the moment, Miss Spooner, and I merely wish to smooth the path a little for her. I have found two decent knitting machines and a woman who is willing to train you and—"

"What are tha' tellin' me for? Why can't tha' speak ter Molly about it? Not that I'm not grateful, like, but wi' you an' Molly bein' . . . well, related, why don't tha' . . .?"

"We had a . . . falling out, Mrs Broadbent and I. Oh, nothing to be alarmed at, but I think it best to keep out of her way. She has enough to contend with at the moment," and again his face jerked before he clamped it rigidly back into a manageable expression. "Besides, she will not feel like troubling herself with all the necessary arrangements which will be needed to set up a new business. That is why I came to you. If you could take on some of the bothersome details, when Mrs Broadbent is ready for it, the venture will have been assembled and ready to take off. She will need something, Miss Spooner, to help her to get over . . . to take her mind off . . . off her terrible loss. Now I have made some enquiries about the yarn needed for the manufacture of the stockinette and if you have the time I would be glad if you would accompany me to the mill where it might be obtained. I mention it not to seem high-handed, Miss Spooner, but if you were to be seen with me by these businessmen, at least the first time we visit them, it will stand you in good stead."

It made sense and Betty said so, her excitement beginning to show in the smooth, flushed skin of her face. She was not a pretty girl, in fact she was really quite plain, but there was a sparkle to her, a strength of character in the set of her jaw, a glint of humour in her pale hazel eyes and a tendency for laughter in the curl of her plump, pink mouth which was her best feature. She had a good figure, of medium height, well rounded, which she liked to show off in the short, tight-fitting clothes she wore.

"But wharram I ter say ter Molly?"

"Tell her the truth about the machines and the yarn for the stockinette and where they came from but that's all."

"What d'yer mean, that's all?"

"Miss Spooner, where were you to get the money for these machines?"

"Well, Molly . . ."

"Mrs Broadbent has none."

"But she must've known they'd ter be paid for when she come ter me about it. Where . . .?"

Neither Betty Spooner nor Joel Greenwood knew of the small box of jewellery Molly had in the safety deposit box at the bank.

"And then there is the yarn, the setting up of the machines, lighting, heating, wages, delivery costs . . ."

"Bloody 'ell!"

"So you see it will take a great deal more than determination and hard work to get your business going. I am prepared to provide you with the necessary funds which you will say came from the bank when Mrs Broadbent asks. In other words you will lie. A document will be drawn up showing the amount of your debt and how you are to repay it."

"Oh, God, I know nowt—"

"No, but I do, Miss Spooner, and I am prepared to back you, to guide you, on the condition that Mrs Broadbent does not know where that backing and guidance came from. Is that clear?"

"Why can't we just go to't bank ourselves?"

"Because they do not lend money without security."

"What's that?" Betty moaned.

"Something . . . like property, say, that the bank can claim if the debt is not repaid."

"She's got that 'ouse. Meddins."

"Miss Spooner, Mrs Broadbent would sell her soul to the devil before she'd let that house go. If you don't know that by now you don't know her very well."

"Aye," Betty said sadly. "She does set great store by it."

"And besides, there is another reason why Meddins can't be used as security. A reason I'm afraid I'm not at liberty to divulge."

It had worked, though sometimes Betty wondered at Molly's total acceptance of the "backing" the bank was prepared to advance them, of Betty's insistence that every month she go alone to the "bank" where their account was held to discuss finances with Mr Barton and to repay part of the loan which was decreasing nicely thanks to their success. She never failed to be amazed at Molly's complete trust in Betty's grasp and control of the financial side of their small business and even when shown the books which Mr Greenwood had advised her on how to set up and keep, books which, apart from repayments to the "bank", were completely valid, she showed little interest in those first months of trading.

What Betty completely failed to recognise was that though Molly walked and talked, worked and played with her children, went about her new life with seeming composure, she was still in a state of deep shock which kept her normally receptive brain in an almost drugged state. Betty was aware that Molly was far from being the bright, ambitious girl she had been before Tim Broadbent's death. She was just – *just* – hanging on to the lifeline Betty provided. That and her sons' need of her kept her above the waterline of her grief. She worked beside Betty and Cissie on the knitting frame in the tack room, Liam and Joss in the care of Elspeth, driving herself to a point of exhaustion which she confessed to Betty helped her to sleep but it seemed in those first months her mind was not capable of tackling yardage and profit, invoices and delivery dates and repayments of loans.

That was fourteen months ago. This afternoon, to Betty's complete satisfaction, she had arrived at exactly halfway in repayment of the loan Joel Greenwood had made them. It had not been a large loan, Betty realised that now, after fourteen months in business and the knowledge and experience that had come with it, though at the time it had seemed enormous to her, but they could not have done it without the man who sat opposite her.

She studied the dark, sombre face of Joel Greenwood, telling herself that she had never in all her life seen a more forbidding or humourless set of features. They were totally without expression, as though inside the man there was nothing to put life or even a flicker of vitality on to his countenance. No feelings of any sort, not anger, compassion, hope, pleasure, excitement, boredom or interest in anything beyond what was spread out on his desk and what went on in his mill. No emotion showed in the deep, dark brown eyes, nor did he smile except in polite greeting or equally polite farewell and yet he was a handsome man. A lot leaner than when she had first met him, she suddenly realised, his face somewhat gaunt but which in no way detracted from his dark good looks.

"And Mrs Broadbent's sons?" he was saying. "They are

progressing well, I hope. In good health I mean. Let me see, they'll be – what? – Liam three in September and . . . and Joss . . . fifteen months . . . walking, I suppose."

His voice broke on Joss's name and it was then that the truth was revealed to Betty Spooner. It was as simple as that. A quite ordinary, courteous question which anyone might ask but as he looked at her, his face doing its best to hold its casual expression of polite interest, the expression any acquaintance of Mrs Broadbent's might reveal, Betty knew what was driving this man and her friend Molly Broadbent to the far edge of sanity, and with the knowledge she wondered why it had taken her so long to arrive at it.

And he knew she knew.

They continued to stare at one another, frozen together in the shared, appalled certainty that they were welded suddenly in a secret that Betty, at least, was horrified to be privy to. All these months, fourteen of them, once every four weeks, she had sat opposite him, handed him his cheque, shown him the monthly figures, the profits, the expenditure, listened to his advice about this or that, advice which had always proved beneficial and she had not taken any particular notice of the strange feeling that she had seen his likeness in someone else. They said everyone had a double and she supposed, if she had thought of it at all, which she hadn't, at least not consciously, that she had met someone with the same darkly scowling, arrogant good looks of Mr Greenwood. And she had, in his son. Joss Broadbent.

She cleared her throat. Her usual ebullient confidence had totally deserted her and it seemed he had nothing further to say on the matter, or if he had, was unable to say it. She became aware that behind his mask of inscrutable, unfeeling coldness was an explosion waiting to explode, a volcano waiting to erupt and by all that was holy, she didn't want to be here when it did. He was suffering – Blessed Mother why hadn't she seen it before – suffering the torture of the damned, in purgatory, a strong, powerful man who had been brought down by his simple need to speak his son's name.

Jesus God . . . Molly, she had the same, exactly the same look about her . . . no wonder . . .

Betty stood up abruptly and so did Mr Greenwood. "I must go, Mr Greenwood," she said harshly. "I promised Mr Connelly at Williamsons I'd see 'im this afternoon. 'E's promised ter tekk on another . . . an' you'll never believe this, Buckley an' Prockters . . . aye . . . an' we're thinkin' of gettin' a little van . . ."

She was babbling, she knew she was, devastated by the expression of raw suffering on the face of the man opposite, a face which, up to ten minutes ago had shown nothing but cool pride, a kind of impassive unconcern in anything that was not to do with business. His eyes were hot, glowing coals that begged her, though he hated himself for doing so, to give him a word, no more, on the son he had not seen since before Tim Broadbent was killed.

Betty sat down again heavily and bowed her head. That was it, then. The mystery, long forgotten now by most, of why Tim Broadbent had been thundering about in the dark of night high up on the moors in Joel Greenwood's motor car.

"'E's thy son." Her voice was harsh, unforgiving.

"Yes . . . Joss . . ."

"I know which bloody one, for God's sake. 'E's tha' spit an' if anyone saw thi' together they'd know."

"They never will, Miss Spooner."

There was a long, anguished silence.

"She said nowt," Betty blurted out.

"She wouldn't. When . . . when Tim found out . . ." He passed a trembling hand across his face, leaning his forehead in it for a moment before continuing. "When Tim found out he . . . damnation, Miss Spooner, this is bloody hard."

"I'm sure it is, Mr Greenwood. I don't know 'ow tha' sleep at night, tha' pair o' yer." Betty, like Molly, had begun to refine slightly her broad Lancashire accent but now, in her distress, she fell back into it.

"I don't sleep, Miss Spooner. I believe . . . we killed him, you see, Molly and me." He paused, his lips caressing her name in a way which made Betty want to weep. "Molly and me . . . we did kill him, so you see, we can never be anything to one another again. It was . . . Jesus, why am I telling you this?"

"Nay, I don't know. I don't want to 'ear it, I can tell thi'."

"It was not a light thing, Betty." He called her by her Christian name for the first time and somehow it seemed to melt the hard shell of horror which had formed about her heart and it went out to this suffering man.

"I'm often shocked, lass, for I'm a self-contained man, by

the power that the loss of one person in my life is able to exercise over me. We . . . loved one another, you see . . . for my part I still do, naturally."

"'E'd 've found out eventually."

"Pardon?"

"Mr Broadbent'd 've found out eventually."

"I don't understand."

"Joss."

"Yes?" He leaned forward eagerly, his face for the first time showing warmth, a love that encompassed not only the child's mother, but the child.

"'E's like thee. The image. Dark, wi' brown eyes but it's not just that. It's in't shape of 'is face, the set of 'is chin. I dunno. Anyone seein' tha' together would 'ave ter be blind . . ."

"Would you . . . tell me about him, Betty?" he pleaded. "And about . . . her? How is she? Does she still grieve? Of course she does . . . I know she loved Tim. Who didn't?" he finished simply.

The office staff were flabbergasted when their employer, who had several important customers waiting to see him, put his head round his office door and shouted for tea, telling them he was not to be disturbed until he said so.

They talked for over an hour. He wanted to support not only his son but Tim's son as well, he confided to Betty, staring blindly out of the window at the row of windows on the other side of the yard, his tea going cold in his cup. It was another reason why he had been so keen to help in the budding business, but he knew that Molly – again murmuring her name with a caress which made Betty feel as though she were spying on some private moment between lovers – would never agree. Did Betty have a young man, he asked her politely, but Betty could see that her broken engagement to the tram driver, caused by her determination to be a woman of business and his to prevent her, did not really interest him. He only wanted to hear about Joss . . . Joss . . . Joss and Joss's mother and had Betty not got to her feet indicating she had a business to run, even if he didn't, would have meandered on for ever. Talk about besotted and talk about the irony of the likes of the godlike Joel Greenwood opening up his heart to Betty Spooner who had once been a ring frame spinner in his cousin's mill!

She would have liked to tell her mam about it but she

couldn't. Betty enjoyed nothing better than a good gossip, a wringing out of every juicy tit-bit of rumour and scandal, but this was different. She was astonished that Mr Greenwood had confided in her in the first place, but something in him, and in her, she supposed, had given him the instinct to trust her, plus his own driven need to talk about his son and his son's mother. Now, here she was with this great burden of sadness and grief to carry about with her and no one to share it with. They wouldn't understand. She wasn't sure she did. She only knew that the confidence she had been made privy to this day was one she must keep to herself for the rest of her life.

The dinner party at Birch Hall was an enormous success, Mrs Holden told herself, preening somewhat, not least because of the marked attention Joel Greenwood had paid to her daughter Sybil. Everyone had noticed it and Totty Roper, who had three daughters of her own still to be married, had drawn Ruth Holden to one side, ready to congratulate her, for Joel was the catch of the county.

Joel had been a visitor at Birch Hall for years, of course, to dinner parties and tennis parties and picnics and it was only last year that he had taken a great deal of interest in a litter of Sybil's labrador puppies, even picking one out for the little Broadbent boys. Strange that. Tim had been over the very same day, cadging, as he so endearingly put it, a ride on Ginger, Sybil's roan, but Ginger had had an injured fetlock and so Tim had stayed no more than fifteen minutes. When Sybil told him about the puppy he'd leaped on that bicycle of his and headed off home, poor old Tim, with his face alight with eagerness to share his sons' pleasure in Joel's gift. And the next day he'd been dead. Sybil had been devastated but Joel's attentions seemed to take her mind off it. Sybil was twenty-nine and, though a handsome, good-natured woman who longed for marriage and children and would make a splendid wife, had been overlooked in the devastation of the loss of the thousands upon thousands of young men of breeding in the war.

Now would you look at her, glowing like some lovely, mature rose under Joel's smiling regard.

"Any word from dear Muriel?" Totty asked Ruth Holden as they both watched Sybil flower in the sun of Joel's smile.

"She's staying with Tessa for a while longer, she writes, but if you ask me she'll never come back to Meddins. At least while that woman insists they live in the gatehouse."

"Poor Muriel. How dreadfully life has treated her. It must tear her to pieces knowing Tim's children are being brought up by a working-class woman in what can only be called a working-class environment. One presumes they are even speaking in the awful broad accents of her family. And do you know she's put some sort of machinery in the stable block and is knitting . . . oh, Lord knows what, but it's said she and some woman from her past are seen all over town selling whatever it is to shopkeepers. Ada Murchison told me she and the woman had been as far as Sam Murchison's Bolton store. You know Sam's in hardware and he has a chain – is that what they call it? – yes, well, one can only suppose she is selling her . . . wares to him in vast quantities. It was a sad, sad day when Tim took up with her."

"I absolutely agree. Has anyone been to see her?" meaning of their sort, naturally.

"Oh, no, though I believe Helen Herbert – you know what a soft heart she has – did say we ought."

"I wonder what will become of it all. I suppose the elder boy . . . what was he called? Some outlandish name Muriel loathed . . . Irish, I think."

"Was it Liam?"

"That's it, Liam, I ask you, for a grandson of Muriel Broadbent's. I suppose you've not heard any . . . well, gossip about her. Men, I mean."

"No, have you?"

"No." Both Totty and Ruth seemed quite crestfallen that they could find no blemish to smear on the good name of the lovely young woman who had so astonishingly flashed across their orbit and, though they would not admit it, made such a success of it. Well, she'd fizzled out now and returned to that way of life which was natural to her. A mill girl who, though she had not exactly gone back to the mill, had brought it instead into the rare and lovely atmosphere which Muriel Broadbent and well-bred women before her had created within the walls of Meddins. The loveliest house in Lancashire, it was said of it, and now there was machinery clanking where there had been only the stamp and wicker of thoroughbred horses. Men, of what sort no one could imagine, were blundering up and down the wide driveway in their horrid little vans, where once only splendid motor cars such as Muriel's Silver Ghost Rolls-Royce had whispered, and before that the elegant brougham in which she and her predecessors had ventured out.

Poor Tim, poor Will and Charlie and even old Joshua. They would all turn in their graves if they knew.

31

It was in September, eighteen months after her husband's death, that Mary Angelina Broadbent knew she was beginning to recover. To be, if only to a small degree, the woman she had been before Tim died. She heard herself laughing as once she had done as she ran after her two sons down the slope of lawn in front of Meddins, racing to catch Joss who was, it seemed, determined to join the ducks which scattered at his approach. The water was a kaleidoscope of shining colours ranging from dark, rippled pewter beneath the trees, to silver where the sun stroked it, to copper and gold where the reflection of the house flickered and her heart swelled with pleasure.

She admitted it was Betty and the work they did together that had accomplished it. She gave thanks every hour that her days were full. She did not thank Our Lady or Her Blessed Son to whom she had prayed ever since she was a child, for somehow it seemed to her that she could not address herself to the Queen of Heaven. It was not that she no longer believed but that she was not worthy to do so after what had happened to Tim. She blamed herself and Joel for what had happened and every night as she lay, wide-eyed with grief, in the bed she had once shared with her husband, she went over and over that day in her mind, watching again and again the pictures that formed on the inside of her closed eyelids. For months she had suffered it, glad that she suffered it since it was only right that she should. She must be punished for what she had done, try to make atonement as her religion had taught her and only in the scourging of her soul, her spirit, her mind, her heart, even her body which still craved Joel Greenwood's, could she eventually find peace.

She genuinely mourned Tim. She missed the enduring

warmth of his love and his complete and unswerving belief that she was the most perfect woman on earth. His belief had transferred a confidence to her which had allowed her to overcome much of the contemptuous scorn she had suffered at the hands of his mother's friends since she had become his wife. He had not been a strong man, as Joel was strong, but the sweetness in him had far outweighed the weakness he had brought back from the war. She had not realised how much she had leaned on him, thinking in her ignorance that it was he who had leaned on her. She had not realised how much she had depended on his infectious good humour, his unconditional love, to put her world to rights again when his mother had sneered at her efforts to be worthy as his wife.

His face was still as clear in her memory as though he had just left the room, or held his photograph in her hand. His face as it had been on the day he had cycled over to Birch Hall, smiling, a little penitent since he knew he really should not "slope off" to beg a ride on Sybil Holden's roan when there was work to be done in the garden. But he so missed Hal and Prince and Major, and Sybil was such a good sort, a lovely, kind-hearted woman who wouldn't mind at all and his darling Molly understood, didn't she? Laughing, boyish, kissing her neck until she laughed too and told him to be off and leave her in peace.

And the other face. The one which had stared, blank and uncomprehending at first, then dying as she turned towards him. Eyes unfocused and yet flaring in unbelieving horror at what they saw in the elegant carriage which his mother would not allow him to get rid of. The carriage had gone now, dragged out into the empty paddock by a bewildered Jud and a couple of labourers to whom she had given a few bob.

"Nay, Mrs Broadbent, tha' can't mean it," Jud had protested as, white-faced, eyes glittering like blue ice in it, her hair, she was well aware, in a tangle of wild curls about her head since she often forgot to brush it, she had ordered him to set fire to it. They didn't know why, naturally, the astonished men, only Joel in all the world would know why and he was gone, lost for ever to her as Tim was, for how could two people, no matter the depth of the love they shared, live in peace with the ghost of the man they had killed living with them? That hour, that rapturous, blind, insane hour in the coachhouse had killed two men really, at least for her, since Joel Greenwood was as dead to her as Tim. She had killed them both with her wickedness and she must live with it and suffer it until the end of her days when, she presumed, she would go straight to hell.

Well and good. It was what she deserved but in the meantime, and Betty had made her see it, she must provide her sons with a mother, a parent, since she was the only one they had. And she must find some way to live her life, at least until they were men and old enough to fend for themselves, a way that would give her, through them, a reason to continue. It was like a mist spreading before her, her future life, with no knowing what was in it, or how she was to get through it but she must not multiply the sin she had committed by letting it threaten her boys.

She grew thinner and all her lovely clothes hung on her like sheets on a line so she discarded them, wearing her riding breeches tightly belted and, strangely, Tim's shirts and jumpers. When she first put them on she had surprised herself but she felt such a wealth of comfort wrap about her, as though she were in Tim's arms, she took to wearing them all the time, though Rosie, Maggie and Flo agreed among themselves it was not healthy. But Molly could smell Tim in their folds, the male fragrance he had left behind of lemon soap and cigarettes and she clung to it, not wanting to let him ago, keeping him and his presence with her during her empty days and nights. Apart from bathing, washing and brushing her growing crop of wild curls she took no interest in her appearance until Betty brought her up short, her expression grimly disapproving.

"Yer not comin' out with me like that, Molly O'Dowd," she pronounced, dipping her head in the direction of the breeches, the polo-neck jumper and the old tweed jacket Molly had on.

It was the first time Molly had felt able to accompany Betty on one of her "selling" calls and to meet people outside her own family and the few friends, Robert and Millicent, Loll, and Sarah Lucas who called on her faithfully. It was September, six months since Tim's death and she had not once gone beyond the gates of Meddins, even to see Mammy, Aunty Flo or Aunty Maggie, begging that they come to see her, which of course they could now whenever they wanted to.

Molly eyed the blatantly coloured skirt and jacket Betty had on as though to say what gave Betty the right to criticise her? The outfit was a vivid scarlet with black velvet frogging and put her in mind of the uniform worn by the ringmaster of a circus Tim had once taken her to. Betty did not so much wear it as trumpet it to the world, tossing her head to which a scarlet, feather-infested cloche hat clung. She was so completely sure of herself and that the outfit suited her, Molly envied her.

"Why not?" she said. "I'm perfectly clean and respectable."

"Aye, fer muckin' out stable, 'appen, or on't back of a horse, but not ter go calling on Mr Emery of Buckley and Prockters. We're ladies of business now, my lass, and we're dressing like one."

"Betty, believe me, there is not a woman in the world who looks less like business than you and I."

Betty took umbrage. "Is that so? Well, let me tell you, madam, looking like I do 'as got us orders from some o't biggest hardware shops in Owd'am. Now, we're off to Buckley an' Prockters today, an' termorrow it's on't train ter Manchester an' if tha' thinks I'm tekkin' someone who looks as if she just fell off an 'orse, then tha' can think again." Her voice and expression softened. "Molly, love, tha' want this thing ter be a success, don't tha'?"

"Yes, of course."

"Well then, yer can't go inter 'ardware . . . hardware shops lookin' as if yer off ter join the bloody hunt or whatever it is the gentry do dressed like that. This is business, lass, an' we must look businesslike. Go an' put summat on. Oh, I dunno, yer must have dozens of outfits in them wardrobes o' thine up at the big house. Tha' spent enough money when . . ."

She stopped abruptly and her face crumpled as Molly's seemed to dissolve, white and strained about the bones of it.

"I'm sorry, chuck. I didn't mean ter remind yer but we're . . . we've medd such a good start an' really, it's time fer yer ter get out a bit. Meet these blokes I meet. Let 'em see what yer medd of, what a team we mekk, thi' an' me. There's summat about thi', always 'as bin, that fellers like, tha' knows, an' we might as well use it if we're ter expand."

So Molly had put on one of her elegant outfits, a perfectly plain suit in a pale blue and grey check, a long-waisted jacket with a low belt and a pleated skirt to her knee. She tied a pale blue silk scarf in the neck, pulled a simple helmet hat of the same colour down over her hair, which needed cutting, grey suede shoes and handbag to match, a smear of poppy red lipstick and she and Betty had run for the tram at the end of Huddersfield Road.

For the first time since March she had felt a little frisson of anticipation run through her as they walked briskly along Mumps Road, turning into the bustle of Buckley and Prockters. Mr Emery, as head of the hardware department where the mistress of a house like Meddins would never venture, had not met her personally but he knew that Mrs Broadbent had once been an important customer, and she might be again! She and her family had fallen on hard times, indeed terrible times and she was now, apparently, forced to earn her own living, but she still looked every inch a lady.

"You see," Betty had exulted, squeezing her arm as they swung out of Buckley and Prockters and back into the busy street. "I told thi', didn't I? You 'ad 'im eatin' outer yer 'and. Sixty dozen an' in only half an hour, thanks ter thee."

"Me? I didn't do anything."

"That's it, tha' don't need to. They just tekk one look at thi' an' can't 'elp themselves, like Tim did an' . . . Oh, Jesus, Mary an' Joseph, there I go again . . . me an' me big gob. I'm sorry, love. Gawd, tha've gone as white as a sheet."

Betty was mortified. She knew she was pushing Molly as best she could, further and further away from the terrible happenings of last March and closer and closer to what Betty wanted for her, and for herself too, but was she going too fast? Was she expecting too much of the frail shell Molly was building round herself? Was it strong enough to withstand the knockabout ups and downs of their small business and what they must do to make it successful? She was fine at her machine in the stable but was she ready to go out into the world of business which Betty had already learned was very competitive?

Strangely, it was one of Molly's "posh" friends who had encouraged her. Old Doctor Taylor had finally retired and, knowing no other, Molly had asked Robert Chard to be her family physician. It was he, catching Betty one late summer day on her way from the workroom, as they were beginning to call it, to the gatehouse, who had congratulated her on her support and the restorative balm of their work together which was doing Molly so much good.

"Keep it up, Miss Spooner," he told her. "It's a better cure for Molly's condition, which is, of course, a desperate mourning for Tim, than I could myself prescribe."

"It's all right, Betty . . . really," Molly said now.

"All right, chuck. I'll try an' be more careful. Let's go an' get us a cup o' tea. How about Monico's?"

"No, not Monico's. I . . . Tim and I . . ."

"Rightio, shall we try Prince's?"

"Yes, that'd be grand."

After that, slowly, little by little, Molly had begun to go about with Betty, even on what Betty called "cold" calling, laughing when Molly questioned her on how she learned all these terms.

"Eeh, I'm gettin' a real old hand now, Molly O'Dowd," she twinkled. "Me an' t'other salesmen in't business speak a different language to't rest o' yer an' yer'd best learn it if tha's ter go out."

"I shan't need it if I'm with you."

"Who ses yer'll be wi' me? I reckon between us, if we 'ad us a motor car apiece, could cover the whole o' Lancashire."

"Oh, Betty, a motor car . . ."

"An' why not? Yer've got ter speculate ter accumulate . . ." then stopped when she realised that she was repeating something Joel Greenwood had said to her.

"Who told you that, Betty Spooner?" Molly smiled.

"Oh, someone I met in't trade."

And so it had gone, through the autumn of 1928 when the trees had shed the last of their leaves and the October sun had cast bright rays on the gold and copper and bronze of the multicoloured carpet which spread about the grounds of Meddins. Jud did his best on his own, building great bonfires from which the woodsmoke rose into the clear air and the poignant aroma, proclaiming the end of the summer, drifted into the stable where Betty, Molly and Cissie worked on their machines. Cissie was very polite with Molly now, grateful for the job she had been given, only too glad to "look after things" when her employers, Betty Spooner and Molly O'Dowd, for goodness sake, were out on business. She was happy to answer the telephone which had been installed, once she had mastered the bally thing, and was overwhelmed by the bonus she got at Christmas.

Molly got through Christmas by the simple expedient of

filling her little house and the days she was not working with her family and her good friends, Robert and Millicent, Loll and her husband and Sarah, with whom Mammy and Aunty Flo and Aunty Maggie were by now completely at ease. For some reason she did not want to go to Mammy's though she was asked. It was as though this was a milestone . . . no, a hurdle she must get over, climbing painfully from one side to the other in the still desolate wasteland of her life. As though this festivity which last year she and Tim had shared must be got through as best she could. It was a penance, she supposed. It would have been so easy to pack up her children and get the tram over to Mammy's and bury herself beneath Mammy's loving kindness, Aunty Flo's sharp but not ill-disposed comments and Aunty Maggie's sympathetic affection. To let it all flow round her with no effort on her part in a state of half-stunned awareness.

She made a good Christmas for them all, for her children, for Mammy and Eileen, Gracie and Archie who was, in Aunty Flo's stringent opinion, a holy terror now, God love 'im. For Clare who, at twelve, was quite the young lady and for Kathleen who had never married.

She took Clare over to see Meddins, just the two of them, for somehow she knew Clare would consider it as special as she did. They went on a tour, drifting from room to room, lifting off dustsheets here and there for Clare to exclaim over the treasures hidden there and she was aware that in her little sister she had a small understanding of what the house meant to her and why, which she sometimes thought the others could never comprehend.

Aunty Maggie and Uncle Alf looked in, perfectly at home in Molly's small cosy house. They all spread from parlour – drawing room had been dropped – to kitchen quite naturally. They wore paper hats and pulled crackers and ate the magnificent turkey which Betty had given her, telling Molly it was a gift from a satisfied customer, she wouldn't say who. It was a success and Molly realised that part of the reason for it was because they saw her now as she had been before she married Tim. She was their Molly. Molly O'Dowd. She had been playing a part as Mrs Tim Broadbent. Now she was herself again. Quieter, certainly, and without that temper she once had, but Rosie and Seamus O'Dowd's daughter again.

Afterwards she felt a small ripple of pride move through

her. It was nine months now – she counted them assiduously as though each was a marker towards the tranquillity she craved – she told herself, determined not to spare herself but she was clawing her way through her guilt and grief and desolation and some day, perhaps in the new year to come, she might find what she searched for. What a mess she was, she often thought, struggling to get on, to survive, to win through this despair, and yet at the same time clinging to it, using it to flagellate herself in true Catholic fashion. Had she felt able to go to church, to confess to Father O'Toole the immensity of her sins and been absolved would she have been different? she wondered but she would never know because she was not fit to enter the place where the blameless Holy Mother reigned.

Spring came and the anniversary of the day Tim had died was got through. She spent it alone, leaving her children with Elspeth, taking a bus to Delph and from there going north, walking for miles and wearying miles up beyond Delph to Ox Hey Top, past Crawshaw Hey and the fine stand of woodland there which was beginning to mist with spring growth and explode into a dazzling spread of wild daffodils. She followed the path round to Blea Green and Millstone Edge, then down again, stopping for a glass of cider at the public house in the hamlet of Grange. She was totally unaware of the stares of the farmers and labourers who were about to take their first pint of the evening, her mind drugged with memories of Tim and his sweetness, her body exhausted but no longer painful with guilt.

She had thought of another man, too, up on the tops and her tears had run silently down her face and on to her husband's tweed jacket and for a long time she had stumbled, blinded and tortured with memories of both men about her.

She went nowhere near Badger's Edge where a man with deep brown eyes sat with his back to a rock. He was a thin-faced man with deep grooves etched from his nostrils to the corners of his mouth. His hair was dark, needing a barber's attention and in it were threads of grey.

In September, on the day her elder son was three years old, Molly O'Dowd went with Betty Spooner to the second-hand car dealers on Shaw Road and they purchased a motor car each. The cars were old, 1922, the first of the Austin Sevens, similar in shape to her own beloved Swallow which Tim had bought her, but not half as expensive. Tim had paid one hundred and ninety pounds for the Swallow but she and Betty got the two for less than one hundred pounds. Only Betty knew that Joel Greenwood had found them, had had them checked and serviced and guaranteed fit for the road and arranged with the dealer a decent price for their sale.

"Right, kid," Betty chirped, showing a great deal of leg to the appreciative dealer as she climbed inside hers, which was, like Molly's, a dull but glossy grey. "Show me what ter do an' I'll foller you 'ome."

Molly began to laugh and Betty realised that it was the first time she had seen her do so quite without reserve since Tim Broadbent died, a real natural "belly" laugh as her dad called it, one which lit up her face and eyes as though the sun shone inside her.

"What?" she asked truculently. "What yer laughin' at?"

"You, you great daft lump. You can't just get in, switch on and drive away."

"Why not? You did."

"I had lessons. Tim taught me." Again it was a first. The first time his name had been spoken easily, without the shadow of grief which always accompanied it.

"Right then! You teach me."

"What, right here on the main road?" Molly turned her smile on the dealer who was nearly knocked for six by the brilliance of it. When she'd come in he'd thought she was a "looker" but a bit on the quiet side for his taste, but with that smile she was like a Christmas tree on which the candles had just been lit and his wide, gawping mouth and the admiration in his eyes told her so.

"Aw, come on, Molly, be a sport. Gerrin an' show me. We can come back tomorrer fer thine. Or 'appen this nice chap'll drive it 'ome fer thi'. What d'yer say?"

Betty winked and the "nice chap" sprang to attention and said just let him get his mechanic and then he was all theirs.

"Eeh, d'yer hear that, Molly," Betty giggled, "'e's all ours," nudging Molly as they climbed into Betty's vehicle, willing to do anything to keep that look of shining laughter on Molly's face.

"Aye, I heard, but you keep your eyes on that road, not him and do exactly, *exactly* what I tell you, d'you understand? Now, switch on the engine."

"Bloody 'ell, Molly, tha's worse than Sister Ursula at school. Right, I'm switched on. What next?"

It was a month later when the tiny wisp of cloud appeared on Betty Spooner's and Molly O'Dowd's business world and it was uncertain whether either of them even noticed, or, if they did, they could not imagine what it was to do with them. They had taken on two more girls, both fresh from school and, being in awe of Cissie, willing to do exactly what she told them to do as she taught them the skills of the stocking frame. Cissie, Betty and Molly were all the same age, which was twenty-three, and from the viewpoint of the fourteen-year-olds seemed positively ancient.

Both Molly and Betty, eighteen months now into their new business and becoming more confident with every passing, profit-filled week, spent most of their time looking for new customers, since they meant to expand and were already talking of converting a second stable into a workroom, buying more machines and taking on more girls. Bert, Betty's dad, was busy from morning till night, and happy with it, helping with anything he was asked to do and was capable of, which was most things since he was a handy chap with a machine. They'd bought an old Ford van for thirty pounds, one that had seen more service than him, he said cheerfully and Betty had taught him to drive it. He was made up, taking to it like a duck to water, rattling round Oldham and Delph, Mossley and Royton, Lees and Chadderton, delivering dishcloths to "his" customers, and back in Sidney Street Bea Spooner thanked her God every night for bringing Molly O'Dowd to their door and into their kitchen which was warm and cosy again now and where tea was in constant supply.

It was the end of October and Betty was going into town but she wouldn't be long, she shouted to Molly as she climbed into her motor car, switched on the engine and revved it up with that particular verve which was part of her nature. She was confident, intrepid, afraid of nothing and nobody and she drove the same way, expecting every other vehicle on the road to get out of her way, which they usually did.

But at the same time there was an almost imperceptible change in the way she dressed and spoke. It was as though eighteen months of being in Molly's company, of noticing what Molly wore, however unconsciously, had given her a brush of refinement. She was still the same cheeky Betty who liked nothing better than a laugh and what she called a "good time" with one of the numerous gentlemen who asked her out, but Molly's influence had given her a touch of polish, which Molly had picked up in the years she had been Tim's wife. It suited her.

"Where are you going?" Molly appeared at the workroom door, still wearing the overall they all put on to work at a machine. She had a ledger in her hand and on her face was an expression Betty had not seen for a long time. In fact she really couldn't have said what it was except that it was keen and yet at the same time uncertain.

"Oh, only to't bank. It's that time o' the month, yer know."

"Won't you want this then?" Molly enquired, holding out the ledger. "It's the record of our repayments and Mr Atkinson will want to make a note of it."

"Aye, yer right. Ta, love."

"Nice chap, Mr Atkinson, don't you think so, Betty? In fact I wouldn't mind coming with you. He was good to me and Tim when the mill closed."

"Oh, aye." Betty, for reasons best known to herself, began to look uneasy. "Look, Molly, I'm in a tearin' hurry so I'd best be off. Next time, 'appen?"

"Yes, you're right. Well, here's the ledger. Give my best to Mr Atkinson."

"Thanks, Moll, I will that."

When Betty glanced in her rearview mirror as she drove out of the stable yard Molly was still standing in the doorway, her hand shading her eyes as she watched the Austin speed through the gate.

Mr Greenwood, polite as ever, got to his feet as Betty entered his office.

"Good morning, Miss Spooner. On time as usual, I see."

From that day when he had talked of Joss Broadbent and his mother, Joel Greenwood had never mentioned either of them again, nor had he called Betty by her Christian name. It was as though the dam which had burst its bank over six months ago had been rigorously plugged, allowing not even a trickle of the turbulence which remained inside to find an escape. They did not drink tea or do more than remark on the weather as Betty gave him his cash and he noted it, in her records and in his, but today his caller seemed anxious, fidgety and he could not help but notice it.

"Is there something wrong, Miss Spooner?" he asked courteously.

From beyond the closed door came the clackety clack of a typewriter and a voice asked what time it was. The window was half open. A male voice in the mill yard was singing "It ain't gonner rain no more, no more" and Betty, her skin beginning to prickle with some dread she did not understand, wanted to whisper, "I'm not so sure about that!"

"Well . . ." She licked her lips.

"If it is something to do with . . . your partner, or . . . well, I'd be obliged if you'd tell me."

"Well, I dunno. It's . . ." She took a deep breath as though to steady herself. "What's the name of the bank manager? The one what I'm supposed to 'ave borrowed brass off? I did know but I've forgot."

"Mr Barton."

"Not Atkinson?"

"No, why?"

"Oh, Jesus!" Her manner was so appalled Joel stood up, her repayment still in his hand, his face, which in the last few months had begun to look better, losing its colour.

"What? What is it?"

"She's suspicious, Mr Greenwood."

"Who?"

"Oh, fer mercy, sake, 'Oo else but Molly?"

"How, in what way?"

"She ran after me wi't ledger which, as tha' knows, is all straight up an' above board, an' which, by the way, she's takin' an interest in now, an' asked me ter give 'er regards ter Mr Atkinson."

"Perhaps there is a Mr Atkinson there. A clerk she knows or . . ."

"She said 'e were't manager."

There was a long and tension-filled silence into which the deep tick of the clock and the cheerful crackle of the fire in the grate fell. They stared at one another, Joel Greenwood and Betty Spooner who had guarded Molly Broadbent's fragile state for eighteen long months, and had one of Joel's clerks entered the room he would have been hard put to understand what they were up to.

Betty studied the apparently calm, impassive face of the man opposite. When he had stood up she could not help but notice and admire his tall, athletic figure, the width of his shoulders, the length of his legs in which the thigh muscles stood out. He was dressed in a dark grey jacket and waistcoat with striped trousers, every inch the businessman but Betty sensed that beneath the gentlemanly attire he put on each morning for the world to see, there was a man none would have recognised. A vibrant, full-blooded pirate of a man who would not have looked out of place with earrings and a cutlass. A man who took what he wanted when he saw it and to hell with the consequences. Was that how he had got Molly into his bed, and if so, glory be to God, could you wonder at it?

"Has she ever questioned you before?"

"Never, all I 'ope is that this will all be done with when she gets round to it."

"That can be arranged. We'll settle it now."

"Gerroff, I 'aven't the cash ter spare. I'll tekk a few more months of tradin', steady tradin' like we're doin' now before there'll be enough cash ter pay thi' off."

"That, with the way things are at the moment, might be tricky."

"What does that mean?"

"Haven't you seen the newspapers today?"

"No. What . . .?"

"There's been a financial crash in the United States which is going to affect us, I'm afraid." He passed a hand through his hair, then shoved it into his trouser pocket, something Betty had seen him do when he was disturbed.

"I don't know what you're talkin' about."

"Miss Spooner, we rely in this country, and indeed the rest of the world, on American loans and American prosperity and if American money ceases to flow then . . ."

Joel shrugged and, pulling his hand from his pocket, raised both emphatically, the expression on his face, scowling and dark, directed at her, she felt, as though it were all Betty Spooner's fault.

"What?" She was completely mystified.

"If they cease to buy British goods, Miss Spooner, they will cease to need the service of British ships. Markets will disappear, unemployment will rise . . ."

"But how will that effect me an' Molly?" Betty's heart was

beginning to thump with painful irregularity and she could physically feel the blood drain from her face. The machines, their little motor cars, her dad's van, the girls, all the cash outlay she and Molly had considered well spent flashed like meteors across the limit of her panic-stricken brain and she wanted to beg Mr Greenwood to reassure her that she and Molly would be all right. Bugger America and the rest. If she and Molly could manage she didn't give a damn about them. Surely this man would know. He was a shrewd businessman who, when other mills had gone under, had kept his going. They said he had – what was the word? – diversified, designing cloth as well as spinning it. He had moved onwards, keeping his finger on the pulse of the cotton trade at all times, and, particularly in view of his relationship with Molly, would be bound to direct them, guide them and their fledgeling business in the right way to go until this crisis, whatever it was, was over.

"I don't honestly know, Miss Spooner," he mused. "Perhaps it won't. But there is trouble ahead. Men who are unemployed will have to tighten their belts since there will be little money about. They will buy only the bare necessities since that is all they will be able to afford, so you see . . ."

"They won't be needin' new dishcloths then?"

"I may be wrong. I sincerely hope so. My own business will be affected."

"Aye . . ." Betty sighed, then stood up jerkily. "I'd best get back if tha'll just see to't ledger."

"Perhaps in view of what I've just told you we might consider the repayment paid up."

"Thanks, but would the bank do that?"

"Well, no."

"Then if tha' don't want Molly to find out you've bin 'elpin' us, tha'd best tekk it."

"Miss Spooner, if . . . if she needs anything, anything at all, or the boys, will you promise to let me know? If your business suffers then . . . then I must find some other way to help her, you understand?"

"Aye, I do, Mr Greenwood."

Betty felt the compassion flood through her as Joel Greenwood allowed her to see, for a moment or two, that his love for Molly Broadbent had in no way diminished with the passage of time. It was really quite amazing, she thought, how this man's face altered when Molly was mentioned. The ferocious, almost angry scowl which normally dipped his eyebrows and tightened his mouth vanished and though it sounded daft when describing such a strong, forbidding face, his features softened, warmed, relaxed and his eyes filled with some light which she had seen in no man's eyes before.

"Promise me, Betty?" he said softly.

"I will, I promise."

"Thank you."

He would have said more, she thought, but there was a knock at the door and without waiting for an answer a tall, handsome woman of about thirty entered the room. She was elegantly and simply dressed in a costume of mole grey gaberdine. Around her shoulders was slung a cape of rich, pale grey fur. She looked and smelled expensive, and very, very sure of herself.

"Joel, I'm sorry. I thought as it was nearly one . . ."

"Sybil, it's quite all right. Miss Spooner was just leaving."

He seemed to hesitate and Betty wondered at the sudden haggard look of pain about his eyes and mouth then, as though making a decision, he held out his hand to the woman who moved to his side.

"Miss Spooner is a business acquaintance of mine, Sybil."

"Really." Sybil smiled coolly as he turned back to Betty.

"This is my fiancée, Miss Sybil Holden, Miss Spooner. Now, if that is all I'll bid you good-day."

32

Molly knew there was something wrong with Betty though Betty denied it every time she questioned her. In fact, she became quite aggressive, almost snapping her head off when Molly begged her to tell her what it was.

"It's nowt, nowt, I tell yer. There's this . . . this Wall Street crash thing everyone keeps goin' on about."

"What?" Molly was ready to smile in genuine amusement. "When did you take any interest in such things?"

"I'm not the bloody 'alf-wit tha' tekk me for, Molly O'Dowd. I 'ave got eyes in me 'ead. I can read an' . . . well, wherever I go they're talkin' about British exports goin' down an' . . ."

"But we don't export our goods, Betty, so how can we be affected?"

"Oh, I dunno." Betty gave the appearance of an animal which has been cornered and Molly's concern deepened. Perhaps she was right. Perhaps this American thing would affect trade, their trade, though she didn't know how. Since they had started in business their output had doubled and then doubled again and they were going further afield each week in their search for fresh markets. Their three girls were working every hour God sent and they could barely keep up with the demand but when she had suggested taking on another girl and either buying another machine or starting some sort of shift work on the three they had, Betty had looked quite haunted. She seemed to have lost her complete and considerable trust in her own judgment and worth, begging caution, saying they'd best wait and see.

"But why, for God's sake?" Molly asked her. Christmas was over. It was nearly a new year now, 1930 and getting on for two years since Tim died and she had gradually come to realise that she was almost whole again. That the wounds his death and the manner of his death had inflicted on her were practically healed. The scabs had gone, now that she no longer picked at them, now that she allowed herself to be restored and though there were still raw and tender spots where those wounds had been, she was recovered. She had fought the battle and it was won. She had wrestled with her mind and taught it to behave, allowing no memory to take her back to the picture of another man who had died, at least for her, on the same day as Tim and should, for an indefinable moment out of her control, her mind open the door she had closed against him on that March day, she slammed it shut again with such force it often frightened her. He no longer existed. She heard nothing from him, or of him and her heart was calm. Dead, it sometimes whispered, but she ignored it and if, in the night, she woke crying broken-heartedly she had only to throw on a coat, take the keys from the back door of the kitchen, walk across the dark lawns and let herself into the house and she was comforted again. Meddins was peace. Meddins was order. Meddins was gentleness and strength which provided her with a carapace of shelter inside which to hide her broken heart.

She was still grieving badly for Tim and knew that he would always lie in a special place in her heart but she had forgiven herself for what she had done to him. Meddins was Tim and Meddins was forgiveness.

"Because," Betty answered irritably, "well, I were told if British goods aren't sold abroad an' British ships weren't . . . oh bloody 'ell, I forget 'is exact words but 'e said unemployment would rise and . . ."

"Who did?"

Molly and Betty had just seen their three employees go tramping off into the gathering gloom of the December afternoon. It was only half past three but already the sky was bruised and darkened, the dull greyness of it heavy and hanging low over the stable roof and there were a few drifting, spiralling flakes of snow in the air. Above the tack room a square of solitary light could be seen streaming from a window, the shaft of it picking out the growing tumble of the snowflakes and Molly knew Jud would be heaping coal on the fire, pottering round his small domain in preparation for the tea he would cook and eat, and the pleasurable, peaceful evening he and his marmalade cat, called Marmy by her two boys, would share.

"Who did, Betty? Who told you these things? No one's said anything to me about exports and unemployment and I've been in the Cotton Exchange in Manchester today."

Betty's head shot up and her mouth opened with a plop.

"Yer what?"

"You heard. As I was in Manchester seeing the buyer in Kendalls I thought I'd just go in and . . . well, see what happens there. The Exchange I mean. Our stockinette is made from cotton and if there's any way we can buy it cheaper then we ought to check it out. I know there is the carding and roving, but there are a hundred women in Oldham, with the proper machines, who could do it for us right here on our premises. There were traders there who . . . I spoke to one or two, and was introduced to a man who ships raw cotton."

"Molly O'Dowd, tha' cheeky little devil." Betty's gasp of admiration was explosive and genuine. "An' what did 'e say?"

"About what?"

"About gettin' cheaper cotton since that's what we'd be after."

Molly looked smug. "He said he'd call on us, or send his agent, in the new year. He was sure we could do business depending on the quantity we'd require."

"An' nowt about . . . about depression in trade or owt like that?"

"Not a word."

Betty spun on her heel and did a little dance on the stone-flagged floor. The room was still warm though they had allowed the coal fire almost to go out. The fireplace was directly below the one in the room Jud occupied, which had been a boon in the winter months since it meant the small staff had the means to keep warm. It glowed cosily and Molly moved towards it, standing with her back to it, her hands clasped behind her. The machines had been unplugged and cleaned in readiness for the next day's work and she watched as Betty moved about the workroom from bench to bench doing the end-of-the-day check either she or Molly carried out. They had been mill girls, both of them, and were well used to machinery. When they had worked at Broadbents this is what they had done at the end of each day and it was a habit neither of them could break.

"So what about this chap who's been telling you that the bottom's about to fall out of the market? Where did he get his information from?" Molly's voice was casual but, though Betty did not notice it, she was watching her carefully.

"I dunno. Read it in't papers, 'e said."

"Was it one of our customers?"

Betty lifted a neat pile of dishcloths which were ready to be packed and moved them to the bench where her father would mark them for delivery.

"No . . . no."

"Then who was it, Betty? It must have been someone of importance to make such an impression on you."

Molly didn't know why she was plaguing poor Betty like this. Betty was being strange, secretive, had been for weeks now and it had begun to bother her though she could not have said why. If Betty wanted to keep something to herself that was her business, but not if it had anything to do with *their* business, a voice inside her head argued. If it involved some aspect of what she and Betty were doing together then Molly had a right to know. If this man, whoever he was, was a man of substance, of credibility, a man who knew what he was talking about then perhaps they should be listening to him, though what they could do about it she was not quite sure.

"Perhaps it was the bank manager?" she said, her voice silky and Betty at once remembered that day in October when Molly had run after her with the ledger. She had talked about Mr Atkinson, said he'd been kind to her and she'd like to meet him again but there was no Mr Atkinson who was a bank manager and now they both knew it. For some reason she had set Betty a trap and Betty had fallen into it but strangely nothing had been said or done about it since. Betty had seen Joel Greenwood twice since then on her monthly visits to him, each time expecting Molly to ask to come with her as she had hinted but it had not happened.

"What's going on, Betty?" Molly asked calmly though, she supposed, even then, she knew who "the man" was. Not to admit to herself, of course, the clear-headed, businesslike Molly who had dragged herself back from the boundaries of madness by the skin of her teeth, but the woman who had sighed and stretched languorously in the arms of the man who was not her husband.

"I don't know what yer on about an' if that's it, I'm off 'ome before this snow sticks. I don't want ter get stuck out 'ere fer't night. I've a hot date wi' the buyer from—"

"Stop it . . . stop it. I'm not interested in your hot dates with anyone. I want to know the name of this man who is so free with his gloomy omens about trade and how it will affect you and me. So free he's scared you half to death. Now, if it's not the bank manager, who, by the way, is called Barton and who, since you meet him every month, a meeting from which you are desperately keen to bar me, you should know, and it's not a customer, then who is it?"

"Look, Molly O'Dowd, I don't know what's up wi' you but I'm purrin' up wi' no more o' tha' nonsense. I bin goin' every month ter pay off this loan from't bank, seein' to't cash, payin' interest, fetching wages and all t'other 'undred an' one things what 'ave ter be dealt with an' which you didn't want ter be . . . ter be bothered with after what 'appened. Oh, chuck, yer weren't well, admit it. Yer weren't fit fer owt but workin' machines an' I were glad ter do it until yer were right again. Thi' an' me go back a long way, Molly. We bin pals, real pals since we were kids an' . . . an' yer mean a lot ter me. Eeh, yer'll 'ave me blubbin' in a minute, but Molly if tha' don't trust me . . ."

"No . . . oh, no, Betty." Molly's voice was passionate in her denial. "There's no one more honest than you and I'm more than grateful for what you've done to . . . to protect me."

"Listen, lovey." Betty was beginning to breathe more easily. She could see that Molly, though she was not quite sure what had happened over the loan from the bank, was prepared to give Betty the benefit of the doubt. As she said, they had been friends for so long there could not possibly be anything underhand in Betty's dealings. If it hadn't been for the bloody "Atkinson" thing there would have been no need for this but it seemed everything was all right again.

"Yes?" Molly questioned, ready to smile and forget it, whatever it was, ready to forget the strange man who was forecasting doom and disaster to small businesses such as hers.

"Why don't tha' come wi' me next month an' 'ave a chat wi' . . ." Betty paused and on her face was an expression of such dismay Molly was ready to smile.

"Who?"

"Mr . . . Mr Atkinson . . . er, no . . . Barton."

It was one of those rare moments which affect the mind when the simplest name, perhaps of something which is totally familiar, slips away on the tongue and the speaker is left foolishly searching for it. For the life of her Betty couldn't remember whether the correct name was Atkinson or Barton and she felt her heart lurch in her chest.

"Betty, you really are the limit. Can't you remember?"

"Oh, dear sweet Mary, I can't keep this up, I can't. It's not fair of 'im to ask." Betty began to weep helplessly, hanging her head so that the tears fell straight from her eyes and on to the neatly cut and stitched dishcloths, marking them with big, wet rings. She simply stood there, sobbing as though her heart were broken, or if not yet, shortly would be. She lifted the dishcloths and buried her face in them and on the other side of the room Molly felt herself slip sideways against the narrow mantelpiece above the fireplace. She had time to be thankful, in one of those strange moments which come in the midst of crisis, that the fire was almost out or she would certainly have set fire to her calf-length overall.

Betty continued to sob helplessly, her hair hanging down on either side of her face. She wore clogs, as they all did in the workroom since they were the best footwear to keep the cold from striking the sole of the foot. She also had on a plain overall and a scarf tied round her head to prevent her hair from being caught in the machinery. She was a far cry from the imperious and confident Miss Spooner who dragged orders out of men who were known to be hard and unmanageable.

Molly watched her, frozen in that strange paralysis which was curiously similar to the one she had fallen into when Tim had found her with . . .

Oh, no . . . Blessed Mother, don't do this to me just when I'm beginning to pick up the pieces of my life and glue them back into some semblance of normality. Some shape that is pleasing to me, something I can live with, take pleasure from and pride in. Not . . . not . . . *him* . . . please, don't let his name be mentioned, Holy Mary, not ever again. I cannot bear it, not now, but it was too late.

"'E medd me promise, yer see," Betty wailed, shaken to the core of her nature which had always inclined towards the stoic. As a child she'd let no one see her cry, even the big lads who teased little girls like her. They could beat her to pulp, her defiant expression had told them, her and Molly O'Dowd who was also a bit dangerous when it came to being bullied, which was why Betty had liked her . . . loved her, but they'd not cry. No, not Betty Spooner and Molly O'Dowd.

"'E come ter Sidney Street to our 'ouse. Me an' me mam were . . . yer'd told 'im yer wanted a knittin' frame an' . . . e'd found a couple, 'e said an' . . . Oh, God, Moll, I swear I didn't want ter deceive yer but . . . yer needed it, lass, an' so did I an' we both knew, 'im an' me, yer wouldn't 'ave it from 'im."

"I'd sooner have starved and let my children starve than accept help from that man."

Betty's head reared up. Her face was blotched and wet with tears and her nose was running. She looked quite dreadful but no more dreadful than the expression of horror on her face.

"May the Holy Mother forgive thee, Molly O'Dowd, for that's a bloody awful thing ter say. 'E wasn't totally ter blame, yer know, fer what 'appened ter Tim."

"That's true, but I still loathe and detest the very air he breathes and want nothing to do with him or any help he thinks to give me. Tell him that he shall have every penny back that he has lent us since I presume it was him and not the bank."

"Now you listen 'ere, madam. Most o' debt's repaid anyroad an' if yer think I'm throwin' away a bloody good business just because tha's too 'igh an' mighty ter—"

"It's all yours, Betty." Molly's voice grated like fingernails on glass. "You can take it and good riddance to it, and to you."

Betty gasped and backed away, suddenly afraid of the menacing woman who stood by the fireplace. Molly's face, even her mouth, was white, as white as the walls Bert had so assiduously painted. Her eyebrows stood out like dark slashes in it and her eyes burned with the cold fire of her hatred and yet in her expression was a thread of what looked strangely like fear to Betty. What should Molly O'Dowd fear, she wondered, and when it came to her she could only marvel at her own failure to recognise it.

She was afraid of Joel Greenwood and their love for one

another which still burned them both as painfully as red-hot metal on flesh.

"Molly, don't torture thisenn, love," Betty said at last, her voice soft, putting out a conciliatory hand. "'E . . . 'e meant no 'arm, ter thi' or Joss."

Molly leaped back as though she had been stung, again nearly falling into the dying embers of the fire. She put out a hand to the mantelpiece to save herself and knocked the bone of her wrist with such a crack Betty was convinced she heard it break but Molly did not even appear to notice it.

"Dear sweet heaven," she whispered, "you two did get matey, didn't you? He told you Joss was his son, did he? Did he? Well, he's wrong." Her voice was high and bitter. "Joss is Tim's son, as Liam is."

"Oh, come off it, Moll." Betty shook a weary head. "Anyone wi' 'alf an eye can see't likeness an' if you was ter put 'em together the whole o' bloody Oldham'd realise."

"Don't you dare say that. Joss is Tim's boy and that man should be horsewhipped for his lies."

"'E's not lyin', Moll. 'E doesn't even mention 'im now. It were just that once, right at start when . . . God, 'e were in such a bloody state, as you are now. 'E was frettin' fer thi' an't lad. 'E wanted ter know 'ow tha' both were. If tha' could've seen 'im, lass. It broke me 'eart ter watch a strong man like 'im beggin' fer a word, just a bloody word, no more, about 'is boy."

"Don't, Betty," Molly moaned. "I can't bear it. I've nothing for him, don't you see?"

"You mun forgive one another, Molly. Can yer not do that?"

"Oh, yes, but it's ourselves neither of us can forgive. We can never truly forgive ourselves for what we did, that's the horror of it."

Molly's eyes were blind and tortured and she reeled with what looked like such pain Betty took a step towards her. "We did love one another . . . once, but it's dead now, as Tim is dead."

Betty sighed. "Well lass, yours might be but 'is isn't."

"It makes no difference. We can never be anything to one another again."

"Yer probably right, Molly O'Dowd, so tha' might as well know, 'e's engaged ter be married."

Betty leaped across the room but was only just in time to catch Molly as she fell, almost senseless with weeping, into her compassionate arms.

She became quiet as the afternoon wore on. Betty had rekindled the small fire and outside the snow, which had started with a little flurry as Cissie and Pauline and Jenny left, settled itself into a full-blown blizzard, slanting as the wind drove it against the door of the workroom, a solid, moving, dangerous curtain which neither woman noticed. They sat before the fire while Molly talked and talked, much as Joel Greenwood had done, whispering over his name, caressing it as he had done hers, dredging up from within herself all that she had tamped down, battened down for the past two years.

Betty listened patiently. She made tea on the small stove and they drank it, telling one another they must go soon. Betty's mam would be worried and her "hot date" as mad as hell. Elspeth would not be alarmed but would have given the boys their tea and put them to bed. Molly was sometimes late back and her nursemaid and housekeeper, which is what the placid young woman had now become, would simply put Molly's meal in the oven and settle down to listen to the wireless which was her constant pleasure.

Elspeth particularly enjoyed a programme called *Woman's Hour* which, if her charges were taking a nap, she managed to listen to in the afternoon. There were many tips on how to make a tasty meal out of next to nothing which, when Mrs Broadbent had first moved to the gatehouse and money was short, had been of prime importance. There would be an interesting talk by some well-known person and then a story read by someone with the most cultured voice. Elspeth loved it. But tonight it was a play, a murder mystery she was engrossed in. She was knitting a garment for Liam who was three and a bit. Joss, at twenty-two months, was the liveliest, merriest, most lovable child imaginable and though she adored both her charges, he was the apple of Elspeth's eye. His charm was such that he'd only to show the little pearls of his teeth in an infectious grin and everyone was his willing slave. His Aunty Flo called him a little tinker as she cuddled him on her knee and his grandmother, Rosie Watson, couldn't get over his likeness to his dead granddaddy who had been the handsomest, the most endearing man you could ever wish to meet, to hear her talk at any rate.

The boys had gone down as good as gold, Liam a bit fretful because his mummy was not yet in but Elspeth had tucked him in, kissed him and promised that the moment she came home Elspeth would send her up to see him. Though he'd been only eighteen months old when his father had suddenly gone out of his life, he had since then become vaguely alarmed if any member of his small world was gone for longer than he liked. He was quieter than Joss, shy with strangers, clinging to those he loved with a tenacity which was sometimes desperate and which often reminded Elspeth of his father. Albert had died in the autumn at the great age of nineteen and Liam had taken it hard. Albert had been Mr Broadbent's dog and then Liam's and though Liam joined in the games his brother and Tizzy loved, Tizzy was very definitely Joss's dog.

"Tell her to wake me, Elly," he begged her, his little face screwed up anxiously. "I won't settle till I know she's home," he added in that old-fashioned way he had.

"Well, I don't know about that, sweetheart."

"Please, Elly, promise you'll tell her to wake me."

"Yeah," said Joss, whose favourite word it was and the only one he spoke, among his infant babble, with a modicum of clarity.

"Well, snuggle down, pet, and you get into bed, Joss, and I promise I'll ask Mummy when she comes in."

"Yeah," said Joss, struggling up on to the narrow bed he slept in. He had only just come out of his cot and in the small room the two beds were so close there was scarcely space between them to stand. She hoisted him up and helped him to cuddle down beneath the covers, kissed them both again and left the room.

"Leave the door open, Elly," Liam begged.

"Yeah," Joss echoed and Elspeth smiled as she made for the steep and narrow staircase which led to the equally narrow hallway. She settled herself in front of the fire, took up her knitting and was soon absorbed in the play.

The young dog which dozed beside her chair opened one eye and cast it in her direction, then, when she deemed it to be the right moment, rose to her feet and padded quietly out of the room. The stairs were carpeted and her paws made no sound as she raced up them. She was not yet two years old and as supple and light as a feather. Nosing into the boys' room she sniffed at each sleeping face, giving them a lick with a loving tongue, then, light as air, jumped up on to Joss's bed and settled herself against him, sighing with deep content.

It was just gone seven thirty. Molly and Betty had their coats on, shivering since the fire had gone out, and were staring in awed disbelief at the solid bank of snow which had mysteriously appeared in the stable yard. They were just about to take their first tentative lurch into its clutching depths when they heard the scream.

"Dear God, what were that?" Betty gasped, staring out into the strange black and white nightmare of what seemed to be a landscape from hell. Was it some sort of wild animal, which, being a city girl, she knew nothing about, and which roamed about shrieking into the night?

"I don't know," but already, her maternal instincts pricking a warning which ran through the length of her body, Molly had begun to fight her way through the almost waist-high snow which barred her way. The blizzard still raged, great blinding whirlwinds of snow which resembled a tornado, a picture of which she had seen at school. But not just one. There were half a dozen lashing about the yard filled with icy pellets which bit at her and in no way resembled the soft feathery stuff of three hours ago.

"Molly," Betty shrieked, "wait fer me," then her voice was lost as the violent wind tore it away and Molly disappeared into the white, whirling curtain.

The scream came again, nearer this time, a high demented sound which brought goose-pimples to the back of Betty's neck and down her arms. It was a woman's voice, Betty recognised that now and it was calling someone's name over and over again.

"What's goin' on?" an anxious voice said in her ear and Betty felt her poor, overworked heart, which could really take no more shocks this day, stop for a minute before leaping on but it was only Jud.

"I dunno," she shouted above the moan of the wind. "Someone's shoutin' 'er 'ead off and Molly's ... Saints preserve us, where the 'ell's Molly?"

"Now then, don't tha' fret, lass." Jud, always calm in a crisis, spoke soothingly as though Betty were one of the restive animals which had once occupied the stable block at their back. "See, tekk 'old of me arm. If Mrs Broadbent's out there we'll find 'er. Now, 'old on ter me. We don't want ter

lose anyone else, do we? See, pick up tha' feet out o't snow,"
eyeing with some alarm Betty's smart court shoes which she
had put on to go home in. Already the pair of them resembled
a couple of shambling snowmen as they struggled away from
the warmth, the light, the safety of the stable block, edging
their way in the general direction of the yard gate which led
out to the drive round the house. Betty thanked God for Jud
who knew this place like the seams in his own face.

"Molly, where are tha'?" she screamed into the teeth of the
gale and was rewarded by Molly's voice which answered
from up ahead. She couldn't make out what she said but
somehow, with Jud as precise as one of those searching
dogs she'd heard about, they found the gate, following now
the ragged indentations Molly had made in her demented,
staggering progress towards the voice.

"Molly . . . Molly, where are tha'?"

"Here . . . come . . . quick."

Betty knew Molly was trying to tell them something of
crisis proportions. Even with the wind tearing every other
word out into the void she could hear it in her voice and
there was another voice, a woman shrieking and shrieking
in high terror but which, though it frightened the life out of
her and Jud, made her easier to find.

It took them, the half-frozen Elspeth who was still shouting
at them to be quick, Betty and Jud, almost fifteen minutes
to battle down the drive towards the gatehouse but Molly
Broadbent, throwing off the hands which tried to hang on
to her, was there five minutes before they were. The light
streamed out from the open door of the gatehouse, turning
the driving flakes of icy snow to a golden explosion which
dazzled them.

"Holy Mother . . . Holy Mother . . . Holy Mother," Betty
heard someone repeating again and again, wishing whoever
it was would give over before she realised it was her. They
blundered, the three of them, stiff with snow, so top heavy
with it they could barely stand, into the hallway which led
to the bottom of the stairs. Molly knelt there and beside her
lay her son, her elder son, a small crumpled figure in a white
sleeping suit, quiet and still and guarding him with a savagery
that was terrifying was the dog.

33

The party at Birch Hall was in full swing. It was a combined New Year's Eve and engagement party and everyone who was anyone was there. If you had not been invited to Sybil Holden's and Joel Greenwood's engagement "bash" then you might as well commit suicide, someone said jocularly, for it meant your social worth was positively zero. Herberts and Forresters, Knights and Ropers, Davidsons and Bowmans, and even the Murchisons, Sam and Ada, whose daughter Daphne had married a baronet.

Ruth Holden, who was a very wealthy widow and of good family, could scarcely contain her elation that not only had she got Sybil off her hands, which she'd long given up any hope of doing, but that she was to marry such a suitable gentleman. Everyone, meaning of her social standing, naturally, and some who were not quite up to it, must be invited to share her triumph. She had been forced, and had not cared for it very much but what could she do, she asked Totty Roper who understood her predicament since she herself was well bred, to invite some of dear Joel's rather radical friends, since they were his friends and he was Sybil's fiancé. They included Mr and Mrs Andrew Thomas, little Mrs Thomas going by the curious name of Loll which she begged everyone to call her, Ruth said, and could Totty imagine it? Totty sympathised. It seemed Mr Thomas was Joel's manager, a man of some importance and so, of course, when Joel asked for his name to be added to the guest list she could not refuse, nor could she say no to a Doctor and Mrs Robert Chard. Doctor Chard had a practice hereabouts, she was not entirely sure where, not a very smart one, she feared, and his wife was a teacher, but they were polite enough and if *Loll*, pulling a face at

Totty, could only be kept in the background by her rather shy husband, all would be well.

It was to be an informal affair. Sybil and Joel had asked that they might have a buffet supper, since it was New Year's Eve which was traditionally not a night for standing on ceremony, and that their guests might be allowed to mix freely sitting where they liked and with whom.

The supper had been set out on long, damask-covered, flower-bedecked tables round the perimeter of the dining room, enormous platters of whole salmon, ribs of lamb cut and ready to eat, tongue, deep veal and ham pies, dishes of lobster, also cut up, fowl and game. There were fruit and jellies and tarts, cheesecakes and chocolate gateaux and ice-cream of every possible flavour. Small tables, decorated tastefully and with immaculately laundered tablecloths to match the main table, had flowers and candle lamps set on each one and fancy gilt chairs where the guests might eat their . . . well, Ruth called it a "picnic" meal since she would have preferred a formal dinner party but it was what Sybil and Joel wanted, so, since it was their night she must give in to them, raising her eyebrows at Totty and sighing. Mind you, it did mean she could invite twice as many guests to witness her success, though she did not say this to Totty. Of course she was well aware that it was Joel who had wanted the buffet and Sybil, who was walking on air in her joy, could deny him nothing and the sooner the wedding took place the better, in Ruth's opinion, again keeping this thought to herself. Perhaps early spring, she told Totty, glancing with a fond but watchful eye to where Sybil circled the ballroom in the arms of her attractive fiancé.

Ruth sometimes felt just a tiny bit anxious whenever she saw Sybil and Joel together. Was there something lacking perhaps in Joel's attitude towards her daughter? He was always the perfect gentleman, naturally, and after all, he and Sybil were not youngsters, so anything of an ardent nature would perhaps not be appropriate but just a shade more warmth would not go amiss, she thought. Not that it mattered. He had bought Sybil the most glorious ring costing thousands, Ruth was sure, though Ruth had heard that his grandmother, Laurel Greenwood, had passed down to her son's wife and thence to Joel, some of the most spectacular jewellery ever to be seen. Emeralds, it was said, since Laurel was known to have green eyes, and an indulgent husband. It would have been rather nice, more personal, Ruth reflected, if dear Joel had given Sybil a family ring, but then, what difference would it have made? He had put a ring on Sybil's finger and that was all that mattered.

The Hall looked quite wonderful, especially against the background of the white storm which raged about it. Thank goodness most of the guests, those who were not staying the night, had managed to get here before it blew up into a blizzard and how they were to get home with motor cars buried up to the top of their bonnets was a laughing topic of conversation. But they'd think about that when the time came, they told one another. After all, it was New Year's Eve and good old Joel and Sybil's engagement party. They moved from room to room admiring the great bowls of flowers which stood on every available surface, even on the polished floor of the wide hallway and up the stairs. Lamps and candles burned since electric light was a little harsh on the older ladies, Ruth privately thought. Candles were very flattering to a woman, especially when she was beyond thirty, Ruth was well aware, and she wanted her girl to look beautiful tonight.

Sybil wore a straight sheath dress of silver lamé, very expensive and perfectly plain, the hem just touching her ankle bone where it was cut into the fashionable handkerchief points. The front of the bodice was high beneath her chin and the back a deep V which showed rather more of Sybil's white flesh than her mother liked, but after all she was dancing with her fiancé and times had changed since Ruth was a girl. Sybil had a splendid figure. A deep bosom and good hips, childbearing hips, and Ruth hoped most fervently that by this time next year she herself would be well on the way to being a grandmother.

It was all so lovely, the occasion, her daughter's joy, the gleaming splendour of the furniture, the deep-piled magnificence of the carpets in most of the rooms, the colour and scent of the flowers, the enormous log fires burning in every fireplace, the multi-hued drifts of the ladies' gowns and the immaculate black and white of the gentlemen's evening dress. There was laughter and the babble of cultured voices. Champagne in tall fluted glasses, smiles and shouted congratulations to the happy couple. Sybil was radiant. Perhaps just a shade more ebullient than Ruth cared for, but the dear girl had waited so long for this and could hardly be blamed for being excited. Joel Greenwood was the most sought-after bachelor in the county and Sybil was a very lucky girl. Ruth knew they were saying that, perhaps wondering why Joel had chosen her, which, to be honest, Ruth had herself. But Sybil would make a wonderful wife, hostess and mother since she had been trained for it and at Joel's age that was what he needed. Not some bright young thing, one of the "flappers" as they had been called, who would have been a disaster for a man of Joel Greenwood's social standing.

The band were taking a breather and in the corner of the ballroom Rupert Lucas was busy with the phonograph, unable to do without music for even five minutes, Ruth thought disapprovingly, while his silly young wife, who had once been Sarah Bowman, was cavorting about dancing the charleston on her own. She had always been a bit wild, Ruth thought, remembering the dreadful incident a few years ago at Meddins. How mortifying it must have been for poor Delia and Peter but at least she was married to the man. Thank goodness for the good sense and behaviour of her own dear Sybil who was at last to be rewarded for it.

Atkins the butler had just announced that supper was being served in the dining room when Ruth heard the upstairs telephone ring. She and Totty, who was her special friend, were standing up, ready to move out of the ballroom and on to the wide landing which led to the staircase and when Atkins came towards her she had no premonition of the horror that lay ahead.

"What is it, Atkins?" she enquired calmly. Perhaps Elizabeth Castle and her husband, who should have been here hours ago, were ringing to apologise but really, with the weather as it was, it was a wonder anyone had been able to get through.

"It's a call for a Doctor Chard, madam."

"Doctor Chard. Have we a Doctor Chard, Atkins?"

"I believe so, madam."

"Ah, yes, I remember now, he's a friend of Mr Greenwood's, Atkins. A tall gentleman with a beard. Yes, there he is at the foot of the stairs with Mr Greenwood and Miss Sybil. Is something wrong?"

"I couldn't say, madam. There is a . . . a . . . person on the line asking for him."

Ruth Holden knew that when Atkins called someone a "person" they were not likely to be a lady or a gentleman. It must be one of his patients, one of those from the working-class homes about Oldham which the doctor treated, she supposed.

"Very well, you had better tell him, Atkins. He can take the call on the telephone in the cloakroom."

She turned to smile at Totty as they prepared to follow Atkins's ponderous progress down the stairs.

She was there when it happened. It was like being in the front row of the stalls at the theatre as a drama takes place on the stage. The best seat in the house, she was to say hysterically later as she wept in Totty's arms in the privacy of her bedroom.

Sybil, as recently engaged girls did, was proudly showing Totty her ring as the doctor came out of the cloakroom. He was carrying his medical bag which he took everywhere with him. His cook/general, a competent woman of over fifty, had instructions to answer his telephone and, if it was an urgent call, and she was well able to judge since she had been with him for many years, she was either to ring him or give the telephone number where he might be found to the caller. Millicent often moaned about the number of second halves he had missed at the theatre and second courses at dinner parties but she did it laughingly, for she was as dedicated as he was himself to the service of his calling.

Already he was looking frantically about him for his coat, his face not only drawn with some medical worry, but uneasy, Ruth thought.

"What is it, my dear?" Ruth heard a woman she took to be his wife ask, helping him on with his coat. "I hope it isn't far since I fear you'll never get through the snow."

"The snow has stopped falling, I believe, madam," Atkins informed her politely, waiting to see if anything further might be needed of him.

"I'm terribly sorry to leave like this, Mrs Holden, Miss Holden," the doctor was saying, bowing in Sybil's direction. "I do apologise."

"Of course, I understand," Ruth said graciously, not at all troubled by his departure.

"Where is it, Robert?" Joel asked mildly, concerned for his friend on such a dreadful night, but turning away courteously to Sybil who clung to his arm like a limpet.

Robert hesitated and it was then that the strange feeling of something she could not bring herself to call dread came over Ruth.

"It's . . . it's one of the Broadbent boys." Robert was aware that the name of Broadbent, when connected to the woman who had married Tim Broadbent, was as bitter as aloe on the tongues of these county people who were behind Tim's poor mother to a man, or woman! He and Millicent, and Andrew and Loll, and, strangely, Sarah Lucas, were the only ones still to visit Molly of whom they were all fond, and of course, now that he was the family doctor he had been called out a time or two to one of the boys' childish ailments. But there was no warmth here, in the heartland of the society Molly Broadbent had threatened.

It was as though every member of the small group at the foot of the stairs had been turned to stone, frozen in the attitudes they had been in before Robert spoke. Even Millicent was somewhat embarrassed, though she quickly took his arm as though to support him in this.

"What?" she asked hesitantly. "Did . . ."

"I don't know who it was on the telephone," though he suspected it was that friend of Molly's who had gone into partnership with her. A nice girl, not the sort Mrs Holden would care to be associated with, of course, but on the several occasions Robert had met her he had liked her devotion to Molly and her straightfoward manner which called a spade a bloody spade.

"There's been an accident."

Joel, who had been leaning casually against the newel post at the foot of the stairs, his left hand in his trouser pocket, at the mention of the Broadbent name had frozen like the rest of them but for a different reason. Now he straightened slowly, withdrawing his hand, not only the one in his pocket but the one on the arm to which Sybil clung.

"Who?" was all he managed to say. They all turned to stare at him, bewildered, even Atkins, since his voice sounded so hollow it might have come from the bottom of a well, but Ruth Holden, who would have nothing spoil this night for her, and Sybil, of course, began to pull her daughter and future son-in-law towards the dining room. She had been entertaining for forty years and was an old hand at moving guests from one place to another, sometimes when they didn't

447

want to go, mixing and matching, pairing off or splitting up, but she might have tried to shift the Town Hall in Oldham as get Joel Greenwood on his way. His face had lost all its colour and his eyes glared for some reason best known to himself into Robert Chard's face as though he'd best answer and be quick about it or he might be sorry.

"Joel, dear, let's leave Doctor Chard to get to his patient," Ruth said smoothly, doing her best to link Joel and Sybil again. They all knew the set-up at Meddins, of course, with that coarse woman and her even coarser friend, it was said, and the business they had begun in the stable of that beautiful house. Dear God, it had been a sorry day for the Broadbents when Tim had taken up with one of his own mill girls and one could only feel deep sorrow for Muriel and Tessa. Since Tim and Muriel had gone not one of them had seen neither hair nor hide of Tim's widow, and didn't want to either, little upstart that she was. Joel and Tim had been cousins of sorts and as far as Sybil was aware even he had been nowhere near the place since Tim died. It was natural, she supposed, that he should be concerned about Tim's son, but really there was no need for this melodrama which seemed to be developing. Ruth would send a couple of the outside men to guide the doctor through the snow-choked lanes from here to the Broadbent place and it seemed only right to her that this working-man's doctor should attend a working-man's daughter.

"Dammit, Robert, who is it who is ill?" Joel snarled, his jaw so tightly clenched he was barely able to get the words out. His hands twitched and clenched and Millicent Chard tried to draw her husband away as though she were afraid Joel might hit him. In Joel's eyes there was a terrible blankness and yet in the very depths of them, like a torch under water, was a mad glow which seriously alarmed them all.

"It's all right, lad," Doctor Chard said, surprisingly, soothingly, as though he were privy to something none of the rest knew. "I'll just borrow one of Mrs Holden's men to guide me."

"Of course, Doctor," Ruth said, doing her best to remain gracious, nodding at Atkins to see to it at once, but she might as well have whistled out of the window for all the notice Joel took of her.

"If you don't answer my question, I'll break your bloody

neck, man." Fierce, knife-edged anger tore at Joel Greenwood's gaunt face and he was unsteady with something he
could barely contain and a visible menace to anyone who
stood in his path, that was obvious. Heads were beginning
to turn. Faces appeared in doorways, curious faces which
wondered what was going on and it was then that Ruth
Holden felt it all slip away from her.

Still she tried. "Joel, dear, why don't you take Sybil into the
dining room and perhaps Mrs . . . er . . . Mrs Chard could go
with you."

"Oh, do let's, darling," Sybil moaned, like her mother
beginning to be badly frightened. She really had no idea
what she was frightened of, only that Joel's face and Joel's
manner threatened something she held very precious which
she'd only just found. She loved him. This was her last
chance. She wanted desperately to be a wife and mother
but some dreadful thing had happened here, something she
didn't understand and she longed for it to go away and be
returned to the rapture of ten minutes ago.

She took hold of his arm, trying to draw him away from
the doctor who had caused all this, the doctor who was now
doing his best to get to the front door, but Joel flung her off
with such force she almost fell.

"What's happened?" he roared. "And who the bloody hell
is it? Robert, I swear if you don't answer . . ."

"Joel, be quiet, lad. All I know is the woman said there
had been an accident to one of the boys. It wasn't Molly on
the telephone so I . . ."

"Oh, Jesus . . . Jesus," Joel moaned. He threw back his head
and the strong brown column of his throat worked in ripples
of anguish and for one horrified moment Ruth Holden thought
he was about to weep, then, with a force which almost had the
doctor off his feet, he took his arm and began to hurry him
out into the hushed beauty of the snow-shrouded garden.

"Come on, man, I know the quickest way. No, we can't
wait for men, for Christ's sake. I know the bloody way, lad,
for haven't I lived in these parts all my life? Oh, damn this
sodding snow, damn it, damn it. Jesus Christ, I could be there
in five minutes in the car. She'll be afraid, out there on her
own. Come on, Robert, for God's sake hurry."

"You'll need a coat, Joel."

"Bugger a coat. I've no need of a coat."

"Joel, oh Joel, darling . . . please . . ." Sybil screamed after him, ready to follow, ready to do anything to keep him there just as though she knew it was the end of everything if he went. "Joel, there's no need for you to go, is there? Doctor Chard can . . ."

In the porch Joel turned on her, a cornered, maddened beast who could stand no more of his tormentors.

"Leave me alone, you silly bitch," he snarled, his face ugly and dangerous. "It could be my son . . . *my son!*"

Grabbing Robert Chard's arm he began to flounder with him across the garden, watched by the silent, appalled, open-mouthed guests who had come to celebrate his engagement to Sybil Holden.

It took them over two hours to cover what, in normal circumstances, could have been walked in fifteen minutes and but for Joel Greenwood's knowledge of the countryside and his inhuman strength it is doubtful Robert would have made it. The snow which had settled in graceful drifts against every hedge and wall clung to their trousers, weighing them down, dragging at them, dragging them down to their knees and they were forced to stop a dozen times to scrape it off. The moon gleamed fitfully through the last of the drifting clouds, a halo of silvery light which thankfully showed them their way. It was a white, silent world with no sound but their laboured breathing, empty of any human or animal stirrings. Even the wind had gone, leaving the icy stillness which froze every hedgerow within its grasp. Joel carried Robert's medical bag and almost carried Robert himself as they stumbled, at the end of their strength in the last few hundred yards, falling again and again now, until, there it was, the tiny lighted window of the gatehouse at the entrance to Meddins.

There was a strange gabbling woman in the open doorway, young, white-faced, who grabbed at Joel's arm since she didn't know which of the exhausted men was the doctor.

"It were my fault, my fault . . . it were my fault. I didn't notice the dog go . . . it were my fault."

"Where is he?" Joel knocked her aside with one swipe, like a bull maddened by a troublesome wasp, but she continued with her strange litany of guilt, moving on to Robert as Joel pushed past her.

"Joel, for God's sake . . . Joel . . ." Robert did his best to capture and control the demented man who had virtually carried him across field after field, so many of them he had lost count. Who had hauled him over hedges and stiles, lifted him bodily a dozen times from snowdrifts and ditches and who was now ready to do murder to anyone who stood in his way.

"Where is he, where? For pity's sake, woman, where?" He was ready to shake the truth out of poor Elspeth as though she personally were to blame for his son's plight, snarling into her face like a madman.

"Joel Greenwood, who is the doctor here, lad, you or me? Will you shut up and let me get to my patient?"

The quiet voice stopped him. Those words, the only ones which made sense to him, stopped him. He sagged against the wall, his head lowered like some goaded beast, allowing Robert to get by him in the tiny hallway, waiting to hear the state of his son whom he had not seen for the past twenty months. Twenty months. He could have told you the exact number of weeks, the days, the hours, the minutes, had you asked him, since he last saw his son and his son's mother but now, as then, he was not needed. He had done his part in bringing Robert here and he should go. She would not want him but he must find out, make certain, reassure himself that the boy and the boy's mother were all right.

Robert Chard entered the room that the young woman indicated, her hand shaking, her face blurred with tears. There was an old man, perched on the edge of a chair, who stood up as the doctor entered. There were two women, both nursing a child, one on either side of the leaping fire. One of them was Molly Broadbent. At her feet, so close it actually lay on them, was a young, shivering labrador.

Joel stood in the doorway, quiet now, like some gaunt shadow, his face grey, his eyes filled with such agony the young woman who had met them at the door put a hand of comfort on his arm, then turned, as they were all turned, to the woman and the doctor at her feet.

"What happened, Molly?" he asked quietly.

"He fell, Robert. He . . . we think he stumbled over the dog at the top of the stairs. Elspeth said he was worried about me . . . he must have got out of bed. Tizzy would follow him . . . she was very protective of both of them."

Molly cradled the limp figure of her son in tender, careful arms. His small arm hung down, the baby hand uncurled and defenceless. His legs, sturdy in his white sleeping suit, lay limply from her lap and his pale face was turned to her breast. His hair, thick and curling, was glossy in the firelight. His pouting lips were slightly parted but he was totally still.

The woman beside Joel turned her face to the wall and moaned.

"May I look at him?"

"He's asleep . . . we couldn't wake him."

Joel Greenwood wanted to moan too, for it seemed to him that he was to see his son, but too late. Then, as the light from the lamp beside Molly fell fully on the child in her arms he realised, with a great leap of delirious joy, that the boy was too big to be his son. That the head resting against Molly's breast had fair curls, not dark, that it was Liam, Tim's boy, and not his and at once a bolt of shame ran through him, for though it was natural to be relieved that it was not Joss who was injured surely he should not be so relieved that Liam was?

"We didn't touch him, Robert. We covered him up and left him where he was, didn't we, Betty? I remember you telling me that once. Never move someone who is hurt . . . but it was so cold in the hall and somehow . . . it seemed to me that whatever it was that . . . well, that he had . . . that he was asleep and not . . ."

"Good girl, but let me have a look at him."

In the other chair Betty held on tightly to Joss Broadbent whose big eyes were bright with alarm. This was not something that he cared for and his baby face said so and in his quiet space by the door Joel longed to go to him, cradle him against his broad chest and tell him there was nothing to be afraid of because his father was here to see nothing ever frightened him again.

Though the room was fiercely hot, Betty shivered. Her feet and legs, her skirt as far as her thighs were wet and steaming in the heat, since it was she who had made the journey, not once, but three times from the workroom to the gatehouse.

"We have no telephone here, you see, so Betty ran – well, it took her a long time – back to the workroom. I needed you, Robert, but you weren't there."

She sounded like a child who has woken to find herself alone in the dark and Joel felt the tears begin to clog at the back of his throat.

"I'm sorry, my dear."

"They gave Betty a number to call."

"Good . . . good."

All the time Molly was speaking Robert Chard's clever hands, which were familiar with children who had not been kindly treated, moved gently over the still and silent figure in her arms.

At last he drew back. "Well, you're right, Molly, he is sleeping. Probably a slight concussion by the bump on his head but not dangerously so. Let him sleep it off."

"Oh, great God . . . Oh, Jesus . . . thank God, thank God."

In the doorway Joel began to weep, since it came to him with a great blast of realisation that he could not have borne it if Tim's boy had been damaged. Tim's boy was just as precious as his own and the loss of either would be devastating. He did not weep like a man weeps but with great noisy gulping sobs that threatened to tear him to pieces. He bent his head and back, placing his hands on his knees, his distress so terrible they all turned to look at him with great compassion, even the dog.

"I'm sorry . . . I'm sorry," he groaned. "I'm sorry . . . I don't know . . ."

"Bloody hell," Betty whispered, then bent to lean her cheek on the dark curls of Joel Greenwood's son.

Molly's gaze rested on the racked figure of the man in the doorway and she seemed not at all surprised to see him there. Perhaps she was still in the state of shock her son's still figure at the foot of the stairs had flung her into but her eyes studied him as though, at this moment of crisis, it was absolutely natural for him to be here.

"Joel," she said, her voice soft so as not to wake her son and when he lifted his shaggy head to look at her she held out her free hand to him.

For the last time in his life Joel Greenwood wept like a child, flinging himself like a child who seeks his mother's comfort across the room to kneel beside her, to be drawn against her, his face in her shoulder, her gentle hand in his rough, wet-tangled hair.

"You thought it was Joss?"

"I didn't know. It didn't matter . . . whichever one, he was your son."

*　　*　　*

They were all in bed. It had been tricky finding a resting place for four adults since Jud did not feel up to going back to his place, he said. Betty sorted it all out, taking over the arranging of it, since Molly was not fit for it and besides, she and Joel and their two sons, for that was how it was going to be, wanted a bit of time to themselves. Molly was not fit for owt except to sit in the circle of Joel Greenwood's trembling arm, it appeared, their sons somehow cradled between them. It had been a bit difficult, for when Liam woke he had not cared for the sight of his mother and brother with that big man who, astonishingly, had cried like Liam sometimes did, but the man had taken him on his knee, asking him in a kind voice if there was anything he wanted more than anything else in the world. When, tentatively, he had mentioned a pony the man had promised he would have one the very next day.

"What about the snow?" piped Tim Broadbent's son, ready to be worried, but the man said the snow was no problem, son – yes, he had called him son – and he should have his pony first thing in the morning.

"And Joss, too."

"Yeah," said Joss, wishing he could sit on the big man's knee, scrambling from his mother's lap with every intention of doing do.

"There's no room for you," Liam said loftily, but it seemed there was and for several minutes Joel Greenwood discussed the colours and sizes of ponies with Tim Broadbent's boy while his own drowsed against him.

"Can Joss have one too?" Liam repeated.

"Of course, Joss too, but now you must go with Elspeth and get some sleep. Do you know what time it is?"

"No." A pair of big brown eyes stared up trustingly into those which were strangely the same colour as his.

"It's ten minutes past midnight which means it's a new year, Liam. Happy new year, son," but his eyes had gone to Liam's mother when he said it.

Liam settled himself against this interesting stranger who somehow seemed familiar.

"A new year. What's that?"

"I promise to tell you tomorrow. Will that do?"

"When we go to get the ponies?"

"When we go to get the ponies."

Betty was in Molly's bed, Robert in what had been Muriel

Broadbent's and Jud was happy to kip down on the sofa in the parlour, he said. That there snow was melting already and would be well thawed by morning, but he didn't relish the journey back to his own quarters, at least not until daylight. Elspeth would go in with Liam, she told the curiously tense couple in the kitchen, just to make sure he was all right, though it sounded as though she'd not get much sleep with him that excited about the pony he was going to get tomorrow and which he was going to call Barney. He'd think of a name for Joss's in the morning, he said solemnly to the big man.

"Yeah," Joss agreed.

Hot-water bottles had been filled and the nursemaid was everywhere, making sure the guests were warm and comfortable, walking on air now that she knew her baby was deemed fit and well, though the doctor said he must go up to hospital in the morning for X-rays, just to be on the safe side. It was amazing, he smiled, how kids bounced, tumbling but recovering from falls that would injure an adult. They would never know the exact circumstances of the fall but Molly's description seemed to be the most likely.

When they were alone Molly and Joel looked at one another and in their eyes was the forgiveness for one another, and for themselves, they could at last acknowledge. Perhaps Tim Broadbent might live on between them, sharing their lives through his son but he would be a kindly ghost who would, as he had in his lifetime, be sweet-natured and generous.

"Well, Mary Angelina." Joel's eyes never left hers.

"Well, Joel Greenwood." She lifted her head in a fair imitation of the spirited young woman he had loved from the moment he had seen her on the day she married Tim Broadbent.

"What is it to be?" he asked her sternly, as though he would brook no argument if she was thinking of giving him one.

"What about your fine fiancée, then?" she demanded to know, ready to fight with him over something, but her eyes were deep warm pools of lovely blue telling him it was really nothing to do with Joel Greenwood or Molly Broadbent. Sybil Holden was one of those who had turned contemptuous eyes on Molly Broadbent in the past and as far as Molly Broadbent was concerned could go to the devil.

"She'll recover. I'd have made her a dreadful husband

anyway. Now you . . ." His eyes glowed in that certain way she remembered and her breathing deepened.

"There'll be one unholy scandal."

"There already is. I believe I told them that Joss is my son." He grinned in great delight.

"Glory!"

"That's what it will be for us, Mary Angelina."

"I'll not give up my business. I owe it to Betty. Besides, I enjoy it."

"Anything else?"

"I'll not sell Meddins." Her voice was defiant.

"Did you honestly think I would expect it of you? But we'll live at Greenacres."

"As long as I can keep Meddins."

"Dear God in heaven, is that all that concerns you?"

"No." Her eyes narrowed.

"Then come over here, woman, and tell me what does."